Stephen Crane

The Complete Novels & Novellas of Stephen Crane

The Red Badge of Courage, Maggie, George's Mother, The Third Violet, Active Service, The Monster...

e-artnow, 2021
Contact: info@e-artnow.org

ISBN 978-80-273-4176-4

Stephen Crane

The Complete Novels & Novellas of Stephen Crane

e-artnow 2021

Contents

The Red Badge of Courage	11
Maggie: A Girl of the Streets	89
George's Mother	133
The Third Violet	171
Active Service	241
The Monster	361
The O'Ruddy	403

The Red Badge of Courage

CHAPTER I.

The cold passed reluctantly from the earth, and the retiring fogs revealed an army stretched out on the hills, resting. As the landscape changed from brown to green, the army awakened, and began to tremble with eagerness at the noise of rumors. It cast its eyes upon the roads, which were growing from long troughs of liquid mud to proper thoroughfares. A river, amber-tinted in the shadow of its banks, purled at the army's feet; and at night, when the stream had become of a sorrowful blackness, one could see across it the red, eyelike gleam of hostile camp-fires set in the low brows of distant hills.

Once a certain tall soldier developed virtues and went resolutely to wash a shirt. He came flying back from a brook waving his garment bannerlike. He was swelled with a tale he had heard from a reliable friend, who had heard it from a truthful cavalryman, who had heard it from his trustworthy brother, one of the orderlies at division headquarters. He adopted the important air of a herald in red and gold. "We're goin' t' move t'morrah—sure," he said pompously to a group in the company street. "We're goin' 'way up the river, cut across, an' come around in behint 'em."

To his attentive audience he drew a loud and elaborate plan of a very brilliant campaign. When he had finished, the blue-clothed men scattered into small arguing groups between the rows of squat brown huts. A negro teamster who had been dancing upon a cracker box with the hilarious encouragement of twoscore soldiers was deserted. He sat mournfully down. Smoke drifted lazily from a multitude of quaint chimneys.

"It's a lie! that's all it is—a thunderin' lie!" said another private loudly. His smooth face was flushed, and his hands were thrust sulkily into his trousers' pockets. He took the matter as an affront to him. "I don't believe the derned old army's ever going to move. We're set. I've got ready to move eight times in the last two weeks, and we ain't moved yet."

The tall soldier felt called upon to defend the truth of a rumor he himself had introduced. He and the loud one came near to fighting over it.

A corporal began to swear before the assemblage. He had just put a costly board floor in his house, he said. During the early spring he had refrained from adding extensively to the comfort of his environment because he had felt that the army might start on the march at any moment. Of late, however, he had been impressed that they were in a sort of eternal camp.

Many of the men engaged in a spirited debate. One outlined in a peculiarly lucid manner all the plans of the commanding general. He was opposed by men who advocated that there were other plans of campaign. They clamored at each other, numbers making futile bids for the popular attention. Meanwhile, the soldier who had fetched the rumor bustled about with much importance. He was continually assailed by questions.

"What's up, Jim?"

"Th' army's goin' t' move."

"Ah, what yeh talkin' about? How yeh know it is?"

"Well, yeh kin b'lieve me er not, jest as yeh like. I don't care a hang."

There was much food for thought in the manner in which he replied. He came near to convincing them by disdaining to produce proofs. They grew excited over it.

There was a youthful private who listened with eager ears to the words of the tall soldier and to the varied comments of his comrades. After receiving a fill of discussions concerning marches and attacks, he went to his hut and crawled through an intricate hole that served it as a door. He wished to be alone with some new thoughts that had lately come to him.

He lay down on a wide bank that stretched across the end of the room. In the other end, cracker boxes were made to serve as furniture. They were grouped about the fireplace. A picture from an illustrated weekly was upon the log walls, and three rifles were paralleled on pegs. Equipments hunt on handy projections, and some tin dishes lay upon a small pile of firewood. A folded tent was serving as a roof. The sunlight, without, beating upon it, made it glow a light yellow shade. A small window shot an oblique square of whiter light upon the cluttered floor.

The smoke from the fire at times neglected the clay chimney and wreathed into the room, and this flimsy chimney of clay and sticks made endless threats to set ablaze the whole establishment.

The youth was in a little trance of astonishment. So they were at last going to fight. On the morrow, perhaps, there would be a battle, and he would be in it. For a time he was obliged to labor to make himself believe. He could not accept with assurance an omen that he was about to mingle in one of those great affairs of the earth.

He had, of course, dreamed of battles all his life-of vague and bloody conflicts that had thrilled him with their sweep and fire. In visions he had seen himself in many struggles. He had imagined peoples secure in the shadow of his eagle-eyed prowess. But awake he had regarded battles as crimson blotches on the pages of the past. He had put them as things of the bygone with his thought-images of heavy crowns and high castles. There was a portion of the world's history which he had regarded as the time of wars, but it, he thought, had been long gone over the horizon and had disappeared forever.

From his home his youthful eyes had looked upon the war in his own country with distrust. It must be some sort of a play affair. He had long despaired of witnessing a Greeklike struggle. Such would be no more, he had said. Men were better, or more timid. Secular and religious education had effaced the throat-grappling instinct, or else firm finance held in check the passions.

He had burned several times to enlist. Tales of great movements shook the land. They might not be distinctly Homeric, but there seemed to be much glory in them. He had read of marches, sieges, conflicts, and he had longed to see it all. His busy mind had drawn for him large pictures extravagant in color, lurid with breathless deeds.

But his mother had discouraged him. She had affected to look with some contempt upon the quality of his war ardor and patriotism. She could calmly seat herself and with no apparent difficulty give him many hundreds of reasons why he was of vastly more importance on the farm than on the field of battle. She had had certain ways of expression that told him that her statements on the subject came from a deep conviction. Moreover, on her side, was his belief that her ethical motive in the argument was impregnable.

At last, however, he had made firm rebellion against this yellow light thrown upon the color of his ambitions. The newspapers, the gossip of the village, his own picturings had aroused him to an uncheckable degree. They were in truth fighting finely down there. Almost every day the newspapers printed accounts of a decisive victory.

One night, as he lay in bed, the winds had carried to him the clangoring of the church bell as some enthusiast jerked the rope frantically to tell the twisted news of a great battle. This voice of the people rejoicing in the night had made him shiver in a prolonged ecstasy of excitement. Later, he had gone down to his mother's room and had spoken thus: "Ma, I'm going to enlist."

"Henry, don't you be a fool," his mother had replied. She had then covered her face with the quilt. There was an end to the matter for that night.

Nevertheless, the next morning he had gone to a town that was near his mother's farm and had enlisted in a company that was forming there. When he had returned home his mother was milking the brindle cow. Four others stood waiting. "Ma, I've enlisted," he had said to her diffidently. There was a short silence. "The Lord's will be done, Henry," she had finally replied, and had then continued to milk the brindle cow.

When he had stood in the doorway with his soldier's clothes on his back, and with the light of excitement and expectancy in his eyes almost defeating the glow of regret for the home bonds, he had seen two tears leaving their trails on his mother's scarred cheeks.

Still, she had disappointed him by saying nothing whatever about returning with his shield or on it. He had privately primed himself for a beautiful scene. He had prepared certain sentences which he thought could be used with touching effect. But her words destroyed his plans. She had doggedly peeled potatoes and addressed him as follows: "You watch out, Henry, an' take good care of yerself in this here fighting business-you watch out, an' take good care of yerself. Don't go a-thinkin' you can lick the hull rebel army at the start, because yeh can't. Yer jest one little feller amongst a hull lot of others, and yeh've got to keep quiet an' do what they tell yeh. I know how you are, Henry.

"I've knet yeh eight pair of socks, Henry, and I've put in all yer best shirts, because I want my boy to be jest as warm and comf'able as anybody in the army. Whenever they get holes in 'em, I want yeh to send 'em right-away back to me, so's I kin dern 'em.

"An' allus be careful an' choose yer comp'ny. There's lots of bad men in the army, Henry. The army makes 'em wild, and they like nothing better than the job of leading off a young feller like you, as ain't never been away from home much and has allus had a mother, an' a-learning 'em to drink and swear. Keep clear of them folks, Henry. I don't want yeh to ever do anything, Henry, that yeh would be 'shamed to let me know about. Jest think as if I was a-watchin' yeh. If yeh keep that in yer mind allus, I guess yeh'll come out about right.

"Yeh must allus remember yer father, too, child, an' remember he never drunk a drop of licker in his life, and seldom swore a cross oath.

"I don't know what else to tell yeh, Henry, excepting that yeh must never do no shirking, child, on my account. If so be a time comes when yeh have to be kilt or do a mean thing, why, Henry, don't think of anything 'cept what's right, because there's many a woman has to bear up 'ginst sech things these times, and the Lord 'll take keer of us all.

"Don't forgit about the socks and the shirts, child; and I've put a cup of blackberry jam with yer bundle, because I know yeh like it above all things. Good-by, Henry. Watch out, and be a good boy."

He had, of course, been impatient under the ordeal of this speech. It had not been quite what he expected, and he had borne it with an air of irritation. He departed feeling vague relief.

Still, when he had looked back from the gate, he had seen his mother kneeling among the potato parings. Her brown face, upraised, was stained with tears, and her spare form was quivering. He bowed his head and went on, feeling suddenly ashamed of his purposes.

From his home he had gone to the seminary to bid adieu to many schoolmates. They had thronged about him with wonder and admiration. He had felt the gulf now between them and had swelled with calm pride. He and some of his fellows who had donned blue were quite overwhelmed with privileges for all of one afternoon, and it had been a very delicious thing. They had strutted.

A certain light-haired girl had made vivacious fun at his martial spirit, but there was another and darker girl whom he had gazed at steadfastly, and he thought she grew demure and sad at sight of his blue and brass. As he had walked down the path between the rows of oaks, he had turned his head and detected her at a window watching his departure. As he perceived her, she had immediately begun to stare up through the high tree branches at the sky. He had seen a good deal of flurry and haste in her movement as she changed her attitude. He often thought of it.

On the way to Washington his spirit had soared. The regiment was fed and caressed at station after station until the youth had believed that he must be a hero. There was a lavish expenditure of bread and cold meats, coffee, and pickles and cheese. As he basked in the smiles of the girls and was patted and complimented by the old men, he had felt growing within him the strength to do mighty deeds of arms.

After complicated journeyings with many pauses, there had come months of monotonous life in a camp. He had had the belief that real war was a series of death struggles with small time in between for sleep and meals; but since his regiment had come to the field the army had done little but sit still and try to keep warm.

He was brought then gradually back to his old ideas. Greeklike struggles would be no more. Men were better, or more timid. Secular and religious education had effaced the throat-grappling instinct, or else firm finance held in check the passions.

He had grown to regard himself merely as a part of a vast blue demonstration. His province was to look out, as far as he could, for his personal comfort. For recreation he could twiddle his thumbs and speculate on the thoughts which must agitate the minds of the generals. Also, he was drilled and drilled and reviewed, and drilled and drilled and reviewed.

The only foes he had seen were some pickets along the river bank. They were a sun-tanned, philosophical lot, who sometimes shot reflectively at the blue pickets. When reproached for this afterward, they usually expressed sorrow, and swore by their gods that the guns had exploded without their permission. The youth, on guard duty one night, conversed across the stream with one of them. He was a slightly ragged man, who spat skillfully between his shoes and possessed a great fund of bland and infantile assurance. The youth liked him personally.

"Yank," the other had informed him, "yer a right dum good feller." This sentiment, floating to him upon the still air, had made him temporarily regret war.

Various veterans had told him tales. Some talked of gray, bewhiskered hordes who were advancing with relentless curses and chewing tobacco with unspeakable valor; tremendous bodies of fierce soldiery who were sweeping along like the Huns. Others spoke of tattered and eternally hungry men who fired despondent powders. "They'll charge through hell's fire an' brimstone t' git a holt on a haversack, an' sech stomachs ain't a-lastin' long," he was told. From the stories, the youth imagined the red, live bones sticking out through slits in the faded uniforms.

Still, he could not put a whole faith in veterans' tales, for recruits were their prey. They talked much of smoke, fire, and blood, but he could not tell how much might be lies. They persistently yelled "Fresh fish!" at him, and were in no wise to be trusted.

However, he perceived now that it did not greatly matter what kind of soldiers he was going to fight, so long as they fought, which fact no one disputed. There was a more serious problem. He lay in his bunk pondering upon it. He tried to mathematically prove to himself that he would not run from a battle.

Previously he had never felt obliged to wrestle too seriously with this question. In his life he had taken certain things for granted, never challenging his belief in ultimate success, and bothering little about means and roads. But here he was confronted with a thing of moment. It had suddenly appeared to him that perhaps in a battle he might run. He was forced to admit that as far as war was concerned he knew nothing of himself.

A sufficient time before he would have allowed the problem to kick its heels at the outer portals of his mind, but now he felt compelled to give serious attention to it.

A little panic-fear grew in his mind. As his imagination went forward to a fight, he saw hideous possibilities. He contemplated the lurking menaces of the future, and failed in an effort to see himself standing stoutly in the midst of them. He recalled his visions of broken-bladed glory, but in the shadow of the impending tumult he suspected them to be impossible pictures.

He sprang from the bunk and began to pace nervously to and fro. "Good Lord, what's th' matter with me?" he said aloud.

He felt that in this crisis his laws of life were useless. Whatever he had learned of himself was here of no avail. He was an unknown quantity. He saw that he would again be obliged to experiment as he had in early youth. He must accumulate information of himself, and meanwhile he resolved to remain close upon his guard lest those qualities of which he knew nothing should everlastingly disgrace him. "Good Lord!" he repeated in dismay.

After a time the tall soldier slid dexterously through the hole. The loud private followed. They were wrangling.

"That's all right," said the tall soldier as he entered. He waved his hand expressively. "You can believe me or not, jest as you like. All you got to do is to sit down and wait as quiet as you can. Then pretty soon you'll find out I was right."

His comrade grunted stubbornly. For a moment he seemed to be searching for a formidable reply. Finally he said: "Well, you don't know everything in the world, do you?"

"Didn't say I knew everything in the world," retorted the other sharply. He began to stow various articles snugly into his knapsack.

The youth, pausing in his nervous walk, looked down at the busy figure. "Going to be a battle, sure, is there, Jim?" he asked.

"Of course there is," replied the tall soldier. "Of course there is. You jest wait 'til to-morrow, and you'll see one of the biggest battles ever was. You jest wait."

"Thunder!" said the youth.

"Oh, you'll see fighting this time, my boy, what'll be regular out-and-out fighting," added the tall soldier, with the air of a man who is about to exhibit a battle for the benefit of his friends.

"Huh!" said the loud one from a corner.

"Well," remarked the youth, "like as not this story'll turn out jest like them others did."

"Not much it won't," replied the tall soldier, exasperated. "Not much it won't. Didn't the cavalry all start this morning?" He glared about him. No one denied his statement. "The cavalry started this morning," he continued. "They say there ain't hardly any cavalry left in camp. They're going to Richmond, or some place, while we fight all the Johnnies. It's some dodge like that. The regiment's got orders, too. A feller what seen 'em go to headquarters told me a little while ago. And they're raising blazes all over camp-anybody can see that."

"Shucks!" said the loud one.

The youth remained silent for a time. At last he spoke to the tall soldier. "Jim!"

"What?"

"How do you think the reg'ment 'll do?"

"Oh, they'll fight all right, I guess, after they once get into it," said the other with cold judgment. He made a fine use of the third person. "There's been heaps of fun poked at 'em because they're new, of course, and all that; but they'll fight all right, I guess."

"Think any of the boys 'll run?" persisted the youth.

"Oh, there may be a few of 'em run, but there's them kind in every regiment, 'specially when they first goes under fire," said the other in a tolerant way. "Of course it might happen that the hull kit-and-boodle might start and run, if some big fighting came first-off, and then again they might stay and fight like fun. But you can't bet on nothing. Of course they ain't never been under fire yet, and it ain't likely they'll lick the hull rebel army all-to-oncet the first time; but I think they'll fight better than some, if worse than others. That's the way I figger. They call the reg'ment 'Fresh fish' and everything; but the boys come of good stock, and most of 'em 'll fight like sin after they oncet git shootin'," he added, with a mighty emphasis on the last four words.

"Oh, you think you know —" began the loud soldier with scorn.

The other turned savagely upon him. They had a rapid altercation, in which they fastened upon each other various strange epithets.

The youth at last interrupted them. "Did you ever think you might run yourself, Jim?" he asked. On concluding the sentence he laughed as if he had meant to aim a joke. The loud soldier also giggled.

The tall private waved his hand. "Well," said he profoundly, "I've thought it might get too hot for Jim Conklin in some of them scrimmages, and if a whole lot of boys started and run, why, I s'pose I'd start and run. And if I once started to run, I'd run like the devil, and no mistake. But if everybody was a-standing and a-fighting, why, I'd stand and fight. Be jiminey, I would. I'll bet on it."

"Huh!" said the loud one.

The youth of this tale felt gratitude for these words of his comrade. He had feared that all of the untried men possessed a great and correct confidence. He now was in a measure reassured.

CHAPTER II.

The next morning the youth discovered that his tall comrade had been the fast-flying messenger of a mistake. There was much scoffing at the latter by those who had yesterday been firm adherents of his views, and there was even a little sneering by men who had never believed the rumor. The tall one fought with a man from Chatfield Corners and beat him severely.

The youth felt, however, that his problem was in no wise lifted from him. There was, on the contrary, an irritating prolongation. The tale had created in him a great concern for himself. Now, with the newborn question in his mind, he was compelled to sink back into his old place as part of a blue demonstration.

For days he made ceaseless calculations, but they were all wondrously unsatisfactory. He found that he could establish nothing. He finally concluded that the only way to prove himself was to go into the blaze, and then figuratively to watch his legs to discover their merits and faults. He reluctantly admitted that he could not sit still and with a mental slate and pencil derive an answer. To gain it, he must have blaze, blood, and danger, even as a chemist requires this, that, and the other. So he fretted for an opportunity.

Meanwhile he continually tried to measure himself by his comrades. The tall soldier, for one, gave him some assurance. This man's serene unconcern dealt him a measure of confidence, for he had known him since childhood, and from his intimate knowledge he did not see how he could be capable of anything that was beyond him, the youth. Still, he thought that his comrade might be mistaken about himself. Or, on the other hand, he might be a man heretofore doomed to peace and obscurity, but, in reality, made to shine in war.

The youth would have liked to have discovered another who suspected himself. A sympathetic comparison of mental notes would have been a joy to him.

He occasionally tried to fathom a comrade with seductive sentences. He looked about to find men in the proper mood. All attempts failed to bring forth any statement which looked in any way like a confession to those doubts which he privately acknowledged in himself. He was afraid to make an open declaration of his concern, because he dreaded to place some unscrupulous confidant upon the high plane of the unconfessed from which elevation he could be derided.

In regard to his companions his mind wavered between two opinions, according to his mood. Sometimes he inclined to believing them all heroes. In fact, he usually admitted in secret the superior development of the higher qualities in others. He could conceive of men going very insignificantly about the world bearing a load of courage unseen, and although he had known many of his comrades through boyhood, he began to fear that his judgment of them had been blind. Then, in other moments, he flouted these theories, and assured himself that his fellows were all privately wondering and quaking.

His emotions made him feel strange in the presence of men who talked excitedly of a prospective battle as of a drama they were about to witness, with nothing but eagerness and curiosity apparent in their faces. It was often that he suspected them to be liars.

He did not pass such thoughts without severe condemnation of himself. He dinned reproaches at times. He was convicted by himself of many shameful crimes against the gods of traditions.

In his great anxiety his heart was continually clamoring at what he considered the intolerable slowness of the generals. They seemed content to perch tranquilly on the river bank, and leave him bowed down by the weight of a great problem. He wanted it settled forthwith. He could not long bear such a load, he said. Sometimes his anger at the commanders reached an acute stage, and he grumbled about the camp like a veteran.

One morning, however, he found himself in the ranks of his prepared regiment. The men were whispering speculations and recounting the old rumors. In the gloom before the break of the day their uniforms glowed a deep purple hue. From across the river the red eyes were still peering. In the eastern sky there was a yellow patch like a rug laid for the feet of the coming sun; and against it, black and patternlike, loomed the gigantic figure of the colonel on a gigantic horse.

From off in the darkness came the trampling of feet. The youth could occasionally see dark shadows that moved like monsters. The regiment stood at rest for what seemed a long time. The youth grew impatient. It was unendurable the way these affairs were managed. He wondered how long they were to be kept waiting.

As he looked all about him and pondered upon the mystic gloom, he began to believe that at any moment the ominous distance might be aflare, and the rolling crashes of an engagement come to his ears. Staring once at the red eyes across the river, he conceived them to be growing larger, as the orbs of a row of dragons advancing. He turned toward the colonel and saw him lift his gigantic arm and calmly stroke his mustache.

At last he heard from along the road at the foot of the hill the clatter of a horse's galloping hoofs. It must be the coming of orders. He bent forward, scarce breathing. The exciting clickety-click, as it grew louder and louder, seemed to be beating upon his soul. Presently a horseman with jangling equipment drew rein before the colonel of the regiment. The two held a short, sharp-worded conversation. The men in the foremost ranks craned their necks.

As the horseman wheeled his animal and galloped away he turned to shout over his shoulder, "Don't forget that box of cigars!" The colonel mumbled in reply. The youth wondered what a box of cigars had to do with war.

A moment later the regiment went swinging off into the darkness. It was now like one of those moving monsters wending with many feet. The air was heavy, and cold with dew. A mass of wet grass, marched upon, rustled like silk.

There was an occasional flash and glimmer of steel from the backs of all these huge crawling reptiles. From the road came creakings and grumblings as some surly guns were dragged away.

The men stumbled along still muttering speculations. There was a subdued debate. Once a man fell down, and as he reached for his rifle a comrade, unseeing, trod upon his hand. He of the injured fingers swore bitterly and aloud. A low, tittering laugh went among his fellows.

Presently they passed into a roadway and marched forward with easy strides. A dark regiment moved before them, and from behind also came the tinkle of equipments on the bodies of marching men.

The rushing yellow of the developing day went on behind their backs. When the sunrays at last struck full and mellowingly upon the earth, the youth saw that the landscape was streaked with two long, thin, black columns which disappeared on the brow of a hill in front and rearward vanished in a wood. They were like two serpents crawling from the cavern of the night.

The river was not in view. The tall soldier burst into praises of what he thought to be his powers of perception.

Some of the tall one's companions cried with emphasis that they, too, had evolved the same thing, and they congratulated themselves upon it. But there were others who said that the tall one's plan was not the true one at all. They persisted with other theories. There was a vigorous discussion.

The youth took no part in them. As he walked along in careless line he was engaged with his own eternal debate. He could not hinder himself from dwelling upon it. He was despondent and sullen, and threw shifting glances about him. He looked ahead, often expecting to hear from the advance the rattle of firing.

But the long serpents crawled slowly from hill to hill without bluster of smoke. A duncolored cloud of dust floated away to the right. The sky overhead was of a fairy blue.

The youth studied the faces of his companions, ever on the watch to detect kindred emotions. He suffered disappointment. Some ardor of the air which was causing the veteran commands to move with glee-almost with song-had infected the new regiment. The men began to speak of victory as of a thing they knew. Also, the tall soldier received his vindication. They were certainly going to come around in behind the enemy. They expressed commiseration for that part of the army which had been left upon the river bank, felicitating themselves upon being a part of a blasting host.

The youth, considering himself as separated from the others, was saddened by the blithe and merry speeches that went from rank to rank. The company wags all made their best endeavors. The regiment tramped to the tune of laughter.

The blatant soldier often convulsed whole files by his biting sarcasms aimed at the tall one.

And it was not long before all the men seemed to forget their mission. Whole brigades grinned in unison, and regiments laughed.

A rather fat soldier attempted to pilfer a horse from a dooryard. He planned to load his knap-sack upon it. He was escaping with his prize when a young girl rushed from the house and grabbed the animal's mane. There followed a wrangle. The young girl, with pink cheeks and shining eyes, stood like a dauntless statue.

The observant regiment, standing at rest in the roadway, whooped at once, and entered whole-souled upon the side of the maiden. The men became so engrossed in this affair that they entirely ceased to remember their own large war. They jeered the piratical private, and called attention to various defects in his personal appearance; and they were wildly enthusiastic in support of the young girl.

To her, from some distance, came bold advice. "Hit him with a stick."

There were crows and catcalls showered upon him when he retreated without the horse. The regiment rejoiced at his downfall. Loud and vociferous congratulations were showered upon the maiden, who stood panting and regarding the troops with defiance.

At nightfall the column broke into regimental pieces, and the fragments went into the fields to camp. Tents sprang up like strange plants. Camp fires, like red, peculiar blossoms, dotted the night.

The youth kept from intercourse with his companions as much as circumstances would allow him. In the evening he wandered a few paces into the gloom. From this little distance the many fires, with the black forms of men passing to and fro before the crimson rays, made weird and satanic effects.

He lay down in the grass. The blades pressed tenderly against his cheek. The moon had been lighted and was hung in a treetop. The liquid stillness of the night enveloping him made him feel vast pity for himself. There was a caress in the soft winds; and the whole mood of the darkness, he thought, was one of sympathy for himself in his distress.

He wished, without reserve, that he was at home again making the endless rounds from the house to the barn, from the barn to the fields, from the fields to the barn, from the barn to the house. He remembered he had often cursed the brindle cow and her mates, and had sometimes flung milking stools. But, from his present point of view, there was a halo of happiness about each of their heads, and he would have sacrificed all the brass buttons on the continent to have been enabled to return to them. He told himself that he was not formed for a soldier. And he mused seriously upon the radical differences between himself and those men who were dodging imp-like around the fires.

As he mused thus he heard the rustle of grass, and, upon turning his head, discovered the loud soldier. He called out, "Oh, Wilson!"

The latter approached and looked down. "Why, hello, Henry; is it you? What you doing here?"

"Oh, thinking," said the youth.

The other sat down and carefully lighted his pipe. "You're getting blue, my boy. You're looking thundering peeked. What the dickens is wrong with you?"

"Oh, nothing," said the youth.

The loud soldier launched then into the subject of the anticipated fight. "Oh, we've got 'em now!" As he spoke his boyish face was wreathed in a gleeful smile, and his voice had an exultant ring. "We've got 'em now. At last, by the eternal thunders, we'll lick 'em good!"

"If the truth was known," he added, more soberly, "*They've* licked *us* about every clip up to now; but this time-this time-we'll lick 'em good!"

"I thought you was objecting to this march a little while ago," said the youth coldly.

"Oh, it wasn't that," explained the other. "I don't mind marching, if there's going to be fighting at the end of it. What I hate is this getting moved here and moved there, with no good coming of it, as far as I can see, excepting sore feet and damned short rations."

"Well, Jim Conklin says we'll get a plenty of fighting this time."

"He's right for once, I guess, though I can't see how it come. This time we're in for a big battle, and we've got the best end of it, certain sure. Gee rod! how we will thump 'em!"

He arose and began to pace to and fro excitedly. The thrill of his enthusiasm made him walk with an elastic step. He was sprightly, vigorous, fiery in his belief in success. He looked into the future with clear, proud eye, and he swore with the air of an old soldier.

The youth watched him for a moment in silence. When he finally spoke his voice was as bitter as dregs. "Oh, you're going to do great things, I s'pose!"

The loud soldier blew a thoughtful cloud of smoke from his pipe. "Oh, I don't know," he remarked with dignity; "I don't know. I s'pose I'll do as well as the rest. I'm going to try like thunder." He evidently complimented himself upon the modesty of this statement.

"How do you know you won't run when the time comes?" asked the youth.

"Run?" said the loud one; "run? —of course not!" He laughed.

"Well," continued the youth, "lots of good-a-'nough men have thought they was going to do great things before the fight, but when the time come they skedaddled."

"Oh, that's all true, I s'pose," replied the other; "but I'm not going to skedaddle. The man that bets on my running will lose his money, that's all." He nodded confidently.

"Oh, shucks!" said the youth. "You ain't the bravest man in the world, are you?"

"No, I ain't," exclaimed the loud soldier indignantly; "and I didn't say I was the bravest man in the world, neither. I said I was going to do my share of fighting-that's what I said. And I am, too. Who are you, anyhow. You talk as if you thought you was Napoleon Bonaparte." He glared at the youth for a moment, and then strode away.

The youth called in a savage voice after his comrade: "Well, you needn't git mad about it!" But the other continued on his way and made no reply.

He felt alone in space when his injured comrade had disappeared. His failure to discover any mite of resemblance in their view points made him more miserable than before. No one seemed to be wrestling with such a terrific personal problem. He was a mental outcast.

He went slowly to his tent and stretched himself on a blanket by the side of the snoring tall soldier. In the darkness he saw visions of a thousand-tongued fear that would babble at his back and cause him to flee, while others were going coolly about their country's business. He admitted that he would not be able to cope with this monster. He felt that every nerve in his body would be an ear to hear the voices, while other men would remain stolid and deaf.

And as he sweated with the pain of these thoughts, he could hear low, serene sentences. "I'll bid five." "Make it six." "Seven." "Seven goes."

He stared at the red, shivering reflection of a fire on the white wall of his tent until, exhausted and ill from the monotony of his suffering, he fell asleep.

CHAPTER III.

WHEN another night came the columns, changed to purple streaks, filed across two pontoon bridges. A glaring fire wine-tinted the waters of the river. Its rays, shining upon the moving masses of troops, brought forth here and there sudden gleams of silver or gold. Upon the other shore a dark and mysterious range of hills was curved against the sky. The insect voices of the night sang solemnly.

After this crossing the youth assured himself that at any moment they might be suddenly and fearfully assaulted from the caves of the lowering woods. He kept his eyes watchfully upon the darkness.

But his regiment went unmolested to a camping place, and its soldiers slept the brave sleep of wearied men. In the morning they were routed out with early energy, and hustled along a narrow road that led deep into the forest.

It was during this rapid march that the regiment lost many of the marks of a new command.

The men had begun to count the miles upon their fingers, and they grew tired. "Sore feet an' damned short rations, that's all," said the loud soldier. There was perspiration and grumblings. After a time they began to shed their knapsacks. Some tossed them unconcernedly down; others hid them carefully, asserting their plans to return for them at some convenient time. Men extricated themselves from thick shirts. Presently few carried anything but their necessary clothing, blankets, haversacks, canteens, and arms and ammunition. "You can now eat and shoot," said the tall soldier to the youth. "That's all you want to do."

There was sudden change from the ponderous infantry of theory to the light and speedy infantry of practice. The regiment, relieved of a burden, received a new impetus. But there was much loss of valuable knapsacks, and, on the whole, very good shirts.

But the regiment was not yet veteranlike in appearance. Veteran regiments in the army were likely to be very small aggregations of men. Once, when the command had first come to the field, some perambulating veterans, noting the length of their column, had accosted them thus: "Hey, fellers, what brigade is that?" And when the men had replied that they formed a regiment and not a brigade, the older soldiers had laughed, and said, "O Gawd!"

Also, there was too great a similarity in the hats. The hats of a regiment should properly represent the history of headgear for a period of years. And, moreover, there were no letters of faded gold speaking from the colors. They were new and beautiful, and the color bearer habitually oiled the pole.

Presently the army again sat down to think. The odor of the peaceful pines was in the men's nostrils. The sound of monotonous axe blows rang through the forest, and the insects, nodding upon their perches, crooned like old women. The youth returned to his theory of a blue demonstration.

One gray dawn, however, he was kicked in the leg by the tall soldier, and then, before he was entirely awake, he found himself running down a wood road in the midst of men who were panting from the first effects of speed. His canteen banged rhythmically upon his thigh, and his haversack bobbed softly. His musket bounced a trifle from his shoulder at each stride and made his cap feel uncertain upon his head.

He could hear the men whisper jerky sentences: "Say-what's all this-about?" "What th' thunder-we-skedaddlin' this way fer?" "Billie-keep off m' feet. Yeh run-like a cow." And the loud soldier's shrill voice could be heard: "What th' devil they in sich a hurry for?"

The youth thought the damp fog of early morning moved from the rush of a great body of troops. From the distance came a sudden spatter of firing.

He was bewildered. As he ran with his comrades he strenuously tried to think, but all he knew was that if he fell down those coming behind would tread upon him. All his faculties seemed to be needed to guide him over and past obstructions. He felt carried along by a mob.

The sun spread disclosing rays, and, one by one, regiments burst into view like armed men just born of the earth. The youth perceived that the time had come. He was about to be measured. For a moment he felt in the face of his great trial like a babe, and the flesh over his heart seemed very thin. He seized time to look about him calculatingly.

But he instantly saw that it would be impossible for him to escape from the regiment. It inclosed him. And there were iron laws of tradition and law on four sides. He was in a moving box.

As he perceived this fact it occurred to him that he had never wished to come to the war. He had not enlisted of his free will. He had been dragged by the merciless government. And now they were taking him out to be slaughtered.

The regiment slid down a bank and wallowed across a little stream. The mournful current moved slowly on, and from the water, shaded black, some white bubble eyes looked at the men.

As they climbed the hill on the farther side artillery began to boom. Here the youth forgot many things as he felt a sudden impulse of curiosity. He scrambled up the bank with a speed that could not be exceeded by a bloodthirsty man.

He expected a battle scene.

There were some little fields girted and squeezed by a forest. Spread over the grass and in among the tree trunks, he could see knots and waving lines of skirmishers who were running hither and thither and firing at the landscape. A dark battle line lay upon a sunstruck clearing that gleamed orange color. A flag fluttered.

Other regiments floundered up the bank. The brigade was formed in line of battle, and after a pause started slowly through the woods in the rear of the receding skirmishers, who were continually melting into the scene to appear again farther on. They were always busy as bees, deeply absorbed in their little combats.

The youth tried to observe everything. He did not use care to avoid trees and branches, and his forgotten feet were constantly knocking against stones or getting entangled in briers. He was aware that these battalions with their commotions were woven red and startling into the gentle fabric of softened greens and browns. It looked to be a wrong place for a battle field.

The skirmishers in advance fascinated him. Their shots into thickets and at distant and prominent trees spoke to him of tragedies-hidden, mysterious, solemn.

Once the line encountered the body of a dead soldier. He lay upon his back staring at the sky. He was dressed in an awkward suit of yellowish brown. The youth could see that the soles of his shoes had been worn to the thinness of writing paper, and from a great rent in one the dead foot projected piteously. And it was as if fate had betrayed the soldier. In death it exposed to his enemies that poverty which in life he had perhaps concealed from his friends.

The ranks opened covertly to avoid the corpse. The invulnerable dead man forced a way for himself. The youth looked keenly at the ashen face. The wind raised the tawny beard. It moved as if a hand were stroking it. He vaguely desired to walk around and around the body and stare; the impulse of the living to try to read in dead eyes the answer to the Question.

During the march the ardor which the youth had acquired when out of view of the field rapidly faded to nothing. His curiosity was quite easily satisfied. If an intense scene had caught him with its wild swing as he came to the top of the bank, he might have gone roaring on. This advance upon Nature was too calm. He had opportunity to reflect. He had time in which to wonder about himself and to attempt to probe his sensations.

Absurd ideas took hold upon him. He thought that he did not relish the landscape. It threatened him. A coldness swept over his back, and it is true that his trousers felt to him that they were no fit for his legs at all.

A house standing placidly in distant fields had to him an ominous look. The shadows of the woods were formidable. He was certain that in this vista there lurked fierce-eyed hosts. The swift thought came to him that the generals did not know what they were about. It was all a trap. Suddenly those close forests would bristle with rifle barrels. Ironlike brigades would appear in the rear. They were all going to be sacrificed. The generals were stupids. The enemy would presently swallow the whole command. He glared about him, expecting to see the stealthy approach of his death.

He thought that he must break from the ranks and harangue his comrades. They must not all be killed like pigs; and he was sure it would come to pass unless they were informed of these dangers. The generals were idiots to send them marching into a regular pen. There was but one pair of eyes in the corps. He would step forth and make a speech. Shrill and passionate words came to his lips.

The line, broken into moving fragments by the ground, went calmly on through fields and woods. The youth looked at the men nearest him, and saw, for the most part, expressions of deep interest, as if they were investigating something that had fascinated them. One or two stepped with overvaliant airs as if they were already plunged into war. Others walked as upon thin ice. The greater part of the untested men appeared quiet and absorbed. They were going to look at war, the red animal-war, the blood-swollen god. And they were deeply engrossed in this march.

As he looked the youth gripped his outcry at his throat. He saw that even if the men were tottering with fear they would laugh at his warning. They would jeer him, and, if practicable, pelt him with missiles. Admitting that he might be wrong, a frenzied declamation of the kind would turn him into a worm.

He assumed, then, the demeanor of one who knows that he is doomed alone to unwritten responsibilities. He lagged, with tragic glances at the sky.

He was surprised presently by the young lieutenant of his company, who began heartily to beat him with a sword, calling out in a loud and insolent voice: "Come, young man, get up into ranks there. No skulking'll do here." He mended his pace with suitable haste. And he hated the lieutenant, who had no appreciation of fine minds. He was a mere brute.

After a time the brigade was halted in the cathedral light of a forest. The busy skirmishers were still popping. Through the aisles of the wood could be seen the floating smoke from their rifles. Sometimes it went up in little balls, white and compact.

During this halt many men in the regiment began erecting tiny hills in front of them. They used stones, sticks, earth, and anything they thought might turn a bullet. Some built comparatively large ones, while others seemed content with little ones.

This procedure caused a discussion among the men. Some wished to fight like duelists, believing it to be correct to stand erect and be, from their feet to their foreheads, a mark. They said they scorned the devices of the cautious. But the others scoffed in reply, and pointed to the veterans on the flanks who were digging at the ground like terriers. In a short time there was quite a barricade along the regimental fronts. Directly, however, they were ordered to withdraw from that place.

This astounded the youth. He forgot his stewing over the advance movement. "Well, then, what did they march us out here for?" he demanded of the tall soldier. The latter with calm faith began a heavy explanation, although he had been compelled to leave a little protection of stones and dirt to which he had devoted much care and skill.

When the regiment was aligned in another position each man's regard for his safety caused another line of small intrenchments. They ate their noon meal behind a third one. They were moved from this one also. They were marched from place to place with apparent aimlessness.

The youth had been taught that a man became another thing in a battle. He saw his salvation in such a change. Hence this waiting was an ordeal to him. He was in a fever of impatience. He considered that there was denoted a lack of purpose on the part of the generals. He began to complain to the tall soldier. "I can't stand this much longer," he cried. "I don't see what good it does to make us wear out our legs for nothin'." He wished to return to camp, knowing that this affair was a blue demonstration; or else to go into a battle and discover that he had been a fool in his doubts, and was, in truth, a man of traditional courage. The strain of present circumstances he felt to be intolerable.

The philosophical tall soldier measured a sandwich of cracker and pork and swallowed it in a nonchalant manner. "Oh, I suppose we must go reconnoitering around the country jest to keep 'em from getting too close, or to develop 'em, or something."

"Huh!" said the loud soldier.

"Well," cried the youth, still fidgeting, "I'd rather do anything 'most than go tramping 'round the country all day doing no good to nobody and jest tiring ourselves out."

"So would I," said the loud soldier. "It ain't right. I tell you if anybody with any sense was a-runnin' this army it —"

"Oh, shut up!" roared the tall private. "You little fool. You little damn' cuss. You ain't had that there coat and them pants on for six months, and yet you talk as if —"

"Well, I wanta do some fighting anyway," interrupted the other. "I didn't come here to walk. I could 'ave walked to home — 'round an' 'round the barn, if I jest wanted to walk."

The tall one, red-faced, swallowed another sandwich as if taking poison in despair.

But gradually, as he chewed, his face became again quiet and contented. He could not rage in fierce argument in the presence of such sandwiches. During his meals he always wore an air of blissful contemplation of the food he had swallowed. His spirit seemed then to be communing with the viands.

He accepted new environment and circumstance with great coolness, eating from his haversack at every opportunity. On the march he went along with the stride of a hunter, objecting to neither gait nor distance. And he had not raised his voice when he had been ordered away from three little protective piles of earth and stone, each of which had been an engineering feat worthy of being made sacred to the name of his grandmother.

In the afternoon the regiment went out over the same ground it had taken in the morning. The landscape then ceased to threaten the youth. He had been close to it and become familiar with it.

When, however, they began to pass into a new region, his old fears of stupidity and incompetence reassailed him, but this time he doggedly let them babble. He was occupied with his problem, and in his desperation he concluded that the stupidity did not greatly matter.

Once he thought he had concluded that it would be better to get killed directly and end his troubles. Regarding death thus out of the corner of his eye, he conceived it to be nothing but rest, and he was filled with a momentary astonishment that he should have made an extraordinary commotion over the mere matter of getting killed. He would die; he would go to some place where he would be understood. It was useless to expect appreciation of his profound and fine senses from such men as the lieutenant. He must look to the grave for comprehension.

The skirmish fire increased to a long chattering sound. With it was mingled far-away cheering. A battery spoke.

Directly the youth would see the skirmishers running. They were pursued by the sound of musketry fire. After a time the hot, dangerous flashes of the rifles were visible. Smoke clouds went slowly and insolently across the fields like observant phantoms. The din became crescendo, like the roar of an oncoming train.

A brigade ahead of them and on the right went into action with a rending roar. It was as if it had exploded. And thereafter it lay stretched in the distance behind a long gray wall, that one was obliged to look twice at to make sure that it was smoke.

The youth, forgetting his neat plan of getting killed, gazed spell bound. His eyes grew wide and busy with the action of the scene. His mouth was a little ways open.

Of a sudden he felt a heavy and sad hand laid upon his shoulder. Awakening from his trance of observation he turned and beheld the loud soldier.

"It's my first and last battle, old boy," said the latter, with intense gloom. He was quite pale and his girlish lip was trembling.

"Eh?" murmured the youth in great astonishment.

"It's my first and last battle, old boy," continued the loud soldier. "Something tells me —"

"What?"

"I'm a gone coon this first time and-and I w-want you to take these here things-to-my-folks." He ended in a quavering sob of pity for himself. He handed the youth a little packet done up in a yellow envelope.

"Why, what the devil—" began the youth again.

But the other gave him a glance as from the depths of a tomb, and raised his limp hand in a prophetic manner and turned away.

CHAPTER IV.

The brigade was halted in the fringe of a grove. The men crouched among the trees and pointed their restless guns out at the fields. They tried to look beyond the smoke.

Out of this haze they could see running men. Some shouted information and gestured as they hurried.

The men of the new regiment watched and listened eagerly, while their tongues ran on in gossip of the battle. They mouthed rumors that had flown like birds out of the unknown.

"They say Perry has been driven in with big loss."

"Yes, Carrott went t' th' hospital. He said he was sick. That smart lieutenant is commanding 'G' Company. Th' boys say they won't be under Carrott no more if they all have t' desert. They allus knew he was a —"

"Hannises' batt'ry is took."

"It ain't either. I saw Hannises' batt'ry off on th' left not more'n fifteen minutes ago."

"Well —"

"Th' general, he ses he is goin' t' take th' hull cammand of th' 304th when we go inteh action, an' then he ses we'll do sech fightin' as never another one reg'ment done."

"They say we're catchin' it over on th' left. They say th' enemy driv' our line inteh a devil of a swamp an' took Hannises' batt'ry."

"No sech thing. Hannises' batt'ry was 'long here 'bout a minute ago."

"That young Hasbrouck, he makes a good off'cer. He ain't afraid 'a nothin'."

"I met one of th' 148th Maine boys an' he ses his brigade fit th' hull rebel army fer four hours over on th' turnpike road an' killed about five thousand of 'em. He ses one more sech fight as that an' th' war 'll be over."

"Bill wasn't scared either. No, sir! It wasn't that. Bill ain't a-gittin' scared easy. He was jest mad, that's what he was. When that feller trod on his hand, he up an' sed that he was willin' t' give his hand t' his country, but he be dumbed if he was goin' t' have every dumb bushwhacker in th' kentry walkin' 'round on it. Se he went t' th' hospital disregardless of th' fight. Three fingers was crunched. Th' dern doctor wanted t' amputate 'm, an' Bill, he raised a heluva row, I hear. He's a funny feller."

The din in front swelled to a tremendous chorus. The youth and his fellows were frozen to silence. They could see a flag that tossed in the smoke angrily. Near it were the blurred and agitated forms of troops. There came a turbulent stream of men across the fields. A battery changing position at a frantic gallop scattered the stragglers right and left.

A shell screaming like a storm banshee went over the huddled heads of the reserves. It landed in the grove, and exploding redly flung the brown earth. There was a little shower of pine needles.

Bullets began to whistle among the branches and nip at the trees. Twigs and leaves came sailing down. It was as if a thousand axes, wee and invisible, were being wielded. Many of the men were constantly dodging and ducking their heads.

The lieutenant of the youth's company was shot in the hand. He began to swear so wondrously that a nervous laugh went along the regimental line. The officer's profanity sounded conventional. It relieved the tightened senses of the new men. It was as if he had hit his fingers with a tack hammer at home.

He held the wounded member carefully away from his side so that the blood would not drip upon his trousers.

The captain of the company, tucking his sword under his arm, produced a handkerchief and began to bind with it the lieutenant's wound. And they disputed as to how the binding should be done.

The battle flag in the distance jerked about madly. It seemed to be struggling to free itself from an agony. The billowing smoke was filled with horizontal flashes.

Men running swiftly emerged from it. They grew in numbers until it was seen that the whole command was fleeing. The flag suddenly sank down as if dying. Its motion as it fell was a gesture of despair.

Wild yells came from behind the walls of smoke. A sketch in gray and red dissolved into a moblike body of men who galloped like wild horses.

The veteran regiments on the right and left of the 304th immediately began to jeer. With the passionate song of the bullets and the banshee shrieks of shells were mingled loud catcalls and bits of facetious advice concerning places of safety.

But the new regiment was breathless with horror. "Gawd! Saunders's got crushed!" whispered the man at the youth's elbow. They shrank back and crouched as if compelled to await a flood.

The youth shot a swift glance along the blue ranks of the regiment. The profiles were motionless, carven; and afterward he remembered that the color sergeant was standing with his legs apart, as if he expected to be pushed to the ground.

The following throng went whirling around the flank. Here and there were officers carried along on the stream like exasperated chips. They were striking about them with their swords and with their left fists, punching every head they could reach. They cursed like highwaymen.

A mounted officer displayed the furious anger of a spoiled child. He raged with his head, his arms, and his legs.

Another, the commander of the brigade, was galloping about bawling. His hat was gone and his clothes were awry. He resembled a man who has come from bed to go to a fire. The hoofs of his horse often threatened the heads of the running men, but they scampered with singular fortune. In this rush they were apparently all deaf and blind. They heeded not the largest and longest of the oaths that were thrown at them from all directions.

Frequently over this tumult could be heard the grim jokes of the critical veterans; but the retreating men apparently were not even conscious of the presence of an audience.

The battle reflection that shone for an instant in the faces on the mad current made the youth feel that forceful hands from heaven would not have been able to have held him in place if he could have got intelligent control of his legs.

There was an appalling imprint upon these faces. The struggle in the smoke had pictured an exaggeration of itself on the bleached cheeks and in the eyes wild with one desire.

The sight of this stampede exerted a floodlike force that seemed able to drag sticks and stones and men from the ground. They of the reserves had to hold on. They grew pale and firm, and red and quaking.

The youth achieved one little thought in the midst of this chaos. The composite monster which had caused the other troops to flee had not then appeared. He resolved to get a view of it, and then, he thought he might very likely run better than the best of them.

CHAPTER V.

There were moments of waiting. The youth thought of the village street at home before the arrival of the circus parade on a day in the spring. He remembered how he had stood, a small, thrillful boy, prepared to follow the dingy lady upon the white horse, or the band in its faded chariot. He saw the yellow road, the lines of expectant people, and the sober houses. He particularly remembered an old fellow who used to sit upon a cracker box in front of the store and feign to despise such exhibitions. A thousand details of color and form surged in his mind. The old fellow upon the cracker box appeared in middle prominence.

Some one cried, "Here they come!"

There was rustling and muttering among the men. They displayed a feverish desire to have every possible cartridge ready to their hands. The boxes were pulled around into various positions, and adjusted with great care. It was as if seven hundred new bonnets were being tried on.

The tall soldier, having prepared his rifle, produced a red handkerchief of some kind. He was engaged in knitting it about his throat with exquisite attention to its position, when the cry was repeated up and down the line in a muffled roar of sound.

"Here they come! Here they come!" Gun locks clicked.

Across the smoke-infested fields came a brown swarm of running men who were giving shrill yells. They came on, stooping and swinging their rifles at all angles. A flag, tilted forward, sped near the front.

As he caught sight of them the youth was momentarily startled by a thought that perhaps his gun was not loaded. He stood trying to rally his faltering intellect so that he might recollect the moment when he had loaded, but he could not.

A hatless general pulled his dripping horse to a stand near the colonel of the 304th. He shook his fist in the other's face. "You 've got to hold 'em back!" he shouted, savagely; "you 've got to hold 'em back!"

In his agitation the colonel began to stammer. "A-all r-right, General, all right, by Gawd! We-we'll do our-we-we'll d-d-do-do our best, General." The general made a passionate gesture and galloped away. The colonel, perchance to relieve his feelings, began to scold like a wet parrot. The youth, turning swiftly to make sure that the rear was unmolested, saw the commander regarding his men in a highly regretful manner, as if he regretted above everything his association with them.

The man at the youth's elbow was mumbling, as if to himself: "Oh, we 're in for it now! oh, we 're in for it now!"

The captain of the company had been pacing excitedly to and fro in the rear. He coaxed in schoolmistress fashion, as to a congregation of boys with primers. His talk was an endless repetition. "Reserve your fire, boys-don't shoot till I tell you-save your fire-wait till they get close up-don't be damned fools—"

Perspiration streamed down the youth's face, which was soiled like that of a weeping urchin. He frequently, with a nervous movement, wiped his eyes with his coat sleeve. His mouth was still a little ways open.

He got the one glance at the foe-swarming field in front of him, and instantly ceased to debate the question of his piece being loaded. Before he was ready to begin-before he had announced to himself that he was about to fight-he threw the obedient, well-balanced rifle into position and fired a first wild shot. Directly he was working at his weapon like an automatic affair.

He suddenly lost concern for himself, and forgot to look at a menacing fate. He became not a man but a member. He felt that something of which he was a part—a regiment, an army, a cause, or a country-was in a crisis. He was welded into a common personality which was dominated by a single desire. For some moments he could not flee no more than a little finger can commit a revolution from a hand.

If he had thought the regiment was about to be annihilated perhaps he could have amputated himself from it. But its noise gave him assurance. The regiment was like a firework that, once ignited, proceeds superior to circumstances until its blazing vitality fades. It wheezed and banged with a mighty power. He pictured the ground before it as strewn with the discomfited.

There was a consciousness always of the presence of his comrades about him. He felt the subtle battle brotherhood more potent even than the cause for which they were fighting. It was a mysterious fraternity born of the smoke and danger of death.

He was at a task. He was like a carpenter who has made many boxes, making still another box, only there was furious haste in his movements. He, in his thought, was careering off in other places, even as the carpenter who as he works whistles and thinks of his friend or his enemy, his home or a saloon. And these jolted dreams were never perfect to him afterward, but remained a mass of blurred shapes.

Presently he began to feel the effects of the war atmosphere —a blistering sweat, a sensation that his eyeballs were about to crack like hot stones. A burning roar filled his ears.

Following this came a red rage. He developed the acute exasperation of a pestered animal, a well-meaning cow worried by dogs. He had a mad feeling against his rifle, which could only be used against one life at a time. He wished to rush forward and strangle with his fingers. He craved a power that would enable him to make a world-sweeping gesture and brush all back. His impotency appeared to him, and made his rage into that of a driven beast.

Buried in the smoke of many rifles his anger was directed not so much against the men whom he knew were rushing toward him as against the swirling battle phantoms which were choking him, stuffing their smoke robes down his parched throat. He fought frantically for respite for his senses, for air, as a babe being smothered attacks the deadly blankets.

There was a blare of heated rage mingled with a certain expression of intentness on all faces. Many of the men were making low-toned noises with their mouths, and these subdued cheers, snarls, imprecations, prayers, made a wild, barbaric song that went as an undercurrent of sound, strange and chantlike with the resounding chords of the war march. The man at the youth's elbow was babbling. In it there was something soft and tender like the monologue of a babe. The tall soldier was swearing in a loud voice. From his lips came a black procession of curious oaths. Of a sudden another broke out in a querulous way like a man who has mislaid his hat. "Well, why don't they support us? Why don't they send supports? Do they think—"

The youth in his battle sleep heard this as one who dozes hears.

There was a singular absence of heroic poses. The men bending and surging in their haste and rage were in every impossible attitude. The steel ramrods clanked and clanged with incessant din as the men pounded them furiously into the hot rifle barrels. The flaps of the cartridge boxes were all unfastened, and bobbed idiotically with each movement. The rifles, once loaded, were jerked to the shoulder and fired without apparent aim into the smoke or at one of the blurred and shifting forms which upon the field before the regiment had been growing larger and larger like puppets under a magician's hand.

The officers, at their intervals, rearward, neglected to stand in picturesque attitudes. They were bobbing to and fro roaring directions and encouragements. The dimensions of their howls were extraordinary. They expended their lungs with prodigal wills. And often they nearly stood upon their heads in their anxiety to observe the enemy on the other side of the tumbling smoke.

The lieutenant of the youth's company had encountered a soldier who had fled screaming at the first volley of his comrades. Behind the lines these two were acting a little isolated scene. The man was blubbering and staring with sheeplike eyes at the lieutenant, who had seized him by the collar and was pommeling him. He drove him back into the ranks with many blows. The soldier went mechanically, dully, with his animal-like eyes upon the officer. Perhaps there was to him a divinity expressed in the voice of the other-stern, hard, with no reflection of fear in it. He tried to reload his gun, but his shaking hands prevented. The lieutenant was obliged to assist him.

The men dropped here and there like bundles. The captain of the youth's company had been killed in an early part of the action. His body lay stretched out in the position of a tired man resting, but upon his face there was an astonished and sorrowful look, as if he thought some friend had done him an ill turn. The babbling man was grazed by a shot that made the blood stream widely down his face. He clapped both hands to his head. "Oh!" he said, and ran. Another grunted suddenly as if he had been struck by a club in the stomach. He sat down and gazed ruefully. In his eyes there was mute, indefinite reproach. Farther up the line a man, standing behind a tree, had had his knee joint splintered by a ball. Immediately he had dropped his rifle and gripped the tree with both arms. And there he remained, clinging desperately and crying for assistance that he might withdraw his hold upon the tree.

At last an exultant yell went along the quivering line. The firing dwindled from an uproar to a last vindictive popping. As the smoke slowly eddied away, the youth saw that the charge had been repulsed. The enemy were scattered into reluctant groups. He saw a man climb to the top of the fence, straddle the rail, and fire a parting shot. The waves had receded, leaving bits of dark *débris* upon the ground.

Some in the regiment began to whoop frenziedly. Many were silent. Apparently they were trying to contemplate themselves.

After the fever had left his veins, the youth thought that at last he was going to suffocate. He became aware of the foul atmosphere in which he had been struggling. He was grimy and dripping like a laborer in a foundry. He grasped his canteen and took a long swallow of the warmed water.

A sentence with variations went up and down the line. "Well, we 've helt 'em back. We 've helt 'em back; derned if we haven't." The men said it blissfully, leering at each other with dirty smiles.

The youth turned to look behind him and off to the right and off to the left. He experienced the joy of a man who at last finds leisure in which to look about him.

Under foot there were a few ghastly forms motionless. They lay twisted in fantastic contortions. Arms were bent and heads were turned in incredible ways. It seemed that the dead men must have fallen from some great height to get into such positions. They looked to be dumped out upon the ground from the sky.

From a position in the rear of the grove a battery was throwing shells over it. The flash of the guns startled the youth at first. He thought they were aimed directly at him. Through the trees he watched the black figures of the gunners as they worked swiftly and intently. Their labor seemed a complicated thing. He wondered how they could remember its formula in the midst of confusion.

The guns squatted in a row like savage chiefs. They argued with abrupt violence. It was a grim pow-wow. Their busy servants ran hither and thither.

A small procession of wounded men were going drearily toward the rear. It was a flow of blood from the torn body of the brigade.

To the right and to the left were the dark lines of other troops. Far in front he thought he could see lighter masses protruding in points from the forest. They were suggestive of unnumbered thousands.

Once he saw a tiny battery go dashing along the line of the horizon. The tiny riders were beating the tiny horses.

From a sloping hill came the sound of cheerings and clashes. Smoke welled slowly through the leaves.

Batteries were speaking with thunderous oratorical effort. Here and there were flags, the red in the stripes dominating. They splashed bits of warm color upon the dark lines of troops.

The youth felt the old thrill at the sight of the emblem. They were like beautiful birds strangely undaunted in a storm.

As he listened to the din from the hillside, to a deep pulsating thunder that came from afar to the left, and to the lesser clamors which came from many directions, it occurred to him that they were fighting, too, over there, and over there, and over there. Heretofore he had supposed that all the battle was directly under his nose.

As he gazed around him the youth felt a flash of astonishment at the blue, pure sky and the sun gleamings on the trees and fields. It was surprising that Nature had gone tranquilly on with her golden process in the midst of so much devilment.

CHAPTER VI.

The youth awakened slowly. He came gradually back to a position from which he could regard himself. For moments he had been scrutinizing his person in a dazed way as if he had never before seen himself. Then he picked up his cap from the ground. He wriggled in his jacket to make a more comfortable fit, and kneeling relaced his shoe. He thoughtfully mopped his reeking features.

So it was all over at last! The supreme trial had been passed. The red, formidable difficulties of war had been vanquished.

He went into an ecstasy of self-satisfaction. He had the most delightful sensations of his life. Standing as if apart from himself, he viewed that last scene. He perceived that the man who had fought thus was magnificent.

He felt that he was a fine fellow. He saw himself even with those ideals which he had considered as far beyond him. He smiled in deep gratification.

Upon his fellows he beamed tenderness and good will. "Gee! ain't it hot, hey?" he said affably to a man who was polishing his streaming face with his coat sleeves.

"You bet!" said the other, grinning sociably. "I never seen sech dumb hotness." He sprawled out luxuriously on the ground. "Gee, yes! An' I hope we don't have no more fightin' till a week from Monday."

There were some handshakings and deep speeches with men whose features were familiar, but with whom the youth now felt the bonds of tied hearts. He helped a cursing comrade to bind up a wound of the shin.

But, of a sudden, cries of amazement broke out along the ranks of the new regiment. "Here they come ag'in! Here they come ag'in!" The man who had sprawled upon the ground started up and said, "Gosh!"

The youth turned quick eyes upon the field. He discerned forms begin to swell in masses out of a distant wood. He again saw the tilted flag speeding forward.

The shells, which had ceased to trouble the regiment for a time, came swirling again, and exploded in the grass or among the leaves of the trees. They looked to be strange war flowers bursting into fierce bloom.

The men groaned. The luster faded from their eyes. Their smudged countenances now expressed a profound dejection. They moved their stiffened bodies slowly, and watched in sullen mood the frantic approach of the enemy. The slaves toiling in the temple of this god began to feel rebellion at his harsh tasks.

They fretted and complained each to each. "Oh, say, this is too much of a good thing! Why can't somebody send us supports?"

"We ain't never goin' to stand this second banging. I didn't come here to fight the hull damn' rebel army."

There was one who raised a doleful cry. "I wish Bill Smithers had trod on my hand, insteader me treddin' on his'n." The sore joints of the regiment creaked as it painfully floundered into position to repulse.

The youth stared. Surely, he thought, this impossible thing was not about to happen. He waited as if he expected the enemy to suddenly stop, apologize, and retire bowing. It was all a mistake.

But the firing began somewhere on the regimental line and ripped along in both directions. The level sheets of flame developed great clouds of smoke that tumbled and tossed in the mild wind near the ground for a moment, and then rolled through the ranks as through a gate. The clouds were tinged an earthlike yellow in the sunrays and in the shadow were a sorry blue. The flag was sometimes eaten and lost in this mass of vapor, but more often it projected, suntouched, resplendent.

Into the youth's eyes there came a look that one can see in the orbs of a jaded horse. His neck was quivering with nervous weakness and the muscles of his arms felt numb and bloodless.

His hands, too, seemed large and awkward as if he was wearing invisible mittens. And there was a great uncertainty about his knee joints.

The words that comrades had uttered previous to the firing began to recur to him. "Oh, say, this is too much of a good thing! What do they take us for—why don't they send supports? I didn't come here to fight the hull damned rebel army."

He began to exaggerate the endurance, the skill, and the valor of those who were coming. Himself reeling from exhaustion, he was astonished beyond measure at such persistency. They must be machines of steel. It was very gloomy struggling against such affairs, wound up perhaps to fight until sundown.

He slowly lifted his rifle and catching a glimpse of the thickspread field he blazed at a cantering cluster. He stopped then and began to peer as best he could through the smoke. He caught changing views of the ground covered with men who were all running like pursued imps, and yelling.

To the youth it was an onslaught of redoubtable dragons. He became like the man who lost his legs at the approach of the red and green monster. He waited in a sort of a horrified, listening attitude. He seemed to shut his eyes and wait to be gobbled.

A man near him who up to this time had been working feverishly at his rifle suddenly stopped and ran with howls. A lad whose face had borne an expression of exalted courage, the majesty of he who dares give his life, was, at an instant, smitten abject. He blanched like one who has come to the edge of a cliff at midnight and is suddenly made aware. There was a revelation. He, too, threw down his gun and fled. There was no shame in his face. He ran like a rabbit.

Others began to scamper away through the smoke. The youth turned his head, shaken from his trance by this movement as if the regiment was leaving him behind. He saw the few fleeting forms.

He yelled then with fright and swung about. For a moment, in the great clamor, he was like a proverbial chicken. He lost the direction of safety. Destruction threatened him from all points.

Directly he began to speed toward the rear in great leaps. His rifle and cap were gone. His unbuttoned coat bulged in the wind. The flap of his cartridge box bobbed wildly, and his canteen, by its slender cord, swung out behind. On his face was all the horror of those things which he imagined.

The lieutenant sprang forward bawling. The youth saw his features wrathfully red, and saw him make a dab with his sword. His one thought of the incident was that the lieutenant was a peculiar creature to feel interested in such matters upon this occasion.

He ran like a blind man. Two or three times he fell down. Once he knocked his shoulder so heavily against a tree that he went headlong.

Since he had turned his back upon the fight his fears had been wondrously magnified. Death about to thrust him between the shoulder blades was far more dreadful than death about to smite him between the eyes. When he thought of it later, he conceived the impression that it is better to view the appalling than to be merely within hearing. The noises of the battle were like stones; he believed himself liable to be crushed.

As he ran he mingled with others. He dimly saw men on his right and on his left, and he heard footsteps behind him. He thought that all the regiment was fleeing, pursued by these ominous crashes.

In his flight the sound of these following footsteps gave him his one meager relief. He felt vaguely that death must make a first choice of the men who were nearest; the initial morsels for the dragons would be then those who were following him. So he displayed the zeal of an insane sprinter in his purpose to keep them in the rear. There was a race.

As he, leading, went across a little field, he found himself in a region of shells. They hurtled over his head with long wild screams. As he listened he imagined them to have rows of cruel teeth that grinned at him. Once one lit before him and the livid lightning of the explosion effectually barred the way in his chosen direction. He groveled on the ground and then springing up went careering off through some bushes.

He experienced a thrill of amazement when he came within view of a battery in action. The men there seemed to be in conventional moods, altogether unaware of the impending annihilation. The battery was disputing with a distant antagonist and the gunners were wrapped in admiration of their shooting. They were continually bending in coaxing postures over the guns. They seemed to be patting them on the back and encouraging them with words. The guns, stolid and undaunted, spoke with dogged valor.

The precise gunners were coolly enthusiastic. They lifted their eyes every chance to the smoke-wreathed hillock from whence the hostile battery addressed them. The youth pitied them as he ran. Methodical idiots! Machine-like fools! The refined joy of planting shells in the midst of the other battery's formation would appear a little thing when the infantry came swooping out of the woods.

The face of a youthful rider, who was jerking his frantic horse with an abandon of temper he might display in a placid barnyard, was impressed deeply upon his mind. He knew that he looked upon a man who would presently be dead.

Too, he felt a pity for the guns, standing, six good comrades, in a bold row.

He saw a brigade going to the relief of its pestered fellows. He scrambled upon a wee hill and watched it sweeping finely, keeping formation in difficult places. The blue of the line was crusted with steel color, and the brilliant flags projected. Officers were shouting.

This sight also filled him with wonder. The brigade was hurrying briskly to be gulped into the infernal mouths of the war god. What manner of men were they, anyhow? Ah, it was some wondrous breed! Or else they didn't comprehend-the fools.

A furious order caused commotion in the artillery. An officer on a bounding horse made maniacal motions with his arms. The teams went swinging up from the rear, the guns were whirled about, and the battery scampered away. The cannon with their noses poked slantingly at the ground grunted and grumbled like stout men, brave but with objections to hurry.

The youth went on, moderating his pace since he had left the place of noises.

Later he came upon a general of division seated upon a horse that pricked its ears in an interested way at the battle. There was a great gleaming of yellow and patent leather about the saddle and bridle. The quiet man astride looked mouse-colored upon such a splendid charger.

A jingling staff was galloping hither and thither. Sometimes the general was surrounded by horsemen and at other times he was quite alone. He looked to be much harassed. He had the appearance of a business man whose market is swinging up and down.

The youth went slinking around this spot. He went as near as he dared trying to overhear words. Perhaps the general, unable to comprehend chaos, might call upon him for information. And he could tell him. He knew all concerning it. Of a surety the force was in a fix, and any fool could see that if they did not retreat while they had opportunity-why —

He felt that he would like to thrash the general, or at least approach and tell him in plain words exactly what he thought him to be. It was criminal to stay calmly in one spot and make no effort to stay destruction. He loitered in a fever of eagerness for the division commander to apply to him.

As he warily moved about, he heard the general call out irritably: "Tompkins, go over an' see Taylor, an' tell him not t' be in such an all-fired hurry; tell him t' halt his brigade in th' edge of th' woods; tell him t' detach a reg'ment-say I think th' center 'll break if we don't help it out some; tell him t' hurry up."

A slim youth on a fine chestnut horse caught these swift words from the mouth of his superior. He made his horse bound into a gallop almost from a walk in his haste to go upon his mission. There was a cloud of dust.

A moment later the youth saw the general bounce excitedly in his saddle.

"Yes, by heavens, they have!" The officer leaned forward. His face was aflame with excitement. "Yes, by heavens, they 've held 'im! They 've held 'im!"

He began to blithely roar at his staff: "We'll wallop 'im now. We'll wallop 'im now. We've got 'em sure." He turned suddenly upon an aid: "Here-you-Jones-quick-ride after Tompkins-see Taylor-tell him t' go in-everlastingly-like blazes-anything."

As another officer sped his horse after the first messenger, the general beamed upon the earth like a sun. In his eyes was a desire to chant a paean. He kept repeating, "They've held 'em, by heavens!"

His excitement made his horse plunge, and he merrily kicked and swore at it. He held a little carnival of joy on horseback.

CHAPTER VII.

The youth cringed as if discovered in a crime. By heavens, they had won after all! The imbecile line had remained and become victors. He could hear cheering.

He lifted himself upon his toes and looked in the direction of the fight. A yellow fog lay wallowing on the treetops. From beneath it came the clatter of musketry. Hoarse cries told of an advance.

He turned away amazed and angry. He felt that he had been wronged.

He had fled, he told himself, because annihilation approached. He had done a good part in saving himself, who was a little piece of the army. He had considered the time, he said, to be one in which it was the duty of every little piece to rescue itself if possible. Later the officers could fit the little pieces together again, and make a battle front. If none of the little pieces were wise enough to save themselves from the flurry of death at such a time, why, then, where would be the army? It was all plain that he had proceeded according to very correct and commendable rules. His actions had been sagacious things. They had been full of strategy. They were the work of a master's legs.

Thoughts of his comrades came to him. The brittle blue line had withstood the blows and won. He grew bitter over it. It seemed that the blind ignorance and stupidity of those little pieces had betrayed him. He had been overturned and crushed by their lack of sense in holding the position, when intelligent deliberation would have convinced them that it was impossible. He, the enlightened man who looks afar in the dark, had fled because of his superior perceptions and knowledge. He felt a great anger against his comrades. He knew it could be proved that they had been fools.

He wondered what they would remark when later he appeared in camp. His mind heard howls of derision. Their density would not enable them to understand his sharper point of view.

He began to pity himself acutely. He was ill used. He was trodden beneath the feet of an iron injustice. He had proceeded with wisdom and from the most righteous motives under heaven's blue only to be frustrated by hateful circumstances.

A dull, animal-like rebellion against his fellows, war in the abstract, and fate grew within him. He shambled along with bowed head, his brain in a tumult of agony and despair. When he looked loweringly up, quivering at each sound, his eyes had the expression of those of a criminal who thinks his guilt and his punishment great, and knows that he can find no words.

He went from the fields into a thick woods, as if resolved to bury himself. He wished to get out of hearing of the crackling shots which were to him like voices.

The ground was cluttered with vines and bushes, and the trees grew close and spread out like bouquets. He was obliged to force his way with much noise. The creepers, catching against his legs, cried out harshly as their sprays were torn from the barks of trees. The swishing saplings tried to make known his presence to the world. He could not conciliate the forest. As he made his way, it was always calling out protestations. When he separated embraces of trees and vines the disturbed foliages waved their arms and turned their face leaves toward him. He dreaded lest these noisy motions and cries should bring men to look at him. So he went far, seeking dark and intricate places.

After a time the sound of musketry grew faint and the cannon boomed in the distance. The sun, suddenly apparent, blazed among the trees. The insects were making rhythmical noises. They seemed to be grinding their teeth in unison. A woodpecker stuck his impudent head around the side of a tree. A bird flew on lighthearted wing.

Off was the rumble of death. It seemed now that Nature had no ears.

This landscape gave him assurance. A fair field holding life. It was the religion of peace. It would die if its timid eyes were compelled to see blood. He conceived Nature to be a woman with a deep aversion to tragedy.

He threw a pine cone at a jovial squirrel, and he ran with chattering fear. High in a treetop he stopped, and, poking his head cautiously from behind a branch, looked down with an air of trepidation.

The youth felt triumphant at this exhibition. There was the law, he said. Nature had given him a sign. The squirrel, immediately upon recognizing danger, had taken to his legs without ado. He did not stand stolidly baring his furry belly to the missile, and die with an upward glance at the sympathetic heavens. On the contrary, he had fled as fast as his legs could carry him; and he was but an ordinary squirrel, too-doubtless no philosopher of his race. The youth wended, feeling that Nature was of his mind. She re-enforced his argument with proofs that lived where the sun shone.

Once he found himself almost into a swamp. He was obliged to walk upon bog tufts and watch his feet to keep from the oily mire. Pausing at one time to look about him he saw, out at some black water, a small animal pounce in and emerge directly with a gleaming fish.

The youth went again into the deep thickets. The brushed branches made a noise that drowned the sounds of cannon. He walked on, going from obscurity into promises of a greater obscurity.

At length he reached a place where the high, arching boughs made a chapel. He softly pushed the green doors aside and entered. Pine needles were a gentle brown carpet. There was a religious half light.

Near the threshold he stopped, horror-stricken at the sight of a thing.

He was being looked at by a dead man who was seated with his back against a columnlike tree. The corpse was dressed in a uniform that once had been blue, but was now faded to a melancholy shade of green. The eyes, staring at the youth, had changed to the dull hue to be seen on the side of a dead fish. The mouth was open. Its red had changed to an appalling yellow. Over the gray skin of the face ran little ants. One was trundling some sort of a bundle along the upper lip.

The youth gave a shriek as he confronted the thing. He was for moments turned to stone before it. He remained staring into the liquid-looking eyes. The dead man and the living man exchanged a long look. Then the youth cautiously put one hand behind him and brought it against a tree. Leaning upon this he retreated, step by step, with his face still toward the thing. He feared that if he turned his back the body might spring up and stealthily pursue him.

The branches, pushing against him, threatened to throw him over upon it. His unguided feet, too, caught aggravatingly in brambles; and with it all he received a subtle suggestion to touch the corpse. As he thought of his hand upon it he shuddered profoundly.

At last he burst the bonds which had fastened him to the spot and fled, unheeding the underbrush. He was pursued by a sight of the black ants swarming greedily upon the gray face and venturing horribly near to the eyes.

After a time he paused, and, breathless and panting, listened. He imagined some strange voice would come from the dead throat and squawk after him in horrible menaces.

The trees about the portal of the chapel moved soughingly in a soft wind. A sad silence was upon the little guarding edifice.

CHAPTER VIII.

The trees began softly to sing a hymn of twilight. The sun sank until slanted bronze rays struck the forest. There was a lull in the noises of insects as if they had bowed their beaks and were making a devotional pause. There was silence save for the chanted chorus of the trees.

Then, upon this stillness, there suddenly broke a tremendous clangor of sounds. A crimson roar came from the distance.

The youth stopped. He was transfixed by this terrific medley of all noises. It was as if worlds were being rended. There was the ripping sound of musketry and the breaking crash of the artillery.

His mind flew in all directions. He conceived the two armies to be at each other panther fashion. He listened for a time. Then he began to run in the direction of the battle. He saw that it was an ironical thing for him to be running thus toward that which he had been at such pains to avoid. But he said, in substance, to himself that if the earth and the moon were about to clash, many persons would doubtless plan to get upon the roofs to witness the collision.

As he ran, he became aware that the forest had stopped its music, as if at last becoming capable of hearing the foreign sounds. The trees hushed and stood motionless. Everything seemed to be listening to the crackle and clatter and earshaking thunder. The chorus pealed over the still earth.

It suddenly occurred to the youth that the fight in which he had been was, after all, but perfunctory popping. In the hearing of this present din he was doubtful if he had seen real battle scenes. This uproar explained a celestial battle; it was tumbling hordes a-struggle in the air.

Reflecting, he saw a sort of a humor in the point of view of himself and his fellows during the late encounter. They had taken themselves and the enemy very seriously and had imagined that they were deciding the war. Individuals must have supposed that they were cutting the letters of their names deep into everlasting tablets of brass, or enshrining their reputations forever in the hearts of their countrymen, while, as to fact, the affair would appear in printed reports under a meek and immaterial title. But he saw that it was good, else, he said, in battle every one would surely run save forlorn hopes and their ilk.

He went rapidly on. He wished to come to the edge of the forest that he might peer out.

As he hastened, there passed through his mind pictures of stupendous conflicts. His accumulated thought upon such subjects was used to form scenes. The noise was as the voice of an eloquent being, describing.

Sometimes the brambles formed chains and tried to hold him back. Trees, confronting him, stretched out their arms and forbade him to pass. After its previous hostility this new resistance of the forest filled him with a fine bitterness. It seemed that Nature could not be quite ready to kill him.

But he obstinately took roundabout ways, and presently he was where he could see long gray walls of vapor where lay battle lines. The voices of cannon shook him. The musketry sounded in long irregular surges that played havoc with his ears. He stood regardant for a moment. His eyes had an awestruck expression. He gawked in the direction of the fight.

Presently he proceeded again on his forward way. The battle was like the grinding of an immense and terrible machine to him. Its complexities and powers, its grim processes, fascinated him. He must go close and see it produce corpses.

He came to a fence and clambered over it. On the far side, the ground was littered with clothes and guns. A newspaper, folded up, lay in the dirt. A dead soldier was stretched with his face hidden in his arm. Farther off there was a group of four or five corpses keeping mournful company. A hot sun had blazed upon the spot.

In this place the youth felt that he was an invader. This forgotten part of the battle ground was owned by the dead men, and he hurried, in the vague apprehension that one of the swollen forms would rise and tell him to begone.

He came finally to a road from which he could see in the distance dark and agitated bodies of troops, smoke-fringed. In the lane was a blood-stained crowd streaming to the rear. The wounded men were cursing, groaning, and wailing. In the air, always, was a mighty swell of sound that it seemed could sway the earth. With the courageous words of the artillery and the spiteful sentences of the musketry mingled red cheers. And from this region of noises came the steady current of the maimed.

One of the wounded men had a shoeful of blood. He hopped like a schoolboy in a game. He was laughing hysterically.

One was swearing that he had been shot in the arm through the commanding general's mismanagement of the army. One was marching with an air imitative of some sublime drum major. Upon his features was an unholy mixture of merriment and agony. As he marched he sang a bit of doggerel in a high and quavering voice:

> "Sing a song 'a vic'try,
> A pocketful 'a bullets,
> Five an' twenty dead men
> Baked in a—pie."

Parts of the procession limped and staggered to this tune.

Another had the gray seal of death already upon his face. His lips were curled in hard lines and his teeth were clinched. His hands were bloody from where he had pressed them upon his wound. He seemed to be awaiting the moment when he should pitch headlong. He stalked like the specter of a soldier, his eyes burning with the power of a stare into the unknown.

There were some who proceeded sullenly, full of anger at their wounds, and ready to turn upon anything as an obscure cause.

An officer was carried along by two privates. He was peevish. "Don't joggle so, Johnson, yeh fool," he cried. "Think m' leg is made of iron? If yeh can't carry me decent, put me down an' let some one else do it."

He bellowed at the tottering crowd who blocked the quick march of his bearers. "Say, make way there, can't yeh? Make way, dickens take it all."

They sulkily parted and went to the roadsides. As he was carried past they made pert remarks to him. When he raged in reply and threatened them, they told him to be damned.

The shoulder of one of the tramping bearers knocked heavily against the spectral soldier who was staring into the unknown.

The youth joined this crowd and marched along with it. The torn bodies expressed the awful machinery in which the men had been entangled.

Orderlies and couriers occasionally broke through the throng in the roadway, scattering wounded men right and left, galloping on followed by howls. The melancholy march was continually disturbed by the messengers, and sometimes by bustling batteries that came swinging and thumping down upon them, the officers shouting orders to clear the way.

There was a tattered man, fouled with dust, blood and powder stain from hair to shoes, who trudged quietly at the youth's side. He was listening with eagerness and much humility to the lurid descriptions of a bearded sergeant. His lean features wore an expression of awe and admiration. He was like a listener in a country store to wondrous tales told among the sugar barrels. He eyed the story-teller with unspeakable wonder. His mouth was agape in yokel fashion.

The sergeant, taking note of this, gave pause to his elaborate history while he administered a sardonic comment. "Be keerful, honey, you'll be a-ketchin' flies," he said.

The tattered man shrank back abashed.

After a time he began to sidle near to the youth, and in a different way try to make him a friend. His voice was gentle as a girl's voice and his eyes were pleading. The youth saw with surprise that the soldier had two wounds, one in the head, bound with a blood-soaked rag, and the other in the arm, making that member dangle like a broken bough.

After they had walked together for some time the tattered man mustered sufficient courage to speak. "Was pretty good fight, wa'n't it?" he timidly said. The youth, deep in thought, glanced up at the bloody and grim figure with its lamblike eyes. "What?"

"Was pretty good fight, wa'n't it?

"Yes," said the youth shortly. He quickened his pace.

But the other hobbled industriously after him. There was an air of apology in his manner, but he evidently thought that he needed only to talk for a time, and the youth would perceive that he was a good fellow.

"Was pretty good fight, wa'n't it?" he began in a small voice, and then he achieved the fortitude to continue. "Dern me if I ever see fellers fight so. Laws, how they did fight! I knowed th' boys 'd like when they onct got square at it. Th' boys ain't had no fair chanct up t' now, but this time they showed what they was. I knowed it 'd turn out this way. Yeh can't lick them boys. No, sir! They're fighters, they be."

He breathed a deep breath of humble admiration. He had looked at the youth for encouragement several times. He received none, but gradually he seemed to get absorbed in his subject.

"I was talkin' 'cross pickets with a boy from Georgie, onct, an' that boy, he ses, 'Your fellers 'll all run like hell when they onct hearn a gun,' he ses. 'Mebbe they will,' I ses, 'but I don't b'lieve none of it,' I ses; 'an' b'jiminey,' I ses back t' 'um, 'mebbe your fellers 'll all run like hell when they onct hearn a gun,' I ses. He larfed. Well, they didn't run t' day, did they, hey? No, sir! They fit, an' fit, an' fit."

His homely face was suffused with a light of love for the army which was to him all things beautiful and powerful.

After a time he turned to the youth. "Where yeh hit, ol' boy?" he asked in a brotherly tone.

The youth felt instant panic at this question, although at first its full import was not borne in upon him.

"What?" he asked.

"Where yeh hit?" repeated the tattered man.

"Why," began the youth, "I—I—that is-why—I—"

He turned away suddenly and slid through the crowd. His brow was heavily flushed, and his fingers were picking nervously at one of his buttons. He bent his head and fastened his eyes studiously upon the button as if it were a little problem.

The tattered man looked after him in astonishment.

CHAPTER IX.

The youth fell back in the procession until the tattered soldier was not in sight. Then he started to walk on with the others.

But he was amid wounds. The mob of men was bleeding. Because of the tattered soldier's question he now felt that his shame could be viewed. He was continually casting sidelong glances to see if the men were contemplating the letters of guilt he felt burned into his brow.

At times he regarded the wounded soldiers in an envious way. He conceived persons with torn bodies to be peculiarly happy. He wished that he, too, had a wound, a red badge of courage.

The spectral soldier was at his side like a stalking reproach. The man's eyes were still fixed in a stare into the unknown. His gray, appalling face had attracted attention in the crowd, and men, slowing to his dreary pace, were walking with him. They were discussing his plight, questioning him and giving him advice.

In a dogged way he repelled them, signing to them to go on and leave him alone. The shadows of his face were deepening and his tight lips seemed holding in check the moan of great despair. There could be seen a certain stiffness in the movements of his body, as if he were taking infinite care not to arouse the passion of his wounds. As he went on, he seemed always looking for a place, like one who goes to choose a grave.

Something in the gesture of the man as he waved the bloody and pitying soldiers away made the youth start as if bitten. He yelled in horror. Tottering forward he laid a quivering hand upon the man's arm. As the latter slowly turned his waxlike features toward him, the youth screamed:

"Gawd! Jim Conklin!"

The tall soldier made a little commonplace smile. "Hello, Henry," he said.

The youth swayed on his legs and glared strangely. He stuttered and stammered. "Oh, Jim-oh, Jim-oh, Jim —"

The tall soldier held out his gory hand. There was a curious red and black combination of new blood and old blood upon it. "Where yeh been, Henry?" he asked. He continued in a monotonous voice, "I thought mebbe yeh got keeled over. There 's been thunder t' pay t'-day. I was worryin' about it a good deal."

The youth still lamented. "Oh, Jim-oh, Jim-oh, Jim —"

"Yeh know," said the tall soldier, "I was out there." He made a careful gesture. "An', Lord, what a circus! An', b'jiminey, I got shot — I got shot. Yes, b'jiminey, I got shot." He reiterated this fact in a bewildered way, as if he did not know how it came about.

The youth put forth anxious arms to assist him, but the tall soldier went firmly on as if propelled. Since the youth's arrival as a guardian for his friend, the other wounded men had ceased to display much interest. They occupied themselves again in dragging their own tragedies toward the rear.

Suddenly, as the two friends marched on, the tall soldier seemed to be overcome by a terror. His face turned to a semblance of gray paste. He clutched the youth's arm and looked all about him, as if dreading to be overheard. Then he began to speak in a shaking whisper:

"I tell yeh what I'm 'fraid of, Henry — I 'll tell yeh what I 'm 'fraid of. I 'm 'fraid I 'll fall down-an' then yeh know-them damned artillery wagons-they like as not 'll run over me. That 's what I 'm 'fraid of—"

The youth cried out to him hysterically: "I 'll take care of yeh, Jim! I'll take care of yeh! I swear t' Gawd I will!"

"Sure-will yeh, Henry?" the tall soldier beseeched.

"Yes-yes — I tell yeh — I'll take care of yeh, Jim!" protested the youth. He could not speak accurately because of the gulpings in his throat.

But the tall soldier continued to beg in a lowly way. He now hung babelike to the youth's arm. His eyes rolled in the wildness of his terror. "I was allus a good friend t' yeh, wa'n't I, Henry? I 've allus been a pretty good feller, ain't I? An' it ain't much t' ask, is it? Jest t' pull me along outer th' road? I 'd do it fer you, Wouldn't I, Henry?"

He paused in piteous anxiety to await his friend's reply.

The youth had reached an anguish where the sobs scorched him. He strove to express his loyalty, but he could only make fantastic gestures.

However, the tall soldier seemed suddenly to forget all those fears. He became again the grim, stalking specter of a soldier. He went stonily forward. The youth wished his friend to lean upon him, but the other always shook his head and strangely protested. "No-no-no-leave me be-leave me be —"

His look was fixed again upon the unknown. He moved with mysterious purpose, and all of the youth's offers he brushed aside. "No-no-leave me be-leave me be —"

The youth had to follow.

Presently the latter heard a voice talking softly near his shoulders. Turning he saw that it belonged to the tattered soldier. "Ye 'd better take 'im outa th' road, pardner. There 's a batt'ry comin' helitywhoop down th' road an' he 'll git runned over. He 's a goner anyhow in about five minutes-yeh kin see that. Ye 'd better take 'im outa th' road. Where th' blazes does he git his stren'th from?"

"Lord knows!" cried the youth. He was shaking his hands helplessly.

He ran forward presently and grasped the tall soldier by the arm. "Jim! Jim!" he coaxed, "come with me."

The tall soldier weakly tried to wrench himself free. "Huh," he said vacantly. He stared at the youth for a moment. At last he spoke as if dimly comprehending. "Oh! Inteh th' fields? Oh!"

He started blindly through the grass.

The youth turned once to look at the lashing riders and jouncing guns of the battery. He was startled from this view by a shrill outcry from the tattered man.

"Gawd! He's runnin'!"

Turning his head swiftly, the youth saw his friend running in a staggering and stumbling way toward a little clump of bushes. His heart seemed to wrench itself almost free from his body at this sight. He made a noise of pain. He and the tattered man began a pursuit. There was a singular race.

When he overtook the tall soldier he began to plead with all the words he could find. "Jim-Jim-what are you doing-what makes you do this way-you 'll hurt yourself."

The same purpose was in the tall soldier's face. He protested in a dulled way, keeping his eyes fastened on the mystic place of his intentions. "No-no-don't tech me-leave me be-leave me be —"

The youth, aghast and filled with wonder at the tall soldier, began quaveringly to question him. "Where yeh goin', Jim? What you thinking about? Where you going? Tell me, won't you, Jim?"

The tall soldier faced about as upon relentless pursuers. In his eyes there was a great appeal. "Leave me be, can't yeh? Leave me be fer a minnit."

The youth recoiled. "Why, Jim," he said, in a dazed way, "what's the matter with you?"

The tall soldier turned and, lurching dangerously, went on. The youth and the tattered soldier followed, sneaking as if whipped, feeling unable to face the stricken man if he should again confront them. They began to have thoughts of a solemn ceremony. There was something rite-like in these movements of the doomed soldier. And there was a resemblance in him to a devotee of a mad religion, blood-sucking, muscle-wrenching, bone-crushing. They were awed and afraid. They hung back lest he have at command a dreadful weapon.

At last, they saw him stop and stand motionless. Hastening up, they perceived that his face wore an expression telling that he had at last found the place for which he had struggled. His spare figure was erect; his bloody hands were quietly at his side. He was waiting with patience for something that he had come to meet. He was at the rendezvous. They paused and stood, expectant.

There was a silence.

Finally, the chest of the doomed soldier began to heave with a strained motion. It increased in violence until it was as if an animal was within and was kicking and tumbling furiously to be free.

This spectacle of gradual strangulation made the youth writhe, and once as his friend rolled his eyes, he saw something in them that made him sink wailing to the ground. He raised his voice in a last supreme call.

"Jim-Jim-Jim —"

The tall soldier opened his lips and spoke. He made a gesture. "Leave me be-don't tech me-leave me be —"

There was another silence while he waited.

Suddenly, his form stiffened and straightened. Then it was shaken by a prolonged ague. He stared into space. To the two watchers there was a curious and profound dignity in the firm lines of his awful face.

He was invaded by a creeping strangeness that slowly enveloped him. For a moment the tremor of his legs caused him to dance a sort of hideous hornpipe. His arms beat wildly about his head in expression of implike enthusiasm.

His tall figure stretched itself to its full height. There was a slight rending sound. Then it began to swing forward, slow and straight, in the manner of a falling tree. A swift muscular contortion made the left shoulder strike the ground first.

The body seemed to bounce a little way from the earth. "God!" said the tattered soldier.

The youth had watched, spellbound, this ceremony at the place of meeting. His face had been twisted into an expression of every agony he had imagined for his friend.

He now sprang to his feet and, going closer, gazed upon the pastelike face. The mouth was open and the teeth showed in a laugh.

As the flap of the blue jacket fell away from the body, he could see that the side looked as if it had been chewed by wolves.

The youth turned, with sudden, livid rage, toward the battlefield. He shook his fist. He seemed about to deliver a philippic.

"Hell —"

The red sun was pasted in the sky like a wafer.

CHAPTER X.

The tattered man stood musing.

"Well, he was reg'lar jim-dandy fer nerve, wa'n't he," said he finally in a little awestruck voice. "A reg'lar jim-dandy." He thoughtfully poked one of the docile hands with his foot. "I wonner where he got 'is stren'th from? I never seen a man do like that before. It was a funny thing. Well, he was a reg'lar jim-dandy."

The youth desired to screech out his grief. He was stabbed, but his tongue lay dead in the tomb of his mouth. He threw himself again upon the ground and began to brood.

The tattered man stood musing.

"Look-a-here, pardner," he said, after a time. He regarded the corpse as he spoke. "He 's up an' gone, ain't 'e, an' we might as well begin t' look out fer ol' number one. This here thing is all over. He 's up an' gone, ain't 'e? An' he 's all right here. Nobody won't bother 'im. An' I must say I ain't enjoying any great health m'self these days."

The youth, awakened by the tattered soldier's tone, looked quickly up. He saw that he was swinging uncertainly on his legs and that his face had turned to a shade of blue.

"Good Lord!" he cried, "you ain't goin' t'—not you, too?"

The tattered man waved his hand. "Nary die," he said. "All I want is some pea soup an' a good bed. Some pea soup," he repeated dreamfully.

The youth arose from the ground. "I wonder where he came from. I left him over there." He pointed. "And now I find 'im here. And he was coming from over there, too." He indicated a new direction. They both turned toward the body as if to ask of it a question.

"Well," at length spoke the tattered man, "there ain't no use in our stayin' here an' tryin' t' ask him anything."

The youth nodded an assent wearily. They both turned to gaze for a moment at the corpse.

The youth murmured something.

"Well, he was a jim-dandy, wa'n't 'e?" said the tattered man as if in response.

They turned their backs upon it and started away. For a time they stole softly, treading with their toes. It remained laughing there in the grass.

"I'm commencin' t' feel pretty bad," said the tattered man, suddenly breaking one of his little silences. "I'm commencin' t' feel pretty damn' bad."

The youth groaned. "O Lord!" He wondered if he was to be the tortured witness of another grim encounter.

But his companion waved his hand reassuringly. "Oh, I'm not goin' t' die yit! There too much dependin' on me fer me t' die yit. No, sir! Nary die! I *can't*! Ye'd oughta see th' swad a' chil'ren I've got, an' all like that."

The youth glancing at his companion could see by the shadow of a smile that he was making some kind of fun.

As they plodded on the tattered soldier continued to talk. "Besides, if I died, I wouldn't die th' way that feller did. That was th' funniest thing. I'd jest flop down, I would. I never seen a feller die th' way that feller did.

"Yeh know Tom Jamison, he lives next door t' me up home. He's a nice feller, he is, an' we was allus good friends. Smart, too. Smart as a steel trap. Well, when we was a-fightin' this atternoon, all-of-a-sudden he begin t' rip up an' cuss an' beller at me. 'Yer shot, yeh blamed infernal!'—he swear horrible-he ses t' me. I put up m' hand t' m' head an' when I looked at m' fingers, I seen, sure 'nough, I was shot. I give a holler an' begin t' run, but b'fore I could git away another one hit me in th' arm an' whirl' me clean 'round. I got skeared when they was all a-shootin' b'hind me an' I run t' beat all, but I cotch it pretty bad. I've an idee I'd a' been fightin' yit, if t'was n't fer Tom Jamison."

Then he made a calm announcement: "There's two of 'em-little ones-but they 're beginnin' t' have fun with me now. I don't b'lieve I kin walk much furder."

They went slowly on in silence. "Yeh look pretty peek-ed yerself," said the tattered man at last. "I bet yeh 've got a worser one than yeh think. Ye'd better take keer of yer hurt. It don't do t' let sech things go. It might be inside mostly, an' them plays thunder. Where is it located?" But he continued his harangue without waiting for a reply. "I see 'a feller git hit plum in th' head when my reg'ment was a-standin' at ease onct. An' everybody yelled out to 'im: Hurt, John? Are yeh hurt much? 'No,' ses he. He looked kinder surprised, an' he went on tellin' 'em how he felt. He sed he didn't feel nothin'. But, by dad, th' first thing that feller knowed he was dead. Yes, he was dead-stone dead. So, yeh wanta watch out. Yeh might have some queer kind 'a hurt yerself. Yeh can't never tell. Where is your'n located?"

The youth had been wriggling since the introduction of this topic. He now gave a cry of exasperation and made a furious motion with his hand. "Oh, don't bother me!" he said. He was enraged against the tattered man, and could have strangled him. His companions seemed ever to play intolerable parts. They were ever upraising the ghost of shame on the stick of their curiosity. He turned toward the tattered man as one at bay. "Now, don't bother me," he repeated with desperate menace.

"Well, Lord knows I don't wanta bother anybody," said the other. There was a little accent of despair in his voice as he replied, "Lord knows I 've gota 'nough m' own t' tend to."

The youth, who had been holding a bitter debate with himself and casting glances of hatred and contempt at the tattered man, here spoke in a hard voice. "Good-by," he said.

The tattered man looked at him in gaping amazement. "Why-why, pardner, where yeh goin'?" he asked unsteadily. The youth looking at him, could see that he, too, like that other one, was beginning to act dumb and animal-like. His thoughts seemed to be floundering about in his head. "Now-now-look—a—here, you Tom Jamison-now—I won't have this-this here won't do. Where-where yeh goin'?"

The youth pointed vaguely. "Over there," he replied.

"Well, now look—a—here-now," said the tattered man, rambling on in idiot fashion. His head was hanging forward and his words were slurred. "This thing won't do, now, Tom Jamison. It won't do. I know yeh, yeh pig-headed devil. Yeh wanta go trompin' off with a bad hurt. It ain't right-now-Tom Jamison-it ain't. Yeh wanta leave me take keer of yeh, Tom Jamison. It ain't—right-it ain't—fer yeh t' go-trompin' off-with a bad hurt-it ain't—ain't—ain't right-it ain't."

In reply the youth climbed a fence and started away. He could hear the tattered man bleating plaintively.

Once he faced about angrily. "What?"

"Look—a—here, now, Tom Jamison-now-it ain't—"

The youth went on. Turning at a distance he saw the tattered man wandering about helplessly in the field.

He now thought that he wished he was dead. He believed that he envied those men whose bodies lay strewn over the grass of the fields and on the fallen leaves of the forest.

The simple questions of the tattered man had been knife thrusts to him. They asserted a society that probes pitilessly at secrets until all is apparent. His late companion's chance persistency made him feel that he could not keep his crime concealed in his bosom. It was sure to be brought plain by one of those arrows which cloud the air and are constantly pricking, discovering, proclaiming those things which are willed to be forever hidden. He admitted that he could not defend himself against this agency. It was not within the power of vigilance.

CHAPTER XI.

He became aware that the furnace roar of the battle was growing louder. Great brown clouds had floated to the still heights of air before him. The noise, too, was approaching. The woods filtered men and the fields became dotted.

As he rounded a hillock, he perceived that the roadway was now a crying mass of wagons, teams, and men. From the heaving tangle issued exhortations, commands, imprecations. Fear was sweeping it all along. The cracking whips bit and horses plunged and tugged. The white-topped wagons strained and stumbled in their exertions like fat sheep.

The youth felt comforted in a measure by this sight. They were all retreating. Perhaps, then, he was not so bad after all. He seated himself and watched the terror-stricken wagons. They fled like soft, ungainly animals. All the roarers and lashers served to help him to magnify the dangers and horrors of the engagement that he might try to prove to himself that the thing with which men could charge him was in truth a symmetrical act. There was an amount of pleasure to him in watching the wild march of this vindication.

Presently the calm head of a forward-going column of infantry appeared in the road. It came swiftly on. Avoiding the obstructions gave it the sinuous movement of a serpent. The men at the head butted mules with their musket stocks. They prodded teamsters indifferent to all howls. The men forced their way through parts of the dense mass by strength. The blunt head of the column pushed. The raving teamsters swore many strange oaths.

The commands to make way had the ring of a great importance in them. The men were going forward to the heart of the din. They were to confront the eager rush of the enemy. They felt the pride of their onward movement when the remainder of the army seemed trying to dribble down this road. They tumbled teams about with a fine feeling that it was no matter so long as their column got to the front in time. This importance made their faces grave and stern. And the backs of the officers were very rigid.

As the youth looked at them the black weight of his woe returned to him. He felt that he was regarding a procession of chosen beings. The separation was as great to him as if they had marched with weapons of flame and banners of sunlight. He could never be like them. He could have wept in his longings.

He searched about in his mind for an adequate malediction for the indefinite cause, the thing upon which men turn the words of final blame. It-whatever it was-was responsible for him, he said. There lay the fault.

The haste of the column to reach the battle seemed to the forlorn young man to be something much finer than stout fighting. Heroes, he thought, could find excuses in that long seething lane. They could retire with perfect self-respect and make excuses to the stars.

He wondered what those men had eaten that they could be in such haste to force their way to grim chances of death. As he watched his envy grew until he thought that he wished to change lives with one of them. He would have liked to have used a tremendous force, he said, throw off himself and become a better. Swift pictures of himself, apart, yet in himself, came to him —a blue desperate figure leading lurid charges with one knee forward and a broken blade high —a blue, determined figure standing before a crimson and steel assault, getting calmly killed on a high place before the eyes of all. He thought of the magnificent pathos of his dead body.

These thoughts uplifted him. He felt the quiver of war desire. In his ears, he heard the ring of victory. He knew the frenzy of a rapid successful charge. The music of the trampling feet, the sharp voices, the clanking arms of the column near him made him soar on the red wings of war. For a few moments he was sublime.

He thought that he was about to start for the front. Indeed, he saw a picture of himself, dust-stained, haggard, panting, flying to the front at the proper moment to seize and throttle the dark, leering witch of calamity.

Then the difficulties of the thing began to drag at him. He hesitated, balancing awkwardly on one foot.

He had no rifle; he could not fight with his hands, said he resentfully to his plan. Well, rifles could be had for the picking. They were extraordinarily profuse.

Also, he continued, it would be a miracle if he found his regiment. Well, he could fight with any regiment.

He started forward slowly. He stepped as if he expected to tread upon some explosive thing. Doubts and he were struggling.

He would truly be a worm if any of his comrades should see him returning thus, the marks of his flight upon him. There was a reply that the intent fighters did not care for what happened rearward saving that no hostile bayonets appeared there. In the battle-blur his face would, in a way be hidden, like the face of a cowled man.

But then he said that his tireless fate would bring forth, when the strife lulled for a moment, a man to ask of him an explanation. In imagination he felt the scrutiny of his companions as he painfully labored through some lies.

Eventually, his courage expended itself upon these objections. The debates drained him of his fire.

He was not cast down by this defeat of his plan, for, upon studying the affair carefully, he could not but admit that the objections were very formidable.

Furthermore, various ailments had begun to cry out. In their presence he could not persist in flying high with the wings of war; they rendered it almost impossible for him to see himself in a heroic light. He tumbled headlong.

He discovered that he had a scorching thirst. His face was so dry and grimy that he thought he could feel his skin crackle. Each bone of his body had an ache in it, and seemingly threatened to break with each movement. His feet were like two sores. Also, his body was calling for food. It was more powerful than a direct hunger. There was a dull, weight like feeling in his stomach, and, when he tried to walk, his head swayed and he tottered. He could not see with distinctness. Small patches of green mist floated before his vision.

While he had been tossed by many emotions, he had not been aware of ailments. Now they beset him and made clamor. As he was at last compelled to pay attention to them, his capacity for self-hate was multiplied. In despair, he declared that he was not like those others. He now conceded it to be impossible that he should ever become a hero. He was a craven loon. Those pictures of glory were piteous things. He groaned from his heart and went staggering off.

A certain mothlike quality within him kept him in the vicinity of the battle. He had a great desire to see, and to get news. He wished to know who was winning.

He told himself that, despite his unprecedented suffering, he had never lost his greed for a victory, yet, he said, in a half-apologetic manner to his conscience, he could not but know that a defeat for the army this time might mean many favorable things for him. The blows of the enemy would splinter regiments into fragments. Thus, many men of courage, he considered, would be obliged to desert the colors and scurry like chickens. He would appear as one of them. They would be sullen brothers in distress, and he could then easily believe he had not run any farther or faster than they. And if he himself could believe in his virtuous perfection, he conceived that there would be small trouble in convincing all others.

He said, as if in excuse for this hope, that previously the army had encountered great defeats and in a few months had shaken off all blood and tradition of them, emerging as bright and valiant as a new one; thrusting out of sight the memory of disaster, and appearing with the valor and confidence of unconquered legions. The shrilling voices of the people at home would pipe dismally for a time, but various generals were usually compelled to listen to these ditties. He of course felt no compunctions for proposing a general as a sacrifice. He could not tell who the chosen for the barbs might be, so he could center no direct sympathy upon him. The people were afar and he did not conceive public opinion to be accurate at long range. It was quite probable they would hit the wrong man who, after he had recovered from his amazement would perhaps spend the rest of his days in writing replies to the songs of his alleged failure. It would be very unfortunate, no doubt, but in this case a general was of no consequence to the youth.

In a defeat there would be a roundabout vindication of himself. He thought it would prove, in a manner, that he had fled early because of his superior powers of perception. A serious prophet upon predicting a flood should be the first man to climb a tree. This would demonstrate that he was indeed a seer.

A moral vindication was regarded by the youth as a very important thing. Without salve, he could not, he thought, wear the sore badge of his dishonor through life. With his heart continually assuring him that he was despicable, he could not exist without making it, through his actions, apparent to all men.

If the army had gone gloriously on he would be lost. If the din meant that now his army's flags were tilted forward he was a condemned wretch. He would be compelled to doom himself to isolation. If the men were advancing, their indifferent feet were trampling upon his chances for a successful life.

As these thoughts went rapidly through his mind, he turned upon them and tried to thrust them away. He denounced himself as a villain. He said that he was the most unutterably selfish man in existence. His mind pictured the soldiers who would place their defiant bodies before the spear of the yelling battle fiend, and as he saw their dripping corpses on an imagined field, he said that he was their murderer.

Again he thought that he wished he was dead. He believed that he envied a corpse. Thinking of the slain, he achieved a great contempt for some of them, as if they were guilty for thus becoming lifeless. They might have been killed by lucky chances, he said, before they had had opportunities to flee or before they had been really tested. Yet they would receive laurels from tradition. He cried out bitterly that their crowns were stolen and their robes of glorious memories were shams. However, he still said that it was a great pity he was not as they.

A defeat of the army had suggested itself to him as a means of escape from the consequences of his fall. He considered, now, however, that it was useless to think of such a possibility. His education had been that success for that mighty blue machine was certain; that it would make victories as a contrivance turns out buttons. He presently discarded all his speculations in the other direction. He returned to the creed of soldiers.

When he perceived again that it was not possible for the army to be defeated, he tried to bethink him of a fine tale which he could take back to his regiment, and with it turn the expected shafts of derision.

But, as he mortally feared these shafts, it became impossible for him to invent a tale he felt he could trust. He experimented with many schemes, but threw them aside one by one as flimsy. He was quick to see vulnerable places in them all.

Furthermore, he was much afraid that some arrow of scorn might lay him mentally low before he could raise his protecting tale.

He imagined the whole regiment saying: "Where's Henry Fleming? He run, didn't 'e? Oh, my!" He recalled various persons who would be quite sure to leave him no peace about it. They would doubtless question him with sneers, and laugh at his stammering hesitation. In the next engagement they would try to keep watch of him to discover when he would run.

Wherever he went in camp, he would encounter insolent and lingeringly cruel stares. As he imagined himself passing near a crowd of comrades, he could hear some one say, "There he goes!"

Then, as if the heads were moved by one muscle, all the faces were turned toward him with wide, derisive grins. He seemed to hear some one make a humorous remark in a low tone. At it the others all crowed and cackled. He was a slang phrase.

CHAPTER XII.

The column that had butted stoutly at the obstacles in the roadway was barely out of the youth's sight before he saw dark waves of men come sweeping out of the woods and down through the fields. He knew at once that the steel fibers had been washed from their hearts. They were bursting from their coats and their equipments as from entanglements. They charged down upon him like terrified buffaloes.

Behind them blue smoke curled and clouded above the treetops, and through the thickets he could sometimes see a distant pink glare. The voices of the cannon were clamoring in interminable chorus.

The youth was horrorstricken. He stared in agony and amazement. He forgot that he was engaged in combating the universe. He threw aside his mental pamphlets on the philosophy of the retreated and rules for the guidance of the damned.

The fight was lost. The dragons were coming with invincible strides. The army, helpless in the matted thickets and blinded by the overhanging night, was going to be swallowed. War, the red animal, war, the blood-swollen god, would have bloated fill.

Within him something bade to cry out. He had the impulse to make a rallying speech, to sing a battle hymn, but he could only get his tongue to call into the air: "Why-why-what-what 's th' matter?"

Soon he was in the midst of them. They were leaping and scampering all about him. Their blanched faces shone in the dusk. They seemed, for the most part, to be very burly men. The youth turned from one to another of them as they galloped along. His incoherent questions were lost. They were heedless of his appeals. They did not seem to see him.

They sometimes gabbled insanely. One huge man was asking of the sky: "Say, where de plank road? Where de plank road!" It was as if he had lost a child. He wept in his pain and dismay.

Presently, men were running hither and thither in all ways. The artillery booming, forward, rearward, and on the flanks made jumble of ideas of direction. Landmarks had vanished into the gathered gloom. The youth began to imagine that he had got into the center of the tremendous quarrel, and he could perceive no way out of it. From the mouths of the fleeing men came a thousand wild questions, but no one made answers.

The youth, after rushing about and throwing interrogations at the heedless bands of retreating infantry, finally clutched a man by the arm. They swung around face to face.

"Why-why—" stammered the youth struggling with his balking tongue.

The man screamed: "Let go me! Let go me!" His face was livid and his eyes were rolling uncontrolled. He was heaving and panting. He still grasped his rifle, perhaps having forgotten to release his hold upon it. He tugged frantically, and the youth being compelled to lean forward was dragged several paces.

"Let go me! Let go me!"

"Why-why—" stuttered the youth.

"Well, then!" bawled the man in a lurid rage. He adroitly and fiercely swung his rifle. It crushed upon the youth's head. The man ran on.

The youth's fingers had turned to paste upon the other's arm. The energy was smitten from his muscles. He saw the flaming wings of lightning flash before his vision. There was a deafening rumble of thunder within his head.

Suddenly his legs seemed to die. He sank writhing to the ground. He tried to arise. In his efforts against the numbing pain he was like a man wrestling with a creature of the air.

There was a sinister struggle.

Sometimes he would achieve a position half erect, battle with the air for a moment, and then fall again, grabbing at the grass. His face was of a clammy pallor. Deep groans were wrenched from him.

At last, with a twisting movement, he got upon his hands and knees, and from thence, like a babe trying to walk, to his feet. Pressing his hands to his temples he went lurching over the grass.

He fought an intense battle with his body. His dulled senses wished him to swoon and he opposed them stubbornly, his mind portraying unknown dangers and mutilations if he should fall upon the field. He went tall soldier fashion. He imagined secluded spots where he could fall and be unmolested. To search for one he strove against the tide of his pain.

Once he put his hand to the top of his head and timidly touched the wound. The scratching pain of the contact made him draw a long breath through his clinched teeth. His fingers were dabbled with blood. He regarded them with a fixed stare.

Around him he could hear the grumble of jolted cannon as the scurrying horses were lashed toward the front. Once, a young officer on a besplashed charger nearly ran him down. He turned and watched the mass of guns, men, and horses sweeping in a wide curve toward a gap in a fence. The officer was making excited motions with a gauntleted hand. The guns followed the teams with an air of unwillingness, of being dragged by the heels.

Some officers of the scattered infantry were cursing and railing like fishwives. Their scolding voices could be heard above the din. Into the unspeakable jumble in the roadway rode a squadron of cavalry. The faded yellow of their facings shone bravely. There was a mighty altercation.

The artillery were assembling as if for a conference.

The blue haze of evening was upon the field. The lines of forest were long purple shadows. One cloud lay along the western sky partly smothering the red.

As the youth left the scene behind him, he heard the guns suddenly roar out. He imagined them shaking in black rage. They belched and howled like brass devils guarding a gate. The soft air was filled with the tremendous remonstrance. With it came the shattering peal of opposing infantry. Turning to look behind him, he could see sheets of orange light illumine the shadowy distance. There were subtle and sudden lightnings in the far air. At times he thought he could see heaving masses of men.

He hurried on in the dusk. The day had faded until he could barely distinguish place for his feet. The purple darkness was filled with men who lectured and jabbered. Sometimes he could see them gesticulating against the blue and somber sky. There seemed to be a great ruck of men and munitions spread about in the forest and in the fields.

The little narrow roadway now lay lifeless. There were overturned wagons like sun-dried bowlders. The bed of the former torrent was choked with the bodies of horses and splintered parts of war machines.

It had come to pass that his wound pained him but little. He was afraid to move rapidly, however, for a dread of disturbing it. He held his head very still and took many precautions against stumbling. He was filled with anxiety, and his face was pinched and drawn in anticipation of the pain of any sudden mistake of his feet in the gloom.

His thoughts, as he walked, fixed intently upon his hurt. There was a cool, liquid feeling about it and he imagined blood moving slowly down under his hair. His head seemed swollen to a size that made him think his neck to be inadequate.

The new silence of his wound made much worriment. The little blistering voices of pain that had called out from his scalp were, he thought, definite in their expression of danger. By them he believed that he could measure his plight. But when they remained ominously silent he became frightened and imagined terrible fingers that clutched into his brain.

Amid it he began to reflect upon various incidents and conditions of the past. He bethought him of certain meals his mother had cooked at home, in which those dishes of which he was particularly fond had occupied prominent positions. He saw the spread table. The pine walls of the kitchen were glowing in the warm light from the stove. Too, he remembered how he and his companions used to go from the schoolhouse to the bank of a shaded pool. He saw his clothes in disorderly array upon the grass of the bank. He felt the swash of the fragrant water upon his body. The leaves of the overhanging maple rustled with melody in the wind of youthful summer.

He was overcome presently by a dragging weariness. His head hung forward and his shoulders were stooped as if he were bearing a great bundle. His feet shuffled along the ground.

He held continuous arguments as to whether he should lie down and sleep at some near spot, or force himself on until he reached a certain haven. He often tried to dismiss the question, but his body persisted in rebellion and his senses nagged at him like pampered babies.

At last he heard a cheery voice near his shoulder: "Yeh seem t' be in a pretty bad way, boy?" The youth did not look up, but he assented with thick tongue. "Uh!"

The owner of the cheery voice took him firmly by the arm. "Well," he said, with a round laugh, "I'm goin' your way. Th' hull gang is goin' your way. An' I guess I kin give yeh a lift." They began to walk like a drunken man and his friend.

As they went along, the man questioned the youth and assisted him with the replies like one manipulating the mind of a child. Sometimes he interjected anecdotes. "What reg'ment do yeh b'long teh? Eh? What's that? Th' 304th N' York? Why, what corps is that in? Oh, it is? Why, I thought they wasn't engaged t'-day-they're 'way over in th' center. Oh, they was, eh? Well, pretty nearly everybody got their share 'a fightin' t'-day. By dad, I give myself up fer dead any number 'a times. There was shootin' here an' shootin' there, an' hollerin' here an' hollerin' there, in th' damn' darkness, until I couldn't tell t' save m' soul which side I was on. Sometimes I thought I was sure 'nough from Ohier, an' other times I could 'a swore I was from th' bitter end of Florida. It was th' most mixed up dern thing I ever see. An' these here hull woods is a reg'lar mess. It'll be a miracle if we find our reg'ments t'-night. Pretty soon, though, we 'll meet a-plenty of guards an' provost-guards, an' one thing an' another. Ho! there they go with an off'cer, I guess. Look at his hand a-draggin'. He's got all th' war he wants, I bet. He won't be talkin' so big about his reputation an' all when they go t' sawin' off his leg. Poor feller! My brother 's got whiskers jest like that. How did yeh git 'way over here, anyhow? Your reg'ment is a long way from here, ain't it? Well, I guess we can find it. Yeh know there was a boy killed in my comp'ny t'-day that I thought th' world an' all of. Jack was a nice feller. By ginger, it hurt like thunder t' see ol' Jack jest git knocked flat. We was a-standin' purty peaceable fer a spell, 'though there was men runnin' ev'ry way all 'round us, an' while we was a-standin' like that, 'long come a big fat feller. He began t' peck at Jack's elbow, an' he ses: 'Say, where 's th' road t' th' river?' An' Jack, he never paid no attention, an' th' feller kept on a-peckin' at his elbow an' sayin': 'Say, where 's th' road t' th' river?' Jack was a-lookin' ahead all th' time tryin' t' see th' Johnnies comin' through th' woods, an' he never paid no attention t' this big fat feller fer a long time, but at last he turned 'round an' he ses: 'Ah, go t' hell an' find th' road t' th' river!' An' jest then a shot slapped him bang on th' side th' head. He was a sergeant, too. Them was his last words. Thunder, I wish we was sure 'a findin' our reg'ments t'-night. It's goin' t' be long huntin'. But I guess we kin do it."

In the search which followed, the man of the cheery voice seemed to the youth to possess a wand of a magic kind. He threaded the mazes of the tangled forest with a strange fortune. In encounters with guards and patrols he displayed the keenness of a detective and the valor of a gamin. Obstacles fell before him and became of assistance. The youth, with his chin still on his breast, stood woodenly by while his companion beat ways and means out of sullen things.

The forest seemed a vast hive of men buzzing about in frantic circles, but the cheery man conducted the youth without mistakes, until at last he began to chuckle with glee and self-satisfaction. "Ah, there yeh are! See that fire?"

The youth nodded stupidly.

"Well, there 's where your reg'ment is. An' now, good-by, ol' boy, good luck t' yeh."

A warm and strong hand clasped the youth's languid fingers for an instant, and then he heard a cheerful and audacious whistling as the man strode away. As he who had so befriended him was thus passing out of his life, it suddenly occurred to the youth that he had not once seen his face.

51

CHAPTER XIII.

The youth went slowly toward the fire indicated by his departed friend. As he reeled, he bethought him of the welcome his comrades would give him. He had a conviction that he would soon feel in his sore heart the barbed missiles of ridicule. He had no strength to invent a tale; he would be a soft target.

He made vague plans to go off into the deeper darkness and hide, but they were all destroyed by the voices of exhaustion and pain from his body. His ailments, clamoring, forced him to seek the place of food and rest, at whatever cost.

He swung unsteadily toward the fire. He could see the forms of men throwing black shadows in the red light, and as he went nearer it became known to him in some way that the ground was strewn with sleeping men.

Of a sudden he confronted a black and monstrous figure. A rifle barrel caught some glinting beams. "Halt! halt!" He was dismayed for a moment, but he presently thought that he recognized the nervous voice. As he stood tottering before the rifle barrel, he called out: "Why, hello, Wilson, you-you here?"

The rifle was lowered to a position of caution and the loud soldier came slowly forward. He peered into the youth's face. "That you, Henry?"

"Yes, it's—it's me."

"Well, well, ol' boy," said the other, "by ginger, I'm glad t' see yeh! I give yeh up fer a goner. I thought yeh was dead sure enough." There was husky emotion in his voice.

The youth found that now he could barely stand upon his feet. There was a sudden sinking of his forces. He thought he must hasten to produce his tale to protect him from the missiles already at the lips of his redoubtable comrades. So, staggering before the loud soldier, he began: "Yes, yes. I've—I've had an awful time. I've been all over. Way over on th' right. Ter'ble fightin' over there. I had an awful time. I got separated from th' reg'ment. Over on th' right, I got shot. In th' head. I never see sech fightin'. Awful time. I don't see how I could 'a got separated from th' reg'ment. I got shot, too."

His friend had stepped forward quickly. "What? Got shot? Why didn't yeh say so first? Poor ol' boy, we must-hol' on a minnit; what am I doin'. I'll call Simpson."

Another figure at that moment loomed in the gloom. They could see that it was the corporal. "Who yeh talkin' to, Wilson?" he demanded. His voice was anger-toned. "Who yeh talkin' to? Yeh th' derndest sentinel-why-hello, Henry, you here? Why, I thought you was dead four hours ago! Great Jerusalem, they keep turnin' up every ten minutes or so! We thought we'd lost forty-two men by straight count, but if they keep on a-comin' this way, we'll git th' comp'ny all back by mornin' yit. Where was yeh?"

"Over on th' right. I got separated"—began the youth with considerable glibness.

But his friend had interrupted hastily. "Yes, an' he got shot in th' head an' he's in a fix, an' we must see t' him right away." He rested his rifle in the hollow of his left arm and his right around the youth's shoulder.

"Gee, it must hurt like thunder!" he said.

The youth leaned heavily upon his friend. "Yes, it hurts-hurts a good deal," he replied. There was a faltering in his voice.

"Oh," said the corporal. He linked his arm in the youth's and drew him forward. "Come on, Henry. I'll take keer 'a yeh."

As they went on together the loud private called out after them: "Put 'im t' sleep in my blanket, Simpson. An'—hol' on a minnit-here's my canteen. It's full 'a coffee. Look at his head by th' fire an' see how it looks. Maybe it's a pretty bad un. When I git relieved in a couple 'a minnits, I'll be over an' see t' him."

The youth's senses were so deadened that his friend's voice sounded from afar and he could scarcely feel the pressure of the corporal's arm. He submitted passively to the latter's directing strength. His head was in the old manner hanging forward upon his breast. His knees wobbled.

The corporal led him into the glare of the fire. "Now, Henry," he said, "let's have look at yer ol' head."

The youth sat down obediently and the corporal, laying aside his rifle, began to fumble in the bushy hair of his comrade. He was obliged to turn the other's head so that the full flush of the fire light would beam upon it. He puckered his mouth with a critical air. He drew back his lips and whistled through his teeth when his fingers came in contact with the splashed blood and the rare wound.

"Ah, here we are!" he said. He awkwardly made further investigations. "Jest as I thought," he added, presently. "Yeh've been grazed by a ball. It's raised a queer lump jest as if some feller had lammed yeh on th' head with a club. It stopped a-bleedin' long time ago. Th' most about it is that in th' mornin' yeh'll feel that a number ten hat wouldn't fit yeh. An' your head'll be all het up an' feel as dry as burnt pork. An' yeh may git a lot 'a other sicknesses, too, by mornin'. Yeh can't never tell. Still, I don't much think so. It's jest a damn' good belt on th' head, an' nothin' more. Now, you jest sit here an' don't move, while I go rout out th' relief. Then I'll send Wilson t' take keer 'a yeh."

The corporal went away. The youth remained on the ground like a parcel. He stared with a vacant look into the fire.

After a time he aroused, for some part, and the things about him began to take form. He saw that the ground in the deep shadows was cluttered with men, sprawling in every conceivable posture. Glancing narrowly into the more distant darkness, he caught occasional glimpses of visages that loomed pallid and ghostly, lit with a phosphorescent glow. These faces expressed in their lines the deep stupor of the tired soldiers. They made them appear like men drunk with wine. This bit of forest might have appeared to an ethereal wanderer as a scene of the result of some frightful debauch.

On the other side of the fire the youth observed an officer asleep, seated bolt upright, with his back against a tree. There was something perilous in his position. Badgered by dreams, perhaps, he swayed with little bounces and starts, like an old toddy-stricken grandfather in a chimney corner. Dust and stains were upon his face. His lower jaw hung down as if lacking strength to assume its normal position. He was the picture of an exhausted soldier after a feast of war.

He had evidently gone to sleep with his sword in his arms. These two had slumbered in an embrace, but the weapon had been allowed in time to fall unheeded to the ground. The brass-mounted hilt lay in contact with some parts of the fire.

Within the gleam of rose and orange light from the burning sticks were other soldiers, snoring and heaving, or lying deathlike in slumber. A few pairs of legs were stuck forth, rigid and straight. The shoes displayed the mud or dust of marches and bits of rounded trousers, protruding from the blankets, showed rents and tears from hurried pitchings through the dense brambles.

The fire crackled musically. From it swelled light smoke. Overhead the foliage moved softly. The leaves, with their faces turned toward the blaze, were colored shifting hues of silver, often edged with red. Far off to the right, through a window in the forest could be seen a handful of stars lying, like glittering pebbles, on the black level of the night.

Occasionally, in this low-arched hall, a soldier would arouse and turn his body to a new position, the experience of his sleep having taught him of uneven and objectionable places upon the ground under him. Or, perhaps, he would lift himself to a sitting posture, blink at the fire for an unintelligent moment, throw a swift glance at his prostrate companion, and then cuddle down again with a grunt of sleepy content.

The youth sat in a forlorn heap until his friend the loud young soldier came, swinging two canteens by their light strings. "Well, now, Henry, ol' boy," said the latter, "we'll have yeh fixed up in jest about a minnit."

He had the bustling ways of an amateur nurse. He fussed around the fire and stirred the sticks to brilliant exertions. He made his patient drink largely from the canteen that contained the coffee. It was to the youth a delicious draught. He tilted his head afar back and held the canteen long to his lips. The cool mixture went caressingly down his blistered throat. Having finished, he sighed with comfortable delight.

The loud young soldier watched his comrade with an air of satisfaction. He later produced an extensive handkerchief from his pocket. He folded it into a manner of bandage and soused water from the other canteen upon the middle of it. This crude arrangement he bound over the youth's head, tying the ends in a queer knot at the back of the neck.

"There," he said, moving off and surveying his deed, "yeh look like th' devil, but I bet yeh feel better."

The youth contemplated his friend with grateful eyes. Upon his aching and swelling head the cold cloth was like a tender woman's hand.

"Yeh don't holler ner say nothin'," remarked his friend approvingly. "I know I'm a blacksmith at takin' keer 'a sick folks, an' yeh never squeaked. Yer a good un, Henry. Most 'a men would a' been in th' hospital long ago. A shot in th' head ain't foolin' business."

The youth made no reply, but began to fumble with the buttons of his jacket.

"Well, come, now," continued his friend, "come on. I must put yeh t' bed an' see that yeh git a good night's rest."

The other got carefully erect, and the loud young soldier led him among the sleeping forms lying in groups and rows. Presently he stooped and picked up his blankets. He spread the rubber one upon the ground and placed the woolen one about the youth's shoulders.

"There now," he said, "lie down an' git some sleep."

The youth, with his manner of doglike obedience, got carefully down like a crone stooping. He stretched out with a murmur of relief and comfort. The ground felt like the softest couch.

But of a sudden he ejaculated: "Hol' on a minnit! Where you goin' t' sleep?"

His friend waved his hand impatiently. "Right down there by yeh."

"Well, but hol' on a minnit," continued the youth. "What yeh goin' t' sleep in? I've got your —"

The loud young soldier snarled: "Shet up an' go on t' sleep. Don't be makin' a damn' fool 'a yerself," he said severely.

After the reproof the youth said no more. An exquisite drowsiness had spread through him. The warm comfort of the blanket enveloped him and made a gentle languor. His head fell forward on his crooked arm and his weighted lids went softly down over his eyes. Hearing a splatter of musketry from the distance, he wondered indifferently if those men sometimes slept. He gave a long sigh, snuggled down into his blanket, and in a moment was like his comrades.

CHAPTER XIV.

When the youth awoke it seemed to him that he had been asleep for a thousand years, and he felt sure that he opened his eyes upon an unexpected world. Gray mists were slowly shifting before the first efforts of the sun rays. An impending splendor could be seen in the eastern sky. An icy dew had chilled his face, and immediately upon arousing he curled farther down into his blanket. He stared for a while at the leaves overhead, moving in a heraldic wind of the day.

The distance was splintering and blaring with the noise of fighting. There was in the sound an expression of a deadly persistency, as if it had not begun and was not to cease.

About him were the rows and groups of men that he had dimly seen the previous night. They were getting a last draught of sleep before the awakening. The gaunt, careworn features and dusty figures were made plain by this quaint light at the dawning, but it dressed the skin of the men in corpselike hues and made the tangled limbs appear pulseless and dead. The youth started up with a little cry when his eyes first swept over this motionless mass of men, thick-spread upon the ground, pallid, and in strange postures. His disordered mind interpreted the hall of the forest as a charnel place. He believed for an instant that he was in the house of the dead, and he did not dare to move lest these corpses start up, squalling and squawking. In a second, however, he achieved his proper mind. He swore a complicated oath at himself. He saw that this somber picture was not a fact of the present, but a mere prophecy.

He heard then the noise of a fire crackling briskly in the cold air, and, turning his head, he saw his friend pottering busily about a small blaze. A few other figures moved in the fog, and he heard the hard cracking of axe blows.

Suddenly there was a hollow rumble of drums. A distant bugle sang faintly. Similar sounds, varying in strength, came from near and far over the forest. The bugles called to each other like brazen gamecocks. The near thunder of the regimental drums rolled.

The body of men in the woods rustled. There was a general uplifting of heads. A murmuring of voices broke upon the air. In it there was much bass of grumbling oaths. Strange gods were addressed in condemnation of the early hours necessary to correct war. An officer's peremptory tenor rang out and quickened the stiffened movement of the men. The tangled limbs unraveled. The corpse-hued faces were hidden behind fists that twisted slowly in the eye sockets.

The youth sat up and gave vent to an enormous yawn. "Thunder!" he remarked petulantly. He rubbed his eyes, and then putting up his hand felt carefully of the bandage over his wound. His friend, perceiving him to be awake, came from the fire. "Well, Henry, ol' man, how do yeh feel this mornin'?" he demanded.

The youth yawned again. Then he puckered his mouth to a little pucker. His head, in truth, felt precisely like a melon, and there was an unpleasant sensation at his stomach.

"Oh, Lord, I feel pretty bad," he said.

"Thunder!" exclaimed the other. "I hoped ye'd feel all right this mornin'. Let's see th' bandage — I guess it's slipped." He began to tinker at the wound in rather a clumsy way until the youth exploded.

"Gosh-dern it!" he said in sharp irritation; "you're the hangdest man I ever saw! You wear muffs on your hands. Why in good thunderation can't you be more easy? I'd rather you'd stand off an' throw guns at it. Now, go slow, an' don't act as if you was nailing down carpet."

He glared with insolent command at his friend, but the latter answered soothingly. "Well, well, come now, an' git some grub," he said. "Then, maybe, yeh'll feel better."

At the fireside the loud young soldier watched over his comrade's wants with tenderness and care. He was very busy marshaling the little black vagabonds of tin cups and pouring into them the streaming, iron colored mixture from a small and sooty tin pail. He had some fresh meat, which he roasted hurriedly upon a stick. He sat down then and contemplated the youth's appetite with glee.

The youth took note of a remarkable change in his comrade since those days of camp life upon the river bank. He seemed no more to be continually regarding the proportions of his personal prowess. He was not furious at small words that pricked his conceits. He was no more a loud young soldier. There was about him now a fine reliance. He showed a quiet belief in his purposes and his abilities. And this inward confidence evidently enabled him to be indifferent to little words of other men aimed at him.

The youth reflected. He had been used to regarding his comrade as a blatant child with an audacity grown from his inexperience, thoughtless, headstrong, jealous, and filled with a tinsel courage. A swaggering babe accustomed to strut in his own dooryard. The youth wondered where had been born these new eyes; when his comrade had made the great discovery that there were many men who would refuse to be subjected by him. Apparently, the other had now climbed a peak of wisdom from which he could perceive himself as a very wee thing. And the youth saw that ever after it would be easier to live in his friend's neighborhood.

His comrade balanced his ebony coffee-cup on his knee. "Well, Henry," he said, "what d'yeh think th' chances are? D'yeh think we'll wallop 'em?"

The youth considered for a moment. "Day-b'fore-yesterday," he finally replied, with boldness, "you would 'a' bet you'd lick the hull kit-an'-boodle all by yourself."

His friend looked a trifle amazed. "Would I?" he asked. He pondered. "Well, perhaps I would," he decided at last. He stared humbly at the fire.

The youth was quite disconcerted at this surprising reception of his remarks. "Oh, no, you wouldn't either," he said, hastily trying to retrace.

But the other made a deprecating gesture. "Oh, yeh needn't mind, Henry," he said. "I believe I was a pretty big fool in those days." He spoke as after a lapse of years.

There was a little pause.

"All th' officers say we've got th' rebs in a pretty tight box," said the friend, clearing his throat in a commonplace way. "They all seem t' think we've got 'em jest where we want 'em."

"I don't know about that," the youth replied. "What I seen over on th' right makes me think it was th' other way about. From where I was, it looked as if we was gettin' a good poundin' yestirday."

"D'yeh think so?" inquired the friend. "I thought we handled 'em pretty rough yestirday."

"Not a bit," said the youth. "Why, lord, man, you didn't see nothing of the fight. Why!" Then a sudden thought came to him. "Oh! Jim Conklin's dead."

His friend started. "What? Is he? Jim Conklin?"

The youth spoke slowly. "Yes. He's dead. Shot in th' side."

"Yeh don't say so. Jim Conklin. . . . poor cuss!"

All about them were other small fires surrounded by men with their little black utensils. From one of these near came sudden sharp voices in a row. It appeared that two light-footed soldiers had been teasing a huge, bearded man, causing him to spill coffee upon his blue knees. The man had gone into a rage and had sworn comprehensively. Stung by his language, his tormentors had immediately bristled at him with a great show of resenting unjust oaths. Possibly there was going to be a fight.

The friend arose and went over to them, making pacific motions with his arms. "Oh, here, now, boys, what's th' use?" he said. "We'll be at th' rebs in less'n an hour. What's th' good fightin' 'mong ourselves?"

One of the light-footed soldiers turned upon him red-faced and violent. "Yeh needn't come around here with yer preachin'. I s'pose yeh don't approve 'a fightin' since Charley Morgan licked yeh; but I don't see what business this here is 'a yours or anybody else."

"Well, it ain't," said the friend mildly. "Still I hate t' see —"

There was a tangled argument.

"Well, he —," said the two, indicating their opponent with accusative forefingers.

The huge soldier was quite purple with rage. He pointed at the two soldiers with his great hand, extended clawlike. "Well, they —"

But during this argumentative time the desire to deal blows seemed to pass, although they said much to each other. Finally the friend returned to his old seat. In a short while the three antagonists could be seen together in an amiable bunch.

"Jimmie Rogers ses I'll have t' fight him after th' battle t'-day," announced the friend as he again seated himself. "He ses he don't allow no interferin' in his business. I hate t' see th' boys fightin' 'mong themselves."

The youth laughed. "Yer changed a good bit. Yeh ain't at all like yeh was. I remember when you an' that Irish feller —" He stopped and laughed again.

"No, I didn't use t' be that way," said his friend thoughtfully. "That's true 'nough."

"Well, I didn't mean —" began the youth.

The friend made another deprecatory gesture. "Oh, yeh needn't mind, Henry."

There was another little pause.

"Th' reg'ment lost over half th' men yestirday," remarked the friend eventually. "I thought a course they was all dead, but, laws, they kep' a-comin' back last night until it seems, after all, we didn't lose but a few. They'd been scattered all over, wanderin' around in th' woods, fightin' with other reg'ments, an' everything. Jest like you done."

"So?" said the youth.

CHAPTER XV.

The regiment was standing at order arms at the side of a lane, waiting for the command to march, when suddenly the youth remembered the little packet enwrapped in a faded yellow envelope which the loud young soldier with lugubrious words had intrusted to him. It made him start. He uttered an exclamation and turned toward his comrade.

"Wilson!"

"What?"

His friend, at his side in the ranks, was thoughtfully staring down the road. From some cause his expression was at that moment very meek. The youth, regarding him with sidelong glances, felt impelled to change his purpose. "Oh, nothing," he said.

His friend turned his head in some surprise, "Why, what was yeh goin' t' say?"

"Oh, nothing," repeated the youth.

He resolved not to deal the little blow. It was sufficient that the fact made him glad. It was not necessary to knock his friend on the head with the misguided packet.

He had been possessed of much fear of his friend, for he saw how easily questionings could make holes in his feelings. Lately, he had assured himself that the altered comrade would not tantalize him with a persistent curiosity, but he felt certain that during the first period of leisure his friend would ask him to relate his adventures of the previous day.

He now rejoiced in the possession of a small weapon with which he could prostrate his comrade at the first signs of a cross-examination. He was master. It would now be he who could laugh and shoot the shafts of derision.

The friend had, in a weak hour, spoken with sobs of his own death. He had delivered a melancholy oration previous to his funeral, and had doubtless in the packet of letters, presented various keepsakes to relatives. But he had not died, and thus he had delivered himself into the hands of the youth.

The latter felt immensely superior to his friend, but he inclined to condescension. He adopted toward him an air of patronizing good humor.

His self-pride was now entirely restored. In the shade of its flourishing growth he stood with braced and self-confident legs, and since nothing could now be discovered he did not shrink from an encounter with the eyes of judges, and allowed no thoughts of his own to keep him from an attitude of manfulness. He had performed his mistakes in the dark, so he was still a man.

Indeed, when he remembered his fortunes of yesterday, and looked at them from a distance he began to see something fine there. He had license to be pompous and veteranlike.

His panting agonies of the past he put out of his sight.

In the present, he declared to himself that it was only the doomed and the damned who roared with sincerity at circumstance. Few but they ever did it. A man with a full stomach and the respect of his fellows had no business to scold about anything that he might think to be wrong in the ways of the universe, or even with the ways of society. Let the unfortunates rail; the others may play marbles.

He did not give a great deal of thought to these battles that lay directly before him. It was not essential that he should plan his ways in regard to them. He had been taught that many obligations of a life were easily avoided. The lessons of yesterday had been that retribution was a laggard and blind. With these facts before him he did not deem it necessary that he should become feverish over the possibilities of the ensuing twenty-four hours. He could leave much to chance. Besides, a faith in himself had secretly blossomed. There was a little flower of confidence growing within him. He was now a man of experience. He had been out among the dragons, he said, and he assured himself that they were not so hideous as he had imagined them. Also, they were inaccurate; they did not sting with precision. A stout heart often defied, and defying, escaped.

And, furthermore, how could they kill him who was the chosen of gods and doomed to greatness?

He remembered how some of the men had run from the battle. As he recalled their terror-struck faces he felt a scorn for them. They had surely been more fleet and more wild than was absolutely necessary. They were weak mortals. As for himself, he had fled with discretion and dignity.

He was aroused from this reverie by his friend, who, having hitched about nervously and blinked at the trees for a time, suddenly coughed in an introductory way, and spoke.

"Fleming!"

"What?"

The friend put his hand up to his mouth and coughed again. He fidgeted in his jacket.

"Well," he gulped, at last, "I guess yeh might as well give me back them letters." Dark, prickling blood had flushed into his cheeks and brow.

"All right, Wilson," said the youth. He loosened two buttons of his coat, thrust in his hand, and brought forth the packet. As he extended it to his friend the latter's face was turned from him.

He had been slow in the act of producing the packet because during it he had been trying to invent a remarkable comment upon the affair. He could conjure nothing of sufficient point. He was compelled to allow his friend to escape unmolested with his packet. And for this he took unto himself considerable credit. It was a generous thing.

His friend at his side seemed suffering great shame. As he contemplated him, the youth felt his heart grow more strong and stout. He had never been compelled to blush in such manner for his acts; he was an individual of extraordinary virtues.

He reflected, with condescending pity: "Too bad! Too bad! The poor devil, it makes him feel tough!"

After this incident, and as he reviewed the battle pictures he had seen, he felt quite competent to return home and make the hearts of the people glow with stories of war. He could see himself in a room of warm tints telling tales to listeners. He could exhibit laurels. They were insignificant; still, in a district where laurels were infrequent, they might shine.

He saw his gaping audience picturing him as the central figure in blazing scenes. And he imagined the consternation and the ejaculations of his mother and the young lady at the seminary as they drank his recitals. Their vague feminine formula for beloved ones doing brave deeds on the field of battle without risk of life would be destroyed.

CHAPTER XVI.

A sputtering of musketry was always to be heard. Later, the cannon had entered the dispute. In the fog-filled air their voices made a thudding sound. The reverberations were continued. This part of the world led a strange, battleful existence.

The youth's regiment was marched to relieve a command that had lain long in some damp trenches. The men took positions behind a curving line of rifle pits that had been turned up, like a large furrow, along the line of woods. Before them was a level stretch, peopled with short, deformed stumps. From the woods beyond came the dull popping of the skirmishers and pickets, firing in the fog. From the right came the noise of a terrific fracas.

The men cuddled behind the small embankment and sat in easy attitudes awaiting their turn. Many had their backs to the firing. The youth's friend lay down, buried his face in his arms, and almost instantly, it seemed, he was in a deep sleep.

The youth leaned his breast against the brown dirt and peered over at the woods and up and down the line. Curtains of trees interfered with his ways of vision. He could see the low line of trenches but for a short distance. A few idle flags were perched on the dirt hills. Behind them were rows of dark bodies with a few heads sticking curiously over the top.

Always the noise of skirmishers came from the woods on the front and left, and the din on the right had grown to frightful proportions. The guns were roaring without an instant's pause for breath. It seemed that the cannon had come from all parts and were engaged in a stupendous wrangle. It became impossible to make a sentence heard.

The youth wished to launch a joke —a quotation from newspapers. He desired to say, "All quiet on the Rappahannock," but the guns refused to permit even a comment upon their uproar. He never successfully concluded the sentence. But at last the guns stopped, and among the men in the rifle pits rumors again flew, like birds, but they were now for the most part black creatures who flapped their wings drearily near to the ground and refused to rise on any wings of hope. The men's faces grew doleful from the interpreting of omens. Tales of hesitation and uncertainty on the part of those high in place and responsibility came to their ears. Stories of disaster were borne into their minds with many proofs. This din of musketry on the right, growing like a released genie of sound, expressed and emphasized the army's plight.

The men were disheartened and began to mutter. They made gestures expressive of the sentence: "Ah, what more can we do?" And it could always be seen that they were bewildered by the alleged news and could not fully comprehend a defeat.

Before the gray mists had been totally obliterated by the sun rays, the regiment was marching in a spread column that was retiring carefully through the woods. The disordered, hurrying lines of the enemy could sometimes be seen down through the groves and little fields. They were yelling, shrill and exultant.

At this sight the youth forgot many personal matters and became greatly enraged. He exploded in loud sentences. "B'jiminey, we're generaled by a lot 'a lunkheads."

"More than one feller has said that t'-day," observed a man.

His friend, recently aroused, was still very drowsy. He looked behind him until his mind took in the meaning of the movement. Then he sighed. "Oh, well, I s'pose we got licked," he remarked sadly.

The youth had a thought that it would not be handsome for him to freely condemn other men. He made an attempt to restrain himself, but the words upon his tongue were too bitter. He presently began a long and intricate denunciation of the commander of the forces.

"Mebbe, it wa'n't all his fault-not all together. He did th' best he knowed. It's our luck t' git licked often," said his friend in a weary tone. He was trudging along with stooped shoulders and shifting eyes like a man who has been caned and kicked.

"Well, don't we fight like the devil? Don't we do all that men can?" demanded the youth loudly.

He was secretly dumfounded at this sentiment when it came from his lips. For a moment his face lost its valor and he looked guiltily about him. But no one questioned his right to deal in such words, and presently he recovered his air of courage. He went on to repeat a statement he had heard going from group to group at the camp that morning. "The brigadier said he never saw a new reg'ment fight the way we fought yestirday, didn't he? And we didn't do better than many another reg'ment, did we? Well, then, you can't say it's th' army's fault, can you?"

In his reply, the friend's voice was stern. "'A course not," he said. "No man dare say we don't fight like th' devil. No man will ever dare say it. Th' boys fight like hell-roosters. But still-still, we don't have no luck."

"Well, then, if we fight like the devil an' don't ever whip, it must be the general's fault," said the youth grandly and decisively. "And I don't see any sense in fighting and fighting and fighting, yet always losing through some derned old lunkhead of a general."

A sarcastic man who was tramping at the youth's side, then spoke lazily. "Mebbe yeh think yeh fit th' hull battle yestirday, Fleming," he remarked.

The speech pierced the youth. Inwardly he was reduced to an abject pulp by these chance words. His legs quaked privately. He cast a frightened glance at the sarcastic man.

"Why, no," he hastened to say in a conciliating voice, "I don't think I fought the whole battle yesterday."

But the other seemed innocent of any deeper meaning. Apparently, he had no information. It was merely his habit. "Oh!" he replied in the same tone of calm derision.

The youth, nevertheless, felt a threat. His mind shrank from going near to the danger, and thereafter he was silent. The significance of the sarcastic man's words took from him all loud moods that would make him appear prominent. He became suddenly a modest person.

There was low-toned talk among the troops. The officers were impatient and snappy, their countenances clouded with the tales of misfortune. The troops, sifting through the forest, were sullen. In the youth's company once a man's laugh rang out. A dozen soldiers turned their faces quickly toward him and frowned with vague displeasure.

The noise of firing dogged their footsteps. Sometimes, it seemed to be driven a little way, but it always returned again with increased insolence. The men muttered and cursed, throwing black looks in its direction.

In a clear space the troops were at last halted. Regiments and brigades, broken and detached through their encounters with thickets, grew together again and lines were faced toward the pursuing bark of the enemy's infantry.

This noise, following like the yellings of eager, metallic hounds, increased to a loud and joyous burst, and then, as the sun went serenely up the sky, throwing illuminating rays into the gloomy thickets, it broke forth into prolonged pealings. The woods began to crackle as if afire.

"Whoop-a-dadee," said a man, "here we are! Everybody fightin'. Blood an' destruction."

"I was willin' t' bet they'd attack as soon as th' sun got fairly up," savagely asserted the lieutenant who commanded the youth's company. He jerked without mercy at his little mustache. He strode to and fro with dark dignity in the rear of his men, who were lying down behind whatever protection they had collected.

A battery had trundled into position in the rear and was thoughtfully shelling the distance. The regiment, unmolested as yet, awaited the moment when the gray shadows of the woods before them should be slashed by the lines of flame. There was much growling and swearing.

"Good Gawd," the youth grumbled, "we're always being chased around like rats! It makes me sick. Nobody seems to know where we go or why we go. We just get fired around from pillar to post and get licked here and get licked there, and nobody knows what it's done for. It makes a man feel like a damn' kitten in a bag. Now, I'd like to know what the eternal thunders we was marched into these woods for anyhow, unless it was to give the rebs a regular pot shot at us. We came in here and got our legs all tangled up in these cussed briers, and then we begin to fight and the rebs had an easy time of it. Don't tell me it's just luck! I know better. It's this derned old —"

The friend seemed jaded, but he interrupted his comrade with a voice of calm confidence. "It'll turn out all right in th' end," he said.

"Oh, the devil it will! You always talk like a dog-hanged parson. Don't tell me! I know —"

At this time there was an interposition by the savage-minded lieutenant, who was obliged to vent some of his inward dissatisfaction upon his men. "You boys shut right up! There no need 'a your wastin' your breath in long-winded arguments about this an' that an' th' other. You've been jawin' like a lot 'a old hens. All you've got t' do is to fight, an' you'll get plenty 'a that t' do in about ten minutes. Less talkin' an' more fightin' is what's best for you boys. I never saw sech gabbling jackasses."

He paused, ready to pounce upon any man who might have the temerity to reply. No words being said, he resumed his dignified pacing.

"There's too much chin music an' too little fightin' in this war, anyhow," he said to them, turning his head for a final remark.

The day had grown more white, until the sun shed his full radiance upon the thronged forest. A sort of a gust of battle came sweeping toward that part of the line where lay the youth's regiment. The front shifted a trifle to meet it squarely. There was a wait. In this part of the field there passed slowly the intense moments that precede the tempest.

A single rifle flashed in a thicket before the regiment. In an instant it was joined by many others. There was a mighty song of clashes and crashes that went sweeping through the woods. The guns in the rear, aroused and enraged by shells that had been thrown burlike at them, suddenly involved themselves in a hideous altercation with another band of guns. The battle roar settled to a rolling thunder, which was a single, long explosion.

In the regiment there was a peculiar kind of hesitation denoted in the attitudes of the men. They were worn, exhausted, having slept but little and labored much. They rolled their eyes toward the advancing battle as they stood awaiting the shock. Some shrank and flinched. They stood as men tied to stakes.

CHAPTER XVII.

This advance of the enemy had seemed to the youth like a ruthless hunting. He began to fume with rage and exasperation. He beat his foot upon the ground, and scowled with hate at the swirling smoke that was approaching like a phantom flood. There was a maddening quality in this seeming resolution of the foe to give him no rest, to give him no time to sit down and think. Yesterday he had fought and had fled rapidly. There had been many adventures. For to-day he felt that he had earned opportunities for contemplative repose. He could have enjoyed portraying to uninitiated listeners various scenes at which he had been a witness or ably discussing the processes of war with other proved men. Too it was important that he should have time for physical recuperation. He was sore and stiff from his experiences. He had received his fill of all exertions, and he wished to rest.

But those other men seemed never to grow weary; they were fighting with their old speed.

He had a wild hate for the relentless foe. Yesterday, when he had imagined the universe to be against him, he had hated it, little gods and big gods; to-day he hated the army of the foe with the same great hatred. He was not going to be badgered of his life, like a kitten chased by boys, he said. It was not well to drive men into final corners; at those moments they could all develop teeth and claws.

He leaned and spoke into his friend's ear. He menaced the woods with a gesture. "If they keep on chasing us, by Gawd, they'd better watch out. Can't stand *too* much."

The friend twisted his head and made a calm reply. "If they keep on a-chasin' us they'll drive us all inteh th' river."

The youth cried out savagely at this statement. He crouched behind a little tree, with his eyes burning hatefully and his teeth set in a curlike snarl. The awkward bandage was still about his head, and upon it, over his wound, there was a spot of dry blood. His hair was wondrously tousled, and some straggling, moving locks hung over the cloth of the bandage down toward his forehead. His jacket and shirt were open at the throat, and exposed his young bronzed neck. There could be seen spasmodic gulpings at his throat.

His fingers twined nervously about his rifle. He wished that it was an engine of annihilating power. He felt that he and his companions were being taunted and derided from sincere convictions that they were poor and puny. His knowledge of his inability to take vengeance for it made his rage into a dark and stormy specter, that possessed him and made him dream of abominable cruelties. The tormentors were flies sucking insolently at his blood, and he thought that he would have given his life for a revenge of seeing their faces in pitiful plights.

The winds of battle had swept all about the regiment, until the one rifle, instantly followed by others, flashed in its front. A moment later the regiment roared forth its sudden and valiant retort. A dense wall of smoke settled slowly down. It was furiously slit and slashed by the knifelike fire from the rifles.

To the youth the fighters resembled animals tossed for a death struggle into a dark pit. There was a sensation that he and his fellows, at bay, were pushing back, always pushing fierce onslaughts of creatures who were slippery. Their beams of crimson seemed to get no purchase upon the bodies of their foes; the latter seemed to evade them with ease, and come through, between, around, and about with unopposed skill.

When, in a dream, it occurred to the youth that his rifle was an impotent stick, he lost sense of everything but his hate, his desire to smash into pulp the glittering smile of victory which he could feel upon the faces of his enemies.

The blue smoke-swallowed line curled and writhed like a snake stepped upon. It swung its ends to and fro in an agony of fear and rage.

The youth was not conscious that he was erect upon his feet. He did not know the direction of the ground. Indeed, once he even lost the habit of balance and fell heavily. He was up again immediately. One thought went through the chaos of his brain at the time. He wondered if he had fallen because he had been shot. But the suspicion flew away at once. He did not think more of it.

He had taken up a first position behind the little tree, with a direct determination to hold it against the world. He had not deemed it possible that his army could that day succeed, and from this he felt the ability to fight harder. But the throng had surged in all ways, until he lost directions and locations, save that he knew where lay the enemy.

The flames bit him, and the hot smoke broiled his skin. His rifle barrel grew so hot that ordinarily he could not have borne it upon his palms; but he kept on stuffing cartridges into it, and pounding them with his clanking, bending ramrod. If he aimed at some changing form through the smoke, he pulled his trigger with a fierce grunt, as if he were dealing a blow of the fist with all his strength.

When the enemy seemed falling back before him and his fellows, he went instantly forward, like a dog who, seeing his foes lagging, turns and insists upon being pursued. And when he was compelled to retire again, he did it slowly, sullenly, taking steps of wrathful despair.

Once he, in his intent hate, was almost alone, and was firing, when all those near him had ceased. He was so engrossed in his occupation that he was not aware of a lull.

He was recalled by a hoarse laugh and a sentence that came to his ears in a voice of contempt and amazement. "Yeh infernal fool, don't yeh know enough t' quit when there ain't anything t' shoot at? Good Gawd!"

He turned then and, pausing with his rifle thrown half into position, looked at the blue line of his comrades. During this moment of leisure they seemed all to be engaged in staring with astonishment at him. They had become spectators. Turning to the front again he saw, under the lifted smoke, a deserted ground.

He looked bewildered for a moment. Then there appeared upon the glazed vacancy of his eyes a diamond point of intelligence. "Oh," he said, comprehending.

He returned to his comrades and threw himself upon the ground. He sprawled like a man who had been thrashed. His flesh seemed strangely on fire, and the sounds of the battle continued in his ears. He groped blindly for his canteen.

The lieutenant was crowing. He seemed drunk with fighting. He called out to the youth: "By heavens, if I had ten thousand wild cats like you I could tear th' stomach outa this war in less'n a week!" He puffed out his chest with large dignity as he said it.

Some of the men muttered and looked at the youth in awe-struck ways. It was plain that as he had gone on loading and firing and cursing without the proper intermission, they had found time to regard him. And they now looked upon him as a war devil.

The friend came staggering to him. There was some fright and dismay in his voice. "Are yeh all right, Fleming? Do yeh feel all right? There ain't nothin' th' matter with yeh, Henry, is there?"

"No," said the youth with difficulty. His throat seemed full of knobs and burs.

These incidents made the youth ponder. It was revealed to him that he had been a barbarian, a beast. He had fought like a pagan who defends his religion. Regarding it, he saw that it was fine, wild, and, in some ways, easy. He had been a tremendous figure, no doubt. By this struggle he had overcome obstacles which he had admitted to be mountains. They had fallen like paper peaks, and he was now what he called a hero. And he had not been aware of the process. He had slept and, awakening, found himself a knight.

He lay and basked in the occasional stares of his comrades. Their faces were varied in degrees of blackness from the burned powder. Some were utterly smudged. They were reeking with perspiration, and their breaths came hard and wheezing. And from these soiled expanses they peered at him.

"Hot work! Hot work!" cried the lieutenant deliriously. He walked up and down, restless and eager. Sometimes his voice could be heard in a wild, incomprehensible laugh.

When he had a particularly profound thought upon the science of war he always unconsciously addressed himself to the youth.

There was some grim rejoicing by the men.
"By thunder, I bet this army'll never see another new reg'ment like us!"
"You bet!"

"A dog, a woman, an' a walnut tree,
Th' more yeh beat 'em, th' better they be!

That's like us."
"Lost a piler men, they did. If an' ol' woman swep' up th' woods she'd git a dustpanful."
"Yes, an' if she'll come around ag'in in 'bout an' hour she'll git a pile more."
The forest still bore its burden of clamor. From off under the trees came the rolling clatter of the musketry. Each distant thicket seemed a strange porcupine with quills of flame. A cloud of dark smoke, as from smoldering ruins, went up toward the sun now bright and gay in the blue, enameled sky.

CHAPTER XVIII.

The ragged line had respite for some minutes, but during its pause the struggle in the forest became magnified until the trees seemed to quiver from the firing and the ground to shake from the rushing of the men. The voices of the cannon were mingled in a long and interminable row. It seemed difficult to live in such an atmosphere. The chests of the men strained for a bit of freshness, and their throats craved water.

There was one shot through the body, who raised a cry of bitter lamentation when came this lull. Perhaps he had been calling out during the fighting also, but at that time no one had heard him. But now the men turned at the woeful complaints of him upon the ground.

"Who is it? Who is it?"

"It's Jimmie Rogers. Jimmie Rogers."

When their eyes first encountered him there was a sudden halt, as if they feared to go near. He was thrashing about in the grass, twisting his shuddering body into many strange postures. He was screaming loudly. This instant's hesitation seemed to fill him with a tremendous, fantastic contempt, and he damned them in shrieked sentences.

The youth's friend had a geographical illusion concerning a stream, and he obtained permission to go for some water. Immediately canteens were showered upon him. "Fill mine, will yeh?" "Bring me some, too." "And me, too." He departed, ladened. The youth went with his friend, feeling a desire to throw his heated body onto the stream and, soaking there, drink quarts.

They made a hurried search for the supposed stream, but did not find it. "No water here," said the youth. They turned without delay and began to retrace their steps.

From their position as they again faced toward the place of the fighting, they could of course comprehend a greater amount of the battle than when their visions had been blurred by the hurling smoke of the line. They could see dark stretches winding along the land, and on one cleared space there was a row of guns making gray clouds, which were filled with large flashes of orange-colored flame. Over some foliage they could see the roof of a house. One window, glowing a deep murder red, shone squarely through the leaves. From the edifice a tall leaning tower of smoke went far into the sky.

Looking over their own troops, they saw mixed masses slowly getting into regular form. The sunlight made twinkling points of the bright steel. To the rear there was a glimpse of a distant roadway as it curved over a slope. It was crowded with retreating infantry. From all the interwoven forest arose the smoke and bluster of the battle. The air was always occupied by a blaring.

Near where they stood shells were flip-flapping and hooting. Occasional bullets buzzed in the air and spanged into tree trunks. Wounded men and other stragglers were slinking through the woods.

Looking down an aisle of the grove, the youth and his companion saw a jangling general and his staff almost ride upon a wounded man, who was crawling on his hands and knees. The general reined strongly at his charger's opened and foamy mouth and guided it with dexterous horsemanship past the man. The latter scrambled in wild and torturing haste. His strength evidently failed him as he reached a place of safety. One of his arms suddenly weakened, and he fell, sliding over upon his back. He lay stretched out, breathing gently.

A moment later the small, creaking cavalcade was directly in front of the two soldiers. Another officer, riding with the skillful abandon of a cowboy, galloped his horse to a position directly before the general. The two unnoticed foot soldiers made a little show of going on, but they lingered near in the desire to overhear the conversation. Perhaps, they thought, some great inner historical things would be said.

The general, whom the boys knew as the commander of their division, looked at the other officer and spoke coolly, as if he were criticising his clothes. "Th' enemy's formin' over there for another charge," he said. "It'll be directed against Whiterside, an' I fear they'll break through there unless we work like thunder t' stop them."

The other swore at his restive horse, and then cleared his throat. He made a gesture toward his cap. "It'll be hell t' pay stoppin' them," he said shortly.

"I presume so," remarked the general. Then he began to talk rapidly and in a lower tone. He frequently illustrated his words with a pointing finger. The two infantrymen could hear nothing until finally he asked: "What troops can you spare?"

The officer who rode like a cowboy reflected for an instant. "Well," he said, "I had to order in th' 12th to help th' 76th, an' I haven't really got any. But there's th' 304th. They fight like a lot 'a mule drivers. I can spare them best of any."

The youth and his friend exchanged glances of astonishment.

The general spoke sharply. "Get 'em ready, then. I'll watch developments from here, an' send you word when t' start them. It'll happen in five minutes."

As the other officer tossed his fingers toward his cap and wheeling his horse, started away, the general called out to him in a sober voice: "I don't believe many of your mule drivers will get back."

The other shouted something in reply. He smiled.

With scared faces, the youth and his companion hurried back to the line.

These happenings had occupied an incredibly short time, yet the youth felt that in them he had been made aged. New eyes were given to him. And the most startling thing was to learn suddenly that he was very insignificant. The officer spoke of the regiment as if he referred to a broom. Some part of the woods needed sweeping, perhaps, and he merely indicated a broom in a tone properly indifferent to its fate. It was war, no doubt, but it appeared strange.

As the two boys approached the line, the lieutenant perceived them and swelled with wrath. "Fleming-Wilson-how long does it take yeh to git water, anyhow-where yeh been to."

But his oration ceased as he saw their eyes, which were large with great tales. "We're goin' t' charge-we're goin' t' charge!" cried the youth's friend, hastening with his news.

"Charge?" said the lieutenant. "Charge? Well, b'Gawd! Now, this is real fightin'." Over his soiled countenance there went a boastful smile. "Charge? Well, b'Gawd!"

A little group of soldiers surrounded the two youths. "Are we, sure 'nough? Well, I'll be derned! Charge? What fer? What at? Wilson, you're lyin'."

"I hope to die," said the youth, pitching his tones to the key of angry remonstrance. "Sure as shooting, I tell you."

And his friend spoke in re-enforcement. "Not by a blame sight, he ain't lyin'. We heard 'em talkin'."

They caught sight of two mounted figures a short distance from them. One was the colonel of the regiment and the other was the officer who had received orders from the commander of the division. They were gesticulating at each other. The soldier, pointing at them, interpreted the scene.

One man had a final objection: "How could yeh hear 'em talkin'?" But the men, for a large part, nodded, admitting that previously the two friends had spoken truth.

They settled back into reposeful attitudes with airs of having accepted the matter. And they mused upon it, with a hundred varieties of expression. It was an engrossing thing to think about. Many tightened their belts carefully and hitched at their trousers.

A moment later the officers began to bustle among the men, pushing them into a more compact mass and into a better alignment. They chased those that straggled and fumed at a few men who seemed to show by their attitudes that they had decided to remain at that spot. They were like critical shepherds struggling with sheep.

Presently, the regiment seemed to draw itself up and heave a deep breath. None of the men's faces were mirrors of large thoughts. The soldiers were bended and stooped like sprinters before a signal. Many pairs of glinting eyes peered from the grimy faces toward the curtains of the deeper woods. They seemed to be engaged in deep calculations of time and distance.

They were surrounded by the noises of the monstrous altercation between the two armies. The world was fully interested in other matters. Apparently, the regiment had its small affair to itself.

The youth, turning, shot a quick, inquiring glance at his friend. The latter returned to him the same manner of look. They were the only ones who possessed an inner knowledge. "Mule drivers-hell t' pay-don't believe many will get back." It was an ironical secret. Still, they saw no hesitation in each other's faces, and they nodded a mute and unprotesting assent when a shaggy man near them said in a meek voice: "We'll git swallowed."

CHAPTER XIX.

The youth stared at the land in front of him. Its foliages now seemed to veil powers and horrors. He was unaware of the machinery of orders that started the charge, although from the corners of his eyes he saw an officer, who looked like a boy a-horseback, come galloping, waving his hat. Suddenly he felt a straining and heaving among the men. The line fell slowly forward like a toppling wall, and, with a convulsive gasp that was intended for a cheer, the regiment began its journey. The youth was pushed and jostled for a moment before he understood the movement at all, but directly he lunged ahead and began to run.

He fixed his eye upon a distant and prominent clump of trees where he had concluded the enemy were to be met, and he ran toward it as toward a goal. He had believed throughout that it was a mere question of getting over an unpleasant matter as quickly as possible, and he ran desperately, as if pursued for a murder. His face was drawn hard and tight with the stress of his endeavor. His eyes were fixed in a lurid glare. And with his soiled and disordered dress, his red and inflamed features surmounted by the dingy rag with its spot of blood, his wildly swinging rifle and banging accouterments, he looked to be an insane soldier.

As the regiment swung from its position out into a cleared space the woods and thickets before it awakened. Yellow flames leaped toward it from many directions. The forest made a tremendous objection.

The line lurched straight for a moment. Then the right wing swung forward; it in turn was surpassed by the left. Afterward the center careered to the front until the regiment was a wedge-shaped mass, but an instant later the opposition of the bushes, trees, and uneven places on the ground split the command and scattered it into detached clusters.

The youth, light-footed, was unconsciously in advance. His eyes still kept note of the clump of trees. From all places near it the clannish yell of the enemy could be heard. The little flames of rifles leaped from it. The song of the bullets was in the air and shells snarled among the tree-tops. One tumbled directly into the middle of a hurrying group and exploded in crimson fury. There was an instant's spectacle of a man, almost over it, throwing up his hands to shield his eyes.

Other men, punched by bullets, fell in grotesque agonies. The regiment left a coherent trail of bodies.

They had passed into a clearer atmosphere. There was an effect like a revelation in the new appearance of the landscape. Some men working madly at a battery were plain to them, and the opposing infantry's lines were defined by the gray walls and fringes of smoke.

It seemed to the youth that he saw everything. Each blade of the green grass was bold and clear. He thought that he was aware of every change in the thin, transparent vapor that floated idly in sheets. The brown or gray trunks of the trees showed each roughness of their surfaces. And the men of the regiment, with their starting eyes and sweating faces, running madly, or falling, as if thrown headlong, to queer, heaped-up corpses-all were comprehended. His mind took a mechanical but firm impression, so that afterward everything was pictured and explained to him, save why he himself was there.

But there was a frenzy made from this furious rush. The men, pitching forward insanely, had burst into cheerings, moblike and barbaric, but tuned in strange keys that can arouse the dullard and the stoic. It made a mad enthusiasm that, it seemed, would be incapable of checking itself before granite and brass. There was the delirium that encounters despair and death, and is heedless and blind to the odds. It is a temporary but sublime absence of selfishness. And because it was of this order was the reason, perhaps, why the youth wondered, afterward, what reasons he could have had for being there.

Presently the straining pace ate up the energies of the men. As if by agreement, the leaders began to slacken their speed. The volleys directed against them had had a seeming windlike effect. The regiment snorted and blew. Among some stolid trees it began to falter and hesitate. The men, staring intently, began to wait for some of the distant walls of smoke to move and disclose to them the scene. Since much of their strength and their breath had vanished, they returned to caution. They were become men again.

The youth had a vague belief that he had run miles, and he thought, in a way, that he was now in some new and unknown land.

The moment the regiment ceased its advance the protesting splutter of musketry became a steadied roar. Long and accurate fringes of smoke spread out. From the top of a small hill came level belchings of yellow flame that caused an inhuman whistling in the air.

The men, halted, had opportunity to see some of their comrades dropping with moans and shrieks. A few lay under foot, still or wailing. And now for an instant the men stood, their rifles slack in their hands, and watched the regiment dwindle. They appeared dazed and stupid. This spectacle seemed to paralyze them, overcome them with a fatal fascination. They stared woodenly at the sights, and, lowering their eyes, looked from face to face. It was a strange pause, and a strange silence.

Then, above the sounds of the outside commotion, arose the roar of the lieutenant. He strode suddenly forth, his infantile features black with rage.

"Come on, yeh fools!" he bellowed. "Come on! Yeh can't stay here. Yeh must come on." He said more, but much of it could not be understood.

He started rapidly forward, with his head turned toward the men. "Come on," he was shouting. The men stared with blank and yokel-like eyes at him. He was obliged to halt and retrace his steps. He stood then with his back to the enemy and delivered gigantic curses into the faces of the men. His body vibrated from the weight and force of his imprecations. And he could string oaths with the facility of a maiden who strings beads.

The friend of the youth aroused. Lurching suddenly forward and dropping to his knees, he fired an angry shot at the persistent woods. This action awakened the men. They huddled no more like sheep. They seemed suddenly to bethink them of their weapons, and at once commenced firing. Belabored by their officers, they began to move forward. The regiment, involved like a cart involved in mud and muddle, started unevenly with many jolts and jerks. The men stopped now every few paces to fire and load, and in this manner moved slowly on from trees to trees.

The flaming opposition in their front grew with their advance until it seemed that all forward ways were barred by the thin leaping tongues, and off to the right an ominous demonstration could sometimes be dimly discerned. The smoke lately generated was in confusing clouds that made it difficult for the regiment to proceed with intelligence. As he passed through each curling mass the youth wondered what would confront him on the farther side.

The command went painfully forward until an open space interposed between them and the lurid lines. Here, crouching and cowering behind some trees, the men clung with desperation, as if threatened by a wave. They looked wild-eyed, and as if amazed at this furious disturbance they had stirred. In the storm there was an ironical expression of their importance. The faces of the men, too, showed a lack of a certain feeling of responsibility for being there. It was as if they had been driven. It was the dominant animal failing to remember in the supreme moments the forceful causes of various superficial qualities. The whole affair seemed incomprehensible to many of them.

As they halted thus the lieutenant again began to bellow profanely. Regardless of the vindictive threats of the bullets, he went about coaxing, berating, and bedamning. His lips, that were habitually in a soft and childlike curve, were now writhed into unholy contortions. He swore by all possible deities.

Once he grabbed the youth by the arm. "Come on, yeh lunkhead!" he roared. "Come on! We'll all git killed if we stay here. We've on'y got t' go across that lot. An' then"—the remainder of his idea disappeared in a blue haze of curses.

The youth stretched forth his arm. "Cross there?" His mouth was puckered in doubt and awe.

"Certainly. Jest 'cross th' lot! We can't stay here," screamed the lieutenant. He poked his face close to the youth and waved his bandaged hand. "Come on!" Presently he grappled with him as if for a wrestling bout. It was as if he planned to drag the youth by the ear on to the assault.

The private felt a sudden unspeakable indignation against his officer. He wrenched fiercely and shook him off.

"Come on yerself, then," he yelled. There was a bitter challenge in his voice.

They galloped together down the regimental front. The friend scrambled after them. In front of the colors the three men began to bawl: "Come on! come on!" They danced and gyrated like tortured savages.

The flag, obedient to these appeals, bended its glittering form and swept toward them. The men wavered in indecision for a moment, and then with a long, wailful cry the dilapidated regiment surged forward and began its new journey.

Over the field went the scurrying mass. It was a handful of men splattered into the faces of the enemy. Toward it instantly sprang the yellow tongues. A vast quantity of blue smoke hung before them. A mighty banging made ears valueless.

The youth ran like a madman to reach the woods before a bullet could discover him. He ducked his head low, like a football player. In his haste his eyes almost closed, and the scene was a wild blur. Pulsating saliva stood at the corners of his mouth.

Within him, as he hurled himself forward, was born a love, a despairing fondness for this flag which was near him. It was a creation of beauty and invulnerability. It was a goddess, radiant, that bended its form with an imperious gesture to him. It was a woman, red and white, hating and loving, that called him with the voice of his hopes. Because no harm could come to it he endowed it with power. He kept near, as if it could be a saver of lives, and an imploring cry went from his mind.

In the mad scramble he was aware that the color sergeant flinched suddenly, as if struck by a bludgeon. He faltered, and then became motionless, save for his quivering knees.

He made a spring and a clutch at the pole. At the same instant his friend grabbed it from the other side. They jerked at it, stout and furious, but the color sergeant was dead, and the corpse would not relinquish its trust. For a moment there was a grim encounter. The dead man, swinging with bended back, seemed to be obstinately tugging, in ludicrous and awful ways, for the possession of the flag.

It was past in an instant of time. They wrenched the flag furiously from the dead man, and, as they turned again, the corpse swayed forward with bowed head. One arm swung high, and the curved hand fell with heavy protest on the friend's unheeding shoulder.

CHAPTER XX.

When the two youths turned with the flag they saw that much of the regiment had crumbled away, and the dejected remnant was coming slowly back. The men, having hurled themselves in projectile fashion, had presently expended their forces. They slowly retreated, with their faces still toward the spluttering woods, and their hot rifles still replying to the din. Several officers were giving orders, their voices keyed to screams.

"Where in hell yeh goin'?" the lieutenant was asking in a sarcastic howl. And a red-bearded officer, whose voice of triple brass could plainly be heard, was commanding: "Shoot into 'em! Shoot into 'em, Gawd damn their souls!" There was a *melée* of screeches, in which the men were ordered to do conflicting and impossible things.

The youth and his friend had a small scuffle over the flag. "Give it t' me!" "No, let me keep it!" Each felt satisfied with the other's possession of it, but each felt bound to declare, by an offer to carry the emblem, his willingness to further risk himself. The youth roughly pushed his friend away.

The regiment fell back to the stolid trees. There it halted for a moment to blaze at some dark forms that had begun to steal upon its track. Presently it resumed its march again, curving among the tree trunks. By the time the depleted regiment had again reached the first open space they were receiving a fast and merciless fire. There seemed to be mobs all about them.

The greater part of the men, discouraged, their spirits worn by the turmoil, acted as if stunned. They accepted the pelting of the bullets with bowed and weary heads. It was of no purpose to strive against walls. It was of no use to batter themselves against granite. And from this consciousness that they had attempted to conquer an unconquerable thing there seemed to arise a feeling that they had been betrayed. They glowered with bent brows, but dangerously, upon some of the officers, more particularly upon the red-bearded one with the voice of triple brass.

However, the rear of the regiment was fringed with men, who continued to shoot irritably at the advancing foes. They seemed resolved to make every trouble. The youthful lieutenant was perhaps the last man in the disordered mass. His forgotten back was toward the enemy. He had been shot in the arm. It hung straight and rigid. Occasionally he would cease to remember it, and be about to emphasize an oath with a sweeping gesture. The multiplied pain caused him to swear with incredible power.

The youth went along with slipping, uncertain feet. He kept watchful eyes rearward. A scowl of mortification and rage was upon his face. He had thought of a fine revenge upon the officer who had referred to him and his fellows as mule drivers. But he saw that it could not come to pass. His dreams had collapsed when the mule drivers, dwindling rapidly, had wavered and hesitated on the little clearing, and then had recoiled. And now the retreat of the mule drivers was a march of shame to him.

A dagger-pointed gaze from without his blackened face was held toward the enemy, but his greater hatred was riveted upon the man, who, not knowing him, had called him a mule driver.

When he knew that he and his comrades had failed to do anything in successful ways that might bring the little pangs of a kind of remorse upon the officer, the youth allowed the rage of the baffled to possess him. This cold officer upon a monument, who dropped epithets unconcernedly down, would be finer as a dead man, he thought. So grievous did he think it that he could never possess the secret right to taunt truly in answer.

He had pictured red letters of curious revenge. "We *are* mule drivers, are we?" And now he was compelled to throw them away.

He presently wrapped his heart in the cloak of his pride and kept the flag erect. He harangued his fellows, pushing against their chests with his free hand. To those he knew well he made frantic appeals, beseeching them by name. Between him and the lieutenant, scolding and near to losing his mind with rage, there was felt a subtle fellowship and equality. They supported each other in all manner of hoarse, howling protests.

But the regiment was a machine run down. The two men babbled at a forceless thing. The soldiers who had heart to go slowly were continually shaken in their resolves by a knowledge that comrades were slipping with speed back to the lines. It was difficult to think of reputation when others were thinking of skins. Wounded men were left crying on this black journey.

The smoke fringes and flames blustered always. The youth, peering once through a sudden rift in a cloud, saw a brown mass of troops, interwoven and magnified until they appeared to be thousands. A fierce-hued flag flashed before his vision.

Immediately, as if the uplifting of the smoke had been prearranged, the discovered troops burst into a rasping yell, and a hundred flames jetted toward the retreating band. A rolling gray cloud again interposed as the regiment doggedly replied. The youth had to depend again upon his misused ears, which were trembling and buzzing from the *melée* of musketry and yells.

The way seemed eternal. In the clouded haze men became panicstricken with the thought that the regiment had lost its path, and was proceeding in a perilous direction. Once the men who headed the wild procession turned and came pushing back against their comrades, screaming that they were being fired upon from points which they had considered to be toward their own lines. At this cry a hysterical fear and dismay beset the troops. A soldier, who heretofore had been ambitious to make the regiment into a wise little band that would proceed calmly amid the huge-appearing difficulties, suddenly sank down and buried his face in his arms with an air of bowing to a doom. From another a shrill lamentation rang out filled with profane allusions to a general. Men ran hither and thither, seeking with their eyes roads of escape. With serene regularity, as if controlled by a schedule, bullets buffed into men.

The youth walked stolidly into the midst of the mob, and with his flag in his hands took a stand as if he expected an attempt to push him to the ground. He unconsciously assumed the attitude of the color bearer in the fight of the preceding day. He passed over his brow a hand that trembled. His breath did not come freely. He was choking during this small wait for the crisis.

His friend came to him. "Well, Henry, I guess this is good-by—John."

"Oh, shut up, you damned fool!" replied the youth, and he would not look at the other.

The officers labored like politicians to beat the mass into a proper circle to face the menaces. The ground was uneven and torn. The men curled into depressions and fitted themselves snugly behind whatever would frustrate a bullet.

The youth noted with vague surprise that the lieutenant was standing mutely with his legs far apart and his sword held in the manner of a cane. The youth wondered what had happened to his vocal organs that he no more cursed.

There was something curious in this little intent pause of the lieutenant. He was like a babe which, having wept its fill, raises its eyes and fixes upon a distant toy. He was engrossed in this contemplation, and the soft under lip quivered from self-whispered words.

Some lazy and ignorant smoke curled slowly. The men, hiding from the bullets, waited anxiously for it to lift and disclose the plight of the regiment.

The silent ranks were suddenly thrilled by the eager voice of the youthful lieutenant bawling out: "Here they come! Right onto us, b'Gawd!" His further words were lost in a roar of wicked thunder from the men's rifles.

The youth's eyes had instantly turned in the direction indicated by the awakened and agitated lieutenant, and he had seen the haze of treachery disclosing a body of soldiers of the enemy. They were so near that he could see their features. There was a recognition as he looked at the types of faces. Also he perceived with dim amazement that their uniforms were rather gay in effect, being light gray, accented with a brilliant-hued facing. Too, the clothes seemed new.

These troops had apparently been going forward with caution, their rifles held in readiness, when the youthful lieutenant had discovered them and their movement had been interrupted by the volley from the blue regiment. From the moment's glimpse, it was derived that they had been unaware of the proximity of their dark-suited foes or had mistaken the direction. Almost instantly they were shut utterly from the youth's sight by the smoke from the energetic rifles of his companions. He strained his vision to learn the accomplishment of the volley, but the smoke hung before him.

The two bodies of troops exchanged blows in the manner of a pair of boxers. The fast angry firings went back and forth. The men in blue were intent with the despair of their circumstances and they seized upon the revenge to be had at close range. Their thunder swelled loud and valiant. Their curving front bristled with flashes and the place resounded with the clangor of their ramrods. The youth ducked and dodged for a time and achieved a few unsatisfactory views of the enemy. There appeared to be many of them and they were replying swiftly. They seemed moving toward the blue regiment, step by step. He seated himself gloomily on the ground with his flag between his knees.

As he noted the vicious, wolflike temper of his comrades he had a sweet thought that if the enemy was about to swallow the regimental broom as a large prisoner, it could at least have the consolation of going down with bristles forward.

But the blows of the antagonist began to grow more weak. Fewer bullets ripped the air, and finally, when the men slackened to learn of the fight, they could see only dark, floating smoke. The regiment lay still and gazed. Presently some chance whim came to the pestering blur, and it began to coil heavily away. The men saw a ground vacant of fighters. It would have been an empty stage if it were not for a few corpses that lay thrown and twisted into fantastic shapes upon the sward.

At sight of this tableau, many of the men in blue sprang from behind their covers and made an ungainly dance of joy. Their eyes burned and a hoarse cheer of elation broke from their dry lips.

It had begun to seem to them that events were trying to prove that they were impotent. These little battles had evidently endeavored to demonstrate that the men could not fight well. When on the verge of submission to these opinions, the small duel had showed them that the proportions were not impossible, and by it they had revenged themselves upon their misgivings and upon the foe.

The impetus of enthusiasm was theirs again. They gazed about them with looks of uplifted pride, feeling new trust in the grim, always confident weapons in their hands. And they were men.

CHAPTER XXI.

Presently they knew that no firing threatened them. All ways seemed once more opened to them. The dusty blue lines of their friends were disclosed a short distance away. In the distance there were many colossal noises, but in all this part of the field there was a sudden stillness.

They perceived that they were free. The depleted band drew a long breath of relief and gathered itself into a bunch to complete its trip.

In this last length of journey the men began to show strange emotions. They hurried with nervous fear. Some who had been dark and unfaltering in the grimmest moments now could not conceal an anxiety that made them frantic. It was perhaps that they dreaded to be killed in insignificant ways after the times for proper military deaths had passed. Or, perhaps, they thought it would be too ironical to get killed at the portals of safety. With backward looks of perturbation, they hastened.

As they approached their own lines there was some sarcasm exhibited on the part of a gaunt and bronzed regiment that lay resting in the shade of trees. Questions were wafted to them.

"Where th' hell yeh been?"

"What yeh comin' back fer?"

"Why didn't yeh stay there?"

"Was it warm out there, sonny?"

"Goin' home now, boys?"

One shouted in taunting mimicry: "Oh, mother, come quick an' look at th' sojers!"

There was no reply from the bruised and battered regiment, save that one man made broadcast challenges to fist fights and the red-bearded officer walked rather near and glared in great swashbuckler style at a tall captain in the other regiment. But the lieutenant suppressed the man who wished to fist fight, and the tall captain, flushing at the little fanfare of the red-bearded one, was obliged to look intently at some trees.

The youth's tender flesh was deeply stung by these remarks. From under his creased brows he glowered with hate at the mockers. He meditated upon a few revenges. Still, many in the regiment hung their heads in criminal fashion, so that it came to pass that the men trudged with sudden heaviness, as if they bore upon their bended shoulders the coffin of their honor. And the youthful lieutenant, recollecting himself, began to mutter softly in black curses.

They turned when they arrived at their old position to regard the ground over which they had charged.

The youth in this contemplation was smitten with a large astonishment. He discovered that the distances, as compared with the brilliant measurings of his mind, were trivial and ridiculous. The stolid trees, where much had taken place, seemed incredibly near. The time, too, now that he reflected, he saw to have been short. He wondered at the number of emotions and events that had been crowded into such little spaces. Elfin thoughts must have exaggerated and enlarged everything, he said.

It seemed, then, that there was bitter justice in the speeches of the gaunt and bronzed veterans. He veiled a glance of disdain at his fellows who strewed the ground, choking with dust, red from perspiration, misty-eyed, disheveled.

They were gulping at their canteens, fierce to wring every mite of water from them, and they polished at their swollen and watery features with coat sleeves and bunches of grass.

However, to the youth there was a considerable joy in musing upon his performances during the charge. He had had very little time previously in which to appreciate himself, so that there was now much satisfaction in quietly thinking of his actions. He recalled bits of color that in the flurry had stamped themselves unawares upon his engaged senses.

As the regiment lay heaving from its hot exertions the officer who had named them as mule drivers came galloping along the line. He had lost his cap. His tousled hair streamed wildly, and his face was dark with vexation and wrath. His temper was displayed with more clearness by the way in which he managed his horse. He jerked and wrenched savagely at his bridle, stopping the hard-breathing animal with a furious pull near the colonel of the regiment. He immediately exploded in reproaches which came unbidden to the ears of the men. They were suddenly alert, being always curious about black words between officers.

"Oh, thunder, MacChesnay, what an awful bull you made of this thing!" began the officer. He attempted low tones, but his indignation caused certain of the men to learn the sense of his words. "What an awful mess you made! Good Lord, man, you stopped about a hundred feet this side of a very pretty success! If your men had gone a hundred feet farther you would have made a great charge, but as it is-what a lot of mud diggers you've got anyway!"

The men, listening with bated breath, now turned their curious eyes upon the colonel. They had a ragamuffin interest in this affair.

The colonel was seen to straighten his form and put one hand forth in oratorical fashion. He wore an injured air; it was as if a deacon had been accused of stealing. The men were wiggling in an ecstasy of excitement.

But of a sudden the colonel's manner changed from that of a deacon to that of a Frenchman. He shrugged his shoulders. "Oh, well, general, we went as far as we could," he said calmly.

"As far as you could? Did you, b'Gawd?" snorted the other. "Well, that wasn't very far, was it?" he added, with a glance of cold contempt into the other's eyes. "Not very far, I think. You were intended to make a diversion in favor of Whiterside. How well you succeeded your own ears can now tell you." He wheeled his horse and rode stiffly away.

The colonel, bidden to hear the jarring noises of an engagement in the woods to the left, broke out in vague damnations.

The lieutenant, who had listened with an air of impotent rage to the interview, spoke suddenly in firm and undaunted tones. "I don't care what a man is-whether he is a general or what-if he says th' boys didn't put up a good fight out there he's a damned fool."

"Lieutenant," began the colonel, severely, "this is my own affair, and I'll trouble you —"

The lieutenant made an obedient gesture. "All right, colonel, all right," he said. He sat down with an air of being content with himself.

The news that the regiment had been reproached went along the line. For a time the men were bewildered by it. "Good thunder!" they ejaculated, staring at the vanishing form of the general. They conceived it to be a huge mistake.

Presently, however, they began to believe that in truth their efforts had been called light. The youth could see this conviction weigh upon the entire regiment until the men were like cuffed and cursed animals, but withal rebellious.

The friend, with a grievance in his eye, went to the youth. "I wonder what he does want," he said. "He must think we went out there an' played marbles! I never see sech a man!"

The youth developed a tranquil philosophy for these moments of irritation. "Oh, well," he rejoined, "he probably didn't see nothing of it at all and got mad as blazes, and concluded we were a lot of sheep, just because we didn't do what he wanted done. It's a pity old Grandpa Henderson got killed yestirday-he'd have known that we did our best and fought good. It's just our awful luck, that's what."

"I should say so," replied the friend. He seemed to be deeply wounded at an injustice. "I should say we did have awful luck! There's no fun in fightin' fer people when everything yeh do-no matter what-ain't done right. I have a notion t' stay behind next time an' let 'em take their ol' charge an' go t' th' devil with it."

The youth spoke soothingly to his comrade. "Well, we both did good. I'd like to see the fool what'd say we both didn't do as good as we could!"

"Of course we did," declared the friend stoutly. "An' I'd break th' feller's neck if he was as big as a church. But we're all right, anyhow, for I heard one feller say that we two fit th' best in th' reg'ment, an' they had a great argument 'bout it. Another feller, 'a course, he had t' up an' say it was a lie-he seen all what was goin' on an' he never seen us from th' beginnin' t' th' end. An' a lot more struck in an' ses it wasn't a lie-we did fight like thunder, an' they give us quite a send-off. But this is what I can't stand-these everlastin' ol' soldiers, titterin' an' laughin', an' then that general, he's crazy."

The youth exclaimed with sudden exasperation: "He's a lunkhead! He makes me mad. I wish he'd come along next time. We'd show 'im what —"

He ceased because several men had come hurrying up. Their faces expressed a bringing of great news.

"O Flem, yeh jest oughta heard!" cried one, eagerly.

"Heard what?" said the youth.

"Yeh jest oughta heard!" repeated the other, and he arranged himself to tell his tidings. The others made an excited circle. "Well, sir, th' colonel met your lieutenant right by us-it was damnedest thing I ever heard-an' he ses: 'Ahem! ahem!' he ses. 'Mr. Hasbrouck!' he ses, 'by th' way, who was that lad what carried th' flag?' he ses. There, Flemin', what d' yeh think 'a that? 'Who was th' lad what carried th' flag?' he ses, an' th' lieutenant, he speaks up right away: 'That's Flemin', an' he's a jimhickey,' he ses, right away. What? I say he did. 'A jim-hickey,' he ses-those 'r his words. He did, too. I say he did. If you kin tell this story better than I kin, go ahead an' tell it. Well, then, keep yer mouth shet. Th' lieutenant, he ses: 'He's a jimhickey,' an' th' colonel, he ses: 'Ahem! ahem! he is, indeed, a very good man t' have, ahem! He kep' th' flag 'way t' th' front. I saw 'im. He's a good un,' ses th' colonel. 'You bet,' ses th' lieutenant, 'he an' a feller named Wilson was at th' head 'a th' charge, an' howlin' like Indians all th' time,' he ses. 'Head 'a th' charge all th' time,' he ses. 'A feller named Wilson,' he ses. There, Wilson, m'boy, put that in a letter an' send it hum t' yer mother, hay? 'A feller named Wilson,' he ses. An' th' colonel, he ses: 'Were they, indeed? Ahem! ahem! My sakes!' he ses. 'At th' head 'a th' reg'ment?' he ses. 'They were,' ses th' lieutenant. 'My sakes!' ses th' colonel. He ses: 'Well, well, well,' he ses, 'those two babies?' 'They were,' ses th' lieutenant. 'Well, well,' ses th' colonel, 'they deserve t' be major generals,' he ses. 'They deserve t' be major-generals.'"

The youth and his friend had said: "Huh!" "Yer lyin', Thompson." "Oh, go t' blazes!" "He never sed it." "Oh, what a lie!" "Huh!" But despite these youthful scoffings and embarrassments, they knew that their faces were deeply flushing from thrills of pleasure. They exchanged a secret glance of joy and congratulation.

They speedily forgot many things. The past held no pictures of error and disappointment. They were very happy, and their hearts swelled with grateful affection for the colonel and the youthful lieutenant.

CHAPTER XXII.

When the woods again began to pour forth the dark-hued masses of the enemy the youth felt serene self-confidence. He smiled briefly when he saw men dodge and duck at the long screechings of shells that were thrown in giant handfuls over them. He stood, erect and tranquil, watching the attack begin against a part of the line that made a blue curve along the side of an adjacent hill. His vision being unmolested by smoke from the rifles of his companions, he had opportunities to see parts of the hard fight. It was a relief to perceive at last from whence came some of these noises which had been roared into his ears.

Off a short way he saw two regiments fighting a little separate battle with two other regiments. It was in a cleared space, wearing a set-apart look. They were blazing as if upon a wager, giving and taking tremendous blows. The firings were incredibly fierce and rapid. These intent regiments apparently were oblivious of all larger purposes of war, and were slugging each other as if at a matched game.

In another direction he saw a magnificent brigade going with the evident intention of driving the enemy from a wood. They passed in out of sight and presently there was a most awe-inspiring racket in the wood. The noise was unspeakable. Having stirred this prodigious uproar, and, apparently, finding it too prodigious, the brigade, after a little time, came marching airily out again with its fine formation in nowise disturbed. There were no traces of speed in its movements. The brigade was jaunty and seemed to point a proud thumb at the yelling wood.

On a slope to the left there was a long row of guns, gruff and maddened, denouncing the enemy, who, down through the woods, were forming for another attack in the pitiless monotony of conflicts. The round red discharges from the guns made a crimson flare and a high, thick smoke. Occasional glimpses could be caught of groups of the toiling artillerymen. In the rear of this row of guns stood a house, calm and white, amid bursting shells. A congregation of horses, tied to a long railing, were tugging frenziedly at their bridles. Men were running hither and thither.

The detached battle between the four regiments lasted for some time. There chanced to be no interference, and they settled their dispute by themselves. They struck savagely and powerfully at each other for a period of minutes, and then the lighter-hued regiments faltered and drew back, leaving the dark-blue lines shouting. The youth could see the two flags shaking with laughter amid the smoke remnants.

Presently there was a stillness, pregnant with meaning. The blue lines shifted and changed a trifle and stared expectantly at the silent woods and fields before them. The hush was solemn and churchlike, save for a distant battery that, evidently unable to remain quiet, sent a faint rolling thunder over the ground. It irritated, like the noises of unimpressed boys. The men imagined that it would prevent their perched ears from hearing the first words of the new battle.

Of a sudden the guns on the slope roared out a message of warning. A spluttering sound had begun in the woods. It swelled with amazing speed to a profound clamor that involved the earth in noises. The splitting crashes swept along the lines until an interminable roar was developed. To those in the midst of it it became a din fitted to the universe. It was the whirring and thumping of gigantic machinery, complications among the smaller stars. The youth's ears were filled up. They were incapable of hearing more.

On an incline over which a road wound he saw wild and desperate rushes of men perpetually backward and forward in riotous surges. These parts of the opposing armies were two long waves that pitched upon each other madly at dictated points. To and fro they swelled. Sometimes, one side by its yells and cheers would proclaim decisive blows, but a moment later the other side would be all yells and cheers. Once the youth saw a spray of light forms go in houndlike leaps toward the waving blue lines. There was much howling, and presently it went away with a vast mouthful of prisoners. Again, he saw a blue wave dash with such thunderous force against a gray obstruction that it seemed to clear the earth of it and leave nothing but trampled sod. And always in their swift and deadly rushes to and fro the men screamed and yelled like maniacs.

Particular pieces of fence or secure positions behind collections of trees were wrangled over, as gold thrones or pearl bedsteads. There were desperate lunges at these chosen spots seemingly every instant, and most of them were bandied like light toys between the contending forces. The youth could not tell from the battle flags flying like crimson foam in many directions which color of cloth was winning.

His emaciated regiment bustled forth with undiminished fierceness when its time came. When assaulted again by bullets, the men burst out in a barbaric cry of rage and pain. They bent their heads in aims of intent hatred behind the projected hammers of their guns. Their ramrods clanged loud with fury as their eager arms pounded the cartridges into the rifle barrels. The front of the regiment was a smoke-wall penetrated by the flashing points of yellow and red.

Wallowing in the fight, they were in an astonishingly short time resmudged. They surpassed in stain and dirt all their previous appearances. Moving to and fro with strained exertion, jabbering the while, they were, with their swaying bodies, black faces, and glowing eyes, like strange and ugly friends jigging heavily in the smoke.

The lieutenant, returning from a tour after a bandage, produced from a hidden receptacle of his mind new and portentous oaths suited to the emergency. Strings of expletives he swung lashlike over the backs of his men, and it was evident that his previous efforts had in nowise impaired his resources.

The youth, still the bearer of the colors, did not feel his idleness. He was deeply absorbed as a spectator. The crash and swing of the great drama made him lean forward, intent-eyed, his face working in small contortions. Sometimes he prattled, words coming unconsciously from him in grotesque exclamations. He did not know that he breathed; that the flag hung silently over him, so absorbed was he.

A formidable line of the enemy came within dangerous range. They could be seen plainly-tall, gaunt men with excited faces running with long strides toward a wandering fence.

At sight of this danger the men suddenly ceased their cursing monotone. There was an instant of strained silence before they threw up their rifles and fired a plumping volley at the foes. There had been no order given; the men, upon recognizing the menace, had immediately let drive their flock of bullets without waiting for word of command.

But the enemy were quick to gain the protection of the wandering line of fence. They slid down behind it with remarkable celerity, and from this position they began briskly to slice up the blue men.

These latter braced their energies for a great struggle. Often, white clinched teeth shone from the dusky faces. Many heads surged to and fro, floating upon a pale sea of smoke. Those behind the fence frequently shouted and yelped in taunts and gibelike cries, but the regiment maintained a stressed silence. Perhaps, at this new assault the men recalled the fact that they had been named mud diggers, and it made their situation thrice bitter. They were breathlessly intent upon keeping the ground and thrusting away the rejoicing body of the enemy. They fought swiftly and with a despairing savageness denoted in their expressions.

The youth had resolved not to budge whatever should happen. Some arrows of scorn that had buried themselves in his heart had generated strange and unspeakable hatred. It was clear to him that his final and absolute revenge was to be achieved by his dead body lying, torn and gluttering, upon the field. This was to be a poignant retaliation upon the officer who had said "mule drivers," and later "mud diggers," for in all the wild graspings of his mind for a unit responsible for his sufferings and commotions he always seized upon the man who had dubbed him wrongly. And it was his idea, vaguely formulated, that his corpse would be for those eyes a great and salt reproach.

The regiment bled extravagantly. Grunting bundles of blue began to drop. The orderly sergeant of the youth's company was shot through the cheeks. Its supports being injured, his jaw hung afar down, disclosing in the wide cavern of his mouth a pulsing mass of blood and teeth. And with it all he made attempts to cry out. In his endeavor there was a dreadful earnestness, as if he conceived that one great shriek would make him well.

The youth saw him presently go rearward. His strength seemed in nowise impaired. He ran swiftly, casting wild glances for succor.

Others fell down about the feet of their companions. Some of the wounded crawled out and away, but many lay still, their bodies twisted into impossible shapes.

The youth looked once for his friend. He saw a vehement young man, powder-smeared and frowzled, whom he knew to be him. The lieutenant, also, was unscathed in his position at the rear. He had continued to curse, but it was now with the air of a man who was using his last box of oaths.

For the fire of the regiment had begun to wane and drip. The robust voice, that had come strangely from the thin ranks, was growing rapidly weak.

CHAPTER XXIII.

The colonel came running along back of the line. There were other officers following him. "We must charge'm!" they shouted. "We must charge'm!" they cried with resentful voices, as if anticipating a rebellion against this plan by the men.

The youth, upon hearing the shouts, began to study the distance between him and the enemy. He made vague calculations. He saw that to be firm soldiers they must go forward. It would be death to stay in the present place, and with all the circumstances to go backward would exalt too many others. Their hope was to push the galling foes away from the fence.

He expected that his companions, weary and stiffened, would have to be driven to this assault, but as he turned toward them he perceived with a certain surprise that they were giving quick and unqualified expressions of assent. There was an ominous, clanging overture to the charge when the shafts of the bayonets rattled upon the rifle barrels. At the yelled words of command the soldiers sprang forward in eager leaps. There was new and unexpected force in the movement of the regiment. A knowledge of its faded and jaded condition made the charge appear like a paroxysm, a display of the strength that comes before a final feebleness. The men scampered in insane fever of haste, racing as if to achieve a sudden success before an exhilarating fluid should leave them. It was a blind and despairing rush by the collection of men in dusty and tattered blue, over a green sward and under a sapphire sky, toward a fence, dimly outlined in smoke, from behind which spluttered the fierce rifles of enemies.

The youth kept the bright colors to the front. He was waving his free arm in furious circles, the while shrieking mad calls and appeals, urging on those that did not need to be urged, for it seemed that the mob of blue men hurling themselves on the dangerous group of rifles were again grown suddenly wild with an enthusiasm of unselfishness. From the many firings starting toward them, it looked as if they would merely succeed in making a great sprinkling of corpses on the grass between their former position and the fence. But they were in a state of frenzy, perhaps because of forgotten vanities, and it made an exhibition of sublime recklessness. There was no obvious questioning, nor figurings, nor diagrams. There was, apparently, no considered loopholes. It appeared that the swift wings of their desires would have shattered against the iron gates of the impossible.

He himself felt the daring spirit of a savage religion mad. He was capable of profound sacrifices, a tremendous death. He had no time for dissections, but he knew that he thought of the bullets only as things that could prevent him from reaching the place of his endeavor. There were subtle flashings of joy within him that thus should be his mind.

He strained all his strength. His eyesight was shaken and dazzled by the tension of thought and muscle. He did not see anything excepting the mist of smoke gashed by the little knives of fire, but he knew that in it lay the aged fence of a vanished farmer protecting the snuggled bodies of the gray men.

As he ran a thought of the shock of contact gleamed in his mind. He expected a great concussion when the two bodies of troops crashed together. This became a part of his wild battle madness. He could feel the onward swing of the regiment about him and he conceived of a thunderous, crushing blow that would prostrate the resistance and spread consternation and amazement for miles. The flying regiment was going to have a catapultian effect. This dream made him run faster among his comrades, who were giving vent to hoarse and frantic cheers.

But presently he could see that many of the men in gray did not intend to abide the blow. The smoke, rolling, disclosed men who ran, their faces still turned. These grew to a crowd, who retired stubbornly. Individuals wheeled frequently to send a bullet at the blue wave.

But at one part of the line there was a grim and obdurate group that made no movement. They were settled firmly down behind posts and rails. A flag, ruffled and fierce, waved over them and their rifles dinned fiercely.

The blue whirl of men got very near, until it seemed that in truth there would be a close and frightful scuffle. There was an expressed disdain in the opposition of the little group, that changed the meaning of the cheers of the men in blue. They became yells of wrath, directed, personal. The cries of the two parties were now in sound an interchange of scathing insults.

They in blue showed their teeth; their eyes shone all white. They launched themselves as at the throats of those who stood resisting. The space between dwindled to an insignificant distance.

The youth had centered the gaze of his soul upon that other flag. Its possession would be high pride. It would express bloody minglings, near blows. He had a gigantic hatred for those who made great difficulties and complications. They caused it to be as a craved treasure of mythology, hung amid tasks and contrivances of danger.

He plunged like a mad horse at it. He was resolved it should not escape if wild blows and darings of blows could seize it. His own emblem, quivering and aflare, was winging toward the other. It seemed there would shortly be an encounter of strange beaks and claws, as of eagles.

The swirling body of blue men came to a sudden halt at close and disastrous range and roared a swift volley. The group in gray was split and broken by this fire, but its riddled body still fought. The men in blue yelled again and rushed in upon it.

The youth, in his leapings, saw, as through a mist, a picture of four or five men stretched upon the ground or writhing upon their knees with bowed heads as if they had been stricken by bolts from the sky. Tottering among them was the rival color bearer, whom the youth saw had been bitten vitally by the bullets of the last formidable volley. He perceived this man fighting a last struggle, the struggle of one whose legs are grasped by demons. It was a ghastly battle. Over his face was the bleach of death, but set upon it was the dark and hard lines of desperate purpose. With this terrible grin of resolution he hugged his precious flag to him and was stumbling and staggering in his design to go the way that led to safety for it.

But his wounds always made it seem that his feet were retarded, held, and he fought a grim fight, as with invisible ghouls fastened greedily upon his limbs. Those in advance of the scampering blue men, howling cheers, leaped at the fence. The despair of the lost was in his eyes as he glanced back at them.

The youth's friend went over the obstruction in a tumbling heap and sprang at the flag as a panther at prey. He pulled at it and, wrenching it free, swung up its red brilliancy with a mad cry of exultation even as the color bearer, gasping, lurched over in a final throe and, stiffening convulsively, turned his dead face to the ground. There was much blood upon the grass blades.

At the place of success there began more wild clamorings of cheers. The men gesticulated and bellowed in an ecstasy. When they spoke it was as if they considered their listener to be a mile away. What hats and caps were left to them they often slung high in the air.

At one part of the line four men had been swooped upon, and they now sat as prisoners. Some blue men were about them in an eager and curious circle. The soldiers had trapped strange birds, and there was an examination. A flurry of fast questions was in the air.

One of the prisoners was nursing a superficial wound in the foot. He cuddled it, baby-wise, but he looked up from it often to curse with an astonishing utter abandon straight at the noses of his captors. He consigned them to red regions; he called upon the pestilential wrath of strange gods. And with it all he was singularly free from recognition of the finer points of the conduct of prisoners of war. It was as if a clumsy clod had trod upon his toe and he conceived it to be his privilege, his duty, to use deep, resentful oaths.

Another, who was a boy in years, took his plight with great calmness and apparent good nature. He conversed with the men in blue, studying their faces with his bright and keen eyes. They spoke of battles and conditions. There was an acute interest in all their faces during this exchange of view points. It seemed a great satisfaction to hear voices from where all had been darkness and speculation.

The third captive sat with a morose countenance. He preserved a stoical and cold attitude. To all advances he made one reply without variation, "Ah, go t' hell!"

The last of the four was always silent and, for the most part, kept his face turned in unmolested directions. From the views the youth received he seemed to be in a state of absolute dejection. Shame was upon him, and with it profound regret that he was, perhaps, no more to be counted in the ranks of his fellows. The youth could detect no expression that would allow him to believe that the other was giving a thought to his narrowed future, the pictured dungeons, perhaps, and starvations and brutalities, liable to the imagination. All to be seen was shame for captivity and regret for the right to antagonize.

After the men had celebrated sufficiently they settled down behind the old rail fence, on the opposite side to the one from which their foes had been driven. A few shot perfunctorily at distant marks.

There was some long grass. The youth nestled in it and rested, making a convenient rail support the flag. His friend, jubilant and glorified, holding his treasure with vanity, came to him there. They sat side by side and congratulated each other.

CHAPTER XXIV.

The roarings that had stretched in a long line of sound across the face of the forest began to grow intermittent and weaker. The stentorian speeches of the artillery continued in some distant encounter, but the crashes of the musketry had almost ceased. The youth and his friend of a sudden looked up, feeling a deadened form of distress at the waning of these noises, which had become a part of life. They could see changes going on among the troops. There were marchings this way and that way. A battery wheeled leisurely. On the crest of a small hill was the thick gleam of many departing muskets.

The youth arose. "Well, what now, I wonder?" he said. By his tone he seemed to be preparing to resent some new monstrosity in the way of dins and smashes. He shaded his eyes with his grimy hand and gazed over the field.

His friend also arose and stared. "I bet we're goin' t' git along out of this an' back over th' river," said he.

"Well, I swan!" said the youth.

They waited, watching. Within a little while the regiment received orders to retrace its way. The men got up grunting from the grass, regretting the soft repose. They jerked their stiffened legs, and stretched their arms over their heads. One man swore as he rubbed his eyes. They all groaned "O Lord!" They had as many objections to this change as they would have had to a proposal for a new battle.

They trampled slowly back over the field across which they had run in a mad scamper.

The regiment marched until it had joined its fellows. The reformed brigade, in column, aimed through a wood at the road. Directly they were in a mass of dust-covered troops, and were trudging along in a way parallel to the enemy's lines as these had been defined by the previous turmoil.

They passed within view of a stolid white house, and saw in front of it groups of their comrades lying in wait behind a neat breastwork. A row of guns were booming at a distant enemy. Shells thrown in reply were raising clouds of dust and splinters. Horsemen dashed along the line of intrenchments.

At this point of its march the division curved away from the field and went winding off in the direction of the river. When the significance of this movement had impressed itself upon the youth he turned his head and looked over his shoulder toward the trampled and *débris*-strewed ground. He breathed a breath of new satisfaction. He finally nudged his friend. "Well, it's all over," he said to him.

His friend gazed backward. "B'Gawd, it is," he assented. They mused.

For a time the youth was obliged to reflect in a puzzled and uncertain way. His mind was undergoing a subtle change. It took moments for it to cast off its battleful ways and resume its accustomed course of thought. Gradually his brain emerged from the clogged clouds, and at last he was enabled to more closely comprehend himself and circumstance.

He understood then that the existence of shot and counter-shot was in the past. He had dwelt in a land of strange, squalling upheavals and had come forth. He had been where there was red of blood and black of passion, and he was escaped. His first thoughts were given to rejoicings at this fact.

Later he began to study his deeds, his failures, and his achievements. Thus, fresh from scenes where many of his usual machines of reflection had been idle, from where he had proceeded sheeplike, he struggled to marshal all his acts.

At last they marched before him clearly. From this present view point he was enabled to look upon them in spectator fashion and to criticise them with some correctness, for his new condition had already defeated certain sympathies.

Regarding his procession of memory he felt gleeful and unregretting, for in it his public deeds were paraded in great and shining prominence. Those performances which had been witnessed by his fellows marched now in wide purple and gold, having various deflections. They went gayly with music. It was pleasure to watch these things. He spent delightful minutes viewing the gilded images of memory.

He saw that he was good. He recalled with a thrill of joy the respectful comments of his fellows upon his conduct.

Nevertheless, the ghost of his flight from the first engagement appeared to him and danced. There were small shoutings in his brain about these matters. For a moment he blushed, and the light of his soul flickered with shame.

A specter of reproach came to him. There loomed the dogging memory of the tattered soldier-he who, gored by bullets and faint for blood, had fretted concerning an imagined wound in another; he who had loaned his last of strength and intellect for the tall soldier; he who, blind with weariness and pain, had been deserted in the field.

For an instant a wretched chill of sweat was upon him at the thought that he might be detected in the thing. As he stood persistently before his vision, he gave vent to a cry of sharp irritation and agony.

His friend turned. "What's the matter, Henry?" he demanded. The youth's reply was an outburst of crimson oaths.

As he marched along the little branch-hung roadway among his prattling companions this vision of cruelty brooded over him. It clung near him always and darkened his view of these deeds in purple and gold. Whichever way his thoughts turned they were followed by the somber phantom of the desertion in the fields. He looked stealthily at his companions, feeling sure that they must discern in his face evidences of this pursuit. But they were plodding in ragged array, discussing with quick tongues the accomplishments of the late battle.

"Oh, if a man should come up an' ask me, I'd say we got a dum good lickin'."

"Lickin'—in yer eye! We ain't licked, sonny. We're goin' down here aways, swing aroun', an' come in behint 'em."

"Oh, hush, with your comin' in behint 'em. I've seen all 'a that I wanta. Don't tell me about comin' in behint—"

"Bill Smithers, he ses he'd rather been in ten hundred battles than been in that heluva hospital. He ses they got shootin' in th' night-time, an' shells dropped plum among 'em in th' hospital. He ses sech hollerin' he never see."

"Hasbrouck? He's th' best off'cer in this here reg'ment. He's a whale."

"Didn't I tell yeh we'd come aroun' in behint 'em? Didn't I tell yeh so? We—"

"Oh, shet yeh mouth!"

For a time this pursuing recollection of the tattered man took all elation from the youth's veins. He saw his vivid error, and he was afraid that it would stand before him all his life. He took no share in the chatter of his comrades, nor did he look at them or know them, save when he felt sudden suspicion that they were seeing his thoughts and scrutinizing each detail of the scene with the tattered soldier.

Yet gradually he mustered force to put the sin at a distance. And at last his eyes seemed to open to some new ways. He found that he could look back upon the brass and bombast of his earlier gospels and see them truly. He was gleeful when he discovered that he now despised them.

With this conviction came a store of assurance. He felt a quiet manhood, nonassertive but of sturdy and strong blood. He knew that he would no more quail before his guides wherever they should point. He had been to touch the great death, and found that, after all, it was but the great death. He was a man.

So it came to pass that as he trudged from the place of blood and wrath his soul changed. He came from hot plowshares to prospects of clover tranquilly, and it was as if hot plowshares were not. Scars faded as flowers.

It rained. The procession of weary soldiers became a bedraggled train, despondent and muttering, marching with churning effort in a trough of liquid brown mud under a low, wretched sky. Yet the youth smiled, for he saw that the world was a world for him, though many discovered it to be made of oaths and walking sticks. He had rid himself of the red sickness of battle. The sultry nightmare was in the past. He had been an animal blistered and sweating in the heat and pain of war. He turned now with a lover's thirst to images of tranquil skies, fresh meadows, cool brooks-an existence of soft and eternal peace.

Over the river a golden ray of sun came through the hosts of leaden rain clouds.

Maggie: A Girl of the Streets

Chapter I

A very little boy stood upon a heap of gravel for the honor of Rum Alley. He was throwing stones at howling urchins from Devil's Row who were circling madly about the heap and pelting at him.

His infantile countenance was livid with fury. His small body was writhing in the delivery of great, crimson oaths.

"Run, Jimmie, run! Dey'll get yehs," screamed a retreating Rum Alley child.

"Naw," responded Jimmie with a valiant roar, "dese micks can't make me run."

Howls of renewed wrath went up from Devil's Row throats. Tattered gamins on the right made a furious assault on the gravel heap. On their small, convulsed faces there shone the grins of true assassins. As they charged, they threw stones and cursed in shrill chorus.

The little champion of Rum Alley stumbled precipitately down the other side. His coat had been torn to shreds in a scuffle, and his hat was gone. He had bruises on twenty parts of his body, and blood was dripping from a cut in his head. His wan features wore a look of a tiny, insane demon.

On the ground, children from Devil's Row closed in on their antagonist. He crooked his left arm defensively about his head and fought with cursing fury. The little boys ran to and fro, dodging, hurling stones and swearing in barbaric trebles.

From a window of an apartment house that upreared its form from amid squat, ignorant stables, there leaned a curious woman. Some laborers, unloading a scow at the dock at the river, paused for a moment and regarded the fight. The engineer of a passive tugboat hung lazily to a railing and watched. Over on the Island, a worm of yellow convicts came from the shadow of a building and crawled slowly along the river's bank.

A stone had smashed into Jimmie's mouth. Blood was bubbling over his chin and down upon his ragged shirt. Tears made furrows on his dirt-stained cheeks. His thin legs had begun to tremble and turn weak, causing his small body to reel. His roaring curses of the first part of the fight had changed to a blasphemous chatter.

In the yells of the whirling mob of Devil's Row children there were notes of joy like songs of triumphant savagery. The little boys seemed to leer gloatingly at the blood upon the other child's face.

Down the avenue came boastfully sauntering a lad of sixteen years, although the chronic sneer of an ideal manhood already sat upon his lips. His hat was tipped with an air of challenge over his eye. Between his teeth, a cigar stump was tilted at the angle of defiance. He walked with a certain swing of the shoulders which appalled the timid. He glanced over into the vacant lot in which the little raving boys from Devil's Row seethed about the shrieking and tearful child from Rum Alley.

"Gee!" he murmured with interest. "A scrap. Gee!"

He strode over to the cursing circle, swinging his shoulders in a manner which denoted that he held victory in his fists. He approached at the back of one of the most deeply engaged of the Devil's Row children.

"Ah, what deh hell," he said, and smote the deeply-engaged one on the back of the head. The little boy fell to the ground and gave a hoarse, tremendous howl. He scrambled to his feet, and perceiving, evidently, the size of his assailant, ran quickly off, shouting alarms. The entire Devil's Row party followed him. They came to a stand a short distance away and yelled taunting oaths at the boy with the chronic sneer. The latter, momentarily, paid no attention to them.

"What deh hell, Jimmie?" he asked of the small champion.

Jimmie wiped his blood-wet features with his sleeve.

"Well, it was dis way, Pete, see! I was goin' teh lick dat Riley kid and dey all pitched on me."

Some Rum Alley children now came forward. The party stood for a moment exchanging vainglorious remarks with Devil's Row. A few stones were thrown at long distances, and words of challenge passed between small warriors. Then the Rum Alley contingent turned slowly in the direction of their home street. They began to give, each to each, distorted versions of the fight. Causes of retreat in particular cases were magnified. Blows dealt in the fight were enlarged to catapultian power, and stones thrown were alleged to have hurtled with infinite accuracy. Valor grew strong again, and the little boys began to swear with great spirit.

"Ah, we blokies kin lick deh hull damn Row," said a child, swaggering.

Little Jimmie was striving to stanch the flow of blood from his cut lips. Scowling, he turned upon the speaker.

"Ah, where deh hell was yeh when I was doin' all deh fightin?" he demanded. "Youse kids makes me tired."

"Ah, go ahn," replied the other argumentatively.

Jimmie replied with heavy contempt. "Ah, youse can't fight, Blue Billie! I kin lick yeh wid one han'."

"Ah, go ahn," replied Billie again.

"Ah," said Jimmie threateningly.

"Ah," said the other in the same tone.

They struck at each other, clinched, and rolled over on the cobble stones.

"Smash 'im, Jimmie, kick deh damn guts out of 'im," yelled Pete, the lad with the chronic sneer, in tones of delight.

The small combatants pounded and kicked, scratched and tore. They began to weep and their curses struggled in their throats with sobs. The other little boys clasped their hands and wriggled their legs in excitement. They formed a bobbing circle about the pair.

A tiny spectator was suddenly agitated.

"Cheese it, Jimmie, cheese it! Here comes yer fader," he yelled.

The circle of little boys instantly parted. They drew away and waited in ecstatic awe for that which was about to happen. The two little boys fighting in the modes of four thousand years ago, did not hear the warning.

Up the avenue there plodded slowly a man with sullen eyes. He was carrying a dinner pail and smoking an apple-wood pipe.

As he neared the spot where the little boys strove, he regarded them listlessly. But suddenly he roared an oath and advanced upon the rolling fighters.

"Here, you Jim, git up, now, while I belt yer life out, you damned disorderly brat."

He began to kick into the chaotic mass on the ground. The boy Billie felt a heavy boot strike his head. He made a furious effort and disentangled himself from Jimmie. He tottered away, damning.

Jimmie arose painfully from the ground and confronting his father, began to curse him. His parent kicked him. "Come home, now," he cried, "an' stop yer jawin', er I'll lam the everlasting head off yehs."

They departed. The man paced placidly along with the apple-wood emblem of serenity between his teeth. The boy followed a dozen feet in the rear. He swore luridly, for he felt that it was degradation for one who aimed to be some vague soldier, or a man of blood with a sort of sublime license, to be taken home by a father.

Chapter II

Eventually they entered into a dark region where, from a careening building, a dozen gruesome doorways gave up loads of babies to the street and the gutter. A wind of early autumn raised yellow dust from cobbles and swirled it against an hundred windows. Long streamers of garments fluttered from fire-escapes. In all unhandy places there were buckets, brooms, rags and bottles. In the street infants played or fought with other infants or sat stupidly in the way of vehicles. Formidable women, with uncombed hair and disordered dress, gossiped while leaning on railings, or screamed in frantic quarrels. Withered persons, in curious postures of submission to something, sat smoking pipes in obscure corners. A thousand odors of cooking food came forth to the street. The building quivered and creaked from the weight of humanity stamping about in its bowels.

A small ragged girl dragged a red, bawling infant along the crowded ways. He was hanging back, baby-like, bracing his wrinkled, bare legs.

The little girl cried out: "Ah, Tommie, come ahn. Dere's Jimmie and fader. Don't be a-pullin' me back."

She jerked the baby's arm impatiently. He fell on his face, roaring. With a second jerk she pulled him to his feet, and they went on. With the obstinacy of his order, he protested against being dragged in a chosen direction. He made heroic endeavors to keep on his legs, denounce his sister and consume a bit of orange peeling which he chewed between the times of his infantile orations.

As the sullen-eyed man, followed by the blood-covered boy, drew near, the little girl burst into reproachful cries. "Ah, Jimmie, youse bin fightin' agin."

The urchin swelled disdainfully.

"Ah, what deh hell, Mag. See?"

The little girl upbraided him, "Youse allus fightin', Jimmie, an' yeh knows it puts mudder out when yehs come home half dead, an' it's like we'll all get a poundin'."

She began to weep. The babe threw back his head and roared at his prospects.

"Ah, what deh hell!" cried Jimmie. "Shut up er I'll smack yer mout'. See?"

As his sister continued her lamentations, he suddenly swore and struck her. The little girl reeled and, recovering herself, burst into tears and quaveringly cursed him. As she slowly retreated her brother advanced dealing her cuffs. The father heard and turned about.

"Stop that, Jim, d'yeh hear? Leave yer sister alone on the street. It's like I can never beat any sense into yer damned wooden head."

The urchin raised his voice in defiance to his parent and continued his attacks. The babe bawled tremendously, protesting with great violence. During his sister's hasty manoeuvres, he was dragged by the arm.

Finally the procession plunged into one of the gruesome doorways. They crawled up dark stairways and along cold, gloomy halls. At last the father pushed open a door and they entered a lighted room in which a large woman was rampant.

She stopped in a career from a seething stove to a pan-covered table. As the father and children filed in she peered at them.

"Eh, what? Been fightin' agin, by Gawd!" She threw herself upon Jimmie. The urchin tried to dart behind the others and in the scuffle the babe, Tommie, was knocked down. He protested with his usual vehemence, because they had bruised his tender shins against a table leg.

The mother's massive shoulders heaved with anger. Grasping the urchin by the neck and shoulder she shook him until he rattled. She dragged him to an unholy sink, and, soaking a rag in water, began to scrub his lacerated face with it. Jimmie screamed in pain and tried to twist his shoulders out of the clasp of the huge arms.

The babe sat on the floor watching the scene, his face in contortions like that of a woman at a tragedy. The father, with a newly-ladened pipe in his mouth, crouched on a backless chair near the stove. Jimmie's cries annoyed him. He turned about and bellowed at his wife:

"Let the damned kid alone for a minute, will yeh, Mary? Yer allus poundin' 'im. When I come nights I can't git no rest 'cause yer allus poundin' a kid. Let up, d'yeh hear? Don't be allus poundin' a kid."

The woman's operations on the urchin instantly increased in violence. At last she tossed him to a corner where he limply lay cursing and weeping.

The wife put her immense hands on her hips and with a chieftain-like stride approached her husband.

"Ho," she said, with a great grunt of contempt. "An' what in the devil are you stickin' your nose for?"

The babe crawled under the table and, turning, peered out cautiously. The ragged girl retreated and the urchin in the corner drew his legs carefully beneath him.

The man puffed his pipe calmly and put his great mudded boots on the back part of the stove.

"Go teh hell," he murmured, tranquilly.

The woman screamed and shook her fists before her husband's eyes. The rough yellow of her face and neck flared suddenly crimson. She began to howl.

He puffed imperturbably at his pipe for a time, but finally arose and began to look out at the window into the darkening chaos of back yards.

"You've been drinkin', Mary," he said. "You'd better let up on the bot', ol' woman, or you'll git done."

"You're a liar. I ain't had a drop," she roared in reply.

They had a lurid altercation, in which they damned each other's souls with frequence.

The babe was staring out from under the table, his small face working in his excitement.

The ragged girl went stealthily over to the corner where the urchin lay.

"Are yehs hurted much, Jimmie?" she whispered timidly.

"Not a damn bit! See?" growled the little boy.

"Will I wash deh blood?"

"Naw!"

"Will I—"

"When I catch dat Riley kid I'll break 'is face! Dat's right! See?"

He turned his face to the wall as if resolved to grimly bide his time.

In the quarrel between husband and wife, the woman was victor. The man grabbed his hat and rushed from the room, apparently determined upon a vengeful drunk. She followed to the door and thundered at him as he made his way down stairs.

She returned and stirred up the room until her children were bobbing about like bubbles.

"Git outa deh way," she persistently bawled, waving feet with their dishevelled shoes near the heads of her children. She shrouded herself, puffing and snorting, in a cloud of steam at the stove, and eventually extracted a frying-pan full of potatoes that hissed.

She flourished it. "Come teh yer suppers, now," she cried with sudden exasperation. "Hurry up, now, er I'll help yeh!"

The children scrambled hastily. With prodigious clatter they arranged themselves at table. The babe sat with his feet dangling high from a precarious infant chair and gorged his small stomach. Jimmie forced, with feverish rapidity, the grease-enveloped pieces between his wounded lips. Maggie, with side glances of fear of interruption, ate like a small pursued tigress.

The mother sat blinking at them. She delivered reproaches, swallowed potatoes and drank from a yellow-brown bottle. After a time her mood changed and she wept as she carried little Tommie into another room and laid him to sleep with his fists doubled in an old quilt of faded red and green grandeur. Then she came and moaned by the stove. She rocked to and fro upon a chair, shedding tears and crooning miserably to the two children about their "poor mother" and "yer fader, damn 'is soul."

The little girl plodded between the table and the chair with a dish-pan on it. She tottered on her small legs beneath burdens of dishes.

Jimmie sat nursing his various wounds. He cast furtive glances at his mother. His practised eye perceived her gradually emerge from a muddled mist of sentiment until her brain burned in drunken heat. He sat breathless.

Maggie broke a plate.

The mother started to her feet as if propelled.

"Good Gawd," she howled. Her eyes glittered on her child with sudden hatred. The fervent red of her face turned almost to purple. The little boy ran to the halls, shrieking like a monk in an earthquake.

He floundered about in darkness until he found the stairs. He stumbled, panic-stricken, to the next floor. An old woman opened a door. A light behind her threw a flare on the urchin's quivering face.

"Eh, Gawd, child, what is it dis time? Is yer fader beatin' yer mudder, or yer mudder beatin' yer fader?"

Chapter III

Jimmie and the old woman listened long in the hall. Above the muffled roar of conversation, the dismal wailings of babies at night, the thumping of feet in unseen corridors and rooms, mingled with the sound of varied hoarse shoutings in the street and the rattling of wheels over cobbles, they heard the screams of the child and the roars of the mother die away to a feeble moaning and a subdued bass muttering.

The old woman was a gnarled and leathery personage who could don, at will, an expression of great virtue. She possessed a small music-box capable of one tune, and a collection of "God bless yehs" pitched in assorted keys of fervency. Each day she took a position upon the stones of Fifth Avenue, where she crooked her legs under her and crouched immovable and hideous, like an idol. She received daily a small sum in pennies. It was contributed, for the most part, by persons who did not make their homes in that vicinity.

Once, when a lady had dropped her purse on the sidewalk, the gnarled woman had grabbed it and smuggled it with great dexterity beneath her cloak. When she was arrested she had cursed the lady into a partial swoon, and with her aged limbs, twisted from rheumatism, had almost kicked the stomach out of a huge policeman whose conduct upon that occasion she referred to when she said: "The police, damn 'em."

"Eh, Jimmie, it's cursed shame," she said. "Go, now, like a dear an' buy me a can, an' if yer mudder raises 'ell all night yehs can sleep here."

Jimmie took a tendered tin-pail and seven pennies and departed. He passed into the side door of a saloon and went to the bar. Straining up on his toes he raised the pail and pennies as high as his arms would let him. He saw two hands thrust down and take them. Directly the same hands let down the filled pail and he left.

In front of the gruesome doorway he met a lurching figure. It was his father, swaying about on uncertain legs.

"Give me deh can. See?" said the man, threateningly.

"Ah, come off! I got dis can fer dat ol' woman an' it 'ud be dirt teh swipe it. See?" cried Jimmie.

The father wrenched the pail from the urchin. He grasped it in both hands and lifted it to his mouth. He glued his lips to the under edge and tilted his head. His hairy throat swelled until it seemed to grow near his chin. There was a tremendous gulping movement and the beer was gone.

The man caught his breath and laughed. He hit his son on the head with the empty pail. As it rolled clanging into the street, Jimmie began to scream and kicked repeatedly at his father's shins.

"Look at deh dirt what yeh done me," he yelled. "Deh ol' woman 'ill be raisin' hell."

He retreated to the middle of the street, but the man did not pursue. He staggered toward the door.

"I'll club hell outa yeh when I ketch yeh," he shouted, and disappeared.

During the evening he had been standing against a bar drinking whiskies and declaring to all comers, confidentially: "My home reg'lar livin' hell! Damndes' place! Reg'lar hell! Why do I come an' drin' whisk' here thish way? 'Cause home reg'lar livin' hell!"

Jimmie waited a long time in the street and then crept warily up through the building. He passed with great caution the door of the gnarled woman, and finally stopped outside his home and listened.

He could hear his mother moving heavily about among the furniture of the room. She was chanting in a mournful voice, occasionally interjecting bursts of volcanic wrath at the father, who, Jimmie judged, had sunk down on the floor or in a corner.

"Why deh blazes don' chere try teh keep Jim from fightin'? I'll break her jaw," she suddenly bellowed.

The man mumbled with drunken indifference. "Ah, wha' deh hell. W'a's odds? Wha' makes kick?"

"Because he tears 'is clothes, yeh damn fool," cried the woman in supreme wrath.

The husband seemed to become aroused. "Go teh hell," he thundered fiercely in reply. There was a crash against the door and something broke into clattering fragments. Jimmie partially suppressed a howl and darted down the stairway. Below he paused and listened. He heard howls and curses, groans and shrieks, confusingly in chorus as if a battle were raging. With all was the crash of splintering furniture. The eyes of the urchin glared in fear that one of them would discover him.

Curious faces appeared in doorways, and whispered comments passed to and fro. "Ol' Johnson's raisin' hell agin."

Jimmie stood until the noises ceased and the other inhabitants of the tenement had all yawned and shut their doors. Then he crawled upstairs with the caution of an invader of a panther den. Sounds of labored breathing came through the broken door-panels. He pushed the door open and entered, quaking.

A glow from the fire threw red hues over the bare floor, the cracked and soiled plastering, and the overturned and broken furniture.

In the middle of the floor lay his mother asleep. In one corner of the room his father's limp body hung across the seat of a chair.

The urchin stole forward. He began to shiver in dread of awakening his parents. His mother's great chest was heaving painfully. Jimmie paused and looked down at her. Her face was inflamed and swollen from drinking. Her yellow brows shaded eyelids that had brown blue. Her tangled hair tossed in waves over her forehead. Her mouth was set in the same lines of vindictive hatred that it had, perhaps, borne during the fight. Her bare, red arms were thrown out above her head in positions of exhaustion, something, mayhap, like those of a sated villain.

The urchin bended over his mother. He was fearful lest she should open her eyes, and the dread within him was so strong, that he could not forbear to stare, but hung as if fascinated over the woman's grim face.

Suddenly her eyes opened. The urchin found himself looking straight into that expression, which, it would seem, had the power to change his blood to salt. He howled piercingly and fell backward.

The woman floundered for a moment, tossed her arms about her head as if in combat, and again began to snore.

Jimmie crawled back in the shadows and waited. A noise in the next room had followed his cry at the discovery that his mother was awake. He grovelled in the gloom, the eyes from out his drawn face riveted upon the intervening door.

He heard it creak, and then the sound of a small voice came to him. "Jimmie! Jimmie! Are yehs dere?" it whispered. The urchin started. The thin, white face of his sister looked at him from the door-way of the other room. She crept to him across the floor.

The father had not moved, but lay in the same death-like sleep. The mother writhed in uneasy slumber, her chest wheezing as if she were in the agonies of strangulation. Out at the window a florid moon was peering over dark roofs, and in the distance the waters of a river glimmered pallidly.

The small frame of the ragged girl was quivering. Her features were haggard from weeping, and her eyes gleamed from fear. She grasped the urchin's arm in her little trembling hands and they huddled in a corner. The eyes of both were drawn, by some force, to stare at the woman's face, for they thought she need only to awake and all fiends would come from below.

They crouched until the ghost-mists of dawn appeared at the window, drawing close to the panes, and looking in at the prostrate, heaving body of the mother.

Chapter IV

The babe, Tommie, died. He went away in a white, insignificant coffin, his small waxen hand clutching a flower that the girl, Maggie, had stolen from an Italian.

She and Jimmie lived.

The inexperienced fibres of the boy's eyes were hardened at an early age. He became a young man of leather. He lived some red years without laboring. During that time his sneer became chronic. He studied human nature in the gutter, and found it no worse than he thought he had reason to believe it. He never conceived a respect for the world, because he had begun with no idols that it had smashed.

He clad his soul in armor by means of happening hilariously in at a mission church where a man composed his sermons of "yous." While they got warm at the stove, he told his hearers just where he calculated they stood with the Lord. Many of the sinners were impatient over the pictured depths of their degradation. They were waiting for soup-tickets.

A reader of words of wind-demons might have been able to see the portions of a dialogue pass to and fro between the exhorter and his hearers.

"You are damned," said the preacher. And the reader of sounds might have seen the reply go forth from the ragged people: "Where's our soup?"

Jimmie and a companion sat in a rear seat and commented upon the things that didn't concern them, with all the freedom of English gentlemen. When they grew thirsty and went out their minds confused the speaker with Christ.

Momentarily, Jimmie was sullen with thoughts of a hopeless altitude where grew fruit. His companion said that if he should ever meet God he would ask for a million dollars and a bottle of beer.

Jimmie's occupation for a long time was to stand on streetcorners and watch the world go by, dreaming blood-red dreams at the passing of pretty women. He menaced mankind at the intersections of streets.

On the corners he was in life and of life. The world was going on and he was there to perceive it.

He maintained a belligerent attitude toward all well-dressed men. To him fine raiment was allied to weakness, and all good coats covered faint hearts. He and his order were kings, to a certain extent, over the men of untarnished clothes, because these latter dreaded, perhaps, to be either killed or laughed at.

Above all things he despised obvious Christians and ciphers with the chrysanthemums of aristocracy in their button-holes. He considered himself above both of these classes. He was afraid of neither the devil nor the leader of society.

When he had a dollar in his pocket his satisfaction with existence was the greatest thing in the world. So, eventually, he felt obliged to work. His father died and his mother's years were divided up into periods of thirty days.

He became a truck driver. He was given the charge of a painstaking pair of horses and a large rattling truck. He invaded the turmoil and tumble of the down-town streets and learned to breathe maledictory defiance at the police who occasionally used to climb up, drag him from his perch and beat him.

In the lower part of the city he daily involved himself in hideous tangles. If he and his team chanced to be in the rear he preserved a demeanor of serenity, crossing his legs and bursting forth into yells when foot passengers took dangerous dives beneath the noses of his champing horses. He smoked his pipe calmly for he knew that his pay was marching on.

If in the front and the key-truck of chaos, he entered terrifically into the quarrel that was raging to and fro among the drivers on their high seats, and sometimes roared oaths and violently got himself arrested.

After a time his sneer grew so that it turned its glare upon all things. He became so sharp that he believed in nothing. To him the police were always actuated by malignant impulses and the rest of the world was composed, for the most part, of despicable creatures who were all trying to take advantage of him and with whom, in defense, he was obliged to quarrel on all possible occasions. He himself occupied a down-trodden position that had a private but distinct element of grandeur in its isolation.

The most complete cases of aggravated idiocy were, to his mind, rampant upon the front platforms of all the street cars. At first his tongue strove with these beings, but he eventually was superior. He became immured like an African cow. In him grew a majestic contempt for those strings of street cars that followed him like intent bugs.

He fell into the habit, when starting on a long journey, of fixing his eye on a high and distant object, commanding his horses to begin, and then going into a sort of a trance of observation. Multitudes of drivers might howl in his rear, and passengers might load him with opprobrium, he would not awaken until some blue policeman turned red and began to frenziedly tear bridles and beat the soft noses of the responsible horses.

When he paused to contemplate the attitude of the police toward himself and his fellows, he believed that they were the only men in the city who had no rights. When driving about, he felt that he was held liable by the police for anything that might occur in the streets, and was the common prey of all energetic officials. In revenge, he resolved never to move out of the way of anything, until formidable circumstances, or a much larger man than himself forced him to it.

Foot-passengers were mere pestering flies with an insane disregard for their legs and his convenience. He could not conceive their maniacal desires to cross the streets. Their madness smote him with eternal amazement. He was continually storming at them from his throne. He sat aloft and denounced their frantic leaps, plunges, dives and straddles.

When they would thrust at, or parry, the noses of his champing horses, making them swing their heads and move their feet, disturbing a solid dreamy repose, he swore at the men as fools, for he himself could perceive that Providence had caused it clearly to be written, that he and his team had the unalienable right to stand in the proper path of the sun chariot, and if they so minded, obstruct its mission or take a wheel off.

And, perhaps, if the god-driver had an ungovernable desire to step down, put up his flame-colored fists and manfully dispute the right of way, he would have probably been immediately opposed by a scowling mortal with two sets of very hard knuckles.

It is possible, perhaps, that this young man would have derided, in an axle-wide alley, the approach of a flying ferry boat. Yet he achieved a respect for a fire engine. As one charged toward his truck, he would drive fearfully upon a sidewalk, threatening untold people with annihilation. When an engine would strike a mass of blocked trucks, splitting it into fragments, as a blow annihilates a cake of ice, Jimmie's team could usually be observed high and safe, with whole wheels, on the sidewalk. The fearful coming of the engine could break up the most intricate muddle of heavy vehicles at which the police had been swearing for the half of an hour.

A fire engine was enshrined in his heart as an appalling thing that he loved with a distant dog-like devotion. They had been known to overturn street-cars. Those leaping horses, striking sparks from the cobbles in their forward lunge, were creatures to be ineffably admired. The clang of the gong pierced his breast like a noise of remembered war.

When Jimmie was a little boy, he began to be arrested. Before he reached a great age, he had a fair record.

He developed too great a tendency to climb down from his truck and fight with other drivers. He had been in quite a number of miscellaneous fights, and in some general barroom rows that had become known to the police. Once he had been arrested for assaulting a Chinaman. Two women in different parts of the city, and entirely unknown to each other, caused him considerable annoyance by breaking forth, simultaneously, at fateful intervals, into wailings about marriage and support and infants.

Nevertheless, he had, on a certain star-lit evening, said wonderingly and quite reverently: "Deh moon looks like hell, don't it?"

Chapter V

The girl, Maggie, blossomed in a mud puddle. She grew to be a most rare and wonderful production of a tenement district, a pretty girl.

None of the dirt of Rum Alley seemed to be in her veins. The philosophers up-stairs, down-stairs and on the same floor, puzzled over it.

When a child, playing and fighting with gamins in the street, dirt disguised her. Attired in tatters and grime, she went unseen.

There came a time, however, when the young men of the vicinity said: "Dat Johnson goil is a puty good looker." About this period her brother remarked to her: "Mag, I'll tell yeh dis! See? Yeh've edder got teh go teh hell or go teh work!" Whereupon she went to work, having the feminine aversion of going to hell.

By a chance, she got a position in an establishment where they made collars and cuffs. She received a stool and a machine in a room where sat twenty girls of various shades of yellow discontent. She perched on the stool and treadled at her machine all day, turning out collars, the name of whose brand could be noted for its irrelevancy to anything in connection with collars. At night she returned home to her mother.

Jimmie grew large enough to take the vague position of head of the family. As incumbent of that office, he stumbled up-stairs late at night, as his father had done before him. He reeled about the room, swearing at his relations, or went to sleep on the floor.

The mother had gradually arisen to that degree of fame that she could bandy words with her acquaintances among the police-justices. Court-officials called her by her first name. When she appeared they pursued a course which had been theirs for months. They invariably grinned and cried out: "Hello, Mary, you here again?" Her grey head wagged in many a court. She always besieged the bench with voluble excuses, explanations, apologies and prayers. Her flaming face and rolling eyes were a sort of familiar sight on the island. She measured time by means of sprees, and was eternally swollen and dishevelled.

One day the young man, Pete, who as a lad had smitten the Devil's Row urchin in the back of the head and put to flight the antagonists of his friend, Jimmie, strutted upon the scene. He met Jimmie one day on the street, promised to take him to a boxing match in Williamsburg, and called for him in the evening.

Maggie observed Pete.

He sat on a table in the Johnson home and dangled his checked legs with an enticing non-chalance. His hair was curled down over his forehead in an oiled bang. His rather pugged nose seemed to revolt from contact with a bristling moustache of short, wire-like hairs. His blue double-breasted coat, edged with black braid, buttoned close to a red puff tie, and his patent-leather shoes looked like murder-fitted weapons.

His mannerisms stamped him as a man who had a correct sense of his personal superiority. There was valor and contempt for circumstances in the glance of his eye. He waved his hands like a man of the world, who dismisses religion and philosophy, and says "Fudge." He had certainly seen everything and with each curl of his lip, he declared that it amounted to nothing. Maggie thought he must be a very elegant and graceful bartender.

He was telling tales to Jimmie.

Maggie watched him furtively, with half-closed eyes, lit with a vague interest.

"Hully gee! Dey makes me tired," he said. "Mos' e'ry day some farmer comes in an' tries teh run deh shop. See? But dey gits t'rowed right out! I jolt dem right out in deh street before dey knows where dey is! See?"

"Sure," said Jimmie.

"Dere was a mug come in deh place deh odder day wid an idear he wus goin' teh own deh place! Hully gee, he wus goin' teh own deh place! I see he had a still on an' I didn' wanna giv 'im no stuff, so I says: 'Git deh hell outa here an' don' make no trouble,' I says like dat! See? 'Git deh hell outa here an' don' make no trouble'; like dat. 'Git deh hell outa here,' I says. See?"

Jimmie nodded understandingly. Over his features played an eager desire to state the amount of his valor in a similar crisis, but the narrator proceeded.

"Well, deh blokie he says: 'T'hell wid it! I ain' lookin' for no scrap,' he says (See?), 'but' he says, 'I'm 'spectable cit'zen an' I wanna drink an' purtydamnsoon, too.' See? 'Deh hell,' I says. Like dat! 'Deh hell,' I says. See? 'Don' make no trouble,' I says. Like dat. 'Don' make no trouble.' See? Den deh mug he squared off an' said he was fine as silk wid his dukes (See?) an' he wanned a drink damnquick. Dat's what he said. See?"

"Sure," repeated Jimmie.

Pete continued. "Say, I jes' jumped deh bar an' deh way I plunked dat blokie was great. See? Dat's right! In deh jaw! See? Hully gee, he t'rowed a spittoon true deh front windee. Say, I taut I'd drop dead. But deh boss, he comes in after an' he says, 'Pete, yehs done jes' right! Yeh've gota keep order an' it's all right.' See? 'It's all right,' he says. Dat's what he said."

The two held a technical discussion.

"Dat bloke was a dandy," said Pete, in conclusion, "but he hadn' oughta made no trouble. Dat's what I says teh dem: 'Don' come in here an' make no trouble,' I says, like dat. 'Don' make no trouble.' See?"

As Jimmie and his friend exchanged tales descriptive of their prowess, Maggie leaned back in the shadow. Her eyes dwelt wonderingly and rather wistfully upon Pete's face. The broken furniture, grimey walls, and general disorder and dirt of her home of a sudden appeared before her and began to take a potential aspect. Pete's aristocratic person looked as if it might soil. She looked keenly at him, occasionally, wondering if he was feeling contempt. But Pete seemed to be enveloped in reminiscence.

"Hully gee," said he, "dose mugs can't phase me. Dey knows I kin wipe up deh street wid any t'ree of dem."

When he said, "Ah, what deh hell," his voice was burdened with disdain for the inevitable and contempt for anything that fate might compel him to endure.

Maggie perceived that here was the beau ideal of a man. Her dim thoughts were often searching for far away lands where, as God says, the little hills sing together in the morning. Under the trees of her dream-gardens there had always walked a lover.

Chapter VI

Pete took note of Maggie.

"Say, Mag, I'm stuck on yer shape. It's outa sight," he said, parenthetically, with an affable grin.

As he became aware that she was listening closely, he grew still more eloquent in his descriptions of various happenings in his career. It appeared that he was invincible in fights.

"Why," he said, referring to a man with whom he had had a misunderstanding, "dat mug scrapped like a damn dago. Dat's right. He was dead easy. See? He tau't he was a scrapper. But he foun' out diff'ent! Hully gee."

He walked to and fro in the small room, which seemed then to grow even smaller and unfit to hold his dignity, the attribute of a supreme warrior. That swing of the shoulders that had frozen the timid when he was but a lad had increased with his growth and education at the ratio of ten to one. It, combined with the sneer upon his mouth, told mankind that there was nothing in space which could appall him. Maggie marvelled at him and surrounded him with greatness. She vaguely tried to calculate the altitude of the pinnacle from which he must have looked down upon her.

"I met a chump deh odder day way up in deh city," he said. "I was goin' teh see a frien' of mine. When I was a-crossin' deh street deh chump runned plump inteh me, an' den he turns aroun' an' says, 'Yer insolen' ruffin,' he says, like dat. 'Oh, gee,' I says, 'oh, gee, go teh hell and git off deh eart',' I says, like dat. See? 'Go teh hell an' git off deh eart',' like dat. Den deh blokie he got wild. He says I was a contempt'ble scoun'el, er somet'ing like dat, an' he says I was doom' teh everlastin' pe'dition an' all like dat. 'Gee,' I says, 'gee! Deh hell I am,' I says. 'Deh hell I am,' like dat. An' den I slugged 'im. See?"

With Jimmie in his company, Pete departed in a sort of a blaze of glory from the Johnson home. Maggie, leaning from the window, watched him as he walked down the street.

Here was a formidable man who disdained the strength of a world full of fists. Here was one who had contempt for brass-clothed power; one whose knuckles could defiantly ring against the granite of law. He was a knight.

The two men went from under the glimmering street-lamp and passed into shadows.

Turning, Maggie contemplated the dark, dust-stained walls, and the scant and crude furniture of her home. A clock, in a splintered and battered oblong box of varnished wood, she suddenly regarded as an abomination. She noted that it ticked raspingly. The almost vanished flowers in the carpet-pattern, she conceived to be newly hideous. Some faint attempts she had made with blue ribbon, to freshen the appearance of a dingy curtain, she now saw to be piteous.

She wondered what Pete dined on.

She reflected upon the collar and cuff factory. It began to appear to her mind as a dreary place of endless grinding. Pete's elegant occupation brought him, no doubt, into contact with people who had money and manners. It was probable that he had a large acquaintance of pretty girls. He must have great sums of money to spend.

To her the earth was composed of hardships and insults. She felt instant admiration for a man who openly defied it. She thought that if the grim angel of death should clutch his heart, Pete would shrug his shoulders and say: "Oh, ev'ryt'ing goes."

She anticipated that he would come again shortly. She spent some of her week's pay in the purchase of flowered cretonne for a lambrequin. She made it with infinite care and hung it to the slightly-careening mantel, over the stove, in the kitchen. She studied it with painful anxiety from different points in the room. She wanted it to look well on Sunday night when, perhaps, Jimmie's friend would come. On Sunday night, however, Pete did not appear.

Afterward the girl looked at it with a sense of humiliation. She was now convinced that Pete was superior to admiration for lambrequins.

A few evenings later Pete entered with fascinating innovations in his apparel. As she had seen him twice and he had different suits on each time, Maggie had a dim impression that his wardrobe was prodigiously extensive.

"Say, Mag," he said, "put on yer bes' duds Friday night an' I'll take yehs teh deh show. See?"

He spent a few moments in flourishing his clothes and then vanished, without having glanced at the lambrequin.

Over the eternal collars and cuffs in the factory Maggie spent the most of three days in making imaginary sketches of Pete and his daily environment. She imagined some half dozen women in love with him and thought he must lean dangerously toward an indefinite one, whom she pictured with great charms of person, but with an altogether contemptible disposition.

She thought he must live in a blare of pleasure. He had friends, and people who were afraid of him.

She saw the golden glitter of the place where Pete was to take her. An entertainment of many hues and many melodies where she was afraid she might appear small and mouse-colored.

Her mother drank whiskey all Friday morning. With lurid face and tossing hair she cursed and destroyed furniture all Friday afternoon. When Maggie came home at half-past six her mother lay asleep amidst the wreck of chairs and a table. Fragments of various household utensils were scattered about the floor. She had vented some phase of drunken fury upon the lambrequin. It lay in a bedraggled heap in the corner.

"Hah," she snorted, sitting up suddenly, "where deh hell yeh been? Why deh hell don' yeh come home earlier? Been loafin' 'round deh streets. Yer gettin' teh be a reg'lar devil."

When Pete arrived Maggie, in a worn black dress, was waiting for him in the midst of a floor strewn with wreckage. The curtain at the window had been pulled by a heavy hand and hung by one tack, dangling to and fro in the draft through the cracks at the sash. The knots of blue ribbons appeared like violated flowers. The fire in the stove had gone out. The displaced lids and open doors showed heaps of sullen grey ashes. The remnants of a meal, ghastly, like dead flesh, lay in a corner. Maggie's red mother, stretched on the floor, blasphemed and gave her daughter a bad name.

Chapter VII

An orchestra of yellow silk women and bald-headed men on an elevated stage near the centre of a great green-hued hall, played a popular waltz. The place was crowded with people grouped about little tables. A battalion of waiters slid among the throng, carrying trays of beer glasses and making change from the inexhaustible vaults of their trousers pockets. Little boys, in the costumes of French chefs, paraded up and down the irregular aisles vending fancy cakes. There was a low rumble of conversation and a subdued clinking of glasses. Clouds of tobacco smoke rolled and wavered high in air about the dull gilt of the chandeliers.

The vast crowd had an air throughout of having just quitted labor. Men with calloused hands and attired in garments that showed the wear of an endless trudge for a living, smoked their pipes contentedly and spent five, ten, or perhaps fifteen cents for beer. There was a mere sprinkling of kid-gloved men who smoked cigars purchased elsewhere. The great body of the crowd was composed of people who showed that all day they strove with their hands. Quiet Germans, with maybe their wives and two or three children, sat listening to the music, with the expressions of happy cows. An occasional party of sailors from a war-ship, their faces pictures of sturdy health, spent the earlier hours of the evening at the small round tables. Very infrequent tipsy men, swollen with the value of their opinions, engaged their companions in earnest and confidential conversation. In the balcony, and here and there below, shone the impassive faces of women. The nationalities of the Bowery beamed upon the stage from all directions.

Pete aggressively walked up a side aisle and took seats with Maggie at a table beneath the balcony.

"Two beehs!"

Leaning back he regarded with eyes of superiority the scene before them. This attitude affected Maggie strongly. A man who could regard such a sight with indifference must be accustomed to very great things.

It was obvious that Pete had been to this place many times before, and was very familiar with it. A knowledge of this fact made Maggie feel little and new.

He was extremely gracious and attentive. He displayed the consideration of a cultured gentleman who knew what was due.

"Say, what deh hell? Bring deh lady a big glass! What deh hell use is dat pony?"

"Don't be fresh, now," said the waiter, with some warmth, as he departed.

"Ah, git off deh eart'," said Pete, after the other's retreating form.

Maggie perceived that Pete brought forth all his elegance and all his knowledge of high-class customs for her benefit. Her heart warmed as she reflected upon his condescension.

The orchestra of yellow silk women and bald-headed men gave vent to a few bars of anticipatory music and a girl, in a pink dress with short skirts, galloped upon the stage. She smiled upon the throng as if in acknowledgment of a warm welcome, and began to walk to and fro, making profuse gesticulations and singing, in brazen soprano tones, a song, the words of which were inaudible. When she broke into the swift rattling measures of a chorus some half-tipsy men near the stage joined in the rollicking refrain and glasses were pounded rhythmically upon the tables. People leaned forward to watch her and to try to catch the words of the song. When she vanished there were long rollings of applause.

Obedient to more anticipatory bars, she reappeared amidst the half-suppressed cheering of the tipsy men. The orchestra plunged into dance music and the laces of the dancer fluttered and flew in the glare of gas jets. She divulged the fact that she was attired in some half dozen skirts. It was patent that any one of them would have proved adequate for the purpose for which skirts are intended. An occasional man bent forward, intent upon the pink stockings. Maggie wondered at the splendor of the costume and lost herself in calculations of the cost of the silks and laces.

The dancer's smile of stereotyped enthusiasm was turned for ten minutes upon the faces of her audience. In the finale she fell into some of those grotesque attitudes which were at the time popular among the dancers in the theatres up-town, giving to the Bowery public the phantasies of the aristocratic theatre-going public, at reduced rates.

"Say, Pete," said Maggie, leaning forward, "dis is great."

"Sure," said Pete, with proper complacence.

A ventriloquist followed the dancer. He held two fantastic dolls on his knees. He made them sing mournful ditties and say funny things about geography and Ireland.

"Do dose little men talk?" asked Maggie.

"Naw," said Pete, "it's some damn fake. See?"

Two girls, on the bills as sisters, came forth and sang a duet that is heard occasionally at concerts given under church auspices. They supplemented it with a dance which of course can never be seen at concerts given under church auspices.

After the duettists had retired, a woman of debatable age sang a negro melody. The chorus necessitated some grotesque waddlings supposed to be an imitation of a plantation darkey, under the influence, probably, of music and the moon. The audience was just enthusiastic enough over it to have her return and sing a sorrowful lay, whose lines told of a mother's love and a sweetheart who waited and a young man who was lost at sea under the most harrowing circumstances. From the faces of a score or so in the crowd, the self-contained look faded. Many heads were bent forward with eagerness and sympathy. As the last distressing sentiment of the piece was brought forth, it was greeted by that kind of applause which rings as sincere.

As a final effort, the singer rendered some verses which described a vision of Britain being annihilated by America, and Ireland bursting her bonds. A carefully prepared crisis was reached in the last line of the last verse, where the singer threw out her arms and cried, "The star-spangled banner." Instantly a great cheer swelled from the throats of the assemblage of the masses. There was a heavy rumble of booted feet thumping the floor. Eyes gleamed with sudden fire, and calloused hands waved frantically in the air.

After a few moments' rest, the orchestra played crashingly, and a small fat man burst out upon the stage. He began to roar a song and stamp back and forth before the foot-lights, wildly waving a glossy silk hat and throwing leers, or smiles, broadcast. He made his face into fantastic grimaces until he looked like a pictured devil on a Japanese kite. The crowd laughed gleefully. His short, fat legs were never still a moment. He shouted and roared and bobbed his shock of red wig until the audience broke out in excited applause.

Pete did not pay much attention to the progress of events upon the stage. He was drinking beer and watching Maggie.

Her cheeks were blushing with excitement and her eyes were glistening. She drew deep breaths of pleasure. No thoughts of the atmosphere of the collar and cuff factory came to her.

When the orchestra crashed finally, they jostled their way to the sidewalk with the crowd. Pete took Maggie's arm and pushed a way for her, offering to fight with a man or two.

They reached Maggie's home at a late hour and stood for a moment in front of the gruesome doorway.

"Say, Mag," said Pete, "give us a kiss for takin' yeh teh deh show, will yer?"

Maggie laughed, as if startled, and drew away from him.

"Naw, Pete," she said, "dat wasn't in it."

"Ah, what deh hell?" urged Pete.

The girl retreated nervously.

"Ah, what deh hell?" repeated he.

Maggie darted into the hall, and up the stairs. She turned and smiled at him, then disappeared.

Pete walked slowly down the street. He had something of an astonished expression upon his features. He paused under a lamp-post and breathed a low breath of surprise.

"Gawd," he said, "I wonner if I've been played fer a duffer."

Chapter VIII

As thoughts of Pete came to Maggie's mind, she began to have an intense dislike for all of her dresses.

"What deh hell ails yeh? What makes yeh be allus fixin' and fussin'? Good Gawd," her mother would frequently roar at her.

She began to note, with more interest, the well-dressed women she met on the avenues. She envied elegance and soft palms. She craved those adornments of person which she saw every day on the street, conceiving them to be allies of vast importance to women.

Studying faces, she thought many of the women and girls she chanced to meet, smiled with serenity as though forever cherished and watched over by those they loved.

The air in the collar and cuff establishment strangled her. She knew she was gradually and surely shrivelling in the hot, stuffy room. The begrimed windows rattled incessantly from the passing of elevated trains. The place was filled with a whirl of noises and odors.

She wondered as she regarded some of the grizzled women in the room, mere mechanical contrivances sewing seams and grinding out, with heads bended over their work, tales of imagined or real girlhood happiness, past drunks, the baby at home, and unpaid wages. She speculated how long her youth would endure. She began to see the bloom upon her cheeks as valuable.

She imagined herself, in an exasperating future, as a scrawny woman with an eternal grievance. Too, she thought Pete to be a very fastidious person concerning the appearance of women.

She felt she would love to see somebody entangle their fingers in the oily beard of the fat foreigner who owned the establishment. He was a detestable creature. He wore white socks with low shoes.

He sat all day delivering orations, in the depths of a cushioned chair. His pocketbook deprived them of the power to retort.

"What een hell do you sink I pie fife dolla a week for? Play? No, py damn!" Maggie was anxious for a friend to whom she could talk about Pete. She would have liked to discuss his admirable mannerisms with a reliable mutual friend. At home, she found her mother often drunk and always raving. It seems that the world had treated this woman very badly, and she took a deep revenge upon such portions of it as came within her reach. She broke furniture as if she were at last getting her rights. She swelled with virtuous indignation as she carried the lighter articles of household use, one by one under the shadows of the three gilt balls, where Hebrews chained them with chains of interest.

Jimmie came when he was obliged to by circumstances over which he had no control. His well-trained legs brought him staggering home and put him to bed some nights when he would rather have gone elsewhere.

Swaggering Pete loomed like a golden sun to Maggie. He took her to a dime museum where rows of meek freaks astonished her. She contemplated their deformities with awe and thought them a sort of chosen tribe.

"What een hell do you sink I pie fife dolla a week for? Play? No, py damn!" Maggie was anxious for a friend to whom she could talk about Pete. She would have liked to discuss his admirable mannerisms with a reliable mutual friend. At home, she found her mother often drunk and always raving. It seems that the world had treated this woman very badly, and she took a deep revenge upon such portions of it as came within her reach. She broke furniture as if she were at last getting her rights. She swelled with virtuous indignation as she carried the lighter articles of household use, one by one under the shadows of the three gilt balls, where Hebrews chained them with chains of interest.

Jimmie came when he was obliged to by circumstances over which he had no control. His well-trained legs brought him staggering home and put him to bed some nights when he would rather have gone elsewhere.

Swaggering Pete loomed like a golden sun to Maggie. He took her to a dime museum where rows of meek freaks astonished her. She contemplated their deformities with awe and thought them a sort of chosen tribe.

Pete, raking his brains for amusement, discovered the Central Park Menagerie and the Museum of Arts. Sunday afternoons would sometimes find them at these places. Pete did not appear to be particularly interested in what he saw. He stood around looking heavy, while Maggie giggled in glee.

Once at the Menagerie he went into a trance of admiration before the spectacle of a very small monkey threatening to thrash a cageful because one of them had pulled his tail and he had not wheeled about quickly enough to discover who did it. Ever after Pete knew that monkey by sight and winked at him, trying to induce hime to fight with other and larger monkeys. At the Museum, Maggie said, "Dis is outa sight."

"Oh hell," said Pete, "wait 'till next summer an' I'll take yehs to a picnic."

While the girl wandered in the vaulted rooms, Pete occupied himself in returning stony stare for stony stare, the appalling scrutiny of the watch-dogs of the treasures. Occasionally he would remark in loud tones: "Dat jay has got glass eyes," and sentences of the sort.

When he tired of this amusement he would go to the mummies and moralize over them.

Usually he submitted with silent dignity to all which he had to go through, but, at times, he was goaded into comment.

"What deh hell," he demanded once. "Look at all dese little jugs! Hundred jugs in a row! Ten rows in a case an' 'bout a t'ousand cases! What deh blazes use is dem?"

Evenings during the week he took her to see plays in which the brain-clutching heroine was rescued from the palatial home of her guardian, who is cruelly after her bonds, by the hero with the beautiful sentiments. The latter spent most of his time out at soak in pale-green snow storms, busy with a nickel-plated revolver, rescuing aged strangers from villains.

Maggie lost herself in sympathy with the wanderers swooning in snow storms beneath happy-hued church windows. And a choir within singing "Joy to the World." To Maggie and the rest of the audience this was transcendental realism. Joy always within, and they, like the actor, inevitably without. Viewing it, they hugged themselves in ecstatic pity of their imagined or real condition.

The girl thought the arrogance and granite-heartedness of the magnate of the play was very accurately drawn. She echoed the maledictions that the occupants of the gallery showered on this individual when his lines compelled him to expose his extreme selfishness.

Shady persons in the audience revolted from the pictured villainy of the drama. With untiring zeal they hissed vice and applauded virtue. Unmistakably bad men evinced an apparently sincere admiration for virtue.

The loud gallery was overwhelmingly with the unfortunate and the oppressed. They encouraged the struggling hero with cries, and jeered the villain, hooting and calling attention to his whiskers. When anybody died in the pale-green snow storms, the gallery mourned. They sought out the painted misery and hugged it as akin.

In the hero's erratic march from poverty in the first act, to wealth and triumph in the final one, in which he forgives all the enemies that he has left, he was assisted by the gallery, which applauded his generous and noble sentiments and confounded the speeches of his opponents by making irrelevant but very sharp remarks. Those actors who were cursed with villainy parts were confronted at every turn by the gallery. If one of them rendered lines containing the most subtle distinctions between right and wrong, the gallery was immediately aware if the actor meant wickedness, and denounced him accordingly.

The last act was a triumph for the hero, poor and of the masses, the representative of the audience, over the villain and the rich man, his pockets stuffed with bonds, his heart packed with tyrannical purposes, imperturbable amid suffering.

Maggie always departed with raised spirits from the showing places of the melodrama. She rejoiced at the way in which the poor and virtuous eventually surmounted the wealthy and wicked. The theatre made her think. She wondered if the culture and refinement she had seen imitated, perhaps grotesquely, by the heroine on the stage, could be acquired by a girl who lived in a tenement house and worked in a shirt factory.

Chapter IX

A group of urchins were intent upon the side door of a saloon. Expectancy gleamed from their eyes. They were twisting their fingers in excitement.

"Here she comes," yelled one of them suddenly.

The group of urchins burst instantly asunder and its individual fragments were spread in a wide, respectable half circle about the point of interest. The saloon door opened with a crash, and the figure of a woman appeared upon the threshold. Her grey hair fell in knotted masses about her shoulders. Her face was crimsoned and wet with perspiration. Her eyes had a rolling glare.

"Not a damn cent more of me money will yehs ever get, not a damn cent. I spent me money here fer t'ree years an' now yehs tells me yeh'll sell me no more stuff! T'hell wid yeh, Johnnie Murckre! 'Disturbance'? Disturbance be damned! T'hell wid yeh, Johnnie —"

The door received a kick of exasperation from within and the woman lurched heavily out on the sidewalk.

The gamins in the half-circle became violently agitated. They began to dance about and hoot and yell and jeer. Wide dirty grins spread over each face.

The woman made a furious dash at a particularly outrageous cluster of little boys. They laughed delightedly and scampered off a short distance, calling out over their shoulders to her. She stood tottering on the curb-stone and thundered at them.

"Yeh devil's kids," she howled, shaking red fists. The little boys whooped in glee. As she started up the street they fell in behind and marched uproariously. Occasionally she wheeled about and made charges on them. They ran nimbly out of reach and taunted her.

In the frame of a gruesome doorway she stood for a moment cursing them. Her hair straggled, giving her crimson features a look of insanity. Her great fists quivered as she shook them madly in the air.

The urchins made terrific noises until she turned and disappeared. Then they filed quietly in the way they had come.

The woman floundered about in the lower hall of the tenement house and finally stumbled up the stairs. On an upper hall a door was opened and a collection of heads peered curiously out, watching her. With a wrathful snort the woman confronted the door, but it was slammed hastily in her face and the key was turned.

She stood for a few minutes, delivering a frenzied challenge at the panels.

"Come out in deh hall, Mary Murphy, damn yeh, if yehs want a row. Come ahn, yeh overgrown terrier, come ahn."

She began to kick the door with her great feet. She shrilly defied the universe to appear and do battle. Her cursing trebles brought heads from all doors save the one she threatened. Her eyes glared in every direction. The air was full of her tossing fists.

"Come ahn, deh hull damn gang of yehs, come ahn," she roared at the spectators. An oath or two, cat-calls, jeers and bits of facetious advice were given in reply. Missiles clattered about her feet.

"What deh hell's deh matter wid yeh?" said a voice in the gathered gloom, and Jimmie came forward. He carried a tin dinner-pail in his hand and under his arm a brown truckman's apron done in a bundle. "What deh hell's wrong?" he demanded.

"Come out, all of yehs, come out," his mother was howling. "Come ahn an' I'll stamp her damn brains under me feet."

"Shet yer face, an' come home, yeh damned old fool," roared Jimmie at her. She strided up to him and twirled her fingers in his face. Her eyes were darting flames of unreasoning rage and her frame trembled with eagerness for a fight.

"T'hell wid yehs! An' who deh hell are yehs? I ain't givin' a snap of me fingers fer yehs," she bawled at him. She turned her huge back in tremendous disdain and climbed the stairs to the next floor.

Jimmie followed, cursing blackly. At the top of the flight he seized his mother's arm and started to drag her toward the door of their room.

"Come home, damn yeh," he gritted between his teeth.

"Take yer hands off me! Take yer hands off me," shrieked his mother.

She raised her arm and whirled her great fist at her son's face. Jimmie dodged his head and the blow struck him in the back of the neck. "Damn yeh," gritted he again. He threw out his left hand and writhed his fingers about her middle arm. The mother and the son began to sway and struggle like gladiators.

"Whoop!" said the Rum Alley tenement house. The hall filled with interested spectators.

"Hi, ol' lady, dat was a dandy!"

"T'ree to one on deh red!"

"Ah, stop yer damn scrappin'!"

The door of the Johnson home opened and Maggie looked out. Jimmie made a supreme cursing effort and hurled his mother into the room. He quickly followed and closed the door. The Rum Alley tenement swore disappointedly and retired.

The mother slowly gathered herself up from the floor. Her eyes glittered menacingly upon her children.

"Here, now," said Jimmie, "we've had enough of dis. Sit down, an' don' make no trouble."

He grasped her arm, and twisting it, forced her into a creaking chair.

"Keep yer hands off me," roared his mother again.

"Damn yer ol' hide," yelled Jimmie, madly. Maggie shrieked and ran into the other room. To her there came the sound of a storm of crashes and curses. There was a great final thump and Jimmie's voice cried: "Dere, damn yeh, stay still." Maggie opened the door now, and went warily out. "Oh, Jimmie."

He was leaning against the wall and swearing. Blood stood upon bruises on his knotty forearms where they had scraped against the floor or the walls in the scuffle. The mother lay screeching on the floor, the tears running down her furrowed face.

Maggie, standing in the middle of the room, gazed about her. The usual upheaval of the tables and chairs had taken place. Crockery was strewn broadcast in fragments. The stove had been disturbed on its legs, and now leaned idiotically to one side. A pail had been upset and water spread in all directions.

The door opened and Pete appeared. He shrugged his shoulders. "Oh, Gawd," he observed.

He walked over to Maggie and whispered in her ear. "Ah, what deh hell, Mag? Come ahn and we'll have a hell of a time."

The mother in the corner upreared her head and shook her tangled locks.

"Teh hell wid him and you," she said, glowering at her daughter in the gloom. Her eyes seemed to burn balefully. "Yeh've gone teh deh devil, Mag Johnson, yehs knows yehs have gone teh deh devil. Yer a disgrace teh yer people, damn yeh. An' now, git out an' go ahn wid dat doe-faced jude of yours. Go teh hell wid him, damn yeh, an' a good riddance. Go teh hell an' see how yeh likes it."

Maggie gazed long at her mother.

"Go teh hell now, an' see how yeh likes it. Git out. I won't have sech as yehs in me house! Get out, d'yeh hear! Damn yeh, git out!"

The girl began to tremble.

At this instant Pete came forward. "Oh, what deh hell, Mag, see," whispered he softly in her ear. "Dis all blows over. See? Deh ol' woman 'ill be all right in deh mornin'. Come ahn out wid me! We'll have a hell of a time."

The woman on the floor cursed. Jimmie was intent upon his bruised fore-arms. The girl cast a glance about the room filled with a chaotic mass of debris, and at the red, writhing body of her mother.

"Go teh hell an' good riddance."

She went.

Chapter X

Jimmie had an idea it wasn't common courtesy for a friend to come to one's home and ruin one's sister. But he was not sure how much Pete knew about the rules of politeness.

The following night he returned home from work at rather a late hour in the evening. In passing through the halls he came upon the gnarled and leathery old woman who possessed the music box. She was grinning in the dim light that drifted through dust-stained panes. She beckoned to him with a smudged forefinger.

"Ah, Jimmie, what do yehs t'ink I got onto las' night. It was deh funnies' t'ing I ever saw," she cried, coming close to him and leering. She was trembling with eagerness to tell her tale. "I was by me door las' night when yer sister and her jude feller came in late, oh, very late. An' she, the dear, she was a-cryin' as if her heart would break, she was. It was deh funnies' t'ing I ever saw. An' right out here by me door she asked him did he love her, did he. An' she was a-cryin' as if her heart would break, poor t'ing. An' him, I could see by deh way what he said it dat she had been askin' orften, he says: 'Oh, hell, yes,' he says, says he, 'Oh, hell, yes.'"

Storm-clouds swept over Jimmie's face, but he turned from the leathery old woman and plodded on up-stairs.

"Oh, hell, yes," called she after him. She laughed a laugh that was like a prophetic croak. "'Oh, hell, yes,' he says, says he, 'Oh, hell, yes.'"

There was no one in at home. The rooms showed that attempts had been made at tidying them. Parts of the wreckage of the day before had been repaired by an unskilful hand. A chair or two and the table, stood uncertainly upon legs. The floor had been newly swept. Too, the blue ribbons had been restored to the curtains, and the lambrequin, with its immense sheaves of yellow wheat and red roses of equal size, had been returned, in a worn and sorry state, to its position at the mantel. Maggie's jacket and hat were gone from the nail behind the door.

Jimmie walked to the window and began to look through the blurred glass. It occurred to him to vaguely wonder, for an instant, if some of the women of his acquaintance had brothers.

Suddenly, however, he began to swear.

"But he was me frien'! I brought 'im here! Dat's deh hell of it!"

He fumed about the room, his anger gradually rising to the furious pitch.

"I'll kill deh jay! Dat's what I'll do! I'll kill deh jay!"

He clutched his hat and sprang toward the door. But it opened and his mother's great form blocked the passage.

"What deh hell's deh matter wid yeh?" exclaimed she, coming into the rooms.

Jimmie gave vent to a sardonic curse and then laughed heavily.

"Well, Maggie's gone teh deh devil! Dat's what! See?"

"Eh?" said his mother.

"Maggie's gone teh deh devil! Are yehs deaf?" roared Jimmie, impatiently.

"Deh hell she has," murmured the mother, astounded.

Jimmie grunted, and then began to stare out at the window. His mother sat down in a chair, but a moment later sprang erect and delivered a maddened whirl of oaths. Her son turned to look at her as she reeled and swayed in the middle of the room, her fierce face convulsed with passion, her blotched arms raised high in imprecation.

"May Gawd curse her forever," she shrieked. "May she eat nothin' but stones and deh dirt in deh street. May she sleep in deh gutter an' never see deh sun shine agin. Deh damn —"

"Here, now," said her son. "Take a drop on yourself."

The mother raised lamenting eyes to the ceiling.

"She's deh devil's own chil', Jimmie," she whispered. "Ah, who would t'ink such a bad girl could grow up in our fambly, Jimmie, me son. Many deh hour I've spent in talk wid dat girl an' tol' her if she ever went on deh streets I'd see her damned. An' after all her bringin' up an' what I tol' her and talked wid her, she goes teh deh bad, like a duck teh water."

The tears rolled down her furrowed face. Her hands trembled.

"An' den when dat Sadie MacMallister next door to us was sent teh deh devil by dat feller what worked in deh soap-factory, didn't I tell our Mag dat if she —"

"Ah, dat's annuder story," interrupted the brother. "Of course, dat Sadie was nice an' all dat-but-see-it ain't dessame as if-well, Maggie was diff'ent-see-she was diff'ent."

He was trying to formulate a theory that he had always unconsciously held, that all sisters, excepting his own, could advisedly be ruined.

He suddenly broke out again. "I'll go t'ump hell outa deh mug what did her deh harm. I'll kill 'im! He t'inks he kin scrap, but when he gits me a-chasin' 'im he'll fin' out where he's wrong, deh damned duffer. I'll wipe up deh street wid 'im."

In a fury he plunged out of the doorway. As he vanished the mother raised her head and lifted both hands, entreating.

"May Gawd curse her forever," she cried.

In the darkness of the hallway Jimmie discerned a knot of women talking volubly. When he strode by they paid no attention to him.

"She allus was a bold thing," he heard one of them cry in an eager voice. "Dere wasn't a feller come teh deh house but she'd try teh mash 'im. My Annie says deh shameless t'ing tried teh ketch her feller, her own feller, what we useter know his fader."

"I could a' tol' yehs dis two years ago," said a woman, in a key of triumph. "Yessir, it was over two years ago dat I says teh my ol' man, I says, 'Dat Johnson girl ain't straight,' I says. 'Oh, hell,' he says. 'Oh, hell.' 'Dat's all right,' I says, 'but I know what I knows,' I says, 'an' it 'ill come out later. You wait an' see,' I says, 'you see.'"

"Anybody what had eyes could see dat dere was somethin' wrong wid dat girl. I didn't like her actions."

On the street Jimmie met a friend. "What deh hell?" asked the latter.

Jimmie explained. "An' I'll t'ump 'im till he can't stand."

"Oh, what deh hell," said the friend. "What's deh use! Yeh'll git pulled in! Everybody 'ill be onto it! An' ten plunks! Gee!"

Jimmie was determined. "He t'inks he kin scrap, but he'll fin' out diff'ent."

"Gee," remonstrated the friend. "What deh hell?"

Chapter XI

On a corner a glass-fronted building shed a yellow glare upon the pavements. The open mouth of a saloon called seductively to passengers to enter and annihilate sorrow or create rage.

The interior of the place was papered in olive and bronze tints of imitation leather. A shining bar of counterfeit massiveness extended down the side of the room. Behind it a great mahogany-appearing sideboard reached the ceiling. Upon its shelves rested pyramids of shimmering glasses that were never disturbed. Mirrors set in the face of the sideboard multiplied them. Lemons, oranges and paper napkins, arranged with mathematical precision, sat among the glasses. Many-hued decanters of liquor perched at regular intervals on the lower shelves. A nickel-plated cash register occupied a position in the exact centre of the general effect. The elementary senses of it all seemed to be opulence and geometrical accuracy.

Across from the bar a smaller counter held a collection of plates upon which swarmed frayed fragments of crackers, slices of boiled ham, dishevelled bits of cheese, and pickles swimming in vinegar. An odor of grasping, begrimed hands and munching mouths pervaded.

Pete, in a white jacket, was behind the bar bending expectantly toward a quiet stranger. "A beeh," said the man. Pete drew a foam-topped glassful and set it dripping upon the bar.

At this moment the light bamboo doors at the entrance swung open and crashed against the siding. Jimmie and a companion entered. They swaggered unsteadily but belligerently toward the bar and looked at Pete with bleared and blinking eyes.

"Gin," said Jimmie.

"Gin," said the companion.

Pete slid a bottle and two glasses along the bar. He bended his head sideways as he assiduously polished away with a napkin at the gleaming wood. He had a look of watchfulness upon his features.

Jimmie and his companion kept their eyes upon the bartender and conversed loudly in tones of contempt.

"He's a dindy masher, ain't he, by Gawd?" laughed Jimmie.

"Oh, hell, yes," said the companion, sneering widely. "He's great, he is. Git onto deh mug on deh blokie. Dat's enough to make a feller turn hand-springs in 'is sleep."

The quiet stranger moved himself and his glass a trifle further away and maintained an attitude of oblivion.

"Gee! ain't he hot stuff!"

"Git onto his shape! Great Gawd!"

"Hey," cried Jimmie, in tones of command. Pete came along slowly, with a sullen dropping of the under lip.

"Well," he growled, "what's eatin' yehs?"

"Gin," said Jimmie.

"Gin," said the companion.

As Pete confronted them with the bottle and the glasses, they laughed in his face. Jimmie's companion, evidently overcome with merriment, pointed a grimy forefinger in Pete's direction.

"Say, Jimmie," demanded he, "what deh hell is dat behind deh bar?"

"Damned if I knows," replied Jimmie. They laughed loudly. Pete put down a bottle with a bang and turned a formidable face toward them. He disclosed his teeth and his shoulders heaved restlessly.

"You fellers can't guy me," he said. "Drink yer stuff an' git out an' don' make no trouble."

Instantly the laughter faded from the faces of the two men and expressions of offended dignity immediately came.

"Who deh hell has said anyt'ing teh you," cried they in the same breath.

The quiet stranger looked at the door calculatingly.

"Ah, come off," said Pete to the two men. "Don't pick me up for no jay. Drink yer rum an' git out an' don' make no trouble."

"Oh, deh hell," airily cried Jimmie.

"Oh, deh hell," airily repeated his companion.

"We goes when we git ready! See!" continued Jimmie.

"Well," said Pete in a threatening voice, "don' make no trouble."

Jimmie suddenly leaned forward with his head on one side. He snarled like a wild animal.

"Well, what if we does? See?" said he.

Dark blood flushed into Pete's face, and he shot a lurid glance at Jimmie.

"Well, den we'll see whose deh bes' man, you or me," he said.

The quiet stranger moved modestly toward the door.

Jimmie began to swell with valor.

"Don' pick me up fer no tenderfoot. When yeh tackles me yeh tackles one of deh bes' men in deh city. See? I'm a scrapper, I am. Ain't dat right, Billie?"

"Sure, Mike," responded his companion in tones of conviction.

"Oh, hell," said Pete, easily. "Go fall on yerself."

The two men again began to laugh.

"What deh hell is dat talkin'?" cried the companion.

"Damned if I knows," replied Jimmie with exaggerated contempt.

Pete made a furious gesture. "Git outa here now, an' don' make no trouble. See? Youse fellers er lookin' fer a scrap an' it's damn likely yeh'll fin' one if yeh keeps on shootin' off yer mout's. I know yehs! See? I kin lick better men dan yehs ever saw in yer lifes. Dat's right! See? Don' pick me up fer no stuff er yeh might be jolted out in deh street before yeh knows where yeh is. When I comes from behind dis bar, I t'rows yehs bote inteh deh street. See?"

"Oh, hell," cried the two men in chorus.

The glare of a panther came into Pete's eyes. "Dat's what I said! Unnerstan'?"

He came through a passage at the end of the bar and swelled down upon the two men. They stepped promptly forward and crowded close to him.

They bristled like three roosters. They moved their heads pugnaciously and kept their shoulders braced. The nervous muscles about each mouth twitched with a forced smile of mockery.

"Well, what deh hell yer goin' teh do?" gritted Jimmie.

Pete stepped warily back, waving his hands before him to keep the men from coming too near.

"Well, what deh hell yer goin' teh do?" repeated Jimmie's ally. They kept close to him, taunting and leering. They strove to make him attempt the initial blow.

"Keep back, now! Don' crowd me," ominously said Pete.

Again they chorused in contempt. "Oh, hell!"

In a small, tossing group, the three men edged for positions like frigates contemplating battle.

"Well, why deh hell don' yeh try teh t'row us out?" cried Jimmie and his ally with copious sneers.

The bravery of bull-dogs sat upon the faces of the men. Their clenched fists moved like eager weapons.

The allied two jostled the bartender's elbows, glaring at him with feverish eyes and forcing him toward the wall.

Suddenly Pete swore redly. The flash of action gleamed from his eyes. He threw back his arm and aimed a tremendous, lightning-like blow at Jimmie's face. His foot swung a step forward and the weight of his body was behind his fist. Jimmie ducked his head, Bowery-like, with the quickness of a cat. The fierce, answering blows of him and his ally crushed on Pete's bowed head.

The quiet stranger vanished.

The arms of the combatants whirled in the air like flails. The faces of the men, at first flushed to flame-colored anger, now began to fade to the pallor of warriors in the blood and heat of a battle. Their lips curled back and stretched tightly over the gums in ghoul-like grins. Through their white, gripped teeth struggled hoarse whisperings of oaths. Their eyes glittered with murderous fire.

Each head was huddled between its owner's shoulders, and arms were swinging with marvelous rapidity. Feet scraped to and fro with a loud scratching sound upon the sanded floor. Blows left crimson blotches upon pale skin. The curses of the first quarter minute of the fight died away. The breaths of the fighters came wheezingly from their lips and the three chests were straining and heaving. Pete at intervals gave vent to low, labored hisses, that sounded like a desire to kill. Jimmie's ally gibbered at times like a wounded maniac. Jimmie was silent, fighting with the face of a sacrificial priest. The rage of fear shone in all their eyes and their blood-colored fists swirled.

At a tottering moment a blow from Pete's hand struck the ally and he crashed to the floor. He wriggled instantly to his feet and grasping the quiet stranger's beer glass from the bar, hurled it at Pete's head.

High on the wall it burst like a bomb, shivering fragments flying in all directions. Then missiles came to every man's hand. The place had heretofore appeared free of things to throw, but suddenly glass and bottles went singing through the air. They were thrown point blank at bobbing heads. The pyramid of shimmering glasses, that had never been disturbed, changed to cascades as heavy bottles were flung into them. Mirrors splintered to nothing.

The three frothing creatures on the floor buried themselves in a frenzy for blood. There followed in the wake of missiles and fists some unknown prayers, perhaps for death.

The quiet stranger had sprawled very pyrotechnically out on the sidewalk. A laugh ran up and down the avenue for the half of a block.

"Dey've trowed a bloke inteh deh street."

People heard the sound of breaking glass and shuffling feet within the saloon and came running. A small group, bending down to look under the bamboo doors, watching the fall of glass, and three pairs of violent legs, changed in a moment to a crowd.

A policeman came charging down the sidewalk and bounced through the doors into the saloon. The crowd bended and surged in absorbing anxiety to see.

Jimmie caught first sight of the on-coming interruption. On his feet he had the same regard for a policeman that, when on his truck, he had for a fire engine. He howled and ran for the side door.

The officer made a terrific advance, club in hand. One comprehensive sweep of the long night stick threw the ally to the floor and forced Pete to a corner. With his disengaged hand he made a furious effort at Jimmie's coat-tails. Then he regained his balance and paused.

"Well, well, you are a pair of pictures. What in hell yeh been up to?"

Jimmie, with his face drenched in blood, escaped up a side street, pursued a short distance by some of the more law-loving, or excited individuals of the crowd.

Later, from a corner safely dark, he saw the policeman, the ally and the bartender emerge from the saloon. Pete locked the doors and then followed up the avenue in the rear of the crowd-encompassed policeman and his charge.

On first thoughts Jimmie, with his heart throbbing at battle heat, started to go desperately to the rescue of his friend, but he halted.

"Ah, what deh hell?" he demanded of himself.

Chapter XII

In a hall of irregular shape sat Pete and Maggie drinking beer. A submissive orchestra dictated to by a spectacled man with frowsy hair and a dress suit, industriously followed the bobs of his head and the waves of his baton. A ballad singer, in a dress of flaming scarlet, sang in the inevitable voice of brass. When she vanished, men seated at the tables near the front applauded loudly, pounding the polished wood with their beer glasses. She returned attired in less gown, and sang again. She received another enthusiastic encore. She reappeared in still less gown and danced. The deafening rumble of glasses and clapping of hands that followed her exit indicated an overwhelming desire to have her come on for the fourth time, but the curiosity of the audience was not gratified.

Maggie was pale. From her eyes had been plucked all look of self-reliance. She leaned with a dependent air toward her companion. She was timid, as if fearing his anger or displeasure. She seemed to beseech tenderness of him.

Pete's air of distinguished valor had grown upon him until it threatened stupendous dimensions. He was infinitely gracious to the girl. It was apparent to her that his condescension was a marvel.

He could appear to strut even while sitting still and he showed that he was a lion of lordly characteristics by the air with which he spat.

With Maggie gazing at him wonderingly, he took pride in commanding the waiters who were, however, indifferent or deaf.

"Hi, you, git a russle on yehs! What deh hell yehs lookin' at? Two more beehs, d'yeh hear?"

He leaned back and critically regarded the person of a girl with a straw-colored wig who upon the stage was flinging her heels in somewhat awkward imitation of a well-known danseuse.

At times Maggie told Pete long confidential tales of her former home life, dwelling upon the escapades of the other members of the family and the difficulties she had to combat in order to obtain a degree of comfort. He responded in tones of philanthropy. He pressed her arm with an air of reassuring proprietorship.

"Dey was damn jays," he said, denouncing the mother and brother.

The sound of the music which, by the efforts of the frowsy-headed leader, drifted to her ears through the smoke-filled atmosphere, made the girl dream. She thought of her former Rum Alley environment and turned to regard Pete's strong protecting fists. She thought of the collar and cuff manufactory and the eternal moan of the proprietor: "What een hell do you sink I pie fife dolla a week for? Play? No, py damn." She contemplated Pete's man-subduing eyes and noted that wealth and prosperity was indicated by his clothes. She imagined a future, rose-tinted, because of its distance from all that she previously had experienced.

As to the present she perceived only vague reasons to be miserable. Her life was Pete's and she considered him worthy of the charge. She would be disturbed by no particular apprehensions, so long as Pete adored her as he now said he did. She did not feel like a bad woman. To her knowledge she had never seen any better.

At times men at other tables regarded the girl furtively. Pete, aware of it, nodded at her and grinned. He felt proud.

"Mag, yer a bloomin' good-looker," he remarked, studying her face through the haze. The men made Maggie fear, but she blushed at Pete's words as it became apparent to her that she was the apple of his eye.

Grey-headed men, wonderfully pathetic in their dissipation, stared at her through clouds. Smooth-cheeked boys, some of them with faces of stone and mouths of sin, not nearly so pathetic as the grey heads, tried to find the girl's eyes in the smoke wreaths. Maggie considered she was not what they thought her. She confined her glances to Pete and the stage.

The orchestra played negro melodies and a versatile drummer pounded, whacked, clattered and scratched on a dozen machines to make noise.

Those glances of the men, shot at Maggie from under half-closed lids, made her tremble. She thought them all to be worse men than Pete.

"Come, let's go," she said.

As they went out Maggie perceived two women seated at a table with some men. They were painted and their cheeks had lost their roundness. As she passed them the girl, with a shrinking movement, drew back her skirts.

Chapter XIII

Jimmie did not return home for a number of days after the fight with Pete in the saloon. When he did, he approached with extreme caution.

He found his mother raving. Maggie had not returned home. The parent continually wondered how her daughter could come to such a pass. She had never considered Maggie as a pearl dropped unstained into Rum Alley from Heaven, but she could not conceive how it was possible for her daughter to fall so low as to bring disgrace upon her family. She was terrific in denunciation of the girl's wickedness.

The fact that the neighbors talked of it, maddened her. When women came in, and in the course of their conversation casually asked, "Where's Maggie dese days?" the mother shook her fuzzy head at them and appalled them with curses. Cunning hints inviting confidence she rebuffed with violence.

"An' wid all deh bringin' up she had, how could she?" moaningly she asked of her son. "Wid all deh talkin' wid her I did an' deh t'ings I tol' her to remember? When a girl is bringed up deh way I bringed up Maggie, how kin she go teh deh devil?"

Jimmie was transfixed by these questions. He could not conceive how under the circumstances his mother's daughter and his sister could have been so wicked.

His mother took a drink from a squdgy bottle that sat on the table. She continued her lament.

"She had a bad heart, dat girl did, Jimmie. She was wicked teh deh heart an' we never knowed it."

Jimmie nodded, admitting the fact.

"We lived in deh same house wid her an' I brought her up an' we never knowed how bad she was."

Jimmie nodded again.

"Wid a home like dis an' a mudder like me, she went teh deh bad," cried the mother, raising her eyes.

One day, Jimmie came home, sat down in a chair and began to wriggle about with a new and strange nervousness. At last he spoke shamefacedly.

"Well, look-a-here, dis t'ing queers us! See? We're queered! An' maybe it 'ud be better if I —well, I t'ink I kin look 'er up an' —maybe it 'ud be better if I fetched her home an' —"

The mother started from her chair and broke forth into a storm of passionate anger.

"What! Let 'er come an' sleep under deh same roof wid her mudder agin! Oh, yes, I will, won't I? Sure? Shame on yehs, Jimmie Johnson, for sayin' such a t'ing teh yer own mudder-teh yer own mudder! Little did I t'ink when yehs was a babby playin' about me feet dat ye'd grow up teh say sech a t'ing teh yer mudder-yer own mudder. I never taut —"

Sobs choked her and interrupted her reproaches.

"Dere ain't nottin' teh raise sech hell about," said Jimmie. "I on'y says it 'ud be better if we keep dis t'ing dark, see? It queers us! See?"

His mother laughed a laugh that seemed to ring through the city and be echoed and re-echoed by countless other laughs. "Oh, yes, I will, won't I! Sure!"

"Well, yeh must take me fer a damn fool," said Jimmie, indignant at his mother for mocking him. "I didn't say we'd make 'er inteh a little tin angel, ner nottin', but deh way it is now she can queer us! Don' che see?"

"Aye, she'll git tired of deh life atter a while an' den she'll wanna be a-comin' home, won' she, deh beast! I'll let 'er in den, won' I?"

"Well, I didn' mean none of dis prod'gal bus'ness anyway," explained Jimmie.

"It wasn't no prod'gal dauter, yeh damn fool," said the mother. "It was prod'gal son, anyhow."

"I know dat," said Jimmie.

For a time they sat in silence. The mother's eyes gloated on a scene her imagination could call before her. Her lips were set in a vindictive smile.

"Aye, she'll cry, won' she, an' carry on, an' tell how Pete, or some odder feller, beats 'er an' she'll say she's sorry an' all dat an' she ain't happy, she ain't, an' she wants to come home agin, she does."

With grim humor, the mother imitated the possible wailing notes of the daughter's voice.

"Den I'll take 'er in, won't I, deh beast. She kin cry 'er two eyes out on deh stones of deh street before I'll dirty deh place wid her. She abused an' ill-treated her own mudder-her own mudder what loved her an' she'll never git anodder chance dis side of hell."

Jimmie thought he had a great idea of women's frailty, but he could not understand why any of his kin should be victims.

"Damn her," he fervidly said.

Again he wondered vaguely if some of the women of his acquaintance had brothers. Nevertheless, his mind did not for an instant confuse himself with those brothers nor his sister with theirs. After the mother had, with great difficulty, suppressed the neighbors, she went among them and proclaimed her grief. "May Gawd forgive dat girl," was her continual cry. To attentive ears she recited the whole length and breadth of her woes.

"I bringed 'er up deh way a dauter oughta be bringed up an' dis is how she served me! She went teh deh devil deh first chance she got! May Gawd forgive her."

When arrested for drunkenness she used the story of her daughter's downfall with telling effect upon the police justices. Finally one of them said to her, peering down over his spectacles: "Mary, the records of this and other courts show that you are the mother of forty-two daughters who have been ruined. The case is unparalleled in the annals of this court, and this court thinks —"

The mother went through life shedding large tears of sorrow. Her red face was a picture of agony.

Of course Jimmie publicly damned his sister that he might appear on a higher social plane. But, arguing with himself, stumbling about in ways that he knew not, he, once, almost came to a conclusion that his sister would have been more firmly good had she better known why. However, he felt that he could not hold such a view. He threw it hastily aside.

Chapter XIV

In a hilarious hall there were twenty-eight tables and twenty-eight women and a crowd of smoking men. Valiant noise was made on a stage at the end of the hall by an orchestra composed of men who looked as if they had just happened in. Soiled waiters ran to and fro, swooping down like hawks on the unwary in the throng; clattering along the aisles with trays covered with glasses; stumbling over women's skirts and charging two prices for everything but beer, all with a swiftness that blurred the view of the cocoanut palms and dusty monstrosities painted upon the walls of the room. A bouncer, with an immense load of business upon his hands, plunged about in the crowd, dragging bashful strangers to prominent chairs, ordering waiters here and there and quarreling furiously with men who wanted to sing with the orchestra.

The usual smoke cloud was present, but so dense that heads and arms seemed entangled in it. The rumble of conversation was replaced by a roar. Plenteous oaths heaved through the air. The room rang with the shrill voices of women bubbling o'er with drink-laughter. The chief element in the music of the orchestra was speed. The musicians played in intent fury. A woman was singing and smiling upon the stage, but no one took notice of her. The rate at which the piano, cornet and violins were going, seemed to impart wildness to the half-drunken crowd. Beer glasses were emptied at a gulp and conversation became a rapid chatter. The smoke eddied and swirled like a shadowy river hurrying toward some unseen falls. Pete and Maggie entered the hall and took chairs at a table near the door. The woman who was seated there made an attempt to occupy Pete's attention and, failing, went away.

Three weeks had passed since the girl had left home. The air of spaniel-like dependence had been magnified and showed its direct effect in the peculiar off-handedness and ease of Pete's ways toward her.

She followed Pete's eyes with hers, anticipating with smiles gracious looks from him.

A woman of brilliance and audacity, accompanied by a mere boy, came into the place and took seats near them.

At once Pete sprang to his feet, his face beaming with glad surprise.

"By Gawd, there's Nellie," he cried.

He went over to the table and held out an eager hand to the woman.

"Why, hello, Pete, me boy, how are you," said she, giving him her fingers.

Maggie took instant note of the woman. She perceived that her black dress fitted her to perfection. Her linen collar and cuffs were spotless. Tan gloves were stretched over her well-shaped hands. A hat of a prevailing fashion perched jauntily upon her dark hair. She wore no jewelry and was painted with no apparent paint. She looked clear-eyed through the stares of the men.

"Sit down, and call your lady-friend over," she said cordially to Pete. At his beckoning Maggie came and sat between Pete and the mere boy.

"I thought yeh were gone away fer good," began Pete, at once. "When did yeh git back? How did dat Buff'lo bus'ness turn out?"

The woman shrugged her shoulders. "Well, he didn't have as many stamps as he tried to make out, so I shook him, that's all."

"Well, I'm glad teh see yehs back in deh city," said Pete, with awkward gallantry.

He and the woman entered into a long conversation, exchanging reminiscences of days together. Maggie sat still, unable to formulate an intelligent sentence upon the conversation and painfully aware of it.

She saw Pete's eyes sparkle as he gazed upon the handsome stranger. He listened smilingly to all she said. The woman was familiar with all his affairs, asked him about mutual friends, and knew the amount of his salary.

She paid no attention to Maggie, looking toward her once or twice and apparently seeing the wall beyond.

The mere boy was sulky. In the beginning he had welcomed with acclamations the additions.

"Let's all have a drink! What'll you take, Nell? And you, Miss what's-your-name. Have a drink, Mr. ——-, you, I mean."

He had shown a sprightly desire to do the talking for the company and tell all about his family. In a loud voice he declaimed on various topics. He assumed a patronizing air toward Pete. As Maggie was silent, he paid no attention to her. He made a great show of lavishing wealth upon the woman of brilliance and audacity.

"Do keep still, Freddie! You gibber like an ape, dear," said the woman to him. She turned away and devoted her attention to Pete.

"We'll have many a good time together again, eh?"

"Sure, Mike," said Pete, enthusiastic at once.

"Say," whispered she, leaning forward, "let's go over to Billie's and have a heluva time."

"Well, it's dis way! See?" said Pete. "I got dis lady frien' here."

"Oh, t'hell with her," argued the woman.

Pete appeared disturbed.

"All right," said she, nodding her head at him. "All right for you! We'll see the next time you ask me to go anywheres with you."

Pete squirmed.

"Say," he said, beseechingly, "come wid me a minit an' I'll tell yer why."

The woman waved her hand.

"Oh, that's all right, you needn't explain, you know. You wouldn't come merely because you wouldn't come, that's all there is of it."

To Pete's visible distress she turned to the mere boy, bringing him speedily from a terrific rage. He had been debating whether it would be the part of a man to pick a quarrel with Pete, or would he be justified in striking him savagely with his beer glass without warning. But he recovered himself when the woman turned to renew her smilings. He beamed upon her with an expression that was somewhat tipsy and inexpressibly tender.

"Say, shake that Bowery jay," requested he, in a loud whisper.

"Freddie, you are so droll," she replied.

Pete reached forward and touched the woman on the arm.

"Come out a minit while I tells yeh why I can't go wid yer. Yer doin' me dirt, Nell! I never taut ye'd do me dirt, Nell. Come on, will yer?" He spoke in tones of injury.

"Why, I don't see why I should be interested in your explanations," said the woman, with a coldness that seemed to reduce Pete to a pulp.

His eyes pleaded with her. "Come out a minit while I tells yeh."

The woman nodded slightly at Maggie and the mere boy, "'Scuse me."

The mere boy interrupted his loving smile and turned a shrivelling glare upon Pete. His boyish countenance flushed and he spoke, in a whine, to the woman:

"Oh, I say, Nellie, this ain't a square deal, you know. You aren't goin' to leave me and go off with that duffer, are you? I should think —"

"Why, you dear boy, of course I'm not," cried the woman, affectionately. She bended over and whispered in his ear. He smiled again and settled in his chair as if resolved to wait patiently.

As the woman walked down between the rows of tables, Pete was at her shoulder talking earnestly, apparently in explanation. The woman waved her hands with studied airs of indifference. The doors swung behind them, leaving Maggie and the mere boy seated at the table.

Maggie was dazed. She could dimly perceive that something stupendous had happened. She wondered why Pete saw fit to remonstrate with the woman, pleading for forgiveness with his eyes. She thought she noted an air of submission about her leonine Pete. She was astounded.

The mere boy occupied himself with cock-tails and a cigar. He was tranquilly silent for half an hour. Then he bestirred himself and spoke.

"Well," he said, sighing, "I knew this was the way it would be." There was another stillness. The mere boy seemed to be musing.

"She was pulling m'leg. That's the whole amount of it," he said, suddenly. "It's a bloomin' shame the way that girl does. Why, I've spent over two dollars in drinks to-night. And she goes off with that plug-ugly who looks as if he had been hit in the face with a coin-die. I call it rocky treatment for a fellah like me. Here, waiter, bring me a cock-tail and make it damned strong."

Maggie made no reply. She was watching the doors. "It's a mean piece of business," complained the mere boy. He explained to her how amazing it was that anybody should treat him in such a manner. "But I'll get square with her, you bet. She won't get far ahead of yours truly, you know," he added, winking. "I'll tell her plainly that it was bloomin' mean business. And she won't come it over me with any of her 'now-Freddie-dears.' She thinks my name is Freddie, you know, but of course it ain't. I always tell these people some name like that, because if they got onto your right name they might use it sometime. Understand? Oh, they don't fool me much."

Maggie was paying no attention, being intent upon the doors. The mere boy relapsed into a period of gloom, during which he exterminated a number of cock-tails with a determined air, as if replying defiantly to fate. He occasionally broke forth into sentences composed of invectives joined together in a long string.

The girl was still staring at the doors. After a time the mere boy began to see cobwebs just in front of his nose. He spurred himself into being agreeable and insisted upon her having a charlotte-russe and a glass of beer.

"They's gone," he remarked, "they's gone." He looked at her through the smoke wreaths. "Shay, lil' girl, we mightish well make bes' of it. You ain't such bad-lookin' girl, y'know. Not half bad. Can't come up to Nell, though. No, can't do it! Well, I should shay not! Nell fine-lookin' girl! F—i—n—ine. You look damn bad longsider her, but by y'self ain't so bad. Have to do anyhow. Nell gone. On'y you left. Not half bad, though."

Maggie stood up.

"I'm going home," she said.

The mere boy started.

"Eh? What? Home," he cried, struck with amazement. "I beg pardon, did hear say home?"

"I'm going home," she repeated.

"Great Gawd, what hava struck," demanded the mere boy of himself, stupefied.

In a semi-comatose state he conducted her on board an up-town car, ostentatiously paid her fare, leered kindly at her through the rear window and fell off the steps.

Chapter XV

A forlorn woman went along a lighted avenue. The street was filled with people desperately bound on missions. An endless crowd darted at the elevated station stairs and the horse cars were thronged with owners of bundles.

The pace of the forlorn woman was slow. She was apparently searching for some one. She loitered near the doors of saloons and watched men emerge from them. She scanned furtively the faces in the rushing stream of pedestrians. Hurrying men, bent on catching some boat or train, jostled her elbows, failing to notice her, their thoughts fixed on distant dinners.

The forlorn woman had a peculiar face. Her smile was no smile. But when in repose her features had a shadowy look that was like a sardonic grin, as if some one had sketched with cruel forefinger indelible lines about her mouth.

Jimmie came strolling up the avenue. The woman encountered him with an aggrieved air.

"Oh, Jimmie, I've been lookin' all over fer yehs —," she began.

Jimmie made an impatient gesture and quickened his pace.

"Ah, don't bodder me! Good Gawd!" he said, with the savageness of a man whose life is pestered.

The woman followed him along the sidewalk in somewhat the manner of a suppliant.

"But, Jimmie," she said, "yehs told me ye'd —"

Jimmie turned upon her fiercely as if resolved to make a last stand for comfort and peace.

"Say, fer Gawd's sake, Hattie, don' foller me from one end of deh city teh deh odder. Let up, will yehs! Give me a minute's res', can't yehs? Yehs makes me tired, allus taggin' me. See? Ain' yehs got no sense. Do yehs want people teh get onto me? Go chase yerself, fer Gawd's sake."

The woman stepped closer and laid her fingers on his arm. "But, look-a-here —"

Jimmie snarled. "Oh, go teh hell."

He darted into the front door of a convenient saloon and a moment later came out into the shadows that surrounded the side door. On the brilliantly lighted avenue he perceived the forlorn woman dodging about like a scout. Jimmie laughed with an air of relief and went away.

When he arrived home he found his mother clamoring. Maggie had returned. She stood shivering beneath the torrent of her mother's wrath.

"Well, I'm damned," said Jimmie in greeting.

His mother, tottering about the room, pointed a quivering forefinger.

"Lookut her, Jimmie, lookut her. Dere's yer sister, boy. Dere's yer sister. Lookut her! Lookut her!"

She screamed in scoffing laughter.

The girl stood in the middle of the room. She edged about as if unable to find a place on the floor to put her feet.

"Ha, ha, ha," bellowed the mother. "Dere she stands! Ain' she purty? Lookut her! Ain' she sweet, deh beast? Lookut her! Ha, ha, lookut her!"

She lurched forward and put her red and seamed hands upon her daughter's face. She bent down and peered keenly up into the eyes of the girl.

"Oh, she's jes' dessame as she ever was, ain' she? She's her mudder's purty darlin' yit, ain' she? Lookut her, Jimmie! Come here, fer Gawd's sake, and lookut her."

The loud, tremendous sneering of the mother brought the denizens of the Rum Alley tenement to their doors. Women came in the hallways. Children scurried to and fro.

"What's up? Dat Johnson party on anudder tear?"

"Naw! Young Mag's come home!"

"Deh hell yeh say?"

Through the open door curious eyes stared in at Maggie. Children ventured into the room and ogled her, as if they formed the front row at a theatre. Women, without, bended toward each other and whispered, nodding their heads with airs of profound philosophy. A baby, overcome with curiosity concerning this object at which all were looking, sidled forward and touched her dress, cautiously, as if investigating a red-hot stove. Its mother's voice rang out like a warning trumpet. She rushed forward and grabbed her child, casting a terrible look of indignation at the girl.

Maggie's mother paced to and fro, addressing the doorful of eyes, expounding like a glib showman at a museum. Her voice rang through the building.

"Dere she stands," she cried, wheeling suddenly and pointing with dramatic finger. "Dere she stands! Lookut her! Ain' she a dindy? An' she was so good as to come home teh her mudder, she was! Ain' she a beaut'? Ain' she a dindy? Fer Gawd's sake!"

The jeering cries ended in another burst of shrill laughter.

The girl seemed to awaken. "Jimmie —"

He drew hastily back from her.

"Well, now, yer a hell of a t'ing, ain' yeh?" he said, his lips curling in scorn. Radiant virtue sat upon his brow and his repelling hands expressed horror of contamination.

Maggie turned and went.

The crowd at the door fell back precipitately. A baby falling down in front of the door, wrenched a scream like a wounded animal from its mother. Another woman sprang forward and picked it up, with a chivalrous air, as if rescuing a human being from an oncoming express train.

As the girl passed down through the hall, she went before open doors framing more eyes strangely microscopic, and sending broad beams of inquisitive light into the darkness of her path. On the second floor she met the gnarled old woman who possessed the music box.

"So," she cried, "'ere yehs are back again, are yehs? An' dey've kicked yehs out? Well, come in an' stay wid me teh-night. I ain' got no moral standin'."

From above came an unceasing babble of tongues, over all of which rang the mother's derisive laughter.

Chapter XVI

Pete did not consider that he had ruined Maggie. If he had thought that her soul could never smile again, he would have believed the mother and brother, who were pyrotechnic over the affair, to be responsible for it.

Besides, in his world, souls did not insist upon being able to smile. "What deh hell?"

He felt a trifle entangled. It distressed him. Revelations and scenes might bring upon him the wrath of the owner of the saloon, who insisted upon respectability of an advanced type.

"What deh hell do dey wanna raise such a smoke about it fer?" demanded he of himself, disgusted with the attitude of the family. He saw no necessity for anyone's losing their equilibrium merely because their sister or their daughter had stayed away from home.

Searching about in his mind for possible reasons for their conduct, he came upon the conclusion that Maggie's motives were correct, but that the two others wished to snare him. He felt pursued.

The woman of brilliance and audacity whom he had met in the hilarious hall showed a disposition to ridicule him.

"A little pale thing with no spirit," she said. "Did you note the expression of her eyes? There was something in them about pumpkin pie and virtue. That is a peculiar way the left corner of her mouth has of twitching, isn't it? Dear, dear, my cloud-compelling Pete, what are you coming to?"

Pete asserted at once that he never was very much interested in the girl. The woman interrupted him, laughing.

"Oh, it's not of the slightest consequence to me, my dear young man. You needn't draw maps for my benefit. Why should I be concerned about it?"

But Pete continued with his explanations. If he was laughed at for his tastes in women, he felt obliged to say that they were only temporary or indifferent ones.

The morning after Maggie had departed from home, Pete stood behind the bar. He was immaculate in white jacket and apron and his hair was plastered over his brow with infinite correctness. No customers were in the place. Pete was twisting his napkined fist slowly in a beer glass, softly whistling to himself and occasionally holding the object of his attention between his eyes and a few weak beams of sunlight that had found their way over the thick screens and into the shaded room.

With lingering thoughts of the woman of brilliance and audacity, the bartender raised his head and stared through the varying cracks between the swaying bamboo doors. Suddenly the whistling pucker faded from his lips. He saw Maggie walking slowly past. He gave a great start, fearing for the previously-mentioned eminent respectability of the place.

He threw a swift, nervous glance about him, all at once feeling guilty. No one was in the room.

He went hastily over to the side door. Opening it and looking out, he perceived Maggie standing, as if undecided, on the corner. She was searching the place with her eyes.

As she turned her face toward him Pete beckoned to her hurriedly, intent upon returning with speed to a position behind the bar and to the atmosphere of respectability upon which the proprietor insisted.

Maggie came to him, the anxious look disappearing from her face and a smile wreathing her lips.

"Oh, Pete —," she began brightly.

The bartender made a violent gesture of impatience.

"Oh, my Gawd," cried he, vehemently. "What deh hell do yeh wanna hang aroun' here fer? Do yeh wanna git me inteh trouble?" he demanded with an air of injury.

Astonishment swept over the girl's features. "Why, Pete! yehs tol' me —"

Pete glanced profound irritation. His countenance reddened with the anger of a man whose respectability is being threatened.

"Say, yehs makes me tired. See? What deh hell deh yeh wanna tag aroun' atter me fer? Yeh'll git me inteh trouble wid deh ol' man an' dey'll be hell teh pay! If he sees a woman roun' here he'll go crazy an' I'll lose me job! See? Yer brudder come in here an' raised hell an' deh ol' man hada put up fer it! An' now I'm done! See? I'm done."

The girl's eyes stared into his face. "Pete, don't yeh remem —"

"Oh, hell," interrupted Pete, anticipating.

The girl seemed to have a struggle with herself. She was apparently bewildered and could not find speech. Finally she asked in a low voice: "But where kin I go?"

The question exasperated Pete beyond the powers of endurance. It was a direct attempt to give him some responsibility in a matter that did not concern him. In his indignation he volunteered information.

"Oh, go teh hell," cried he. He slammed the door furiously and returned, with an air of relief, to his respectability.

Maggie went away.

She wandered aimlessly for several blocks. She stopped once and asked aloud a question of herself: "Who?"

A man who was passing near her shoulder, humorously took the questioning word as intended for him.

"Eh? What? Who? Nobody! I didn't say anything," he laughingly said, and continued his way.

Soon the girl discovered that if she walked with such apparent aimlessness, some men looked at her with calculating eyes. She quickened her step, frightened. As a protection, she adopted a demeanor of intentness as if going somewhere.

After a time she left rattling avenues and passed between rows of houses with sternness and stolidity stamped upon their features. She hung her head for she felt their eyes grimly upon her.

Suddenly she came upon a stout gentleman in a silk hat and a chaste black coat, whose decorous row of buttons reached from his chin to his knees. The girl had heard of the Grace of God and she decided to approach this man.

His beaming, chubby face was a picture of benevolence and kind-heartedness. His eyes shone good-will.

But as the girl timidly accosted him, he gave a convulsive movement and saved his respectability by a vigorous side-step. He did not risk it to save a soul. For how was he to know that there was a soul before him that needed saving?

Chapter XVII

Upon a wet evening, several months after the last chapter, two interminable rows of cars, pulled by slipping horses, jangled along a prominent side-street. A dozen cabs, with coat-enshrouded drivers, clattered to and fro. Electric lights, whirring softly, shed a blurred radiance. A flower dealer, his feet tapping impatiently, his nose and his wares glistening with rain-drops, stood behind an array of roses and chrysanthemums. Two or three theatres emptied a crowd upon the storm-swept pavements. Men pulled their hats over their eyebrows and raised their collars to their ears. Women shrugged impatient shoulders in their warm cloaks and stopped to arrange their skirts for a walk through the storm. People having been comparatively silent for two hours burst into a roar of conversation, their hearts still kindling from the glowings of the stage.

The pavements became tossing seas of umbrellas. Men stepped forth to hail cabs or cars, raising their fingers in varied forms of polite request or imperative demand. An endless procession wended toward elevated stations. An atmosphere of pleasure and prosperity seemed to hang over the throng, born, perhaps, of good clothes and of having just emerged from a place of forgetfulness.

In the mingled light and gloom of an adjacent park, a handful of wet wanderers, in attitudes of chronic dejection, was scattered among the benches.

A girl of the painted cohorts of the city went along the street. She threw changing glances at men who passed her, giving smiling invitations to men of rural or untaught pattern and usually seeming sedately unconscious of the men with a metropolitan seal upon their faces.

Crossing glittering avenues, she went into the throng emerging from the places of forgetfulness. She hurried forward through the crowd as if intent upon reaching a distant home, bending forward in her handsome cloak, daintily lifting her skirts and picking for her well-shod feet the dryer spots upon the pavements.

The restless doors of saloons, clashing to and fro, disclosed animated rows of men before bars and hurrying barkeepers.

A concert hall gave to the street faint sounds of swift, machine-like music, as if a group of phantom musicians were hastening.

A tall young man, smoking a cigarette with a sublime air, strolled near the girl. He had on evening dress, a moustache, a chrysanthemum, and a look of ennui, all of which he kept carefully under his eye. Seeing the girl walk on as if such a young man as he was not in existence, he looked back transfixed with interest. He stared glassily for a moment, but gave a slight convulsive start when he discerned that she was neither new, Parisian, nor theatrical. He wheeled about hastily and turned his stare into the air, like a sailor with a search-light.

A stout gentleman, with pompous and philanthropic whiskers, went stolidly by, the broad of his back sneering at the girl.

A belated man in business clothes, and in haste to catch a car, bounced against her shoulder. "Hi, there, Mary, I beg your pardon! Brace up, old girl." He grasped her arm to steady her, and then was away running down the middle of the street.

The girl walked on out of the realm of restaurants and saloons. She passed more glittering avenues and went into darker blocks than those where the crowd travelled.

A young man in light overcoat and derby hat received a glance shot keenly from the eyes of the girl. He stopped and looked at her, thrusting his hands in his pockets and making a mocking smile curl his lips. "Come, now, old lady," he said, "you don't mean to tel me that you sized me up for a farmer?"

A labouring man marched along; with bundles under his arms. To her remarks, he replied, "It's a fine evenin', ain't it?"

She smiled squarely into the face of a boy who was hurrying by with his hands buried in his overcoat pockets, his blonde locks bobbing on his youthful temples, and a cheery smile of unconcern upon his lips. He turned his head and smiled back at her, waving his hands.

"Not this eve-some other eve!"

A drunken man, reeling in her pathway, began to roar at her. "I ain' ga no money!" he shouted, in a dismal voice. He lurched on up the street, wailing to himself: "I ain' ga no money. Ba' luck. Ain' ga no more money."

The girl went into gloomy districts near the river, where the tall black factories shut in the street and only occasional broad beams of light fell across the pavements from saloons. In front of one of these places, whence came the sound of a violin vigorously scraped, the patter of feet on boards and the ring of loud laughter, there stood a man with blotched features.

Further on in the darkness she met a ragged being with shifting, bloodshot eyes and grimy hands.

She went into the blackness of the final block. The shutters of the tall buildings were closed like grim lips. The structures seemed to have eyes that looked over them, beyond them, at other things. Afar off the lights of the avenues glittered as if from an impossible distance. Street-car bells jingled with a sound of merriment.

At the feet of the tall buildings appeared the deathly black hue of the river. Some hidden factory sent up a yellow glare, that lit for a moment the waters lapping oilily against timbers. The varied sounds of life, made joyous by distance and seeming unapproachableness, came faintly and died away to a silence.

Chapter XVIII

In a partitioned-off section of a saloon sat a man with a half dozen women, gleefully laughing, hovering about him. The man had arrived at that stage of drunkenness where affection is felt for the universe.

"I'm good f'ler, girls," he said, convincingly. "I'm damn good f'ler. An'body treats me right, I allus trea's zem right! See?"

The women nodded their heads approvingly. "To be sure," they cried out in hearty chorus. "You're the kind of a man we like, Pete. You're outa sight! What yeh goin' to buy this time, dear?"

"An't'ing yehs wants, damn it," said the man in an abandonment of good will. His countenance shone with the true spirit of benevolence. He was in the proper mode of missionaries. He would have fraternized with obscure Hottentots. And above all, he was overwhelmed in tenderness for his friends, who were all illustrious.

"An't'ing yehs wants, damn it," repeated he, waving his hands with beneficent recklessness. "I'm good f'ler, girls, an' if an'body treats me right I—here," called he through an open door to a waiter, "bring girls drinks, damn it. What 'ill yehs have, girls? An't'ing yehs wants, damn it!"

The waiter glanced in with the disgusted look of the man who serves intoxicants for the man who takes too much of them. He nodded his head shortly at the order from each individual, and went.

"Damn it," said the man, "we're havin' heluva time. I like you girls! Damn'd if I don't! Yer right sort! See?"

He spoke at length and with feeling, concerning the excellencies of his assembled friends.

"Don' try pull man's leg, but have a heluva time! Das right! Das way teh do! Now, if I sawght yehs tryin' work me fer drinks, wouldn' buy damn t'ing! But yer right sort, damn it! Yehs know how ter treat a f'ler, an' I stays by yehs 'til spen' las' cent! Das right! I'm good f'ler an' I knows when an'body treats me right!"

Between the times of the arrival and departure of the waiter, the man discoursed to the women on the tender regard he felt for all living things. He laid stress upon the purity of his motives in all dealings with men in the world and spoke of the fervor of his friendship for those who were amiable. Tears welled slowly from his eyes. His voice quavered when he spoke to them.

Once when the waiter was about to depart with an empty tray, the man drew a coin from his pocket and held it forth.

"Here," said he, quite magnificently, "here's quar'."

The waiter kept his hands on his tray.

"I don' want yer money," he said.

The other put forth the coin with tearful insistence.

"Here, damn it," cried he, "tak't! Yer damn goo' f'ler an' I wan' yehs tak't!"

"Come, come, now," said the waiter, with the sullen air of a man who is forced into giving advice. "Put yer mon in yer pocket! Yer loaded an' yehs on'y makes a damn fool of yerself."

As the latter passed out of the door the man turned pathetically to the women.

"He don' know I'm damn goo' f'ler," cried he, dismally.

"Never you mind, Pete, dear," said a woman of brilliance and audacity, laying her hand with great affection upon his arm. "Never you mind, old boy! We'll stay by you, dear!"

"Das ri'," cried the man, his face lighting up at the soothing tones of the woman's voice. "Das ri', I'm damn goo' f'ler an' w'en anyone trea's me ri', I treats zem ri'! Shee!"

"Sure!" cried the women. "And we're not goin' back on you, old man."

The man turned appealing eyes to the woman of brilliance and audacity. He felt that if he could be convicted of a contemptible action he would die.

"Shay, Nell, damn it, I allus trea's yehs shquare, didn' I? I allus been goo' f'ler wi' yehs, ain't I, Nell?"

"Sure you have, Pete," assented the woman. She delivered an oration to her companions. "Yessir, that's a fact. Pete's a square fellah, he is. He never goes back on a friend. He's the right kind an' we stay by him, don't we, girls?"

"Sure," they exclaimed. Looking lovingly at him they raised their glasses and drank his health.

"Girlsh," said the man, beseechingly, "I allus trea's yehs ri', didn' I? I'm goo' f'ler, ain' I, girlsh?"

"Sure," again they chorused.

"Well," said he finally, "le's have nozzer drink, zen."

"That's right," hailed a woman, "that's right. Yer no bloomin' jay! Yer spends yer money like a man. Dat's right."

The man pounded the table with his quivering fists.

"Yessir," he cried, with deep earnestness, as if someone disputed him. "I'm damn goo' f'ler, an' w'en anyone trea's me ri', I allus trea's—le's have nozzer drink."

He began to beat the wood with his glass.

"Shay," howled he, growing suddenly impatient. As the waiter did not then come, the man swelled with wrath.

"Shay," howled he again.

The waiter appeared at the door.

"Bringsh drinksh," said the man.

The waiter disappeared with the orders.

"Zat f'ler damn fool," cried the man. "He insul' me! I'm ge'man! Can' stan' be insul'! I'm goin' lickim when comes!"

"No, no," cried the women, crowding about and trying to subdue him. "He's all right! He didn't mean anything! Let it go! He's a good fellah!"

"Din' he insul' me?" asked the man earnestly.

"No," said they. "Of course he didn't! He's all right!"

"Sure he didn' insul' me?" demanded the man, with deep anxiety in his voice.

"No, no! We know him! He's a good fellah. He didn't mean anything."

"Well, zen," said the man, resolutely, "I'm go' 'pol'gize!"

When the waiter came, the man struggled to the middle of the floor.

"Girlsh shed you insul' me! I shay damn lie! I 'pol'gize!"

"All right," said the waiter.

The man sat down. He felt a sleepy but strong desire to straighten things out and have a perfect understanding with everybody.

"Nell, I allus trea's yeh shquare, din' I? Yeh likes me, don' yehs, Nell? I'm goo' f'ler?"

"Sure," said the woman of brilliance and audacity.

"Yeh knows I'm stuck on yehs, don' yehs, Nell?"

"Sure," she repeated, carelessly.

Overwhelmed by a spasm of drunken adoration, he drew two or three bills from his pocket, and, with the trembling fingers of an offering priest, laid them on the table before the woman.

"Yehs knows, damn it, yehs kin have all got, 'cause I'm stuck on yehs, Nell, damn't, I—I'm stuck on yehs, Nell-buy drinksh-damn't—we're havin' heluva time—w'en anyone trea's me ri'—I—damn't, Nell-we're havin' heluva-time."

Shortly he went to sleep with his swollen face fallen forward on his chest.

The women drank and laughed, not heeding the slumbering man in the corner. Finally he lurched forward and fell groaning to the floor.

The women screamed in disgust and drew back their skirts.

"Come ahn," cried one, starting up angrily, "let's get out of here."

The woman of brilliance and audacity stayed behind, taking up the bills and stuffing them into a deep, irregularly-shaped pocket. A guttural snore from the recumbent man caused her to turn and look down at him.

She laughed. "What a damn fool," she said, and went.

The smoke from the lamps settled heavily down in the little compartment, obscuring the way out. The smell of oil, stifling in its intensity, pervaded the air. The wine from an overturned glass dripped softly down upon the blotches on the man's neck.

Chapter XIX

In a room a woman sat at a table eating like a fat monk in a picture.

A soiled, unshaven man pushed open the door and entered.

"Well," said he, "Mag's dead."

"What?" said the woman, her mouth filled with bread.

"Mag's dead," repeated the man.

"Deh hell she is," said the woman. She continued her meal. When she finished her coffee she began to weep.

"I kin remember when her two feet was no bigger dan yer t'umb, and she weared worsted boots," moaned she.

"Well, whata dat?" said the man.

"I kin remember when she weared worsted boots," she cried.

The neighbors began to gather in the hall, staring in at the weeping woman as if watching the contortions of a dying dog. A dozen women entered and lamented with her. Under their busy hands the rooms took on that appalling appearance of neatness and order with which death is greeted.

Suddenly the door opened and a woman in a black gown rushed in with outstretched arms. "Ah, poor Mary," she cried, and tenderly embraced the moaning one.

"Ah, what ter'ble affliction is dis," continued she. Her vocabulary was derived from mission churches. "Me poor Mary, how I feel fer yehs! Ah, what a ter'ble affliction is a disobed'ent chil'."

Her good, motherly face was wet with tears. She trembled in eagerness to express her sympathy. The mourner sat with bowed head, rocking her body heavily to and fro, and crying out in a high, strained voice that sounded like a dirge on some forlorn pipe.

"I kin remember when she weared worsted boots an' her two feets was no bigger dan yer t'umb an' she weared worsted boots, Miss Smith," she cried, raising her streaming eyes.

"Ah, me poor Mary," sobbed the woman in black. With low, coddling cries, she sank on her knees by the mourner's chair, and put her arms about her. The other women began to groan in different keys.

"Yer poor misguided chil' is gone now, Mary, an' let us hope it's fer deh bes'. Yeh'll fergive her now, Mary, won't yehs, dear, all her disobed'ence? All her t'ankless behavior to her mudder an' all her badness? She's gone where her ter'ble sins will be judged."

The woman in black raised her face and paused. The inevitable sunlight came streaming in at the windows and shed a ghastly cheerfulness upon the faded hues of the room. Two or three of the spectators were sniffling, and one was loudly weeping. The mourner arose and staggered into the other room. In a moment she emerged with a pair of faded baby shoes held in the hollow of her hand.

"I kin remember when she used to wear dem," cried she. The women burst anew into cries as if they had all been stabbed. The mourner turned to the soiled and unshaven man.

"Jimmie, boy, go git yer sister! Go git yer sister an' we'll put deh boots on her feets!"

"Dey won't fit her now, yeh damn fool," said the man.

"Go git yer sister, Jimmie," shrieked the woman, confronting him fiercely.

The man swore sullenly. He went over to a corner and slowly began to put on his coat. He took his hat and went out, with a dragging, reluctant step.

The woman in black came forward and again besought the mourner.

"Yeh'll fergive her, Mary! Yeh'll fergive yer bad, bad, chil'! Her life was a curse an' her days were black an' yeh'll fergive yer bad girl? She's gone where her sins will be judged."

"She's gone where her sins will be judged," cried the other women, like a choir at a funeral.

"Deh Lord gives and deh Lord takes away," said the woman in black, raising her eyes to the sunbeams.

"Deh Lord gives and deh Lord takes away," responded the others.

"Yeh'll fergive her, Mary!" pleaded the woman in black. The mourner essayed to speak but her voice gave way. She shook her great shoulders frantically, in an agony of grief. Hot tears seemed to scald her quivering face. Finally her voice came and arose like a scream of pain.

"Oh, yes, I'll fergive her! I'll fergive her!"

George's Mother

CHAPTER I

In the swirling rain that came at dusk the broad avenue glistened with that deep bluish tint which is so widely condemned when it is put into pictures. There were long rows of shops, whose fronts shone with full, golden light. Here and there, from druggists' windows, or from the red street-lamps that indicated the positions of fire-alarm boxes, a flare of uncertain, wavering crimson was thrown upon the wet pavements.

The lights made shadows, in which the buildings loomed with a new and tremendous massiveness, like castles and fortresses. There were endless processions of people, mighty hosts, with umbrellas waving, banner-like, over them. Horse-cars, aglitter with new paint, rumbled in steady array between the pillars that supported the elevated railroad. The whole street resounded with the tinkle of bells, the roar of iron-shod wheels on the cobbles, the ceaseless trample of the hundreds of feet. Above all, too, could be heard the loud screams of the tiny newsboys, who scurried in all directions. Upon the corners, standing in from the dripping eaves, were many loungers, descended from the world that used to prostrate itself before pageantry.

A brown young man went along the avenue. He held a tin lunch-pail under his arm in a manner that was evidently uncomfortable. He was puffing at a corncob pipe. His shoulders had a self-reliant poise, and the hang of his arms and the raised veins of his hands showed him to be a man who worked with his muscles.

As he passed a street-corner, a man in old clothes gave a shout of surprise, and, rushing impetuously forward, grasped his hand.

'Hello, Kelcey, ol boy!' cried the man in old clothes. 'How's th' boy, anyhow? Where in thunder yeh been fer th' last seventeen years? I'll be hanged if you ain't th' last man I ever expected t' see!'

The brown youth put his pail to the ground and grinned. 'Well, if it ain't ol' Charley Jones,' he said ecstatically, shaking hands. 'How are yeh, anyhow? Where yeh been keepin' yerself? I ain't seen yeh fer a year.'

'Well, I should say so. Why, th' last time I saw you was up in Handyville!'

'Sure! On Sunday, we —'

'Sure. Out at Bill Sickles' place. Let's go get a drink.'

They made toward a little glass-fronted saloon that sat blinking jovially at the crowds. It engulfed them with a gleeful motion of its too widely-smiling lips.

'What'll yeh take, Kelcey?'

'Oh, I guess I'll take a beer.'

'Gimme little whisky, John.'

The two friends leaned against the bar, and looked with enthusiasm upon each other.

'Well, well, I'm thunderin' glad t' see yeh,' said Jones.

'Well, I guess,' replied Kelcey. 'Here's to yeh, ol' man.'

'Let 'er go.'

They lifted their glasses, glanced fervidly at each other, and drank.

'Yeh ain't changed much, on'y yeh've growed like th' devil,' said Jones reflectively, as he put down his glass; 'I'd know yeh anywheres.'

'Certainly yeh would,' said Kelcey; 'an' I knew you, too, th' minute I saw yeh. Yer changed, though.'

'Yes,' admitted Jones with some complacency; 'I s'pose I am.' He regarded himself in the mirror that multiplied the bottles on the shelf back of the bar. He should have seen a grinning face with a rather pink nose. His derby was perched carelessly on the back part of his head. Two wisps of hair straggled down over his hollow temples. There was something very worldly and wise about him. Life did not seem to confuse him. Evidently he understood its complications. His hand thrust into his trousers-pocket, where he jingled keys, and his hat perched back on his head, expressed a young man of vast knowledge. His extensive acquaintance with bar-tenders aided him materially in this habitual expression of wisdom.

Having finished, he turned to the barkeeper. 'John, has any of th' gang been in t'-night yet?'

'No-not yet,' said the barkeeper; 'ol Bleecker was aroun' this afternoon about four. He said if I seen any of th' boys t' tell 'em he'd be up t'-night if he could get away. I saw Connor an' that other fellah goin' down th' avenyeh about an hour ago. I guess they'll be back after awhile.'

'This is th' hang-out fer a great gang,' said Jones, turning to Kelcey. 'They're a great crowd, I tell yeh. We own th' place when we get started. Come aroun' some night. Any night, almost — t'-night, b' jiminy! They'll almost all be here, an' I'd like t' interduce yeh. They're a great gang-gre-e-at!'

'I'd like teh,' said Kelcey.

'Well, come ahead, then,' cried the other cordially. 'Ye'd like t' know 'em. It's an outa sight crowd. Come aroun' t'-night!'

'I will if I can.'

'Well, yeh ain't got anything t' do, have yeh?' demanded Jones. 'Well, come along, then. Yeh might just as well spend yer time with a good crowd 'a fellahs. An' it's a great gang-great-gre-e-at!'

'Well, I must make fer home now, anyhow,' said Kelcey. 'It's late as blazes. What'll yeh take this time, ol' man?'

'Gimme little more whisky, John.'

'Guess I'll take another beer.'

Jones emptied the whisky into his large mouth, and then put the glass upon the bar.

'Been in th' city long?' he asked. 'Um-well, three years is a good deal fer a slick man. Doin' well? Oh! well, nobody's doin' well these days.' He looked down mournfully at his shabby clothes. 'Father's dead, ain't 'ee? Yeh don't say so? Fell off a scaffoldin', didn't 'ee? I heard it somewheres. Mother's livin', of course? I thought she was. Fine ol' lady-fi-i-ine! Well, you're th' last of her boys. Was five of yeh onct, wasn't there? I knew four m'self. Yes, five. I thought so. An' all gone but you, hey? Well, you'll have t' brace up an' be a comfort t' th' ol' mother. Well, well, well, who would 'a thought that on'y you'd be left out 'a all that mob 'a tow-headed kids! Well, well, well, it's a queer world, ain't it?'

A contemplation of this thought made him sad. He sighed, and moodily watched the other sip beer.

'Well, well, it's a queer world — a damn queer world.'

'Yes,' said Kelcey, 'I'm th' on'y one left!' There was an accent of discomfort in his voice. He did not like this dwelling upon a sentiment that was connected with himself.

'How is th' ol' lady, anyhow?' continued Jones. Th' last time I remember she was as spry as a little ol' cricket, an' was helpeltin' aroun' th' country lecturin' before W. C. T. U.'s an' one thing an' another.'

'Oh, she's pretty well,' said Kelcey.

'An' outa five boys you're th' on'y one she's got left? Well, well-have another drink before yeh go.'

'Oh, I guess I've had enough.'

A wounded expression came into Jones's eyes. 'Oh, come on,' he said.

'Well, I'll take another beer!'

'Gimme little more whisky, John!'

When they had concluded this ceremony, Jones went with his friend to the door of the saloon. 'Good-bye, of man,' he said genially. His homely features shone with friendliness. 'Come aroun', now, sure. T'-night! See? They're a great crowd. Gre-e-at!'

CHAPTER II

A man with a red, mottled face put forth his head from a window and cursed violently. He flung a bottle high across two backyards at a window of the opposite tenement. It broke against the bricks of the house, and the fragments fell crackling upon the stones below. The man shook his fist.

A bare-armed woman, making an array of clothes on a line in one of the yards glanced casually up at the man and listened' to his words. Her eyes followed his to the other tenement. From a distant window a youth with a pipe yelled some comments upon the poor aim. Two children, being in the proper yard, picked up the bits of broken glass and began to fondle them as new toys.

From the window at which the man raged came the sound of an old voice, singing. It quavered and trembled out into the air as if a sound-spirit had a broken wing.

> 'Should I be car-reed tew th' skies
> O-on flow'ry be-eds of ee-ease,
> While others fought tew win th' prize
> An' sailed through blood-ee seas?'

The man in the opposite window was greatly enraged. He continued to swear.

A little old woman was the owner of the voice. In a fourth-story room of the red and black tenement she was trudging on a journey. In her arms she bore pots and pans, and sometimes a broom and dust-pan. She wielded them like weapons. Their weight seemed to have bended her back and crooked her arms until she walked with difficulty. Often she plunged her hands into water at a sink. She splashed about, the dwindled muscles working to and fro under the loose skin of her arms. She came from the sink, steaming and bedraggled as if she had crossed a flooded river.

There was the flurry of a battle in this room. Through the clouded dust or steam one could see the thin figure dealing mighty blows. Always her way seemed beset. Her broom was continually poised, lance-wise, at dust demons. There came clashings and clangings as she strove with her tireless foes.

It was a picture of indomitable courage. And as she went on her way her voice was often raised in a long cry, a strange war-chant, a shout of battle and defiance, that rose and fell in harsh screams, and exasperated the ears of the man with the red, mottled face.

> 'Should I be car-reed tew th' skies
> O-on flow'ry be-eds of ee-ease —'

Finally she halted for a moment. Going to the window, she sat down and mopped her face with her apron. It was a lull, a moment of respite. Still it could be seen that she even then was planning skirmishes, charges, campaigns. She gazed thoughtfully about the room, and noted the strength and position of her enemies. She was very alert.

At last she returned to the mantel. 'Five o'clock,' she murmured, scrutinizing a little, swaggering, nickel-plated clock.

She looked out at chimneys growing thickly on the roofs. A man at work on one seemed like a bee. In the intricate yards below, vine-like lines had strange leaves of cloth. To her ears there came the howl of the man with the red, mottled face. He was engaged in a furious altercation with the youth who had called attention to his poor aim. They were like animals in a jungle.

In the distance an enormous brewery towered over the other buildings. Great gilt letters advertised a brand of beer. Thick smoke came from funnels and spread near it like vast and powerful wings. The structure seemed a great bird, flying. The letters of the sign made a chain of gold hanging from its neck. The little old woman looked at the brewery. It vaguely interested her, for a moment, as a stupendous affair, a machine of mighty strength.

Presently she sprang from her rest and began to buffet with her shrivelled arms. In a moment the battle was again in full swing. Terrific blows were given and received. There arose the clattering uproar of a new fight. The little intent warrior never hesitated nor faltered. She fought with a strong and relentless will. Beads and lines of perspiration stood upon her forehead.

Three blue plates were leaning in a row on the shelf back of the stove. The little old woman had seen it done somewhere. In front of them swaggered the round nickel-plated clock. Her son had stuck many cigarette pictures in the rim of a looking-glass that hung near. Occasional chromos were tacked upon the yellowed walls of the room. There was one in a gilt frame. It was quite an affair in reds and greens. They all seemed like trophies.

It began to grow dark. A mist came winding. Rain plashed softly upon the window-sill. A lamp had been lighted in the opposite tenement; the strong orange glare revealed the man with a red, mottled face. He was seated by a table, smoking and reflecting.

The little old woman looked at the clock again. 'Quarter 'a six.'

She had paused for a moment, but she now hurled herself fiercely at the stove that lurked in the gloom, red-eyed, like a dragon. It hissed, and there was renewed clangour of blows. The little old woman dashed to and fro.

CHAPTER III

As it grew toward seven o'clock the little old woman became nervous. She often would drop into a chair and sit staring at the little clock.

'I wonder why he don't come,' she continually repeated. There was a small, curious note of despair in her voice. As she sat thinking and staring at the clock, the expressions of her face changed swiftly. All manner of emotions flickered in her eyes and about her lips. She was evidently perceiving in her imagination the journey of a loved person. She dreamed for him mishaps and obstacles. Something tremendous and irritating was hindering him from coming to her.

She had lighted an oil-lamp. It flooded the room with vivid yellow glare. The table, in its oil-cloth covering, had previously appeared like a bit of bare, brown desert. It now was a white garden, growing the fruits of her labour.

'Seven o'clock!' she murmured finally. She was aghast.

Then suddenly she heard a step upon the stair. She sprang up and began to bustle about the room. The little fearful emotions passed at once from her face. She seemed now to be ready to scold.

Young Kelcey entered the room. He gave a sigh of relief, and dropped his pail in a corner. He was evidently greatly wearied by a hard day of toil.

The little old woman hobbled over to him and raised her wrinkled lips. She seemed on the verge of tears and an outburst of reproaches.

'Hello!' he cried, in a voice of cheer. 'Been gettin' anxious?'

'Yes,' she said, hovering about him.

'Where yeh been, George? What made yeh so late? I've been waitin' th' longest while. Don't throw your coat down there. Hang it up behind th' door.'

The son put his coat on the proper hook, and then went to splatter water in a tin wash-basin at the sink.

'Well, yeh see, I met Jones-you remember Jones? Ol' Handyville fellah. An' we had t' stop an' talk over of times. Jones is quite a boy.'

The little old woman's mouth set in a sudden straight line. 'Oh, that Jones!' she said. 'I don't like him.'

The youth interrupted a flurry of white towel to give a glance of irritation.

'Well, now, what's th' use of talkin' that way?' he said to her. 'What do yeh know 'bout 'im? Ever spoke to 'im in yer life?'

'Well, I don't know as I ever did since he grew up,' replied the little old woman. 'But I know he ain't th' kind 'a man I'd like t' have you go around with. He ain't a good man. I'm sure he ain't. He drinks.'

Her son began to laugh. 'Th' dickens he does!'

He seemed amazed, but not shocked, at this information.

She nodded her head with the air of one who discloses a dreadful thing. 'I'm sure of it! Once I saw 'im comin' outa Simpson's Hotel, up in Handyville, an' he could hardly walk. He drinks! I'm sure he drinks!'

'Holy smoke!' said Kelcey.

They sat down at the table and began to wreck the little white garden. The youth leaned back in his chair, in the manner of a man who is paying for things. His mother bended alertly forward, apparently watching each mouthful. She perched on the edge of her chair, ready to spring to her feet and run to the closet or the stove for anything that he might need. She was as anxious as a young mother with a babe. In the careless and comfortable attitude of the son there was denoted a great deal of dignity.

'Yeh ain't eatin' much t'-night, George?'

'Well, I ain't very hungry, t' tell th' truth.'

'Don't yeh like yer supper, dear? Yeh must eat somethin', chile. Yeh mustn't go without.'

'Well, I'm eatin' somethin', ain't I?'

He wandered aimlessly through the meal. She sat over behind the little blackened coffee-pot and gazed affectionately upon him.

After a time she began to grow agitated. Her worn fingers were gripped. It could be seen that a great thought was within her. She was about to venture something. She had arrived at a supreme moment. 'George,' she said suddenly, 'come t' prayer-meetin' with me t'-night.'

The young man dropped his fork.

'Say, you must be crazy!' he said in amazement.

'Yes, dear,' she continued rapidly, in a small, pleading voice, 'I'd like t' have yeh go with me onct in a while. Yeh never go with me any more, dear, an' I d like t' have yeh go. Yeh ain't been anywheres at all with me in th' longest while.'

'Well,' he said —'well; but what th' blazes —'

'Ah, come on!' said the little old woman. She went to him, and put her arms about his neck. She began to coax him with caresses.

The young man grinned. 'Thunderation!' he said; 'what would I do at a prayer-meetin'?'

The mother considered him to be consenting. She did a little antique caper.

Well, yeh can come an' take care 'a yer mother,' she cried gleefully. 'It's such a long walk every Thursday night alone, an' don't yeh s'pose that when I have such a big, fine, strappin' boy I want 'im t' beau me aroun' some? Ah, I knew ye'd come!'

He smiled for a moment, indulgent of her humour. But presently his face turned a shade of discomfort. 'But —' he began, protesting.

'Ah, come on!' she continually repeated.

He began to be vexed. He frowned into the air. A vision came to him of dreary blackness arranged in solemn rows. A mere dream of it was depressing.

'But —' he said again. He was obliged to make great search for an argument. Finally he concluded: 'But what th' blazes would I do at prayer-meetin'?'

In his ears was the sound of a hymn, made by people who tilted their heads at a prescribed angle of devotion. It would be too apparent that they were all better than he. When he entered they would turn their heads and regard him with suspicion. This would be an enormous aggravation, since he was certain that he was as good as they.

'Well, now, y' see,' he said, quite gently, 'I don't wanta go, an' it wouldn't do me no good t' go if I didn't wanta go.'

His mother's face swiftly changed. She breathed a huge sigh, the counterpart of ones he had heard upon like occasions. She put a tiny black bonnet on her head, and wrapped her figure in an old shawl. She cast a martyr-like glance upon her son, and went mournfully away. She resembled a limited funeral procession.

The young man writhed under it to an extent. He kicked moodily at a table-leg. When the sound of her footfalls died away he felt distinctly relieved.

CHAPTER IV

That night, when Kelcey arrived at the little smiling saloon, he found his friend Jones standing before the bar engaged in a violent argument with a stout man.

'Oh, well,' this latter person was saying, 'you can make a lot of noise, Charley, for a man that never says anything—let's have a drink!'

Jones was waving his arms and delivering splintering blows upon some distant theories. The stout man chuckled fatly and winked at the bar-tender.

The orator ceased for a moment to say, 'Gimme little whisky, John.' At the same time he perceived young Kelcey. He sprang forward with a welcoming cry. 'Hello, of man! didn't much think ye'd come.' He led him to the stout man.

'Mr. Bleecker—my friend Mr. Kelcey!'

'How d'yeh do?'

'Mr. Kelcey, I'm happy to meet you, sir; have a drink.'

They drew up in line and waited. The busy hands of the bar-tender made glasses clink. Mr. Bleecker, in a very polite way, broke the waiting silence.

'Never been here before, I believe, have you, Mr. Kelcey?'

The young man felt around for a highbred reply. 'Er-no—I've never had that-er-pleasure,' he said.

After a time the strained and wary courtesy of their manners wore away. It became evident to Bleecker that his importance slightly dazzled the young man. He grew warmer. Obviously, the youth was one whose powers of perception were developed. Directly, then, he launched forth into a tale of bygone days, when the world was better. He had known all the great men of that age. He reproduced his conversations with them. There were traces of pride and of mournfulness in his voice. He rejoiced at the glory of the world of dead spirits. He grieved at the youth and flippancy of the present one. He lived with his head in the clouds of the past, and he seemed obliged to talk of what he saw there.

Jones nudged Kelcey ecstatically in the ribs. 'You've got th' of man started in great shape,' he whispered.

Kelcey was proud that the prominent character of the place talked at him, glancing into his eyes for appreciation of fine points.

Presently they left the bar, and going into a little rear room, took seats about a table. A gas-jet with a coloured globe shed a crimson radiance. The polished wood of walls and furniture gleamed with faint rose-coloured reflections. Upon the floor sawdust was thickly sprinkled.

Two other men presently came. By the time Bleecker had told three tales of the grand past, Kelcey was slightly acquainted with everybody.

He admired Bleecker immensely. He developed a brotherly feeling for the others, who were all gentle-spoken. He began to feel that he was passing the happiest evening of his life. His companions were so jovial and good-natured; and everything they did was marked by such courtesy.

For a time the two men who had come in late did not presume to address him directly. They would say: 'Jones, won't your friend have so and so, or so and so?' And Bleecker would begin his orations: 'Now, Mr. Kelcey, don't you think —'

Presently he began to believe that he was a most remarkably fine fellow, who had at last found his place in a crowd of most remarkably fine fellows.

Jones occasionally breathed comments into his ear.

'I tell yeh, Bleecker's an ol'-timer. He was a husky guy in his day, yeh can bet. He was one 'a th' best known men in N' York once. Yeh ought to hear him tell about —'

Kelcey listened intently. He was profoundly interested in these intimate tales of men who had gleamed in the rays of old suns.

'That O'Connor's a damn fine fellah,' interjected Jones once, referring to one of the others; 'he's one 'a th' best fellahs I ever knowed. He's always on th' dead level, an' he's always jest th' same as yeh see him now-good-natured an' grinnin'.'

Kelcey nodded. He could well believe it.

When he offered to buy drinks there came a loud volley of protests. 'No, no, Mr. Kelcey,' cried Bleecker; 'no, no. To-night you are our guest. Some other time —'

'Here,' said O'Connor; 'it's my turn now.'

He called and pounded for the bar-tender. He then sat with a coin in hand warily eyeing the others. He was ready to frustrate them if they offered to pay.

After a time Jones began to develop qualities of great eloquence and wit. His companions laughed. 'It's the whisky talking now,' said Bleecker.

He grew earnest and impassioned; he delivered speeches on various subjects. His lectures were to him very imposing. The force of his words thrilled him. Sometimes he was overcome.

The others agreed with him in all things. Bleecker grew almost tender, and considerately placed words here and there for his use. As Jones became fiercely energetic the others became more docile in agreeing. They soothed him with friendly interjections.

His mode changed directly. He began to sing popular airs with enthusiasm. He congratulated his companions upon being in his society. They were excited by his frenzy. They began to fraternize in jovial fashion. It was understood that they were true and tender spirits. They had come away from a grinding world filled with men who were harsh.

When one of them chose to divulge some place where the world had pierced him, there was a chorus of violent sympathy. They rejoiced at their temporary isolation and safety.

Once a man, completely drunk, stumbled along the floor of the saloon. He opened the door of the little room and made a show of entering. The men sprang instantly to their feet. They were ready to throttle any invader of their island. They elbowed each other in rivalry as to who should take upon himself the brunt of an encounter.

'Oh!' said the drunken individual, swaying on his legs and blinking at the party' oh! thish private room?'

'That's what it is, Willie,' said Jones. 'An' you git outa here, er we'll throw yeh out.'

'That's what we will,' said the others.

'Oh!' said the drunken man. He blinked at them aggrievedly for an instant and then went away.

They sat down again. Kelcey felt in a way that he would have liked to display his fidelity to the others by whipping the intruder.

The bar-tender came often. 'Gee, you fellahs er tanks!' he said in a jocular manner, as he gathered empty glasses and polished the table with his little towel.

Through the exertions of Jones, the little room began to grow clamorous. The tobacco smoke eddied about the forms of the men in ropes and wreaths. Near the ceiling there was a thick gray cloud.

Each man explained in his way that he was totally out of place in the before-mentioned world. They were possessed of various virtues, which were unappreciated by those with whom they were commonly obliged to mingle-they were fitted for a tree-shaded land, where everything was peace.

Now that five of them had congregated, it gave them happiness to speak their inmost thoughts without fear of being misunderstood.

As he drank more beer Kelcey felt his breast expand with manly feeling. He knew that he was capable of sublime things. He wished that some day one of his present companions would come to him for relief. His mind pictured a little scene. In it he was magnificent in his friendship.

He looked upon the beaming faces and knew that if at that instant there should come a time for a great sacrifice he would blissfully make it. He would pass tranquilly into the unknown, or into bankruptcy, amid the ejaculations of his companions upon his many virtues.

They had no bickerings during the evening. If one chose to momentarily assert himself, the others instantly submitted.

They exchanged compliments. Once old Bleecker stared at Jones for a few moments. Suddenly he broke out:

'Jones, you're one of the finest fellows I ever knew!'

A flush of pleasure went over the other's face, and then he made a modest gesture, the protest of a humble man.

'Don't flimflam me, ol' boy,' he said with earnestness.

But Bleecker roared that he was serious about it.

The two men arose and shook hands emotionally. Jones butted against the table and knocked off a glass.

Afterward a general hand-shaking was inaugurated. Brotherly sentiments flew about the room. There was an uproar of fraternal feeling.

Jones began to sing. He beat time with precision and dignity. He gazed into the eyes of his companions, trying to call music from their souls. O'Connor joined in heartily, but with another tune. Off in a corner old Bleecker was making a speech.

The bar-tender came to the door. 'Gee, you fellahs er making a row. It's time fer me t' shut up th' front th' place, an' you mugs better sit on yerselves. It's one o'clock.'

They began to argue with him. Kelcey, however, sprang to his feet. 'One o'clock?' he said. 'Holy smoke, I mus' be flyin'!'

There came protesting howls from Jones. Bleecker ceased his oration.

'My dear boy —' he began.

Kelcey searched for his hat.

'I've gota go t' work at seven,' he said.

The others watched him with discomfort in their eyes.

'Well,' said O'Connor, 'if one goes we might as well all go.'

They sadly took their hats and filed out.

The cold air of the street filled Kelcey with vague surprise. It made his head feel hot. As for his legs, they were like willow-twigs.

A few yellow lights blinked. In front of an all-night restaurant a huge red electric lamp hung and sputtered. Horse-car bells jingled far down the street. Overhead a train thundered on the elevated road.

On the sidewalk the men took fervid leave. They clutched hands with extraordinary force, and proclaimed, for the last time, ardent and admiring friendships.

When he arrived at his home Kelcey proceeded with caution. His mother had left a light burning low. He stumbled once in his voyage across the floor. As he paused to listen he heard the sound of little snores coming from her room.

He lay awake for a few moments and thought of the evening. He had a pleasurable consciousness that he had made a good impression upon those fine fellows. He felt that he had spent the most delightful evening of his life.

CHAPTER V

Kelcey was cross in the morning. His mother had been obliged to shake him a great deal, and it had seemed to him a most unjust thing. Also, when he, blinking his eyes, had entered the kitchen, she had said: 'Yeh left th' lamp burnin' all night last night, George. How many times must I tell yeh never t' leave th' lamp burnin'?'

He ate the greater part of his breakfast in silence, moodily stirring his coffee, and glaring at a remote corner of the room with eyes that felt as if they had been baked. When he moved his eyelids there was a sensation that they were cracking. In his mouth there was a singular taste. It seemed to him that he had been sucking the end of a wooden spoon. Moreover, his temper was rampant within him. It sought something to devour.

Finally he said savagely: 'Damn these early hours!'

His mother jumped as if he had flung a missile at her. 'Why, George —' she began.

Kelcey broke in again. 'Oh, I know all that; but this gettin' up in th' mornin' so early makes me sick. Jest when a man is gettin' his mornin' nap he's gota get up. I —'

'George, dear,' said his mother, 'yeh know how I hate yeh t' swear, dear. Now, please don't.' She looked beseechingly at him.

He made a swift gesture. 'Well, I ain't swearin', am I?' he demanded. 'I was on'y sayin' that this gettin'-up business gives me a pain, wasn't I?'

Well, yeh know how swearin' hurts me,' protested the little old woman. She seemed about to sob. She gazed off retrospectively. She apparently was recalling persons who had never been profane.

'I don't see where yeh ever caught this way 'a swearin' out at everything,' she continued presently. 'Fred, ner John, ner Willie never swore a bit. Ner Tom neither, except when he was real mad.'

The son made another gesture. It was directed into the air, as if he saw there a phantom injustice. 'Oh, good thunder!' he said, with an accent of despair. Thereupon he relapsed into a mood of silence. He sombrely regarded his plate.

This demeanour speedily reduced his mother to meekness. When she spoke again it was in a conciliatory voice. 'George, dear, won't yeh bring some sugar home t'-night?' It could be seen that she was asking for a crown of gold.

Kelcey aroused from his semi-slumber.

'Yes, if I kin remember it,' he said.

The little old woman arose to stow her son's lunch into the pail. When he had finished his breakfast he stalked for a time about the room in a dignified way. He put on his coat and hat, and, taking his lunch-pail, went to the door. There he halted, and without turning his head, stiffly said:

'Well, good-bye.'

The little old woman saw that she had offended her son. She did not seek an explanation. She was accustomed to these phenomena. She made haste to surrender.

'Ain't yeh goin' t' kiss me good-bye?' she asked in a little woful voice.

The youth made a pretence of going on deaf-heartedly. He wore the dignity of an injured monarch.

Then the little old woman called again in forsaken accents: 'George-George! ain't yeh goin' t' kiss me good-bye?' When he moved he found that she was hanging to his coat-tails.

He turned eventually with a murmur of a sort of tenderness. 'Why, 'a course I am,' he said. He kissed her. Withal, there was an undertone of superiority in his voice, as if he were granting an astonishing suit. She looked at him with reproach and gratitude and affection.

She stood at the head of the stairs and watched his hand sliding along the rail as he went down. Occasionally she could see his arm and part of his shoulder. When he reached the first-floor she called to him 'Good-bye!'

The little old woman went back to her work in the kitchen with a frown of perplexity upon her brow. 'I wonder what was th' matter with George this mornin',' she mused. 'He didn't seem a bit like himself!'

As she trudged to and fro at her labour she began to speculate. She was much worried. She surmised in a vague way that he was a sufferer from a great internal disease. It was something, no doubt, that devoured the kidneys or quietly fed upon the lungs. Later, she imagined a woman, wicked and fair, who had fascinated him, and was turning his life into a bitter thing. Her mind created many wondrous influences that were swooping like green dragons at him. They were changing him to a morose man, who suffered silently. She longed to discover them, that she might go bravely to the rescue of her heroic son. She knew that he, generous in his pain, would keep it from her. She racked her mind for knowledge.

However, when he came home at night he was extraordinarily blithe. He seemed to be a lad of ten. He capered all about the room. When she was bringing the coffee-pot from the stove to the table he made show of waltzing with her, so that she spilled some of the coffee. She was obliged to scold him.

All through the meal he made jokes. She occasionally was compelled to laugh, despite the fact that she believed that she should not laugh at her own son's jokes. She uttered reproofs at times, but he did not regard them.

'Golly,' he said once, 'I feel fine as silk. I didn't think I'd get over feelin' bad so quick. It —' He stopped abruptly.

During the evening he sat content. He smoked his pipe and read from an evening paper. She bustled about at her work. She seemed utterly happy with him there, lazily puffing out little clouds of smoke and giving frequent brilliant dissertations upon the news of the day. It seemed to her that she must be a model mother to have such a son, one who came home to her at night and sat contented, in a languor of the muscles after a good day's toil. She pondered upon the science of her management.

The week thereafter, too, she was joyous, for he stayed at home each night of it, and was sunny-tempered. She became convinced that she was a perfect mother, rearing a perfect son. There came often a lovelight into her eyes. The wrinkled, yellow face frequently warmed into a smile of the kind that a maiden bestows upon him who to her is first and perhaps last.

CHAPTER VI

The little old woman habitually discouraged all outbursts of youthful vanity on the part of her son. She feared that he would get to think too much of himself, and she knew that nothing could do more harm. Great self-esteem was always passive, she thought, and if he grew to regard his qualities of mind as forming a dazzling constellation, he would tranquilly sit still and not do those wonders she expected of him. So she was constantly on the alert to suppress even a shadow of such a thing. As for him, he ruminated with the savage, vengeful bitterness of a young man, and decided that she did not comprehend him.

But, despite her precautions, he often saw that she believed him to be the most marvellous young man on the earth. He had only to look at those two eyes that became lighted with a glow from her heart whenever he did some excessively brilliant thing. On these occasions he could see her glance triumphantly at a neighbour, or whoever happened to be present. He grew to plan for these glances. And then he took a vast satisfaction in detecting and appropriating them.

Nevertheless, he could not understand why, directly after a scene of this kind, his mother was liable to call to him to hang his coat on the hook under the mantel, her voice in a key of despair, as if he were negligent and stupid in what was, after all, the only important thing in life.

'If yeh'll only get in the habit of doin' it, it'll be jest as easy as throwin' it down anywheres,' she would say to him. 'When ye pitch it down anywheres, somebody's got t' pick it up, an' that'll most likely be your poor of mother. Yeh can hang it up yerself, if yeh'll on'y think.' This was intolerable. He usually went then and hurled his coat savagely at the hook. The correctness of her position was maddening.

It seemed to him that anyone who had a son of his glowing attributes should overlook the fact that he seldom hung up his coat. It was impossible to explain this situation to his mother. She was unutterably narrow. He grew sullen.

There came a time, too, that, even in all his mother's tremendous admiration for him, he did not entirely agree with her. He was delighted that she liked his great wit. He spurred himself to new and flashing effort because of this appreciation.

But for the greater part he could see that his mother took pride in him in quite a different way from that in which he took pride in himself. She rejoiced at qualities in him that indicated that he was going to become a white and looming king among men. From these she made pictures, in which he appeared as a benign personage, blessed by the filled hands of the poor-one whose brain could hold massive thoughts, and awe certain men about whom she had read. She was fêted as the mother of this enormous man. These dreams were her solace. She spoke of them to no one, because she knew that, worded, they would be ridiculous. But she dwelt with them, and they shed a radiance of gold upon her long days, her sorry labour. Upon the dead altars of her life she had built the little fires of hope for another.

Kelcey had a complete sympathy for as much as he understood of these thoughts of his mother. They were so wise that he admired her foresight. As for himself, however, most of his dreams were of a nearer time. He had many of the distant future when he would be a man with a cloak of coldness concealing his gentleness and his faults, and of whom the men, and more particularly the women, would think with reverence. He agreed with his mother that at that time he would go through what were obstacles to other men, like a flung stone. And then he would have power, and he would enjoy having his bounty and his wrath alike fall swiftly upon those below. They would be awed. And, above all, he would mystify them.

But then his nearer dreams were a multitude. He had begun to look at the great world revolving near to his nose. He had a vast curiosity concerning this city in whose complexities he was buried. It was an impenetrable mystery, this city. It was a blend of many enticing colours. He longed to comprehend it completely, that he might walk understandingly in its greatest marvels, its mightiest march of life, of sin. He dreamed of a comprehension whose pay was the admirable attitude of a man of knowledge. He remembered Jones. He could not help admiring a man who knew so many bartenders.

CHAPTER VII

An indefinite woman was in all of Kelcey's dreams. As a matter of fact, it was not himself he pictured as wedding her. It was a vision of a man, greater, finer, more terrible. It was himself as he expected to be. In scenes which he took mainly from pictures, this vision conducted a courtship, strutting, posing, and lying through a drama which was magnificent from glow of purple. In it he was icy, self-possessed; but she, the dream-girl, was consumed by wild, torrential passion. He went to the length of having her display it before the people.

He saw them wonder at his tranquillity. It amazed them infinitely to see him remain cold before the glory of this peerless woman's love. She was to him as beseeching for affection as a pet animal, but still he controlled appearances, and none knew of his deep, abiding love. Some day, at the critical romantic time, he was going to divulge it. In these long dreams there were accessories of castle-like houses, wide lands, servants, horses, clothes.

They began somewhere in his childhood. When he ceased to see himself as a stern general pointing a sword at the nervous and abashed horizon, he became this sublime king of a vague woman's heart. Later, when he had read some books, it all achieved clearer expression. He was told in them that there was a goddess in the world whose business it was to wait until he should exchange a glance with her. It became a creed, subtly powerful. It saved discomfort for him and for several women who flitted by him. He used her as a standard.

Often he saw the pathos of her long wait, but his faith did not falter. The world was obliged to turn gold in time. His life was to be fine and heroic, else he would not have been born. He believed that the commonplace lot was the sentence, the doom of certain people who did not know how to feel. His blood was a tender current of life. He thought that the usual should fall to others whose nerves were of lead.

Occasionally he wondered how fate was going to begin in making an enormous figure of him; but he had no doubt of the result. A chariot of pink clouds was coming for him. His faith was his reason for existence. Meanwhile, he could dream of the indefinite woman and the fragrance of roses that came from her hair.

One day he met Maggie Johnson on the stairs. She had a can of beer in one hand and a brown-paper parcel under her arm. She glanced at him. He discovered that it would wither his heart to see another man signally successful in the smiles of her. And the glance that she gave him was so indifferent and so unresponsive to the sudden vivid admiration in his own eyes that he immediately concluded that she was magnificent in two ways.

As she came to the landing, the light from a window passed in a silver gleam over the girlish roundness of her cheek. It was a thing that he remembered.

He was silent for the most part at supper that night. He was particularly unkind when he did speak. His mother, observing him apprehensively, tried in vain to picture the new terrible catastrophe. She eventually concluded that he did not like the beef-stew. She put more salt in it.

He saw Maggie quite frequently after the meeting upon the stairs. He reconstructed his dreams and placed her in the full glory of that sun. The dream-woman, the goddess, pitched from her pedestal, lay prostrate, unheeded, save when he brought her forth to call her insipid and childish in the presence of his new religion.

He was relatively happy sometimes when Maggie's mother would get drunk and make terrific uproars. He used then to sit in the dark and make scenes in which he rescued the girl from her hideous environment.

He laid clever plans by which he encountered her in the halls, at the door, on the street. When he succeeded in meeting her he was always overcome by the thought that the whole thing was obvious to her. He could feel the shame of it burn his face and neck.

To prove to her that she was mistaken he would turn away his head or regard her with a granite stare.

After a time he became impatient of the distance between them. He saw looming princes who would aim to seize her. Hours of his leisure and certain hours of his labour he spent in contriving. The shade of this girl was with him continually. With her he built his grand dramas so that he trod in clouds, the matters of his daily life obscured and softened by a mist.

He saw that he need only break down the slight conventional barriers, and she would soon discover his noble character. Sometimes he could see it all in his mind. It was very skilful; but then his courage flew away at the supreme moment. Perhaps the whole affair was humorous to her. Perhaps she was watching his mental contortions. She might laugh. He felt that he would then die or kill her. He could not approach the dread moment. He sank often from the threshold of knowledge. Directly after these occasions it was his habit to avoid her, to prove that she was a cipher to him.

He reflected that if he could only get a chance to rescue her from something, the whole tragedy would speedily unwind.

He met a young man in the halls one evening who said to him: 'Say, me frien', where d' d' Johnson birds live in, heh? I can't fin' me feet in dis bloomin' joint. I been battin' round heh fer a half hour.'

'Two flights up,' said Kelcey stonily. He had felt a sudden quiver of his heart. The grandeur of the clothes, the fine worldly air, the experience, the self-reliance, the courage that shone in the countenance of this other young man, made him suddenly sink to the depths of woe. He stood listening in the hall, flushing and ashamed of it, until he heard them coming downstairs together. He slunk away then. It would have been a horror to him if she had discovered him there. She might have felt sorry for him.

They were going out to a show, perhaps. That pig of the world in his embroidered cloak was going to dazzle her with splendour. He mused upon how unrighteous it was for other men to dazzle women with splendour.

As he appreciated his handicap, he swore with savage, vengeful bitterness. In his home his mother raised her voice in a high key of monotonous irritability.

'Hang up yer coat, cant yeh, George?' she cried at him; 'I can't go round after yeh all th' time. It's jest as easy t' hang it up as it is t' throw it down that way. Don't yeh ever git tired 'a hearing me yell at yeh?'

'Yes!' he exploded. In this word he put a profundity of sudden anger. He turned toward his mother a face red, seamed, hard with hate and rage. They stared a moment in silence. Then she turned and staggered toward her room. Her hip struck violently against the corner of the table during this blind passage. A moment later the door closed.

Kelcey sank down in a chair with his legs thrust out straight and his hands deep in his trousers-pockets. His chin was forward upon his breast, and his eyes stared before him. There swept over him all the self-pity that comes when the soul is turned back from a road.

CHAPTER VIII

During the next few days Kelcey suffered from his first gloomy conviction that the earth was not grateful to him for his presence upon it. When sharp words were said to him, he interpreted them with what seemed to be a lately acquired insight. He could now perceive that the universe hated him. He sank to the most sublime depths of despair.

One evening of this period he met Jones. The latter rushed upon him with enthusiasm.

'Why, yer jest th' man I wanted t' see! I was comin' round t' your place t'-night. Lucky I met yeh! Ol' Bleecker's goin' t' give a blow-out t'-morrah night. Anything yeh want t' drink! All th' boys'll be there, an' everything. He tol' me expressly that he wanted yeh t' be there. Great time! Great! Can yeh come?'

Kelcey grasped the other's hand with fervour. He felt now that there was some solacing friendship in space.

'You bet I will, of man,' he said huskily. 'I'd like nothin' better in th' world!'

As he walked home he thought that he was a very grim figure. He was about to taste the delicious revenge of a partial self-destruction. The universe would regret its position when it saw him drunk. He was a little late in getting to Bleecker's lodging. He was delayed while his mother read aloud a letter from an old uncle, who wrote in one place: 'God bless th' boy! Bring him up to be the man his father was.'

Bleecker lived in an old three-storied house on a side-street. A Jewish tailor lived and worked in the front parlour, and old Bleecker lived in the back parlour. A German, whose family took care of the house, occupied the basement. Another German, with a wife and eight children, rented the dining-room. The two upper floors were inhabited by tailors, dressmakers, a pedlar, and mysterious people who were seldom seen. The door of the little hall-bedroom, at the foot of the second flight, was always open, and in there could be seen two bended men who worked at mending opera-glasses.

The German woman in the dining-room was not friends with the little dressmaker in the rear room of the third floor, and frequently they yelled the vilest names up and down between the balusters. Each part of the woodwork was scratched and rubbed by the contact of innumerable persons. In one wall there was a long slit with chipped edges, celebrating the time when a man had thrown a hatchet at his wife. In the lower hall there was an eternal woman, with a rag and a pail of suds, who knelt over the worn oilcloth. Old Bleecker felt that he had quite respectable and high-class apartments. He was glad to invite his friends.

Bleecker met Kelcey in the hall. He wore a collar that was cleaner and higher than his usual one. It changed his appearance greatly. He was now formidably aristocratic.

'How are yeh, of man?' he shouted. He grasped Kelcey's arm, and, babbling jovially, conducted him down the hall and into the ex-parlour.

A group of standing men made vast shadows in the yellow glare of the lamp. They turned their heads as the two entered.

'Why, hello, Kelcey, of man!' Jones exclaimed, coming rapidly forward. 'Good fer you! Glad yeh come! Yeh know O'Connor, 'a course! an' Schmidt! an' Woods! Then there's Zeusentell! Mr. Zeusentell-my friend Mr. Kelcey! Shake hands-both good fellows, damnitall! Then here is-oh, gentlemen, my friend Mr. Kelcey! A good fellow he is, too. I've known 'im since I was a kid. Come, have a drink!'

Everybody was excessively amiable. Kelcey felt that he had social standing. The strangers were cautious and respectful.

'By all means,' said old Bleecker. 'Mr. Kelcey, have a drink! An' by th' way, gentlemen, while we're about it, let's all have a drink!' There was much laughter. Bleecker was so droll at times.

With mild and polite gesturing they marched up to the table. There were upon it a keg of beer, a long row of whisky bottles, a little heap of corn-cob pipes, some bags of tobacco, a box of cigars, and a mighty collection of glasses, cups, and mugs. Old Bleecker had arranged them so deftly that they resembled a primitive bar. There was considerable scuffling for possession of the cracked cups.

Jones politely but vehemently insisted upon drinking from the worst of the assortment. He was quietly opposed by others. Everybody showed that they were awed by Bleecker's lavish hospitality. Their demeanours expressed their admiration at the cast of this entertainment.

Kelcey took his second mug of beer away to a corner and sat down with it. He wished to socially reconnoitre. Over in a corner a man was telling a story, in which at intervals he grunted like a pig. A half-dozen men were listening. Two or three others sat alone in isolated places. They looked expectantly bright, ready to burst out cordially if anyone should address them.

The row of bottles made quaint shadows upon the table, and upon a side-wall the keg of beer created a portentous black figure that reared toward the ceiling, hovering over the room and its inmates with spectral stature. Tobacco-smoke lay in lazy cloud-banks overhead.

Jones and O'Connor stayed near the table, occasionally being affable in all directions. Kelcey saw old Bleecker go to them, and heard him whisper:

'Come, we must git th' thing started. Git th' thing started.'

Kelcey saw that the host was fearing that all were not having a good time. Jones conferred with O'Connor, and then O'Connor went to the man named Zeusentell. O'Connor evidently proposed something. Zeusentell refused at once. O'Connor beseeched. Zeusentell remained implacable.

At last O'Connor broke off his argument, and going to the centre of the room, held up his hand.

'Gentlemen!' he shouted loudly, 'we will now have a recitation by Mr. Zeusentell, entitled "Patrick Clancy's Pig!" He then glanced triumphantly at Zeusentell and said: 'Come on!'

Zeusentell had been twisting and making pantomimic appeals. He said in a reproachful whisper:

'You son of a gun!'

The men turned their heads to glance at Zeusentell for a moment, and then burst into a sustained clamour.

'Hurray! Let 'er go! Come-give it t' us! Spring it! Spring it! Let it come!'

As Zeusentell made no advances, they appealed personally.

'Come, ol' man, let 'er go! Whatter yeh 'fraid of? Let 'er go! Go ahn! Hurry up!'

Zeusentell was protesting with almost frantic modesty. O'Connor took him by the lapel and tried to drag him; but he leaned back, pulling at his coat and shaking his head.

'No, no! I don't know it, I tell yeh! I can't! I don't know it! I tell yeh I don't know it! I've forgotten it, I tell yeh! No-no-no-no! Ah, say, lookahere, le' go me, can't yeh? What's th' matter with yeh? I tell yeh I don't know it!'

The men applauded violently. O'Connor did not relent. A little battle was waged until all of a sudden Zeusentell was seen to grow wondrously solemn. A hush fell upon the men. He was about to begin. He paused in the middle of the floor and nervously adjusted his collar and cravat. The audience became grave.

'"Patrick Clancy's Pig,"' announced Zeusentell in a shrill, dry, unnatural tone. And then he began in a rapid sing-song:

'"Patrick Clancy had a pig Th' pride uv all th' nation, The half uv him was half as big As half uv all creation—"'

When he concluded the others looked at each other to convey their appreciation. They then wildly clapped their hands or tinkled their glasses. As Zeusentell went toward his seat a man leaned over and asked:

'Can yeh tell me where I kin git that?'

He had made a great success. After an enormous pressure he was induced to recite two more tales. Old Bleecker finally led him forward and pledged him in a large drink. He declared that they were the best things he had ever heard.

The efforts of Zeusentell imparted a gaiety to the company. The men having laughed together were better acquainted, and there was now a universal topic. Some of the party, too, began to be quite drunk.

The invaluable O'Connor brought forth a man who could play the mouth-organ. The latter, after wiping his instrument upon his coat-sleeve, played all the popular airs. The men's heads swayed to and fro in the clouded smoke. They grinned and beat time with their feet. A valour, barbaric and wild, began to show in their poses and in their faces, red and glistening from perspiration.

The conversation resounded in a hoarse roar. The beer would not run rapidly enough for Jones; so he remained behind to tilt the keg. This caused the black shadow on the wall to retreat and advance, sinking mystically, to loom forward again with sudden menace —a huge dark figure, controlled as by some unknown emotion. The glasses, mugs, and cups travelled swift and regular, catching orange reflections from the lamp-light. Two or three men were grown so careless that they were continually spilling their drinks. Old Bleecker, cackling with pleasure, seized time to glance triumphantly at Jones. His party was going to be a success.

CHAPTER IX

Of a sudden Kelcey felt the buoyant thought that he was having a good time. He was all at once an enthusiast, as if he were at a festival of a religion. He felt that there was something fine and thrilling in this affair, isolated from a stern world, and from which the laughter arose like incense. He knew that old sentiment of brotherly regard for those about him. He began to converse tenderly with them.

He was not sure of his drift of thought, but he knew that he was immensely sympathetic. He rejoiced at their faces, shining red and wrinkled with smiles. He was capable of heroisms.

His pipe irritated him by going out frequently. He was too busy in amiable conversations to attend to it. When he arose to go for a match he discovered that his legs were a trifle uncertain under him. They bended, and did not precisely obey his intent.

At the table he lit a match, and then, in laughing at a joke made near him, forgot to apply it to the bowl of his pipe. He succeeded with the next match, after annoying trouble. He swayed so that the match would appear first on one side of the bowl and then on the other. At last he happily got it directly over the tobacco. He had burned his fingers. He inspected them, laughing vaguely.

Jones came and slapped him on the shoulder.

'Well, ol' man, let's take a drink fer ol' Handyville's sake!'

Kelcey was deeply affected. He looked at Jones with moist eyes.

'I'll go yeh,' he said.

With an air of profound melancholy, Jones poured out some whisky. They drank reverently. They exchanged a glistening look of tender recollections, and then went over to where Bleecker was telling a humorous story to a circle of giggling listeners. The old man sat like a fat, jolly god.

'And just at that moment th' old woman put her head out of th' window an' said: "Mike, yez lezy divil, fer phwat do yez be slapin' in me new geranium bid?" An' Mike woke up an' said: "Domn a wash-woman thot do niver wash her own bid-clues. Here do I be slapin' in nothin' but dhirt an' wades."'

The men slapped their knees, roaring loudly. They begged him to tell another. A clamour of comment arose concerning the anecdote, so that when old Bleecker began a fresh one nobody was heeding.

It occurred to Jones to sing. Suddenly he burst forth with a ballad that had a rippling waltz movement, and, seizing Kelcey, made a furious attempt to dance. They sprawled over a pair of outstretched legs and pitched headlong. Kelcey fell with a yellow crash. Blinding lights flashed before his vision, but he arose immediately, laughing. He did not feel at all hurt. The pain in his head was rather pleasant.

Old Bleecker, O'Connor, and Jones, who now limped and drew breath through his teeth, were about to lead him with much care and tenderness to the table for another drink, but he laughingly pushed them away and went unassisted. Bleecker told him: 'Great Gawd, your head struck hard enough t' break a trunk.'

He laughed again, and with a show of steadiness and courage he poured out an extravagant portion of whisky. With cold muscles he put it to his lips and drank it. It chanced that this addition dazed him like a powerful blow. A moment later it affected him, with blinding and numbing power.

Suddenly unbalanced, he felt the room sway. His blurred sight could only distinguish a tumbled mass of shadow through which the beams from the light ran like swords of flame, The sound of the many voices was to him like the roar of a distant river.

Still, he felt that if he could only annul the force of these million winding figures that gripped his senses, he was capable of most brilliant and entertaining things.

He was at first of the conviction that his feelings were only temporary. He waited for them to pass away, but the mental and physical pause only caused a new reeling and swinging of the room. Chasms with inclined approaches were before him; peaks leaned toward him. And withal he was blind and numb with surprise. He understood vaguely in his stupefaction that it would disgrace him to fall down a chasm.

At last he perceived a shadow, a form, which he knew to be Jones. The adorable Jones, the supremely wise Jones, was walking in this strange land without fear or care, erect and tranquil. Kelcey murmured in admiration and affection, and fell toward his friend. Jones's voice sounded as from the shores of the unknown.

'Come, come, of man, this will never do. Brace up.'

It appeared after all that Jones was not wholly wise.

'Oh, I'm —all ri', Jones! I'm all ri'! I wan' shing song! T ha's all —I wan' shing song!' Jones was stupid.

'Come, now, sit down an' shut up.'

It made Kelcey burn with fury.

'Jones, le' me alone, I tell yeh! Le' me alone! I wan' shing song er te' story! G'l'm'n, I lovsh girl live down my shtreet. Thash reason 'm drunk —'tis! She —'

Jones seized him and dragged him toward a chair. He heard him laugh. He could not endure these insults from his friend. He felt a blazing desire to strangle his companion.

He threw out his hand violently, but Jones grappled him close, and he was no more than a dried leaf. He was amazed to find that Jones possessed the strength of twenty horses. He was forced skilfully to the floor.

As he lay he reflected in great astonishment upon Jones's muscle. It was singular that he had never before discovered it. The whole incident had impressed him immensely. An idea struck him that he might denounce Jones for it. It would be a sage thing. There would be a thrilling and dramatic moment in which he would dazzle all the others.

But at this moment he was assailed by a mighty desire to sleep. Sombre and soothing clouds of slumber were heavily upon him. He closed his eyes with a sigh that was yet like that of a babe.

When he awoke there was still the battleful clamour of the revel. He half arose, with a plan of participating, when O'Connor came and pushed him down again, throwing out his chin in affectionate remonstrance, and saying, 'Now, now!' as to a child.

The change that had come over these men mystified Kelcey in a great degree. He had never seen anything so vastly stupid as their idea of his state. He resolved to prove to them that they were dealing with one whose mind was very clear.

He kicked and squirmed in O'Connor's arms, until, with a final wrench, he scrambled to his feet and stood tottering in the middle of the room. He would let them see that he had a strangely lucid grasp of events.

'G'l'm'n, I lovsh girl! I ain' drunker'n yeh all are! She —'

He felt them hurl him to a corner of the room and pile chairs and tables upon him until he was buried beneath a stupendous mountain. Far above, as up a mine's shaft, there were voices, lights, and vague figures. He was not hurt physically, but his feelings were unutterably injured.

He, the brilliant, the good, the sympathetic, had been thrust fiendishly from the party. They had had the comprehension of red lobsters. It was an unspeakable barbarism. Tears welled piteously from his eyes. He planned long diabolical explanations!

CHAPTER X

At first the gray lights of dawn came timidly into the room, remaining near the windows, afraid to approach certain sinister corners. Finally, mellow streams of sunshine poured in, undraping the shadows to disclose the putrefaction, making pitiless revelation. Kelcey awoke with a groan of undirected misery. He tossed his stiffened arms about his head for a moment, and then, leaning heavily upon his elbow, stared blinking at his environment. The grim truthfulness of the day showed disaster and death. After the tumults of the previous night the interior of this room resembled a decaying battlefield. The air hung heavy and stifling with the odours of tobacco, men's breaths, and beer half filling forgotten glasses. There was ruck of broken tumblers, pipes, bottles, spilled tobacco, cigar stumps. The chairs and tables were pitched this way and that way, as after some terrible struggle. In the midst of it all lay old Bleecker, stretched upon a couch in deepest sleep, as abandoned in attitude, as motionless, as ghastly, as if it were a corpse that had been flung there.

A knowledge of the thing came gradually into Kelcey's eyes. He looked about him with an expression of utter woe, regret, and loathing. He was compelled to lie down again. A pain above his eyebrows was like that from an iron clamp.

As he lay pondering, his bodily condition created for him a bitter philosophy, and he perceived all the futility of a red existence. He saw his life-problems confronting him like granite giants, and he was no longer erect to meet them. He had made a calamitous retrogression in his war. Spectres were to him now as large as clouds.

Inspired by the pitiless ache in his head, he was prepared to reform and live a white life. His stomach informed him that a good man was the only being who was wise. But his perception of his future was hopeless. He was aghast at the prospect of the old routine. It was impossible. He trembled before its exactions.

Turning toward the other way, he saw that the gold portals of vice no longer enticed him. He could not hear the strains of alluring music. The beckoning sirens of drink had been killed by this pain in his head. The desires of his life suddenly lay dead, like mullein stalks. Upon reflection, he saw, therefore, that he was perfectly willing to be virtuous if somebody would come and make it easy for him.

When he stared over at old Bleecker, he felt a sudden contempt and dislike for him. He considered him to be a tottering old beast. It was disgusting to perceive aged men so weak in sin. He dreaded to see him awaken, lest he should be required to be somewhat civil to him.

Kelcey wished for a drink of water. For some time he had dreamed of the liquid, deliciously cool. It was an abstract, uncontained thing that poured upon him and tumbled him, taking away his pain like a kind of surgery. He arose and staggered slowly toward a little sink in a corner of the room. He understood that any rapid movement might cause his head to split.

The little sink was filled with a chaos of broken glass and spilled liquids. A sight of it filled him with horror, but he rinsed a glass with scrupulous care, and, filling it, took an enormous drink. The water was an intolerable disappointment. It was insipid and weak to his scorched throat, and not at all cool. He put down the glass with a gesture of despair. His face became fixed in the stony and sullen expression of a man who waits for the recuperative power of morrows.

Old Bleecker awakened. He rolled over and groaned loudly. For awhile he thrashed about in a fury of displeasure at his bodily stiffness and pain. Kelcey watched him as he would have watched a death agony.

'Good Gawd!' said the old man, 'beer an' whisky make th' devil of a mix! Did yeh see th' fight?'

'No,' said Kelcey stolidly.

'Why, Zeusentell an' O'Connor had a great old mill. They were scrappin' all over th' place. I thought we were all goin' t' get pulled. Thompson, that fellah over in th' corner, though, he sat down on th' whole business. He was a dandy! He had t' poke Zeusentell! He was a bird! Lord, I wish I had a Manhattan!'

Kelcey remained in bitter silence while old Bleecker dressed. 'Come an' get a cocktail,' said the latter briskly. This was part of his aristocracy. He was the only man of them who knew much about cocktails. He perpetually referred to them. 'It'll brace yeh right up! Come along! Say, you get full too soon. You oughter wait until later, me boy! You're too speedy!' Kelcey wondered vaguely where his companion had lost his zeal for polished sentences, his iridescent mannerisms.

'Come along,' said Bleecker.

Kelcey made a movement of disdain for cocktails, but he followed the other to the street. At the corner they separated. Kelcey attempted a friendly parting smile and then went on up the street. He had to reflect to know that he was erect and using his own muscles in walking. He felt like a man of paper, blown by the winds. Withal, the dust of the avenue was galling to his throat, eyes and nostrils, and the roar of traffic cracked his head. He was glad, however, to be alone, to be rid of old Bleecker. The sight of him had been as the contemplation of a disease.

His mother was not at home. In his little room he mechanically undressed and bathed his head, arms and shoulders. When he crawled between the two white sheets he felt a first lifting of his misery. His pillow was soothingly soft. There was an effect that was like the music of tender voices.

When he awoke again his mother was bending over him giving vent to alternate cries of grief and joy. Her hands trembled so that they were useless to her. 'Oh, George, George, where have yeh been? What has happened t' yeh? Oh, George, I've been so worried! I didn't sleep a wink all night!'

Kelcey was instantly wide awake. With a moan of suffering he turned his face to the wall before he spoke. 'Never mind, mother, I'm all right. Don't fret now! I was knocked down by a truck last night in th' street, an' they took me t' th' hospital; but it's all right now. I got out jest a little while ago. They told me I'd better go home an' rest up.'

His mother screamed in pity, horror, joy and self-reproach for something unknown. She frenziedly demanded the details. He sighed with unutterable weariness. 'Oh-wait-wait-wait!' he said, shutting his eyes as from the merciless monotony of a pain. 'Wait-wait-please wait! I can't talk now. I want t' rest.'

His mother condemned herself with a little cry. She adjusted his pillow, her hands shaking with love and tenderness.

'There, there, don't mind, dearie! But yeh can't think how worried I was-an' crazy. I was near frantic. I went down t' th' shop, an' they said they hadn't seen anything 'a yeh there. The foreman was awful good t' me. He said he'd come up this afternoon t' see if yeh had come home yet. He tol' me not t' worry. Are yeh sure yer all right? Ain't there anythin' I kin git fer yeh? What did th' doctor say?'

Kelcey's patience was worn. He gestured, and then spoke querulously. 'Now-now-mother, it's all right, I tell yeh! All I need is a little rest, an' I'll be as well as ever. But it makes it all th' worse if yeh stand there an' ask me questions an' make me think. Jest leave me alone fer a little while, an' I'll be as well as ever. Can't yeh do that?'

The little old woman puckered her lips funnily. 'My, what an old bear th' boy is!' She kissed him blithely. Presently she went out, upon her face a bright and glad smile that must have been a reminiscence of some arming girlhood.

CHAPTER XI

At one time Kelcey had a friend who was struck in the head by the pole of a truck and knocked senseless. He was taken to the hospital, from which he emerged in the morning an astonished man, with rather a dim recollection of the accident. He used to hold an old brierwood pipe in his teeth in a manner peculiar to himself, and, with a brown derby hat tilted back on his head, recount his strange sensations. Kelcey had always remembered it as a bit of curious history. When his mother cross-examined him in regard to the accident, he told this story with barely a variation. Its truthfulness was incontestable.

At the shop he was welcomed on the following day with considerable enthusiasm. The foreman had told the story, and there were already jokes created concerning it. Mike O'Donnell, whose wit was famous, had planned a humorous campaign, in which he made charges against Kelcey which were, as a matter of fact, almost the exact truth. Upon hearing it, Kelcey looked at him suddenly from the corners of his eyes, but otherwise remained imperturbable. O'Donnell eventually despaired. 'Yez can't goiy that kid! He tekes ut all loike mate an' dhrink.' Kelcey often told the story, his pipe held in his teeth peculiarly, and his derby tilted back on his head.

He remained at home for several evenings, content to read the papers and talk with his mother. She began to look around for the tremendous reason for it. She suspected that his nearness to death in the recent accident had sobered his senses and made him think of high things. She mused upon it continually. When he sat moodily pondering she watched him. She said to herself that she saw the light breaking in upon his spirit. She felt that it was a very critical period of his existence. She resolved to use all her power and skill to turn his eyes toward the lights in the sky. Accordingly, she addressed him one evening:

'Come, go t' prayer-meetin' t'-night with me, will yeh, George?' It sounded more blunt than she intended.

He glanced at her in sudden surprise. 'Huh?'

As she repeated her request, her voice quavered. She felt that it was a supreme moment.

'Come, go t' prayer-meetin' t'-night, won't yeh?'

He seemed amazed.

'Oh, I don't know,' he began. He was fumbling in his mind for a reason for refusing. 'I don't wanta go. I'm tired as the dickens!'

His obedient shoulders sank down languidly. His head mildly drooped.

The little old woman, with a quick perception of her helplessness, felt a motherly rage at her son. It was intolerable that she could not impart motion to him in a chosen direction. The waves of her desires were puny against the rocks of his indolence. She had a great wish to beat him.

'I don't know what I'm ever goin' t' do with yeh,' she told him in a choking voice. 'Yeh won't do anything I ask yeh to. Yeh never pay th' least bit 'a attention t' what I say. Yeh don't mind me any more than yeh would a fly. Whatever am I goin' t' do with yeh?'

She faced him in a battleful way, her eyes blazing with a sombre light of despairing rage.

He looked up at her ironically. 'I don't know,' he said, with calmness. 'What are yeh?' He had traced her emotions and seen her fear of his rebellion. He thrust out his legs in the easy scorn of a rapier-bravo. 'What are yeh?'

The little old woman began to weep. They were tears without a shame of grief. She allowed them to run unheeded down her cheeks. As she stared into space her son saw her regarding there the powers and influences that she had held in her younger life. She was in some way acknowledging to fate that she was now but withered grass, with no power but the power to feel the winds. He was smitten with a sudden shame. Besides, in the last few days he had gained quite a character for amiability. He saw something grand in relenting at this point. 'Well,' he said, trying to remove a sulky quality from his voice, 'well, if yer bound t' have me go, I s'pose I'll have t' go.'

His mother, with strange, immobile face, went to him and kissed him on the brow. 'All right, George!' There was in her wet eyes an emotion which he could not fathom.

She put on her bonnet and shawl, and they went out together. She was unusually silent, and made him wonder why she did not appear gleeful at his coming. He was resentful because she did not display more appreciation of his sacrifice. Several times he thought of halting and refusing to go further, to see if that would not wring from her some acknowledgment.

In a dark street the little chapel sat humbly between two towering apartment-houses. A red street-lamp stood in front. It threw a. marvellous reflection upon the wet pavements. It was like the death-stain of a spirit. Further up the brilliant lights of an avenue made a span of gold across the black street. A roar of wheels and a clang of bells came from this point, interwoven into a sound emblematic of the life of the city. It seemed somehow to affront this solemn and austere little edifice. It suggested an approaching barbaric invasion. The little church, pierced, would die with a fine, illimitable scorn for its slayers.

When Kelcey entered with his mother he felt a sudden quaking. His knees shook. It was an awesome place to him. There was a menace in the red padded carpet and the leather doors, studded with little brass tacks that penetrated his soul with their pitiless glances. As for his mother, she had acquired such a new air that he would have been afraid to address her. He felt completely alone and isolated at this formidable time.

There was a man in the vestibule who looked at them blandly. From within came the sound of singing. To Kelcey there were a million voices. He dreaded the terrible moment when the doors should swing back. He wished to recoil, but at that instant the bland man pushed the doors aside, and he followed his mother up the centre aisle of the little chapel. To him there was a riot of lights that made him transparent. The multitudinous pairs of eyes that turned toward him were implacable in their cool valuations.

They had just ceased singing. He who conducted the meeting motioned that the service should wait until the new-comers found seats. The little old woman went slowly on toward the first rows. Occasionally she paused to scrutinize vacant places, but they did not seem to meet her requirements. Kelcey was in agony. He thought the moment of her decision would never come. In his unspeakable haste he walked a little faster than his mother.

Once she paused to glance in her calculating way at some seats and he forged ahead. He halted abruptly and returned, but by that time she had resumed her thoughtful march up the aisle. He could have assassinated her. He felt that everybody must have seen his torture, during which his hands were to him like monstrous swollen hides. He was wild with a rage in which his lips turned slightly livid. He was capable of doing some furious, unholy thing.

When the little old woman at last took a seat, her son sat down beside her slowly and stiffly. He was opposing his strong desire to drop.

When from the mists of his shame and humiliation the scene came before his vision, he was surprised to find that all eyes were not fastened upon his face. The leader of the meeting seemed to be the only one who saw him. He stared gravely, solemnly, regretfully. He was a pale-faced but plump young man in a black coat that buttoned to his chin. It was evident to Kelcey that his mother had spoken of him to the young clergyman, and that the latter was now impressing upon him the sorrow caused by the con- templation of his sin. Kelcey hated the man.

A man seated alone over in a corner began to sing. He closed his eyes and threw back his head. Others, scattered sparsely throughout the innumerable light-wood chairs, joined him as they caught the air.

Kelcey heard his mother's frail, squeaking soprano. The chandelier in the centre was the only one lighted, and far at the end of the room one could discern the pulpit swathed in gloom, solemn and mystic as a bier. It was surrounded by vague shapes of darkness on which at times was the glint of brass, or of glass that shone like steel, until one could feel there the presence of the army of the unknown, possessors of the great eternal truths, and silent listeners at this ceremony. High up, the stained glass windows loomed in leaden array like dull-hued banners, merely catching occasional splashes of dark wine-colour from the lights. Kelcey fell to brooding concerning this indefinable presence which he felt in a church.

One by one people arose and told little tales of their religious faith. Some were tearful, and others calm, emotionless, and convincing.

Kelcey listened closely for a time. These people filled him with a great curiosity. He was not familiar with their types.

At last the young clergyman spoke at some length.

Kelcey was amazed, because, from the young man's appearance, he would not have suspected him of being so glib; but the speech had no effect on Kelcey, excepting to prove to him again that he was damned.

CHAPTER XII

Kelcey sometimes wondered whether he liked beer. He had been obliged to cultivate a talent for imbibing it. He was born with an abhorrence which he had steadily battled until it had come to pass that he could drink from ten to twenty glasses of beer without the act of swallowing causing him to shiver. He understood that drink was an essential to joy, to the coveted position of a man of the world and of the streets. The saloons contained the mystery of a street for him. When he knew its saloons he comprehended the street.

Drink and its surroundings were the eyes of a superb green dragon to him. He followed a fascinating glitter, and the glitter required no explanation.

Directly after old Bleecker's party he almost reformed. He was tired and worn from the tumult of it, and he saw it as one might see a skeleton emerged from a crimson cloak. He wished then to turn his face away.

Gradually, however, he recovered his mental balance. Then he admitted again by his point of view that the thing was not so terrible. His headache had caused him to exaggerate. A 'drunk' was not the blight which he had once remorsefully named it. On the contrary, it was a mere unpleasant incident. He resolved, however, to be more cautious.

When prayer-meeting night came again his mother approached him hopefully. She smiled like one whose request is already granted.

'Well, will yeh go t' prayer-meetin' with me t'-night again?'

He turned toward her with eloquent suddenness, and then riveted his eyes upon a corner of the floor.

'Well, I guess not,' he said.

His mother tearfully tried to comprehend his state of mind.

'What has come over yeh?' she said tremblingly. 'Yeh never used t' be this way, George. Yeh never used t' be so cross an' mean t' me —'

'Oh, I ain't cross an' mean t' yeh,' he interpolated, exasperated and violent.

'Yes, yeh are, too! I ain't hardly had a decent word from yeh in ever so long. Yer as cross an' as mean as yeh can be. I don't know what t' make of it. It can't be'—there came a look in her eyes that told that she was going to shock and alarm him with her heaviest sentence —'it can't be that yeh've got t' drinkin'.'

Kelcey grunted with disgust at the ridiculous thing. 'Why, what an old goose yer gettin' t' be!'

She was compelled to laugh a little, as a child laughs between tears at a hurt. She had not been serious. She was only trying to display to him how she regarded his horrifying mental state. 'Oh, of course I didn't mean that, but I think yeh act jest as bad as if yeh did drink. I wish yeh would do better, George!'

She had grown so much less frigid and stern in her censure that Kelcey seized the opportunity to try to make a joke of it. He laughed at her, but she shook her head and continued: 'I do wish yeh would do better. I don't know what's t' become 'a yeh, George. Yeh don't mind what I say no more'n if I was th' wind in th' chimbly. Yeh don't care about nothin' 'cept goin out nights. I can't ever get yeh t' prayermeetin' ner church; yeh never go out with me anywheres unless yeh can't get out of it; yeh swear an' take on sometimes like everything; yeh never —'

He gestured wrathfully in interruption. 'Say, lookahere, can't yeh think 'a something I do?'

She ended her oration then in the old way —'An' I don't know what's goin' t' become 'a yeh.'

She put on her bonnet and shawl and then came and stood near him expectantly. She imparted to her attitude a subtle threat of unchangeableness. He pretended to be engrossed in his newspaper. The little swaggering clock on the mantel became suddenly evident, ticking with loud monotony. Presently she said firmly, 'Well, are yeh comin'?'

He was reading.

'Well, are yeh comin'?'

He threw his paper down angrily. 'Oh, why don't yeh go on an' leave me alone?' he demanded in supreme impatience. 'What do yeh wanta pester me fer? Ye'd think there was robbers. Why can't yeh go alone or else stay home? You wanta go, an' I don't wanta go, an' yeh keep all time tryin' t' drag me. Yeh know I don't wanta go.' He concluded in a last defiant wounding of her. 'What do I care 'bout those of bags-'a-wind, anyhow? They gimme a pain!'

His mother turned her face and went from him. He sat staring with a mechanical frown. Presently he went and picked up his newspaper.

Jones told him that night that everybody had had such a good time at old Bleecker's party that they were going to form a club. They waited at the little smiling saloon, and then, amid much enthusiasm, all signed a membership-roll. Old Bleecker, late that night, was violently elected president. He made speeches of thanks and gratification during the remainder of the meeting. Kelcey went home rejoicing. He felt that at any rate he would have true friends. The dues were a dollar for each week.

He was deeply interested. For a number of evenings he fairly gobbled his supper in order that he might be off to the little smiling saloon to discuss the new organization. All the men were wildly enthusiastic. One night the saloon-keeper announced that he would donate half the rent of quite a large room over his saloon. It was an occasion for great cheering. Kelcey's legs were like whalebone when he tried to go upstairs upon his return home, and the edge of each step was moved curiously forward.

His mother's questions made him snarl. 'Oh, nowheres!' At other times he would tell her, 'Oh, t' see some friends 'a mine! Where d' yeh s'pose?'

Finally, some of the women of the tenement concluded that the little old mother had a wild son. They came to condole with her. They sat in the kitchen for hours. She told them of his wit, his cleverness, his kind heart.

CHAPTER XIII

At a certain time Kelcey discovered that some young men who stood in the cinders between a brick wall and the pavement, and near the side-door of a corner saloon, knew more about life than other people. They used to lean there smoking and chewing, and comment upon events and persons. They knew the neighbourhood extremely well. They debated upon small typical things that transpired before them, until they had extracted all the information that existence contained. They sometimes inaugurated little fights with foreigners or well-dressed men. It was here that Sapristi Glielmi, the pedlar, stabbed Pete Brady to death, for which he got a life-sentence. Each patron of the saloon was closely scrutinized as he entered the place.

Sometimes they used to throng upon the heels of a man, and in at the bar assert that he had asked them in to drink. When he objected, they would claim with one voice that it was too deep an insult, and gather about to thrash him. When they had caught chance customers and absolute strangers, the barkeeper had remained in stolid neutrality, ready to serve one or seven, but two or three times they had encountered the wrong men. Finally, the proprietor had come out one morning and told them in the fearless way of his class that their pastime must cease.

'It quits right here! See? Right here! Th' nex' time yeh try t' work it, I come with th' bung-starter, an' th' mugs I miss with it git pulled. See? It quits!' Infrequently, however, men did ask them in to drink.

The policeman of that beat grew dignified and shrewd whenever he approached this corner. Sometimes he stood with his hands behind his back and cautiously conversed with them. It was understood on both sides that it was a good thing to be civil.

In winter this band, a trifle diminished in numbers, huddled in their old coats and stamped little flat places in the snow, their faces turned always toward the changing life in the streets. In the summer they became more lively. Sometimes, then, they walked out to the kerb to look up and down the street.

Over in a trampled vacant lot, surrounded by high tenement-houses, there was a sort of a den among some boulders. An old truck was made to form a shelter. The small hoodlums of that vicinity all avoided the spot-so many of them had been thrashed upon being caught near it. It was the summer-time lounging place of the band from the corner.

They were all too clever to work. Some of them had worked, but these used their experiences as stores from which to draw tales. They were like veterans with their wars. One lad in particular used to recount how he whipped his employer, proprietor of a large grain and feed establishment. He described his victim's features and form and clothes with minute exactness. He bragged of his wealth and social position. It had been a proud moment of the lad's life. He was like a savage who had killed a great chief.

Their feeling for contemporaneous life was one of contempt. Their philosophy taught that in a large part the whole thing was idle and a great bore. With fine scorn they sneered at the futility of it. Work was done by men who had not the courage to stand still and let the skies clap together if they willed.

The vast machinery of the popular law indicated to them that there were people in the world who wished to remain quiet. They awaited the moment when they could prove to them that a riotous upheaval, a cloud-burst of destruction, would be a delicious thing. They thought of their fingers buried in the lives of these people. They longed dimly for a time when they could run through decorous streets with crash and roar of war, an army of revenge for pleasures long possessed by others, a wild sweeping compensation for their years without crystal and gilt, women and wine. This thought slumbered in them, as the image of Rome might have lain small in the hearts of the barbarians.

Kelcey respected these youths so much that he ordinarily used the other side of the street. He could not go near to them, because if a passer minded his own business he was a disdainful prig and had insulted them; if he showed that he was aware of them they were likely to resent his not minding his own business and prod him into a fight if the opportunity were good. Kelcey longed for their acquaintance and friendship, for with it came social safety and ease; they were respected so universally.

Once, in another street, Fidsey Corcoran was whipped by a short, heavy man. Fidsey picked himself up, and in the fury of defeat hurled pieces of brick at his opponent. The short man dodged with skill, and then pursued Fidsey for over a block. Sometimes he got near enough to punch him. Fidsey raved in maniacal fury. The moment the short man would attempt to resume his own affairs, Fidsey would turn upon him again, tears and blood upon his face, with the lashed rage of a vanquished animal. The short man used to turn about, swear madly, and make little dashes. Fidsey always ran, and then returned as pursuit ceased.

The short man apparently wondered if this maniac was ever going to allow him to finish whipping him. He looked helplessly up and down the street. People were there who knew Fidsey, and they remonstrated with him; but he continued to confront the short man, gibbering like a wounded ape, using all the eloquence of the street in his wild oaths.

Finally, the short man was exasperated to black fury. He decided to end the fight. With low snarls, ominous as death, he plunged at Fidsey.

Kelcey happened there then. He grasped the short man's shoulder. He cried out, in the peculiar whine of the man who interferes:

'Oh, hol' on! Yeh don't wanta hit 'im any more! Yeh've done enough to 'im now! Leave 'im be!'

The short man wrenched and tugged. He turned his face until his teeth were almost at Kelcey's cheek.

'Le' go me! Le' go me, you —'

The rest of his sentence was screamed curses.

Kelcey's face grew livid from fear, but he somehow managed to keep his grip. Fidsey, with but an instant's pause, plunged into the new fray.

They beat the short man. They forced him against a high board-fence, where for a few seconds their blows sounded upon his head in swift thuds. A moment later Fidsey descried a running policeman. He made off, fleet as a shadow. Kelcey noted his going. He ran after him.

Three or four blocks away they halted. Fidsey said:

'I'd 'a licked dat big stuff in 'bout a minute more,' and wiped the blood from his eyes.

At the gang's corner they asked: 'Who soaked yeh, Fidsey?' His description was burning. Everybody laughed. 'Where is 'e now?'

Later they began to question Kelcey. He recited a tale in which he allowed himself to appear prominent and redoubtable. They looked at him then as if they thought he might be quite a man.

Once when the little old woman was going out to buy something for her son's supper, she discovered him standing at the side-door of the saloon engaged intimately with Fidsey and the others. She slunk away, for she understood that it would be a terrible thing to confront him and his pride there with youths who were superior to mothers.

When he arrived home, he threw down his hat with a weary sigh, as if he had worked long hours, but she attacked him before he had time to complete the falsehood. He listened to her harangue with a curled lip. In defence he merely made a gesture of supreme exasperation. She never understood the advanced things in life. He felt the hopelessness of ever making her comprehend. His mother was not modern.

CHAPTER XIV

The little old woman arose early and bustled in the preparation of breakfast. At times she looked anxiously at the clock. An hour before her son should leave for work she went to his room, and called him in the usual tone of sharpness:

'George! George!'

A sleepy growl came to her.

'Come, come, it's time t' git up,' she continued. 'Come, now, git right up!' Later she went again to the door.

'George, are yeh gittin' up?'

'Huh?'

'Are yeh gittin' up?'

'Yes, I'll git right up!'

He had introduced a valour into his voice which she detected to be false. She went to his bedside and took him by the shoulder.

'George-George-git up!'

From the mist-lands of sleep he began to protest incoherently. 'Oh le' me be, won' yeh? 'M sleepy!'

She continued to shake him. 'Well, it's time t' git up. Come-come-come on, now!'

Her voice, shrill with annoyance, pierced his ears in a slender, piping thread of sound. He turned over on the pillow to bury his head in his arms. When he expostulated, his tones came half-smothered.

'Oh, le' me be, can't yeh? There's plenty 'a time! Jest fer ten minutes! 'M sleepy!'

She was implacable. 'No, yeh must git up now! Yeh ain't got more'n time enough t' eat yer breakfast an' git t' work.'

Eventually he arose, sullen and grumbling. Later he came to his breakfast, blinking his dry eyelids, his stiffened features set in a mechanical scowl.

Each morning his mother went to his room, and fought a battle to arouse him. She was like a soldier. Despite his pleadings, his threats, she remained at her post, imperturbable and unyielding.

These affairs assumed large proportions in his life. Sometimes he grew beside himself with a bland, unformulated wrath. The whole thing was a consummate imposition. He felt that he was being cheated of his sleep. It was an injustice to compel him to arise morning after morning with bitter regularity, before the sleep-gods had at all loosened their grasp. He hated that unknown force which directed his life.

One morning he swore a tangled mass of oaths, aimed into the air, as if the injustice poised there. His mother flinched at first; then her mouth set in the little straight line. She saw that the momentous occasion had come. It was the time of the critical battle. She turned upon him valorously.

'Stop your swearin', George Kelcey; I won't have yeh talk so before me! I won't have it! Stop this minute! Not another word! Do yeh think I'll allow yeh t' swear b'fore me like that? Not another word! I won't have it! I declare I won't have it another minute!'

At first her projected words had slid from his mind as if striking against ice, but at last he heeded her. His face grew sour with passion and misery-he spoke in tones dark with dislike.

'Th' 'ell yeh won't? Whatter yeh goin' t' do 'bout it?' Then, as if he considered that he had not been sufficiently impressive, he arose and slowly walked over to her. Having arrived at point-blank range he spoke again. 'Whatter yeh goin' t' do 'bout it?' He regarded her then with an unaltering scowl, albeit his mien was as dark and cowering as that of a condemned criminal.

She threw out her hands in the gesture of an impotent one. He was acknowledged victor. He took his hat and slowly left her.

For three days they lived in silence. He brooded upon his mother's agony and felt a singular joy in it. As opportunity offered, he did little despicable things. He was going to make her abject. He was now uncontrolled, ungoverned; he wished to be an emperor. Her suffering was all a sort of compensation for his own dire pains.

She went about with a gray, impassive face. It was as if she had survived a massacre in which all that she loved had been torn from her by the brutality of savages.

One evening at six he entered and stood looking at his mother as she peeled potatoes. She had hearkened to his coming listlessly, without emotion, and at his entrance she did not raise her eyes.

'Well, I'm fired!' he said suddenly.

It seemed to be the final blow. Her body gave a convulsive movement in the chair. When she finally lifted her eyes, horror possessed her face. Her underjaw had fallen. 'Fired? Outa work? Why-George?'

He went over to the window and stood with his back to her. He could feel her gray stare upon him.

'Yes! Fired!'

At last she said:

'Well, whatter yeh goin' t' do?'

He tapped the pane with his finger-nail.

He answered in a tone made hoarse and unnatural by an assumption of gay carelessness:

'Oh, nothin'!'

She began, then, her first weeping. 'Oh-George-George-George —'

He looked at her, scowling.

'Ah, whatter yeh givin' us? Is this all I git when I come home f'm being fired? Anybody 'ud think it was my fault. I couldn't help it.'

She continued to sob in a dull, shaking way. In the pose of her head there was an expression of her conviction that comprehension of her pain was impossible to the universe.

He paused for a moment, and then, with his usual tactics, went out, slamming the door. A pale flood of sunlight, imperturbable at its vocation, streamed upon the little old woman, bowed with pain, forlorn in her chair.

CHAPTER XV

Kelcey was standing on the corner next day when three little boys came running. Two halted some distance away, and the other came forward.

He halted before Kelcey, and spoke importantly.

'Hey, your ol' woman's sick.'

'What?'

'Your ol' woman's sick.'

'Git out!'

'She is, too!'

'Who tol' yeh?'

'Mis' Callahan. She said fer me t' run an' tell yeh. Dey want yeh.'

A swift dread struck Kelcey. Like flashes of light little scenes from the past shot through his brain. He had thoughts of a vengeance from the clouds.

As he glanced about him the familiar view assumed a meaning that was ominous and dark. There was prophecy of disaster in the street, the buildings, the sky, the people. Something tragic and terrible in the air was known to his nervous, quivering nostrils. He spoke to the little boy in a tone that quavered.

'All right!'

Behind him he felt the sudden contemplative pause of his companions of the gang. They were watching him. As he went rapidly up the street he knew that they had come out to the middle of the walk and were staring after him. He was glad that they could not see his face, his trembling lips, his eyes quavering in fear.

He stopped at the door of his home and stared at the panel as if he saw written thereon a word. A moment later he entered. His eye comprehended the room in a frightened glance.

His mother sat gazing out at the opposite walls and windows. She was leaning her head upon the back of the chair. Her face was overspread with a singular pallor, but the glance of her eyes was strong, and the set of her lips was tranquil.

He felt an unspeakable thrill of thanksgiving at seeing her seated there calmly.

'Why, mother, they said yeh was sick,' he cried, going toward her impetuously. 'What's th' matter?'

She smiled at him.

'Oh, it ain't nothin'! I on'y got kinda dizzy, that's all.'

Her voice was sober, and had the ring of vitality in it.

He noted her commonplace air. There was no alarm or pain in her tones, but the misgivings of the street, the prophetic twinges of his nerves, made him still hesitate.

'Well–are you sure it ain't? They scared me 'bout t' death.'

'No, it ain't anything, o'ny some sorta dizzy feelin'. I fell down b'hind th' stove. Missis Calahan, she came an' picked me up. I must 'a laid there fer quite a while. Th' doctor said he guessed I'd be all right in a couple 'a hours. I don't feel nothin'!'

Kelcey heaved a great sigh of relief.

'Lord, I was scared!' He began to beam joyously, since he was escaped from his fright. 'Why, I couldn't think what had happened,' he told her.

'Well, it ain't nothin',' she said.

He stood about awkwardly, keeping his eyes fastened upon her in a sort of surprise, as if he had expected to discover that she had vanished. The reaction from his panic was a thrill of delicious contentment. He took a chair and sat down near her, but presently he jumped up to ask:

'There ain't nothin' I can get for yeh, is ther?'

He looked at her eagerly. In his eyes shone love and joy. If it were not for the shame of it, he would have called her endearing names.

'No, ther ain't nothin',' she answered. Presently she continued, in a conversational way: 'Yeh ain't found no work yit, have yeh?'

The shadow of his past fell upon him then, and he became suddenly morose. At last he spoke in a sentence that was a vow, a declaration of change.

'No, I ain't, but I'm going t' hunt fer it hard, you bet.'

She understood from his tone that he was making peace with her. She smiled at him gladly.

'Yer a good boy, George!' A rediance from the stars lit her face.

Presently she asked:

'D' yeh think yer old boss would take yeh on ag'in if I went t' see him?'

'No,' said Kelcey at once. 'It wouldn't do no good! They got all th' men they want. There ain't no room there. It wouldn't do no good.' He ceased to beam for a moment as he thought of certain disclosures. 'I'm goin' t' try to git work everywheres. I'm going t' make a wild break t' get a job, an' if there's one anywheres I'll get it.'

She smiled at him again.

'That's right, George!'

When it came supper-time he dragged her in her chair over to the table, and then scurried to and fro to prepare a meal for her. She laughed gleefully at him. He was awkward and densely ignorant. He exaggerated his helplessness sometimes until she was obliged to lean back in her chair to laugh. Afterward they sat by the window. Her hand rested upon his hair.

CHAPTER XVI

When Kelcey went to borrow money from old Bleecker, Jones and the others, he discovered that he was below them in social position. Old Bleecker said gloomily that he did not see how he could loan money at that time. When Jones asked him to have a drink, his tone was careless.

O'Connor recited at length some bewildering financial troubles of his own. In them all he saw that something had been reversed. They remained silent upon many occasions when they might have grunted in sympathy for him.

As he passed along the street near his home he perceived Fidsey Corcoran and another of the gang. They made eloquent signs.

'Are yeh wid us?'

He stopped and looked at them.

'What's wrong with yeh?'

'Are yeh wid us er not?' demanded Fidsey. 'New barkeep'! Big can! We got it over in d' lot. Big can, I tell yeh.'

He drew a picture in the air, so to speak, with his enthusiastic fingers.

Kelcey turned dejectedly homeward.

'Oh, I guess not, this roun'.'

'What's d' matter wi'che?' said Fidsey. Yer gittin' t' be a reg'lar willie! Come ahn, I tell yeh! Youse gits one smoke at d' can b'cause yeh b'longs t' d' gang, an' yeh don't wanta give it up widout er scrap! See? Some udder john 'll get yer smoke. Come ahn!'

When they arrived at the place among the boulders in the vacant lot, one of the band had a huge and battered tin can tilted afar up. His throat worked convulsively. He was watched keenly and anxiously by five or six others. Their eyes followed carefully each fraction of distance that the can was lifted. They were very silent.

Fidsey burst out violently as he perceived what was in progress:

'Heh, Tim, yeh big sojer, let go d' can! What 'a yeh tink! Wese er in dis! Le' go dat!'

He who was drinking made several angry protesting contortions of his throat. Then he put down the can and swore.

'Who's a big sojer? I ain't gittin' more'n me own smoke! Yer too bloomin' swift I Ye'd tink yeh was d' on'y mug what owned dis can! Close yer face while I gits me smoke!'

He took breath for a moment, and then returned the can to its tilted position.

Fidsey went to him and worried and clamoured. He interfered so seriously with the action of drinking that the other was obliged to release the can again for fear of choking.

Fidsey grabbed it, and glanced swiftly at the contents.

'Dere! Dat's what I was hollerin' at! Lookut d' beer! Not 'nough t' wet yer t'roat! Yehs can't have notin' on d' level wid youse damn' tanks! Youse was a reg'lar resevoiy, Tim Connigan! Look what yeh lef' us! Ah, say, youse was a dandy! What 'a yeh tink we ah? Willies? Don' we want no smoke? Say, lookut dat can! It's drier'n hell! What 'a yeh tink?'

Tim glanced in at the beer. Then he said:

'Well, d' mug what come b'fore me, he on'y lef' me dat much. Blue Billie, he done d' swallerin'! I on'y had a tas'e!'

Blue Billie, from his seat near, called out in wrathful protest:

'Yeh lie, Tim. I never had more'n a mouf-ful!' An inspiration evidently came to him then, for his countenance suddenly brightened, and, arising, he went toward the can. 'I ain't had me reg'lar smoke yit! Guess I come in aheader Fidsey, don t I?'

Fidsey, with a sardonic smile, swung the can behind him.

'I guess nit! Not dis minnet! Youse hadger smoke. If yeh ain't, yeh don't git none. See?'

Blue Billie confronted Fidsey determinedly.

'D' 'ell I don't!'

'Nit,' said Fidsey.

Billie sat down again.

Fidsey drank his portion. Then he manoeuvred skilfully before the crowd until Kelcey and the other youth took their shares.

'Youse er a mob 'a tanks,' he told the gang. 'Nobody 'ud git not'in' if dey wasn't on t' yehs!'

Blue Billie's soul had been smouldering in hate against Fidsey.

'Ah, shut up! Youse ain't gota take care 'a dose two mugs, dough. Youse badger smoke, ain't yeh? Den yer tr'u. G' home!'

'Well, I hate t' see er bloke use 'imself for a tank,' said Fidsey. 'But youse don't wanta go jollyin' 'round 'bout d' can, Blue, er youse'll git done.'

'Who'll do me?' demanded Blue Billie, casting his eye about him.

'Kel' will,' said Fidsey bravely.

'D' 'el he will!'

'Dat's what he will!'

Blue Billie made the gesture of a warrior.

'He never saw d' day 'a his life dat he could do me little finger. If 'e says much t' me, I'll push 'is face all over d' lot.'

Fidsey called to Kelcey.

'Say, Kel, hear what dis mug is chewin'?'

Kelcey was apparently deep in other matters. His back was half-turned.

Blue Billie spoke to Fidsey in a battleful voice.

'Did 'e ever say 'e could do me?'

Fidsey said:

'Soitenly 'e did. Youse is dead easy, 'e says. He says he kin punch holes in you, Blue!'

'When did 'e say it?'

'Oh-any time. Youse is a cinch, Kel' says.'

Blue Billie walked over to Kelcey. The others of the band followed him, exchanging joyful glances.

'Did youse say yeh could do me?'

Kelcey slowly turned, but he kept his eyes upon the ground. He heard Fidsey darting among the others, telling of his prowess, preparing them for the downfall of Blue Billie. He stood heavily on one foot and moved his hands nervously. Finally he said in a low growl: 'Well, what if I did?'

The sentence sent a happy thrill through the band. It was a formidable question. Blue Billie braced himself. Upon him came the responsibility of the next step. The gang fell back a little upon all sides. They looked expectantly at Blue Billie.

He walked forward with a deliberate step until his face was close to Kelcey.

'Well, if you did,' he said, with a snarl between his teeth, 'I'm goin' t' t'ump d' life outa yeh right heh!'

A little boy, wild of eye and puffing, came down the slope as from an explosion. He burst out in a rapid treble:

'Is dat Kelcey feller here? Say, yeh ol' woman's sick again. Dey want yeh! Yeh's better run! She's awful sick!'

The gang turned with loud growls. 'Ah, git outa here!' Fidsey threw a stone at the little boy and chased him a short distance, but he continued to clamour:

'Youse better come, Kelcey feller! She's awful sick! She was hollerin'! Dey been lookin' for yeh over'n hour!'

In his eagerness he returned part way, regardless of Fidsey.

Kelcey had moved away from Blue Billie. He said:

'I guess I'd better go.' They howled at him. 'Well,' he continued, 'I can't —I don't wanta —I don't wanta leave me mother be-she —'

His words were drowned in the chorus of their derision. 'Well, looka-here,' he would begin, and at each time their cries and screams ascended. They dragged at Blue Billie. 'Go for 'im, Blue! Slug 'im! Go ahn!'

Kelcey went slowly away while they were urging Blue Billie to do a decisive thing.

Billie stood fuming and blustering and explaining himself. When Kelcey had achieved a considerable distance from him, he stepped forward a few paces and hurled a terrible oath. Kelcey looked back darkly.

CHAPTER XVII

When he entered the chamber of death he was brooding over the recent encounter and devising extravagant revenges upon Blue Billie and the others.

The little old woman was stretched upon her bed. Her face and hands were of the hue of the blankets. Her hair, seemingly of a new and wondrous grayness, hung over her temples in whips and tangles. She was sickeningly motionless, save for her eyes, which rolled and swayed in maniacal glances.

A young doctor had just been administering medicine.

'There,' he said, with a great satisfaction, 'I guess that'll do her good!' As he went briskly towards the door he met Kelcey. 'Oh,' he said. 'Son?'

Kelcey had that in his throat which was like fur. When he forced his voice the words came first low and then high, as if they had broken through something.

'Will she—will she —'

The doctor glanced back at the bed. She was watching them as she would have watched ghouls, and muttering.

'Can't tell,' he said. 'She's a wonderful woman! Got more vitality than you and I together! Can't tell! May-may not! Good-day! Back in two hours.'

In the kitchen Mrs. Calahan was feverishly dusting the furniture, polishing this and that. She arranged everything in decorous rows. She was preparing for the coming of death. She looked at the floor as if she longed to scrub it.

The doctor paused to speak in an undertone to her, glancing at the bed. When he departed she laboured with a renewed speed.

Kelcey approached his mother. From a little distance he called to her: 'Mother-mother —' He proceeded with caution lest this mystic being upon the bed should clutch at him. 'Mother-mother-don't yeh know me?' He put forth apprehensive, shaking fingers and touched her hand.

There were two brilliant steel-coloured points upon her eyeballs. She was staring off at something sinister.

Suddenly she turned to her son in a wild babbling appeal:

'Help me! Help me! Oh, help me! I see them coming.'

Kelcey called to her as to a distant place. 'Mother! Mother!' She looked at him, and then there began within her a struggle to reach him with her mind. She fought with some implacable power whose fingers were in her brain. She called to Kelcey in stammering, incoherent cries for help. Then she again looked away.

'Ah, there they come! There they come! Ah, look-look-loo —' She arose to a sitting posture without the use of her arms.

Kelcey felt himself being choked. When her voice pealed forth in a scream he saw crimson curtains moving before his eyes.

'Mother-oh, mother-there's nothin'—there's nothin' —'

She was at a kitchen-door with a dishcloth in her hand. Within there had just been a clatter of crockery. Down through the trees of the orchard she could see a man in a field ploughing.

'Bill —o-o-oh, Bill-have yeh seen Georgie? Is he out there with you? Georgie! Georgie! Come right here this minnet! Right-this-minnet!'

She began to talk to some people in the room:

'I want t' know what yeh want here! I want yeh t' git out! I don't want yeh here! I don't feel good t'-day, an' I don't want yeh here! I don't feel good t'-day! I want yeh t' git out!' Her voice became peevish. 'Go away! Go away! Go away!'

Kelcey lay in a chair. His nerveless arms allowed his fingers to sweep the floor. He became so that he could not hear the chatter from the bed, but he was always conscious of the ticking of the little clock out on the kitchen shelf.

When he aroused, the pale-faced but plump young clergyman was before him.

'My poor lad!' began this latter.

The little old woman lay still with her eyes closed. On the table at the head of the bed was a glass containing a water-like medicine. The reflected lights made a silver star on its side. The two men sat side by side, waiting. Out in the kitchen Mrs. Calahan had taken a chair by the stove and was waiting.

Kelcey began to stare at the wall-paper. The pattern was clusters of brown roses. He felt them like hideous crabs crawling upon his brain.

Through the doorway he saw the oilcloth covering of the table catching a glimmer from the warm afternoon sun. The window disclosed a fair, soft sky, like blue enamel, and a fringe of chimneys and roofs, resplendent here and there. An endless roar, the eternal trample of the marching city, came mingled with vague cries. At intervals the woman out by the stove moved restlessly and coughed.

Over the transom from the hall-way came two voices.

'Johnnie!'

'Wot!'

'You come right here t' me! I want yehs t' go t' d' store fer me!'

'Ah, ma, send Sally!'

'No, I will not! You come right here!'

'All right, in a minnet!'

'Johnnie!'

'In a minnet, I tell yeh!'

'Johnnie —' There was the sound of a heavy tread, and later a boy squealed. Suddenly the clergyman started to his feet. He rushed forward and peered. The little old woman was dead.

The Third Violet

CHAPTER I.

The engine bellowed its way up the slanting, winding valley. Grey crags, and trees with roots fastened cleverly to the steeps looked down at the struggles of the black monster.

When the train finally released its passengers they burst forth with the enthusiasm of escaping convicts. A great bustle ensued on the platform of the little mountain station. The idlers and philosophers from the village were present to examine the consignment of people from the city. These latter, loaded with bundles and children, thronged at the stage drivers. The stage drivers thronged at the people from the city.

Hawker, with his clothes case, his paint-box, his easel, climbed awkwardly down the steps of the car. The easel swung uncontrolled and knocked against the head of a little boy who was disembarking backward with fine caution. "Hello, little man," said Hawker, "did it hurt?" The child regarded him in silence and with sudden interest, as if Hawker had called his attention to a phenomenon. The young painter was politely waiting until the little boy should conclude his examination, but a voice behind him cried, "Roger, go on down!" A nursemaid was conducting a little girl where she would probably be struck by the other end of the easel. The boy resumed his cautious descent.

The stage drivers made such great noise as a collection that as individuals their identities were lost. With a highly important air, as a man proud of being so busy, the baggageman of the train was thundering trunks at the other employees on the platform. Hawker, prowling through the crowd, heard a voice near his shoulder say, "Do you know where is the stage for Hemlock Inn?" Hawker turned and found a young woman regarding him. A wave of astonishment whirled into his hair, and he turned his eyes quickly for fear that she would think that he had looked at her. He said, "Yes, certainly, I think I can find it." At the same time he was crying to himself: "Wouldn't I like to paint her, though! What a glance-oh, murder! The-the-the distance in her eyes!"

He went fiercely from one driver to another. That obdurate stage for Hemlock Inn must appear at once. Finally he perceived a man who grinned expectantly at him. "Oh," said Hawker, "you drive the stage for Hemlock Inn?" The man admitted it. Hawker said, "Here is the stage." The young woman smiled.

The driver inserted Hawker and his luggage far into the end of the vehicle. He sat there, crooked forward so that his eyes should see the first coming of the girl into the frame of light at the other end of the stage. Presently she appeared there. She was bringing the little boy, the little girl, the nursemaid, and another young woman, who was at once to be known as the mother of the two children. The girl indicated the stage with a small gesture of triumph. When they were all seated uncomfortably in the huge covered vehicle the little boy gave Hawker a glance of recognition. "It hurted then, but it's all right now," he informed him cheerfully.

"Did it?" replied Hawker. "I'm sorry."

"Oh, I didn't mind it much," continued the little boy, swinging his long, red-leather leggings bravely to and fro. "I don't cry when I'm hurt, anyhow." He cast a meaning look at his tiny sister, whose soft lips set defensively.

The driver climbed into his seat, and after a scrutiny of the group in the gloom of the stage he chirped to his horses. They began a slow and thoughtful trotting. Dust streamed out behind the vehicle. In front, the green hills were still and serene in the evening air. A beam of gold struck them aslant, and on the sky was lemon and pink information of the sun's sinking. The driver knew many people along the road, and from time to time he conversed with them in yells.

The two children were opposite Hawker. They sat very correctly mucilaged to their seats, but their large eyes were always upon Hawker, calmly valuing him.

"Do you think it nice to be in the country? I do," said the boy.

"I like it very well," answered Hawker.

"I shall go fishing, and hunting, and everything. Maybe I shall shoot a bears."

"I hope you may."

"Did you ever shoot a bears?"

"No."

"Well, I didn't, too, but maybe I will. Mister Hollanden, he said he'd look around for one. Where I live — —"

"Roger," interrupted the mother from her seat at Hawker's side, "perhaps every one is not interested in your conversation." The boy seemed embarrassed at this interruption, for he leaned back in silence with an apologetic look at Hawker. Presently the stage began to climb the hills, and the two children were obliged to take grip upon the cushions for fear of being precipitated upon the nursemaid.

Fate had arranged it so that Hawker could not observe the girl with the-the-the distance in her eyes without leaning forward and discovering to her his interest. Secretly and impiously he wriggled in his seat, and as the bumping stage swung its passengers this way and that way, he obtained fleeting glances of a cheek, an arm, or a shoulder.

The driver's conversation tone to his passengers was also a yell. "Train was an hour late t'night," he said, addressing the interior. "It'll be nine o'clock before we git t' th' inn, an' it'll be perty dark travellin'."

Hawker waited decently, but at last he said, "Will it?"

"Yes. No moon." He turned to face Hawker, and roared, "You're ol' Jim Hawker's son, hain't yeh?"

"Yes."

"I thort I'd seen yeh b'fore. Live in the city now, don't yeh?"

"Yes."

"Want t' git off at th' cross-road?"

"Yes."

"Come up fer a little stay doorin' th' summer?"

"Yes."

"On'y charge yeh a quarter if yeh git off at cross-road. Useter charge 'em fifty cents, but I ses t' th' ol' man. 'Tain't no use. Goldern 'em, they'll walk ruther'n put up fifty cents.' Yep. On'y a quarter."

In the shadows Hawker's expression seemed assassinlike. He glanced furtively down the stage. She was apparently deep in talk with the mother of the children.

CHAPTER II.

When Hawker pushed at the old gate, it hesitated because of a broken hinge. A dog barked with loud ferocity and came headlong over the grass.

"Hello, Stanley, old man!" cried Hawker. The ardour for battle was instantly smitten from the dog, and his barking swallowed in a gurgle of delight. He was a large orange and white setter, and he partly expressed his emotion by twisting his body into a fantastic curve and then dancing over the ground with his head and his tail very near to each other. He gave vent to little sobs in a wild attempt to vocally describe his gladness. "Well, 'e was a dreat dod," said Hawker, and the setter, overwhelmed, contorted himself wonderfully.

There were lights in the kitchen, and at the first barking of the dog the door had been thrown open. Hawker saw his two sisters shading their eyes and peering down the yellow stream. Presently they shouted, "Here he is!" They flung themselves out and upon him. "Why, Will! why, Will!" they panted.

"We're awful glad to see you!" In a whirlwind of ejaculation and unanswerable interrogation they grappled the clothes case, the paint-box, the easel, and dragged him toward the house.

He saw his old mother seated in a rocking-chair by the table. She had laid aside her paper and was adjusting her glasses as she scanned the darkness. "Hello, mother!" cried Hawker, as he entered. His eyes were bright. The old mother reached her arms to his neck. She murmured soft and half-articulate words. Meanwhile the dog writhed from one to another. He raised his muzzle high to express his delight. He was always fully convinced that he was taking a principal part in this ceremony of welcome and that everybody was heeding him.

"Have you had your supper?" asked the old mother as soon as she recovered herself. The girls clamoured sentences at him. "Pa's out in the barn, Will. What made you so late? He said maybe he'd go up to the cross-roads to see if he could see the stage. Maybe he's gone. What made you so late? And, oh, we got a new buggy!"

The old mother repeated anxiously, "Have you had your supper?"

"No," said Hawker, "but — —"

The three women sprang to their feet. "Well, we'll git you something right away." They bustled about the kitchen and dove from time to time into the cellar. They called to each other in happy voices.

Steps sounded on the line of stones that led from the door toward the barn, and a shout came from the darkness. "Well, William, home again, hey?" Hawker's grey father came stamping genially into the room. "I thought maybe you got lost. I was comin' to hunt you," he said, grinning, as they stood with gripped hands. "What made you so late?"

While Hawker confronted the supper the family sat about and contemplated him with shining eyes. His sisters noted his tie and propounded some questions concerning it. His mother watched to make sure that he should consume a notable quantity of the preserved cherries. "He used to be so fond of 'em when he was little," she said.

"Oh, Will," cried the younger sister, "do you remember Lil' Johnson? Yeh? She's married. Married las' June."

"Is the boy's room all ready, mother?" asked the father.

"We fixed it this mornin'," she said.

"And do you remember Jeff Decker?" shouted the elder sister. "Well, he's dead. Yep. Drowned, pickerel fishin' —poor feller!"

"Well, how are you gitting along, William?" asked the father. "Sell many pictures?"

"An occasional one."

"Saw your illustrations in the May number of Perkinson's." The old man paused for a moment, and then added, quite weakly, "Pretty good."

"How's everything about the place?"

"Oh, just about the same —'bout the same. The colt run away with me last week, but didn't break nothin', though. I was scared, because I had out the new buggy-we got a new buggy-but it didn't break nothin'. I'm goin' to sell the oxen in the fall; I don't want to winter 'em. And then in the spring I'll get a good hoss team. I rented th' back five-acre to John Westfall. I had more'n I could handle with only one hired hand. Times is pickin' up a little, but not much-not much."

"And we got a new school-teacher," said one of the girls.

"Will, you never noticed my new rocker," said the old mother, pointing. "I set it right where I thought you'd see it, and you never took no notice. Ain't it nice? Father bought it at Monticello for my birthday. I thought you'd notice it first thing."

When Hawker had retired for the night, he raised a sash and sat by the window smoking. The odour of the woods and the fields came sweetly to his nostrils. The crickets chanted their hymn of the night. On the black brow of the mountain he could see two long rows of twinkling dots which marked the position of Hemlock Inn.

CHAPTER III.

Hawker had a writing friend named Hollanden. In New York Hollanden had announced his resolution to spend the summer at Hemlock Inn. "I don't like to see the world progressing," he had said; "I shall go to Sullivan County for a time."

In the morning Hawker took his painting equipment, and after manœuvring in the fields until he had proved to himself that he had no desire to go toward the inn, he went toward it. The time was only nine o'clock, and he knew that he could not hope to see Hollanden before eleven, as it was only through rumour that Hollanden was aware that there was a sunrise and an early morning.

Hawker encamped in front of some fields of vivid yellow stubble on which trees made olive shadows, and which was overhung by a china-blue sky and sundry little white clouds. He fiddled away perfunctorily at it. A spectator would have believed, probably, that he was sketching the pines on the hill where shone the red porches of Hemlock Inn.

Finally, a white-flannel young man walked into the landscape. Hawker waved a brush. "Hi, Hollie, get out of the colour-scheme!"

At this cry the white-flannel young man looked down at his feet apprehensively. Finally he came forward grinning. "Why, hello, Hawker, old boy! Glad to find you here." He perched on a boulder and began to study Hawker's canvas and the vivid yellow stubble with the olive shadows. He wheeled his eyes from one to the other. "Say, Hawker," he said suddenly, "why don't you marry Miss Fanhall?"

Hawker had a brush in his mouth, but he took it quickly out, and said, "Marry Miss Fanhall? Who the devil is Miss Fanhall?"

Hollanden clasped both hands about his knee and looked thoughtfully away. "Oh, she's a girl."

"She is?" said Hawker.

"Yes. She came to the inn last night with her sister-in-law and a small tribe of young Fanhalls. There's six of them, I think."

"Two," said Hawker, "a boy and a girl."

"How do you-oh, you must have come up with them. Of course. Why, then you saw her."

"Was that her?" asked Hawker listlessly.

"Was that her?" cried Hollanden, with indignation. "Was that her?"

"Oh!" said Hawker.

Hollanden mused again. "She's got lots of money," he said. "Loads of it. And I think she would be fool enough to have sympathy for you in your work. They are a tremendously wealthy crowd, although they treat it simply. It would be a good thing for you. I believe-yes, I am sure she could be fool enough to have sympathy for you in your work. And now, if you weren't such a hopeless chump — —"

"Oh, shut up, Hollie," said the painter.

For a time Hollanden did as he was bid, but at last he talked again. "Can't think why they came up here. Must be her sister-in-law's health. Something like that. She — —"

"Great heavens," said Hawker, "you speak of nothing else!"

"Well, you saw her, didn't you?" demanded Hollanden. "What can you expect, then, from a man of my sense? You-you old stick-you — —"

"It was quite dark," protested the painter.

"Quite dark," repeated Hollanden, in a wrathful voice. "What if it was?"

"Well, that is bound to make a difference in a man's opinion, you know."

"No, it isn't. It was light down at the railroad station, anyhow. If you had any sand-thunder, but I did get up early this morning! Say, do you play tennis?"

"After a fashion," said Hawker. "Why?"

"Oh, nothing," replied Hollanden sadly. "Only they are wearing me out at the game. I had to get up and play before breakfast this morning with the Worcester girls, and there is a lot more mad players who will be down on me before long. It's a terrible thing to be a tennis player."

"Why, you used to put yourself out so little for people," remarked Hawker.

"Yes, but up there"—Hollanden jerked his thumb in the direction of the inn—"they think I'm so amiable."

"Well, I'll come up and help you out."

"Do," Hollanden laughed; "you and Miss Fanhall can team it against the littlest Worcester girl and me." He regarded the landscape and meditated. Hawker struggled for a grip on the thought of the stubble.

"That colour of hair and eyes always knocks me kerplunk," observed Hollanden softly.

Hawker looked up irascibly. "What colour hair and eyes?" he demanded. "I believe you're crazy."

"What colour hair and eyes?" repeated Hollanden, with a savage gesture. "You've got no more appreciation than a post."

"They are good enough for me," muttered Hawker, turning again to his work. He scowled first at the canvas and then at the stubble. "Seems to me you had best take care of yourself, instead of planning for me," he said.

"Me!" cried Hollanden. "Me! Take care of myself! My boy, I've got a past of sorrow and gloom. I——"

"You're nothing but a kid," said Hawker, glaring at the other man.

"Oh, of course," said Hollanden, wagging his head with midnight wisdom. "Oh, of course."

"Well, Hollie," said Hawker, with sudden affability, "I didn't mean to be unpleasant, but then you are rather ridiculous, you know, sitting up there and howling about the colour of hair and eyes."

"I'm not ridiculous."

"Yes, you are, you know, Hollie."

The writer waved his hand despairingly. "And you rode in the train with her, and in the stage."

"I didn't see her in the train," said Hawker.

"Oh, then you saw her in the stage. Ha-ha, you old thief! I sat up here, and you sat down there and lied." He jumped from his perch and belaboured Hawker's shoulders.

"Stop that!" said the painter.

"Oh, you old thief, you lied to me! You lied——Hold on-bless my life, here she comes now!"

CHAPTER IV.

One day Hollanden said: "There are forty-two people at Hemlock Inn, I think. Fifteen are middle-aged ladies of the most aggressive respectability. They have come here for no discernible purpose save to get where they can see people and be displeased at them. They sit in a large group on that porch and take measurements of character as importantly as if they constituted the jury of heaven. When I arrived at Hemlock Inn I at once cast my eye searchingly about me. Perceiving this assemblage, I cried, 'There they are!' Barely waiting to change my clothes, I made for this formidable body and endeavoured to conciliate it. Almost every day I sit down among them and lie like a machine. Privately I believe they should be hanged, but publicly I glisten with admiration. Do you know, there is one of 'em who I know has not moved from the inn in eight days, and this morning I said to her, 'These long walks in the clear mountain air are doing you a world of good.' And I keep continually saying, 'Your frankness is so charming!' Because of the great law of universal balance, I know that this illustrious corps will believe good of themselves with exactly the same readiness that they will believe ill of others. So I ply them with it. In consequence, the worst they ever say of me is, 'Isn't that Mr. Hollanden a peculiar man?' And you know, my boy, that's not so bad for a literary person." After some thought he added: "Good people, too. Good wives, good mothers, and everything of that kind, you know. But conservative, very conservative. Hate anything radical. Can not endure it. Were that way themselves once, you know. They hit the mark, too, sometimes. Such general volleyings can't fail to hit everything. May the devil fly away with them!"

Hawker regarded the group nervously, and at last propounded a great question: "Say, I wonder where they all are recruited? When you come to think that almost every summer hotel——"

"Certainly," said Hollanden, "almost every summer hotel. I've studied the question, and have nearly established the fact that almost every summer hotel is furnished with a full corps of——"

"To be sure," said Hawker; "and if you search for them in the winter, you can find barely a sign of them, until you examine the boarding houses, and then you observe——"

"Certainly," said Hollanden, "of course. By the way," he added, "you haven't got any obviously loose screws in your character, have you?"

"No," said Hawker, after consideration, "only general poverty-that's all."

"Of course, of course," said Hollanden. "But that's bad. They'll get on to you, sure. Particularly since you come up here to see Miss Fanhall so much."

Hawker glinted his eyes at his friend. "You've got a deuced open way of speaking," he observed.

"Deuced open, is it?" cried Hollanden. "It isn't near so open as your devotion to Miss Fanhall, which is as plain as a red petticoat hung on a hedge."

Hawker's face gloomed, and he said, "Well, it might be plain to you, you infernal cat, but that doesn't prove that all those old hens can see it."

"I tell you that if they look twice at you they can't fail to see it. And it's bad, too. Very bad. What's the matter with you? Haven't you ever been in love before?"

"None of your business," replied Hawker.

Hollanden thought upon this point for a time. "Well," he admitted finally, "that's true in a general way, but I hate to see you managing your affairs so stupidly."

Rage flamed into Hawker's face, and he cried passionately, "I tell you it is none of your business!" He suddenly confronted the other man.

Hollanden surveyed this outburst with a critical eye, and then slapped his knee with emphasis. "You certainly have got it—a million times worse than I thought. Why, you-you-you're heels over head."

"What if I am?" said Hawker, with a gesture of defiance and despair.

Hollanden saw a dramatic situation in the distance, and with a bright smile he studied it. "Say," he exclaimed, "suppose she should not go to the picnic to-morrow? She said this morning she did not know if she could go. Somebody was expected from New York, I think. Wouldn't it break you up, though! Eh?"

"You're so dev'lish clever!" said Hawker, with sullen irony.

Hollanden was still regarding the distant dramatic situation. "And rivals, too! The woods must be crowded with them. A girl like that, you know. And then all that money! Say, your rivals must number enough to make a brigade of militia. Imagine them swarming around! But then it doesn't matter so much," he went on cheerfully; "you've got a good play there. You must appreciate them to her-you understand? —appreciate them kindly, like a man in a watch-tower. You must laugh at them only about once a week, and then very tolerantly-you understand? —and kindly, and-and appreciatively."

"You're a colossal ass, Hollie!" said Hawker. "You——"

"Yes, yes, I know," replied the other peacefully; "a colossal ass. Of course." After looking into the distance again, he murmured: "I'm worried about that picnic. I wish I knew she was going. By heavens, as a matter of fact, she must be made to go!"

"What have you got to do with it?" cried the painter, in another sudden outburst.

"There! there!" said Hollanden, waving his hand. "You fool! Only a spectator, I assure you."

Hawker seemed overcome then with a deep dislike of himself. "Oh, well, you know, Hollie, this sort of thing——" He broke off and gazed at the trees. "This sort of thing——It——"

"How?" asked Hollanden.

"Confound you for a meddling, gabbling idiot!" cried Hawker suddenly.

Hollanden replied, "What did you do with that violet she dropped at the side of the tennis court yesterday?"

CHAPTER V.

Mrs. Fanhall, with the two children, the Worcester girls, and Hollanden, clambered down the rocky path. Miss Fanhall and Hawker had remained on top of the ledge. Hollanden showed much zeal in conducting his contingent to the foot of the falls. Through the trees they could see the cataract, a great shimmering white thing, booming and thundering until all the leaves gently shuddered.

"I wonder where Miss Fanhall and Mr. Hawker have gone?" said the younger Miss Worcester. "I wonder where they've gone?"

"Millicent," said Hollander, looking at her fondly, "you always had such great thought for others."

"Well, I wonder where they've gone?"

At the foot of the falls, where the mist arose in silver clouds and the green water swept into the pool, Miss Worcester, the elder, seated on the moss, exclaimed, "Oh, Mr. Hollanden, what makes all literary men so peculiar?"

"And all that just because I said that I could have made better digestive organs than Providence, if it is true that he made mine," replied Hollanden, with reproach. "Here, Roger," he cried, as he dragged the child away from the brink, "don't fall in there, or you won't be the full-back at Yale in 1907, as you have planned. I'm sure I don't know how to answer you, Miss Worcester. I've inquired of innumerable literary men, and none of 'em know. I may say I have chased that problem for years. I might give you my personal history, and see if that would throw any light on the subject." He looked about him with chin high until his glance had noted the two vague figures at the top of the cliff. "I might give you my personal history——"

Mrs. Fanhall looked at him curiously, and the elder Worcester girl cried, "Oh, do!"

After another scanning of the figures at the top of the cliff, Hollanden established himself in an oratorical pose on a great weather-beaten stone. "Well-you must understand—I started my career-my career, you understand-with a determination to be a prophet, and, although I have ended in being an acrobat, a trained bear of the magazines, and a juggler of comic paragraphs, there was once carved upon my lips a smile which made many people detest me, for it hung before them like a banshee whenever they tried to be satisfied with themselves. I was informed from time to time that I was making no great holes in the universal plan, and I came to know that one person in every two thousand of the people I saw had heard of me, and that four out of five of these had forgotten it. And then one in every two of those who remembered that they had heard of me regarded the fact that I wrote as a great impertinence. I admitted these things, and in defence merely built a maxim that stated that each wise man in this world is concealed amid some twenty thousand fools. If you have eyes for mathematics, this conclusion should interest you. Meanwhile I created a gigantic dignity, and when men saw this dignity and heard that I was a literary man they respected me. I concluded that the simple campaign of existence for me was to delude the populace, or as much of it as would look at me. I did. I do. And now I can make myself quite happy concocting sneers about it. Others may do as they please, but as for me," he concluded ferociously, "I shall never disclose to anybody that an acrobat, a trained bear of the magazines, a juggler of comic paragraphs, is not a priceless pearl of art and philosophy."

"I don't believe a word of it is true," said Miss Worcester.

"What do you expect of autobiography?" demanded Hollanden, with asperity.

"Well, anyhow, Hollie," exclaimed the younger sister, "you didn't explain a thing about how literary men came to be so peculiar, and that's what you started out to do, you know."

"Well," said Hollanden crossly, "you must never expect a man to do what he starts to do, Millicent. And besides," he went on, with the gleam of a sudden idea in his eyes, "literary men are not peculiar, anyhow."

The elder Worcester girl looked angrily at him. "Indeed? Not you, of course, but the others."

"They are all asses," said Hollanden genially.

The elder Worcester girl reflected. "I believe you try to make us think and then just tangle us up purposely!"

The younger Worcester girl reflected. "You are an absurd old thing, you know, Hollie!"

Hollanden climbed offendedly from the great weather-beaten stone. "Well, I shall go and see that the men have not spilled the luncheon while breaking their necks over these rocks. Would you like to have it spread here, Mrs. Fanhall? Never mind consulting the girls. I assure you I shall spend a great deal of energy and temper in bullying them into doing just as they please. Why, when I was in Brussels——"

"Oh, come now, Hollie, you never were in Brussels, you know," said the younger Worcester girl.

"What of that, Millicent?" demanded Hollanden. "This is autobiography."

"Well, I don't care, Hollie. You tell such whoppers."

With a gesture of despair he again started away; whereupon the Worcester girls shouted in chorus, "Oh, I say, Hollie, come back! Don't be angry. We didn't mean to tease you, Hollie-really, we didn't!"

"Well, if you didn't," said Hollanden, "why did you——"

The elder Worcester girl was gazing fixedly at the top of the cliff. "Oh, there they are! I wonder why they don't come down?"

CHAPTER VI.

Stanley, the setter, walked to the edge of the precipice and, looking over at the falls, wagged his tail in friendly greeting. He was braced warily, so that if this howling white animal should reach up a hand for him he could flee in time.

The girl stared dreamily at the red-stained crags that projected from the pines of the hill across the stream. Hawker lazily aimed bits of moss at the oblivious dog and missed him.

"It must be fine to have something to think of beyond just living," said the girl to the crags.

"I suppose you mean art?" said Hawker.

"Yes, of course. It must be finer, at any rate, than the ordinary thing."

He mused for a time. "Yes. It is-it must be," he said. "But then —I'd rather just lie here."

The girl seemed aggrieved. "Oh, no, you wouldn't. You couldn't stop. It's dreadful to talk like that, isn't it? I always thought that painters were ——"

"Of course. They should be. Maybe they are. I don't know. Sometimes I am. But not to-day."

"Well, I should think you ought to be so much more contented than just ordinary people. Now, I——"

"You!" he cried —"you are not 'just ordinary people.'"

"Well, but when I try to recall what I have thought about in my life, I can't remember, you know. That's what I mean."

"You shouldn't talk that way," he told her.

"But why do you insist that life should be so highly absorbing for me?"

"You have everything you wish for," he answered, in a voice of deep gloom.

"Certainly not. I am a woman."

"But ——"

"A woman, to have everything she wishes for, would have to be Providence. There are some things that are not in the world."

"Well, what are they?" he asked of her.

"That's just it," she said, nodding her head, "no one knows. That's what makes the trouble."

"Well, you are very unreasonable."

"What?"

"You are very unreasonable. If I were you-an heiress ——"

The girl flushed and turned upon him angrily.

"Well!" he glowered back at her. "You are, you know. You can't deny it."

She looked at the red-stained crags. At last she said, "You seemed really contemptuous."

"Well, I assure you that I do not feel contemptuous. On the contrary, I am filled with admiration. Thank Heaven, I am a man of the world. Whenever I meet heiresses I always have the deepest admiration." As he said this he wore a brave hang-dog expression. The girl surveyed him coldly from his chin to his eyebrows. "You have a handsome audacity, too."

He lay back in the long grass and contemplated the clouds.

"You should have been a Chinese soldier of fortune," she said.

He threw another little clod at Stanley and struck him on the head.

"You are the most scientifically unbearable person in the world," she said.

Stanley came back to see his master and to assure himself that the clump on the head was not intended as a sign of serious displeasure. Hawker took the dog's long ears and tried to tie them into a knot.

"And I don't see why you so delight in making people detest you," she continued.

Having failed to make a knot of the dog's ears, Hawker leaned back and surveyed his failure admiringly. "Well, I don't," he said.

"You do."

"No, I don't."

"Yes, you do. You just say the most terrible things as if you positively enjoyed saying them."

"Well, what did I say, now? What did I say?"

"Why, you said that you always had the most extraordinary admiration for heiresses whenever you met them."

"Well, what's wrong with that sentiment?" he said. "You can't find fault with that!"

"It is utterly detestable."

"Not at all," he answered sullenly. "I consider it a tribute—a graceful tribute."

Miss Fanhall arose and went forward to the edge of the cliff. She became absorbed in the falls. Far below her a bough of a hemlock drooped to the water, and each swirling, mad wave caught it and made it nod-nod-nod. Her back was half turned toward Hawker.

After a time Stanley, the dog, discovered some ants scurrying in the moss, and he at once began to watch them and wag his tail.

"Isn't it curious," observed Hawker, "how an animal as large as a dog will sometimes be so entertained by the very smallest things?"

Stanley pawed gently at the moss, and then thrust his head forward to see what the ants did under the circumstances.

"In the hunting season," continued Hawker, having waited a moment, "this dog knows nothing on earth but his master and the partridges. He is lost to all other sound and movement. He moves through the woods like a steel machine. And when he scents the bird-ah, it is beautiful! Shouldn't you like to see him then?"

Some of the ants had perhaps made war-like motions, and Stanley was pretending that this was a reason for excitement. He reared aback, and made grumbling noises in his throat.

After another pause Hawker went on: "And now see the precious old fool! He is deeply interested in the movements of the little ants, and as childish and ridiculous over them as if they were highly important. —There, you old blockhead, let them alone!"

Stanley could not be induced to end his investigations, and he told his master that the ants were the most thrilling and dramatic animals of his experience.

"Oh, by the way," said Hawker at last, as his glance caught upon the crags across the river, "did you ever hear the legend of those rocks yonder? Over there where I am pointing? Where I'm pointing? Did you ever hear it? What? Yes? No? Well, I shall tell it to you." He settled comfortably in the long grass.

CHAPTER VII.

"Once upon a time there was a beautiful Indian maiden, of course. And she was, of course, beloved by a youth from another tribe who was very handsome and stalwart and a mighty hunter, of course. But the maiden's father was, of course, a stern old chief, and when the question of his daughter's marriage came up, he, of course, declared that the maiden should be wedded only to a warrior of her tribe. And, of course, when the young man heard this he said that in such case he would, of course, fling himself headlong from that crag. The old chief was, of course, obdurate, and, of course, the youth did, of course, as he had said. And, of course, the maiden wept." After Hawker had waited for some time, he said with severity, "You seem to have no great appreciation of folklore."

The girl suddenly bent her head. "Listen," she said, "they're calling. Don't you hear Hollie's voice?"

They went to another place, and, looking down over the shimmering tree-tops, they saw Hollanden waving his arms. "It's luncheon," said Hawker. "Look how frantic he is!"

The path required that Hawker should assist the girl very often. His eyes shone at her whenever he held forth his hand to help her down a blessed steep place. She seemed rather pensive. The route to luncheon was very long. Suddenly he took a seat on an old tree, and said: "Oh, I don't know why it is, whenever I'm with you, I —I have no wits, nor good nature, nor anything. It's the worst luck!"

He had left her standing on a boulder, where she was provisionally helpless. "Hurry!" she said; "they're waiting for us."

Stanley, the setter, had been sliding down cautiously behind them. He now stood wagging his tail and waiting for the way to be cleared.

Hawker leaned his head on his hand and pondered dejectedly. "It's the worst luck!"

"Hurry!" she said; "they're waiting for us."

At luncheon the girl was for the most part silent. Hawker was superhumanly amiable. Somehow he gained the impression that they all quite fancied him, and it followed that being clever was very easy. Hollanden listened, and approved him with a benign countenance.

There was a little boat fastened to the willows at the edge of the black pool. After the spread, Hollanden navigated various parties around to where they could hear the great hollow roar of the falls beating against the sheer rocks. Stanley swam after sticks at the request of little Roger.

Once Hollanden succeeded in making the others so engrossed in being amused that Hawker and Miss Fanhall were left alone staring at the white bubbles that floated solemnly on the black water. After Hawker had stared at them a sufficient time, he said, "Well, you are an heiress, you know."

In return she chose to smile radiantly. Turning toward him, she said, "If you will be good now-always-perhaps I'll forgive you."

They drove home in the sombre shadows of the hills, with Stanley padding along under the wagon. The Worcester girls tried to induce Hollanden to sing, and in consequence there was quarrelling until the blinking lights of the inn appeared above them as if a great lantern hung there.

Hollanden conveyed his friend some distance on the way home from the inn to the farm. "Good time at the picnic?" said the writer.

"Yes."

"Picnics are mainly places where the jam gets on the dead leaves, and from thence to your trousers. But this was a good little picnic." He glanced at Hawker. "But you don't look as if you had such a swell time."

Hawker waved his hand tragically. "Yes-no —I don't know."

"What's wrong with you?" asked Hollanden.

"I tell you what it is, Hollie," said the painter darkly, "whenever I'm with that girl I'm such a blockhead. I'm not so stupid, Hollie. You know I'm not. But when I'm with her I can't be clever to save my life."

Hollanden pulled contentedly at his pipe. "Maybe she don't notice it."

"Notice it!" muttered Hawker, scornfully; "of course she notices it. In conversation with her, I tell you, I am as interesting as an iron dog." His voice changed as he cried, "I don't know why it is. I don't know why it is."

Blowing a huge cloud of smoke into the air, Hollanden studied it thoughtfully. "Hits some fellows that way," he said. "And, of course, it must be deuced annoying. Strange thing, but now, under those circumstances, I'm very glib. Very glib, I assure you."

"I don't care what you are," answered Hawker. "All those confounded affairs of yours-they were not——"

"No," said Hollanden, stolidly puffing, "of course not. I understand that. But, look here, Billie," he added, with sudden brightness, "maybe you are not a blockhead, after all. You are on the inside, you know, and you can't see from there. Besides, you can't tell what a woman will think. You can't tell what a woman will think."

"No," said Hawker, grimly, "and you suppose that is my only chance?"

"Oh, don't be such a chump!" said Hollanden, in a tone of vast exasperation.

They strode for some time in silence. The mystic pines swaying over the narrow road made talk sibilantly to the wind. Stanley, the setter, took it upon himself to discover some menacing presence in the woods. He walked on his toes and with his eyes glinting sideways. He swore half under his breath.

"And work, too," burst out Hawker, at last. "I came up here this season to work, and I haven't done a thing that ought not be shot at."

"Don't you find that your love sets fire to your genius?" asked Hollanden gravely.

"No, I'm hanged if I do."

Hollanden sighed then with an air of relief. "I was afraid that a popular impression was true," he said, "but it's all right. You would rather sit still and moon, wouldn't you?"

"Moon-blast you! I couldn't moon to save my life."

"Oh, well, I didn't mean moon exactly."

CHAPTER VIII.

The blue night of the lake was embroidered with black tree forms. Silver drops sprinkled from the lifted oars. Somewhere in the gloom of the shore there was a dog, who from time to time raised his sad voice to the stars.

"But still, the life of the studios——" began the girl.

Hawker scoffed. "There were six of us. Mainly we smoked. Sometimes we played hearts and at other times poker-on credit, you know-credit. And when we had the materials and got something to do, we worked. Did you ever see these beautiful red and green designs that surround the common tomato can?"

"Yes."

"Well," he said proudly, "I have made them. Whenever you come upon tomatoes, remember that they might once have been encompassed in my design. When first I came back from Paris I began to paint, but nobody wanted me to paint. Later, I got into green corn and asparagus——"

"Truly?"

"Yes, indeed. It is true."

"But still, the life of the studios——"

"There were six of us. Fate ordained that only one in the crowd could have money at one time. The other five lived off him and despised themselves. We despised ourselves five times as long as we had admiration."

"And was this just because you had no money?"

"It was because we had no money in New York," said Hawker.

"Well, after a while something happened——"

"Oh, no, it didn't. Something impended always, but it never happened."

"In a case like that one's own people must be such a blessing. The sympathy——"

"One's own people!" said Hawker.

"Yes," she said, "one's own people and more intimate friends. The appreciation——"

"'The appreciation!'" said Hawker. "Yes, indeed!"

He seemed so ill-tempered that she became silent. The boat floated through the shadows of the trees and out to where the water was like a blue crystal. The dog on the shore thrashed about in the reeds and waded in the shallows, mourning his unhappy state in an occasional cry. Hawker stood up and sternly shouted. Thereafter silence was among the reeds. The moon slipped sharply through the little clouds.

The girl said, "I liked that last picture of yours."

"What?"

"At the last exhibition, you know, you had that one with the cows-and things-in the snow-and-and a haystack."

"Yes," he said, "of course. Did you like it, really? I thought it about my best. And you really remembered it? Oh," he cried, "Hollanden perhaps recalled it to you."

"Why, no," she said. "I remembered it, of course."

"Well, what made you remember it?" he demanded, as if he had cause to be indignant.

"Why—I just remembered it because—I liked it, and because-well, the people with me said-said it was about the best thing in the exhibit, and they talked about it a good deal. And then I remember that Hollie had spoken of you, and then I—I——"

"Never mind," he said. After a moment, he added, "The confounded picture was no good, anyhow!"

The girl started. "What makes you speak so of it? It was good. Of course, I don't know—I can't talk about pictures, but," she said in distress, "everybody said it was fine."

"It wasn't any good," he persisted, with dogged shakes of the head.

From off in the darkness they heard the sound of Hollanden's oars splashing in the water. Sometimes there was squealing by the Worcester girls, and at other times loud arguments on points of navigation.

"Oh," said the girl suddenly, "Mr. Oglethorpe is coming to-morrow!"

"Mr. Oglethorpe?" said Hawker. "Is he?"

"Yes." She gazed off at the water.

"He's an old friend of ours. He is always so good, and Roger and little Helen simply adore him. He was my brother's chum in college, and they were quite inseparable until Herbert's death. He always brings me violets. But I know you will like him."

"I shall expect to," said Hawker.

"I'm so glad he is coming. What time does that morning stage get here?"

"About eleven," said Hawker.

"He wrote that he would come then. I hope he won't disappoint us."

"Undoubtedly he will be here," said Hawker.

The wind swept from the ridge top, where some great bare pines stood in the moonlight. A loon called in its strange, unearthly note from the lakeshore. As Hawker turned the boat toward the dock, the flashing rays from the boat fell upon the head of the girl in the rear seat, and he rowed very slowly.

The girl was looking away somewhere with a mystic, shining glance. She leaned her chin in her hand. Hawker, facing her, merely paddled subconsciously. He seemed greatly impressed and expectant.

At last she spoke very slowly. "I wish I knew Mr. Oglethorpe was not going to disappoint us."

Hawker said, "Why, no, I imagine not."

"Well, he is a trifle uncertain in matters of time. The children-and all of us-shall be anxious. I know you will like him."

CHAPTER IX.

"Eh?" said Hollanden. "Oglethorpe? Oglethorpe? Why, he's that friend of the Fanhalls! Yes, of course, I know him! Deuced good fellow, too! What about him?"

"Oh, nothing, only he's coming here to-morrow," answered Hawker. "What kind of a fellow did you say he was?"

"Deuced good fellow! What are you so——Say, by the nine mad blacksmiths of Donawhiroo, he's your rival! Why, of course! Glory, but I must be thick-headed to-night!"

Hawker said, "Where's your tobacco?"

"Yonder, in that jar. Got a pipe?"

"Yes. How do you know he's my rival?"

"Know it? Why, hasn't he been——Say, this is getting thrilling!" Hollanden sprang to his feet and, filling a pipe, flung himself into the chair and began to rock himself madly to and fro. He puffed clouds of smoke.

Hawker stood with his face in shadow. At last he said, in tones of deep weariness, "Well, I think I'd better be going home and turning in."

"Hold on!" Hollanden exclaimed, turning his eyes from a prolonged stare at the ceiling, "don't go yet! Why, man, this is just the time when——Say, who would ever think of Jem Oglethorpe's turning up to harrie you! Just at this time, too!"

"Oh," cried Hawker suddenly, filled with rage, "you remind me of an accursed duffer! Why can't you tell me something about the man, instead of sitting there and gibbering those crazy things at the ceiling?"

"By the piper——"

"Oh, shut up! Tell me something about Oglethorpe, can't you? I want to hear about him. Quit all that other business!"

"Why, Jem Oglethorpe, he-why, say, he's one of the best fellows going. If he were only an ass! If he were only an ass, now, you could feel easy in your mind. But he isn't. No, indeed. Why, blast him, there isn't a man that knows him who doesn't like Jem Oglethorpe! Excepting the chumps!"

The window of the little room was open, and the voices of the pines could be heard as they sang of their long sorrow. Hawker pulled a chair close and stared out into the darkness. The people on the porch of the inn were frequently calling, "Good-night! Good-night!"

Hawker said, "And of course he's got train loads of money?"

"You bet he has! He can pave streets with it. Lordie, but this is a situation!"

A heavy scowl settled upon Hawker's brow, and he kicked at the dressing case. "Say, Hollie, look here! Sometimes I think you regard me as a bug and like to see me wriggle. But——"

"Oh, don't be a fool!" said Hollanden, glaring through the smoke. "Under the circumstances, you are privileged to rave and ramp around like a wounded lunatic, but for heaven's sake don't swoop down on me like that! Especially when I'm —when I'm doing all I can for you."

"Doing all you can for me! Nobody asked you to. You talk as if I were an infant."

"There! That's right! Blaze up like a fire balloon just because I said that, will you? A man in your condition-why, confound you, you are an infant!"

Hawker seemed again overwhelmed in a great dislike of himself. "Oh, well, of course, Hollie, it——" He waved his hand. "A man feels like-like——"

"Certainly he does," said Hollanden. "That's all right, old man."

"And look now, Hollie, here's this Oglethorpe——"

"May the devil fly away with him!"

"Well, here he is, coming along when I thought maybe-after a while, you know—I might stand some show. And you are acquainted with him, so give me a line on him."

"Well, I should advise you to——"

"Blow your advice! I want to hear about Oglethorpe."

"Well, in the first place, he is a rattling good fellow, as I told you before, and this is what makes it so ——"

"Oh, hang what it makes it! Go on."

"He is a rattling good fellow and he has stacks of money. Of course, in this case his having money doesn't affect the situation much. Miss Fanhall ——"

"Say, can you keep to the thread of the story, you infernal literary man!"

"Well, he's popular. He don't talk money-ever. And if he's wicked, he's not sufficiently proud of it to be perpetually describing his sins. And then he is not so hideously brilliant, either. That's great credit to a man in these days. And then he-well, take it altogether, I should say Jem Oglethorpe was a smashing good fellow."

"I wonder how long he is going to stay?" murmured Hawker.

During this conversation his pipe had often died out. It was out at this time. He lit another match. Hollanden had watched the fingers of his friend as the match was scratched. "You're nervous, Billie," he said.

Hawker straightened in his chair. "No, I'm not."

"I saw your fingers tremble when you lit that match."

"Oh, you lie!"

Hollanden mused again. "He's popular with women, too," he said ultimately; "and often a woman will like a man and hunt his scalp just because she knows other women like him and want his scalp."

"Yes, but not ——"

"Hold on! You were going to say that she was not like other women, weren't you?"

"Not exactly that, but ——"

"Well, we will have all that understood."

After a period of silence Hawker said, "I must be going."

As the painter walked toward the door Hollanden cried to him: "Heavens! Of all pictures of a weary pilgrim!" His voice was very compassionate.

Hawker wheeled, and an oath spun through the smoke clouds.

CHAPTER X.

"Where's Mr. Hawker this morning?" asked the younger Miss Worcester. "I thought he was coming up to play tennis?"

"I don't know. Confound him! I don't see why he didn't come," said Hollanden, looking across the shining valley. He frowned questioningly at the landscape. "I wonder where in the mischief he is?"

The Worcester girls began also to stare at the great gleaming stretch of green and gold. "Didn't he tell you he was coming?" they demanded.

"He didn't say a word about it," answered Hollanden. "I supposed, of course, he was coming. We will have to postpone the *mêlée*."

Later he met Miss Fanhall. "You look as if you were going for a walk?"

"I am," she said, swinging her parasol. "To meet the stage. Have you seen Mr. Hawker to-day?"

"No," he said. "He is not coming up this morning. He is in a great fret about that field of stubble, and I suppose he is down there sketching the life out of it. These artists-they take such a fiendish interest in their work. I dare say we won't see much of him until he has finished it. Where did you say you were going to walk?"

"To meet the stage."

"Oh, well, I won't have to play tennis for an hour, and if you insist———"

"Of course."

As they strolled slowly in the shade of the trees Hollanden began, "Isn't that Hawker an ill-bred old thing?"

"No, he is not." Then after a time she said, "Why?"

"Oh, he gets so absorbed in a beastly smudge of paint that I really suppose he cares nothing for anything else in the world. Men who are really artists —I don't believe they are capable of deep human affections. So much of them is occupied by art. There's not much left over, you see."

"I don't believe it at all," she exclaimed.

"You don't, eh?" cried Hollanden scornfully. "Well, let me tell you, young woman, there is a great deal of truth in it. Now, there's Hawker-as good a fellow as ever lived, too, in a way, and yet he's an artist. Why, look how he treats-look how he treats that poor setter dog!"

"Why, he's as kind to him as he can be," she declared.

"And I tell you he is not!" cried Hollanden.

"He is, Hollie. You-you are unspeakable when you get in these moods."

"There-that's just you in an argument. I'm not in a mood at all. Now, look-the dog loves him with simple, unquestioning devotion that fairly brings tears to one's eyes———"

"Yes," she said.

"And he-why, he's as cold and stern———"

"He isn't. He isn't, Holly. You are awf'ly unfair."

"No, I'm not. I am simply a liberal observer. And Hawker, with his people, too," he went on darkly; "you can't tell-you don't know anything about it-but I tell you that what I have seen proves my assertion that the artistic mind has no space left for the human affections. And as for the dog———"

"I thought you were his friend, Hollie?"

"Whose?"

"No, not the dog's. And yet you-really, Hollie, there is something unnatural in you. You are so stupidly keen in looking at people that you do not possess common loyalty to your friends. It is because you are a writer, I suppose. That has to explain so many things. Some of your traits are very disagreeable."

"There! there!" plaintively cried Hollanden. "This is only about the treatment of a dog, mind you. Goodness, what an oration!"

"It wasn't about the treatment of a dog. It was about your treatment of your friends."

"Well," he said sagely, "it only goes to show that there is nothing impersonal in the mind of a woman. I undertook to discuss broadly ——

"Oh, Hollie!"

"At any rate, it was rather below you to do such scoffing at me."

"Well, I didn't mean-not all of it, Hollie."

"Well, I didn't mean what I said about the dog and all that, either."

"You didn't?" She turned toward him, large-eyed.

"No. Not a single word of it."

"Well, what did you say it for, then?" she demanded indignantly.

"I said it," answered Hollanden placidly, "just to tease you." He looked abstractedly up to the trees.

Presently she said slowly, "Just to tease me?"

At this time Hollanden wore an unmistakable air of having a desire to turn up his coat collar. "Oh, come now——" he began nervously.

"George Hollanden," said the voice at his shoulder, "you are not only disagreeable, but you are hopelessly ridiculous. I—I wish you would never speak to me again!"

"Oh, come now, Grace, don't—don't—— Look! There's the stage coming, isn't it?"

"No, the stage is not coming. I wish—I wish you were at the bottom of the sea, George Hollanden. And-and Mr. Hawker, too. There!"

"Oh, bless my soul! And all about an infernal dog," wailed Hollanden. "Look! Honest, now, there's the stage. See it? See it?"

"It isn't there at all," she said.

Gradually he seemed to recover his courage. "What made you so tremendously angry? I don't see why."

After consideration, she said decisively, "Well, because."

"That's why I teased you," he rejoined.

"Well, because-because ——"

"Go on," he told her finally. "You are doing very well." He waited patiently.

"Well," she said, "it is dreadful to defend somebody so-so excitedly, and then have it turned out just a tease. I don't know what he would think."

"Who would think?"

"Why-he."

"What could he think? Now, what could he think? Why," said Hollanden, waxing eloquent, "he couldn't under any circumstances think-think anything at all. Now, could he?"

She made no reply.

"Could he?"

She was apparently reflecting.

"Under any circumstances," persisted Hollanden, "he couldn't think anything at all. Now, could he?"

"No," she said.

"Well, why are you angry at me, then?"

CHAPTER XI.

"John," said the old mother, from the profound mufflings of the pillow and quilts.

"What?" said the old man. He was tugging at his right boot, and his tone was very irascible.

"I think William's changed a good deal."

"Well, what if he has?" replied the father, in another burst of ill-temper. He was then tugging at his left boot.

"Yes, I'm afraid he's changed a good deal," said the muffled voice from the bed. "He's got a good many fine friends, now, John-folks what put on a good many airs; and he don't care for his home like he did."

"Oh, well, I don't guess he's changed very much," said the old man cheerfully. He was now free of both boots.

She raised herself on an elbow and looked out with a troubled face. "John, I think he likes that girl."

"What girl?" said he.

"What girl? Why, that awful handsome girl you see around-of course."

"Do you think he likes 'er?"

"I'm afraid so—I'm afraid so," murmured the mother mournfully.

"Oh, well," said the old man, without alarm, or grief, or pleasure in his tone.

He turned the lamp's wick very low and carried the lamp to the head of the stairs, where he perched it on the step. When he returned he said, "She's mighty good-look-in'!"

"Well, that ain't everything," she snapped. "How do we know she ain't proud, and selfish, and-everything?"

"How do you know she is?" returned the old man.

"And she may just be leading him on."

"Do him good, then," said he, with impregnable serenity. "Next time he'll know better."

"Well, I'm worried about it," she said, as she sank back on the pillow again. "I think William's changed a good deal. He don't seem to care about-us-like he did."

"Oh, go to sleep!" said the father drowsily.

She was silent for a time, and then she said, "John?"

"What?"

"Do you think I better speak to him about that girl?"

"No."

She grew silent again, but at last she demanded, "Why not?"

"'Cause it's none of your business. Go to sleep, will you?" And presently he did, but the old mother lay blinking wild-eyed into the darkness.

In the morning Hawker did not appear at the early breakfast, eaten when the blue glow of dawn shed its ghostly lights upon the valley. The old mother placed various dishes on the back part of the stove. At ten o'clock he came downstairs. His mother was sweeping busily in the parlour at the time, but she saw him and ran to the back part of the stove. She slid the various dishes on to the table. "Did you oversleep?" she asked.

"Yes. I don't feel very well this morning," he said. He pulled his chair close to the table and sat there staring.

She renewed her sweeping in the parlour. When she returned he sat still staring undeviatingly at nothing.

"Why don't you eat your breakfast?" she said anxiously.

"I tell you, mother, I don't feel very well this morning," he answered quite sharply.

"Well," she said meekly, "drink some coffee and you'll feel better."

Afterward he took his painting machinery and left the house. His younger sister was at the well. She looked at him with a little smile and a little sneer. "Going up to the inn this morning?" she said.

"I don't see how that concerns you, Mary?" he rejoined, with dignity.

"Oh, my!" she said airily.

"But since you are so interested, I don't mind telling you that I'm not going up to the inn this morning."

His sister fixed him with her eye. "She ain't mad at you, is she, Will?"

"I don't know what you mean, Mary." He glared hatefully at her and strode away.

Stanley saw him going through the fields and leaped a fence jubilantly in pursuit. In a wood the light sifted through the foliage and burned with a peculiar reddish lustre on the masses of dead leaves. He frowned at it for a while from different points. Presently he erected his easel and began to paint. After a a time he threw down his brush and swore. Stanley, who had been solemnly staring at the scene as if he too was sketching it, looked up in surprise.

In wandering aimlessly through the fields and the forest Hawker once found himself near the road to Hemlock Inn. He shied away from it quickly as if it were a great snake.

While most of the family were at supper, Mary, the younger sister, came charging breathlessly into the kitchen. "Ma-sister," she cried, "I know why-why Will didn't go to the inn to-day. There's another fellow come. Another fellow."

"Who? Where? What do you mean?" exclaimed her mother and her sister.

"Why, another fellow up at the inn," she shouted, triumphant in her information. "Another fellow come up on the stage this morning. And she went out driving with him this afternoon."

"Well," exclaimed her mother and her sister.

"Yep. And he's an awful good-looking fellow, too. And she-oh, my-she looked as if she thought the world and all of him."

"Well," exclaimed her mother and her sister again.

"Sho!" said the old man. "You wimen leave William alone and quit your gabbling."

The three women made a combined assault upon him. "Well, we ain't a-hurting him, are we, pa? You needn't be so snifty. I guess we ain't a-hurting him much."

"Well," said the old man. And to this argument he added, "Sho!"

They kept him out of the subsequent consultations.

CHAPTER XII.

The next day, as little Roger was going toward the tennis court, a large orange and white setter ran effusively from around the corner of the inn and greeted him. Miss Fanhall, the Worcester girls, Hollanden, and Oglethorpe faced to the front like soldiers. Hollanden cried, "Why, Billie Hawker must be coming!" Hawker at that moment appeared, coming toward them with a smile which was not overconfident.

Little Roger went off to perform some festivities of his own on the brown carpet under a clump of pines. The dog, to join him, felt obliged to circle widely about the tennis court. He was much afraid of this tennis court, with its tiny round things that sometimes hit him. When near it he usually slunk along at a little sheep trot and with an eye of wariness upon it.

At her first opportunity the younger Worcester girl said, "You didn't come up yesterday, Mr. Hawker."

Hollanden seemed to think that Miss Fanhall turned her head as if she wished to hear the explanation of the painter's absence, so he engaged her in swift and fierce conversation.

"No," said Hawker. "I was resolved to finish a sketch of a stubble field which I began a good many days ago. You see, I was going to do such a great lot of work this summer, and I've done hardly a thing. I really ought to compel myself to do some, you know."

"There," said Hollanden, with a victorious nod, "just what I told you!"

"You didn't tell us anything of the kind," retorted the Worcester girls with one voice.

A middle-aged woman came upon the porch of the inn, and after scanning for a moment the group at the tennis court she hurriedly withdrew. Presently she appeared again, accompanied by five more middle-aged women. "You see," she said to the others, "it is as I said. He has come back."

The five surveyed the group at the tennis court, and then said: "So he has. I knew he would. Well, I declare! Did you ever?" Their voices were pitched at low keys and they moved with care, but their smiles were broad and full of a strange glee.

"I wonder how he feels," said one in subtle ecstasy.

Another laughed. "You know how you would feel, my dear, if you were him and saw yourself suddenly cut out by a man who was so hopelessly superior to you. Why, Oglethorpe's a thousand times better looking. And then think of his wealth and social position!"

One whispered dramatically, "They say he never came up here at all yesterday."

Another replied: "No more he did. That's what we've been talking about. Stayed down at the farm all day, poor fellow!"

"Do you really think she cares for Oglethorpe?"

"Care for him? Why, of course she does. Why, when they came up the path yesterday morning I never saw a girl's face so bright. I asked my husband how much of the Chambers Street Bank stock Oglethorpe owned, and he said that if Oglethorpe took his money out there wouldn't be enough left to buy a pie."

The youngest woman in the corps said: "Well, I don't care. I think it is too bad. I don't see anything so much in that Mr. Oglethorpe."

The others at once patronized her. "Oh, you don't, my dear? Well, let me tell you that bank stock waves in the air like a banner. You would see it if you were her."

"Well, she don't have to care for his money."

"Oh, no, of course she don't have to. But they are just the ones that do, my dear. They are just the ones that do."

"Well, it's a shame."

"Oh, of course it's a shame."

The woman who had assembled the corps said to one at her side: "Oh, the commonest kind of people, my dear, the commonest kind. The father is a regular farmer, you know. He drives oxen. Such language! You can really hear him miles away bellowing at those oxen. And the girls are shy, half-wild things–oh, you have no idea! I saw one of them yesterday when we were out driving. She dodged as we came along, for I suppose she was ashamed of her frock, poor child! And the mother-well, I wish you could see her! A little, old, dried-up thing. We saw her carrying a pail of water from the well, and, oh, she bent and staggered dreadfully, poor thing!"

"And the gate to their front yard, it has a broken hinge, you know. Of course, that's an awful bad sign. When people let their front gate hang on one hinge you know what that means."

After gazing again at the group at the court, the youngest member of the corps said, "Well, he's a good tennis player anyhow."

The others smiled indulgently. "Oh, yes, my dear, he's a good tennis player."

CHAPTER XIII.

One day Hollanden said, in greeting, to Hawker, "Well, he's gone."

"Who?" asked Hawker.

"Why, Oglethorpe, of course. Who did you think I meant?"

"How did I know?" said Hawker angrily.

"Well," retorted Hollanden, "your chief interest was in his movements, I thought."

"Why, of course not, hang you! Why should I be interested in his movements?"

"Well, you weren't, then. Does that suit you?"

After a period of silence Hawker asked, "What did he-what made him go?"

"Who?"

"Why-Oglethorpe."

"How was I to know you meant him? Well, he went because some important business affairs in New York demanded it, he said; but he is coming back again in a week. They had rather a late interview on the porch last evening."

"Indeed," said Hawker stiffly.

"Yes, and he went away this morning looking particularly elated. Aren't you glad?"

"I don't see how it concerns me," said Hawker, with still greater stiffness.

In a walk to the lake that afternoon Hawker and Miss Fanhall found themselves side by side and silent. The girl contemplated the distant purple hills as if Hawker were not at her side and silent. Hawker frowned at the roadway. Stanley, the setter, scouted the fields in a genial gallop.

At last the girl turned to him. "Seems to me," she said, "seems to me you are dreadfully quiet this afternoon."

"I am thinking about my wretched field of stubble," he answered, still frowning.

Her parasol swung about until the girl was looking up at his inscrutable profile. "Is it, then, so important that you haven't time to talk to me?" she asked with an air of what might have been timidity.

A smile swept the scowl from his face. "No, indeed," he said, instantly; "nothing is so important as that."

She seemed aggrieved then. "Hum-you didn't look so," she told him.

"Well, I didn't mean to look any other way," he said contritely. "You know what a bear I am sometimes. Hollanden says it is a fixed scowl from trying to see uproarious pinks, yellows, and blues."

A little brook, a brawling, ruffianly little brook, swaggered from side to side down the glade, swirling in white leaps over the great dark rocks and shouting challenge to the hillsides. Hollanden and the Worcester girls had halted in a place of ferns and wet moss. Their voices could be heard quarrelling above the clamour of the stream. Stanley, the setter, had soused himself in a pool and then gone and rolled in the dust of the road. He blissfully lolled there, with his coat now resembling an old door mat.

"Don't you think Jem is a wonderfully good fellow?" said the girl to the painter.

"Why, yes, of course," said Hawker.

"Well, he is," she retorted, suddenly defensive.

"Of course," he repeated loudly.

She said, "Well, I don't think you like him as well as I like him."

"Certainly not," said Hawker.

"You don't?" She looked at him in a kind of astonishment.

"Certainly not," said Hawker again, and very irritably. "How in the wide world do you expect me to like him as well as you like him?"

"I don't mean as well," she explained.

"Oh!" said Hawker.

"But I mean you don't like him the way I do at all-the way I expected you to like him. I thought men of a certain pattern always fancied their kind of men wherever they met them, don't you know? And I was so sure you and Jem would be friends."

"Oh!" cried Hawker. Presently he added, "But he isn't my kind of a man at all."

"He is. Jem is one of the best fellows in the world."

Again Hawker cried "Oh!"

They paused and looked down at the brook. Stanley sprawled panting in the dust and watched them. Hawker leaned against a hemlock. He sighed and frowned, and then finally coughed with great resolution. "I suppose, of course, that I am unjust to him. I care for you myself, you understand, and so it becomes ——"

He paused for a moment because he heard a rustling of her skirts as if she had moved suddenly. Then he continued: "And so it becomes difficult for me to be fair to him. I am not able to see him with a true eye." He bitterly addressed the trees on the opposite side of the glen. "Oh, I care for you, of course. You might have expected it." He turned from the trees and strode toward the roadway. The uninformed and disreputable Stanley arose and wagged his tail.

As if the girl had cried out at a calamity, Hawker said again, "Well, you might have expected it."

CHAPTER XIV.

At the lake, Hollanden went pickerel fishing, lost his hook in a gaunt, gray stump, and earned much distinction by his skill in discovering words to express his emotion without resorting to the list ordinarily used in such cases. The younger Miss Worcester ruined a new pair of boots, and Stanley sat on the bank and howled the song of the forsaken. At the conclusion of the festivities Hollanden said, "Billie, you ought to take the boat back."

"Why had I? You borrowed it."

"Well, I borrowed it and it was a lot of trouble, and now you ought to take it back."

Ultimately Hawker said, "Oh, let's both go!"

On this journey Hawker made a long speech to his friend, and at the end of it he exclaimed: "And now do you think she cares so much for Oglethorpe? Why, she as good as told me that he was only a very great friend."

Hollanden wagged his head dubiously. "What a woman says doesn't amount to shucks. It's the way she says it-that's what counts. Besides," he cried in a brilliant afterthought, "she wouldn't tell you, anyhow, you fool!"

"You're an encouraging brute," said Hawker, with a rueful grin.

Later the Worcester girls seized upon Hollanden and piled him high with ferns and mosses. They dragged the long gray lichens from the chins of venerable pines, and ran with them to Hollanden, and dashed them into his arms. "Oh, hurry up, Hollie!" they cried, because with his great load he frequently fell behind them in the march. He once positively refused to carry these things another step. Some distance farther on the road he positively refused to carry this old truck another step. When almost to the inn he positively refused to carry this senseless rubbish another step. The Worcester girls had such vivid contempt for his expressed unwillingness that they neglected to tell him of any appreciation they might have had for his noble struggle.

As Hawker and Miss Fanhall proceeded slowly they heard a voice ringing through the foliage: "Whoa! Haw! Git-ap, blast you! Haw! Haw, drat your hides! Will you haw? Git-ap! Gee! Whoa!"

Hawker said, "The others are a good ways ahead. Hadn't we better hurry a little?"

The girl obediently mended her pace.

"Whoa! haw! git-ap!" shouted the voice in the distance. "Git over there, Red, git over! Gee! Git-ap!" And these cries pursued the man and the maid.

At last Hawker said, "That's my father."

"Where?" she asked, looking bewildered.

"Back there, driving those oxen."

The voice shouted: "Whoa! Git-ap! Gee! Red, git over there now, will you? I'll trim the shin off'n you in a minute. Whoa! Haw! Haw! Whoa! Git-ap!"

Hawker repeated, "Yes, that's my father."

"Oh, is it?" she said. "Let's wait for him."

"All right," said Hawker sullenly.

Presently a team of oxen waddled into view around the curve of the road. They swung their heads slowly from side to side, bent under the yoke, and looked out at the world with their great eyes, in which was a mystic note of their humble, submissive, toilsome lives. An old wagon creaked after them, and erect upon it was the tall and tattered figure of the farmer swinging his whip and yelling: "Whoa! Haw there! Git-ap!" The lash flicked and flew over the broad backs of the animals.

"Hello, father!" said Hawker.

"Whoa! Back! Whoa! Why, hello, William, what you doing here?"

"Oh, just taking a walk. Miss Fanhall, this is my father. Father——"

"How d' you do?" The old man balanced himself with care and then raised his straw hat from his head with a quick gesture and with what was perhaps a slightly apologetic air, as if he feared that he was rather over-doing the ceremonial part.

The girl later became very intent upon the oxen. "Aren't they nice old things?" she said, as she stood looking into the faces of the team. "But what makes their eyes so very sad?"

"I dunno," said the old man.

She was apparently unable to resist a desire to pat the nose of the nearest ox, and for that purpose she stretched forth a cautious hand. But the ox moved restlessly at the moment and the girl put her hand apprehensively behind herself and backed away. The old man on the wagon grinned. "They won't hurt you," he told her.

"They won't bite, will they?" she asked, casting a glance of inquiry at the old man and then turning her eyes again upon the fascinating animals.

"No," said the old man, still grinning, "just as gentle as kittens."

She approached them circuitously. "Sure?" she said.

"Sure," replied the old man. He climbed from the wagon and came to the heads of the oxen. With him as an ally, she finally succeeded in patting the nose of the nearest ox. "Aren't they solemn, kind old fellows? Don't you get to think a great deal of them?"

"Well, they're kind of aggravating beasts sometimes," he said. "But they're a good yoke — a good yoke. They can haul with anything in this region."

"It doesn't make them so terribly tired, does it?" she said hopefully. "They are such strong animals."

"No-o-o," he said. "I dunno. I never thought much about it."

With their heads close together they became so absorbed in their conversation that they seemed to forget the painter. He sat on a log and watched them.

Ultimately the girl said, "Won't you give us a ride?"

"Sure," said the old man. "Come on, and I'll help you up." He assisted her very painstakingly to the old board that usually served him as a seat, and he clambered to a place beside her. "Come on, William," he called. The painter climbed into the wagon and stood behind his father, putting his hand on the old man's shoulder to preserve his balance.

"Which is the near ox?" asked the girl with a serious frown.

"Git-ap! Haw! That one there," said the old man.

"And this one is the off ox?"

"Yep."

"Well, suppose you sat here where I do; would this one be the near ox and that one the off ox, then?"

"Nope. Be just same."

"Then the near ox isn't always the nearest one to a person, at all? That ox there is always the near ox?"

"Yep, always. 'Cause when you drive 'em a-foot you always walk on the left side."

"Well, I never knew that before."

After studying them in silence for a while, she said, "Do you think they are happy?"

"I dunno," said the old man. "I never thought." As the wagon creaked on they gravely discussed this problem, contemplating profoundly the backs of the animals. Hawker gazed in silence at the meditating two before him. Under the wagon Stanley, the setter, walked slowly, wagging his tail in placid contentment and ruminating upon his experiences.

At last the old man said cheerfully, "Shall I take you around by the inn?"

Hawker started and seemed to wince at the question. Perhaps he was about to interrupt, but the girl cried: "Oh, will you? Take us right to the door? Oh, that will be awfully good of you!"

"Why," began Hawker, "you don't want-you don't want to ride to the inn on an-on an ox wagon, do you?"

"Why, of course I do," she retorted, directing a withering glance at him.

"Well——" he protested.

"Let 'er be, William," interrupted the old man. "Let 'er do what she wants to. I guess everybody in th' world ain't even got an ox wagon to ride in. Have they?"

"No, indeed," she returned, while withering Hawker again.

"Gee! Gee! Whoa! Haw! Git-ap! Haw! Whoa! Back!"

After these two attacks Hawker became silent.

"Gee! Gee! Gee there, blast—s'cuse me. Gee! Whoa! Git-ap!"

All the boarders of the inn were upon its porches waiting for the dinner gong. There was a surge toward the railing as a middle-aged woman passed the word along her middle-aged friends that Miss Fanhall, accompanied by Mr. Hawker, had arrived on the ox cart of Mr. Hawker's father.

"Whoa! Ha! Git-ap!" said the old man in more subdued tones. "Whoa there, Red! Whoa, now! Wh-o-a!"

Hawker helped the girl to alight, and she paused for a moment conversing with the old man about the oxen. Then she ran smiling up the steps to meet the Worcester girls.

"Oh, such a lovely time! Those dear old oxen-you should have been with us!"

CHAPTER XV.

"Oh, Miss Fanhall!"

"What is it, Mrs. Truscot?"

"That was a great prank of yours last night, my dear. We all enjoyed the joke so much."

"Prank?"

"Yes, your riding on the ox cart with that old farmer and that young Mr. What's-his-name, you know. We all thought it delicious. Ah, my dear, after all-don't be offended-if we had your people's wealth and position we might do that sort of unconventional thing, too; but, ah, my dear, we can't, we can't! Isn't the young painter a charming man?"

Out on the porch Hollanden was haranguing his friends. He heard a step and glanced over his shoulder to see who was about to interrupt him. He suddenly ceased his oration, and said, "Hello! what's the matter with Grace?" The heads turned promptly.

As the girl came toward them it could be seen that her cheeks were very pink and her eyes were flashing general wrath and defiance.

The Worcester girls burst into eager interrogation. "Oh, nothing!" she replied at first, but later she added in an undertone, "That wretched Mrs. Truscot ——"

"What did she say?" whispered the younger Worcester girl.

"Why, she said-oh, nothing!"

Both Hollanden and Hawker were industriously reflecting.

Later in the morning Hawker said privately to the girl, "I know what Mrs. Truscot talked to you about."

She turned upon him belligerently. "You do?"

"Yes," he answered with meekness. "It was undoubtedly some reference to your ride upon the ox wagon."

She hesitated a moment, and then said, "Well?"

With still greater meekness he said, "I am very sorry."

"Are you, indeed?" she inquired loftily. "Sorry for what? Sorry that I rode upon your father's ox wagon, or sorry that Mrs. Truscot was rude to me about it?"

"Well, in some ways it was my fault."

"Was it? I suppose you intend to apologize for your father's owning an ox wagon, don't you?"

"No, but ——"

"Well, I am going to ride in the ox wagon whenever I choose. Your father, I know, will always be glad to have me. And if it so shocks you, there is not the slightest necessity of your coming with us."

They glowered at each other, and he said, "You have twisted the question with the usual ability of your sex."

She pondered as if seeking some particularly destructive retort. She ended by saying bluntly, "Did you know that we were going home next week?"

A flush came suddenly to his face. "No. Going home? Who? You?"

"Why, of course." And then with an indolent air she continued, "I meant to have told you before this, but somehow it quite escaped me."

He stammered, "Are-are you, honestly?"

She nodded. "Why, of course. Can't stay here forever, you know."

They were then silent for a long time.

At last Hawker said, "Do you remember what I told you yesterday?"

"No. What was it?"

He cried indignantly, "You know very well what I told you!"

"I do not."

"No," he sneered, "of course not! You never take the trouble to remember such things. Of course not! Of course not!"

"You are a very ridiculous person," she vouchsafed, after eying him coldly.

He arose abruptly. "I believe I am. By heavens, I believe I am!" he cried in a fury.

She laughed. "You are more ridiculous now than I have yet seen you."

After a pause he said magnificently, "Well, Miss Fanhall, you will doubtless find Mr. Hollanden's conversation to have a much greater interest than that of such a ridiculous person."

Hollanden approached them with the blithesome step of an untroubled man. "Hello, you two people, why don't you-oh-ahem! Hold on, Billie, where are you going?"

"I——" began Hawker.

"Oh, Hollie," cried the girl impetuously, "do tell me how to do that slam thing, you know. I've tried it so often, but I don't believe I hold my racket right. And you do it so beautifully."

"Oh, that," said Hollanden. "It's not so very difficult. I'll show it to you. You don't want to know this minute, do you?"

"Yes," she answered.

"Well, come over to the court, then. Come ahead, Billie!"

"No," said Hawker, without looking at his friend, "I can't this morning, Hollie. I've got to go to work. Good-bye!" He comprehended them both in a swift bow and stalked away.

Hollanden turned quickly to the girl. "What was the matter with Billie? What was he grinding his teeth for? What was the matter with him?"

"Why, nothing-was there?" she asked in surprise.

"Why, he was grinding his teeth until he sounded like a stone crusher," said Hollanden in a severe tone. "What was the matter with him?"

"How should I know?" she retorted.

"You've been saying something to him."

"I! I didn't say a thing."

"Yes, you did."

"Hollie, don't be absurd."

Hollanden debated with himself for a time, and then observed, "Oh, well, I always said he was an ugly-tempered fellow——"

The girl flashed him a little glance.

"And now I am sure of it-as ugly-tempered a fellow as ever lived."

"I believe you," said the girl. Then she added: "All men are. I declare, I think you to be the most incomprehensible creatures. One never knows what to expect of you. And you explode and go into rages and make yourselves utterly detestable over the most trivial matters and at the most unexpected times. You are all mad, I think."

"I!" cried Hollanden wildly. "What in the mischief have I done?"

CHAPTER XVI.

"Look here," said Hollanden, at length, "I thought you were so wonderfully anxious to learn that stroke?"

"Well, I am," she said.

"Come on, then." As they walked toward the tennis court he seemed to be plunged into mournful thought. In his eyes was a singular expression, which perhaps denoted the woe of the optimist pushed suddenly from its height. He sighed. "Oh, well, I suppose all women, even the best of them, are that way."

"What way?" she said.

"My dear child," he answered, in a benevolent manner, "you have disappointed me, because I have discovered that you resemble the rest of your sex."

"Ah!" she remarked, maintaining a noncommittal attitude.

"Yes," continued Hollanden, with a sad but kindly smile, "even you, Grace, were not above fooling with the affections of a poor country swain, until he don't know his ear from the tooth he had pulled two years ago."

She laughed. "He would be furious if he heard you call him a country swain."

"Who would?" said Hollanden.

"Why, the country swain, of course," she rejoined.

Hollanden seemed plunged in mournful reflection again. "Well, it's a shame, Grace, anyhow," he observed, wagging his head dolefully. "It's a howling, wicked shame."

"Hollie, you have no brains at all," she said, "despite your opinion."

"No," he replied ironically, "not a bit."

"Well, you haven't, you know, Hollie."

"At any rate," he said in an angry voice, "I have some comprehension and sympathy for the feelings of others."

"Have you?" she asked. "How do you mean, Hollie? Do you mean you have feeling for them in their various sorrows? Or do you mean that you understand their minds?"

Hollanden ponderously began, "There have been people who have not questioned my ability to — —"

"Oh, then, you mean that you both feel for them in their sorrows and comprehend the machinery of their minds. Well, let me tell you that in regard to the last thing you are wrong. You know nothing of anyone's mind. You know less about human nature than anybody I have met."

Hollanden looked at her in artless astonishment. He said, "Now, I wonder what made you say that?" This interrogation did not seem to be addressed to her, but was evidently a statement to himself of a problem. He meditated for some moments. Eventually he said, "I suppose you mean that I do not understand you?"

"Why do you suppose I mean that?"

"That's what a person usually means when he-or she-charges another with not understanding the entire world."

"Well, at any rate, it is not what I mean at all," she said. "I mean that you habitually blunder about other people's affairs, in the belief, I imagine, that you are a great philanthropist, when you are only making an extraordinary exhibition of yourself."

"The dev— —" began Hollanden. Afterward he said, "Now, I wonder what in blue thunder you mean this time?"

"Mean this time? My meaning is very plain, Hollie. I supposed the words were clear enough."

"Yes," he said thoughtfully, "your words were clear enough, but then you were of course referring back to some event, or series of events, in which I had the singular ill fortune to displease you. Maybe you don't know yourself, and spoke only from the emotion generated by the event, or series of events, in which, as I have said, I had the singular ill fortune to displease you."

"How awf'ly clever!" she said.

"But I can't recall the event, or series of events, at all," he continued, musing with a scholarly air and disregarding her mockery. "I can't remember a thing about it. To be sure, it might have been that time when ——"

"I think it very stupid of you to hunt for a meaning when I believe I made everything so perfectly clear," she said wrathfully.

"Well, you yourself might not be aware of what you really meant," he answered sagely. "Women often do that sort of thing, you know. Women often speak from motives which, if brought face to face with them, they wouldn't be able to distinguish from any other thing which they had never before seen."

"Hollie, if there is a disgusting person in the world it is he who pretends to know so much concerning a woman's mind."

"Well, that's because they who know, or pretend to know, so much about a woman's mind are invariably satirical, you understand," said Hollanden cheerfully.

A dog ran frantically across the lawn, his nose high in the air and his countenance expressing vast perturbation and alarm. "Why, Billie forgot to whistle for his dog when he started for home," said Hollanden. "Come here, old man! Well, 'e was a nice dog!" The girl also gave invitation, but the setter would not heed them. He spun wildly about the lawn until he seemed to strike his master's trail, and then, with his nose near to the ground, went down the road at an eager gallop. They stood and watched him.

"Stanley's a nice dog," said Hollanden.

"Indeed he is!" replied the girl fervently.

Presently Hollanden remarked: "Well, don't let's fight any more, particularly since we can't decide what we're fighting about. I can't discover the reason, and you don't know it, so ——"

"I do know it. I told you very plainly."

"Well, all right. Now, this is the way to work that slam: You give the ball a sort of a lift—see! —underhanded and with your arm crooked and stiff. Here, you smash this other ball into the net. Hi! Look out! If you hit it that way you'll knock it over the hotel. Let the ball drop nearer to the ground. Oh, heavens, not on the ground! Well, it's hard to do it from the serve, anyhow. I'll go over to the other court and bat you some easy ones."

Afterward, when they were going toward the inn, the girl suddenly began to laugh.

"What are you giggling at?" said Hollanden.

"I was thinking how furious he would be if he heard you call him a country swain," she rejoined.

"Who?" asked Hollanden.

CHAPTER XVII.

Oglethorpe contended that the men who made the most money from books were the best authors. Hollanden contended that they were the worst. Oglethorpe said that such a question should be left to the people. Hollanden said that the people habitually made wrong decisions on questions that were left to them. "That is the most odiously aristocratic belief," said Oglethorpe.

"No," said Hollanden, "I like the people. But, considered generally, they are a collection of ingenious blockheads."

"But they read your books," said Oglethorpe, grinning.

"That is through a mistake," replied Hollanden.

As the discussion grew in size it incited the close attention of the Worcester girls, but Miss Fanhall did not seem to hear it. Hawker, too, was staring into the darkness with a gloomy and preoccupied air.

"Are you sorry that this is your last evening at Hemlock Inn?" said the painter at last, in a low tone.

"Why, yes-certainly," said the girl.

Under the sloping porch of the inn the vague orange light from the parlours drifted to the black wall of the night.

"I shall miss you," said the painter.

"Oh, I dare say," said the girl.

Hollanden was lecturing at length and wonderfully. In the mystic spaces of the night the pines could be heard in their weird monotone, as they softly smote branch and branch, as if moving in some solemn and sorrowful dance.

"This has been quite the most delightful summer of my experience," said the painter.

"I have found it very pleasant," said the girl.

From time to time Hawker glanced furtively at Oglethorpe, Hollanden, and the Worcester girl. This glance expressed no desire for their well-being.

"I shall miss you," he said to the girl again. His manner was rather desperate. She made no reply, and, after leaning toward her, he subsided with an air of defeat.

Eventually he remarked: "It will be very lonely here again. I dare say I shall return to New York myself in a few weeks."

"I hope you will call," she said.

"I shall be delighted," he answered stiffly, and with a dissatisfied look at her.

"Oh, Mr. Hawker," cried the younger Worcester girl, suddenly emerging from the cloud of argument which Hollanden and Oglethorpe kept in the air, "won't it be sad to lose Grace? Indeed, I don't know what we shall do. Sha'n't we miss her dreadfully?"

"Yes," said Hawker, "we shall of course miss her dreadfully."

"Yes, won't it be frightful?" said the elder Worcester girl. "I can't imagine what we will do without her. And Hollie is only going to spend ten more days. Oh, dear! mamma, I believe, will insist on staying the entire summer. It was papa's orders, you know, and I really think she is going to obey them. He said he wanted her to have one period of rest at any rate. She is such a busy woman in town, you know."

"Here," said Hollanden, wheeling to them suddenly, "you all look as if you were badgering Hawker, and he looks badgered. What are you saying to him?"

"Why," answered the younger Worcester girl, "we were only saying to him how lonely it would be without Grace."

"Oh!" said Hollanden.

As the evening grew old, the mother of the Worcester girls joined the group. This was a sign that the girls were not to long delay the vanishing time. She sat almost upon the edge of her chair, as if she expected to be called upon at any moment to arise and bow "Good-night," and she repaid Hollanden's eloquent attention with the placid and absent-minded smiles of the chaperon who waits.

Once the younger Worcester girl shrugged her shoulders and turned to say, "Mamma, you make me nervous!" Her mother merely smiled in a still more placid and absent-minded manner.

Oglethorpe arose to drag his chair nearer to the railing, and when he stood the Worcester mother moved and looked around expectantly, but Oglethorpe took seat again. Hawker kept an anxious eye upon her.

Presently Miss Fanhall arose.

"Why, you are not going in already, are you?" said Hawker and Hollanden and Oglethorpe. The Worcester mother moved toward the door followed by her daughters, who were protesting in muffled tones. Hollanden pitched violently upon Oglethorpe. "Well, at any rate ——" he said. He picked the thread of a past argument with great agility.

Hawker said to the girl, "I —I —I shall miss you dreadfully."

She turned to look at him and smiled. "Shall you?" she said in a low voice.

"Yes," he said. Thereafter he stood before her awkwardly and in silence. She scrutinized the boards of the floor. Suddenly she drew a violet from a cluster of them upon her gown and thrust it out to him as she turned toward the approaching Oglethorpe.

"Good-night, Mr. Hawker," said the latter. "I am very glad to have met you, I'm sure. Hope to see you in town. Good-night."

He stood near when the girl said to Hawker: "Good-bye. You have given us such a charming summer. We shall be delighted to see you in town. You must come some time when the children can see you, too. Good-bye."

"Good-bye," replied Hawker, eagerly and feverishly, trying to interpret the inscrutable feminine face before him. "I shall come at my first opportunity."

"Good-bye."

"Good-bye."

Down at the farmhouse, in the black quiet of the night, a dog lay curled on the door-mat. Of a sudden the tail of this dog began to thump, thump, on the boards. It began as a lazy movement, but it passed into a state of gentle enthusiasm, and then into one of curiously loud and joyful celebration. At last the gate clicked. The dog uncurled, and went to the edge of the steps to greet his master. He gave adoring, tremulous welcome with his clear eyes shining in the darkness. "Well, Stan, old boy," said Hawker, stooping to stroke the dog's head. After his master had entered the house the dog went forward and sniffed at something that lay on the top step. Apparently it did not interest him greatly, for he returned in a moment to the door-mat.

But he was again obliged to uncurl himself, for his master came out of the house with a lighted lamp and made search of the door-mat, the steps, and the walk, swearing meanwhile in an undertone. The dog wagged his tail and sleepily watched this ceremony. When his master had again entered the house the dog went forward and sniffed at the top step, but the thing that had lain there was gone.

CHAPTER XVIII.

It was evident at breakfast that Hawker's sisters had achieved information. "What's the matter with you this morning?" asked one. "You look as if you hadn't slep' well."

"There is nothing the matter with me," he rejoined, looking glumly at his plate.

"Well, you look kind of broke up."

"How I look is of no consequence. I tell you there is nothing the matter with me."

"Oh!" said his sister. She exchanged meaning glances with the other feminine members of the family. Presently the other sister observed, "I heard she was going home to-day."

"Who?" said Hawker, with a challenge in his tone.

"Why, that New York girl-Miss What's-her-name," replied the sister, with an undaunted smile.

"Did you, indeed? Well, perhaps she is."

"Oh, you don't know for sure, I s'pose."

Hawker arose from the table, and, taking his hat, went away.

"Mary!" said the mother, in the sepulchral tone of belated but conscientious reproof.

"Well, I don't care. He needn't be so grand. I didn't go to tease him. I don't care."

"Well, you ought to care," said the old man suddenly. "There's no sense in you wimen folks pestering the boy all the time. Let him alone with his own business, can't you?"

"Well, ain't we leaving him alone?"

"No, you ain't —'cept when he ain't here. I don't wonder the boy grabs his hat and skips out when you git to going."

"Well, what did we say to him now? Tell us what we said to him that was so dreadful."

"Aw, thunder an' lightnin'!" cried the old man with a sudden great snarl. They seemed to know by this ejaculation that he had emerged in an instant from that place where man endures, and they ended the discussion. The old man continued his breakfast.

During his walk that morning Hawker visited a certain cascade, a certain lake, and some roads, paths, groves, nooks. Later in the day he made a sketch, choosing an hour when the atmosphere was of a dark blue, like powder smoke in the shade of trees, and the western sky was burning in strips of red. He painted with a wild face, like a man who is killing.

After supper he and his father strolled under the apple boughs in the orchard and smoked. Once he gestured wearily. "Oh, I guess I'll go back to New York in a few days."

"Um," replied his father calmly. "All right, William."

Several days later Hawker accosted his father in the barnyard. "I suppose you think sometimes I don't care so much about you and the folks and the old place any more; but I do."

"Um," said the old man. "When you goin'?"

"Where?" asked Hawker, flushing.

"Back to New York."

"Why—I hadn't thought much about—— Oh, next week, I guess."

"Well, do as you like, William. You know how glad me an' mother and the girls are to have you come home with us whenever you can come. You know that. But you must do as you think best, and if you ought to go back to New York now, William, why-do as you think best."

"Well, my work——" said Hawker.

From time to time the mother made wondering speech to the sisters. "How much nicer William is now! He's just as good as he can be. There for a while he was so cross and out of sorts. I don't see what could have come over him. But now he's just as good as he can be."

Hollanden told him, "Come up to the inn more, you fool."

"I was up there yesterday."

"Yesterday! What of that? I've seen the time when the farm couldn't hold you for two hours during the day."

"Go to blazes!"

"Millicent got a letter from Grace Fanhall the other day."

"That so?"

"Yes, she did. Grace wrote —— Say, does that shadow look pure purple to you?"

"Certainly it does, or I wouldn't paint it so, duffer. What did she write?"

"Well, if that shadow is pure purple my eyes are liars. It looks a kind of slate colour to me. Lord! if what you fellows say in your pictures is true, the whole earth must be blazing and burning and glowing and ——"

Hawker went into a rage. "Oh, you don't know anything about colour, Hollie. For heaven's sake, shut up, or I'll smash you with the easel."

"Well, I was going to tell you what Grace wrote in her letter. She said ——"

"Go on."

"Gimme time, can't you? She said that town was stupid, and that she wished she was back at Hemlock Inn."

"Oh! Is that all?"

"Is that all? I wonder what you expected? Well, and she asked to be recalled to you."

"Yes? Thanks."

"And that's all. 'Gad, for such a devoted man as you were, your enthusiasm and interest is stupendous."

The father said to the mother, "Well, William's going back to New York next week."

"Is he? Why, he ain't said nothing to me about it."

"Well, he is, anyhow."

"I declare! What do you s'pose he's going back before September for, John?"

"How do I know?"

"Well, it's funny, John. I bet —I bet he's going back so's he can see that girl."

"He says it's his work."

CHAPTER XIX.

Wrinkles had been peering into the little dry-goods box that acted as a cupboard. "There are only two eggs and half a loaf of bread left," he announced brutally.

"Heavens!" said Warwickson from where he lay smoking on the bed. He spoke in a dismal voice. This tone, it is said, had earned him his popular name of Great Grief.

From different points of the compass Wrinkles looked at the little cupboard with a tremendous scowl, as if he intended thus to frighten the eggs into becoming more than two, and the bread into becoming a loaf. "Plague take it!" he exclaimed.

"Oh, shut up, Wrinkles!" said Grief from the bed.

Wrinkles sat down with an air austere and virtuous. "Well, what are we going to do?" he demanded of the others.

Grief, after swearing, said: "There, that's right! Now you're happy. The holy office of the inquisition! Blast your buttons, Wrinkles, you always try to keep us from starving peacefully! It is two hours before dinner, anyhow, and——"

"Well, but what are you going to do?" persisted Wrinkles.

Pennoyer, with his head afar down, had been busily scratching at a pen-and-ink drawing. He looked up from his board to utter a plaintive optimism. "The Monthly Amazement will pay me to-morrow. They ought to. I've waited over three months now. I'm going down there to-morrow, and perhaps I'll get it."

His friends listened with airs of tolerance. "Oh, no doubt, Penny, old man." But at last Wrinkles giggled pityingly. Over on the bed Grief croaked deep down in his throat. Nothing was said for a long time thereafter.

The crash of the New York streets came faintly to this room.

Occasionally one could hear the tramp of feet in the intricate corridors of the begrimed building which squatted, slumbering, and old, between two exalted commercial structures which would have had to bend afar down to perceive it. The northward march of the city's progress had happened not to overturn this aged structure, and it huddled there, lost and forgotten, while the cloud-veering towers strode on.

Meanwhile the first shadows of dusk came in at the blurred windows of the room. Pennoyer threw down his pen and tossed his drawing over on the wonderful heap of stuff that hid the table. "It's too dark to work." He lit a pipe and walked about, stretching his shoulders like a man whose labour was valuable.

When the dusk came fully the youths grew apparently sad. The solemnity of the gloom seemed to make them ponder. "Light the gas, Wrinkles," said Grief fretfully.

The flood of orange light showed clearly the dull walls lined with sketches, the tousled bed in one corner, the masses of boxes and trunks in another, a little dead stove, and the wonderful table. Moreover, there were wine-coloured draperies flung in some places, and on a shelf, high up, there were plaster casts, with dust in the creases. A long stove-pipe wandered off in the wrong direction and then turned impulsively toward a hole in the wall. There were some elaborate cobwebs on the ceiling.

"Well, let's eat," said Grief.

"Eat," said Wrinkles, with a jeer; "I told you there was only two eggs and a little bread left. How are we going to eat?"

Again brought face to face with this problem, and at the hour for dinner, Pennoyer and Grief thought profoundly. "Thunder and turf!" Grief finally announced as the result of his deliberations.

"Well, if Billie Hawker was only home——" began Pennoyer.

"But he isn't," objected Wrinkles, "and that settles that."

Grief and Pennoyer thought more. Ultimately Grief said, "Oh, well, let's eat what we've got." The others at once agreed to this suggestion, as if it had been in their minds.

Later there came a quick step in the passage and a confident little thunder upon the door. Wrinkles arranging the tin pail on the gas stove, Pennoyer engaged in slicing the bread, and Great Grief affixing the rubber tube to the gas stove, yelled, "Come in!"

The door opened, and Miss Florinda O'Connor, the model, dashed into the room like a gale of obstreperous autumn leaves.

"Why, hello, Splutter!" they cried.

"Oh, boys, I've come to dine with you."

It was like a squall striking a fleet of yachts.

Grief spoke first. "Yes, you have?" he said incredulously.

"Why, certainly I have. What's the matter?"

They grinned. "Well, old lady," responded Grief, "you've hit us at the wrong time. We are, in fact, all out of everything. No dinner, to mention, and, what's more, we haven't got a sou."

"What? Again?" cried Florinda.

"Yes, again. You'd better dine home to-night."

"But I'll—I'll stake you," said the girl eagerly. "Oh, you poor old idiots! It's a shame! Say, I'll stake you."

"Certainly not," said Pennoyer sternly.

"What are you talking about, Splutter?" demanded Wrinkles in an angry voice.

"No, that won't go down," said Grief, in a resolute yet wistful tone.

Florinda divested herself of her hat, jacket, and gloves, and put them where she pleased. "Got coffee, haven't you? Well, I'm not going to stir a step. You're a fine lot of birds!" she added bitterly, "You've all pulled me out of a whole lot of scrape-oh, any number of times-and now you're broke, you go acting like a set of dudes."

Great Grief had fixed the coffee to boil on the gas stove, but he had to watch it closely, for the rubber tube was short, and a chair was balanced on a trunk, and two bundles of kindling was balanced on the chair, and the gas stove was balanced on the kindling. Coffee-making was here accounted a feat.

Pennoyer dropped a piece of bread to the floor. "There! I'll have to go shy one."

Wrinkles sat playing serenades on his guitar and staring with a frown at the table, as if he was applying some strange method of clearing it of its litter.

Florinda assaulted Great Grief. "Here, that's not the way to make coffee!"

"What ain't?"

"Why, the way you're making it. You want to take——" She explained some way to him which he couldn't understand.

"For heaven's sake, Wrinkles, tackle that table! Don't sit there like a music box," said Pennoyer, grappling the eggs and starting for the gas stove.

Later, as they sat around the board, Wrinkles said with satisfaction, "Well, the coffee's good, anyhow."

"'Tis good," said Florinda, "but it isn't made right. I'll show you how, Penny. You first——"

"Oh, dry up, Splutter," said Grief. "Here, take an egg."

"I don't like eggs," said Florinda.

"Take an egg," said the three hosts menacingly.

"I tell you I don't like eggs."

"Take-an-egg!" they said again.

"Oh, well," said Florinda, "I'll take one, then; but you needn't act like such a set of dudes-and, oh, maybe you didn't have much lunch. I had such a daisy lunch! Up at Pontiac's studio. He's got a lovely studio."

The three looked to be oppressed. Grief said sullenly, "I saw some of his things over in Stencil's gallery, and they're rotten."

"Yes-rotten," said Pennoyer.

"Rotten," said Grief.

"Oh, well," retorted Florinda, "if a man has a swell studio and dresses-oh, sort of like a Willie, you know, you fellows sit here like owls in a cave and say rotten-rotten-rotten. You're away off. Pontiac's landscapes — —"

"Landscapes be blowed! Put any of his work alongside of Billie Hawker's and see how it looks."

"Oh, well, Billie Hawker's," said Florinda. "Oh, well."

At the mention of Hawker's name they had all turned to scan her face.

CHAPTER XX.

"He wrote that he was coming home this week," said Pennoyer.

"Did he?" asked Florinda indifferently.

"Yes. Aren't you glad?"

They were still watching her face.

"Yes, of course I'm glad. Why shouldn't I be glad?" cried the girl with defiance.

They grinned.

"Oh, certainly. Billie Hawker is a good fellow, Splutter. You have a particular right to be glad."

"You people make me tired," Florinda retorted. "Billie Hawker doesn't give a rap about me, and he never tried to make out that he did."

"No," said Grief. "But that isn't saying that you don't care a rap about Billie Hawker. Ah, Florinda!"

It seemed that the girl's throat suffered a slight contraction. "Well, and what if I do?" she demanded finally.

"Have a cigarette?" answered Grief.

Florinda took a cigarette, lit it, and, perching herself on a divan, which was secretly a coal box, she smoked fiercely.

"What if I do?" she again demanded. "It's better than liking one of you dubs, anyhow."

"Oh, Splutter, you poor little outspoken kid!" said Wrinkle in a sad voice.

Grief searched among the pipes until he found the best one. "Yes, Splutter, don't you know that when you are so frank you defy every law of your sex, and wild eyes will take your trail?"

"Oh, you talk through your hat," replied Florinda. "Billie don't care whether I like him or whether I don't. And if he should hear me now, he wouldn't be glad or give a hang, either way. I know that." The girl paused and looked at the row of plaster casts. "Still, you needn't be throwing it at me all the time."

"We didn't," said Wrinkles indignantly. "You threw it at yourself."

"Well," continued Florinda, "it's better than liking one of you dubs, anyhow. He makes money and——"

"There," said Grief, "now you've hit it! Bedad, you've reached a point in eulogy where if you move again you will have to go backward."

"Of course I don't care anything about a fellow's having money——"

"No, indeed you don't, Splutter," said Pennoyer.

"But then, you know what I mean. A fellow isn't a man and doesn't stand up straight unless he has some money. And Billie Hawker makes enough so that you feel that nobody could walk over him, don't you know? And there isn't anything jay about him, either. He's a thoroughbred, don't you know?"

After reflection, Pennoyer said, "It's pretty hard on the rest of us, Splutter."

"Well, of course I like him, but-but——"

"What?" said Pennoyer.

"I don't know," said Florinda.

Purple Sanderson lived in this room, but he usually dined out. At a certain time in his life, before he came to be a great artist, he had learned the gas-fitter's trade, and when his opinions were not identical with the opinions of the art managers of the greater number of New York publications he went to see a friend who was a plumber, and the opinions of this man he was thereafter said to respect. He frequented a very neat restaurant on Twenty-third Street. It was known that on Saturday nights Wrinkles, Grief, and Pennoyer frequently quarreled with him.

As Florinda ceased speaking Purple entered. "Hello, there, Splutter!" As he was neatly hanging up his coat, he said to the others, "Well, the rent will be due in four days."

"Will it?" asked Pennoyer, astounded.

"Certainly it will," responded Purple, with the air of a superior financial man.

"My soul!" said Wrinkles.

"Oh, shut up, Purple!" said Grief. "You make me weary, coming around here with your chin about rent. I was just getting happy."

"Well, how are we going to pay it? That's the point," said Sanderson.

Wrinkles sank deeper in his chair and played despondently on his guitar. Grief cast a look of rage at Sanderson, and then stared at the wall. Pennoyer said, "Well, we might borrow it from Billie Hawker."

Florinda laughed then.

"Oh," continued Pennoyer hastily, "if those Amazement people pay me when they said they would I'll have the money."

"So you will," said Grief. "You will have money to burn. Did the Amazement people ever pay you when they said they would? You are wonderfully important all of a sudden, it seems to me. You talk like an artist."

Wrinkles, too, smiled at Pennoyer. "The Eminent Magazine people wanted Penny to hire models and make a try for them, too. It would only cost him a stack of blues. By the time he has invested all his money he hasn't got, and the rent is three weeks overdue, he will be able to tell the landlord to wait seven months until the Monday morning after the day of publication. Go ahead, Penny."

After a period of silence, Sanderson, in an obstinate manner, said, "Well, what's to be done? The rent has got to be paid."

Wrinkles played more sad music. Grief frowned deeper. Pennoyer was evidently searching his mind for a plan.

Florinda took the cigarette from between her lips that she might grin with greater freedom.

"We might throw Purple out," said Grief, with an inspired air. "That would stop all this discussion."

"You!" said Sanderson furiously. "You can't keep serious a minute. If you didn't have us to take care of you, you wouldn't even know when they threw you out into the street."

"Wouldn't I?" said Grief.

"Well, look here," interposed Florinda, "I'm going home unless you can be more interesting. I am dead sorry about the rent, but I can't help it, and ——"

"Here! Sit down! Hold on, Splutter!" they shouted. Grief turned to Sanderson: "Purple, you shut up!"

Florinda curled again on the divan and lit another cigarette. The talk waged about the names of other and more successful painters, whose work they usually pronounced "rotten."

CHAPTER XXI.

Pennoyer, coming home one morning with two gigantic cakes to accompany the coffee at the breakfast in the den, saw a young man bounce from a horse car. He gave a shout. "Hello, there, Billie! Hello!"

"Hello, Penny!" said Hawker. "What are you doing out so early?" It was somewhat after nine o'clock.

"Out to get breakfast," said Pennoyer, waving the cakes. "Have a good time, old man?"

"Great."

"Do much work?"

"No. Not so much. How are all the people?"

"Oh, pretty good. Come in and see us eat breakfast," said Pennoyer, throwing open the door of the den. Wrinkles, in his shirt, was making coffee. Grief sat in a chair trying to loosen the grasp of sleep. "Why, Billie Hawker, b'ginger!" they cried.

"How's the wolf, boys? At the door yet?"

"'At the door yet?' He's halfway up the back stairs, and coming fast. He and the landlord will be here to-morrow. 'Mr. Landlord, allow me to present Mr. F. Wolf, of Hunger, N. J. Mr. Wolf-Mr. Landlord.'"

"Bad as that?" said Hawker.

"You bet it is! Easy Street is somewhere in heaven, for all we know. Have some breakfast? — coffee and cake, I mean."

"No, thanks, boys. Had breakfast."

Wrinkles added to the shirt, Grief aroused himself, and Pennoyer brought the coffee. Cheerfully throwing some drawings from the table to the floor, they thus made room for the breakfast, and grouped themselves with beaming smiles at the board.

"Well, Billie, come back to the old gang again, eh? How did the country seem? Do much work?"

"Not very much. A few things. How's everybody?"

"Splutter was in last night. Looking out of sight. Seemed glad to hear that you were coming back soon."

"Did she? Penny, did anybody call wanting me to do a ten-thousand-dollar portrait for them?"

"No. That frame-maker, though, was here with a bill. I told him — —"

Afterward Hawker crossed the corridor and threw open the door of his own large studio. The great skylight, far above his head, shed its clear rays upon a scene which appeared to indicate that some one had very recently ceased work here and started for the country. A distant closet door was open, and the interior showed the effects of a sudden pillage.

There was an unfinished "Girl in Apple Orchard" upon the tall Dutch easel, and sketches and studies were thick upon the floor. Hawker took a pipe and filled it from his friend the tan and gold jar. He cast himself into a chair and, taking an envelope from his pocket, emptied two violets from it to the palm of his hand and stared long at them. Upon the walls of the studio various labours of his life, in heavy gilt frames, contemplated him and the violets.

At last Pennoyer burst impetuously in upon him. "Hi, Billie! come over and — — What's the matter?"

Hawker had hastily placed the violets in the envelope and hurried it to his pocket. "Nothing," he answered.

"Why, I thought —" said Pennoyer, "I thought you looked rather rattled. Didn't you have —I thought I saw something in your hand."

"Nothing, I tell you!" cried Hawker.

"Er-oh, I beg your pardon," said Pennoyer. "Why, I was going to tell you that Splutter is over in our place, and she wants to see you."

"Wants to see me? What for?" demanded Hawker. "Why don't she come over here, then?"

"I'm sure I don't know," replied Pennoyer. "She sent me to call you."

"Well, do you think I'm going to —— Oh, well, I suppose she wants to be unpleasant, and knows she loses a certain mental position if she comes over here, but if she meets me in your place she can be as infernally disagreeable as she —— That's it, I'll bet."

When they entered the den Florinda was gazing from the window. Her back was toward the door.

At last she turned to them, holding herself very straight. "Well, Billie Hawker," she said grimly, "you don't seem very glad to see a fellow."

"Why, heavens, did you think I was going to turn somersaults in the air?"

"Well, you didn't come out when you heard me pass your door," said Florinda, with gloomy resentment.

Hawker appeared to be ruffled and vexed. "Oh, great Scott!" he said, making a gesture of despair.

Florinda returned to the window. In the ensuing conversation she took no part, save when there was an opportunity to harry some speech of Hawker's, which she did in short contemptuous sentences. Hawker made no reply save to glare in her direction. At last he said, "Well, I must go over and do some work." Florinda did not turn from the window. "Well, so-long, boys," said Hawker, "I'll see you later."

As the door slammed Pennoyer apologetically said, "Billie is a trifle off his feed this morning."

"What about?" asked Grief.

"I don't know; but when I went to call him he was sitting deep in his chair staring at some ——" He looked at Florinda and became silent.

"Staring at what?" asked Florinda, turning then from the window.

Pennoyer seemed embarrassed. "Why, I don't know-nothing, I guess — I couldn't see very well. I was only fooling."

Florinda scanned his face suspiciously. "Staring at what?" she demanded imperatively.

"Nothing, I tell you!" shouted Pennoyer.

Florinda looked at him, and wavered and debated. Presently she said, softly: "Ah, go on, Penny. Tell me."

"It wasn't anything at all, I say!" cried Pennoyer stoutly. "I was only giving you a jolly. Sit down, Splutter, and hit a cigarette."

She obeyed, but she continued to cast the dubious eye at Pennoyer. Once she said to him privately: "Go on, Penny, tell me. I know it was something from the way you are acting."

"Oh, let up, Splutter, for heaven's sake!"

"Tell me," beseeched Florinda.

"No."

"Tell me."

"No."

"Pl-e-a-se tell me."

"No."

"Oh, go on."

"No."

"Ah, what makes you so mean, Penny? You know I'd tell you, if it was the other way about."

"But it's none of my business, Splutter. I can't tell you something which is Billie Hawker's private affair. If I did I would be a chump."

"But I'll never say you told me. Go on."

"No."

"Pl-e-a-se tell me."

"No."

CHAPTER XXII.

When Florinda had gone, Grief said, "Well, what was it?" Wrinkles looked curiously from his drawing-board.

Pennoyer lit his pipe and held it at the side of his mouth in the manner of a deliberate man. At last he said, "It was two violets."

"You don't say!" ejaculated Wrinkles.

"Well, I'm hanged!" cried Grief. "Holding them in his hand and moping over them, eh?"

"Yes," responded Pennoyer. "Rather that way."

"Well, I'm hanged!" said both Grief and Wrinkles. They grinned in a pleased, urchin-like manner. "Say, who do you suppose she is? Somebody he met this summer, no doubt. Would you ever think old Billie would get into that sort of a thing? Well, I'll be gol-durned!"

Ultimately Wrinkles said, "Well, it's his own business." This was spoken in a tone of duty.

"Of course it's his own business," retorted Grief. "But who would ever think— —" Again they grinned.

When Hawker entered the den some minutes later he might have noticed something unusual in the general demeanour. "Say, Grief, will you loan me your— — What's up?" he asked.

For answer they grinned at each other, and then grinned at him.

"You look like a lot of Chessy cats," he told them.

They grinned on.

Apparently feeling unable to deal with these phenomena, he went at last to the door. "Well, this is a fine exhibition," he said, standing with his hand on the knob and regarding them. "Won election bets? Some good old auntie just died? Found something new to pawn? No? Well, I can't stand this. You resemble those fish they discover at deep sea. Good-bye!"

As he opened the door they cried out: "Hold on, Billie! Billie, look here! Say, who is she?"

"What?"

"Who is she?"

"Who is who?"

They laughed and nodded. "Why, you know. She. Don't you understand? She."

"You talk like a lot of crazy men," said Hawker. "I don't know what you mean."

"Oh, you don't, eh? You don't? Oh, no! How about those violets you were moping over this morning? Eh, old man! Oh, no, you don't know what we mean! Oh, no! How about those violets, eh? How about 'em?"

Hawker, with flushed and wrathful face, looked at Pennoyer. "Penny— —" But Grief and Wrinkles roared an interruption. "Oh, ho, Mr. Hawker! so it's true, is it? It's true. You are a nice bird, you are. Well, you old rascal! Durn your picture!"

Hawker, menacing them once with his eyes, went away. They sat cackling.

At noon, when he met Wrinkles in the corridor, he said: "Hey, Wrinkles, come here for a minute, will you? Say, old man, I—I— —"

"What?" said Wrinkles.

"Well, you know, I—I—of course, every man is likely to make an accursed idiot of himself once in a while, and I— —"

"And you what?" asked Wrinkles.

"Well, we are a kind of a band of hoodlums, you know, and I'm just enough idiot to feel that I don't care to hear-don't care to hear-well, her name used, you know."

"Bless your heart," replied Wrinkles, "we haven't used her name. We don't know her name. How could we use it?"

"Well, I know," said Hawker. "But you understand what I mean, Wrinkles."

"Yes, I understand what you mean," said Wrinkles, with dignity. "I don't suppose you are any worse of a stuff than common. Still, I didn't know that we were such outlaws."

"Of course, I have overdone the thing," responded Hawker hastily. "But-you ought to understand how I mean it, Wrinkles."

After Wrinkles had thought for a time, he said: "Well, I guess I do. All right. That goes."

Upon entering the den, Wrinkles said, "You fellows have got to quit guying Billie, do you hear?"

"We?" cried Grief. "We've got to quit? What do you do?"

"Well, I quit too."

Pennoyer said: "Ah, ha! Billie has been jumping on you."

"No, he didn't," maintained Wrinkles; "but he let me know it was-well, rather a —rather a —sacred subject." Wrinkles blushed when the others snickered.

In the afternoon, as Hawker was going slowly down the stairs, he was almost impaled upon the feather of a hat which, upon the head of a lithe and rather slight girl, charged up at him through the gloom.

"Hello, Splutter!" he cried. "You are in a hurry."

"That you, Billie?" said the girl, peering, for the hallways of this old building remained always in a dungeonlike darkness.

"Yes, it is. Where are you going at such a headlong gait?"

"Up to see the boys. I've got a bottle of wine and some-some pickles, you know. I'm going to make them let me dine with them to-night. Coming back, Billie?"

"Why, no, I don't expect to."

He moved then accidentally in front of the light that sifted through the dull, gray panes of a little window.

"Oh, cracky!" cried the girl; "how fine you are, Billie! Going to a coronation?"

"No," said Hawker, looking seriously over his collar and down at his clothes. "Fact is-er-well, I've got to make a call."

"A call-bless us! And are you really going to wear those gray gloves you're holding there, Billie? Say, wait until you get around the corner. They won't stand 'em on this street."

"Oh, well," said Hawker, depreciating the gloves —"oh, well."

The girl looked up at him. "Who you going to call on?"

"Oh," said Hawker, "a friend."

"Must be somebody most extraordinary, you look so dreadfully correct. Come back, Billie, won't you? Come back and dine with us."

"Why, I —I don't believe I can."

"Oh, come on! It's fun when we all dine together. Won't you, Billie?"

"Well, I — —"

"Oh, don't be so stupid!" The girl stamped her foot and flashed her eyes at him angrily.

"Well, I'll see —I will if I can —I can't tell — —" He left her rather precipitately.

Hawker eventually appeared at a certain austere house where he rang the bell with quite nervous fingers.

But she was not at home. As he went down the steps his eyes were as those of a man whose fortunes have tumbled upon him. As he walked down the street he wore in some subtle way the air of a man who has been grievously wronged. When he rounded the corner, his lips were set strangely, as if he were a man seeking revenge.

CHAPTER XXIII.

"It's just right," said Grief.

"It isn't quite cool enough," said Wrinkles.

"Well, I guess I know the proper temperature for claret."

"Well, I guess you don't. If it was buttermilk, now, you would know, but you can't tell anything about claret."

Florinda ultimately decided the question. "It isn't quite cool enough," she said, laying her hand on the bottle. "Put it on the window ledge, Grief."

"Hum! Splutter, I thought you knew more than — —"

"Oh, shut up!" interposed the busy Pennoyer from a remote corner. "Who is going after the potato salad? That's what I want to know. Who is going?"

"Wrinkles," said Grief.

"Grief," said Wrinkles.

"There," said Pennoyer, coming forward and scanning a late work with an eye of satisfaction. "There's the three glasses and the little tumbler; and then, Grief, you will have to drink out of a mug."

"I'll be double-dyed black if I will!" cried Grief. "I wouldn't drink claret out of a mug to save my soul from being pinched!"

"You duffer, you talk like a bloomin' British chump on whom the sun never sets! What do you want?"

"Well, there's enough without that-what's the matter with you? Three glasses and the little tumbler."

"Yes, but if Billie Hawker comes — —"

"Well, let him drink out of the mug, then. He — —"

"No, he won't," said Florinda suddenly. "I'll take the mug myself."

"All right, Splutter," rejoined Grief meekly. "I'll keep the mug. But, still, I don't see why Billie Hawker — —"

"I shall take the mug," reiterated Florinda firmly.

"But I don't see why — —"

"Let her alone, Grief," said Wrinkles. "She has decided that it is heroic. You can't move her now."

"Well, who is going for the potato salad?" cried Pennoyer again. "That's what I want to know."

"Wrinkles," said Grief.

"Grief," said Wrinkles.

"Do you know," remarked Florinda, raising her head from where she had been toiling over the *spaghetti*, "I don't care so much for Billie Hawker as I did once?" Her sleeves were rolled above the elbows of her wonderful arms, and she turned from the stove and poised a fork as if she had been smitten at her task with this inspiration.

There was a short silence, and then Wrinkles said politely, "No."

"No," continued Florinda, "I really don't believe I do." She suddenly started. "Listen! Isn't that him coming now?"

The dull trample of a step could be heard in some distant corridor, but it died slowly to silence.

"I thought that might be him," she said, turning to the *spaghetti* again.

"I hope the old Indian comes," said Pennoyer, "but I don't believe he will. Seems to me he must be going to see — —"

"Who?" asked Florinda.

"Well, you know, Hollanden and he usually dine together when they are both in town."

Florinda looked at Pennoyer. "I know, Penny. You must have thought I was remarkably clever not to understand all your blundering. But I don't care so much. Really I don't."

"Of course not," assented Pennoyer.

"Really I don't."

"Of course not."

"Listen!" exclaimed Grief, who was near the door. "There he comes now." Somebody approached, whistling an air from "Traviata," which rang loud and clear, and low and muffled, as the whistler wound among the intricate hallways. This air was as much a part of Hawker as his coat. The *spaghetti* had arrived at a critical stage. Florinda gave it her complete attention.

When Hawker opened the door he ceased whistling and said gruffly, "Hello!"

"Just the man!" said Grief. "Go after the potato salad, will you, Billie? There's a good boy! Wrinkles has refused."

"He can't carry the salad with those gloves," interrupted Florinda, raising her eyes from her work and contemplating them with displeasure.

"Hang the gloves!" cried Hawker, dragging them from his hands and hurling them at the divan. "What's the matter with you, Splutter?"

Pennoyer said, "My, what a temper you are in, Billie!"

"I am," replied Hawker. "I feel like an Apache. Where do you get this accursed potato salad?"

"In Second Avenue. You know where. At the old place."

"No, I don't!" snapped Hawker.

"Why——"

"Here," said Florinda, "I'll go." She had already rolled down her sleeves and was arraying herself in her hat and jacket.

"No, you won't," said Hawker, filled with wrath. "I'll go myself."

"We can both go, Billie, if you are so bent," replied the girl in a conciliatory voice.

"Well, come on, then. What are you standing there for?"

When these two had departed, Wrinkles said: "Lordie! What's wrong with Billie?"

"He's been discussing art with some pot-boiler," said Grief, speaking as if this was the final condition of human misery.

"No, sir," said Pennoyer. "It's something connected with the now celebrated violets."

Out in the corridor Florinda said, "What-what makes you so ugly, Billie?"

"Why, I am not ugly, am I?"

"Yes, you are-ugly as anything."

Probably he saw a grievance in her eyes, for he said, "Well, I don't want to be ugly." His tone seemed tender. The halls were intensely dark, and the girl placed her hand on his arm. As they rounded a turn in the stairs a straying lock of her hair brushed against his temple. "Oh!" said Florinda, in a low voice.

"We'll get some more claret," observed Hawker musingly. "And some cognac for the coffee. And some cigarettes. Do you think of anything more, Splutter?"

As they came from the shop of the illustrious purveyors of potato salad in Second Avenue, Florinda cried anxiously, "Here, Billie, you let me carry that!"

"What infernal nonsense!" said Hawker, flushing. "Certainly not!"

"Well," protested Florinda, "it might soil your gloves somehow."

"In heaven's name, what if it does? Say, young woman, do you think I am one of these cholly boys?"

"No, Billie; but then, you know——"

"Well, if you don't take me for some kind of a Willie, give us peace on this blasted glove business!"

"I didn't mean——"

"Well, you've been intimating that I've got the only pair of gray gloves in the universe, but you are wrong. There are several pairs, and these need not be preserved as unique in history."

"They're not gray. They're——"

"They are gray! I suppose your distinguished ancestors in Ireland did not educate their families in the matter of gloves, and so you are not expected to——"

"Billie!"

"You are not expected to believe that people wear gloves only in cold weather, and then you expect to see mittens."

On the stairs, in the darkness, he suddenly exclaimed, "Here, look out, or you'll fall!" He reached for her arm, but she evaded him. Later he said again: "Look out, girl! What makes you stumble around so? Here, give me the bottle of wine. I can carry it all right. There-now can you manage?"

CHAPTER XXIV.

"Penny," said Grief, looking across the table at his friend, "if a man thinks a heap of two violets, how much would he think of a thousand violets?"

"Two into a thousand goes five hundred times, you fool!" said Pennoyer. "I would answer your question if it were not upon a forbidden subject."

In the distance Wrinkles and Florinda were making Welsh rarebits.

"Hold your tongues!" said Hawker. "Barbarians!"

"Grief," said Pennoyer, "if a man loves a woman better than the whole universe, how much does he love the whole universe?"

"Gawd knows," said Grief piously. "Although it ill befits me to answer your question."

Wrinkles and Florinda came with the Welsh rarebits, very triumphant. "There," said Florinda, "soon as these are finished I must go home. It is after eleven o'clock. —Pour the ale, Grief."

At a later time, Purple Sanderson entered from the world. He hung up his hat and cast a look of proper financial dissatisfaction at the remnants of the feast. "Who has been — —"

"Before you breathe, Purple, you graceless scum, let me tell you that we will stand no reference to the two violets here," said Pennoyer.

"What the — —"

"Oh, that's all right, Purple," said Grief, "but you were going to say something about the two violets, right then. Weren't you, now, you old bat?"

Sanderson grinned expectantly. "What's the row?" said he.

"No row at all," they told him. "Just an agreement to keep you from chattering obstinately about the two violets."

"What two violets?"

"Have a rarebit, Purple," advised Wrinkles, "and never mind those maniacs."

"Well, what is this business about two violets?"

"Oh, it's just some dream. They gibber at anything."

"I think I know," said Florinda, nodding. "It is something that concerns Billie Hawker."

Grief and Pennoyer scoffed, and Wrinkles said: "You know nothing about it, Splutter. It doesn't concern Billie Hawker at all."

"Well, then, what is he looking sideways for?" cried Florinda.

Wrinkles reached for his guitar, and played a serenade, "The silver moon is shining — —"

"Dry up!" said Pennoyer.

Then Florinda cried again, "What does he look sideways for?"

Pennoyer and Grief giggled at the imperturbable Hawker, who destroyed rarebit in silence.

"It's you, is it, Billie?" said Sanderson. "You are in this two-violet business?"

"I don't know what they're talking about," replied Hawker.

"Don't you, honestly?" asked Florinda.

"Well, only a little."

"There!" said Florinda, nodding again. "I knew he was in it."

"He isn't in it at all," said Pennoyer and Grief.

Later, when the cigarettes had become exhausted, Hawker volunteered to go after a further supply, and as he arose, a question seemed to come to the edge of Florinda's lips and pend there. The moment that the door was closed upon him she demanded, "What is that about the two violets?"

"Nothing at all," answered Pennoyer, apparently much aggrieved. He sat back with an air of being a fortress of reticence.

"Oh, go on—tell me! Penny, I think you are very mean. —Grief, you tell me!"

"The silver moon is shining;
Oh, come, my love, to me!
My heart — —"

"Be still, Wrinkles, will you?—What was it, Grief? Oh, go ahead and tell me!"

"What do you want to know for?" cried Grief, vastly exasperated. "You've got more blamed curiosity—— It isn't anything at all, I keep saying to you."

"Well, I know it is," said Florinda sullenly, "or you would tell me."

When Hawker brought the cigarettes, Florinda smoked one, and then announced, "Well, I must go now."

"Who is going to take you home, Splutter?"

"Oh, anyone," replied Florinda.

"I tell you what," said Grief, "we'll throw some poker hands, and the one who wins will have the distinguished honour of conveying Miss Splutter to her home and mother."

Pennoyer and Wrinkles speedily routed the dishes to one end of the table. Grief's fingers spun the halves of a pack of cards together with the pleased eagerness of a good player. The faces grew solemn with the gambling solemnity. "Now, you Indians," said Grief, dealing, "a draw, you understand, and then a show-down."

Florinda leaned forward in her chair until it was poised on two legs. The cards of Purple Sanderson and of Hawker were faced toward her. Sanderson was gravely regarding two pair-aces and queens. Hawker scanned a little pair of sevens. "They draw, don't they?" she said to Grief.

"Certainly," said Grief. "How many, Wrink?"

"Four," replied Wrinkles, plaintively.

"Gimme three," said Pennoyer.

"Gimme one," said Sanderson.

"Gimme three," said Hawker. When he picked up his hand again Florinda's chair was tilted perilously. She saw another seven added to the little pair. Sanderson's draw had not assisted him.

"Same to the dealer," said Grief. "What you got, Wrink?"

"Nothing," said Wrinkles, exhibiting it face upward on the table. "Good-bye, Florinda."

"Well, I've got two small pair," ventured Pennoyer hopefully. "Beat 'em?"

"No good," said Sanderson. "Two pair-aces up."

"No good," said Hawker. "Three sevens."

"Beats me," said Grief. "Billie, you are the fortunate man. Heaven guide you in Third Avenue!"

Florinda had gone to the window. "Who won?" she asked, wheeling about carelessly.

"Billie Hawker."

"What! Did he?" she said in surprise.

"Never mind, Splutter. I'll win sometime," said Pennoyer. "Me too," cried Grief. "Good night, old girl!" said Wrinkles. They crowded in the doorway. "Hold on to Billie. Remember the two steps going up," Pennoyer called intelligently into the Stygian blackness. "Can you see all right?"

Florinda lived in a flat with fire-escapes written all over the front of it. The street in front was being repaired. It had been said by imbecile residents of the vicinity that the paving was never allowed to remain down for a sufficient time to be invalided by the tramping millions, but that it was kept perpetually stacked in little mountains through the unceasing vigilance of a virtuous and heroic city government, which insisted that everything should be repaired. The alderman for the district had sometimes asked indignantly of his fellow-members why this street had not been repaired, and they, aroused, had at once ordered it to be repaired. Moreover, shopkeepers, whose stables were adjacent, placed trucks and other vehicles strategically in the darkness. Into this tangled midnight Hawker conducted Florinda. The great avenue behind them was no more than a level stream of yellow light, and the distant merry bells might have been boats floating down it. Grim loneliness hung over the uncouth shapes in the street which was being repaired.

"Billie," said the girl suddenly, "what makes you so mean to me?"

A peaceful citizen emerged from behind a pile of *débris*, but he might not have been a peaceful citizen, so the girl clung to Hawker.

"Why, I'm not mean to you, am I?"

"Yes," she answered. As they stood on the steps of the flat of innumerable fire-escapes she slowly turned and looked up at him. Her face was of a strange pallour in this darkness, and her eyes were as when the moon shines in a lake of the hills.

He returned her glance. "Florinda!" he cried, as if enlightened, and gulping suddenly at something in his throat. The girl studied the steps and moved from side to side, as do the guilty ones in country schoolhouses. Then she went slowly into the flat.

There was a little red lamp hanging on a pile of stones to warn people that the street was being repaired.

CHAPTER XXV.

"I'll get my check from the Gamin on Saturday," said Grief. "They bought that string of comics."

"Well, then, we'll arrange the present funds to last until Saturday noon," said Wrinkles. "That gives us quite a lot. We can have a *table d'hôte* on Friday night."

However, the cashier of the Gamin office looked under his respectable brass wiring and said: "Very sorry, Mr. —er-Warwickson, but our pay-day is Monday. Come around any time after ten."

"Oh, it doesn't matter," said Grief.

When he plunged into the den his visage flamed with rage. "Don't get my check until Monday morning, any time after ten!" he yelled, and flung a portfolio of mottled green into the danger zone of the casts.

"Thunder!" said Pennoyer, sinking at once into a profound despair

"Monday morning, any time after ten," murmured Wrinkles, in astonishment and sorrow.

While Grief marched to and fro threatening the furniture, Pennoyer and Wrinkles allowed their under jaws to fall, and remained as men smitten between the eyes by the god of calamity.

"Singular thing!" muttered Pennoyer at last. "You get so frightfully hungry as soon as you learn that there are no more meals coming."

"Oh, well——" said Wrinkles. He took up his guitar.

Oh, some folks say dat a niggah won' steal,
'Way down yondeh in d' cohn'-fiel';
But Ah caught two in my cohn'-fiel',
Way down yondeh in d' cohn'-fiel'.

"Oh, let up!" said Grief, as if unwilling to be moved from his despair.

"Oh, let up!" said Pennoyer, as if he disliked the voice and the ballad.

In his studio, Hawker sat braced nervously forward on a little stool before his tall Dutch easel. Three sketches lay on the floor near him, and he glared at them constantly while painting at the large canvas on the easel.

He seemed engaged in some kind of a duel. His hair dishevelled, his eyes gleaming, he was in a deadly scuffle. In the sketches was the landscape of heavy blue, as if seen through powder-smoke, and all the skies burned red. There was in these notes a sinister quality of hopelessness, eloquent of a defeat, as if the scene represented the last hour on a field of disastrous battle. Hawker seemed attacking with this picture something fair and beautiful of his own life, a possession of his mind, and he did it fiercely, mercilessly, formidably. His arm moved with the energy of a strange wrath. He might have been thrusting with a sword.

There was a knock at the door. "Come in." Pennoyer entered sheepishly. "Well?" cried Hawker, with an echo of savagery in his voice. He turned from the canvas precisely as one might emerge from a fight. "Oh!" he said, perceiving Pennoyer. The glow in his eyes slowly changed. "What is it, Penny?"

"Billie," said Pennoyer, "Grief was to get his check to-day, but they put him off until Monday, and so, you know-er-well——"

"Oh!" said Hawker again.

When Pennoyer had gone Hawker sat motionless before his work. He stared at the canvas in a meditation so profound that it was probably unconscious of itself.

The light from above his head slanted more and more toward the east.

Once he arose and lighted a pipe. He returned to the easel and stood staring with his hands in his pockets. He moved like one in a sleep. Suddenly the gleam shot into his eyes again. He dropped to the stool and grabbed a brush. At the end of a certain long, tumultuous period he clinched his pipe more firmly in his teeth and puffed strongly. The thought might have occurred to him that it was not alight, for he looked at it with a vague, questioning glance. There came another knock at the door. "Go to the devil!" he shouted, without turning his head.

Hollanden crossed the corridor then to the den.

"Hi, there, Hollie! Hello, boy! Just the fellow we want to see. Come in-sit down-hit a pipe. Say, who was the girl Billie Hawker went mad over this summer?"

"Blazes!" said Hollanden, recovering slowly from this onslaught. "Who-what-how did you Indians find it out?"

"Oh, we tumbled!" they cried in delight, "we tumbled."

"There!" said Hollanden, reproaching himself. "And I thought you were such a lot of blockheads."

"Oh, we tumbled!" they cried again in their ecstasy. "But who is she? That's the point."

"Well, she was a girl."

"Yes, go on."

"A New York girl."

"Yes."

"A perfectly stunning New York girl."

"Yes. Go ahead."

"A perfectly stunning New York girl of a very wealthy and rather old-fashioned family."

"Well, I'll be shot! You don't mean it! She is practically seated on top of the Matterhorn. Poor old Billie!"

"Not at all," said Hollanden composedly.

It was a common habit of Purple Sanderson to call attention at night to the resemblance of the den to some little ward in a hospital. Upon this night, when Sanderson and Grief were buried in slumber, Pennoyer moved restlessly. "Wrink!" he called softly into the darkness in the direction of the divan which was secretly a coal-box.

"What?" said Wrinkles in a surly voice. His mind had evidently been caught at the threshold of sleep.

"Do you think Florinda cares much for Billie Hawker?"

Wrinkles fretted through some oaths. "How in thunder do I know?" The divan creaked as he turned his face to the wall.

"Well — —" muttered Pennoyer.

CHAPTER XXVI.

The harmony of summer sunlight on leaf and blade of green was not known to the two windows, which looked forth at an obviously endless building of brownstone about which there was the poetry of a prison. Inside, great folds of lace swept down in orderly cascades, as water trained to fall mathematically. The colossal chandelier, gleaming like a Siamese headdress, caught the subtle flashes from unknown places.

Hawker heard a step and the soft swishing of a woman's dress. He turned toward the door swiftly, with a certain dramatic impulsiveness. But when she entered the room he said, "How delighted I am to see you again!"

She had said, "Why, Mr. Hawker, it was so charming in you to come!"

It did not appear that Hawker's tongue could wag to his purpose. The girl seemed in her mind to be frantically shuffling her pack of social receipts and finding none of them made to meet this situation. Finally, Hawker said that he thought Hearts at War was a very good play.

"Did you?" she said in surprise. "I thought it much like the others."

"Well, so did I," he cried hastily —"the same figures moving around in the mud of modern confusion. I really didn't intend to say that I liked it. Fact is, meeting you rather moved me out of my mental track."

"Mental track?" she said. "I didn't know clever people had mental tracks. I thought it was a privilege of the theologians."

"Who told you I was clever?" he demanded.

"Why," she said, opening her eyes wider, "nobody."

Hawker smiled and looked upon her with gratitude. "Of course, nobody. There couldn't be such an idiot. I am sure you should be astonished to learn that I believed such an imbecile existed. But— —"

"Oh!" she said.

"But I think you might have spoken less bluntly."

"Well," she said, after wavering for a time, "you are clever, aren't you?"

"Certainly," he answered reassuringly.

"Well, then?" she retorted, with triumph in her tone. And this interrogation was apparently to her the final victorious argument.

At his discomfiture Hawker grinned.

"You haven't asked news of Stanley," he said. "Why don't you ask news of Stanley?"

"Oh! and how was he?"

"The last I saw of him he stood down at the end of the pasture-the pasture, you know- wagging his tail in blissful anticipation of an invitation to come with me, and when it finally dawned upon him that he was not to receive it, he turned and went back toward the house 'like a man suddenly stricken with age,' as the story-tellers eloquently say. Poor old dog!"

"And you left him?" she said reproachfully. Then she asked, "Do you remember how he amused you playing with the ants at the falls?"

"No."

"Why, he did. He pawed at the moss, and you sat there laughing. I remember it distinctly."

"You remember distinctly? Why, I thought-well, your back was turned, you know. Your gaze was fixed upon something before you, and you were utterly lost to the rest of the world. You could not have known if Stanley pawed the moss and I laughed. So, you see, you are mistaken. As a matter of fact, I utterly deny that Stanley pawed the moss or that I laughed, or that any ants appeared at the falls at all."

"I have always said that you should have been a Chinese soldier of fortune," she observed musingly. "Your daring and ingenuity would be prized by the Chinese."

"There are innumerable tobacco jars in China," he said, measuring the advantages. "Moreover, there is no perspective. You don't have to walk two miles to see a friend. No. He is always there near you, so that you can't move a chair without hitting your distant friend. You— —"

"Did Hollie remain as attentive as ever to the Worcester girls?"

"Yes, of course, as attentive as ever. He dragged me into all manner of tennis games ———"

"Why, I thought you loved to play tennis?"

"Oh, well," said Hawker, "I did until you left."

"My sister has gone to the park with the children. I know she will be vexed when she finds that you have called."

Ultimately Hawker said, "Do you remember our ride behind my father's oxen?"

"No," she answered; "I had forgotten it completely. Did we ride behind your father's oxen?"

After a moment he said: "That remark would be prized by the Chinese. We did. And you most graciously professed to enjoy it, which earned my deep gratitude and admiration. For no one knows better than I," he added meekly, "that it is no great comfort or pleasure to ride behind my father's oxen."

She smiled retrospectively. "Do you remember how the people on the porch hurried to the railing?"

CHAPTER XXVII.

Near the door the stout proprietress sat intrenched behind the cash-box in a Parisian manner. She looked with practical amiability at her guests, who dined noisily and with great fire, discussing momentous problems furiously, making wide, maniacal gestures through the cigarette smoke. Meanwhile the little handful of waiters ran to and fro wildly. Imperious and importunate cries rang at them from all directions. "Gustave! Adolphe!" Their faces expressed a settled despair. They answered calls, commands, oaths in a semi-distraction, fleeting among the tables as if pursued by some dodging animal. Their breaths came in gasps. If they had been convict labourers they could not have surveyed their positions with countenances of more unspeakable injury. Withal, they carried incredible masses of dishes and threaded their ways with skill. They served people with such speed and violence that it often resembled a personal assault. They struck two blows at a table and left there a knife and fork. Then came the viands in a volley. The clatter of this business was loud and bewilderingly rapid, like the gallop of a thousand horses.

In a remote corner a band of mandolins and guitars played the long, sweeping, mad melody of a Spanish waltz. It seemed to go tingling to the hearts of many of the diners. Their eyes glittered with enthusiasm, with abandon, with deviltry. They swung their heads from side to side in rhythmic movement. High in air curled the smoke from the innumerable cigarettes. The long, black claret bottles were in clusters upon the tables. At an end of the hall two men with maudlin grins sang the waltz uproariously, but always a trifle belated.

An unsteady person, leaning back in his chair to murmur swift compliments to a woman at another table, suddenly sprawled out upon the floor. He scrambled to his feet, and, turning to the escort of the woman, heatedly blamed him for the accident. They exchanged a series of tense, bitter insults, which spatted back and forth between them like pellets. People arose from their chairs and stretched their necks. The musicians stood in a body, their faces turned with expressions of keen excitement toward this quarrel, but their fingers still twinkling over their instruments, sending into the middle of this turmoil the passionate, mad, Spanish music. The proprietor of the place came in agitation and plunged headlong into the argument, where he thereafter appeared as a frantic creature harried to the point of insanity, for they buried him at once in long, vociferous threats, explanations, charges, every form of declamation known to their voices. The music, the noise of the galloping horses, the voices of the brawlers, gave the whole thing the quality of war.

There were two men in the *café* who seemed to be tranquil. Hollanden carefully stacked one lump of sugar upon another in the middle of his saucer and poured cognac over them. He touched a match to the cognac and the blue and yellow flames eddied in the saucer. "I wonder what those two fools are bellowing at?" he said, turning about irritably.

"Hanged if I know!" muttered Hawker in reply. "This place makes me weary, anyhow. Hear the blooming din!"

"What's the matter?" said Hollanden. "You used to say this was the one natural, the one truly Bohemian, resort in the city. You swore by it."

"Well, I don't like it so much any more."

"Ho!" cried Hollanden, "you're getting correct-that's it exactly. You will become one of these intensely —— Look, Billie, the little one is going to punch him!"

"No, he isn't. They never do," said Hawker morosely. "Why did you bring me here to-night, Hollie?"

"I? I bring you? Good heavens, I came as a concession to you! What are you talking about? — Hi! the little one is going to punch him, sure!"

He gave the scene his undivided attention for a moment; then he turned again: "You will become correct. I know you will. I have been watching. You are about to achieve a respectability that will make a stone saint blush for himself. What's the matter with you? You act as if you thought falling in love with a girl was a most extraordinary circumstance. —I wish they would put those people out. —Of course I know that you — — There! The little one has swiped at him at last!"

After a time he resumed his oration. "Of course, I know that you are not reformed in the matter of this uproar and this remarkable consumption of bad wine. It is not that. It is a fact that there are indications that some other citizen was fortunate enough to possess your napkin before you; and, moreover, you are sure that you would hate to be caught by your correct friends with any such *consommé* in front of you as we had to-night. You have got an eye suddenly for all kinds of gilt. You are in the way of becoming a most unbearable person. —Oh, look! the little one and the proprietor are having it now. —You are in the way of becoming a most unbearable person. Presently many of your friends will not be fine enough. —In heaven's name, why don't they throw him out? Are you going to howl and gesticulate there all night?"

"Well," said Hawker, "a man would be a fool if he did like this dinner."

"Certainly. But what an immaterial part in the glory of this joint is the dinner! Who cares about dinner? No one comes here to eat; that's what you always claimed. —Well, there, at last they are throwing him out. I hope he lands on his head. —Really, you know, Billie, it is such a fine thing being in love that one is sure to be detestable to the rest of the world, and that is the reason they created a proverb to the other effect. You want to look out."

"You talk like a blasted old granny!" said Hawker. "Haven't changed at all. This place is all right, only — —"

"You are gone," interrupted Hollanden in a sad voice. "It is very plain-you are gone."

CHAPTER XXVIII.

The proprietor of the place, having pushed to the street the little man, who may have been the most vehement, came again and resumed the discussion with the remainder of the men of war. Many of these had volunteered, and they were very enduring.

"Yes, you are gone," said Hollanden, with the sobriety of graves in his voice. "You are gone. — Hi!" he cried, "there is Lucian Pontiac. —Hi, Pontiac! Sit down here."

A man with a tangle of hair, and with that about his mouth which showed that he had spent many years in manufacturing a proper modesty with which to bear his greatness, came toward them, smiling.

"Hello, Pontiac!" said Hollanden. "Here's another great painter. Do you know Mr. Hawker? —Mr. William Hawker-Mr. Pontiac."

"Mr. Hawker-delighted," said Pontiac. "Although I have not known you personally, I can assure you that I have long been a great admirer of your abilities."

The proprietor of the place and the men of war had at length agreed to come to an amicable understanding. They drank liquors, while each firmly, but now silently, upheld his dignity.

"Charming place," said Pontiac. "So thoroughly Parisian in spirit. And from time to time, Mr. Hawker, I use one of your models. Must say she has the best arm and wrist in the universe. Stunning figure-stunning!"

"You mean Florinda?" said Hawker.

"Yes, that's the name. Very fine girl. Lunches with me from time to time and chatters so volubly. That's how I learned you posed her occasionally. If the models didn't gossip we would never know what painters were addicted to profanity. Now that old Thorndike-he told me you swore like a drill-sergeant if the model winked a finger at the critical time. Very fine girl, Florinda. And honest, too-honest as the devil. Very curious thing. Of course honesty among the girl models is very common, very common-quite universal thing, you know-but then it always strikes me as being very curious, very curious. I've been much attracted by your girl Florinda."

"My girl?" said Hawker.

"Well, she always speaks of you in a proprietary way, you know. And then she considers that she owes you some kind of obedience and allegiance and devotion. I remember last week I said to her: 'You can go now. Come again Friday.' But she said: 'I don't think I can come on Friday. Billie Hawker is home now, and he may want me then.' Said I: 'The devil take Billie Hawker! He hasn't engaged you for Friday, has he? Well, then, I engage you now.' But she shook her head. No, she couldn't come on Friday. Billie Hawker was home, and he might want her any day. 'Well, then,' said I, 'you have my permission to do as you please, since you are resolved upon it anyway. Go to your Billie Hawker.' Did you need her on Friday?"

"No," said Hawker.

"Well, then, the minx, I shall scold her. Stunning figure-stunning! It was only last week that old Charley Master said to me mournfully: 'There are no more good models. Great Scott! not a one.' 'You're 'way off, my boy,' I said; 'there is one good model,' and then I named your girl. I mean the girl who claims to be yours."

"Poor little beggar!" said Hollanden.

"Who?" said Pontiac.

"Florinda," answered Hollanden. "I suppose — —"

Pontiac interrupted. "Oh, of course, it is too bad. Everything is too bad. My dear sir, nothing is so much to be regretted as the universe. But this Florinda is such a sturdy young soul! The world is against her, but, bless your heart, she is equal to the battle. She is strong in the manner of a little child. Why, you don't know her. She — —"

"I know her very well."

"Well, perhaps you do, but for my part I think you don't appreciate her formidable character and stunning figure-stunning!"

"Damn it!" said Hawker to his coffee cup, which he had accidentally overturned.

"Well," resumed Pontiac, "she is a stunning model, and I think, Mr. Hawker, you are to be envied."

"Eh?" said Hawker.

"I wish I could inspire my models with such obedience and devotion. Then I would not be obliged to rail at them for being late, and have to badger them for not showing up at all. She has a beautiful figure-beautiful."

CHAPTER XXIX.

When Hawker went again to the house of the great window he looked first at the colossal chandelier, and, perceiving that it had not moved, he smiled in a certain friendly and familiar way.

"It must be a fine thing," said the girl dreamily. "I always feel envious of that sort of life."

"What sort of life?"

"Why—I don't know exactly; but there must be a great deal of freedom about it. I went to a studio tea once, and——"

"A studio tea! Merciful heavens——Go on."

"Yes, a studio tea. Don't you like them? To be sure, we didn't know whether the man could paint very well, and I suppose you think it is an imposition for anyone who is not a great painter to give a tea."

"Go on."

"Well, he had the dearest little Japanese servants, and some of the cups came from Algiers, and some from Turkey, and some from——What's the matter?"

"Go on. I'm not interrupting you."

"Well, that's all; excepting that everything was charming in colour, and I thought what a lazy, beautiful life the man must lead, lounging in such a studio, smoking monogrammed cigarettes, and remarking how badly all the other men painted."

"Very fascinating. But——"

"Oh! you are going to ask if he could draw. I'm sure I don't know, but the tea that he gave was charming."

"I was on the verge of telling you something about artist life, but if you have seen a lot of draperies and drunk from a cup of Algiers, you know all about it."

"You, then, were going to make it something very terrible, and tell how young painters struggled, and all that."

"No, not exactly. But listen: I suppose there is an aristocracy who, whether they paint well or paint ill, certainly do give charming teas, as you say, and all other kinds of charming affairs too; but when I hear people talk as if that was the whole life, it makes my hair rise, you know, because I am sure that as they get to know me better and better they will see how I fall short of that kind of an existence, and I shall probably take a great tumble in their estimation. They might even conclude that I can not paint, which would be very unfair, because I can paint, you know."

"Well, proceed to arrange my point of view, so that you sha'n't tumble in my estimation when I discover that you don't lounge in a studio, smoke monogrammed cigarettes, and remark how badly the other men paint."

"That's it. That's precisely what I wish to do."

"Begin."

"Well, in the first place——"

"In the first place-what?"

"Well, I started to study when I was very poor, you understand. Look here! I'm telling you these things because I want you to know, somehow. It isn't that I'm not ashamed of it. Well, I began very poor, and I—as a matter of fact—I—well, I earned myself over half the money for my studying, and the other half I bullied and badgered and beat out of my poor old dad. I worked pretty hard in Paris, and I returned here expecting to become a great painter at once. I didn't, though. In fact, I had my worst moments then. It lasted for some years. Of course, the faith and endurance of my father were by this time worn to a shadow-this time, when I needed him the most. However, things got a little better and a little better, until I found that by working quite hard I could make what was to me a fair income. That's where I am now, too."

"Why are you so ashamed of this story?"

"The poverty."

"Poverty isn't anything to be ashamed of."

"Great heavens! Have you the temerity to get off that old nonsensical remark? Poverty is everything to be ashamed of. Did you ever see a person not ashamed of his poverty? Certainly not. Of course, when a man gets very rich he will brag so loudly of the poverty of his youth that one would never suppose that he was once ashamed of it. But he was."

"Well, anyhow, you shouldn't be ashamed of the story you have just told me."

"Why not? Do you refuse to allow me the great right of being like other men?"

"I think it was-brave, you know."

"Brave? Nonsense! Those things are not brave. Impression to that effect created by the men who have been through the mill for the greater glory of the men who have been through the mill."

"I don't like to hear you talk that way. It sounds wicked, you know."

"Well, it certainly wasn't heroic. I can remember distinctly that there was not one heroic moment."

"No, but it was-it was ——"

"It was what?"

"Well, somehow I like it, you know."

CHAPTER XXX.

"There's three of them," said Grief in a hoarse whisper.

"Four, I tell you!" said Wrinkles in a low, excited tone.

"Four," breathed Pennoyer with decision.

They held fierce pantomimic argument. From the corridor came sounds of rustling dresses and rapid feminine conversation.

Grief had kept his ear to the panel of the door. His hand was stretched back, warning the others to silence. Presently he turned his head and whispered, "Three."

"Four," whispered Pennoyer and Wrinkles.

"Hollie is there, too," whispered Grief. "Billie is unlocking the door. Now they're going in. Hear them cry out, 'Oh, isn't it lovely!' Jinks!" He began a noiseless dance about the room. "Jinks! Don't I wish I had a big studio and a little reputation! Wouldn't I have my swell friends come to see me, and wouldn't I entertain 'em!" He adopted a descriptive manner, and with his forefinger indicated various spaces of the wall. "Here is a little thing I did in Brittany. Peasant woman in sabots. This brown spot here is the peasant woman, and those two white things are the sabots. Peasant woman in sabots, don't you see? Women in Brittany, of course, all wear sabots, you understand. Convenience of the painters. I see you are looking at that little thing I did in Morocco. Ah, you admire it? Well, not so bad-not so bad. Arab smoking pipe, squatting in doorway. This long streak here is the pipe. Clever, you say? Oh, thanks! You are too kind. Well, all Arabs do that, you know. Sole occupation. Convenience of the painters. Now, this little thing here I did in Venice. Grand Canal, you know. Gondolier leaning on his oar. Convenience of the painters. Oh, yes, American subjects are well enough, but hard to find, you know-hard to find. Morocco, Venice, Brittany, Holland-all oblige with colour, you know-quaint form-all that. We are so hideously modern over here; and, besides, nobody has painted us much. How the devil can I paint America when nobody has done it before me? My dear sir, are you aware that that would be originality? Good heavens! we are not æsthetic, you understand. Oh, yes, some good mind comes along and understands a thing and does it, and after that it is æsthetic. Yes, of course, but then-well —— Now, here is a little Holland thing of mine; it ——"

The others had evidently not been heeding him. "Shut up!" said Wrinkles suddenly. "Listen!" Grief paused his harangue and they sat in silence, their lips apart, their eyes from time to time exchanging eloquent messages. A dulled melodious babble came from Hawker's studio.

At length Pennoyer murmured wistfully, "I would like to see her."

Wrinkles started noiselessly to his feet. "Well, I tell you she's a peach. I was going up the steps, you know, with a loaf of bread under my arm, when I chanced to look up the street and saw Billie and Hollanden coming with four of them."

"Three," said Grief.

"Four; and I tell you I scattered. One of the two with Billie was a peach —a peach."

"O, Lord!" groaned the others enviously. "Billie's in luck."

"How do you know?" said Wrinkles. "Billie is a blamed good fellow, but that doesn't say she will care for him-more likely that she won't."

They sat again in silence, grinning, and listening to the murmur of voices.

There came the sound of a step in the hallway. It ceased at a point opposite the door of Hawker's studio. Presently it was heard again. Florinda entered the den. "Hello!" she cried, "who is over in Billie's place? I was just going to knock ——"

They motioned at her violently. "Sh!" they whispered. Their countenances were very impressive.

"What's the matter with you fellows?" asked Florinda in her ordinary tone; whereupon they made gestures of still greater wildness. "S-s-sh!"

Florinda lowered her voice properly. "Who is over there?"

"Some swells," they whispered.

Florinda bent her head. Presently she gave a little start. "Who is over there?" Her voice became a tone of deep awe. "She?"

Wrinkles and Grief exchanged a swift glance. Pennoyer said gruffly, "Who do you mean?"

"Why," said Florinda, "you know. She. The-the girl that Billie likes."

Pennoyer hesitated for a moment and then said wrathfully: "Of course she is! Who do you suppose?"

"Oh!" said Florinda. She took a seat upon the divan, which was privately a coal-box, and unbuttoned her jacket at the throat. "Is she-is she-very handsome, Wrink?"

Wrinkles replied stoutly, "No."

Grief said: "Let's make a sneak down the hall to the little unoccupied room at the front of the building and look from the window there. When they go out we can pipe 'em off."

"Come on!" they exclaimed, accepting this plan with glee.

Wrinkles opened the door and seemed about to glide away, when he suddenly turned and shook his head. "It's dead wrong," he said, ashamed.

"Oh, go on!" eagerly whispered the others. Presently they stole pattering down the corridor, grinning, exclaiming, and cautioning each other.

At the window Pennoyer said: "Now, for heaven's sake, don't let them see you! —Be careful, Grief, you'll tumble. —Don't lean on me that way, Wrink; think I'm a barn door? Here they come. Keep back. Don't let them see you."

"O-o-oh!" said Grief. "Talk about a peach! Well, I should say so."

Florinda's fingers tore at Wrinkle's coat sleeve. "Wrink, Wrink, is that her? Is that her? On the left of Billie? Is that her, Wrink?"

"What? Yes. Stop punching me! Yes, I tell you! That's her. Are you deaf?"

CHAPTER XXXI.

In the evening Pennoyer conducted Florinda to the flat of many fire-escapes. After a period of silent tramping through the great golden avenue and the street that was being repaired, she said, "Penny, you are very good to me."

"Why?" said Pennoyer.

"Oh, because you are. You-you are very good to me, Penny."

"Well, I guess I'm not killing myself."

"There isn't many fellows like you."

"No?"

"No. There isn't many fellows like you, Penny. I tell you 'most everything, and you just listen, and don't argue with me and tell me I'm a fool, because you know that it-because you know that it can't be helped, anyhow."

"Oh, nonsense, you kid! Almost anybody would be glad to — —"

"Penny, do you think she is very beautiful?" Florinda's voice had a singular quality of awe in it.

"Well," replied Pennoyer, "I don't know."

"Yes, you do, Penny. Go ahead and tell me."

"Well — —"

"Go ahead."

"Well, she is rather handsome, you know."

"Yes," said Florinda, dejectedly, "I suppose she is." After a time she cleared her throat and remarked indifferently, "I suppose Billie cares a lot for her?"

"Oh, I imagine that he does-in a way."

"Why, of course he does," insisted Florinda. "What do you mean by 'in a way'? You know very well that Billie thinks his eyes of her."

"No, I don't."

"Yes, you do. You know you do. You are talking in that way just to brace me up. You know you are."

"No, I'm not."

"Penny," said Florinda thankfully, "what makes you so good to me?"

"Oh, I guess I'm not so astonishingly good to you. Don't be silly."

"But you are good to me, Penny. You don't make fun of me the way-the way the other boys would. You are just as good as you can be. —But you do think she is beautiful, don't you?"

"They wouldn't make fun of you," said Pennoyer.

"But do you think she is beautiful?"

"Look here, Splutter, let up on that, will you? You keep harping on one string all the time. Don't bother me!"

"But, honest now, Penny, you do think she is beautiful?"

"Well, then, confound it-no! no! no!"

"Oh, yes, you do, Penny. Go ahead now. Don't deny it just because you are talking to me. Own up, now, Penny. You do think she is beautiful?"

"Well," said Pennoyer, in a dull roar of irritation, "do you?"

Florinda walked in silence, her eyes upon the yellow flashes which lights sent to the pavement. In the end she said, "Yes."

"Yes, what?" asked Pennoyer sharply.

"Yes, she-yes, she is-beautiful."

"Well, then?" cried Pennoyer, abruptly closing the discussion.

Florinda announced something as a fact. "Billie thinks his eyes of her."

"How do you know he does?"

"Don't scold at me, Penny. You-you — —"

"I'm not scolding at you. There! What a goose you are, Splutter! Don't, for heaven's sake, go to whimpering on the street! I didn't say anything to make you feel that way. Come, pull yourself together."

"I'm not whimpering."

"No, of course not; but then you look as if you were on the edge of it. What a little idiot!"

CHAPTER XXXII.

When the snow fell upon the clashing life of the city, the exiled stones, beaten by myriad strange feet, were told of the dark, silent forests where the flakes swept through the hemlocks and swished softly against the boulders.

In his studio Hawker smoked a pipe, clasping his knee with thoughtful, interlocked fingers. He was gazing sourly at his finished picture. Once he started to his feet with a cry of vexation. Looking back over his shoulder, he swore an insult into the face of the picture. He paced to and fro, smoking belligerently and from time to time eying it. The helpless thing remained upon the easel, facing him.

Hollanden entered and stopped abruptly at sight of the great scowl. "What's wrong now?" he said.

Hawker gestured at the picture. "That dunce of a thing. It makes me tired. It isn't worth a hang. Blame it!"

"What?" Hollanden strode forward and stood before the painting with legs apart, in a properly critical manner. "What? Why, you said it was your best thing."

"Aw!" said Hawker, waving his arms, "it's no good! I abominate it! I didn't get what I wanted, I tell you. I didn't get what I wanted. That?" he shouted, pointing thrust-way at it —"that? It's vile! Aw! it makes me weary."

"You're in a nice state," said Hollanden, turning to take a critical view of the painter. "What has got into you now? I swear, you are more kinds of a chump!"

Hawker crooned dismally: "I can't paint! I can't paint for a damn! I'm no good. What in thunder was I invented for, anyhow, Hollie?"

"You're a fool," said Hollanden. "I hope to die if I ever saw such a complete idiot! You give me a pain. Just because she don't ——"

"It isn't that. She has nothing to do with it, although I know well enough —I know well enough——"

"What?"

"I know well enough she doesn't care a hang for me. It isn't that. It is because-it is because I can't paint. Look at that thing over there! Remember the thought and energy I —— Damn the thing!"

"Why, did you have a row with her?" asked Hollanden, perplexed. "I didn't know——"

"No, of course you didn't know," cried Hawker, sneering; "because I had no row. It isn't that, I tell you. But I know well enough" —he shook his fist vaguely —"that she don't care an old tomato can for me. Why should she?" he demanded with a curious defiance. "In the name of Heaven, why should she?"

"I don't know," said Hollanden; "I don't know, I'm sure. But, then, women have no social logic. This is the great blessing of the world. There is only one thing which is superior to the multiplicity of social forms, and that is a woman's mind —a young woman's mind. Oh, of course, sometimes they are logical, but let a woman be so once, and she will repent of it to the end of her days. The safety of the world's balance lies in woman's illogical mind. I think——"

"Go to blazes!" said Hawker. "I don't care what you think. I am sure of one thing, and that is that she doesn't care a hang for me!"

"I think," Hollanden continued, "that society is doing very well in its work of bravely lawing away at Nature; but there is one immovable thing —a woman's illogical mind. That is our safety. Thank Heaven, it ——"

"Go to blazes!" said Hawker again.

CHAPTER XXXIII.

As Hawker again entered the room of the great windows he glanced in sidelong bitterness at the chandelier. When he was seated he looked at it in open defiance and hatred.

Men in the street were shovelling at the snow. The noise of their instruments scraping on the stones came plainly to Hawker's ears in a harsh chorus, and this sound at this time was perhaps to him a *miserere*.

"I came to tell you," he began, "I came to tell you that perhaps I am going away."

"Going away!" she cried. "Where?"

"Well, I don't know-quite. You see, I am rather indefinite as yet. I thought of going for the winter somewhere in the Southern States. I am decided merely this much, you know—I am going somewhere. But I don't know where. 'Way off, anyhow."

"We shall be very sorry to lose you," she remarked. "We——"

"And I thought," he continued, "that I would come and say 'adios' now for fear that I might leave very suddenly. I do that sometimes. I'm afraid you will forget me very soon, but I want to tell you that——"

"Why," said the girl in some surprise, "you speak as if you were going away for all time. You surely do not mean to utterly desert New York?"

"I think you misunderstand me," he said. "I give this important air to my farewell to you because to me it is a very important event. Perhaps you recollect that once I told you that I cared for you. Well, I still care for you, and so I can only go away somewhere-some place 'way off-where-where——See?"

"New York is a very large place," she observed.

"Yes, New York is a very large——How good of you to remind me! But then you don't understand. You can't understand. I know I can find no place where I will cease to remember you, but then I can find some place where I can cease to remember in a way that I am myself. I shall never try to forget you. Those two violets, you know-one I found near the tennis court and the other you gave me, you remember—I shall take them with me."

"Here," said the girl, tugging at her gown for a moment—"Here! Here's a third one." She thrust a violet toward him.

"If you were not so serenely insolent," said Hawker, "I would think that you felt sorry for me. I don't wish you to feel sorry for me. And I don't wish to be melodramatic. I know it is all commonplace enough, and I didn't mean to act like a tenor. Please don't pity me."

"I don't," she replied. She gave the violet a little fling.

Hawker lifted his head suddenly and glowered at her. "No, you don't," he at last said slowly, "you don't. Moreover, there is no reason why you should take the trouble. But——"

He paused when the girl leaned and peered over the arm of her chair precisely in the manner of a child at the brink of a fountain. "There's my violet on the floor," she said. "You treated it quite contemptuously, didn't you?"

"Yes."

Together they stared at the violet. Finally he stooped and took it in his fingers. "I feel as if this third one was pelted at me, but I shall keep it. You are rather a cruel person, but, Heaven guard us! that only fastens a man's love the more upon a woman."

She laughed. "That is not a very good thing to tell a woman."

"No," he said gravely, "it is not, but then I fancy that somebody may have told you previously."

She stared at him, and then said, "I think you are revenged for my serene insolence."

"Great heavens, what an armour!" he cried. "I suppose, after all, I did feel a trifle like a tenor when I first came here, but you have chilled it all out of me. Let's talk upon indifferent topics." But he started abruptly to his feet. "No," he said, "let us not talk upon indifferent topics. I am not brave, I assure you, and it-it might be too much for me." He held out his hand. "Good-bye."

"You are going?"

"Yes, I am going. Really I didn't think how it would bore you for me to come around here and croak in this fashion."

"And you are not coming back for a long, long time?"

"Not for a long, long time." He mimicked her tone. "I have the three violets now, you know, and you must remember that I took the third one even when you flung it at my head. That will remind you how submissive I was in my devotion. When you recall the two others it will remind you of what a fool I was. Dare say you won't miss three violets."

"No," she said.

"Particularly the one you flung at my head. That violet was certainly freely-given."

"I didn't fling it at your head." She pondered for a time with her eyes upon the floor. Then she murmured, "No more freely-given than the one I gave you that night-that night at the inn."

"So very good of you to tell me so!"

Her eyes were still upon the floor.

"Do you know," said Hawker, "it is very hard to go away and leave an impression in your mind that I am a fool? That is very hard. Now, you do think I am a fool, don't you?"

She remained silent. Once she lifted her eyes and gave him a swift look with much indignation in it.

"Now you are enraged. Well, what have I done?"

It seemed that some tumult was in her mind, for she cried out to him at last in sudden tearfulness: "Oh, do go! Go! Please! I want you to go!"

Under this swift change Hawker appeared as a man struck from the sky. He sprang to his feet, took two steps forward, and spoke a word which was an explosion of delight and amazement. He said, "What?"

With heroic effort she slowly raised her eyes until, alight with anger, defiance, unhappiness, they met his eyes.

Later, she told him that he was perfectly ridiculous.

Active Service

CHAPTER I.

MARJORY walked pensively along the hall. In the cool shadows made by the palms on the window ledge, her face wore the expression of thoughtful melancholy expected on the faces of the devotees who pace in cloistered gloom. She halted before a door at the end of the hall and laid her hand on the knob. She stood hesitating, her head bowed. It was evident that this mission was to require great fortitude.

At last she opened the door. "Father," she began at once. There was disclosed an elderly, narrow-faced man seated at a large table and surrounded by manuscripts and books. The sunlight flowing through curtains of Turkey red fell sanguinely upon the bust of dead-eyed Pericles on the mantle. A little clock was ticking, hidden somewhere among the countless leaves of writing, the maps and broad heavy tomes that swarmed upon the table.

Her father looked up quickly with an ogreish scowl.

Go away!" he cried in a rage. "Go away. Go away. Get out " "He seemed on the point of arising to eject the visitor. It was plain to her that he had been interrupted in the writing of one of his sentences, ponderous, solemn and endless, in which wandered multitudes of homeless and friendless prepositions, adjectives looking for a parent, and quarrelling nouns, sentences which no longer symbolised the languageform of thought but which had about them a quaint aroma from the dens of long-dead scholars. "Get out," snarled the professor.

Father," faltered the girl. Either because his formulated thought was now completely knocked out of his mind by his own emphasis in defending it, or because he detected something of portent in her expression, his manner suddenly changed, and with a petulant glance at his writing he laid down his pen and sank back in his chair to listen. "Well, what is it, my child?"

The girl took a chair near the window and gazed out upon the snow-stricken campus, where at the moment a group of students returning from a class room were festively hurling snow-balls. "I've got something important to tell you, father," said she, but I don't quite know how to say it."

"Something important?" repeated the professor. He was not habitually interested in the affairs of his family, but this proclamation that something important could be connected with them, filled his mind with a capricious interest. "Well, what is it, Marjory?"

She replied calmly: "Rufus Coleman wants to marry me."

"What?" demanded the professor loudly. "Rufus Coleman. What do you mean?"

The girl glanced furtively at him. She did not seem to be able to frame a suitable sentence.

As for the professor, he had, like all men both thoughtless and thoughtful, told himself that one day his daughter would come to him with a tale of this kind. He had never forgotten that the little girl was to be a woman, and he had never forgotten that this tall, lithe creature, the present Marjory, was a woman. He had been entranced and confident or entranced and apprehensive according' to the time. A man focussed upon astronomy, the pig market or social progression, may nevertheless have a secondary mind which hovers like a spirit over his dahlia tubers and dreams upon the mystery of their slow and tender revelations. The professor's secondary mind had dwelt always with his daughter and watched with a faith and delight the changing to a woman of a certain fat and mumbling babe. However, he now saw this machine, this self- sustaining, self-operative love, which had run with the ease of a clock, suddenly crumble to ashes and leave the mind of a great scholar staring at a calamity. "Rufus Coleman," he repeated, stunned. Here was his daughter, very obviously desirous of marrying Rufus Coleman. "Marjory," he cried in amazement and fear, "what possesses, you? Marry Rufus Colman?"

The girl seemed to feel a strong sense of relief at his prompt recognition of a fact. Being freed from the necessity of making a flat declaration, she simply hung her head and blushed impressively. A hush fell upon them. The professor stared long at his daughter. The shadow of unhappiness deepened upon his face. "Marjory, Marjory," he murmured at last. He had tramped heroically upon his panic and devoted his strength to bringing thought into some kind of attitude toward this terrible fact. "I am-I am surprised," he began. Fixing her then with a stern eye, he asked: "Why do you wish to marry this man? You, with your opportunities of meeting persons of intelligence. And you want to marry–" His voice grew tragic. "You want to marry the Sunday editor of the New York Eclipse."

"It is not so very terrible, is it?" said Marjory sullenly.

"Wait a moment; don't talk," cried the professor. He arose and walked nervously to and fro, his hands flying in the air. He was very red behind the ears as when in the Classroom some student offended him. "A gambler, a sporter of fine clothes, an expert on champagne, a polite loafer, a witness knave who edits the Sunday edition of a great outrage upon our sensibilities. You want to marry him, this man? Marjory, you are insane. This fraud who asserts that his work is intelligent, this fool comes here to my house and–"

He became aware that his daughter was regarding him coldly. "I thought we had best have all this part of it over at once," she remarked.

He confronted her in a new kind of surprise. The little keen-eyed professor was at this time imperial, on the verge of a majestic outburst. "Be still," he said. "Don't be clever with your father. Don't be a dodger. Or, if you are, don't speak of it to me. I suppose this fine young man expects to see me personally?"

"He was coming to-morrow," replied Marjory. She began to weep. "He was coming to-morrow."

"Um," said the professor. He continued his pacing while Marjory wept with her head bowed to the arm of the chair. His brow made the three dark vertical crevices well known to his students. Some.times he glowered murderously at the photographs of ancient temples which adorned the walls. "My poor child," he said once, as he paused near her, "to think I never knew you were a fool. I have been deluding myself. It has been my fault as much as it has been yours. I will not readily forgive myself."

The girl raised her face and looked at him. Finally, resolved to disregard the dishevelment wrought by tears, she presented a desperate front with her wet eyes and flushed cheeks. Her hair was disarrayed. "I don't see why you can call me a fool," she said. The pause before this sentence had been so portentous of a wild and rebellious speech that the professor almost laughed now. But still the father for the first time knew that he was being un-dauntedly faced by his child in his own library, in the presence Of 372 pages of the book that was to be his masterpiece. At the back of his mind he felt a great awe as if his own youthful spirit had come from the past and challenged him with a glance. For a moment he was almost a defeated man. He dropped into a chair. " Does your mother know of this " " he asked mournfully.

"Yes," replied the girl. "She knows. She has been trying to make me give up Rufus."

"Rufus," cried the professor rejuvenated by anger.

"Well, his name is Rufus," said the girl.

"But please don't call him so before me," said the father with icy dignity. "I do not recognise him as being named Rufus. That is a contention of yours which does not arouse my interest. I know him very well as a gambler and a drunkard, and if incidentally, he is named Rufus, I fail to see any importance to it."

"He is not a gambler and he is not a drunkard," she said.

"Um. He drinks heavily-that is well known. He gambles. He plays cards for money-more than he possesses-at least he did when he was in college."

"You said you liked him when he was in college."

"So I did. So I did," answered the professor sharply. "I often find myself liking that kind of a boy in college. Don't I know them-those lads with their beer and their poker games in the dead of the night with a towel hung over the keyhole. Their habits are often vicious enough, but something remains in them through it all and they may go away and do great things. This happens. We know it. It happens with confusing insistence. It destroys theo-ries. There-there isn't much to say about it. And sometimes we like this kind of a boy better than we do the-the others. For my part I know of many a pure, pious and fine-minded student that I have positively loathed from a personal point-of-view. But," he added, "this Rufus Coleman, his life in college and his life since, go to prove how often we get off the track. There is no gauge of collegiate conduct whatever, until we can get evidence of the man's work in the world. Your precious scoundrel's evidence is now all in and he is a failure, or worse."

"You are not habitually so fierce in judging people," said the girl.

"I would be if they all wanted to marry my daughter," rejoined the professor. "Rather than let that man make love to you-or even be within a short railway journey of you, I'll cart you off to Europe this winter and keep you there until you forget. If you persist in this silly fancy, I shall at once become medieval."

Marjory had evidently recovered much of her composure. "Yes, father, new climates are alway's supposed to cure one," she remarked with a kind of lightness.

"It isn't so much the old expedient," said the professor musingly, "as it is that I would be afraid to leave you herewith no protection against that drinking gambler and gambling drunkard."

"Father, I have to ask you not to use such terms in speaking of the man that I shall marry."

There was a silence. To all intents, the professor remained unmoved. He smote the tips of his fingers thoughtfully together. "Ye-es," he observed. "That sounds reasonable from your standpoint." His eyes studied her face in a long and steady glance. He arose and went into the hall. When he returned he wore his hat and great coat. He took a book and some papers from the table and went away.

Marjory walked slowly through the halls and up to her room. From a window she could see her father making his way across the campus labouriously against the wind and whirling snow. She watched it, this little black figure, bent forward, patient, steadfast. It was an inferior fact that her father was one of the famous scholars of the generation. To her, he was now a little old man facing the wintry winds. Recollect. ing herself and Rufus Coleman she began to weep again, wailing amid the ruins of her tumbled hopes. Her skies had turned to paper and her trees were mere bits of green sponge. But amid all this woe appeared the little black image of her father making its way against the storm.

CHAPTER II.

IN a high-walled corridor of one of the college buildings, a crowd of students waited amid jostlings and a loud buzz of talk. Suddenly a huge pair of doors flew open and a wedge of young men inserted itself boisterously and deeply into the throng. There was a great scuffle attended by a general banging of books upon heads. The two lower classes engaged in herculean play while members of the two higher classes, standing aloof, devoted themselves strictly to the encouragement of whichever party for a moment lost ground or heart. This was in order to prolong the conflict.

The combat, waged in the desperation of proudest youth, waxed hot and hotter. The wedge had been instantly smitten into a kind of block of men. It had crumpled into an irregular square and on three sides it was now assailed with remarkable ferocity.

It was a matter of wall meet wall in terrific rushes, during which lads could feel their very hearts leaving them in the compress of friends and foes. They on the outskirts upheld the honour of their classes by squeezing into paper thickness the lungs of those of their fellows who formed the centre of the melee

In some way it resembled a panic at a theatre.

The first lance-like attack of the Sophomores had been formidable, but the Freshmen outnumbering their enemies and smarting from continual Sophomoric oppression, had swarmed to the front like drilled collegians and given the arrogant foe the first serious check of the year. Therefore the tall Gothic windows which lined one side of the corridor looked down upon as incomprehensible and enjoyable a tumult as could mark the steps of advanced education. The Seniors and juniors cheered themselves ill. Long freed from the joy of such meetings, their only means for this kind of recreation was to involve the lower classes, and they had never seen the victims fall to with such vigour and courage. Bits of printed leaves, torn note-books, dismantled collars and cravats, all floated to the floor beneath the feet of the warring hordes. There were no blows; it was a battle of pressure. It was a deadly pushing where the leaders on either side often suffered the most cruel and sickening agony caught thus between phalanxes of shoulders with friend as well as foe contributing to the pain.

Charge after charge of Freshmen beat upon the now compact and organised Sophomores. Then, finally, the rock began to give slow way. A roar came from the Freshmen and they hurled themselves in a frenzy upon their betters.

To be under the gaze of the juniors and Seniors is to be in sight of all men, and so the Sophomores at this important moment laboured with the desperation of the half-doomed to stem the terrible Freshmen.

In the kind of game, it was the time when bad tempers came strongly to the front, and in many Sophomores' minds a thought arose of the incomparable insolence of the Freshmen. A blow was struck; an infuriated Sophomore had swung an arm high and smote a Freshman.

Although it had seemed that no greater noise could be made by the given numbers, the din that succeeded this manifestation surpassed everything. The juniors and Seniors immediately set up an angry howl. These veteran classes projected themselves into the middle of the fight, buffeting everybody with small thought as to merit. This method of bringing peace was as militant as a landslide, but they had much trouble before they could separate the central clump of antagonists into its parts. A score of Freshmen had cried out: "It was Coke. Coke punched him. Coke." A dozen of them were tempestuously endeavouring to register their protest against fisticuffs by means of an introduction of more fisticuffs.

The upper classmen were swift, harsh and hard. "Come, now, Freshies, quit it. Get back, get back, d'y'hear?" With a wrench of muscles they forced themselves in front of Coke, who was being blindly defended by his classmates from intensely earnest attacks by outraged Freshmen.

These meetings between the lower classes at the door of a recitation room were accounted quite comfortable and idle affairs, and a blow delivered openly and in hatred fractured a sharply defined rule of conduct. The corridor was in a hubbub. Many Seniors and Juniors, bursting from old and iron discipline, wildly clamoured that some Freshman should be given the privilege of a single encounter with Coke. The Freshmen themselves were frantic. They besieged the tight and dauntless circle of men that encompassed Coke. None dared confront the Seniors openly, but by headlong rushes at auspicious moments they tried to come to quarters with the rings of dark-browed Sophomores. It was no longer a festival, a game; it was a riot. Coke, wild-eyed, pallid with fury, a ribbon of blood on his chin, swayed in the middle of the mob of his classmates, comrades who waived the ethics of the blow under the circumstance of being obliged as a corps to stand against the scorn of the whole college, as well as against the tremendous assaults of the Freshmen. Shamed by their own man, but knowing full well the right time and the wrong time for a palaver of regret and disavowal, this battalion struggled in the desperation of despair. Once they were upon the verge of making unholy campaign against the interfering Seniors. This fiery impertinence was the measure of their state.

It was a critical moment in the play of the college. Four or five defeats from the Sophomores during the fall had taught the Freshmen much. They had learned the comparative measurements, and they knew now that their prowess was ripe to enable them to amply revenge what was, according to their standards, an execrable deed by a man who had not the virtue to play the rough game, but was obliged to resort to uncommon methods. In short, the Freshmen were almost out of control, and the Sophomores debased but defiant, were quite out of control. The Senior and junior classes which, in American colleges dictate in these affrays, found their dignity toppling, and in consequence there was a sudden oncome of the entire force of upper classmen football players naturally in advance. All distinctions were dissolved at once in a general fracas. The stiff and still Gothic windows surveyed a scene of dire carnage.

Suddenly a voice rang brazenly through the tumult. It was not loud, but it was different. "Gentlemen! Gentlemen!'" Instantly there was a remarkable number of haltings, abrupt replacements, quick changes. Prof. Wainwright stood at the door of his recitation room, looking into the eyes of each member of the mob of three hundred. "Ssh! " said the mob. " Ssh! Quit! Stop! It's the Embassador! Stop!" He had once been minister to Austro-Hungary, and forever now to the students of the college his name was Embassador. He stepped into the corridor, and they cleared for him a little respectful zone of floor. He looked about him coldly. "It seems quite a general dishevelment. The Sophomores display an energy in the halls which I do not detect in the class room." A feeble murmur of appreciation arose from the outskirts of the throng. While he had been speaking several remote groups of battling men had been violently signaled and suppressed by other students. The professor gazed into terraces of faces that were still inflamed. "I needn't say that I am surprised," he remarked in the accepted rhetoric of his kind. He added musingly: "There seems to be a great deal of torn linen. Who is the young gentleman with blood on his chin?"

The throng moved restlessly. A manful silence, such as might be in the tombs of stern and honourable knights, fell upon the shadowed corridor. The subdued rustling had fainted to nothing. Then out of the crowd Coke, pale and desperate, delivered himself.

"Oh, Mr. Coke," said the professor, "I would be glad if you would tell the gentlemen they may retire to their dormitories." He waited while the students passed out to the campus.

The professor returned to his room for some books, and then began his own march across the snowy campus. The wind twisted his coat-tails fantastically, and he was obliged to keep one hand firmly on the top of his hat. When he arrived home he met his wife in the hall. "Look here, Mary," he cried. She followed him into the library. "Look here," he said. "What is this all about? Marjory tells me she wants to marry Rufus Coleman."

Mrs. Wainwright was a fat woman who was said to pride herself upon being very wise and if necessary, sly. In addition she laughed continually in an inexplicably personal way, which apparently made everybody who heard her feel offended. Mrs. Wainwright laughed.

"Well," said the professor, bristling, "what do you mean by that?"

"Oh, Harris," she replied. "Oh, Harris."

The professor straightened in his chair. "I do not see any illumination in those remarks, Mary. I understand from Marjory's manner that she is bent upon marrying Rufus Coleman. She said you knew of it."

"Why, of course I knew. It was as plain——"

"Plain!" scoffed the professor. "Plain!"

Why, of course," she cried. "I knew it all along."

There was nothing in her tone which proved that she admired the event itself. She was evidently carried away by the triumph of her penetration. "I knew it all along," she added, nodding.

The professor looked at her affectionately. "You knew it all along, then, Mary? Why didn't you tell me, dear?"

"Because you ought to have known it," she answered blatantly.

The professor was glaring. Finally he spoke in tones of grim reproach. "Mary, whenever you happen to know anything, dear, it seems only a matter of partial recompense that you should tell me."

The wife had been taught in a terrible school that she should never invent any inexpensive retorts concerning bookworms and so she yawed at once. "Really, Harris. Really, I didn't suppose the affair was serious. You could have knocked me down with a feather. Of course he has been here very often, but then Marjory gets a great deal of attention. A great deal of attention." The professor had been thinking. "Rather than let my girl marry that scalawag, I'll take you and her to Greece this winter with the class. Separation. It is a sure cure that has the sanction of antiquity."

"Well," said Mrs. Wainwright, "you know best, Harris. You know best." It was a common remark with her, and it probably meant either approbation or disapprobation if it did not mean simple discretion.

CHAPTER III.

THERE had been a babe with no arms born in one of the western counties of Massachusetts. In place of upper limbs the child had growing from its chest a pair of fin-like hands, mere bits of skin-covered bone. Furthermore, it had only one eye. This phenomenon lived four days, but the news of the birth had travelled up this country road and through that village until it reached the ears of the editor of the Michaelstown Tribune. He was also a correspondent of the New York Eclipse. On the third day he appeared at the home of the parents accompanied by a photographer. While the latter arranged his, instrument, the correspondent talked to the father and mother, two coweyed and yellow-faced people who seemed to suffer a primitive fright of the strangers. Afterwards as the correspondent and the photographer were climbing into their buggy, the mother crept furtively down to the gate and asked, in a foreigner's dialect, if they would send her a copy of the photograph. The correspondent carelessly indulgent, promised it. As the buggy swung away, the father came from behind an apple tree, and the two semi-humans watched it with its burden of glorious strangers until it rumbled across the bridge and disappeared. The correspondent was elate; he told the photographer that the Eclipse would probably pay fifty dollars for the article and the photograph.

The office of the New York Eclipse was at the top of the immense building on Broadway. It was a sheer mountain to the heights of which the interminable thunder of the streets arose faintly. The Hudson was a broad path of silver in the distance. Its edge was marked by the tracery of sailing ships' rigging and by the huge and many-coloured stacks of ocean liners. At the foot of the cliff lay City Hall Park. It seemed no larger than a quilt. The grey walks patterned the snow-covering into triangles and ovals and upon them many tiny people scurried here and there, without sound, like a fish at the bottom of a pool. It was only the vehicles that sent high, unmistakable, the deep bass of their movement. And yet after listening one seemed to hear a singular murmurous note, a pulsation, as if the crowd made noise by its mere living, a mellow hum of the eternal strife. Then suddenly out of the deeps might ring a human voice, a newsboy shout perhaps, the cry of a faraway jackal at night.

From the level of the ordinary roofs, combined in many plateaus, dotted with short iron chimneys from which curled wisps of steam, arose other mountains like the Eclipse Building. They were great peaks, ornate, glittering with paint or polish. Northward they subsided to sun-crowned ranges.

From some of the windows of the Eclipse office dropped the walls of a terrible chasm in the darkness of which could be seen vague struggling figures. Looking down into this appalling crevice one discovered only the tops of hats and knees which in spasmodic jerks seemed to touch the rims of the hats. The scene represented some weird fight or dance or carouse. It was not an exhibition of men hurrying along a narrow street.

It was good to turn one's eyes from that place to the vista of the city's splendid reaches, with spire and spar shining in the clear atmosphere and the marvel of the Jersey shore, pearl-misted or brilliant with detail. From this height the sweep of a snow-storm was defined and majestic. Even a slight summer shower, with swords of lurid yellow sunlight piercing its edges as if warriors were contesting every foot of its advance, was from the Eclipse office something so inspiring that the chance pilgrim felt a sense of exultation as if from this peak he was surveying the worldwide war of the elements and life. The staff of the Eclipse usually worked without coats and amid the smoke from pipes.

To one of the editorial chambers came a photograph and an article from Michaelstown, Massachusetts. A boy placed the packet and many others upon the desk of a young man who was standing before a window and thoughtfully drumming upon the pane. He turned at the thudding of the packets upon his desk. "Blast you," he remarked amiably. "Oh, I guess it won't hurt you to work," answered the boy, grinning with a comrade's Insolence. Baker, an assistant editor for the Sunday paper, took scat at his desk and began the task of examining the packets.

His face could not display any particular interest because he had been at the same work for nearly a fortnight.

The first long envelope he opened was from a woman. There was a neat little manuscript accompanied by a letter which explained that the writer was a widow who was trying to make her living by her pen and who, further, hoped that the generosity of the editor of the Eclipse would lead him to give her article the opportunity which she was sure it deserved. She hoped that the editor would pay her as well as possible for it, as she needed the money greatly. She added that her brother was a reporter on the Little Rock Sentinel and he had declared that her literary style was excellent. Baker really did not read this note. His vast experience of a fortnight had enabled him to detect its kind in two glances. He unfolded the manuscript, looked at it woodenly and then tossed it with the letter to the top of his desk, where it lay with the other corpses. None could think of widows in Arkansas, ambitious from the praise of the reporter on the Little Rock Sentinel, waiting for a crown of literary glory and money. In the next envelope a man using the note-paper of a Boston journal begged to know if the accompanying article would be acceptable; if not it was to be kindly returned in the enclosed stamped envelope. It was a humourous essay on trolley cars. Adventuring through the odd scraps that were come to the great mill, Baker paused occasionally to relight his pipe.

As he went through envelope after envelope, the desks about him gradually were occupied by young men who entered from the hall with their faces still red from the cold of the streets. For the most part they bore the unmistakable stamp of the American college. They had that confident poise which is easily brought from the athletic field. Moreover, their clothes were quite in the way of being of the newest fashion. There was an air of precision about their cravats and linen. But on the other hand there might be with them some indifferent westerner who was obliged to resort to irregular means and harangue startled shop-keepers in order to provide himself with collars of a strange kind. He was usually very quick and brave of eye and noted for his inability to perceive a distinction between his own habit and the habit of others, his western character preserving itself inviolate amid a confusion of manners.

The men, coming one and one, or two and two, flung badinage to all corners of the room. Afterward, as they wheeled from time to time in their chairs, they bitterly insulted each other with the utmost good-nature, taking unerring aim at faults and riddling personalities with the quaint and cynical humour of a newspaper office. Throughout this banter, it was strange to note how infrequently the men smiled, particularly when directly engaged in an encounter.

A wide door opened into another apartment where were many little slanted tables, each under an electric globe with a green shade. Here a curly-headed scoundrel with a corncob pipe was hurling paper balls the size of apples at the head of an industrious man who, under these difficulties, was trying to draw a picture of an awful wreck with ghastly-faced sailors frozen in the rigging. Near this pair a lady was challenging a German artist who resembled Napoleon III. with having been publicly drunk at a music hall on the previous night. Next to the great gloomy corridor of this sixteenth floor was a little office presided over by an austere boy, and here waited in enforced patience a little dismal band of people who wanted to see the Sunday editor.

Baker took a manuscript and after glancing about the room, walked over to a man at another desk, Here is something that. I think might do," he said. The man at the desk read the first two pages. "But where is the photogragh " " he asked then. "There should be a photograph with this thing."

"Oh, I forgot," said Baker. He brought from his desk a photograph of the babe that had been born lacking arms and one eye. Baker's superior braced a knee against his desk and settled back to a judicial attitude. He took the photograph and looked at it impassively. "Yes," he said, after a time, "that's a pretty good thing. You better show that to Coleman when he comes in."

In the little office where the dismal band waited, there had been a sharp hopeful stir when Rufus Coleman, the Sunday editor, passed rapidly from door to door and vanished within the holy precincts. It had evidently been in the minds of some to accost him then, but his eyes did not turn once in their direction. It was as if he had not seen them. Many experiences had taught him that the proper manner of passing through this office was at a blind gallop.

The dismal band turned then upon the austere office boy. Some demanded with terrible dignity that he should take in their cards at once. Others sought to ingratiate themselves by smiles of tender friendliness. He for his part employed what we would have called his knowledge of men and women upon the group, and in consequence blundered and bungled vividly, freezing with a glance an annoyed and importunate Arctic explorer who was come to talk of illustrations for an article that had been lavishly paid for in advance. The hero might have thought he was again in the northern seas. At the next moment the boy was treating almost courteously a German from the east side who wanted the Eclipse to print a grand full page advertising description of his invention, a gun which was supposed to have a range of forty miles and to be able to penetrate anything with equanimity and joy. The gun, as a matter of fact, had once been induced to go off when it had hurled itself passionately upon its back, incidentally breaking its inventor's leg. The projectile had wandered some four hundred yards seaward, where it dug a hole in the water which was really a menace to navigation. Since then there had been nothing tangible save the inventor, in splints and out of splints, as the fortunes of science decreed. In short, this office boy mixed his business in the perfect manner of an underdone lad dealing with matters too large for him, and throughout he displayed the pride and assurance of a god.

As Coleman crossed the large office his face still wore the stern expression which he invariably used to carry him unmolested through the ranks of the dismal band. As he was removing his London overcoat he addressed the imperturbable back of one of his staff, who had a desk against the opposite wall. "Has Hasskins sent in that drawing of the mine accident yet?" The man did not lift his head from his work-, but he answered at once: "No; not yet." Coleman was laying his hat on a chair. "Well, why hasn't he?" he demanded. He glanced toward the door of the room in which the curly-headed scoundrel with the corncob pipe was still hurling paper balls at the man who was trying to invent the postures of dead mariners frozen in the rigging. The office boy came timidly from his post and informed Coleman of the waiting people. "All right," said the editor. He dropped into his chair and began to finger his letters, which had been neatly opened and placed in a little stack by a boy. Baker came in with the photograph of the miserable babe.

It was publicly believed that the Sunday staff of the Eclipse must have a kind of aesthetic delight in pictures of this kind, but Coleman's face betrayed no emotion as he looked at this specimen. He lit a fresh cigar, tilted his chair and surveyed it with a cold and stony stare. "Yes, that's all right," he said slowly. There seemed to be no affectionate relation between him and this picture. Evidently he was weighing its value as a morsel to be flung to a ravenous public, whose wolf-like appetite, could only satisfy itself upon mental entrails, abominations. As for himself, he seemed to be remote, exterior. It was a matter of the Eclipse business.

Suddenly Coleman became executive. "Better give it to Schooner and tell him to make a half-page —-or, no, send him in here and I'll tell him my idea. How's the article? Any good? Well, give it to Smith to rewrite."

An artist came from the other room and presented for inspection his drawing of the seamen dead in the rigging of the wreck, a company of grizzly and horrible figures, bony-fingered, shrunken and with awful eyes. "Hum," said Coleman, after a prolonged study, "that's all right. That's good, Jimmie. But you'd better work 'em up around the eyes a little more." The office boy was deploying in the distance, waiting for the correct moment to present some cards and names.

The artist was cheerfully taking away his corpses when Coleman hailed him. "Oh, Jim, let me see that thing again, will you? Now, how about this spar? This don't look right to me."

"It looks right to me," replied the artist, sulkily.

"But, see. It's going to take up half a page. Can't you change it somehow"

How am I going to change it?" said the other, glowering at Coleman. "That's the way it ought to be. How am I going to change it? That's the way it ought to be."

"No, it isn't at all," said Coleman. "You've got a spar sticking out of the main body of the drawing in a way that will spoil the look of the whole page."

The artist was a man of remarkable popular reputation and he was very stubborn and conceited of it, constantly making himself unbearable with covert, threats that if he was not delicately placated at all points, he would freight his genius over to the office of the great opposition journal.

"That's the way it ought to be," he repeated, in a tone at once sullen and superior. "The spar is all right. I can't rig spars on ships just to suit you."

"And I can't give up the whole paper to your accursed spars, either," said Coleman, with animation. "Don't you see you use about a third of a page with this spar sticking off into space? Now, you were always so clever, Jimmie, in adapting yourself to the page. Can't you shorten it, or cut it off, or something? Or, break it—that's the thing. Make it a broken spar dangling down. See?"

"Yes, I s'pose I could do that," said the artist, mollified by a thought of the ease with which he could make the change, and mollified, too, by the brazen tribute to a part of his cleverness.

"Well, do it, then," said the Sunday editor, turning abruptly away. The artist, with head high, walked majestically back to the other room. Whereat the curly-headed one immediately resumed the rain of paper balls upon him. The office boy came timidly to Coleman and suggested the presence of the people in the outer office. "Let them wait until I read my mail," said Coleman. He shuffled the pack of letters indifferently through his hands. Suddenly he came upon a little grey envelope. He opened it at once and scanned its contents with the speed of his craft. Afterward he laid it down before him on the desk and surveyed it with a cool and musing smile. "So?" he remarked. "That's the case, is it?"

He presently swung around in his chair, and for a time held the entire attention of the men at the various desks. He outlined to them again their various parts in the composition of the next great Sunday edition. In a few brisk sentences he set a complex machine in proper motion. His men no longer thrilled with admiration at the precision with which he grasped each obligation of the campaign toward a successful edition. They had grown to accept it as they accepted his hat or his London clothes. At this time his face was lit with something of the self-contained enthusiasm of a general. Immediately afterward he arose and reached for his coat and hat.

The office boy, coming circuitously forward, presented him with some cards and also with a scrap of paper upon which was scrawled a long and semicoherent word. "What are these? " grumbled Coleman.

"They are waiting outside," answered the boy, with trepidation. It was part of the law that the lion of the ante-room should cringe like a cold monkey, more or less, as soon as he was out of his private jungle. "Oh, Tallerman," cried the Sunday editor, "here's this Arctic man come to arrange about his illustration. I wish you'd go and talk it over with him." By chance he picked up the scrap of paper with its cryptic word. "Oh," he said, scowling at the office boy. "Pity you can't remember that fellow. If you can't remember faces any better than that you should be a detective. Get out now and tell him to go to the devil." The wilted slave turned at once, but Coleman hailed him. "Hold on. Come to think of it, I will see this idiot. Send him in," he commanded, grimly.

Coleman lapsed into a dream over the sheet of grey note paper. Presently, a middle-aged man, a palpable German, came hesitatingly into the room and bunted among the desks as unmanageably as a tempest-tossed scow. Finally he was impatiently towed in the right direction. He came and stood at Coleman's elbow and waited nervously for the engrossed man to raise his eyes. It was plain that this interview meant important things to him. Somehow on his commonplace countenance was to be found the expression of a dreamer, a fashioner of great and absurd projects, a fine, tender fool. He cast hopeful and reverent glances at the man who was deeply contemplative of the grey note. He evidently believed himself on the threshold of a triumph of some kind, and he awaited his fruition with a joy that was only made sharper by the usual human suspicion of coming events.

Coleman glanced up at last and saw his visitor.

"Oh, it's you, is it?" he remarked icily, bending upon the German the stare of a tyrant. "So you've come again, have you? " He wheeled in his chair until he could fully display a contemptuous, merciless smile. "Now, Mr. What's-your-name, you've called here to see me about twenty times already and at last I am going to say something definite about your invention." His listener's face, which had worn for a moment a look of fright and bewilderment, gladdened swiftly to a gratitude that seemed the edge of an outburst of tears. "Yes," continued Coleman, "I am going to say something definite. I am going to say that it is the most imbecile bit of nonsense that has come within the range of my large newspaper experience. It is simply the aberration of a rather remarkable lunatic. It is no good; it is not worth the price of a cheese sandwich. I understand that its one feat has been to break your leg; if it ever goes off again, persuade it to break your neck. And now I want you to take this nursery rhyme of yours and get out. And don't ever come here again. Do You understand? You understand, do you?" He arose and bowed in courteous dismissal.

The German was regarding him with the surprise and horror of a youth shot mortally. He could not find his tongue for a moment. Ultimately he gasped : "But, Mister Editor " — Coleman interrupted him tigerishly. "You heard what I said? Get out." The man bowed his head and went slowly toward the door.

Coleman placed the little grey note in his breast pocket. He took his hat and top coat, and evading the dismal band by a shameless manoeuvre, passed through the halls to the entrance to the elevator shaft. He heard a movement behind him and saw that the German was also waiting for the elevator. Standing in the gloom of the corridor, Coleman felt the mournful owlish eyes of the German resting upon him. He took a case from his pocket and elaborately lit a cigarette. Suddenly there was a flash of light and a cage of bronze, gilt and steel dropped, magically from above. Coleman yelled: "Down!" A door flew open. Coleman, followed by the German, stepped upon the elevator. "Well, Johnnie," he said cheerfully to the lad who operated this machine, "is business good?" "Yes, sir, pretty good," answered the boy, grinning. The little cage sank swiftly; floor after floor seemed to be rising with marvellous speed; the whole building was winging straight into the sky. There were soaring lights, figures and the opalescent glow of ground glass doors marked with black inscriptions. Other lifts were springing heavenward. All the lofty corridors rang with cries. "Up! " Down! " " Down! " " Up! " The boy's hand grasped a lever and his machine obeyed his lightest movement with sometimes an unbalancing swiftness.

Coleman discoursed briskly to the youthful attendant. Once he turned and regarded with a quick stare of insolent annoyance the despairing countenance of the German whose eyes had never left him. When the elevator arrived at the ground floor, Coleman departed with the outraged air of a man who for a time had been compelled to occupy a cell in company with a harmless spectre.

He walked quickly away. Opposite a corner of the City Hall he was impelled to look behind him. Through the hordes of people with cable cars marching like panoplied elephants, he was able to distinguish the German, motionless and gazing after him. Coleman laughed. "That's a comic old boy," he said, to himself.

In the grill-room of a Broadway hotel he was obliged to wait some minutes for the fulfillment of his orders and he spent the time in reading and studying the little grey note. When his luncheon was served he ate with an expression of morose dignity.

CHAPTER IV.

MARJORY paused again at her father's door. After hesitating in the original way she entered the library. Her father almost represented an emblematic figure, seated upon a column of books. "Well," he cried. Then, seeing it was Marjory, he changed his tone. "Ah, under the circumstances, my dear, I admit your privilege of interrupting me at any hour of the day. You have important business with me." His manner was satanically indulgent.

The girl fingered a book. She turned the leaves in absolute semblance of a person reading. "Rufus Coleman called."

"Indeed," said the professor.

"And I've come to you, father, before seeing him."

The professor was silent for a time. "Well, Marjory," he said at last, "what do you want me to say?" He spoke very deliberately. "I am sure this is a singular situation. Here appears the man I formally forbid you to marry. I am sure I do not know what I am to say."

"I wish to see him," said the girl.

"You wish to see him?" enquired the professor. "You wish to see him" Marjory, I may as well tell you now that with all the books and plays I've read, I really don't know how the obdurate father should conduct himself. He is always pictured as an exceedingly dense gentleman with white whiskers, who does all the unintelligent things in the plot. You and I are going to play no drama, are we, Marjory? I admit that I have white whiskers, and I am an obdurate father. I am, as you well may say, a very obdurate father. You are not to marry Rufus Coleman. You understand the rest of the matter. He is here ; you want to see him. What will you say to him when you see him?"

"I will say that you refuse to let me marry him, father and-" She hesitated a moment before she lifted her eyes fully and formidably to her father's face. "And that I shall marry him anyhow."

The professor did not cavort when this statement came from his daughter. He nodded and then passed into a period of reflection. Finally he asked: "But when? That is the point. When?"

The girl made a sad gesture. "I don't know. I don't know. Perhaps when you come to know Rufus better-"

"Know him better. Know that rapscallion better? Why, I know him much better than he knows himself. I know him too well. Do you think I am talking offhand about this affair? Do you think I am talking without proper information?"

Marjory made no reply.

"Well," said the professor, "you may see Coleman on condition that you inform him at once that I forbid your marriage to him. I don't understand at all how to manage these situations. I don't know what to do. I suppose I should go myself and-No, you can't see him, Majory."

Still the girl made no reply. Her head sank forward and she breathed a trifle heavily. "Marjory," cried the professor, it is impossible that you should think so much of this man." He arose and went to his daughter. "Marjory, many wise children have been guided by foolish fathers, but we both suspect that no foolish child has ever been guided by a wise father. Let us change it. I present myself to you as a wise father. Follow my wishes in this affair and you will be at least happier than if you marry this wretched Coleman."

She answered: "He is waiting for me."

The professor turned abruptly from her and dropped into his chair at the table. He resumed a grip on his pen. "Go," he said, wearily. "Go. But if you have a remnant of sense, remember what I have said to you. Go." He waved his hand in a dismissal that was slightly scornful. "I hoped you would have a minor conception of what you were doing. It seems a pity." Drooping in tears, the girl slowly left the room.

Coleman had an idea that he had occupied the chair for several months. He gazed about at the pictures and the odds and ends of a drawing-room in an attempt to take an interest in them. The great garlanded paper shade over the piano lamp consoled his impatience in a mild degree because he knew that Marjory had made it. He noted the clusters of cloth violets which she had pinned upon the yellow paper and he dreamed over the fact. He was able to endow this shade with certain qualities of sentiment that caused his stare to become almost a part of an intimacy, a communion. He looked as if he could have unburdened his soul to this shade over the piano lamp.

Upon the appearance of Marjory he sprang up and came forward rapidly. "Dearest," he murmured, stretching out both hands. She gave him one set of fingers with chilling convention. She said something which he understood to be " Good-afternoon." He started as if the woman before him had suddenly drawn a knife. "Marjory," he cried, "what is the matter?." They walked together toward a window. The girl looked at him in polite enquiry. "Why?" she said. "Do I seem strange?" There was a moment's silence while he gazed into her eyes, eyes full of innocence and tranquillity. At last she tapped her foot upon the floor in expression of mild impatience. " People do not like to be asked what is the matter when there is nothing the matter. What do you mean?"

Coleman's face had gradually hardened. "Well, what is wrong?" he demanded, abruptly. "What has happened? What is it, Marjory?"

She raised her glance in a perfect reality of wonder. "What is wrong? What has happened? How absurd! Why nothing, of course." She gazed out of the window. "Look," she added, brightly, the students are rolling somebody in a drift. Oh, the poor Man ! "

Coleman, now wearing a bewildered air, made some pretense of being occupied with the scene. "Yes," he said, ironically. "Very interesting, indeed."

"Oh," said Marjory, suddenly, "I forgot to tell you. Father is going to take mother and me to Greece this winter with him and the class."

Coleman replied at once. "Ah, indeed? That will be jolly."

"Yes. Won't it be charming?"

"I don't doubt it," he replied. His composure May have displeased her, for she glanced at him furtively and in a way that denoted surprise, perhaps.

"Oh, of course," she said, in a glad voice. "It will be more fun. We expect to nave a fine time. There is such a n ice lot of boys going Sometimes father chooses these dreadfully studious ones. But this time he acts as if he knew precisely how to make up a party."

He reached for her hand and grasped it vise-like. "Marjory," he breathed, passionately, "don't treat me so. Don't treat me-"

She wrenched her hand from him in regal indignation. "One or two rings make it uncomfortable for the hand that is grasped by an angry gentleman." She held her fingers and gazed as if she expected to find them mere debris. "I am sorry that you are not interested in the students rolling that man in the snow. It is the greatest scene our quiet life can afford."

He was regarding her as a judge faces a lying culprit. "I know," he said, after a pause. "Somebody has been telling you some stories. You have been hearing something about me."

"Some stories?" she enquired. "Some stories about you? What do you mean? Do you mean that I remember stories I may happen to hear about people?"

There was another pause and then Coleman's face flared red. He beat his hand violently upon a table. "Good God, Marjory! Don't make a fool of me. Don't make this kind of a fool of me, at any rate. Tell me what you mean. Explain-"

She laughed at him. "Explain? Really, your vocabulary is getting extensive, but it is dreadfully awkward to ask people to explain when there is nothing to explain."

He glanced at her, "I know as well as you do that your father is taking you to Greece in order to get rid of me."

"And do people have to go to Greece in order to get rid of you?" she asked, civilly. "I think you are getting excited."

"Marjory," he began, stormily. She raised her hand. "Hush," she said, "there is somebody coming." A bell had rung. A maid entered the room. "Mr. Coke," she said. Marjory nodded. In the interval of waiting, Coleman gave the girl a glance that mingled despair with rage and pride. Then Coke burst with half-tamed rapture into the room. "Oh, Miss Wainwright," he almost shouted, "I can't tell you how glad I am. I just heard to-day you were going. Imagine it. It will be more-oh, how are you Coleman, how are you " "

Marjory welcomed the new-comer with a cordiality that might not have thrilled Coleman with pleasure. They took chairs that formed a triangle and one side of it vibrated with talk. Coke and Marjory engaged in a tumultuous conversation concerning the prospective trip to Greece. The Sunday editor, as remote as if the apex of his angle was the top of a hill, could only study the girl's clear profile. The youthful voices of the two others rang like bells. He did not scowl at Coke; he merely looked at him as if be gently disdained his mental calibre. In fact all the talk seemed to tire him; it was childish; as for him, he apparently found this babble almost insupportable.

"And, just think of the camel rides we'll have," cried Coke.

"Camel rides," repeated Coleman, dejectedly. "My dear Coke."

Finally he arose like an old man climbing from a sick bed. "Well, I am afraid I must go, Miss Wainwright." Then he said affectionately to Coke: "Good-bye, old boy. I hope you will have a good time."

Marjory walked with him to the door. He shook her hand in a friendly fashion. "Good-bye, Marjory,' he said. "Perhaps it may happen that I shan't see you again before you start for Greece and so I had best bid you God-speed ——-or whatever the term is now. You will have a charming time; Greece must be a delightful place. Really, I envy you, Marjory. And now my dear child "-his voice grew brotherly, filled with the patronage of generous fraternal love, "although I may never see you again let me wish you fifty as happy years as this last one has been for me." He smiled frankly into her eyes; then dropping her hand, he went away.

Coke renewed his tempest of talk as Marjory turned toward him. But after a series of splendid eruptions, whose red fire illumined all of ancient and modem Greece, he too went away.

The professor was in his. library apparently absorbed in a book when a tottering pale-faced woman appeared to him and, in her course toward a couch in a corner of the room, described almost a semi-circle. She flung herself face downward. A thick strand of hair swept over her shoulder. "Oh, my heart is broken! My heart is broken! "

The professor arose, grizzled and thrice-old with pain. He went to the couch, but he found himself a handless, fetless man. "My poor child," he said. "My poor child." He remained listening stupidly to her convulsive sobbing. A ghastly kind of solemnity came upon the room.

Suddenly the girl lifted herself and swept the strand of hair away from her face. She looked at the professor with the wide- open dilated eyes of one who still sleeps. "Father," she said in a hollow voice, "he don't love me. He don't love me. He don't love me. at all. You were right, father." She began to laugh.

"Marjory," said the professor, trembling. "Be quiet, child. Be quiet."

"But," she said, "I thought he loved me —I was sure of it. But it don't-don't matter. I —I can't get over it. Women-women, the- but it don't matter."

"Marjory," said the professor. "Marjory, my poor daughter."

She did not heed his appeal, but continued in a dull whisper. " He was playing with me. He was-was-was flirting with me. He didn't care when I told him —I told him — I was going-going away." She turned her face wildly to the cushions again. Her young shoulders shook as if they might break. "Wo-men-women-they always — —"

CHAPTER V.

By a strange mishap of management the train which bore Coleman back toward New York was fetched into an obscure side-track of some lonely region and there compelled to bide a change of fate. The engine wheezed and sneezed like a paused fat man. The lamps in the cars pervaded a stuffy odor of smoke and oil. Coleman examined his case and found only one cigar. Important brakemen proceeded rapidly along the aisles, and when they swung open the doors, a polar wind circled the legs of the passengers. "Well, now, what is all this for?" demanded Coleman, furiously. "I want to get back to New York."

The conductor replied with sarcasm, "Maybe you think I'm stuck on it " I ain't running the road. I'm running this train, and I run it according to orders." Amid the dismal comforts of the waiting cars, Coleman felt all the profound misery of the rebuffed true lover. He had been sentenced, he thought, to a penal servitude of the heart, as he watched the dusky, vague ribbons of smoke come from the lamps and felt to his knees the cold winds from the brakemen's busy flights. When the train started with a whistle and a jolt, he was elate as if in his abjection his beloved's hand had reached to him from the clouds.

When he had arrived in New York, a cab rattled him to an uptown hotel with speed. In the restaurant he first ordered a large bottle of champagne. The last of the wine he finished in sombre mood like an unbroken and defiant man who chews the straw that litters his prison house. During his dinner he was continually sending out messenger boys. He was arranging a poker party. Through a window he watched the beautiful moving life of upper Broadway at night, with its crowds and clanging cable cars and its electric signs, mammoth and glittering, like the jewels of a giantess.

Word was brought to him that the poker players were arriving. He arose joyfully, leaving his cheese. In the broad hall, occupied mainly by miscellaneous people and actors, all deep in leather chairs, he found some of his friends waiting. They trooped up stairs to Coleman's rooms, where as a preliminary, Coleman began to hurl books and papers from the table to the floor. A boy came with drinks. Most of the men, in order to prepare for the game, removed their coats and cuffs and drew up the sleeves of their shirts. The electric globes shed a blinding light upon the table. The sound of clinking chips arose; the elected banker spun the cards, careless and dexterous.

Later, during a pause of dealing, Coleman said:

"Billie, what kind of a lad is that young Coke up at Washurst?"

He addressed an old college friend.

"Oh, you mean the Sophomore Coke?" asked the friend.

"Seems a decent sort of a fellow. I don't know. Why?"

"Well, who is he? Where does he come from? What do you know about him?"

"He's one of those Ohio Cokes-regular thing — father millionaire-used to be a barber-good old boy -why?"

"Nothin'," said Coleman, looking at his cards. "I know the lad. I thought he was a good deal of an ass. I wondered who his people were."

"Oh, his people are all right-in one way. Father owns rolling mills. Do you raise it, Henry? Well, in order to make vice abhorrent to the young, I'm obliged to raise back."

"I'll see it," observed Coleman, slowly pushing forward two blue chips. Afterward he reached behind him and took another glass of wine.

To the others Coleman seemed to have something bitter upon his mind. He played poker quietly, steadfastly, and, without change of eye, following the mathematical religion of the game. Outside of the play he was savage, almost insupportable. " What's the matter with you, Rufus?" said his old college friend. "Lost your job? Girl gone back on you? You're a hell of-a host. We don't get any. thing but insults and drinks."

Late at night Coleman began to lose steadily. In the meantime he drank glass after glass of wine. Finally he made reckless bets on a mediocre hand and an opponent followed him thoughtfully bet by bet, undaunted, calm, absolutely without emotion. Coleman lost; he hurled down his cards. " Nobody but a damned fool would have seen that last raise on anything less than a full hand."

"Steady. Come off. What's wrong with you, Rufus?" cried his guests.

"You're not drunk, are you?" said his old college friend, puritanically.

"'Drunk'?" repeated Coleman.

"Oh, say," cried a man, "let's play cards. What's all this gabbling?"

It was when a grey, dirty light of dawn evaded the thick curtains and fought on the floor with the feebled electric glow that Coleman, in the midst of play, lurched his chest heavily upon the table. Some chips rattled to the floor. "I'll call you," he murmured, sleepily.

"Well," replied a man, sternly, "three kings."

The other players with difficulty extracted five cards from beneath Coleman's pillowed head. "Not a pair! Come, come, this won't do. Oh, let's stop playing. This is the rottenest game I ever sat in. Let's go home. Why don't you put him to bed, Billie?"

When Coleman awoke next morning, he looked back upon the poker game as something that had transpired in previous years. He dressed and went down to the grill-room. For his breakfast he ordered some eggs on toast and a pint of champagne. A privilege of liberty belonged to a certain Irish waiter, and this waiter looked at him, grinning. "Maybe you had a pretty lively time last night, Mr Coleman?"

"Yes, Pat," answered Coleman, "I did. It was all because of an unrequited affection, Patrick." The man stood near, a napkin over his arm. Coleman went on impressively. "The ways of the modern lover are strange. Now, I, Patrick, am a modern lover, and when, yesterday, the dagger of disappointment was driven deep into my heart, I immediately played poker as hard as I could and incidentally got loaded. This is the modern point of view. I understand on good authority that in old times lovers used to. languish. That is probably a lie, but at any rate we do not, in these times, languish to any great extent. We get drunk. Do you understand, Patrick?" The waiter was used to a harangue at Coleman's breakfast time. He placed his hand over his mouth and giggled. "Yessir."

"Of course," continued Coleman, thoughtfully. "It might be pointed out by uneducated persons that it is difficult to maintain a high standard of drunkenness for the adequate length of time, but in the series of experiments which I am about to make I am sure I can easily prove them to be in the wrong."

"I am sure, sir," said the waiter, "the young ladies would not like to be hearing you talk this way."

"Yes; no doubt, no doubt. The young ladies have still quite medieval ideas. They don't understand. They still prefer lovers to languish."

"At any rate, sir, I don't see that your heart is sure enough broken. You seem to take it very easy. "

"Broken! " cried Coleman. "Easy? Man, my heart is in fragments. Bring me another small bottle."

CHAPTER VI.

Six weeks later, Coleman went to the office of the proprietor of the Eclipse. Coleman was one of those smooth-shaven old-young men who wear upon some occasions a singular air of temperance and purity. At these times, his features lost their quality of worldly shrewdness and endless suspicion and bloomed as the face of some innocent boy. It then would be hard to tell that he had ever encountered even such a crime as a lie or a cigarette. As he walked into the proprietor's office he was a perfect semblance of a fine, inexperienced youth. People usually concluded this change was due to a Turkish bath or some other expedient of recuperation, but it was due probably to the power of a physical characteristic.

"Boss in?" said Coleman.

"Yeh," said the secretary, jerking his thumb toward an inner door. In his private office, Sturgeon sat on the edge of the table dangling one leg and dreamily surveying the wall. As Coleman entered he looked up quickly. "Rufus," he cried, "you're just the man I wanted to see. I've got a scheme. A great scheme." He slid from the table and began to pace briskly to and fro, his hands deep in his trousers' pockets, his chin sunk in his collar, his light blue eyes afire with interest. "Now listen. This is immense. The Eclipse enlists a battalion of men to go to Cuba and fight the Spaniards under its own flag-the Eclipse flag. Collect trained officers from here and there-enlist every young devil we see-drill 'em-best rifles-loads of ammunition- provisions-staff of doctors and nurses -a couple of dynamite guns-everything complete best in the world. Now, isn't that great? What's the matter with that now? Eh? Eh? Isn't that great? It's great, isn't it? Eh? Why, my boy, we'll free-"

Coleman did not seem to ignite. "I have been arrested four or five times already on fool matters connected with the newspaper business," he observed, gloomily, "but I've never yet been hung. I think your scheme is a beauty."

Sturgeon paused in astonishment. "Why, what happens to be the matter with you? What are you kicking about?"

Coleman made a slow gesture. "I'm tired," he answered. "I need a vacation."

"Vacation!" cried Sturgeon. "Why don't you take one then?"

"That's what I've come to see you about. I've had a pretty heavy strain on me for three years now, and I want to get a little rest."

"Well, who in thunder has been keeping you from it? It hasn't been me."

"I know it hasn't been you, but, of course, I wanted the paper to go and I wanted to have my share in its success, but now that everything is all right I think I might go away for a time if you don't mind."

"Mind! " exclaimed Sturgeon falling into his chair and reaching for his check book. "Where do you want to go? How long do you want to be gone? How much money do you want?"

"I don't want very much. And as for where I want to go, I thought I might like to go to Greece for a while."

Sturgeon had been writing a check. He poised his pen in the air and began to laugh. "That's a queer place to go for a rest. Why, the biggest war of modern times —a war that may involve all Europe-is likely to start there at any moment. You are not likely to get any rest in Greece."

"I know that," answered Coleman. "I know there is likely to be a war there. But I think that is exactly what would rest me. I would like to report the war."

"You are a queer bird," answered Sturgeon deeply fascinated with this new idea. He had apparently forgotten his vision of a Cuban volunteer battalion. "War correspondence is about the most original medium for a rest I ever heard of."

"Oh, it may seem funny, but really, any change will be good for me now. I've been whacking at this old Sunday edition until I'm sick of it, and some,. times I wish the Eclipse was in hell."

That's all right," laughed the proprietor of the Eclipse. "But I still don't see how you 'are going to get any vacation out of a war that will upset the whole of Europe. But that's your affair. If you want to become the chief correspondent in the field in case of any such war, why, of course, I would be glad to have you. I couldn't get anybody better. But I don't see where your vacation comes in."

"I'll take care of that," answered Coleman. "When I take a vacation I want to take it my own way, and I think this will be a vacation because it will be different -don't you see-different?"

"No, I don't see any sense in it, but if you think that is the way that suits you, why, go ahead. How much money do you want?"

"I don't want much. just enough to see me through nicely."

Sturgeon scribbled on his check book and then ripped a check from it. "Here's a thousand dollars. Will that do you to start with?"

"That's plenty."

"When do you want to start?"

"To-morrow."

"Oh," said Sturgeon. "You're in a hurry." This impetuous manner of exit from business seemed to appeal to him. "To-morrow," he repeated smiling. In reality he was some kind of a poet using his millions romantically, spending wildly on a sentiment that might be with beauty or without beauty, according to the momentary vacillation. The vaguely-defined desperation in Coleman's last announcement appeared to delight him. He grinned and placed the points of his fingers together stretching out his legs in a careful attitude of indifference which might even mean disapproval. "To-morrow," he murmured teasingly.

"By jiminy," exclaimed Coleman, ignoring the other man's mood, "I'm sick of the whole business. I've got out a Sunday paper once a week for three years and I feel absolutely incapable of getting out another edition. It would be all right if we were running on ordinary lines, but when each issue is more or less of an attempt to beat the previous issue, it becomes rather wearing, you know. If I can't get a vacation now I take one later in a lunatic asylum."

"Why, I'm not objecting to your having a vacation. I'm simply marvelling at the kind of vacation you want to take. And 'to-morrow,' too, eh? " " Well, it suits me," muttered Coleman, sulkily.

"Well, if it suits you, that's enough. Here's your check. Clear out now and don't let me see you again until you are thoroughly rested, even if it takes a year." He arose and stood smiling. He was mightily pleased with himself. He liked to perform in this way. He was almost seraphic as he thrust the check for a thousand dollars toward Coleman.

Then his manner changed abruptly. "Hold on a minute. I must think a little about this thing if you are going to manage the correspondence. Of course it will be a long and bloody war."

"You bet."

"The big chance is that all Europe will be dragged into it. Of course then you would have to come out of Greece and take up a better position-say Vienna."

"No, I wouldn't care to do that," said Coleman positively. "I just want to take care of the Greek end of it."

"It will be an idiotic way to take a vacation," observed Sturgeon.

"Well, it suits me," muttered Coleman again. "I tell you what it is-" he added suddenly. "I've got some private reasons- see?"

Sturgeon was radiant with joy. "Private reasons." He was charmed by the sombre pain in Coleman's eyes and his own ability to eject it. "Good. Go now and be blowed. I will cable final instruction to meet you in London. As soon as you get to Greece, cable me an account of the situation there and we will arrange our plans." He began to laugh. "Private reasons. Come out to dinner with me."

"I can't very well," said Coleman. "If I go tomorrow, I've got to pack-"

But here the real tyrant appeared, emerging suddenly from behind the curtain of sentiment, appearing like a red devil in a pantomine. "You can't?" snapped Sturgeon. "Nonsense — —"

CHAPTER VII.

SWEEPING out from between two remote, half-submerged dunes on which stood slender sentry light. houses, the steamer began to roll with a gentle insinuating motion. Passengers in their staterooms saw at rhythmical intervals the spray racing fleetly past the portholes. The waves grappled hurriedly at the sides of the great flying steamer and boiled discomfited astern in a turmoil of green and white. From the tops of the enormous funnels streamed level masses of smoke which were immediately torn to nothing by the headlong wind. Meanwhile as the steamer rushed into the northeast, men in caps and ulsters comfortably paraded the decks and stewards arranged deck chairs for the reception of various women who were coming from their cabins with rugs.

In the smoking room, old voyagers were settling down comfortably while new voyagers were regarding them with a diffident respect. Among the passengers Coleman found a number of people whom he knew, including a wholesale wine merchant, a Chicago railway magnate and a New York millionaire. They lived practically in the smoking room. Necessity drove them from time to time to the salon, or to their berths. Once indeed the millionaire was absent, from the group while penning a short note to his wife.

When the Irish coast was sighted Coleman came on deck to look at it. A tall young woman immediately halted in her walk until he had stepped up to her. "Well, of all ungallant men, Rufus Coleman, you are the star," she cried laughing and held out her hand.

"Awfully sorry, I'm sure," he murmured. "Been playing poker in the smoking room all voyage. Didn't have a look at the passenger list until just now. Why didn't you send me word?" These lies were told so modestly and sincerely that when the girl flashed her, brilliant eyes full upon their author there was a mixt of admiration in the indignation.

"Send you a card " I don't believe you can read, else you would have known I was to sail on this steamer. If I hadn't been ill until to-day you would have seen me in the salon. I open at the Folly Theatre next week. Dear ol' Lunnon, y' know."

"Of course, I knew you were going," said Coleman. "But I thought you were to go later. What do you open in?"

"Fly by Night. Come walk along with me. See those two old ladies " They've been watching for me like hawks ever since we left New York. They expected me to flirt with every man on board. But I've fooled them. I've been just as g-o-o-d. I had to be."

As the pair moved toward the stern, enormous and radiant green waves were crashing futilely after the steamer. Ireland showed a dreary coast line to the north. A wretched man who had crossed the Atlantic eighty-four times was declaiming to a group of novices. A venerable banker, bundled in rugs, was asleep in his deck chair.

"Well, Nora," said Coleman, "I hope you make a hit in London. You deserve it if anybody does. You've worked hard."

"Worked hard," cried the girl. "I should think so. Eight years ago I was in the rear row. Now I have the centre of the stage whenever I want it. I made Chalmers cut out that great scene in the second act between the queen and Rodolfo. The idea! Did he think I would stand that? And just because he was in love with Clara Trotwood, too."

Coleman was dreamy. "Remember when I was dramatic man for the Gazette and wrote the first notice?"

"Indeed, I do," answered the girl affectionately. " Indeed, I do, Rufus. Ah, that was a great lift. I believe that was the first thing that had an effect on old Oliver. Before that, he never would believe that I was any good. Give me your arm, Rufus. Let's parade before the two old women." Coleman glanced at her keenly. Her voice had trembled slightly. Her eyes were lustrous as if she were about to weep.

"Good heavens," he said. "You are the same old Nora Black. I thought you would be proud and 'aughty by this time."

"Not to my friends," she murmured., "Not to my friends. I'm always the same and I never forget. Rufus."

"Never forget what?" asked Coleman.

"If anybody does me a favour I never forget it as long as I live," she answered fervently.

"Oh, you mustn't be so sentimental, Nora. You remember that play you bought from little Ben Whipple, just because he had once sent you some flowers in the old days when you were poor and happened to bed sick. A sense of gratitude cost you over eight thousand dollars that time, didn't it?" Coleman laughed heartily.

"Oh, it wasn't the flowers at all," she interrupted seriously. " Of course Ben was always a nice boy, but then his play was worth a thousand dollars. That's all I gave him. I lost some more in trying to make it go. But it was too good. That was what was the matter. It was altogether too good for the public. I felt awfully sorry for poor little Ben."

"Too good?" sneered Coleman. "Too good? Too indifferently bad, you mean. My dear girl, you mustn't imagine that you know a good play. You don't, at all."

She paused abruptly and faced him. This regal, creature was looking at him so sternly that Coleman felt awed for a moment as if he, were in the presence of a great mind. "Do you mean to say that I'm not an artist?" she asked.

Coleman remained cool. "I've never been decorated for informing people of their own affairs," he observed, "but I should say that you were about as much of an artist as I am."

Frowning slightly, she reflected upon this reply. Then, of a sudden, she laughed. "There is no use in being angry with you, Rufus. You always were a hopeless scamp. But," she added, childishly wistful, "have you ever seen Fly by Night? Don't you think my dance in the second act is artistic?"

"No," said Coleman, "I haven't seen Fly by Night yet, but of course I know that you are the most beautiful dancer on the stage. Everybody knows that."

It seemed that her hand tightened on his arm. Her face was radiant. "There," she exclaimed. "Now you are forgiven. You are a nice boy, Rufus-some- times."

When Miss Black went to her cabin, Coleman strolled into the smoking room. Every man there covertly or openly surveyed him. He dropped lazily into a chair at a table where the wine merchant, the Chicago railway king and the New York millionaire were playing cards. They made a noble pretense of not being aware of him. On the oil cloth top of the table the cards were snapped down, turn by turn.

Finally the wine merchant, without lifting his head to- address a particular person, said: "New conquest."

Hailing a steward Coleman asked for a brandy and soda.

The millionaire said: "He's a sly cuss, anyhow." The railway man grinned. After an elaborate silence the wine merchant asked: "Know Miss Black long, Rufus?" Coleman looked scornfully at his friends. "What's wrong with you there, fellows, anyhow?" The Chicago man answered airily. "Oh, nothin'. Nothin', whatever."

At dinner in the crowded salon, Coleman was aware that more than one passenger glanced first at Nora Black and then at him, as if connecting them in some train of thought, moved to it by the narrow horizon of shipboard and by a sense of the mystery that surrounds the lives of the beauties of the stage. Near the captain's right hand sat the glowing and splendid Nora, exhibiting under the gaze of the persistent eyes of many meanings, a practiced and profound composure that to the populace was terrifying dignity.

Strolling toward the smoking room after dinner, Coleman met the New York millionaire, who seemed agitated. He took Coleman fraternally by the arm. "Say, old man, introduce me, won't you? I'm crazy to know her."

"Do you mean Miss Black?" asked Coleman.

"Why, I don't know that I have a right. Of course, you know, she hasn't been meeting anybody aboard. I'll ask her, though- certainly."

"Thanks, old man, thanks. I'd be tickled to death. Come along and have a drink. When will you ask her?" " "Why, I don't know when I'll see her. To-morrow, I suppose-"

They had not been long in the smoking room, however, when the deck steward came with a card to Coleman. Upon it was written: "Come for' a stroll?" Everybody, saw Coleman read this card and then look up and whisper to the deck steward. The deck steward bent his head and whispered discreetly in reply. There was an abrupt pause in the hum of conversation. The interest was acute.

Coleman leaned carelessly back in his chair, puffing at his cigar. He mingled calmly in a discussion of the comparative merits of certain trans-Atlantic lines. After a time he threw away his cigar and arose. Men nodded. "Didn't I tell you?" His studiously languid exit was made dramatic by the eagle-eyed attention of the smoking room.

On deck he found Nora pacing to and fro. "You didn't hurry yourself," she said, as he joined her. The lights of Queenstown were twinkling. A warm wind, wet with the moisture of rain-stricken sod, was coming from the land.

"Why," said Coleman, "we've got all these duffers very much excited."

"Well what do you care?" asked hte girl. "You don't, care do you?"

"No, I don't care. Only it's rather absurd to be watched all the time." He said this precisely as if he abhorred being watched in this case. "Oh by the way," he added. Then he paused for a moment. "Aw—a friend of mine-not a bad fellow— he asked me for an introduction. Of course, I told him I'd ask you."

She made a contemptuous gesture. "Oh, another Willie. Tell him no. Tell him to go home to his family. Tell him to run away."

"He isn't a bad fellow. He —" said Coleman diffidently, "he would probably be at the theatre every night in a box."

"yes, and get drunk and throw a wine bottle on the stage instead of a bouquet. No," she declared positively, "I won't see him."

Coleman did not seem to be oppressed by this ultimatum. "Oh, all right. I promised him-that was all."

"Besides, are you in a great hurry to get rid of me?"

"Rid of you? Nonsense."

They walked in the shadow. "How long are you going to be in London, Rufus?" asked Nora softly.

"Who? I? Oh, I'm going right off to Greece. First train. There's going to be a war, you know."

"A war? Why, who is going to fight? The Greeks and the-the-the what?"

"The Turks. I'm going right over there."

"Why, that's dreadful, Rufus," said the girl, mournfull and shocked. "You might get hurt or something." Presently she asked: "And aren't you going to be in London any time at all?"

"Oh," he answered, puffing out his lips, "I may stop in Londom for three or four days on my way home. I'm not sure of it."

"And when will that be?"

"Oh, I can't tell. It may be in three or four months, or it may be a year from now. When the war stops."

There was a long silence as the walked up and down the swaying deck.

"Do you know," said Nora at last, "I like you, Rufus Coleman. I don't know any good reason for it either, unless it is because you are such a brute. Now, when I was asking you if you were to be in London you were perfectly detestable. You know I was anxious."

"I—detestable?" cried Coleman, feigning amazement. "Why, what did I say?"

"It isn't so much what you said —" began Nora slowly. Then she suddenly changed her manner. "Oh, well, don't let's talk about it any more. It's too foolish. Only-you are a disagreeable person sometimes."

In the morning, as the vessel steamed up the Irish channel, Coleman was on deck, keeping furtive watch on the cabin stairs. After two hours of waiting, he scribbled a message on a card and sent it below. He received an answer that Miss Black had a headache, and felt too ill to come on deck. He went to the smoking room. The three card-players glanced up, grinning. "What's the matter?" asked the wine merchant. "You look angry." As a matter of fact, Coleman had purposely wreathed his features in a pleasant and satisfied expression, so he was for a moment furious at the wine merchant.

"Confound the girl," he thought to himself. "She has succeeded in making all these beggars laugh at me." He mused that if he had another chance he would show her how disagreeable or detestable or scampish he was under some circumstances. He reflected ruefully that the complacence with which he had accepted the comradeship of the belle of the voyage might have been somewhat overdone. Perhaps he had got a little out of proportion. He was annoyed at the stares of the other men in the smoking room, who seemed now to be reading his discomfiture. As for Nora Black he thought of her wistfully and angrily as a superb woman whose company was honour and joy, a payment for any sacrifices.

"What's the matter?" persisted the wine merchant. "You look grumpy." Coleman laughed. "Do I?"

At Liverpool, as the steamer was being slowly warped to the landing stage by some tugs, the passengers crowded the deck with their hand-bags. Adieus were falling as dead leaves fall from a great tree. The stewards were handling small hills of luggage marked with flaming red labels. The ship was firmly against the dock before Miss Black came from her cabin. Coleman was at the time gazing shoreward, but his three particular friends instantly nudged him. "What?" "There she is?" "Oh, Miss Black?" He composedly walked toward her. It was impossible to tell whether she saw him coming or whether it was accident, but at any rate she suddenly turned and moved toward the stern of the ship. Ten watchful gossips had noted Coleman's travel in her direction and more than half the passengers noted his defeat. He wheeled casually and returned to his three friends. They were colic-stricken with a coarse and yet silent merriment. Coleman was glad that the voyage was over.

After the polite business of an English custom house, the travellers passed out to the waiting train. A nimble little theatrical agent of some kind, sent from London, dashed forward to receive Miss Black. He had a first-class compartment engaged for her and he bundled her and her maid into it in an exuberance of enthusiasm and admiration.. Coleman passing moodily along the line of coaches heard Nora's voice hailing him.

"Rufus." There she was, framed in a carriage window, beautiful and smiling brightly. Every near. by person turned to contemplate this vision.

"Oh," said Coleman advancing, "I thought I was not going to get a chance to say good-bye to you." He held out his hand. " Good-bye."

She pouted. "Why, there's plenty of room in this compartment." Seeing that some forty people were transfixed in observation of her, she moved a short way back. "Come on in this compartment, Rufus," she said.

"Thanks. I prefer to smoke," said Coleman. He went off abruptly.

On the way to London, he brooded in his corner on the two divergent emotions he had experienced when refusing her invitation. At Euston Station in London, he was directing a porter, who had his luggage, when he heard Nora speak at his shoulder. "Well, Rufus, you sulky boy," she said, "I shall be at the Cecil. If you have time, come and see me."

"Thanks, I'm sure, my dear Nora," answered Coleman effusively. "But honestly, I'm off for Greece."

A brougham was drawn up near them and the nimble little agent was waiting. The maid was directing the establishment of a mass of luggage on and in a four-wheeler cab. "Well, put me into my carriage, anyhow," said Nora. "You will have time for that."

Afterward she addressed him from the dark interior. Now, Rufus, you must come to see me the minute you strike London again- of She hesitated a moment and then smiling gorgeously upon him, she said: "Brute!"

CHAPTER VIII.

As soon as Coleman had planted his belongings in a hotel he was bowled in a hansom briskly along the smoky Strand, through a dark city whose walls dripped like the walls of a cave and whose passages were only illuminated by flaring yellow and red signs.

Walkley the London correspondent of the Eclipse, whirled from his chair with a shout of joy and relief -at sight of Coleman. " Cables," he cried. "Nothin' but cables! All the people in New York are writing cables to you. The wires groan with them. And we groan with them too. They come in here in bales. However, there is no reason why you should read them all. Many are similar in words and many more are similar in spirit. The sense of the whole thing is that you get to Greece quickly, taking with you immense sums of money and enormous powers over nations."

"Well, when does the row begin?"

"The most astute journalists in Europe have been predicting a general European smash-up every year since 1878," said Walkley, "and the prophets weep. The English are the only people who can pull off wars on schedule time, and they have to do it in odd corners of the globe. I fear the war business is getting tuckered. There is sorrow in the lodges of the lone wolves, the war correspondents. However, my boy, don't bury your face in your blanket. This Greek business looks very promising, very promising." He then began to proclaim trains and connections. " Dover, Calais, Paris, Brindisi, Corfu, Patras, Athens. That is your game. You are supposed to sky-rocket yourself over that route in the shortest possible time, but you would gain no time by starting before to-morrow, so you can cool your heels here in London until then. I wish I was going along."

Coleman returned to his hotel, a knight impatient and savage at being kept for a time out of the saddle. He went for a late supper to the grill room and as he was seated there alone, a party of four or five people came to occupy the table directly behind him. They talked a great deal even before they arrayed them. selves at the table, and he at once recognised the voice of Nora Black. She was queening it, apparently, over a little band of awed masculine worshippers.

Either by accident or for some curious reason, she took a chair back to back with Coleman's chair. Her sleeve of fragrant stuff almost touched his shoulder and he felt appealing to him seductively a perfume of orris root and violet. He was drinking bottled stout with his chop; be sat with a face of wood.

"Oh, the little lord?" Nora was crying to some slave. "Now, do you know, he won't do at all. He is too awfully charming. He sits and ruminates for fifteen minutes and then he pays me a lovely compliment. Then he ruminates for another fifteen minutes and cooks up another fine thing. It is too tiresome. Do you know what kind of man. I like?" she asked softly and confidentially. And here she sank back in her chair until. Coleman knew from the tingle that her head was but a few inches from his head. Her, sleeve touched him. He turned more wooden under the spell of the orris root and violet. Her courtiers thought it all a graceful pose, but Coleman believed otherwise. Her voice sank to the liquid, siren note of a succubus. "Do you know what kind of a man I like? Really like? I like a man that a woman can't bend in a thousand different ways in five minutes. He must have some steel in him. He obliges me to admire him the most when he remains stolid; stolid to me lures. Ah, that is the only kind of a man who cap ever break a heart among us women of the world. His stolidity is not real; no; it is mere art, but it is a highly finished art and often enough we can't cut through it. Really we can't. And, then we may actually come to-er-care for the man. Really we may. Isn't it funny?"

Alt the end Coleman arose and strolled out of the. room, smoking a cigarette. He did not betray, a sign. Before. the door clashed softly behind him, Nora laughed a little defiantly, perhaps a little loudly. It made every man in the grill-room perk up his ears. As for her courtiers, they were entranced. In her description of the conquering man, she had easily contrived that each one of them wondered if she might not mean him. Each man was perfectly sure that he had plenty of steel in his composition and that seemed to be a main point.

Coleman delayed for a time in the smoking room and then went to his own quarters. In reality he was somewhat puzzled in his mind by a projection of the beauties of Nora Black upon his desire for Greece and Marjory, His thoughts formed a duality. Once he was on the point of sending his card to Nora Black's parlour, inasmuch as Greece was very distant and he could not start until the morrow. But he suspected that he was holding the interest of the actress because of his recent appearance of impregnable serenity in the presence of her fascinations. If he now sent his card, it was a form of surrender and he knew her to be one to take a merciless advantage. He would not make this tactical mistake. On the contrary he would go to bed and think of war,

In reality he found it easy to fasten his mind upon the prospective war. He regarded himself cynically in most affairs, but he could not be cynical of war, because had he - seen none of it. His rejuvenated imagination began to thrill to the roll of battle, through his thought passing all the lightning in the pictures of Detaille, de Neuville and Morot; lashed battery horse roaring over bridges; grand cuirassiers dashing headlong against stolid invincible red-faced lines of German infantry; furious and bloody grapplings in the streets of little villages of northeastern France. There was one thing at least of which he could still feel the spirit of a debutante. In this matter of war he was not, too, unlike a young girl embarking upon her first season of opera. Walkely, the next morning, saw this mood sitting quaintly upon Coleman and cackled with astonishment and glee. Coleman's usual manner did not return until he detected Walkely's appreciation of his state and then he snubbed him according to the ritual of the Sunday editor of the New York Eclipse. Parenthetically, it might be said that if Coleman now recalled Nora Black to his mind at all, it was only to think of her for a moment with ironical complacence. He had beaten her.

When the train drew out of the station, Coleman felt himself thrill. Was ever fate less perverse? War and love-war and Marjory-were in conjunction both in Greece-and he could tilt with one lance at both gods. It was a great fine game to play and no man was ever so blessed in vacations. He was smiling continually to himself and sometimes actually on the point of talking aloud. This was despite the presence in the compartment of two fellow passengers who preserved in their uncomfortably rigid, icy and uncompromising manners many of the more or less ridiculous traditions of the English first class carriage. Coleman's fine humour betrayed him once into addressing one of these passengers and the man responded simply with a wide look of incredulity, as if he discovered that he was travelling in the same compartment with a zebu. It turned Coleman suddenly to evil temper and he wanted to ask the man questions concerning his education and his present mental condition: and so until the train arrived at Dover, his ballooning soul was in danger of collapsing. On the packet crossing the channel, too, he almost returned to the usual Rufus Coleman since all the world was seasick and he could not get a cabin in which to hide himself from it. However he reaped much consolation by ordering a bottle of champagne and drinking it in sight of the people, which made them still more seasick. From Calais to Brindisi really nothing met his disapproval save the speed of the train, the conduct of some of the passengers, the quality of the food served, the manners of the guards, the temperature of the carriages, the prices charged and the length of the journey.

In time he passed as in a vision from wretched Brindisi to charming Corfu, from Corfu to the little war-bitten city of Patras and from Patras by rail at the speed of an ox-cart to Athens.

With a smile of grim content and surrounded in his carriage with all his beautiful brown luggage, he swept through the dusty streets of the Greek capital. Even as the vehicle arrived in a great terraced square in front of the yellow palace, Greek recruits in garments representing many trades and many characters were marching up cheering for Greece and the king. Officers stood upon the little iron chairs in front of the cafes; all the urchins came running and shouting; ladies waved their handkerchiefs from the balconies; the whole city was vivified with a leaping and joyous enthusiasm. The Athenians-as dragomen or otherwise-had preserved an ardor for their glorious traditions, and it was as if that in the white dust which lifted from the plaza and floated across the old-ivory face of the palace, there were the souls of the capable soldiers of the past. Coleman was almost intoxicated with it. It seemed to celebrate his own reasons, his reasons of love and ambition to conquer in love.

When the carriage arrived in front of the Hotel D'Angleterre, Coleman found the servants of the place with more than one eye upon the scene in the plaza, but they soon paid heed to the arrival of a gentleman with such an amount of beautiful leather luggage, all marked boldly with the initials "R. C." Coleman let them lead him and follow him and conduct him and use bad English upon him without noting either their words, their salaams or their work. His mind had quickly fixed upon the fact that here was the probable headquarters of the Wainwright party and, with the rush of his western race fleeting through his veins, he felt that he would choke and die if he did not learn of the Wainwrights in the first two minutes. It was a tragic venture to attempt to make the Levantine mind understand something off the course, that the new arrival's first thought was to establish a knowlege of the whereabouts of some of his friends rather than to swarm helter-skelter into that part of the hotel for which he was willing to pay rent. In fact he failed to thus impress them; failed in dark wrath, but, nevertheless, failed. At last he was simply forced to concede the travel of files of men up the broad, redcarpeted stair-case, each man being loaded with Coleman's luggage. The men in the hotel-bureau were then able to comprehend that the foreign gentleman might have something else on his mind. They raised their eye-brows languidly when he spoke of the Wainwright party in gentle surprise that he had not yet learned that they were gone some time. They were departed on some excursion. Where? Oh, really-it was almost laughable, indeed-they didn't know. Were they sure? Why, yes-it was almost laughable, indeed -they were quite sure. Where could the gentleman find out about them? Well, they-as they had explained-did not know, but-it was possible-the American minister might know. Where was he to be found? Oh, that was very simple. It was well known that the American minister had apartments in the hotel. Was he in? Ah, that they could not say. So Coleman, rejoicing at his final emancipation and with the grime of travel still upon him, burst in somewhat violently upon the secretary of the Hon. Thomas M. Gordner of Nebraska, the United States minister to Greece. From his desk the secretary arose from behind an accidental bulwark of books and govermental pamphlets. "Yes, certainly. Mr. Gordner is in. If you would give me your card-"

Directly. Coleman was introduced into another room where a quiet man who was rolling a cigarette looked him frankly but carefully in the eye. "The Wainwrights " said the minister immediately after the question. "Why, I myself am immensely concerned about them at present. I'm afraid they've gotten themselves into trouble.'

"Really?" said Coleman.

"Yes. That little professor is ratherer-stubborn; Isn't he? He wanted to make an expedition to Nikopolis and I explained to him all the possibilities of war and begged him to at least not take his wife and daughter with him."

"Daughter," murmured Coleman, as if in his sleep.

"But that little old man had a head like a stone and only laughed at me. Of course those villainous young students were only too delighted at a prospect of war, but it was a stupid and absurd. thing for the man to take his wife and daughter there. They are up there now. I can't get a word from them or get a word to them."

Coleman had been choking. "Where is Nikopolis?" he asked.

The minister gazed suddenly in comprehension of the man before him. "Nikopolis is in Turkey," he answered gently.

Turkey at that time was believed to be a country of delay, corruption, turbulence and massacre. It meant everything. More than a half of the Christians of the world shuddered at the name of Turkey. Coleman's lips tightened and perhaps blanched, and his chin moved out strangely, once, twice, thrice. "How can I get to Nikopolis?" he said.

The minister smiled. "It would take you the better part of four days if you could get there, but as a matter of fact you can't get there at the present time. A Greek army and a Turkish army are looking at each other from the sides of the river at Arta-the river is there the frontier-and Nikopolis happens to be on the wrong side. You can't reach them. The forces at Arta will fight within three days. I know it. Of course I've notified our legation at Constantinople, but, with Turkish methods of communication, Nikopolis is about as far from Constantinople as New York is from Pekin."

Coleman arose. "They've run themselves into a nice mess," he said crossly. "Well, I'm a thousand times obliged to you, I'm sure."

The minister opened his eyes a trifle. You are not going to try to reach them, are you?"

"Yes," answered Coleman, abstractedly. "I'm going to have a try at it. Friends of mine, you know-"

At the bureau of the hotel, the correspondent found several cables awaiting him from the alert office of the New York Eclipse. One of them read: "State Department gives out bad plight of Wainwright party lost somewhere; find them. Eclipse." When Coleman perused the message he began to smile with seraphic bliss. Could fate have ever been less perverse.

Whereupon he whirled himself in Athens. And it was to the considerable astonishment of some Athenians. He discovered and instantly subsidised a young Englishman who, during his absence at the front, would act as correspondent for the Eclipse at the capital. He took unto himself a dragoman and then bought three horses and hired a groom at a speed that caused a little crowd at the horse dealer's place to come out upon the pavement and watch this surprising young man ride back toward his hotel. He had already driven his dragoman into a curious state of Oriental bewilderment and panic in which he could only lumber hastily and helplessly here and there, with his face in the meantime marked with agony. Coleman's own field equipment had been ordered by cable from New York to London, but it was necessary to buy much tinned meats, chocolate, coffee, candles, patent food, brandy, tobaccos, medicine and other things.

He went to bed that night feeling more placid. The train back to Patras was to start in the early morning, and he felt the satisfaction of a man who is at last about to start on his own great quest. Before he dropped off to slumber, he heard crowds cheering exultantly in the streets, and the cheering moved him as it had done in the morning. He felt that the celebration of the people was really an accompaniment to his primal reason, a reason of love and ambition to conquer in love-even as in the theatre, the music accompanies the heroin his progress. He arose once during the night to study a map of the Balkan peninsula and get nailed into his mind the exact position of Nikopolis. It was important.

CHAPTER IX.

COLEMAN'S dragoman aroused him in the blue before dawn. The correspondent arrayed himself in one of his new khaki suits- riding breeches and a tunic well marked with buttoned pockets- and accompanied by some of his beautiful brown luggage, they departed for the station.

The ride to Patras is a terror under ordinary circumstances. It begins in the early morning and ends in the twilight. To Coleman, having just come from Patras to Athens, this journey from Athens to Patras had all the exasperating elements of a forced recantation. Moreover, he had not come prepared to view with awe the ancient city of Corinth nor to view with admiration the limpid beauties of the gulf of that name with its olive grove shore. He was not stirred by Parnassus, a far-away snow-field high on the black shoulders of the mountains across the gulf. No; he wished to go to Nikopolis. He passed over the graves of an ancient race the gleam of whose mighty minds shot, hardly dimmed, through the clouding ages. No; he wished to go to Nikopolis. The train went at a snail's pace, and if Coleman bad an interest it was in the people who lined the route and cheered the soldiers on the train. In Coleman s compartment there was a greasy person who spoke a little English. He explained that he was a poet, a poet who now wrote of nothing but war. When a man is in pursuit of his love and success is known to be at least remote, it often relieves his strain if he is deeply bored from time to time.

The train was really obliged to arrive finally at Patras even if it was a tortoise, and when this happened, a hotel runner appeared, who lied for the benefit of the hotel in saying that there was no boat over to Mesalonghi that night. When, all too late, Coleman discovered the truth of the matter his wretched dragoman came in for a period of infamy and suffering. However, while strolling in the plaza at Patras, amid newsboys from every side, by rumour and truth, Coleman learned things to his advantage. A Greek fleet was bombarding Prevasa. Prevasa was near Nikopolis. The opposing armies at Arta were engaged, principally in an artillery duel. Arta was on the road from Nikopolis into Greece. Hearing this news in the sunlit square made him betray no weakness, but in the darkness of his room at the hotel, he seemed to behold Marjory encircled by insurmountable walls of flame. He could look out of his window into the black night of the north and feel every ounce of a hideous circumstance. It appalled him; here was no power of calling up a score of reporters and sending them scampering to accomplish everything. He even might as well have been without a tongue as far as it could serve him in goodly speech. He was alone, confronting the black ominous Turkish north behind which were the deadly flames; behind the flames was Marjory. It worked upon him until he felt obliged to call in his dragoman, and then, seated upon the edge of his bed and waving his pipe eloquently, he described the plight of some very dear friends who were cut off at Nikopolis in Epirus. Some of his talk was almost wistful in its wish for sympathy from his servant, but at the end he bade the dragoman understand that be, Coleman, was going to their rescue, and he defiantly asked the hireling if he was prepared to go with him. But he did not know the Greek nature. In two minutes the dragoman was weeping tears of enthusiasm, and, for these tears, Coleman was over-grateful, because he had not been told that any of the more crude forms of sentiment arouse the common Greek to the highest pitch, but sometimes, when it comes to what the Americans call a "show down," when he gets backed toward his last corner with a solitary privilege of dying for these sentiments, perhaps he does not always exhibit those talents which are supposed to be possessed by the bulldog. He often then, goes into the cafes and take's it out in oration, like any common Parisian.

In the morning A steamer carried them across the strait and landed them near Mesalonghi at the foot of the railroad that leads to Agrinion. At Agrinion Coleman at last began to feel that he was nearing his goal. There were plenty of soldiers in the town, who received with delight and applause this gentleman in the distinguished-looking khaki clothes with his revolver and his field glasses and his canteen and; his dragoman. The dragoman lied, of course, and vociferated that the gentleman in the distinguished-looking khaki clothes was an English soldier of reputation, who had, naturally, come to help the cross in its fight against, the crescent. He also said that his master had three superb horses coming from Athens in charge of a groom, and was undoubtedly going to join the cavalry. Whereupon the soldiers wished to embrace and kiss the gentleman in the distinguished-looking khaki clothes.

There was more or less of a scuffle. Coleman would have taken to kicking and punching, but he found that by a- series of elusive movements he could dodge the demonstrations of affection without losing his popularity. Escorted by the soldiers, citizens, children and dogs, he went to the diligence which was to take him and others the next stage of the journey. As the diligence proceeded, Coleman's mind suffered another little inroad of ill-fate as to the success of his expedition. In the first place it appeared foolish to expect that this diligence would ever arrive anywhere. Moreover, the accommodations were about equal to what one would endure if one undertook to sleep for a night in a tree. Then there was a devil-dog, a little black-and-tan terrier in a blanket gorgeous and belled, whose duty it was to stand on the top of the coach and bark incessantly to keep the driver fully aroused to the enormity of his occupation. To have this cur silenced either by strangulation or ordinary clubbing, Coleman struggled with his dragoman as Jacob struggled with the angel, but in the first place, the dragoman was a Greek whose tongue could go quite drunk, a Greek who became a slave to the heralding and establishment of one certain fact, or lie, and now he was engaged in describing to every village and to all the country side the prowess of the gentleman in the distinguished-looking khaki clothes. It was the general absurdity of this advance to the frontier and the fighting, to the crucial place where he was resolved to make an attempt to rescue his sweetheart ; it was this ridiculous aspect that caused to come to Coleman a premonition of failure. No knight ever went out to recover a lost love in such a diligence and with such a devil-dog, tinkling his little bells and yelping insanely to keep the driver awake. After night-fall they arrived at a town on the southern coast of the Gulf of Arta and the goaded dragoman was-thrust forth from the little inn into the street to find the first possible means of getting on to Arta. He returned at last to tremulously say that there was no single chance of starting for Arta that night. Where upon he was again thrust into the street with orders, strict orders. In due time, Coleman spread his rugs upon the floor of his little room and thought himself almost asleep,. when the dragoman entered with a really intelligent man who, for some reason, had agreed to consort with him in the business of getting the stranger off to Arta. They announced that there was a brigantine about to sail with a load of soldiers for a little port near Arta, and if Coleman hurried he could catch it, permission from an officer having already been obtained. He was up at once, and the dragoman and the unaccountably intelligent person hastily gathered his chattels. Stepping out into a black street and moving to the edge of black water and embarking in a black boat filled with soldiers whose rifles dimly shone, was as impressive to Coleman as if, really, it had been the first start. He had endured many starts, it was true, but the latest one always touched him as being conclusive.

There were no lights on the brigantine and the men swung precariously up her sides to the deck which was already occupied by a babbling multitude. The dragoman judiciously found a place for his master where during the night the latter had to move quickly everytime the tiller was shifted to starboard.

The craft raised her shadowy sails and swung slowly off into the deep gloom. Forward, some of the soldiers began to sing weird minor melodies. Coleman, enveloped in his rugs, -smoked three or four cigars. He was content and miserable, lying there, hearing these melodies which defined to him his own affairs.

At dawn they were at the little port. First, in the carmine and grey tints from a sleepy sun, they could see little mobs of soldiers working amid boxes of stores. And then from the back in some dun and green hills sounded a deep-throated thunder of artillery An officer gave Coleman and his dragoman positions in one of the first boats, but of course it could not be done without an almost endless amount of palaver. Eventually they landed with their traps. Coleman felt through the sole of his boot his foot upon the shore. He was within striking distance.

But here it was smitten into the head of Coleman's servant to turn into the most inefficient dragoman, probably in the entire East. Coleman discerned it immediately, before any blunder could tell him. He at first thought that it was the voices of the guns which had made a chilly inside for the man, but when he reflected upon the incompetency, or childish courier's falsity, at Patras and his discernible lack of sense from Agrinion onward, he felt that the fault was elemental in his nature. It was a mere basic inability to front novel situations which was somehow in the dragoman; he retreated from everything difficult in a smoke of gibberish and gesticulation. Coleman glared at him with the hatred that sometimes ensues when breed meets breed, but he saw that this man was indeed a golden link in his possible success. This man connected him with Greece and its language. If he destroyed him he delayed what was now his main desire in life. However, this truth did not prevent him from addressing the man in elegant speech.

The two little men who were induced to carry Coleman's luggage as far as the Greek camp were really procured by the correspondent himself, who pantomined vigorously and with unmistakable vividness. Followed by his dragoman and the two little men, he strode off along a road which led straight as a stick to where the guns were at intervals booming. Meanwhile the dragoman and the two little men talked, talked, talked.- Coleman was silent, puffing his cigar and reflecting upon the odd things which happen to chivalry in the modern age.

He knew of many men who would have been astonished if they could have seen into his mind at that time, and he knew of many more men who would have laughed if they had the same privilege of sight. He made no attempt to conceal from himself that the whole thing was romantic, romantic despite the little tinkling dog, the decrepit diligence, the palavering natives, the super-idiotic dragoman. It was fine, It was from another age and even the actors could not deface the purity of the picture. However it was true that upon the brigantine the previous night he had unaccountably wetted all his available matches. This was momentous, important, cruel truth, but Coleman, after all, was taking-as well as he could forget-a solemn and knightly joy of this adventure and there were as many portraits of his lady envisioning. before him as ever held the heart of an armour-encased young gentleman of medieval poetry. If he had been travelling in this region as an ordinary tourist, he would have been apparent mainly for his lofty impatience over trifles, but now there was in him a positive assertion of direction which was undoubtedly one of the reasons for the despair of the accomplished dragoman.

Before them the country slowly opened and opened, the straight white road always piercing it like a lanceshaft. Soon they could see black masses of men marking the green knolls. The artillery thundered loudly and now vibrated augustly through the air. Coleman quickened his pace, to the despair of the little men carrying the traps. They finally came up with one of these black bodies of men and found it to be composed of a considerable number of soldiers who were idly watching some hospital people bury a dead Turk. The dragoman at once dashed forward to peer through the throng and see the face of the corpse. Then he came and supplicated Coleman as if he were hawking him to look at a relic and Coleman moved by a strong, mysterious impulse, went forward to look at the poor little clay-coloured body. At that moment a snake ran out from a tuft of grass at his feet and wriggled wildly over the sod. The dragoman shrieked, of course, but one of the soldiers put his heel upon the head of the reptile and it flung itself into the agonising knot of death. Then the whole crowd powwowed, turning from the dead man to the dead snake. Coleman signaled his contingent and proceeded along the road.

This incident, this paragraph, had seemed a strange introduction to war. The snake, the dead man, the entire sketch, made him shudder of itself, but more than anything he felt an uncanny symbolism. It was no doubt a mere occurrence; nothing but an occurrence; but inasmuch as all the detail of this daily life associated itself with Marjory, he felt a different horror. He had thought of the little devil-dog and Marjory in an interwoven way. Supposing Marjory had been riding in the diligence with the devil-dog-a-top? What would she have said? Of her fund of expressions, a fund uncountable, which would she have innocently projected against the background of the Greek hills? Would it have smitten her nerves badly or would she have laughed? And supposing Marjory could have seen him in his new khaki clothes cursing his dragoman as he listened to the devil-dog?

And now he interwove his memory of Marjory with a dead man and with a snake in the throes of the end of life. They crossed, intersected, tangled, these two thoughts. He perceived it clearly; the incongruity of it. He academically reflected upon the mysteries of the human mind, this homeless machine which lives here and then there and often lives in two or three opposing places at the same instant. He decided that the incident of the snake and the dead man had no more meaning than the greater number of the things which happen to us in our daily lives. Nevertheless it bore upon him.

On a spread of plain they saw a force drawn up in a long line. It was a flagrant inky streak on the verdant prairie. From somewhere near it sounded the timed reverberations of guns. The brisk walk of the next ten minutes was actually exciting to Coleman. He could not but reflect that those guns were being fired with serious purpose at certain human bodies much like his own.

As they drew nearer they saw that the inky streak was composed of cavalry, the troopers standing at their bridles. The sunlight flicked, upon their bright weapons. Now the dragoman developed in one of his extraordinary directions. He announced forsooth that an intimate friend was a captain of cavalry in this command. Coleman at first thought. that this was some kind of mysterious lie, but when he arrived where they could hear the stamping of hoofs, the clank of weapons, and the murmur of men, behold, a most dashing young officer gave a shout of joy and he and the dragoman hurled themselves into a mad embrace. After this first ecstacy was over, the dragoman bethought him of his employer, and looking toward Coleman hastily explained him to the officer. The latter, it appeared, was very affable indeed. Much had happened. The Greeks and the Turks had been fighting over a shallow part of the river nearly opposite this point and the Greeks had driven back the Turks and succeeded in throwing a bridge of casks and planking across the stream. It was now the duty and the delight of this force of cavalry to cross the bridge and, passing, the little force of covering Greek infantry, to proceed into Turkey until they came in touch with the enemy.

Coleman's eyes dilated. Was ever fate less perverse? Partly in wretched French to the officer and partly in idiomatic English to the dragoman, he proclaimed his fiery desire to accompany the expedition. The officer immediately beamed upon him. In fact, he was delighted. The dragoman had naturally told him many falsehoods concerning Coleman, incidentally referring to himself more as a philanthropic guardian and, valuable friend of the correspondent than as, a plain, unvarnished. dragoman with an exceedingly good eye for the financial possibilities of his position.

Coleman wanted to ask his servant if there was any chance of the scout taking them near Nikopolis, but he delayed being informed upon this point until such time as he could find out, secretly, for himself. To ask the dragoman would be mere stupid questioning which would surely make the animal shy. He tried to be content that fate had given him this early opportunity of dealing with a Medieval situation with some show of proper form ; that is to say, armed, a-horse- back, and in danger. Then he could feel that to the gods of the game he was not laughable, as when he rode to rescue his love in a diligence with a devil- dog yelping a-top.

With some flourish, the young captain presented him to the major who commanded the cavalry. This officer stood with his legs wide apart, eating the rind of a fresh lemon and talking betimes to some of his officers. The major also beamed upon Coleman when the captain explained that the gentleman in the distinguished-looking khaki clothes wished to accompany the expedition. He at once said that he would provide two troop horses for Coleman and the dragoman. Coleman thanked fate for his behaviour and his satisfaction was not without a vestige of surprise. At that time he judged it to be a remarkable amiability of individuals, but in later years he came to believe in certain laws which he deemed existent solely for the benefit of war correspondents. In the minds of governments, war offices and generals they have no function save one of disturbance, but Coleman deemed it proven that the common men, and many uncommon men, when they go away to the fighting ground, out of the sight, out of the hearing of the world known to them, and are eager to perform feats of war in this new place, they feel an absolute longing for a spectator. It is indeed the veritable coronation of this world. There is not too much vanity of the street in this desire of men to have some disinterested fellows perceive their deeds. It is merely that a man doing his best in the middle of a sea of war, longs to have people see him doing his best. This feeling is often notably serious if, in peace, a man has done his worst, or part of his worst. Coleman believed that, above everybody, young, proud and brave subalterns had this itch, but it existed, truly enough, from lieutenants to colonels. None wanted to conceal from his left hand that his right hand was performing a manly and valiant thing, although there might be times when an application of the principle would be immensely convenient. The war correspondent arises, then, to become a sort of a cheap telescope for the people at home; further still, there have been fights where the eyes of a solitary man were the eyes of the world; one spectator, whose business it was to transfer, according to his ability, his visual impressions to other minds.

Coleman and his servant were conducted to two saddled troop horses, and beside them, waited decently in the rear of the ranks. The uniform of the troopers was of plain, dark green cloth and they were well and sensibly equipped. The mounts, however, had in no way been picked; there were little horses and big horses, fat horses and thin horses. They looked the result of a wild conscription. Coleman noted the faces of the troopers, and they were calm enough save when a man betrayed himself by perhaps a disproportionate angry jerk at the bridle of his restive horse.

The major, artistically drooping his cloak from his left shoulder and tenderly and musingly fingering his long yellow moustache, rode slowly to the middle of the line and wheeled his horse to face his men. A bugle called attention, and then he addressed them in a loud and rapid speech, which did not seem to have an end. Coleman imagined that the major was paying tribute to the Greek tradition of the power of oratory. Again the trumpet rang out, and this parade front swung off into column formation. Then Coleman and the dragoman trotted at the tail of the squadron, restraining with difficulty their horses, who could not understand their new places in the procession, and worked feverishly to regain what they considered their positions in life.

The column jangled musically over the sod, passing between two hills on one of which a Greek light battery was posted. Its men climbed to the tops of their interenchments to witness the going of the cavalry. Then the column curved along over ditch and through hedge to the shallows of the river. Across this narrow stream was Turkey. Turkey, however, presented nothing to the eye but a muddy bank with fringes of trees back of it. It seemed to be a great plain with sparse collections of foliage marking it, whereas the Greek side, presented in the main a vista of high, gaunt rocks. Perhaps one of the first effects of war upon the mind, is a. new recognition and fear of the circumscribed ability of the eye, making all landscape seem inscrutable. The cavalry drew up in platoon formation on their own. bank of the stream and waited. If Coleman had known anything of war, he would have known, from appearances, that there was nothing in the immediate vicinity to, cause heart- jumping, but as a matter of truth he was deeply moved and wondered what was hidden, what was veiled by those trees. Moreover, the squadrons resembled art old picture of a body of horse awaiting Napoleon's order to charge. In the, meantime his mount fumed at the bit, plunging to get back to the ranks. The sky was, without a cloud, and the sun rays swept down upon them. Sometimes Coleman was on the verge of addressing the dragoman, according to his anxiety, but in the end he simply told him to go to the river and fill the can- teens.

At last an order came, and the first troop moved with muffled tumult across the bridge. Coleman and his dragoman followed the last troop. The horses scrambled up the muddy bank much as if they were merely breaking out of a pasture, but probably all the men felt a sudden tightening of their muscles. Coleman, in his excitement, felt, more than he saw, glossy horse flanks, green-clothed men chumping in their saddles, banging sabres and canteens, and carbines slanted in line.

There were some Greek infantry in a trench. They were heavily overcoated, despite the heat, and some were engaged in eating loaves of round, thick bread. They called out lustily as the cavalry passed them. The troopers smiled slowly, somewhat proudly in response.

Presently there was another halt and Coleman saw the major trotting busily here and there, while troop commanders rode out to meet him. Spreading groups of scouts and flankers moved off and disappeared. Their dashing young officer friend cantered past them with his troop at his heels. He waved a joyful good-bye. It was the doings of cavalry in actual service, horsemen fanning out in all forward directions. There were two troops held in reserve, and as they jangled ahead at a foot pace, Coleman and his dragoman followed them.

The dragoman was now moved to erect many reasons for an immediate return. It was plain that he had no stomach at all for this business, and that he wished himself safely back on the other side of the river. Coleman looked at him askance. When these men talked together Coleman might as well have been a polar bear for all he understood of it. When he saw the trepidation of his dragoman, he did not know what it foreboded. In this situation it was not for him to say that the dragoman's fears were founded on nothing. And ever the dragoman raised his reasons for a retreat. Coleman spoke to himself. "I am just a trifle rattled," he said to his heart, and after he had communed for a time upon the duty of steadiness, he addressed the dragoman in cool language. "Now, my persuasive friend, just quit all that, because business is business, and it may be rather annoying business, but you will have to go through with it." Long afterward, when ruminating over the feelings of that morning, he saw with some astonishment that there was not a single thing within sound or sight to cause a rational being any quaking. He was simply riding with some soldiers over a vast tree-dotted prairie.

Presently the commanding officer turned in his saddle and told the dragoman that he was going to ride forward with his orderly to where he could see the flanking parties and the scouts, and courteously, with the manner of a gentleman entertaining two guests, he asked if the civilians cared to accompany him. The dragoman would not have passed this question correctly on to Coleman if he had thought he could have avoided it, but, with both men regarding him, he considered that a lie probably meant instant detection. He spoke almost the truth, contenting himself with merely communicating to Coleman in a subtle way his sense that a ride forward with the commanding officer and his orderly would be depressing and dangerous occupation. But Coleman immediately accepted the invitation mainly because it was the invitation of the major, and in war it is a brave man who can refuse the invitation of a commanding officer. The little party of four trotted away from the reserves, curving in single file about the water-holes. In time they arrived at where the plain lacked trees and was one great green lake of grass; grass and scrubs. On this expanse they could see the Greek horsemen riding, mainly appearing as little black dots. Far to the left there was a squad said to be composed of only twenty troopers, but in the distance their black mass seemed to be a regiment.

As the officer and his guests advanced they came in view of what one may call the shore of the plain. The rise of ground was heavily clad with trees, and over the tops of them appeared the cupola and part of the walls of a large white house, and there were glimpses of huts near it as if a village was marked. The black specks seemed to be almost to it. The major galloped forward and the others followed at his pace. The house grew larger and larger and they came nearly to the advance scouts who they could now see were not quite close to the village. There had been a deception of the eye precisely as occurs at sea. Herds of unguarded sheep drifted over the plain and little ownerless horses, still cruelly hobbled, leaped painfully away, frightened, as if they understood that an anarchy had come upon them. The party rode until they were very nearly up with the scouts, and then from low down at the very edge of the plain there came a long rattling noise which endured as if some kind of grinding machine had been put in motion. Smoke arose, faintly marking the position of an intrenchment. Sometimes a swift spitting could be heard from the air over the party.

It was Coleman's fortune to think at first that the Turks were not firing in his direction, but as soon as he heard the weird voices in the air he knew that war was upon him. But it was plain that the range was almost excessive, plain even to his ignorance. The major looked at him and laughed; he found no difficulty in smiling in response. If this was war, it could be withstood somehow. He could not at this time understand what a mere trifle was the present incident. He felt upon his cheek a little breeze which was moving the grass-blades. He had tied his canteen in a wrong place on the saddle and every time the horse moved quickly the canteen banged the correspondent, to his annoyance and distress, forcibly on the knee. He had forgotten about his dragoman, but happening to look upon that faithful servitor, he saw him gone white with horror. A bullet at that moment twanged near his head and the slave to fear ducked in a spasm. Coleman called the orderly's attention and they both laughed discreetly. They made no pretension of being heroes, but they saw plainly that they were better than this man. Coleman said to him : "How far is it now to Nikopolis?" The dragoman replied only, with a look of agonized impatience.

But of course there was no going to Nikopolis that day. The officer had advanced his men as far as was intended by his superiors, and presently they were all recalled and trotted back to the bridge. They crossed it to their old camp.

An important part of Coleman's traps was back with his Athenian horses and their groom, but with his present equipment he could at least lie smoking on his blankets and watch the dragoman prepare food. But he reflected that for that day he had only attained the simple discovery that the approach to Nikopolis was surrounded with difficulties.

CHAPTER X.

The same afternoon Coleman and the dragoman rode up to Arta on their borrowed troop horses. The correspondent first went to the telegraph office and found there the usual number of despairing clerks. They were outraged when they found he was going to send messages and thought it preposterous that he insisted upon learning if there were any in the office for him. They had trouble enough with endless official communications without being hounded about private affairs by a confident young man in khaki. But Coleman at last unearthed six cablegrams which collective said that the Eclipse wondered why they did not hear from him, that Walkley had been relieved from duty in London and sent to join the army of the crown prince, that young Point, the artist, had been shipped to Greece, that if he, Coleman, succeeded in finding the Wainwright party the paper was prepared to make a tremendous uproar of a celebration over it and, finally, the paper wondered twice more why they did not hear from him.

When Coleman went forth to enquire if anybody knew of the whereabouts of the Wainwright party he thought first of his fellow correspondents. He found most of them in a cafe where was to be had about the only food in the soldier-laden town. It was a slothful den where even an ordinary boiled egg could be made unpalatable. Such a common matter as the salt men watched with greed and suspicion as if they were always about to grab it from each other. The proprietor, in a dirty shirt, could always be heard whining, evidently telling the world that he was being abused, but he had spirit enough remaining to charge three prices for everything with an almost Jewish fluency.

The correspondents consoled themselves largely upon black-bread and the native wines. Also there were certain little oiled fishes, and some green odds and ends for salads. The correspondents were practically all Englishmen. Some of them were veterans of journalism in the Sudan, in India, in South Africa; and there were others who knew as much of war as they could learn by sitting at a desk and editing the London stock reports. Some were on their own hook; some had horses and dragomen and some had neither the one nor the other; many knew how to write and a few had it yet to learn. The thing in common was a spirit of adventure which found pleasure in the extraordinary business of seeing how men kill each other.

They were talking of an artillery duel which had been fought the previous day between the Greek batteries above the town and the Turkish batteries across the river. Coleman took seat at one of the long tables, and the astute dragoman got somebody in the street to hold the horses in order that he might be present at any feasting.

One of the experienced correspondents was remarking that the fire of the Greek batteries in the engagement had been the finest artillery practice of the century. He spoke a little loudly, perhaps, in the wistful hope that some of the Greek officers would understand enough English to follow his meaning, for it is always good for a correspondent to admire the prowess on his own side of the battlefield. After a time Coleman spoke in a lull, and describing the supposed misfortunes of the Wainwright party, asked if anyone had news of them. The correspondents were surprised; they had none of them heard even of the existence of a Wainwright party. Also none of them seemed to care exceedingly. The conversation soon changed to a discussion of the probable result of the general Greek advance announced for the morrow.

Coleman silently commented that this remarkable appearance of indifference to the mishap of the Wainwrights, a little party, a single group, was a better definition of a real condition of war than that bit of long-range musketry of the morning. He took a certain despatch out of his pocket and again read it. "Find Wainwright party at all hazards; much talk here; success means red fire by ton. Eclipse." It was an important matter. He could imagine how the American people, vibrating for years to stories of the cruelty of the Turk, would tremble-indeed, was now trembling-while the newspapers howled out the dire possibilities. He saw all the kinds of people, from those who would read the Wainwright chapters from day to day as a sort of sensational novel, to those who would work up a gentle sympathy for the woe of others around the table in the evenings. He saw bar keepers and policemen taking a high gallery thrill out of this kind of romance. He saw even the emotion among American colleges over the tragedy of a professor and some students. It certainly was a big affair. Marjory of course was everything in one way, but that, to the world, was not a big affair. It was the romance of the Wainwright party in its simplicity that to the American world was arousing great sensation; one that in the old days would have made his heart leap like a colt.

Still, when batteries had fought each other savagely, and horse, foot and guns were now about to make a general advance, it was difficult, he could see, to stir men to think and feel out of the present zone of action; to adopt for a time in fact the thoughts and feelings of the other side of the world. It made Coleman dejected as he saw clearly that the task was wholly on his own shoulders.

Of course they were men who when at home manifested the most gentle and wide-reaching feelings; most of them could not by any possibility have slapped a kitten merely for the prank and yet all of them who had seen an unknown man shot through the head in battle had little more to think of it than if the man had been a rag-baby. Tender they might be; poets they might be; but they were all horned with a provisional, temporary, but absolutely essential callouse which was formed by their existence amid war with its quality of making them always think of the sights and sounds concealed in their own direct future.

They had been simply polite. "Yes?" said one to Coleman. "How many people in the party? Are they all Americans? Oh, I suppose it will be quite right. Your minister in Constantinople will arrange that easily. Where did you say? At Nikopolis? Well, we conclude that the Turks will make no stand between here and Pentepigadia. In that case your Nikopolis will be uncovered unless the garrison at Prevasa intervenes. That garrison at Prevasa, by the way, may make a deal of trouble. Remember Plevna."

"Exactly how far is it to Nikopolis?" asked Coleman.

"Oh, I think it is about thirty kilometers," replied the others. "There is a good military road as soon as you cross the Louros river. I've got the map of the Austrian general staff. Would you like to look at it?"

Coleman studied the map, speeding with his eye rapidly to and fro between Arta and Nikopolis. To him it was merely a brown lithograph of mystery, but he could study the distances.

He had received a cordial invitation from the com- mander of the cavalry to go with him for another ride into Turkey, and he inclined to believe that his project would be furthered if he stuck close to the cavalry. So he rode back to the cavalry camp and went peacefully to sleep on the sod. He awoke in the morning with chattering teeth to find his dragoman saying that the major had unaccountably withdrawn his loan of the two troop horses. Coleman of course immediately said to himself that the dragoman was lying a-gain in order to prevent another expedition into ominous Turkey, but after all if the commander, of the cavalry had suddenly turned the light of his favour from the correspondent it was only a proceeding consistent with the nature which Coleman now thought he was beginning to discern, a nature which can never think twice in the same place, a gageous mind which drifts, dissolves, combines, vanishes with the ability of an aerial thing until the man of the north feels that when he clutches it with full knowledge of his senses he is only the victim of his ardent imagination. It is the difference in standards, in creeds, which is the more luminous when men call out that they are all alike.

So Coleman and his dragoman loaded their traps and moved out to again invade Turkey. It was not yet clear daylight, but they felt that they might well start early since they were no longer mounted men.

On the way to the bridge, the dragoman, although he was curiously in love with his forty francs a day and his opportunities, ventured a stout protest, based apparently upon the fact that after all this foreigner, four days out from Athens was somewhat at his mercy. "Meester Coleman," he said, stopping suddenly, "I think we make no good if we go there. Much better we wait Arta for our horse. Much better. I think this no good. There is coming one big fight and I think much better we go stay Arta. Much better."

"Oh, come off," said Coleman. And in clear language he began to labour with the man. "Look here, now, if you think you are engaged in steering a bunch of wooden-headed guys about the Acropolis, my dear partner of my joys and sorrows, you are extremely mistaken. As a matter of fact you are now the dragoman of a war correspondent and you were engaged and are paid to be one. It becomes necessary that you make good. Make good, do you understand? I'm not out here to be buncoed by this sort of game." He continued indefinitely in this strain and at intervals he asked sharply Do you understand?

Perhaps the dragoman was dumbfounded that the laconic Coleman could on occasion talk so much, or perhaps he understood everything and was impressed by the argumentative power. At any rate he suddenly wilted. He made a gesture which was a protestation of martyrdom and picking up his burden proceeded on his way.

When they reached the bridge, they saw strong columns of Greek infantry, dead black in the dim light, crossing the stream and slowly deploying on the other shore. It was a bracing sight to the dragoman, who then went into one of his absurd babbling moods, in which he would have talked the head off any man who was not born in a country laved by the childish Mediterranean. Coleman could not understand what he said to the soldiers as they passed, but it was evidently all grandiose nonsense.

Two light batteries had precariously crossed the rickety bridge during the night, and now this force of several thousand infantry, with the two batteries, was moving out over the territory which the cavalry had reconnoitered on the previous day. The ground being familiar to Coleman, he no longer knew a tremour, and, regarding his dragoman, he saw that that invaluable servitor was also in better form. They marched until they found one of the light batteries unlimbered and aligned on the lake of grass about a mile from where parts of the white house appeared above the tree-tops. Here the dragoman talked with the captain of artillery, a tiny man on an immense horse, who for some unknown reason told him that this force was going to raid into Turkey and try to swing around the opposing army's right flank. He announced, as he showed his teeth in a smile, that it would be very, very dangerous work. The dragoman precipitated himself upon Coleman.

"This is much danger. The copten he tell me the trups go now in back of the Turks. It will be much danger. I think much better we go Arta wait for horse. Much better." Coleman, although be believed he despised the dragoman, could not help but be influenced by his fears. They were, so to speak, in a room with one window, and only the dragoman looked forth from the window, so if he said that what he saw outside frightened him, Coleman was perforce frightened also in a measure. But when the correspondent raised his eyes he saw the captain of the battery looking at him, his teeth still showing in a smile, as if his information, whether true or false, had been given to convince the foreigner that the Greeks were a very superior and brave people, notably one little officer of artillery. He had apparently assumed that Coleman would balk from venturing with such a force upon an excursion to trifle with the rear of a hard fighting Ottoman army. He exceedingly disliked that man, sitting up there on his tall horse and grinning like a cruel little ape with a secret. In truth, Coleman was taken back at the outlook, but he could no more refrain from instantly accepting this half-concealed challenge than he could have refrained from resenting an ordinary form of insult. His mind was not at peace, but the small vanities are very large. He was perfectly aware that he was, being misled into the thing by an odd pride, but anyhow, it easily might turn out to be a stroke upon the doors of Nikopolis. He nodded and smiled at the officer in grateful acknowledgment of his service.

The infantry was moving steadily a-field. Black blocks of men were trailing in column slowly over the plain. They were not unlike the backs of dominoes on a green baize table ; they were so vivid, so startling. The correspondent and his servant followed them. Eventually they overtook two companies in command of a captain, who seemed immensely glad to have the strangers with him. As they marched, the captain spoke through the dragoman upon the virtues of his men, announcing with other news the fact that his first sergeant was the bravest man in the world.

A number of columns were moving across the plain parallel to their line of march, and the whole force seemed to have orders to halt when they reached a long ditch about four hundred yards from where the shore of the plain arose to the luxuriant groves with the cupola of the big white house sticking above them. The soldiers lay along the ditch, and the bravest man in the world spread his blanket on the ground for the captain, Coleman and himself. During a long pause Coleman tried to elucidate the question of why the Greek soldiers wore heavy overcoats, even in the bitter heat of midday, but he could only learn that the dews, when they came, were very destructive to the lungs, Further, he convinced himself anew that talking through an interpreter to the minds of other men was as satisfactory as looking at landscape through a stained glass window.

After a time there was, in front, a stir near where a curious hedge of dry brambles seemed to outline some sort of a garden patch. Many of the soldiers exclaimed and raised their guns. But there seemed to come a general understanding to the line that it was wrong to fire. Then presently into the open came a dirty brown figure, and Coleman could see through his glasses that its head was crowned with a dirty fez which had once been white. This indicated that the figure was that of one of the Christian peasants of Epirus. Obedient to the captain, the sergeant arose and waved invitation. The peasant wavered, changed his mind, was obviously terror-stricken, regained confidence and then began to advance circuitously toward the Greek lines. When he arrived within hailing dis- tance, the captain, the sergeant, Coleman's dragoman and many of the soldiers yelled human messages, and a moment later he was seen to be a poor, yellow-faced stripling with a body which seemed to have been first twisted by an ill-birth and afterward maimed by either labour or oppression, these being often identical in their effects.

His reception of the Greek soldiery was no less fervid than their welcome of him to their protection. He threw his grimy fez in the air and croaked out cheers, while tears wet his cheeks. When he had come upon the right side of the ditch he ran capering among them and the captain, the sergeant, the dragoman and a number of soldiers received wild embraces and kisses. He made a dash at Coleman, but Coleman was now wary in the game, and retired dexterously behind different groups with a finished appearance of not noting that the young man wished to greet him.

Behind the hedge of dry brambles there were more indications of life, and the peasant stood up and made beseeching gestures. Soon a whole flock of miserable people had come out to the Greeks, men, women and children, in crude and comic smocks, prancing here and there, uproariously embracing and kissing their deliverers. An old, tearful, toothless hag flung herself rapturously into the arms of the captain, and Coleman's brick-and-iron soul was moved to admiration at the way in which the officer administered a chaste salute upon the furrowed cheek. The dragoman told the correspondent that the Turks had run away from the village on up a valley toward Jannina. Everybody was proud and happy. A major of infantry came from the rear at this time and asked the captain in sharp tones who were the two strangers in civilian attire. When the captain had answered correctly the major was immediately mollified, and had it announced to the correspondent that his battalion was going to move immediately into the village, and that he would be delighted to have his company.

The major strode at the head of his men with the group of villagers singing and dancing about him and looking upon him as if he were a god. Coleman and the dragoman, at the officer's request, marched one on either side of him, and in this manner they entered the village. From all sorts of hedges and thickets, people came creeping out to pass into a delirium of joy. The major borrowed three little pack horses with rope-bridles, and thus mounted and followed by the clanking column, they rode on in triumph.

It was probably more of a true festival than most men experience even in the longest life time. The major with his Greek instinct of drama was a splendid personification of poetic quality; in fact he was himself almost a lyric. From time to time he glanced back at Coleman with eyes half dimmed with appreciation. The people gathered flowers, great blossoms of purple and corn colour. They sprinkled them over the three horsemen and flung them deliriously under the feet of the little nags. Being now mounted Coleman had no difficulty in avoiding the embraces of the peasants, but he felt to the tips of his toes an abandonment to a kind of pleasure with which he was not at all familiar. Riding thus amid cries of thanksgiving addressed at him equally with the others, he felt a burning virtue and quite lost his old self in an illusion of noble be. nignity. And there continued the fragrant hail of blossoms.

Miserable little huts straggled along the sides of the village street as if they were following at the heels of the great white house of the bey. The column proceeded northward, announcing laughingly to the glad villagers that they would never see another Turk. Before them on the road was here and there a fez from the head of a fled Turkish soldier and they lay like drops of blood from some wounded leviathan. Ultimately it grew cloudy. It even rained slightly. In the misty downfall the column of soldiers in blue was dim as if it were merely a long trail of low-hung smoke.

They came to the ruins of a church and there the major halted his battalion. Coleman worried at his dragoman to learn if the halt was only temporary. It was a long time before there was answer from the major, for he had drawn up his men in platoons and was addressing them in a speech as interminable as any that Coleman had heard in Greece. The officer waved his arms and roared out evidently the glories of patriotism and soldierly honour, the glories of their ancient people, and he may have included any subject in this wonderful speech, for the reason that he had plenty of time in which to do it. It was impossible to tell whether the oration was a good one or bad one, because the men stood in their loose platoons without discernible feelings as if to them this appeared merely as one of the inevitable consequences of a campaign, an established rule of warfare. Coleman ate black bread and chocolate tablets while the dragoman hovered near the major with the intention of pouncing upon him for information as soon as his lungs yielded to the strain upon them.

The dragoman at last returned with a very long verbal treatise from the major, who apparently had not been as exhausted after his speech to the men as one would think. The major had said that he had been ordered to halt here to form a junction with some of the troops coming direct from Arta, and that he expected that in the morning the army would be divided and one wing would chase the retreating Turks on toward Jannina, while the other wing would advance upon Prevasa because the enemy had a garrison there which had not retreated an inch, and, although it was cut off, it was necessary to send either a force to hold it in its place or a larger force to go through with the business of capturing it. Else there would be left in the rear of the left flank of a Greek advance upon Jannina a body of the enemy which at any moment might become active. The major said that his battalion would probably form part of the force to advance upon Prevasa. Nikopolis was on the road to Prevasa and only three miles away from it.

CHAPTER XI.

Coleman spent a long afternoon in the drizzle Enveloped in his macintosh he sat on a boulder in the lee of one of the old walls and moodily smoked cigars and listened to the ceaseless clatter of tongues. A ray of light penetrated the mind of the dragoman and he laboured assiduously with wet fuel until he had accomplished a tin mug of coffee. Bits of cinder floated in it, but Coleman rejoiced and was kind to the dragoman.

The night was of cruel monotony. Afflicted by the wind and the darkness, the correspondent sat with nerves keyed high waiting to hear the pickets open fire on a night attack. He was so unaccountably sure that there would be a tumult and panic of this kind at some time of the night that he prevented himself from getting a reasonable amount of rest. He could hear the soldiers breathing in sleep all about him. He wished to arouse them from this slumber which, to his ignorance, seemed stupid. The quality of mysterious menace in the great gloom and the silence would have caused him to pray if prayer would have transported him magically to New York and made him a young man with no coat playing billiards at his club.

The chill dawn came at last and with a fine elation which ever follows a dismal night in war; an elation which bounds in the bosom as soon as day has knocked the shackles from a trembling mind. Although Coleman had slept but a short time he was now as fresh as a total abstainer coming from the bath. He heard the creak of battery wheels; he saw crawling bodies of infantry moving in the dim light like ghostly processions. He felt a tremendous virility come with this new hope in the daylight. He again took satis. faction in his sentimental journey. It was a shining affair. He was on active service, an active service of the heart, and he' felt that he was a strong man ready to conquer difficulty even as the olden heroes conquered difficulty. He imagined himself in a way like them. He, too, had come out to fight for love with giants, dragons and witches. He had never known that he could be so pleased with that kind of a parallel.

The dragoman announced that the major had suddenly lent their horses to some other people, and after cursing this versatility of interest, he summoned his henchmen and they moved out on foot, following the sound of the creaking wheels. They came in time to a bridge, and on the side of this bridge was a hard military road which sprang away in two directions, north and west. Some troops were creeping out the westward way and the dragoman pointing at them said: "They going Prevasa. That is road to Nikopolis." Coleman grinned from ear to car and slapped his dragoman violently on the shoulder. For a moment he intended to hand the man a louis of reward, but he changed his mind.

Their traps were in the way of being heavy, but they minded little since the dragoman was now a victim of the influence of Coleman's enthusiasm. The road wound along the base of the mountain range, sheering around the abutments in wide white curves and then circling into glens where immense trees spread their shade over it. Some of the great trunks were oppressed with vines green as garlands, and these vines even ran like verdant foam over the rocks. Streams of translucent water showered down from the hills, and made pools in which every pebble, every eaf of a water plant shone with magic lustre, and if the bottom of a pool was only of clay, the clay glowed with sapphire light. The day was fair. The country was part of that land which turned the minds of its ancient poets toward a more tender dreaming, so that indeed their nymphs would die, one is sure, in the cold mythology of the north with its storms amid the gloom of pine forests. It was all wine to Coleman's spirit. It enlivened him to think of success with absolute surety. To be sure one of his boots began soon to rasp his toes, but he gave it no share of his attention. They passed at a much faster pace than the troops, and everywhere they met laughter and confidence and the cry. "On to Prevasa! "

At midday they were at the heels of the advance battalion, among its stragglers, taking its white dust into their throats and eyes. The dragoman was waning and he made a number of attempts to stay Coleman, but no one could have had influence upon Coleman's steady rush with his eyes always straight to the front as if thus to symbolize his steadiness of purpose. Rivulets of sweat marked the dust on his face, and two of his toes were now paining as if they were being burned off. He was obliged to concede a privilege of limping, but he would not stop.

At nightfall they halted with the outpost batallion of the infantry. All the cavalry had in the meantirne come up and they saw their old friends. There was a village from which the Christian peasants came and cheered like a trained chorus. Soldiers were driving a great flock of fat sheep into a corral. They had belonged to a Turkish bey and they bleated as if they knew that they were now mere spoils of war. Coleman lay on the steps of the bey's house smoking with his head on his blanket roll. Camp fires glowed off in the fields. He was now about four miles from Nikopolis.

Within the house, the commander of the cavalry was writing dispatches. Officers clanked up and down the stairs. The dashing young captain came and said that there would be a general assault on Prevasa at the dawn of the next day. Afterward the dragoman descended upon the village and in some way wrenched a little grey horse from an inhabitant. Its pack saddle was on its back and it would very handily carry the traps. In this matter the dragoman did not consider his master; he considered his own sore back.

Coleman ate more bread and chocolate tablets and also some tinned sardines. He was content with the day's work. He did not see how he could have improved it. There was only one route by which the Wainwright party could avoid him, and that was by going to Prevasa and thence taking ship. But since Prevasa was blockaded by a Greek fleet, he conceived that event to be impossible. Hence, he had them hedged on this peninsula and they must be either at Nikopolis or Prevasa. He would probably know all early in the morning. He reflected that he was too tired to care if there might be a night attack and then wrapped in his blankets he went peacefully to sleep in the grass under a big tree with the crooning of some soldiers around their fire blending into his slumber.

And now, although the dragoman had performed a number of feats of incapacity, he achieved during the one hour of Coleman's sleeping a blunder which for real finish was simply a perfection of art. When Coleman, much later, extracted the full story, it appeared that ringing. events happened during that single hour of sleep. Ten minutes after he had lain down for a night of oblivion, the battalion of infantry, which had advanced a little beyond the village, was recalled and began a hurried night march back on the way it had so festively come. It was significant enough to appeal to almost any mind, but the dragoman was able to not understand it. He remained jabbering to some acquaintances among the troopers. Coleman had been asleep his hour when the dashing young captain perceived the dragoman, and completely horrified by his presence at that place, ran to him and whispered to him swiftly that the game was to flee, flee, flee. The wing of the army which had advanced northward upon Jannina had already been tumbled back by the Turks and all the other wing had been recalled to the Louros river and there was now nothing practically between him and his sleeping master and the enemy but a cavalry picket. The cavalry was immediately going to make a forced march to the rear. The stricken dragoman could even then see troopers getting into their saddles. He, rushed to, the, tree, and in. a panic simply bundled Coleman upon his feet before he was awake. He stuttered out his tale, and the dazed, correspondent heard it punctuated by the steady trample of the retiring cavalry. The dragoman saw a man's face then turn in a flash from an expression of luxurious drowsiness to an expression of utter malignancy. However, he was in too much of a hurry to be afraid of it; he ran off to the little grey horse and frenziedly but skilfully began to bind the traps upon the packsaddle. He appeared in a moment tugging at the halter. He could only say: "Come! Come! Come! Queek! Queek!" They slid hurriedly down a bank to the road and started to do again that which they had accomplished with considerable expenditure of physical power during the day. The hoof beats of the cavalry had already died away and the mountains shadowed them in lonely silence. They were the rear guard after the rear guard.

The dragoman muttered hastily his last dire rumours. Five hundred Circassian cavalry were coming. The mountains were now infested with the dread Albanian irregulars, Coleman had thought in his daylight tramp that he had appreciated the noble distances, but he found that he knew nothing of their nobility until he tried this night stumbling. And the hoofs of the little horse made on the hard road more noise than could be made by men beating with hammers upon brazen cylinders. The correspondent glanced continually up at the crags. From the other side he could sometimes hear the metallic clink of water deep down in a glen. For the first time in his life he seriously opened the flap of his holster and let his fingers remain on the handle of his revolver. From just in front of him he could hear the chattering of the dragoman's teeth which no attempt at more coolness could seem to prevent. In the meantime the casual manner of the little grey horse struck Coleman with maddening vividness. If the blank darkness was simply filled with ferocious Albanians, the horse did not care a button; he leisurely put his feet down with a resounding ring. Coleman whispered hastily to the dragoman. "If they rush us, jump down the bank, no matter how deep it is. That's our only chance. And try to keep together."

All they saw of the universe was, in front of them, a place faintly luminous near their feet, but fading in six yards to the darkness of a dungeon. This repre- sented the bright white road of the day time. It had no end. Coleman had thought that he could tell from the very feel of the air some of the landmarks of his daytime journey, but he had now no sense of location at all. He would not have denied that he was squirming on his belly like a worm through black mud. They went on and on. Visions of his past were sweeping through Coleman's mind precisely as they are said to sweep through the mind of a drowning person. But he had no regret for any bad deeds; he regretted merely distant hours of peace and protection. He was no longer a hero going to rescue his love. He was a slave making a gasping attempt to escape from the most incredible tyranny of circumstances. He half vowed to himself that if the God whom he had in no wise heeded, would permit him to crawl out of this slavery he would never again venture a yard toward a danger any greater than may be incurred from the police of a most proper metropolis. If his juvenile and uplifting thoughts of other days had reproached him he would simply have repeated and repeated: "Adventure be damned."

It became known to them that the horse had to be led. The debased creature was asserting its right to do as it had been trained, to follow its customs; it was asserting this right during a situation which required conduct superior to all training and custom. It was so grossly conventional that Coleman would have understood that demoniac form of anger which sometimes leads men to jab knives into warm bodies. Coleman from cowardice tried to induce the dragoman to go ahead leading the horse, and the dragoman from cowardice tried to induce Coleman to go ahead leading the horse. Coleman of course had to succumb. The dragoman was only good to walk behind and tearfully whisper maledictions as he prodded the flanks of their tranquil beast.

In the absolute black of the frequent forests, Coleman could not see his feet and he often felt like a man walking forward to fall at any moment down a thousand yards of chasm. He heard whispers; he saw skulking figures, and these frights turned out to be the voice of a little trickle of water or the effects of wind among the leaves, but they were replaced by the same terrors in slightly different forms.

Then the poignant thing interpolated. A volley crashed ahead of them some half of a mile away and another volley answered from a still nearer point. Swishing noises which the correspondent had heard in the air he now know to have been from the passing of bullets. He and the dragoman came stock still. They heard three other volleys sounding with the abrupt clamour of a hail of little stones upon a hollow surface. Coleman and the dragoman came close together and looked into the whites of each other's eyes. The ghastly horse at that moment stretched down his neck and began placidly to pluck the grass at the roadside. The two men were equally blank with fear and each seemed to seek in the other some newly rampant manhood upon which he could lean at this time. Behind them were the Turks. In front of them was a fight in the darkness. In front it was mathematic to suppose in fact were also the Turks. They were barred; enclosed; cut off. The end was come.

Even at that moment they heard from behind them the sound of slow, stealthy footsteps. They both wheeled instantly, choking with this additional terror. Coleman saw the dragoman move swiftly to the side of the road, ready to jump into whatever abyss happened to be there. Coleman still gripped the halter as if it were in truth a straw. The stealthy footsteps were much nearer. Then it was that an insanity came upon him as if fear had flamed up within him until it gave him all the magnificent desperation of a madman. He jerked the grey horse broadside to the approaching mystery, and grabbing out his revolver aimed it from the top of his improvised bulwark. He hailed the darkness.

"Halt. Who's there?" He had expected his voice to sound like a groan, but instead it happened to sound clear, stern, commanding, like the voice of a young sentry at an encampment of volunteers. He did not seem to have any privilege of selection as to the words. They were born of themselves.

He waited then, blanched and hopeless, for death to wing out of the darkness and strike him down. He heard a voice. The voice said: "Do you speak English?" For one or two seconds he could not even understand English, and then the great fact swelled up and within him. This voice with all its new quavers was still undoubtedly the voice of Prof. Harrison B. Wainwright of Washurst College

CHAPTER XII.

A CHANGE flashed over Coleman as if it had come from an electric storage. He had known the professor long, but he had never before heard a quaver in his voice, and it was this little quaver that seemed to impel him to supreme disregard of the dangers which he looked upon as being the final dangers. His own voice had not quavered.

When he spoke, he spoke in a low tone, it was the voice of the master of the situation. He could hear his dupes fluttering there in the darkness. "Yes," he said, "I speak English. There is some danger. Stay where you are and make no noise." He was as cool as an iced drink. To be sure the circumstances had in no wise changed as to his personal danger, but beyond the important fact that there were now others to endure it with him, he seemed able to forget it in a strange, unauthorized sense of victory. It came from the professor's quavers.

Meanwhile he had forgotten the dragoman, but he recalled him in time to bid him wait. Then, as well concealed as a monk hiding in his cowl, he tip-toed back into a group of people who knew him intimately.

He discerned two women mounted on little horses and about them were dim men. He could hear them breathing hard. "It is all right" he began smoothly. "You only need to be very careful —-"

Suddenly out of the blackness projected a half phosphorescent face. It was the face of the little professor. He stammered. "We-we-do you really speak English?" Coleman in his feeling of superb triumph could almost have laughed. His nerves were as steady as hemp, but he was in haste and his haste allowed him to administer rebuke to his old professor.

"Didn't you hear me?" he hissed through his tightening lips. " They are fighting just ahead of us on the road and if you want to save yourselves don't waste time."

Another face loomed faintly like a mask painted in dark grey. It belonged to Coke, and it was a mask figured in profound stupefaction. The lips opened and tensely breathed out the name: "Coleman." Instantly the correspondent felt about him that kind of a tumult which tries to suppress itself. He knew that it was the most theatric moment of his life. He glanced quickly toward the two figures on horseback. He believed that one was making foolish gesticulation while the other sat rigid and silent. This latter one he knew to be Marjory. He was content that she did not move. Only a woman who was glad he had come but did not care for him would have moved. This applied directly to what he thought he knew of Marjory's nature.

There was confusion among the students, but Coleman suppressed it as in such situation might a centurion. "S-s-steady!" He seized the arm of the professor and drew him forcibly close. "The condition is this," he whispered rapidly. "We are in a fix with this fight on up the road. I was sent after you, but I can't get you into the Greek lines to-night. Mrs. Wainwright and Marjory must dismount and I and my man will take the horses on and hide them. All the rest of you must go up about a hundred feet into the woods and hide. When I come back, I'll hail you and you answer low." The professor was like pulp in his grasp. He choked out the word "Coleman" in agony and wonder, but he obeyed with a palpable gratitude. Coleman sprang to the side of the shadowy figure of Marjory. "Come," he said authoritatively. She laid in his palm a little icy cold hand and dropped from her horse. He had an impulse to cling to the small fingers, but he loosened them immediately, im- parting to his manner, as well as the darkness per- mitted him, a kind of casual politeness as if he were too intent upon the business in hand. He bunched the crowd and pushed them into the wood. Then he and the dragoman took the horses a hundred yards onward and tethered them. No one would care if they were stolen; the great point was to get them where their noise would have no power of revealing the whole party. There had been no further firing.

After he had tied the little grey horse to a tree he unroped his luggage and carried the most of it back to the point where the others had left the road. He called out cautiously and received a sibilant answer. He and the dragoman bunted among the trees until they came to where a forlorn company was seated awaiting them lifting their faces like frogs out of a pond. His first question did not give them any assurance. He said at once: "Are any of you armed?" Unanimously they lowly breathed: "No." He searched them out one by one and finally sank down by the professor. He kept sort of a hypnotic handcuff upon the dragoman, because he foresaw that this man was really going to be the key to the best means of escape. To a large neutral party wandering between hostile lines there was technically no danger, but actually there was a great deal. Both armies had too many irregulars, lawless hillsmen come out to fight in their own way, and if they were encountered in the dead of night on such hazardous ground the Greek hillsmen with their white cross on a blue field would be precisely as dangerous as the blood-hungry Albanians. Coleman knew that the rational way was to reach the Greek lines, and he had no intention of reaching the Greek lines without a tongue, and the only tongue was in the mouth of the dragoman. He was correct in thinking that the professor's deep knowledge of the ancient language would give him small clue to the speech of the modern Greek.

As he settled himself by the professor the band of students, eight in number pushed their faces close.

He did not see any reason for speaking. There were thirty seconds of deep silence in which he felt that all were bending to hearken to his words of counsel The professor huskily broke the stillness. Well * * * what are we to do now?"

Coleman was decisive, indeed absolute. "We'll stay here until daylight unless you care to get shot."

"All right," answered the professor. He turned and made a useless remark to his flock. "Stay here."

Coleman asked civilly, "Have you had anything to eat? Have you got anything to wrap around you?"

"We have absolutely nothing," answered the professor. "Our servants ran away and * * and then we left everything behind us * * and I've never been in such a position in my life."

Coleman moved softly in the darkness and unbuckled some of his traps. On his knee he broke the hard cakes of bread and with his fingers he broke the little tablets of chocolate. These he distributed to his people. And at this time he felt fully the appreciation of the conduct of the eight American college students They had not yet said a word-with the exception of the bewildered exclamation from Coke. They all knew him well. In any circumstance of life which as far as he truly believed, they had yet encountered, they would have been privileged to accost him in every form of their remarkable vocabulary. They were as new to this game as, would have been eight newly-caught Apache Indians if such were set to run the elevators in the Tract Society Building. He could see their eyes gazing at him anxiously and he could hear their deep- drawn breaths. But they said no word. He knew that they were looking upon him as their leader, almost as their saviour, and he knew also that they were going to follow him without a murmur in the conviction that he knew ten-fold more than they knew. It occurred to him that his position was ludicrously false, but, anyhow, he was glad. Surely it would be a very easy thing to lead them to safety in the morning and he foresaw the credit which would come to him. He concluded that it was beneath his dignity as preserver to vouchsafe them many words. His business was to be the cold, masterful, enigmatic man. It might be said that these reflections were only half-thoughts in his mind. Meanwhile a section of his intellect was flying hither and thither, speculating upon the Circassian cavalry and the Albanian guerillas and even the Greek outposts.

He unbuckled his blanket roll and taking one blanket placed it about the shoulders of the shadow which was Mrs. Wainwright. The shadow protested incoherently,. hut he muttered "Oh that's all right." Then he took his other blanket and went to the shadow which was Marjory. It was something like putting a wrap about the shoulders of a statue. He was base enough to linger in the hopes that he could detect some slight trembling but as far as lie knew she was of stone. His macintosh he folded around the body of the professor amid quite senile protest, so senile that the professor seemed suddenly proven to him as an old, old man, a fact which had never occurred to Washurst or her children. Then he went to the dragoman and pre-empted half of his blankets, The dragoman grunted but Coleman It would not do to have this dragoman develop a luxurious temperament when eight American college students were, without speech, shivering in the cold night.

Coleman really begun to ruminate upon his glory, but he found that he could not do this well without Smoking, so he crept away some distance from this fireless, encampment, and bending his face to the ground at the foot of a tree he struck a match and lit a cigar. His retun to the others would have been somewhat in the manner of coolness as displayed on the stage if he had not been prevented by the necessity of making no noise. He saw regarding him as before the dimly visible eyes of the eight students and Marjory and her father and mother. Then he whispered the conventional words. "Go to sleep if you can. You'll need your strength in the morning. I and this man here will keep watch." Three of the college students of course crawled up to him and each said: "I'll keep watch, old man." " No. We'll keep watch. You people try to sleep."

He deemed that it might be better to yield the dragoman his blanket, and So he got up and leaned against a tree, holding his hand to cover the brilliant point of his cigar. He knew perfectly well that none of them could sleep. But he stood there somewhat like a sentry without the attitude, but with all the effect of responsibility.

He had no doubt but what escape to civilisation would be easy, but anyhow his heroism should be preserved. He was the rescuer. His thoughts of Marjory were somewhat in a puzzle. The meeting had placed him in such a position that he had expected a lot of condescension on his own part. Instead she had exhibited about as much recognition of him as would a stone fountain on his grandfather's place in Connecticut. This in his opinion was not the way to greet the knight who had come to the rescue of his lady. He had not expected it so to happen. In fact from Athens to this place he had engaged himself with imagery of possible meetings. He was vexed, certainly, but, far beyond that, he knew a deeper adminiration for this girl. To him she represented the sex, and so the sex as embodied in her seemed a mystery to be feared. He wondered if safety came on the morrow he would not surrender to this feminine invulnerability. She had not done anything that he had expected of her and so inasmuch as he loved her he loved her more. It was bewitching. He half considered himself a fool. But at any rate he thought resentfully she should be thankful to him for having rendered her a great service. However, when he came to consider this proposition he knew that on a basis of absolute manly endeavour he had rendered her little or no service.

The night was long.

CHAPTER XIII.

COLEMAN suddenly found himself looking upon his pallid dragoman. He saw that he had been asleep crouched at the foot of the tree. Without any exchange of speech at all he knew there had been alarming noises. Then shots sounded from nearby. Some were from rifles aimed in that direction and some were from rifles opposed to them. This was distinguishable to the experienced man, but all that Coleman knew was that the conditions of danger were now triplicated. Unconsciously he stretched his hands in supplication over his charges. "Don't move! Don't move! And keep close to the ground!" All heeded him but Marjory. She still sat straight. He himself was on his feet, but he now knew the sound of bullets, and he knew that no bullets had spun through the trees. He could not see her distinctly, but it was known to him in some way that she was mutinous. He leaned toward her and spoke as harshly as possible. "Marjory, get down!" She wavered for a moment as if resolved to defy him. As he turned again to peer in the direction of the firing it went through his mind that she must love him very much indeed. He was assured of it. It must have been some small outpour between nervous pickets and eager hillsmen, for it ended in a moment. The party waited in abasement for what seemed to them a time, and the blue dawn began, to laggardly shift the night as they waited. The dawn itself seemed prodigiously long in arriving at anything like discernible landscape. When this was consummated, Coleman, in somewhat the manner of the father of a church, dealt bits of chocolate out to the others. He had already taken the precaution to confer with the dragoman, so he said: "Well, come ahead. We'll make a try for it." They arose at his bidding and followed him to the road. It was the same broad, white road, only that the white was in the dawning something like the grey of a veil. It took some courage to venture upon this thoroughfare, but Coleman stepped out-after looking quickly in both directions. The party tramped to where the horses had been left, and there they were found without change of a rope. Coleman rejoiced to see that his dragoman now followed him in the way of a good lieutenant. They both dashed in among the trees and had the horses out into the road in a twinkle. When Coleman turned to direct that utterly subservient, group he knew that his face was drawn from hardship and anxiety, but he saw everywhere the same style of face with the exception of the face of Marjory, who looked simply of lovely marble. He noted with a curious satisfaction, as if the thing was a tribute to himself, that his macintosh was over the professor's shoulder, that Marjory and her mother were each carrying a blanket, and that, the corps of students had dutifully brought all the traps which his dragoman had forgotten. It was grand.

He addressed them to say: "Now, approaching outposts is very dangerous business at this time in the morning. So my man, who can talk both Greek and Turkish, will go ahead forty yards, and I will follow somewhere between him and you. Try not to crowd forward."

He directed the ladies upon their horses and placed the professor upon the little grey nag. Then they took up their line of march. The dragoman had looked somewhat dubiously upon this plan of having him go forty yards in advance, but he had the utmost confidence in this new Coleman, whom yesterday he had not known. Besides, he himself was a very gallant man indeed, and it befitted him to take the post of danger before the eyes of all these foreigners. In his new position he was as proud and unreasonable as a rooster. He was continually turning his head to scowl back at them, when only the clank of hoofs was sounding. An impenetrable mist lay on the valley and the hill-tops were shrouded. As for the people, they were like mice. Coleman paid no attention to the Wainwright party, but walked steadily along near the dragoman.

Perhaps the whole thing was a trifle absurd, but to a great percentage, of the party it was terrible. For instance, those eight boys, fresh from a school, could in no wise gauge the dimensions. And if this was true of the students, it was more distinctly true of Marjory and her mother. As for the professor, he seemed Weighted to the earth by his love and his responsibility.

Suddenly the dragoman wheeled and made demoniac signs. Coleman half-turned to survey the main body, and then paid his attention swiftly to the front. The white road sped to the top of a hill where it seemed to make a rotund swing into oblivion. The top of the curve was framed in foliage, and therein was a horseman. He had his carbine slanted on his thigh, and his bridle-reins taut. Upon sight of them he immediately wheeled and galloped down the other slope and vanished.

The dragoman was throwing wild gestures into the air. As Coleman looked back at the Wainwright party he saw plainly that to an ordinary eye they might easily appear as a strong advance of troops. The peculiar light would emphasize such theory. The dragoman ran to him jubilantly, but he contained now a form of intelligence which caused him to whisper; " That was one Greek. That was one Greek-what do you call-sentree?"

Coleman addressed the others. He said: "It's all right. Come ahead. That was a Greek picket. There is only one trouble now, and that is to approach them easy-do you see-easy."

His obedient charges came forward at his word. When they arrived at the top of this rise they saw nothing. Coleman was very uncertain. He was not sure that this picket had not carried with him a general alarm, and in that case there would soon occur a certain amount of shooting. However, as far as he understood the business, there was no way but forward. Inasmuch as he did not indicate to the Wainwright party that he wished them to do differently, they followed on doggedly after him and the dragoman. He knew now that the dragoman's heart had for the tenth time turned to dog-biscuit, so he kept abreast of him. And soon together they walked into a cavalry outpost, commanded by no less a person than the dashing young captain, who came laughing out to meet them.

Suddenly losing all colour of war, the condition was now such as might occur in a drawing room. Coleman felt the importance of establishing highly conventional relations between the captain and the Wainwright party. To compass this he first seized his dragoman, and the dragoman, enlightened immediately, spun a series of lies which must have led the captain to believe that the entire heart of the American republic had been taken out of that western continent and transported to Greece. Coleman was proud of the captain, The latter immediately went and bowed in the manner of the French school and asked everybody to have a cup of coffee, although acceptation would have proved his ruin and disgrace. Coleman refused in the name of courtesy. He called his party forward, and now they proceeded merely as one crowd. Marjory had dismounted in the meantime.

The moment was come. Coleman felt it. The first rush was from the students. Immediately he was buried in a thrashing mob of them. "Good boy! Good boy! Great man! Oh, isn't he a peach? How did he do it? He came in strong at the finish ! Good boy, Coleman!" Through this mist of glowing youthful congratulatioin he saw the professor standing at the outskirts with direct formal thanks already moving on his lips, while near him his wife wept joyfully. Marjory was evidently enduring some inscrutable emotion.

After all, it did penetrate his mind that it was indecent to accept all this wild gratitude, but there was built within him no intention of positively declaring himself lacking in all credit, or at least, lacking in all credit in the way their praises defined it. In truth he had assisted them, but he had been at the time largely engaged in assisting himself, and their coming had been more of a boon to his loneliness than an addition to his care. However, he soon had no difficulty in making his conscience appropriate every line in these hymns sung in his honour. The students, curiously wise of men, thought his conduct quite perfect. "Oh, say, come off ! " he protested. "Why, I didn't do anything. You fellows are crazy. You would have gotten in all right by yourselves. Don't act like asses-"

As soon as the professor had opportunity he came to Coleman. He was a changed little man, and his extraordinary bewilderment showed in his face. It was the disillusion and amazement of a stubborn mind that had gone implacably in its one direction and found in the end that the direction was all wrong, and that really a certain mental machine had not been infallible. Coleman remembered what the American minister in Athens had described of his protests against the starting of the professor's party on this journey, and of the complete refusal of the professor to recognise any value in the advice. And here now was the consequent defeat. It was mirrored in the professor's astonished eyes. Coleman went directly to his dazed old teacher.

"Well, you're out of it now, professor," he said warmly. "I congratulate you on your escape, sir." The professor looked at him, helpless to express himself, but the correspondent was at that time suddenly enveloped in the hysterical gratitude of Mrs. Wainwright, who hurled herself upon him with extravagant manifestations. Coleman played his part with skill. To both the professor and Mrs. Wainwright his manner was a combination of modestly filial affection and a pretentious disavowal of his having done anything at all. It seemed to charm everybody but Marjory. It irritated him to see that she was apparently incapable of acknowledging that he was a grand man.

He was actually compelled to go to her and offer congratulations upon her escape, as he had congratulated the professor. If his manner to her parents had been filial, his manner to her was parental. "Well, Marjory," he said kindly, "you have been in considerable danger. I suppose you're glad to be through with it." She at that time made no reply, but by her casual turn he knew that he was expected to walk along by her side. The others knew it, too, and the rest of the party left them free to walk side by side in the rear.

"This is a beautiful country here-abouts if one gets a good chance to see it," he remarked. Then he added: "But I suppose you had a view of it when you were going out to Nikopolis?"

She answered in muffled tones. "Yes, we thought it very beautiful."

Did you note those streams from the mountains " That seemed to me the purest water I'd ever seen, but I bet it would make one ill to drink it. There is, you know, a prominent German chemist who has almost proven that really pure water is practical poison to the human stomach."

"Yes?" she said.

There was a period of silence, during which he was perfectly comfortable because he knew that she was ill at ease. If the silence was awkward, she was suffering from it. As for himself, he had no inclination to break it. His position was, as far as the entire Wainwright party was concerned, a place where he could afford to wait. She turned to him at last. "Of course, I know how much you have done for us, and I want you to feel that we all appreciate it deeply-deeply." There was discernible to the ear a certain note of desperation.

"Oh, not at all," he said generously. "Not at all. I didn't do anything. It was quite an accident. Don't let that trouble you for a moment."

"Well, of course you would say that," she said more steadily. "But I-we-we know how good and how-brave it was in you to come for us, and I —we must never forget it."

As a matter of fact," replied Coleman, with an appearance of ingenuous candor, "I was sent out here by the Eclipse to find you people, and of course I worked rather hard to reach you, but the final meeting was purely accidental and does not redound to my credit in the least."

As he had anticipated, Marjory shot him a little glance of disbelief. "Of course you would say that," she repeated with gloomy but flattering conviction.

"Oh, if I had been a great hero," he said smiling, "no doubt I would have kept up this same manner which now sets so well upon me, but I am telling you the truth when I say that I had no part in your rescue at all."

She became slightly indignant. "Oh, if you care to tell us constantly that you were of no service to us, I don't see what we can do but continue to declare that you were."

Suddenly he felt vulgar. He spoke to her this time with real meaning. "I beg of 'you never to mention it again. That will be the best way."

But to this she would not accede. "No, we will often want to speak of it."

He replied "How do you like Greece? Don't you think that some of these ruins are rather out of shape in the popular mind? Now, for my part, I would rather look at a good strong finish at a horserace than to see ten thousand Parthenons in a bunch."

She was immediately in the position of defending him from himself. "You would rather see no such thing. You shouldn't talk in that utterly trivial way. I like the Parthenon, of course, but I can't think of it now because my head. is too full of my escape from where I was so-so frightened."

Coleman grinned. "Were you really frightened?"

"Naturally," she answered. "I suppose I was more frightened for mother and father, but I was frightened enough for myself. It was not-not a nice thing."

"No, it wasn't," said Coleman. "I could hardly believe my senses, when the minister at Athens told me that, you all had ventured into such a trap, and there is no doubt but what you can be glad that you are well out of it."

She seemed to have some struggle with herself and then she deliberately said: "Thanks to you."

Coleman embarked on what he intended to make a series of high-minded protests. "Not at all-" but at that moment the dragoman whirled back from the van-guard with a great collection of the difficulties which had been gathering upon him. Coleman was obliged to resign Marjory and again take up the active leadership. He disposed of the dragoman's difficulties mainly by declaring that they were not difficulties at all. He had learned that this was the way to deal with dragomen. The fog had already lifted from the valley and, as they passed along the wooded mountain-side the fragrance of leaves and earth came to them. Ahead, along the hooded road, they could see the blue clad figures of Greek infantrymen. Finally they passed an encampment of a battalion whose line was at a right angle to the highway. A hundred yards in advance was the bridge across the Louros river. And there a battery of artillery was encamped. The dragoman became involved in all sorts of discussions with other Greeks, but Coleman stuck to his elbow and stifled all aimless oration. The Wainwright party waited for them in the rear in an observant but patient group.

Across a plain, the hills directly behind Arta loomed up showing the straight yellow scar of a modern entrenchment. To the north of Arta were some grey mountains with a dimly marked road winding to the summit. On one side of this road were two shadows. It took a moment for the eye to find these shadows, but when this was accomplished it was plain that they were men. The captain of the battery explained to the dragoman that he did not know that they were not also Turks. In which case the road to Arta was a dangerous path. It was no good news to Coleman. He waited a moment in order to gain composure and then walked back to the Wainwright party. They must have known at once from his peculiar gravity that all was not well. Five of the students and the professor immediately asked: "What is it?"

He had at first some old-fashioned idea of concealing the ill tidings from the ladies, but he perceived what flagrant nonsense this would be in circumstances in which all were fairly likely to incur equal dangers, and at any rate he did not see his way clear to allow their imagination to run riot over a situation which might not turn out to be too bad. He said slowly: "You see those mountains over there? Well, troops have been seen there and the captain of this battery thinks they are Turks. If they are Turks the road to Arta is distinctly-er-unsafe."

This new blow first affected the Wainwright party as being too much to endure. "They thought they had gone through enough. This was a general sentiment. Afterward the emotion took colour according to the individual character. One student laughed and said: "Well, I see our finish."

Another student piped out: "How do they know they are Turks? What makes them think they are Turks?"

Another student expressed himself with a sigh. "This is a long way from the Bowery."

The professor said nothing but looked annihilated; Mrs. Wainwright wept profoundly; Marjory looked expectantly toward Coleman.

As for the correspondent he was adamantine and reliable and stern, for he had not the slightest idea that those men on the distant hill were Turks at all.

CHAPTER XIV.

"OH," said a student, "this game ought to quit. I feel like thirty cents. We didn't come out here to be pursued about the country by these Turks. Why don't they stop it?"

Coleman was remarking: "Really, the only sensible thing to do now is to have breakfast. There is no use in worrying ourselves silly over this thing until we've got to."

They spread the blankets on the ground and sat about a feast of bread, water cress and tinned beef. Coleman was the real host, but he contrived to make the professor appear as that honourable person. They ate, casting their eyes from time to time at the distant mountain with its two shadows. People began to fly down the road from Jannina, peasants hurriedly driving little flocks, women and children on donkeys and little horses which they clubbed unceasingly. One man rode at a gallop, shrieking and flailing his arms in the air. They were all Christian peasants of Turkey, but they were in flight now because they did not wish to be at home if the Turk was going to return and reap revenge for his mortification. The Wainwright party looked at Coleman in abrupt questioning.

"Oh, it's all right," he said, easily. "They are always taking on that way."

Suddenly the dragoman gave a shout and dashed up the road to the scene of a melee where a little ratfaced groom was vociferously defending three horses from some Greek officers, who as vociferously were stating their right to requisition them. Coleman ran after his dragoman. There was a sickening pow-wow, but in the end Coleman, straight and easy in the saddle, came cantering back on a superb open-mouthed snorting bay horse. He did not mind if the half-wild animal plunged crazily. It was part of his role. "They were trying to steal my horses," he explained. He leaped to the ground, and holding the horse by the bridle, he addressed his admiring companions. "The groom- the man who has charge of the horses -says that he thinks that the people on the mountain-side are Turks, but I don't see how that is possible. You see-" he pointed wisely-" that road leads directly south to Arta, and it is hardly possible that the Greek army would come over here and leave that approach to Arta utterly unguarded. It would be too foolish. They must have left some men to cover it, and that is certainly what those troops are. If you are all ready and willing, I don't see anything to do but make a good, stout-hearted dash for Arta. It would be no more dangerous than to sit here." The professor was at last able to make his formal speech. "Mr. Coleman," he said distinctly, "we place ourselves entirely in your hands." It was some. how pitiful. This man who, for years and years had reigned in a little college town almost as a monarch, passing judgment with the air of one who words the law, dealing criticism upon the universe as one to whom all things are plain, publicly disdaining defeat as one to whom all things are easy-this man was now veritably appealing to Coleman to save his wife, his daughter and himself, and really declared himself de. pendent for safety upon the ingenuity and courage of the correspondent.

The attitude of the students was utterly indifferent. They did not consider themselves helpless at all. they were evidently quite ready to withstand anything but they looked frankly up to Coleman as their intelligent leader. If they suffered any, their only expression of it was in the simple grim slang of their period.

"I wish I was at Coney Island."

"This is not so bad as trigonometry, but it's worse than playing billiards for the beers."

And Coke said privately to Coleman: "Say, what in hell are these two damn peoples fighting for, anyhow?"

When he saw that all opinions were in favour of following him loyally, Coleman was impelled to feel a responsibility. He was now no errant rescuer, but a properly elected leader of fellow beings in distress. While one of the students held his horse, he took the dragoman for another consultation with the captain of the battery. The officer was sitting on a large stone, with his eyes fixed into his field glasses. When again questioned he could give no satisfaction as to the identity of the troops on the distant mountain. He merely shrugged his shoulders and said that if they were Greeks it was very good, but if they were Turks it was very bad. He seemed more occupied in trying to impress the correspondent that it was a matter of soldierly indifference to himself. Coleman, after loathing him sufficiently in silence, returned to the others and said: "Well, we'll chance it."

They looked to him to arrange the caravan. Speaking to the men of the party he said: "Of course, any one of you is welcome to my horse if you can ride it, but-if you're not too tired-I think I had myself better ride, so that I can go ahead at times."

His manner was so fine as he said this that the students seemed fairly to worship him. Of course it had been most improbable that any of them could have ridden that volcanic animal even if one of them had tried it.

He saw Mrs. Wainwright and Marjory upon the backs of their two little natives, and hoisted the professor into the saddle of the groom's horse, leaving instructions with the servant to lead the animal always and carefully. He and the dragoman then mounted at the head of the procession, and amid curious questionings from the soldiery they crossed the bridge and started on the trail to Arta. The rear was brought up by the little grey horse with the luggage, led by one student and flogged by another.

Coleman, checking with difficulty the battling disposition of his horse, was very uneasy in his mind because the last words of the captain of the battery had made him feel that perhaps on this ride he would be placed in a position where only the best courage would count, and he did not see his way clear to feeling very confident about his conduct in such a case. Looking back upon the caravan, he saw it as a most unwieldy thing, not even capable of running away. He hurried it with sudden, sharp contemptuous phrases.

On the march there incidentally flashed upon him a new truth. More than half of that student band were deeply in love with Marjory. Of course, when he had been distant from her he had had an eternal jealous reflection to that effect. It was natural that he should have thought of the intimate camping relations between Marjory and these young students with a great deal of bitterness, grinding his teeth when picturing their opportunities to make Marjory fall in love with some one of them. He had raged particularly about Coke, whose father had millions of dollars. But he had forgotten all these jealousies in the general splendour of his exploits. Now, when he saw the truth, it seemed to bring him back to his common life and he saw himself suddenly as not being frantically superior in any way to those other young men. The more closely he looked at this last fact, the more convinced he was of its truth. He seemed to see that he had been improperly elated over his services to the Wainwrights, and that, in the end, the girl might fancy a man because the man had done her no service at all. He saw his proud position lower itself to be a pawn in the game. Looking back over the students, he wondered which one Marjory might love. This hideous Nikopolis had given eight men chance to win her. His scorn and his malice quite centered upon Coke, for he could never forget that the man's father had millions of dollars. The unfortunate Coke chose that moment to address him querulously: "Look here, Coleman, can't you tell us how far it is to Arta?"

"Coke," said Coleman, "I don't suppose you take me for a tourist agency, but if you can only try to distinguish between me and a map with the scale of miles printed in the lower left- hand corner, you will not contribute so much to the sufferings of the party which you now adorn."

The students within hearing guffawed and Coke retired, in confusion.

The march was not rapid. Coleman almost wore out his arms holding in check his impetuous horse. Often the caravan floundered through mud, while at the same time a hot, yellow dust came from the north.

They were perhaps half way to Arta when Coleman decided that a rest and luncheon were the things to be considered. He halted his troop then in the shade of some great trees, and privately he bade his dragoman prepare the best feast which could come out of those saddle-bags fresh from Athens. The result was rather gorgeous in the eyes of the poor wanderers. First of all there were three knives, three forks, three spoons, three tin cups and three tin plates, which the entire party of twelve used on a most amiable socialistic principle. There were crisp, salty biscuits and olives, for which they speared in the bottle. There was potted turkey, and potted ham, and potted tongue, all tasting precisely alike. There were sardines and the ordinary tinned beef, disguised sometimes with onions, carrots and potatoes. Out of the saddle-bags came pepper and salt and even mustard. The dragoman made coffee over a little fire of sticks that blazed with a white light. The whole thing was prodigal, but any philanthropist would have approved of it if he could have seen the way in which the eight students laid into the spread. When there came a polite remonstrance-notably from Mrs. Wainwright-Coleman merely pointed to a large bundle strapped back of the groom's saddle. During the coffee he was considering how best to get the students one by one out of the sight of the Wainwrights where he could give them good drinks of whisky.

There was an agitation on the road toward Arta. Some people were coming on horses. He paid small heed until he heard a thump of pausing hoofs near him, and a musical voice say: "Rufus! "

He looked up quickly, and then all present saw his eyes really bulge. There on a fat and glossy horse sat Nora Black, dressed in probably one of the most correct riding habits which had ever been seen in the East. She was smiling a radiant smile, which held the eight students simply spell-bound. They would have recognised her if it had not been for this apparitional coming in the wilds of southeastern Europe. Behind her were her people-some servants and an old lady on a very little pony. " Well, Rufus?" she said.

Coleman made the mistake of hesitating. For a fraction of a moment he had acted as if he were embarrassed, and was only going to nod and say: "How d'do?"

He arose and came forward too late. She was looking at him with a menacing glance which meant difficulties for him if he was not skilful. Keen as an eagle, she swept her glance over the face and figure of Marjory. Without further introduction, the girls seemed to understand that they were enemies.

Despite his feeling of awkwardness, Coleman's mind was mainly occupied by pure astonishment. "Nora Black?" he said, as if even then he could not believe his senses. "How in the world did you get down here?

She was not too amiable, evidently, over his reception, and she seemed to know perfectly that it was in her power to make him feel extremely unpleasant. "Oh, it's not so far," she answered. "I don't see where you come in to ask me what I'm doing here. What are you doing here?" She lifted her eyes and shot the half of a glance at Marjory. Into her last question she had interjected a spirit of ownership in which he saw future woe. It turned him cowardly. "Why, you know I was sent up here by the paper to rescue the Wainwright party, and I've got them. I'm taking them to Arta. But why are you here?"

"I am here," she said, giving him the most defiant of glances, "principally to look for you."

Even the horse she rode betrayed an intention of abiding upon that spot forever. She had made her communication with Coleman appear to the Wainwright party as a sort of tender reunion.

Coleman looked at her with a steely eye. "Nora, you can certainly be a devil when you choose."

"Why don't you present me to your friends? Mis,; Nora Black, special correspondent of the New York Daylighi, if you please. I belong to your opposition. I am your rival, Rufus, and I draw a bigger salary-see? Funny looking gang, that. Who is the old Johnnie in the white wig?"

"Er-where you goin'-you can't "-blundered Coleman miserably "Aw-the army is in retreat and you must go back to- don't you see?"

"Is it?" she agked. After a pause she added coolly: "Then I shall go back to Arta with you and your precious Wainwrights."

CHAPTER XV.

GIVING Coleman another glance of subtle menace Nora repeated: "Why don't you present me to your friends? " Coleman had been swiftly searching the whole world for a way clear of this unhappiness, but he knew at last that he could only die at his guns. "Why, certainly," he said quickly, "if you wish it." He sauntered easily back to the luncheon blanket. "This is Miss Black of the New York Daylight and she says that those people on the mountain are Greeks." The students were gaping at him, and Marjory and her father sat in the same silence. But to the relief of Coleman and to the high edification of the students, Mrs. Wainwright cried out: "Why, is she an American woman?" And seeing Coleman's nod of assent she rustled to her feet and advanced hastily upon the complacent horsewoman. "I'm delighted to see you. Who would think of seeing an American woman way over here. Have you been here long? Are you going on further? Oh, we've had such a dreadful time." Coleman remained long enough to hear Nora say: " Thank you very much, but I shan't dismount. I am going to ride back to Arta presently."

Then he heard Mrs. Wainwright cry: "Oh, are you indeed? Why we, too, are going at once to Arta. We can all go together." Coleman fled then to the bosom of the students, who all looked at him with eyes of cynical penetration. He cast a glance at Marjory more than fearing a glare which denoted an implacable resolution never to forgive this thing. On the contrary he had never seen her so content and serene. "You have allowed your coffee to get chilled," she said considerately. "Won't you have the man warm you some more?"

"Thanks, no," he answered with gratitude.

Nora, changing her mind, had dismounted and was coming with Mrs. Wainwright. That worthy lady had long had a fund of information and anecdote the sound of which neither her husband nor her daughter would endure for a moment. Of course the rascally students were out of the question. Here, then, was really the first ear amiably and cheerfully open, and she was talking at what the students called her "thirty knot gait."

"Lost everything. Absolutely everything. Neither of us have even a brush and comb, or a cake of soap, or enough hairpins to hold up our hair. I'm going to take Marjory's away from her and let her braid her hair down her back. You can imagine how dreadful it is —-"

From time to time the cool voice of Nora sounded without effort through this clamour. "Oh, it will be no trouble at all. I have more than enough of everything. We can divide very nicely."

Coleman broke somewhat imperiously into this feminine chat. "Well, we must be moving, you know, "and his voice started the men into activity. When the traps were all packed again on the horse Coleman looked back surprised to see the three women engaged in the most friendly discussion. The combined parties now made a very respectable squadron. Coleman rode off at its head without glancing behind at all. He knew that they were following from the soft pounding of the horses hoofs on the sod and from the mellow hum of human voices.

For a long time he did not think to look upon himself as anything but a man much injured by circumstances. Among his friends he could count numbers who had lived long lives without having this peculiar class of misfortune come to them. In fact it was so unusual a misfortune that men of the world had not found it necessary to pass from mind to mind a perfect formula for dealing with it. But he soon began to consider himself an extraordinarily lucky person inasmuch as Nora Black had come upon him with her saddle bags packed with inflammable substances, so to speak, and there had been as yet only enough fire to boil coffee for luncheon. He laughed tenderly when he thought of the innocence of Mrs. Wainwright, but his face and back flushed with heat when lie thought of the canniness of the eight American college students.

He heard a horse cantering up on his left side and looking he saw Nora Black. She was beaming with satisfaction and good nature. "Well, Rufus," she cried flippantly, "how goes it with the gallant rescuer? You've made a hit, my boy. You are the success of the season."

Coleman reflected upon the probable result of a direct appeal to Nora. He knew of course that such appeals were usually idle, but he did not consider Nora an ordinary person. His decision was to venture it. He drew his horse close to hers. "Nora," he said, "do you know that you are raising the very devil?"

She lifted her finely penciled eyebrows and looked at him with the baby-stare. "How?" she enquired.

"You know well enough," he gritted out wrathfully.

"Raising the very devil?" she asked. "How do you mean?" She was palpably interested for his answer. She waited for his reply for an interval, and then she asked him outright. "Rufus Coleman do you mean that I am not a respectable woman? "

In reality he had meant nothing of the kind, but this direct throttling of a great question stupefied him utterly, for he saw now that she' would probably never understand him in the least and that she would at any rate always pretend not to understand him and that the more he said the more harm he manufactured. She studied him over carefully and then wheeled her horse towards the rear with some parting remarks. "I suppose you should attend more strictly to your own affairs, Rufus. Instead of raising the devil I am lending hairpins. I have seen you insult people, but I have never seen you insult anyone quite for the whim of the thing. Go soak your head."

Not considering it advisable to then indulge in such immersion Coleman rode moodily onward. The hot dust continued to sting the cheeks of the travellers and in some places great clouds of dead leaves roared in circles about them. All of the Wainwright party were utterly fagged. Coleman felt his skin crackle and his throat seemed to be coated with the white dust. He worried his dragoman as to the distance to Arta until the dragoman lied to the point where he always declared that Arta was only off some hundreds of yards.

At their places in the procession Mrs. Wainwright and Marjory were animatedly talking to Nora and the old lady on the little pony. They had at first suffered great amazement at the voluntary presence of the old lady, but she was there really because she knew no better. Her colossal ignorance took the form, mainly, of a most obstreperous patriotism, and indeed she always acted in a foreign country as if she were the special commissioner of the President, or perhaps as a special commissioner could not act at all. She was very aggressive, and when any of the travelling arrangements in Europe did not suit her ideas she was won't to shrilly exclaim: "Well! New York is good enough for me." Nora, morbidly afraid that her ex- pense bill to the Daylight would not be large enough, had dragged her bodily off to Greece as her companion, friend and protection. At Arta they had heard of the grand success of the Greek army. The Turks had not stood for a moment before that gallant and terrible advance; no; they had scampered howling with fear into the north. Jannina would fall-well, Jannina would fall as soon as the Greeks arrived. There was no doubt of it. The correspondent and her friend, deluded and hurried by the light-hearted confidence of the Greeks in Arta, had hastened out then on a regular tourist's excursion to see Jannina after its capture. Nora concealed from her friend the fact that the editor of the Daylight particularly wished her to see a battle so that she might write an article on actual warfare from a woman's point of view. With her name as a queen of comic opera, such an article from her pen would be a burning, sensation.

Coleman had been the first to point out to Nora that instead of going on a picnic to Jannina, she had better run back to Arta. When the old lady heard that they had not been entirely safe, she was furious with Nora. "The idea!" she exclaimed to Mrs. Wainwright. "They might have caught us! They might have caught us!"

"Well," said Mrs. Wainwright. "I verily believe they would have caught us if it had not been for Mr. Coleman."

"Is he the gentleman on the fine horse?"

"Yes; that's him. Oh, he has been sim-plee splendid. I confess I was a little bit-er-surprised. He was in college under my husband. I don't know that we thought very great things of him, but if ever a man won golden opinions he has done so from us."

"Oh, that must be the Coleman who is such a great friend of Nora's."

"Yes?" said Mrs. Wainwright insidiously. "Is he? I didn't know. Of course he knows so many people." Her mind had been suddenly illumined by the old lady and she thought extravagantly of the arrival of Nora upon the scene. She remained all sweetness to the old lady. "Did you know he was here? Did you expect to meet him? I seemed such a delightful coincidence." In truth she was being subterraneously clever.

"Oh, no; I don't think so. I didn't hear Nora mention it. Of course she would have told me. You know, our coming to Greece was such a surprise. Nora had an engagement in London at the Folly Theatre in Fly by Night, but the manager was insufferable, oh, insufferable. So, of course, Nora wouldn't stand it a minute, and then these newspaper people came along and asked her to go to Greece for them and she accepted. I am sure I never expected to find us-aw-fleeing from the Turks or I shouldn't have Come."

"Mrs. Wainwright was gasping. "You don't mean that she is — she is Nora Black, the actress."

"Of course she is," said the old lady jubilantly.

"Why, how strange," choked Mrs. Wainwrignt. Nothing she knew of Nora could account for her stupefaction and grief. What happened glaringly to her was the duplicity of man. Coleman was a ribald deceiver. He must have known and yet he had pretended throughout that the meeting was a pure accident She turned with a nervous impulse to sympathist with her daughter, but despite the lovely tranquillity of the girl's face there was something about her which forbade the mother to meddle. Anyhow Mrs. Wainwright was sorry that she had told nice things of Coleman's behaviour, so she said to the old lady: " Young men of these times get a false age so quickly. We have always thought it a great pity, about Mr. Coleman."

"Why, how so?" asked the old lady.

"Oh, really nothing. Only, to us he seemed rather —er- prematurely experienced or something of that kind. The old lady did not catch the meaning of the phrase. She seemed surprised. "Why, I've never seen any full-grown person in this world who got experience any too quick for his own good."

At the tail of the procession there was talk between the two students who had in charge the little grey horse-one to lead and one to flog. "Billie," said one, "it now becomes necessary to lose this hobby into the hands of some of the other fellows. Whereby we will gain opportunity to pay homage to the great Nora. Why, you egregious thick-head, this is the chance of a life-time. I'm damned if I'm going to tow this beast of burden much further."

"You wouldn't stand a show," said Billie pessimistically. "Look at Coleman."

"That's all right. Do you mean to say that you prefer to continue towing pack horses in the presence of this queen of song and the dance just because you think Coleman can throw out his chest a little more than you. Not so. Think of your bright and sparkling youth. There's Coke and Pete Tounley near Marjory. We'll call 'em." Whereupon he set up a cry. "Say, you people, we're not getting a, salary for this. Supposin' you try for a time. It'll do you good." When the two addressed bad halted to await the arrival of the little grey horse, they took on glum expressions. "You look like poisoned pups," said the student who led the horse. "Too strong for light work. Grab onto the halter, now, Peter, and tow. We are going ahead to talk to Nora Black."

"Good time you'll have," answered Peter Tounley.

"Coleman is cuttin' up scandalous. You won't stand a show."

"What do you think of him?" said Coke. "Seems curious, all 'round. Do you suppose he knew she would show up? It was nervy to —"

"Nervy to what?" asked Billie.

"Well," said Coke, "seems to me he is playing both ends against the middle. I don't know anything about Nora Black, but-"

The three other students expressed themselves with conviction and in chorus. "Coleman's all right."

"Well, anyhow," continued Coke, "I don't see my way free to admiring him introducing Nora Black to the Wainwrights."

"He didn't," said the others, still in chorus.

"Queer game," said Peter Tounley. "He seems to know her pretty well."

"Pretty damn well," said Billie.

"Anyhow he's a brick," said Peter Tounley. "We mustn't forget that. Lo, I begin to feel that our Rufus is a fly guy of many different kinds. Any play that he is in commands my respect. He won't be hit by a chimney in the daytime, for unto him has come much wisdom, I don't think I'll worry."

"Is he stuck on Nora Black, do you know?" asked Billie.

"One thing is plain," replied Coke. "She has got him somehow by the short hair and she intends him to holler murder. Anybody can see that."

"Well, he won't holler murder," said one of them with conviction. "I'll bet you he won't. He'll hammer the war-post and beat the tom-tom until he drops, but he won't holler murder."

"Old Mother Wainwright will be in his wool presently," quoth Peter Tounley musingly, "I could see it coming in her eye. Somebody has given his snap away, or something." "Aw, he had no snap," said Billie. "Couldn't you see how rattled he was? He would have given a lac if dear Nora hadn't turned up."

"Of course," the others assented. "He was rattled."

"Looks queer. And nasty," said Coke.

"Nora herself had an axe ready for him."

They began to laugh. "If she had had an umbrella she would have basted him over the head with it. Oh, my! He was green."

"Nevertheless," said Peter Tounley, "I refuse to worry over our Rufus. When he can't take care of himself the rest of us want to hunt cover. He is a fly guy-"

Coleman in the meantime had become aware that the light of Mrs. Wainwright's countenance was turned from him. The party stopped at a well, and when he offered her a drink from his cup he thought she accepted it with scant thanks. Marjory was still gracious, always gracious, but this did not reassure him, because he felt there was much unfathomable deception in it. When he turned to seek consolation in the manner of the professor he found him as before, stunned with surprise, and the only idea he had was to be as tractable as a child.

When he returned to the head of the column, Nora again cantered forward to join him. "Well, me gay Lochinvar," she cried, "and has your disposition improved?"

"You are very fresh," he said.

She laughed loud enough to be heard the full length of the caravan. It was a beautiful laugh, but full of insolence and confidence. He flashed his eyes malignantly upon her, but then she only laughed more. She could see that he wished to strangle her. "What a disposition!" she said. "What a disposition! You are not. nearly so nice as your friends. Now, they are charming, but you-Rufus, I wish you would get that temper mended. Dear Rufus, do it to please me. You know you like to please me. Don't you now, dear?" He finally laughed. "Confound you, Nora. I would like to kill you."

But at his laugh she was all sunshine. It was as if she. had been trying to taunt him into good humour with her. "Aw, now, Rufus, don't be angry. I'll be good, Rufus. Really, I will. Listen. I want to tell you something. Do you know what I did? Well, you know, I never was cut out for this business, and, back there, when you told me about the Turks being near and all that sort of thing, I was frightened almost to death. Really, I was. So, when nobody was looking, I sneaked two or three little drinks out of my flask. Two or three little drinks-"

CHAPTER XVI.

"GOOD God!" said Coleman. "You don't Mean-"

Nora smiled rosily at him. "Oh, I'm all right," she answered. "Don't worry about your Aunt Nora, my precious boy. Not for a minute."

Coleman was horrified. "But you are not going to-you are not going to-"

"Not at all, me son. Not at all," she answered.

I'm not going to prance. I'm going to be as nice as pie, and just ride quietly along here with dear little Rufus. Only * * you know what I can do when I get started, so you had better be a very good boy. I might take it into my head to say some things, you know."

Bound hand and foot at his stake, he could not even chant his defiant torture song. It might precipitate — in fact, he was sure it would precipitate the grand smash. But to the very core of his soul, he for the time hated Nora Black. He did not dare to remind her that he would revenge himself; he dared only to dream of this revenge, but it fairly made his thoughts flame, and deep in his throat he was swearing an inflexible persecution of Nora Black. The old expression of his sex came to him, "Oh, if she were only a man!" she had been a man, he would have fallen upon her tooth and nail. Her motives for all this impressed him not at all; she was simply a witch who bound him helpless with the pwer of her femininity, and made him eat cinders. He was so sure that his face betrayed him that he did not dare let her see it. "Well, what are you going to do about it?" he asked, over his shoulder.

"0-o-oh," she drawled, impudently. "Nothing." He could see that she was determined not to be confessed. "I may do this or I may do that. It all depends upon your behaviour, my dear Rufus."

As they rode on, he deliberated as to the best means of dealing with this condition. Suddenly he resolved to go with the whole tale direct to Marjory, and to this end he half wheeled his horse. He would reiterate that he loved her and then explain- explain! He groaned when he came to the word, and ceased formulation.

The cavalcade reached at last the bank of the Aracthus river, with its lemon groves and lush grass. A battery wheeled before them over the ancient bridge -a flight of short, broad cobbled steps up as far as the centre of the stream and a similar flight down to the other bank. The returning aplomb of the travellers was well illustrated by the professor, who, upon sighting this bridge, murmured : "Byzantine."

This was the first indication that he had still within him a power to resume the normal.

The steep and narrow street was crowded with soldiers; the smoky little coffee shops were a-babble with people discussing the news from the front. None seemed to heed the remarkable procession that wended its way to the cable office. Here Coleman resolutely took precedence. He knew that there was no good in expecting intelligence out of the chaotic clerks, but he managed to get upon the wires this message :

"Eclipse, New York: Got Wainwright party; all well. Coleman." The students had struggled to send messages to their people in America, but they had only succeeded in deepening the tragic boredom of the clerks.

When Coleman returned to the street he thought that he had seldom looked upon a more moving spectacle than the Wainwright party presented at that moment. Most of the students were seated in a row, dejectedly, upon the kerb. The professor and Mrs. Wainwright looked like two old pictures, which, after an existence in a considerate gloom, had been brought out in their tawdriness to the clear light. Hot white dust covered everybody, and from out the grimy faces the eyes blinked, red-fringed with sleeplessness. Desolation sat upon all, save Marjory. She possessed some marvellous power of looking always fresh. This quality had indeed impressed the old lady on the little pony until she had said to Nora Black: "That girl would look well anywhere." Nora Black had not been amiable in her reply.

Coleman called the professor and the dragoman for a durbar. The dragoman said: "Well, I can get one carriage, and we can go immediate-lee."

"Carriage be blowed!" said Coleman. "What these people need is rest, sleep. You must find a place at once. These people can't remain in the street." He spoke in anger, as if he had previously told the dragoman and the latter had been inattentive. The man immediately departed.

Coleman remarked that there was no course but to remain in the street until his dragoman had found them a habitation. It was a mournful waiting. The students sat on the kerb. Once they whispered to Coleman, suggesting a drink, but he told them that he knew only one cafe, the entrance of which would be in plain sight of the rest of the party. The ladies talked together in a group of four. Nora Black was bursting with the fact that her servant had hired rooms in Arta on their outcoming journey, and she wished Mrs. Wainwright and Marjory to come to them, at least for a time, but she dared not risk a refusal, and she felt something in Mrs. Wainwright's manner which led her to be certain that such would be the answer to her invitation. Coleman and the professor strolled slowly up and down the walk.

"Well, my work is over, sir," said Coleman. "My paper told me to find you, and, through no virtue of my own, I found you. I am very glad of it. I don't know of anything in my life that has given me greater pleasure."

The professor was himself again in so far as he had lost all manner of dependence. But still he could not yet be bumptious. "Mr. Coleman," he said, "I am placed under life-long obligation to you. * * * I am not thinking of myself so much. * * * My wife and daughter —-" His gratitude was so genuine that he could not finish its expression.

"Oh, don't speak of it," said Coleman. "I really didn't do anything at all."

The dragoman finally returned and led them all to a house which he had rented for gold. In the great, bare, upper chamber the students dropped wearily to the floor, while the woman of the house took the Wainwrights to a more secluded apartment., As the door closed on them, Coleman turned like a flash.

"Have a drink," he said. The students arose around him like the wave of a flood. "You bet." In the absence of changes of clothing, ordinary food, the possibility of a bath, and in the presence of great weariness and dust, Coleman's whisky seemed to them a glistening luxury. Afterward they laid down as if to sleep, but in reality they were too dirty and too fagged to sleep. They simply lay murmuring Peter Tounley even developed a small fever.

It was at this time that Coleman. suddenly discovered his acute interest in the progressive troubles of his affair of the heart had placed the business of his newspaper in the rear of his mind. The greater part of the next hour he spent in getting off to New York that dispatch which created so much excitement for him later. Afterward he was free to reflect moodily upon the ability of Nora Black to distress him. She, with her retinue, had disappeared toward her own rooms. At dusk he went into the street, and was edified to see Nora's dragoman dodging along in his wake. He thought that this was simply another manifestation of Nora's interest in his movements, and so he turned a corner, and there pausing, waited until the dragoman spun around directly into his arms. But it seemed that the man had a note to deliver, and this was only his Oriental way of doing it.

The note read: "Come and dine with me to-night." It was, not a request. It was peremptory. "All right," he said, scowling at the man.

He did not go at once, for he wished to reflect for a time and find if he could not evolve some weapons of his own. It seemed to him that all the others were liberally supplied with weapons.

A clear, cold night had come upon the earth when he signified to the lurking dragoman that he was in readiness to depart with him to Nora's abode. They passed finally into a dark court-yard, up a winding staircase, across an embowered balcony, and Coleman entered alone a room where there were lights.

His, feet were scarcely over the threshold before he had concluded that the tigress was now going to try some velvet purring. He noted that the arts of the stage had not been thought too cheaply obvious for use. Nora sat facing the door. A bit of yellow silk had been twisted about the crude shape of the lamp, and it made the play of light, amber-like, shadowy and yet perfectly clear, the light which women love. She was arrayed in a puzzling gown of that kind of Grecian silk which is so docile that one can pull yards of it through a ring. It was of the colour of new straw. Her chin was leaned pensively upon her palm and the light fell on a pearly rounded forearm. She was looking at him with a pair of famous eyes, azure, per- haps-certainly purple at times-and it may be, black at odd moments-a pair of eyes that had made many an honest man's heart jump if he thought they were looking at him. It was a vision, yes, but Coleman's cynical knowledge of drama overpowered his sense of its beauty. He broke out brutally, in the phrases of the American street. "Your dragoman is a rubber-neck. If he keeps darking me I will simply have to kick the stuffing out of him."

She was alone in the room. Her old lady had been instructed to have a headache and send apologies. She was not disturbed by Coleman's words. "Sit down, Rufus, and have a cigarette, and don't be cross, because I won't stand it."

He obeyed her glumly. She had placed his chair where not a charm of her could be lost upon an observant man. Evidently she did not purpose to allow him to irritate her away from her original plan. Purring was now her method, and none of his insolence could achieve a growl from the tigress. She arose, saying softly: "You look tired, almost ill, poor boy. I will give you some brandy. I have almost everything that I could think to make those Daylight people buy." With a sweep of her hand she indicated the astonishing opulence of the possessions in different parts of the room.

As she stood over him with the brandy there came through the smoke of his cigarette the perfume of orris-root and violet.

A servant began to arrange the little cold dinner on a camp table, and Coleman saw with an enthusiasm which he could not fully master, four quart bottles of a notable brand of champagne placed in a rank on the floor.

At dinner Nora was sisterly. She watched him, waited upon him, treated him to an affectionate inti. macy for which he knew a thousand men who would have hated him. The champagne was cold.

Slowly he melted. By the time that the boy came with little cups of Turkish coffee he was at least amiable. Nora talked dreamily. "The dragoman says this room used to be part of the harem long ago." She shot him a watchful glance, as if she had expected the fact to affect him. "Seems curious, doesn't it? A harem. Fancy that." He smoked one cigar and then discarded tobacco, for the perfume of orris-root and violet was making him meditate. Nora talked on in a low voice. She knew that, through half-closed lids, he was looking at her in steady speculation. She knew that she was conquering, but no movement of hers betrayed an elation. With the most exquisite art she aided his contemplation, baring to him, for instance, the glories of a statuesque neck, doing it all with the manner of a splendid and fabulous virgin who knew not that there was such a thing as shame. Her stockings were of black silk.

Coleman presently answered her only in monosyllable, making small distinction between yes and no. He simply sat watching her with eyes in which there were two little covetous steel-coloured flames.

He was thinking, "To go to the devil-to go to the devil-to go to the devil with this girl is not a bad fate-not a bad fate-not a bad fate."

CHAPTER XVII.

" Come out on the balcony," cooed Nora. "There are some funny old storks on top of some chimneys near here and they clatter like mad all day and night."

They moved together out to the balcony, but Nora retreated with a little cry when she felt the coldness of the night. She said that she would get a cloak. Coleman was not unlike a man in a dream. He walked to the rail of the balcony where a great vine climbed toward the roof. He noted that it was dotted with. blossoms, which in the deep purple of the Oriental night were coloured in strange shades of maroon. This truth penetrated his abstraction until when Nora came she found him staring at them as if their colour was a revelation which affected him vitally. She moved to his side without sound and he first knew of her presence from the damning fragrance. She spoke just above her breath. "It's a beautiful evening." " Yes," he answered. She was at his shoulder. If he moved two inches he must come in contact. They remained in silence leaning upon the rail. Finally he began to mutter some commonplaces which meant nothing particularly, but into his tone as he mouthed them was the note of a forlorn and passionate lover. Then as if by accident he traversed the two inches and his shoulder was against the soft and yet firm shoulder of Nora Black. There was something in his throat at this time which changed his voice into a mere choking noise. She did not move. He could see her eyes glowing innocently out of the pallour which the darkness gave to her face. If he was touching her, she did not seem to know it.

"I am awfully tired," said Coleman, thickly. "I think I will go home and turn in."

"You must be, poor boy," said Nora tenderly.

"Wouldn't you like a little more of that champagne?"

"Well, I don't mind another glass."

She left him again and his galloping thought pounded to the old refrain. "To go to the devil-to go to the devil-to go to the devil with this girl is not a bad fate-not a bad fate- not a bad fate." When she returned he drank his glass of champagne. Then he mumbled: "You must be cold. Let me put your cape around you better. It won't do to catch cold here, you know."

She made a sweet pretence of rendering herself to his care. "Oh, thanks * * * I am not really cold * * * There that's better."

Of course all his manipulation of the cloak had been a fervid caress, and although her acting up to this point had remained in the role of the splendid and fabulous virgin she now turned her liquid eyes to his with a look that expressed knowledge, triumph and delight. She was sure of her victory. And she said: "Sweetheart * * * don't you think I am as nice as Marjory?" The impulse had been airily confident. It was as if the silken cords had been parted by the sweep of a sword. Coleman's face had instantly stiffened and he looked like a man suddenly recalled to the ways of light. It may easily have been that in a moment he would have lapsed again to his luxurious dreaming. But in his face the girl had read a fatal character to her blunder and her resentment against him took precedence of any other emotion. She wheeled abruptly from him and said with great contempt: "Rufus, you had better go home. You're tired and sleepy, and more or less drunk."

He knew that the grand tumble of all their little embowered incident could be neither stayed or mended. "Yes," he answered, sulkily, "I think so too." They shook hands huffily and he went away.

When he arrived among the students he found that they had appropriated everything of his which would conduce to their comfort. He was furious over it. But to his bitter speeches they replied in jibes.

"Rufus is himself again. Admire his angelic disposition. See him smile. Gentle soul."

A sleepy voice said from a comer: "I know what pinches him."

"What?" asked several.

"He's been to see Nora and she flung him out bodily."

"Yes?" sneered Coleman. "At times I seem to see in you, Coke, the fermentation of some primeval form of sensation, as if it were possible for you to de- velop a mind in two or three thousand years, and then at other times you appear * * * much as you are now."

As soon as they had well measured Coleman's temper all of the students save Coke kept their mouths tightly closed. Coke either did not understand or his mood was too vindictive for silence. "Well, I know you got a throw-down all right," he muttered.

"And how would you know when I got a throw down? You pimply, milk-fed sophomore."

The others perked up their ears in mirthful appreciation of this language.

"Of course," continued Coleman, "no one would protest against your continued existence, Coke, unless you insist on recalling yourself violently to people's attention in this way. The mere fact of your living would not usually be offensive to people if you weren't eternally turning a sort of calcium light on your prehensile attributes." Coke was suddenly angry, angry much like a peasant, and his anger first evinced itself in a mere sputtering and spluttering. Finally he got out a rather long speech, full of grumbling noises, but he was understood by all to declare that his prehensile attributes had not led him to cart a notorious woman about the world with him. When they quickly looked at Coleman they saw that he was livid. "You-"

But, of course, there immediately arose all sorts of protesting cries from the seven non-combatants. Coleman, as he took two strides toward Coke's corner, looked fully able to break him across his knee, but for this Coke did not seem to care at all. He was on his feet with a challenge in his eye. Upon each cheek burned a sudden hectic spot. The others were clamouring, "Oh, say, this won't do. Quit it. Oh, we mustn't have a fight. He didn't mean it, Coleman." Peter Tounley pressed Coke to the wall saying: "You damned young jackass, be quiet."

They were in the midst of these festivities when a door opened and disclosed the professor. He might have been coming into the middle of a row in one of the corridors of the college at home only this time he carried a candle. His speech, however, was a Washurst speech : "Gentlemen, gentlemen, what does this mean?" All seemed to expect Coleman to make the answer. He was suddenly very cool. "Nothing, professor," he said, "only that this-only that Coke has insulted me. I suppose that it was only the irresponsibility of a boy, and I beg that you will not trouble over it."

"Mr. Coke," said the professor, indignantly, "what have you to say to this?" Evidently he could not clearly see Coke, and he peered around his candle at where the virtuous Peter Tounley was expostulating with the young man. The figures of all the excited group moving in the candle light caused vast and uncouth shadows to have conflicts in the end of the room.

Peter Tounley's task was not light, and beyond that he had the conviction that his struggle with Coke was making him also to appear as a rowdy. This conviction was proven to be true by a sudden thunder from the old professor, "Mr. Tounley, desist ! "

In wrath he desisted and Coke flung himself forward. He paid less attention to the professor than if the latter had been a jack-rabbit. "You say I insulted you? he shouted crazily in Coleman's face.

"Well * * * I meant to, do you see?"

Coleman was glacial and lofty beyond everything. "I am glad to have you admit the truth of what I have said."

Coke was, still suffocating with his peasant rage, which would not allow him to meet the clear, calm expressions of Coleman. "Yes * * * I insulted you * * * I insulted you because what I said was correct * * my prehensile attributes * * yes but I have never — —"

He was interrupted by a chorus from the other students. "Oh, no, that won't do. Don't say that. Don't repeat that, Coke."

Coleman remembered the weak bewilderment of the little professor in hours that had not long passed, and it was with something of an impersonal satisfaction that he said to himself: "The old boy's got his war-paint on again." The professor had stepped sharply up to Coke and looked at him with eyes that seemed to throw out flame and heat. There was a moment's pause, and then the old scholar spoke, biting his words as if they were each a short section of steel wire. "Mr. Coke, your behaviour will end your college career abruptly and in gloom, I promise you. You have been drinking."

Coke, his head simply floating in a sea of universal defiance, at once blurted out: "Yes, sir."

"You have been drinking?" cried the professor, ferociously. "Retire to your-retire to your— —retire—-" And then in a voice of thunder he shouted: "Retire."

Whereupon seven hoodlum students waited a decent moment, then shrieked with laughter. But the old professor would have none of their nonsense. He quelled them all with force and finish.

Coleman now spoke a few words." Professor, I can't tell you how sorry I am that I should be concerned in any such riot as this, and since we are doomed to be bound so closely into each other's society I offer myself without reservation as being willing to repair the damage as well as may be, done. I don t see how I can forget at once that Coke's conduct was insolently unwarranted, but * * * if he has anything to say of a nature that might heal the breach I would be willing to to meet him in the openest manner." As he made these re- marks Coleman's dignity was something grand, and, Morever, there was now upon his face that curious look of temperance and purity which had been noted in New York as a singular physical characteristic. If he. was guilty of anything in this affair at all-in fact, if he had ever at any time been guilty of anything- no mark had come to stain that bloom of innocence. The professor nodded in the fullest appreciation and sympathy. "Of course * * * really there is no other sleeping placeI suppose it would be better-" Then he again attacked Coke. "Young man, you have chosen an unfortunate moment to fill us with a suspicion that you may not be a gentleman. For the time there is nothing to be done with you." He addressed the other students. "There is nothing for me to do, young gentleman, but to leave Mr. Coke in your care. Good-night, sirs. Good-night, Coleman." He left the room with his candle.

When Coke was bade to " Retire " he had, of course, simply retreated fuming to a corner of the room where he remained looking with yellow eyes like an animal from a cave. When the others were able to see through the haze of mental confusion they found that Coleman was with deliberation taking off his boots. "Afterward, when he removed his waist-coat, he took great care to wind his large gold watch.

The students, much subdued, lay again in their places, and when there was any talking it was of an extremely local nature, referring principally to the floor As being unsuitable for beds and also referring from time to time to a real or an alleged selfishness on the part of some one of the recumbent men. Soon there was only the sound of heavy breathing.

When the professor had returned to what he called the Wainwright part of the house he was greeted instantly with the question: "What was it?" His wife and daughter were up in alarm. "What was it " they repeated, wildly.

He was peevish. "Oh, nothing, nothing. But that young Coke is a regular ruffian. He had gotten him. self into some tremendous uproar with Coleman. When I arrived he seemed actually trying to assault him. Revolting! He had been drinking. Coleman's behaviour, I must say, was splendid. Recognised at once the delicacy of my position-he not being a student. If I had found him in the wrong it would have been simpler than finding him in the right. Confound that rascal of a Coke." Then, as he began a partial disrobing, he treated them to grunted scrap of information. " Coke was quite insane * * * I feared that I couldn't control him * * * Coleman was like ice * * * and as much as I have seen to admire in him during the last few days, this quiet beat it all. If he had not recognised my helplessness as far as he was concerned the whole thing might have been a most miserable business. He is a very fine young man." The dissenting voice to this last tribute was the voice of Mrs. Wainwright. She said: "Well, Coleman drinks, too-everybody knows that."

"I know," responded the professor, rather bashfully, but I am confident that he had not touched a drop." Marjory said nothing.

The earlier artillery battles had frightened most of the furniture out of the houses of Arta, and there was left in this room only a few old red cushions, and the Wainwrights were camping upon the floor. Marjory was enwrapped in Coleman's macintosh, and while the professor and his wife maintained some low talk of the recent incident she in silence had turned her cheek into the yellow velvet collar of the coat. She felt something against her bosom, and putting her hand carefully into the top pocket of the coat she found three cigars. These she took in the darkness and laid aside, telling herself to remember their position in the morning. She had no doubt that Coleman: would rejoice over them, before he could get back to, Athens where there were other good cigars.

CHAPTER XVIII.

THE ladies of the Wainwright party had not complained at all when deprived of even such civilised advantages as a shelter and a knife and fork and soap and water, but Mrs. Wainwright complained bitterly amid the half-civilisation of Arta. She could see here no excuse for the absence of several hundred things which she had always regarded as essential to life. She began at 8.30 A. M. to make both the professor and Marjory woeful with an endless dissertation upon the beds in the hotel at Athens. Of course she had not regarded them at the time as being exceptional beds * * * that was quite true, * * * but then one really never knew what one was really missing until one really missed it * * * She would never have thought that she would come to consider those Athenian beds as excellent * * * but experience is a great teacher * * * makes- one reflect upon the people who year in and year out have no beds at all, poor things. * * * Well, it made one glad if one did have a good bed, even if it was at the time on the other side of the world. If she ever reached it she did not know what could ever induce her to leave it again. * * * She would never be induced —

"'Induced!'" snarled the professor. The word represented to him a practiced feminine mis-usage of truth, and at such his white warlock always arose." "Induced!' Out of four American women I have seen lately, you seem to be the only one who would say that you had endured this thing because you had been 'induced' by others to come over here. How absurd!"

Mrs. Wainwright fixed her husband with a steely eye. She saw opportunity for a shattering retort. "You don't mean, Harrison, to include Marjory and I in the same breath with those two women?"

The professor saw no danger ahead for himself. He merely answered: "I had no thought either way. It did not seem important."

"Well, it is important," snapped Mrs. Wainwright.

"Do you know that you are speaking in the same breath of Marjory and Nora Black, the actress? "

"No," said the professor. "Is that so?" He was astonished, but he was not aghast at all. "Do you mean to say that is Nora Black, the comic opera star?"

"That's exactly who she is," said Mrs. Wainwright, dramatically. "And I consider that-I consider that Rufus Coleman has done no less than-misled us."

This last declaration seemed to have no effect upon the professor's pure astonishment, but Marjory looked at her mother suddenly. However, she said no word, exhibiting again that strange and, inscrutable countenance which masked even the tiniest of her maidenly emotions.

Mrs. Wainwright was triumphant, and she immediately set about celebrating her victory. "Men never see those things," she said to her husband. "Men never see those things. You would have gone on forever without finding out that your-your- hospitality was, being abused by that Rufus Coleman."

The professor woke up." Hospitality?" he said, indignantly. "Hospitality? I have not had any hospitality to be abused. Why don't you talk sense? It is not that, but-it might-" He hesitated and then spoke slowly. "It might be very awkward. Of course one never knows anything definite about such people, but I suppose * * * Anyhow, it was strange in Coleman to allow her to meet us. "

"It Was all a pre-arranged plan," announced the triumphant Mrs. Wainwright. "She came here on putpose to meet Rufus Coleman, and he knew it, and I should not wonder if they had not the exact spot picked out where they were going to meet."

"I can hardly believe that," said the professor, in distress. "I can, hardly believe that. It does, not seem to me that Coleman —"

"Oh yes. Your dear Rufus Coleman," cried Mrs. Wainwright. "You think he is very fine now. But I can remember when you didn't think —-"

And the parents turned together an abashed look at their daughter. The professor actually flushed with shame. It seemed to him that he had just committed an atrocity upon the heart of his child. The instinct of each of them was to go to her and console her in their arms. She noted it immediately, and seemed to fear it. She spoke in a clear and even voice. "I don't think, father, that you should distress me by supposing that I am concerned at all if Mr. Coleman cares to get Nora Black over here."

"Not at all," stuttered the professor. "I —-"

Mrs. Wainwright's consternation turned suddenly to, anger. "He is a scapegrace. A rascal. A — a —"

"Oh," said Marjory, coolly, "I don't see why it isn't his own affair. He didn't really present her to you, mother, you remember? She seemed quite to force her way at first, and then you-you did the rest. It should be very easy to avoid her, now that we are out of the wilderness. And then it becomes a private matter of Mr. Coleman's. For my part, I rather liked her. I don't see such a dreadful calamity."

"Marjory!" screamed her mother. "How dreadful. Liked her!Don't let me hear you say such shocking things."

"I fail to see anything shocking," answered Marjory, stolidly.

The professor was looking helplessly from his daughter to his wife, and from his wife to his daughter, like a man who was convinced that his troubles would never end. This new catastrophe created a different kind of difficulty, but he considered that the difficulties were as robust as had been the preceding ones. He put on his hat and went out of the room. He felt an impossibility of saying anything to Coleman, but he felt that he must look upon him. He must look upon this man and try to know from his manner the measure of guilt. And incidentally he longed for the machinery of a finished society which prevents its parts from clashing, prevents it with its great series of I law upon law, easily operative but relentless. Here he felt as a man flung into the jungle with his wife and daughter, where they could become the victims of any sort of savagery. His thought referred once more to what he considered the invaluable services of Coleman, and as he observed them in conjunction with the present accusation, he was simply dazed. It was then possible that one man could play two such divergent parts. He had not learned this at Washurst. But no; the world was not such a bed of putrefaction. He would not believe it; he would not believe it.

After adventures which require great nervous en. durance, it is only upon the second or third night that the common man sleeps hard. The students had expected to slumber like dogs on the first night after their trials. but none slept long, And few slept.

Coleman was the first man to arise. When he left the room the students were just beginning to blink. He took his dragoman among the shops and he bought there all the little odds and ends which might go to make up the best breakfast in Arta. If he had had news of certain talk he probably would not have been buying breakfast for eleven people. Instead, he would have been buying breakfast for one. During his absence the students arose and performed their frugal toilets. Considerable attention was paid to Coke by the others. "He made a monkey of you," said Peter Tounley with unction. "He twisted you until you looked like a wet, grey rag. You had better leave this wise guy alone."

It was not the night nor was it meditation that had taught Coke anything, but he seemed to have learned something from the mere lapse of time. In appearance he was subdued, but he managed to make a temporary jauntiness as he said : "Oh, I don't know."

"Well, you ought to know," said he who was called Billie. "You ought to know. You made an egregious snark of yourself. Indeed, you sometimes resembled a boojum. Anyhow, you were a plain chump. You exploded your face about something of which you knew nothing, and I'm damned if I believe you'd make even a good retriever."

"You're a half-bred water-spaniel," blurted Peter Tounley. "And," he added, musingly, "that is a pretty low animal."

Coke was argumentative. "Why am I?" he asked, turning his head from side to side. "I don't see where I was so wrong."

"Oh, dances, balloons, picnics, parades and ascensions," they retorted, profanely. "You swam voluntarily into water that was too deep for you. Swim out. Get dry. Here's a towel."

Coke, smitten in the face with a wet cloth rolled into a ball, grabbed it and flung it futilely at a well-dodging companion " No," he cried, "I don't see it. Now look here. I don't see why we shouldn't all resent this Nora Black business."

One student said: "Well, what's the matter with Nora B lack, anyhow?"

Another student said "I don't see how you've been issued any license to say things about Nora Black."

Another student said dubiously: "Well, he knows her well."

And then three or four spoke at once. "He was very badly rattled when she appeared upon the scene."

Peter Tounley asked: "Well, which of you people know anything wrong about Nora Black?"

There was a pause, and then Coke said: "Oh, of course-I don't know-but-"

He who was called Billie then addressed his companions. " It wouldn't be right to repeat any old lie about Nora Black, and by the same token it wouldn't be right to see old Mother Wainwright chummin' with her. There is no wisdom in going further than that. Old Mother Wainwright don't know that her fair companion of yesterday is the famous comic opera star. For my part, I believe that Coleman is simply afraid to tell her. I don't think he wished to see Nora Black yesterday any more than he wished to see the devil. The discussion, as I understand it concerned itself only with what Coleman had to do with the thing, and yesterday anybody could see that he was in a panic."

They heard a step on the stair, and directly Coleman entered, followed by his dragoman. They were laden with the raw material for breakfast. The correspondent looked keenly among the students, for it was plain that they had been talking of him. It, filled him with rage, and for a stifling moment he could not think why he failed to immediately decamp in chagrin and leave eleven orphans to whatever fate. their general incompetence might lead them. It struck him as a deep shame that even then he and his paid man were carrying in the breakfast. He wanted to fling it all on the floor and walk out. Then he remembered Marjory. She was the reason. She was the reason for everything.

But he could not repress certain, of his thoughts. "Say, you people," he said, icily, "you had better soon learn to hustle for yourselves. I may be a dragoman, and a butler, and a cook, and a housemaid, but I'm blowed if I'm a wet nurse." In reality, he had taken the most generous pleasure in working for the others before their eyes had even been opened from sleep, but it was now all turned to wormwood. It is certain that even this could not have deviated this executive man from labour and management. because these were his life. But he felt that he was about to walk out of the room, consigning them all to Hades. His glance of angry, reproach fastened itself mainly upon Peter Tounley, because he knew that of all, Peter was the most innocent.

Peter, Tounley was abashed by this glance. So you've brought us something to eat, old man. That is tremendously nice of you-we-appreciate it like everything."

Coleman was mollified by Peter's tone. Peter had had that emotion which is equivalent to a sense of guilt, although in reality he was speckless. Two or three of the other students bobbed up to a sense of the situation. They ran to Coleman, and with polite cries took his provisions from him. One dropped a bunch of lettuce on the floor, and others reproached him with scholastic curses. Coke was seated near the window, half militant, half conciliatory. It was impossible for him to keep up a manner of deadly enmity while Coleman was bringing in his breakfast. He would have much preferred that Coleman had not brought in his breakfast. He would have much preferred to have foregone breakfast altogether. He would have much preferred anything. There seemed to be a conspiracy of circumstance to put him in the wrong and make him appear as a ridiculous young peasant. He was the victim of a benefaction, and he hated Coleman harder now than at any previous time. He saw that if he stalked out and took his breakfast alone in a cafe, the others would consider him still more of an outsider. Coleman had expressed himself like a man of the world and a gentleman, and Coke was convinced that he was a superior man of the world and a superior gentleman, but that he simply had not had words to express his position at the proper time. Coleman was glib. Therefore, Coke had been the victim of an attitude as well as of a benefaction. And so he deeply hated Coleman.

The others were talking cheerfully. "What the deuce are these, Coleman? Sausages? Oh, my. And look at these burlesque fishes. Say, these Greeks don't care what they eat. Them thar things am sardines in the crude state. No? Great God, look at those things. Look. What? Yes, they are. Radishes. Greek synonym for radishes."

The professor entered. "Oh," he said apologetically, as if he were intruding in a boudoir. All his serious desire to probe Coleman to the bottom ended in embarrassment. Mayhap it was not a law of feeling, but it happened at any rate. " He had come in a puzzled frame of mind, even an accusative frame of mind, and almost immediately he found himself suffer. ing like a culprit before his judge. It is a phenomenon of what we call guilt and innocence.

"Coleman welcomed him cordially. "Well, professor, good-morning. I've rounded up some things that at least may be eaten."

"You are very good " very considerate, Mr. Coleman," answered the professor, hastily. "I'am sure we are much indebted to you." He had scanned the correspondent's face, land it had been so devoid of guile that he was fearful that his suspicion, a base suspicion, of this noble soul would be detected. "No, no, we can never thank you enough."

Some of the students began to caper with a sort of decorous hilarity before their teacher. "Look at the sausage, professor. Did you ever see such sausage " Isn't it salubrious " And see these other things, sir. Aren't they curious " I shouldn't wonder if they were alive. Turnips, sir? No, sir. I think they are Pharisees. I have seen a Pharisee look like a pelican, but I have never seen a Pharisee look like a turnip, so I think these turnips must be Pharisees, sir, Yes, they may be walrus. We're not sure. Anyhow, their angles are geometrically all wrong. Peter, look out." Some green stuff was flung across the room. The professor laughed; Coleman laughed. Despite Coke, dark-browed, sulking. and yet desirous of reinstating himself, the room had waxed warm with the old college feeling, the feeling of lads who seemed never to treat anything respectfully and yet at the same time managed to treat the real things with respect. The professor himself contributed to their wild carouse over the strange Greek viands. It was a vivacious moment common to this class in times of relaxation, and it was understood perfectly.

Coke arose. "I don't see that I have any friends here," he said, hoarsely, "and in consequence I don't see why I should remain here."

All looked at him. At the same moment Mrs. Wainwright and Marjory entered the room.

CHAPTER XIX.

"Good-morning," said Mrs. Wainwright jovially to the students and then she stared at Coleman as if he were a sweep at a wedding.

"Good-morning," said Marjory.

Coleman and the students made reply. "Good-morning. Good-morning. Good-morning. Good-morning —"

It was curious to see this greeting, this common phrase, this bit of old ware, this antique, come upon a dramatic scene and pulverise it. Nothing remained but a ridiculous dust. Coke, glowering, with his lips still trembling from heroic speech, was an angry clown, a pantaloon in rage. Nothing was to be done to keep him from looking like an ass. He, strode toward the door mumbling about a walk before breakfast.

Mrs. Wainwright beamed upon him. "Why, Mr. Coke, not before breakfast? You surely won't have time." It was grim punishment. He appeared to go blind, and he fairly staggered out of the door mumbling again, mumbling thanks or apologies or explanations. About the mouth of Coleman played a sinister smile. The professor cast. upon his wife a glance expressing weariness. It was as if he said " There you go again. You can't keep your foot out of it." She understood the glance, and so she asked blankly: "Why, What's the matter? Oh." Her belated mind grasped that it waw an aftermath of the quarrel of Coleman and Coke. Marjory looked as if she was distressed in the belief that her mother had been stupid. Coleman was outwardly serene. It was Peter Tounley who finally laughed a cheery, healthy laugh and they all looked at him with gratitude as if his sudden mirth had been a real statement or reconciliation and consequent peace.

The dragoman and others disported themselves until a breakfast was laid upon the floor. The adventurers squatted upon the floor. They made a large company. The professor and Coleman discussed the means of getting to Athens. Peter Tounley sat next to Marjory. "Peter," she said, privately, "what was all this trouble between Coleman and Coke?"

Peter answered blandly: "Oh, nothing at Nothing at all."

"Well, but —" she persisted, "what was the cause of it?"

He looked at her quaintly. He was not one of those in love with her, but be was interested in the affair. "Don't you know ?" he asked.

She understood from his manner that she had been some kind of an issue in the quarrel. "No," she answered, hastily. "I don't."

"Oh, I don't mean that," said Peter. "I only meant —I only meant-oh, well, it was nothing-really."

"It must have been about something," continued Marjory. She continued, because Peter had denied that she was concerned in it. "Whose fault?"

"I really don't know. It was all rather confusing," lied Peter, tranquilly.

Coleman and the professor decided to accept a plan of the correspondent's dragoman to start soon on the first stage of the journey to Athens. The dragoman had said that he had found two large carriages rentable.

Coke, the outcast, walked alone in the narrow streets. The flight of the crown prince's army from Larissa had just been announced in Arta, but Coke was probably the most woebegone object on the Greek peninsula.

He encountered a strange sight on the streets. A woman garbed in the style for walking of an afternoon on upper Broadway was approaching him through a mass of kilted mountaineers and soldiers in soiled overcoats. Of course he recognised Nora Black.

In his conviction that everybody in the world was at this time considering him a mere worm, he was sure that she would not heed him. Beyond that he had been presented to her notice in but a transient and cursory fashion. But contrary to his conviction, she turned a radiant smile upon him. "Oh," she said, brusquely, "you are one of the students. Good morning." In her manner was all the confidence of an old warrior, a veteran, who addresses the universe with assurance because of his past battles.

Coke grinned at this strange greeting. "Yes, Miss Black," he answered, "I am one of the students."

She did not seem to quite know how to formulate her next speech. "Er-I suppose you're going to Athens at once " You must be glad after your horrid experiences."

"I believe they are going to start for Athens today," said Coke.

Nora was all attention. " 'They?' " she repeated. "Aren't you going with them?"

"Well," he said, "* * Well—"

She saw of course that there had been some kind of trouble. She laughed. "You look as if somebody had kicked you down stairs," she said, candidly. She at once assumed an intimate manner toward him which was like a temporary motherhood. " Come, walk with me and tell me all about it." There was in her tone a most artistic suggestion that whatever had happened she was on his side. He was not loath. The street was full of soldiers whose tongues clattered so loudly that the two foreigners might have been wandering in a great cave of the winds. "Well, what was the row about?" asked Nora. "And who was in it?"

It would have been no solace to Coke to pour out his tale even if it had been a story that he could have told Nora. He was not stopped by the fact that he had gotten himself in the quarrel because he had insulted the name of the girt at his side. He did not think of it at that time. The whole thing was now extremely vague in outline to him and he only had a dull feeling of misery and loneliness. He wanted her to cheer him.

Nora laughed again. "Why, you're a regular little kid. Do you mean to say you've come out here sulking alone because of some nursery quarrel?" He was ruffled by her manner. It did not contain the cheering he required. "Oh, I don't know that I'm such a regular little kid," he said, sullenly. "The quarrel was not a nursery quarrel."

"Why don't you challenge him to a duel?" asked Nora, suddenly. She was watching him closely.

"Who?" said Coke.

"Coleman, you stupid," answered Nora.

They stared at each other, Coke paying her first the tribute of astonishment and then the tribute of admiration. "Why, how did you guess that?" he demanded.

"Oh," said Nora., "I've known Rufus Coleman for years, and he is always rowing with people."

"That is just it," cried Coke eagerly. "That is just it. I fairly hate the man. Almost all of the other fellows will stand his abuse, but it riles me, I tell you. I think he is a beast. And, of course, if you seriously meant what you said about challenging him to a duel —I mean if there is any sense in that sort of thing-I would challenge Coleman. I swear I would. I think he's a great bluffer, anyhow. Shouldn't wonder if he would back out. Really, I shouldn't."

Nora smiled humourously at a house on her side of the narrow way. "I wouldn't wonder if he did either " she answered. After a time she said " Well, do you mean to say that you have definitely shaken them? Aren't you going back to Athens with them or anything?"

"I-I don't see how I can," he said, morosely.

"Oh," she said. She reflected for a time. At last she turned to him archly and asked: "Some words over a lady?"

Coke looked at her blankly. He suddenly remembered the horrible facts. "No-no-not over a lady."

"My dear boy, you are a liar," said Nora, freely. "You are a little unskilful liar. It was some words over a lady, and the lady's name is Marjory Wainwright."

Coke felt as though he had suddenly been let out of a cell, but he continued a mechanical denial. "No, no * * It wasn't truly * * upon my word * * "

"Nonsense," said Nora. "I know better. Don't you think you can fool me, you little cub. I know you're in love with Marjory Wainwright, and you think Coleman is your rival. What a blockhead you are. Can't you understand that people see these things?"

311

"Well-" stammered Coke.

"Nonsense," said Nora again. "Don't try to fool me, you may as well understand that it's useless. I am too wise."

"Well-" stammered Coke.

"Go ahead," urged Nora. "Tell me about it. Have it out."

He began with great importance and solemnity. "Now, to tell you the truth * * that is why I hate him * * I hate him like anything. * * I can't see why everybody admires him so. I don't see anything to him myself. I don't believe he's got any more principle than a wolf. I wouldn't trust him with two dollars. Why, I know stories about him that would make your hair curl. When I think of a girl like Marjory — "

His speech had become a torrent. But here Nora raised her hand. "Oh! Oh! Oh! That will do. That will do. Don't lose your senses. I don't see why this girl Marjory is any too good. She is no chicken, I'll bet. Don't let yourself get fooled with that sort of thing."

Coke was unaware of his incautious expressions. He floundered on. while Nora looked at him as if she wanted to wring his neck. "No-she's too fine and too good-for him or anybody like him-she's too fine and too good-"

"Aw, rats," interrupted Nora, furiously. "You make me tired."

Coke had a wooden-headed conviction that he must make Nora understand Marjory's infinite superiority to all others of her sex, and so he passed into a pariegyric, each word of which was a hot coal to the girl addressed. Nothing would stop him, apparently. He even made the most stupid repetitions. Nora finally stamped her foot formidably. "Will you stop? Will you stop?" she said through her clenched teeth. " Do you think I want to listen to your everlasting twaddle about her? Why, she's-she's no better than other people, you ignorant little mamma's boy. She's no better than other people, you swab! "

Coke looked at her with the eyes of a fish. He did not understand. "But she is better than other people," he persisted.

Nora seemed to decide suddenly that there would be no accomplishment in flying desperately against this rock-walled conviction. "Oh, well," she said, with marvellous good nature, "perhaps you are right, numbskull. But, look here; do you think she cares for him?"

In his heart, his jealous heart, he believed that Marjory loved Coleman, but he reiterated eternally to himself that it was not true. As for speaking it to, another, that was out of the question. "No," he said, stoutly, "she doesn't care a snap for him." If he had admitted it, it would have seemed to him that. he was somehow advancing Coleman's chances.

"'Oh, she doesn't, eh?" said Nora enigmatically.

"She doesn't?" He studied her face with an abrupt, miserable suspicion, but he repeated doggedly: "No, she doesn't."

"Ahem," replied Nora. "Why, she's set her cap for him all right. She's after him for certain. It's as plain as day. Can't you see that, stupidity?"

"No," he said hoarsely.

"You are a fool," said Nora. "It isn't Coleman that's after her. It is she that is after Coleman."

Coke was mulish. "No such thing. Coleman's crazy about her. Everybody has known it ever since he was in college. You ask any of the other fellows."

Nora was now very serious, almost doleful. She remained still for a time, casting at Coke little glances of hatred. "I don't see my way clear to ask any of the other fellows," she said at last, with considerable bitterness. "I'm not in the habit of conducting such enquiries."

Coke felt now that he disliked her, and he read plainly her dislike of him. If they were the two villains of the play, they were not having fun together at all. Each had some kind of a deep knowledge that their aspirations, far from colliding, were of such character that the success of one would mean at least assistance to the other, but neither could see how to confess if. Perhaps it was from shame, perhaps it was because Nora thought Coke to have little wit ; perhaps it was because Coke thought Nora to have little conscience. Their talk was mainly rudderless. From time to time Nora had an inspiration to come boldly at the point, but this inspiration was commonly defeated by, some extraordinary manifestation of Coke's incapacity. To her mind, then, it seemed like a proposition to ally herself to a butcher-boy in a matter purely sentimental. She Wondered indignantly how she was going to conspire With this lad, who puffed out his infantile cheeks in order to conceitedly demonstrate that he did not understand the game at all. She hated Marjory for it. Evidently it was only the weaklings who fell in love with that girl. Coleman was an exception, but then, Coleman was misled, by extraordinary artifices. She meditated for a moment if she should tell Coke to go home and not bother her. What at last decided the question was his unhappiness. She clung to this unhappiness for its value as it stood alone, and because its reason for existence was related to her own unhappiness. "You Say you are not going back to Athens with your party. I don't suppose you're going to stay here. I'm going back to Athens to-day. I came up here to see a battle, but it doesn't seem that there are to be any more battles., The fighting will now all be on the other side of the mountains." Apparent she had learned in some haphazard way that the Greek peninsula was divided by a spine of almost inaccessible mountains, and the war was thus split into two simultaneous campaigns. The Arta campaign was known to be ended. "If you want to go back to Athens without consorting with your friends, you had better go back with me. I can take you in my carriage as far as the beginning of the railroad. Don't you worry. You've got money enough, haven't you? The professor isn't keeping your money?"

"Yes," he said slowly, "I've got money enough." He was apparently dubious over the proposal. In their abstracted walk they had arrived in front of the house occupied by Coleman and the Wainwright party. Two carriages, forlorn in dusty age, stood be- fore the door. Men were carrying out new leather luggage and flinging it into the traps amid a great deal of talk which seemed to refer to nothing. Nora and Coke stood looking at the scene without either thinking of the importance of running away, when out tumbled seven students, followed immediately but in more decorous fashion by the Wainwrights and Coleman.

Some student set up a whoop. "Oh, there he is. There's Coke. Hey, Coke, where you been? Here he is, professor." For a moment after the hoodlum had subsided, the two camps stared at each other in silence.

CHAPTER XX.

NORA and Coke were an odd looking pair at the time. They stood indeed as if rooted to the spot, staring vacuously, like two villagers, at the surprising travellers. It was not an eternity before the practiced girl of the stage recovered her poise, but to the end of the incident the green youth looked like a culprit and a fool. Mrs. Wainwright's glower of offensive incredulity was a masterpiece. Marjory nodded pleasantly; the professor nodded. The seven students clambered boisterously into the forward carriage making it clang with noise like a rook's nest. They shouted to Coke. "Come on; all aboard; come on, Coke; - we're off. Hey, there, Cokey, hurry up." The professor, as soon as he had seated himself on the forward seat of' the second carriage, turned in Coke's general direction and asked formally: "Mr. Coke, you are coming with us?" He felt seemingly much in doubt as to the propriety of abandoning the headstrong young man, and this doubt was not at all decreased by Coke's appearance with Nora Black. As far as he could tell, any assertion of authority on his part would end only in a scene in which Coke would probably insult him with some gross violation of collegiate conduct. As at first the young man made no reply, the professor after waiting spoke again. "You understand, Mr. Coke, that if you separate yourself from the party you encounter my strongest disapproval, and if I did not feel responsible to the college and your father for your safe journey to New York I-I don't know but what I would have you ex- pelled by cable if that were possible."

Although Coke had been silent, and Nora Black had had the appearance of being silent, in reality she had lowered her chin and whispered sideways and swiftly. She had said: "Now, here's your time. Decide quickly, and don't look such a wooden Indian." Coke pulled himself together with a visible effort, and spoke to the professor from an inspiration in which he had no faith. "I understand my duties to you, sir, perfectly. I also understand my duty to the college. But I fail to see where either of these obligations require me to accept the introduction of objectionable people into the party. If I owe a duty to the college and to you, I don't owe any to Coleman, and, as I understand it, Coleman was not in the original plan of this expedition. If such had been the case, I would not have been here. I can't tell what the college may see fit to do, but as for my father I I have no doubt of how he will view it."

The first one to be electrified by the speech was Coke himself. He saw with a kind of subconscious amazement this volley of bird-shot take effect upon the face of the old professor. The face of Marjory flushed crimson as if her mind had sprung to a fear that if Coke could develop ability in this singular fashion he might succeed in humiliating her father in the street in the presence of the seven students, her mother, Coleman and-herself. She had felt the bird- shot sting her father.

When Coke had launched forth, Coleman with his legs stretched far apart had just struck a match on the wall of the house and was about to light a cigar. His groom was leading up his horse. He saw the value of Coke's argument more appreciatively and sooner perhaps than did Coke. The match dropped from his fingers, and in the white sunshine and still air it burnt on the pavement orange coloured and with langour. Coleman held his cigar with all five fingers-in a manner out of all the laws of smoking. He turned toward Coke. There was danger in the moment, but then in a flash it came upon him that his role was not of squabbling with Coke, far less of punching him. On the contrary, he was to act the part of a cool and instructed man who refused to be waylaid into foolishness by the outcries of this pouting youngster and who placed himself in complete deference to the wishes of the professor. Before the professor had time to embark upon any reply to Coke, Coleman was at the side of the carriage and, with a fine assumption of distress, was saying: "Professor, I could very easily ride back to Agrinion alone. It would be all right. I don't want to-"

To his surprise the professor waved at him to be silent as if he were a mere child. The old man's face was set with the resolution of exactly what hewas going to say to Coke. He began in measured tone, speaking with feeling, but with no trace of anger.

"Mr. Coke, it has probably escaped your attention that Mr. Coleman, at what I consider a great deal of peril to himself, came out to rescue this party-you and others-and although he studiously disclaims all merit in his finding us and bringing us in, I do not regard it in that way, and I am surprised that any member of this party should conduct himself in this manner toward a man who has been most devotedly and generously at our service." It was at this time that the professor raised himself and shook his finger at Coke, his voice now ringing with scorn. In such moments words came to him and formed themselves into sentences almost too rapidly for him to speak them. "You are one of the most remarkable products of our civilisation which I have yet come upon. What do you mean, sir? Where are your senses? Do you think that all this pulling and pucking is manhood? I will tell you what I will do with you. I thought I brought out eight students to Greece, but when I find that I brought out, seven students and-er-an-ourang-outang-don't get angry, sir —I don't care for your anger —I say when I discover this I am naturally puzzled for a moment. I will leave you to the judgment of your peers. Young gentlemen! " Of the seven heads of the forward carriage none had to be turned. All had been turned since the beginning of the talk. If the professor's speech had been delivered in one of the class-rooms of Washurst they would have glowed with delight over the butchery of Coke, but they felt its portentous aspect. Butchery here in Greece thousands of miles from home presented to them more of the emphasis of downright death and destruction. The professor called out " Young gentlemen, I have done all that I can do without using force, which, much to my regret, is impracticable. If you will persuade your fellow student to accompany you I think our consciences will be the better for not having left a weak minded brother alone among the by-paths." The valuable aggregation of intelligence and refinement which decorated the interior of the first carriage did not hesitate over answering this appeal. In fact, his fellow students had worried among themselves over Coke, and their desire to see him come out of his troubles in fair condition was intensified by the fact that they had lately concentrated much thought upon him. There was a somewhat comic pretense of speaking so that only Coke could hear. Their chorus was law sung. "Oh, cheese it, Coke. Let up on your-self, you blind ass. Wait till you get to Athens and then go and act like a monkey. All this is no good-"

The advice which came from the carriage was all in one direction, and there was so much of it that the hum of voices sounded like a wind blowing through a forest.

Coke spun suddenly and said something to Nora Black. Nora laughed rather loudly, and then the two turned squarely and the Wainwright party contemplated what were surely at that time the two most insolent backs in the world.

The professor looked as if he might be going to have a fit. Mrs. Wainwright lifted her eyes toward heaven, and flinging out her trembling hands, cried: " Oh, what an outrage. What an outrage! That minx-" The concensus of opinion in the first carriage was perfectly expressed by Peter Tounley, who with a deep drawn breath, said : "Well, I'm damned! " Marjory had moaned and lowered her head as from a sense of complete personal shame. Coleman lit his cigar and mounted his horse. "Well, I suppose there is nothing for it but to be off, professor?" His tone was full of regret, with sort of poetic regret. For a moment the professor looked at him blankly, and then gradually recovered part of his usual manner. "Yes," he said sadly, "there is nothing for it but to go on." At a word from the dragoman, the two impatient drivers spoke gutturally to their horses and the carriages whirled out of Arta. Coleman, his dragoman and the groom trotted in the dust from the wheels of the Wainwright carriage. The correspondent always found his reflective faculties improved by the constant pounding of a horse on the trot, and he was not sorry to have now a period for reflection, as well as this artificial stimulant. As he viewed the game he had in his hand about all the cards that were valuable. In fact, he considered that the only ace against him was Mrs. Wainwright. He had always regarded her as a stupid person, concealing herself behind a mass of trivialities which were all conventional, but he thought now that the more stupid she was and the more conventional in her triviality the more she approached to being the very ace of trumps itself. She was just the sort of a card that would come upon the table mid the neat play of experts and by some inexplicable arrangement of circumstance, lose a whole game for the wrong man. After Mrs. Wainwright he worried over the students. He believed them to be reasonable enough; in fact, he honoured them distinctly in regard to their powers of reason, but he knew that people generally hated a row. It, put them off their balance, made them sweat over a lot of pros and cons, and prevented them from thinking for a time at least only of themselves. Then they came to resent the principals in a row. Of course the principal, who was thought to be in the wrong, was the most resented, but Coleman believed that, after all, people always came to resent the other principal, or at least be impatient and suspicious of him. If he was a correct person, why was he in a row at all? The principal who had been in the right often brought this impatience and suspicion upon himself, no doubt, by never letting the matter end, continuing to yawn about his virtuous suffering, and not allowing people to return to the steady contemplation of their own affairs. As a precautionary measure he decided to say nothing at all about the late trouble, unless some one addressed him upon it. Even then he would be serenely laconic. He felt that he must be popular with the seven students. In the first place, it was nice that in the presence of Marjory they should like him, and in the second place he feared to displease them as a body because he believed that he had some dignity. Hoodlums are seldom dangerous to other hoodlums, but if they catch pomposity alone in the field, pomposity is their prey. They tear him to mere bloody ribbons, amid heartless shrieks. When Coleman put himself on the same basis with the students, he could cope with them easily, but he did not want the wild pack after him when Marjory could see the chase. And so be reasoned that his best attitude was to be one of rather taciturn serenity.

On the hard military road the hoofs of the horses made such clatter that it was practically impossible to hold talk between the carriages and the horsemen without all parties bellowing. The professor, how- ever, strove to overcome the difficulties. He was apparently undergoing a great amiability toward Coleman. Frequently he turned with a bright face, and pointing to some object in the landscape, obviously tried to convey something entertaining to Coleman's mind. Coleman could see his lips mouth the words. He always nodded cheerily in answer and yelled.

The road ultimately became that straight lance-handle which Coleman-it seemed as if many years had passed-had traversed with his dragoman and the funny little carriers. He was fixing in his mind a possible story to the Wainwrights about the snake and his first dead Turk. But suddenly the carriages left this road and began a circuit of the Gulf of Arta, winding about an endless series of promontories. The journey developed into an excess of dust whirling from a road, which half circled the waist of cape after cape. All dramatics were lost in the rumble of wheels and in the click of hoofs. They passed a little soldier leading a prisoner by a string. They passed more frightened peasants, who seemed resolved to flee down into the very boots of Greece. And people looked at them with scowls, envying them their speed. At the little town from which Coleman embarked at one stage of the upward journey, they found crowds in the streets. There was no longer any laughter, any confidence, any vim. All the spirit of the visible Greek nation seemed to have been knocked out of it in two blows. But still they talked and never ceased talking. Coleman noticed that the most curious changes had come upon them since his journey to the frontier. They no longer approved of foreigners. They seemed to blame the travellers for something which had transpired in the past few days. It was not that they really blamed the travellers for the nation's calamity: It was simply that their minds were half stunned by the news of defeats, and, not thinking for a moment to blame themselves, or even not thinking to attribute the defeats to mere numbers and skill, they were savagely eager to fasten it upon something near enough at hand for the operation of vengeance.

Coleman perceived that the dragoman, all his former plumage gone, was whining and snivelling as he argued to a dark-browed crowd that was running beside the cavalcade. The groom, who always had been a miraculously laconic man, was suddenly launched forth garrulously. The, drivers, from their high seats, palavered like mad men, driving with oat hand and gesturing with the other, explaining evidently their own great innocence.

Coleman saw that there was trouble, but he only sat more stiffly in his saddle. The eternal gabble moved him to despise the situation. At any rate, the travellers would soon be out of this town and on to a more sensible region.

However he saw the driver of the first carriage suddenly pull up boforg a little blackened coffee shop and inn. The dragman spurred forward and began wild expostulation. The second carriage pulled close behind the other. The crowd, murmuring like a Roman mob in Nero's time, closed around them.

CHAPTER XXI.

COLEMAN pushed his horse coolly through to the dragoman;s side. "What is it?" he demanded. The dragoman was broken-voiced. "These peoples, they say you are Germans, all Germans, and they are angry," he wailed. "I can do nossing-nossing."

"Well, tell these men to drive on," said Coleman, "tell them they must drive on."

"They will not drive on," wailed the dragoman, still more loudly. "I can do nossing. They say here is place for feed the horse. It is the custom and they will note drive on."

"Make them drive on."

"They will note," shrieked the agonised servitor. Coleman looked from the men waving their arms and chattering on the box-seats to the men of the crowd who also waved their arms and chattered. In this throng far to the rear of the fighting armies there did not seem to be a single man who was not ablebodied, who had not been free to enlist as a soldier. They were of that scurvy behind-the-rear-guard which every nation has in degree proportionate to its worth. The manhood of Greece had gone to the frontier, leaving at home this rabble of talkers, most of whom were armed with rifles for mere pretention. Coleman loathed them to the end of his soul. He thought them a lot of infants who would like to prove their courage upon eleven innocent travellers, all but unarmed, and in this fact he was quick to see a great danger to the Wainwright party. One could deal with soldiers; soldiers would have been ashamed to bait helpless people ; but this rabble-

The fighting blood of the correspondent began to boil, and he really longed for the privilege to run amuck through the multitude. But a look at the Wainwrights kept him in his senses. The professor had turned pale as a dead man. He sat very stiff and still while his wife clung to him, hysterically beseeching him to do something, do something, although what he was to do she could not have even imagined.

Coleman took the dilemma by its beard. He dismounted from his horse into the depths of the crowd and addressed the Wainwrights. "I suppose we had better go into this place and have some coffee while the men feed their horses. There is no use in trying to make them go on." His manner was fairly casual, but they looked at him in glazed horror. "It is the only thing to do. This crowd is not nearly so bad as they think they are. But we've got to look as if we felt confident." He himself had no confidence with this angry buzz in his ears, but be felt certain that the only correct move was to get everybody as quickly as possible within the shelter of the inn. It might not be much of a shelter for them, but it was better than the carriages in the street.

The professor and Mrs. Wainwright seemed to be considering their carriage as a castle, and they looked as if their terror had made them physically incapable of leaving it. Coleman stood waiting. Behind him the clapper-tongued crowd was moving ominously. Marjory arose and stepped calmly down to him. He thrilled to the end of every nerve. It was as if she had said: "I don't think there is great danger, but if there is great danger, why * * here I am * ready * with you." It conceded everything, admitted everything. It was a surrender without a blush, and it was only possible in the shadow of the crisis when they did not know what the next moments might contain for them. As he took her hand and she stepped past him he whispered swiftly and fiercely in her ear, "I love you." She did not look up, but he felt that in this quick incident they had claimed each other, accepted each other with a far deeper meaning and understanding than could be possible in a mere drawing-room. She laid her hand on his arm, and with the strength of four men he twisted his horse into the making of furious prancing side-steps toward the door of the inn, clanking side- steps which mowed a wide lane through the crowd for Marjory, his Marjory. He was as haughty as a new German lieutenant, and although he held the fuming horse with only his left hand, he seemed perfectly capable of hurling the animal over a house without calling into service the arm which was devoted to Marjory.

It was not an exhibition of coolness such as wins applause on the stage when the hero placidly lights a cigarette before the mob which is clamouring for his death. It was, on the contrary, an exhibition of downright classic disdain, a disdain which with the highest arrogance declared itself in every glance of his eye into the faces about him. "Very good * * attack me if you like * * there is nothing to prevent it * * you mongrels." Every step of his progress was made a renewed insult to them. The very air was charged with what this lone man was thinking of this threatening crowd.

His audacity was invincible. They actually made way for it as quickly as children would flee from a ghost. The horse, dancing; with ringing steps, with his glistening neck arched toward the iron hand at his bit, this powerful, quivering animal was a regular engine of destruction, and they gave room until Coleman halted him -at an exclamation from Marjory.

"My mother and father." But they were coming close behind and Coleman resumed this contemptuous journey to the door of the inn. The groom, with his new-born tongue, was clattering there to the populace. Coleman gave him the horse and passed after the Wainwrights into the public room of the inn. He was smiling. What simpletons!

A new actor suddenly appeared in the person of the keeper of the inn. He too had a rifle and a prodigious belt of cartridges, but it was plain at once that he had elected to be a friend of the worried travellers. A large part of the crowd were thinking it necessary to enter the inn and pow-wow more. But the innkeeper stayed at the door with the dragoman, and together they vociferously held back the tide. The spirit of the mob had subsided to a more reasonable feeling. They no longer wished to tear the strangers limb from limb on the suspicion that they were Germans. They now were frantic to talk as if some inexorable law had kept them silent for ten years and this was the very moment of their release. Whereas, their simultaneous and interpolating orations had throughout made noise much like a coal-breaker. Coleman led the Wainwrights to a table in a far part of the room. They took chairs as if he had commanded them. "What an outrage," he said jubilantly. "The apes." He was keeping more than half an eye upon the door, because he knew that the quick coming of the students was important.

Then suddenly the storm broke in wrath. Something had happened in the street. The jabbering crowd at the door had turned and were hurrying upon some central tumult. The dragoman screamed to Coleman. Coleman jumped and grabbed the dragoman. "Tell this man to take them somewhere up stairs," he cried, indicating the Wainwrights with a sweep of his arm. The innkeeper seemed to understand sooner than the dragoman, and he nodded eagerly. The professor was crying: "What is it, Mr. Coleman? What is it? " An instant later, the correspondent was out in the street, buffeting toward a scuffle. Of course it was the students. It appeared, afterward, that those seven young men, with their feelings much ruffled, had been making the best of their way toward the door of the inn, when a large man in the crowd, during a speech which was surely most offensive, had laid an arresting hand on the shoulder of Peter Tounley. Whereupon the excellent Peter Tounley had hit the large man on the jaw in such a swift and skilful manner that the large man had gone spinning through a group of his countrymen to the hard earth, where he lay holding his face together and howling. Instantly, of course, there had been a riot. It might well be said that even then the affair could have ended in a lot of talking, but in the first place the students did not talk modern Greek, and in the second place they were now past all thought of talking. They regarded this affair seriously as a fight, and now that they at last were in it, they were in it for every pint of blood in their bodies. Such a pack of famished wolves had never before been let loose upon men armed with Gras rifles.

They all had been expecting the row, and when Peter Tounley had found it expedient to knock over the man, they had counted it a signal: their arms immediately begun to swing out as if they had been wound up. It was at this time that Coleman swam brutally through the Greeks and joined his countrymen. He was more frightened than any of those novices. When he saw Peter Tounley overthrow a dreadful looking brigand whose belt was full of knives, and who -crashed to the ground amid a clang of cartridges, he was appalled by the utter simplicity with which the lads were treating the crisis. It was to them no common scrimmage at Washurst, of course, but it flashed through Coleman's mind that they had not the slightegt sense of the size of the thing. He expected every instant to see the flash of knives or to hear the deafening intonation of a rifle fired against hst ear. It seemed to him miraculous that the tragedy was so long delayed.

In the meantirne he was in the affray. He jilted one man under the chin with his elbow in a way that reeled him off from Peter Tounley's back; a little person in thecked clothes he smote between the eyes; he recieved a gun-butt emphatically on the aide of the neck; he felt hands tearing at him; he kicked the pins out from under three men in rapid succession. He was always yelling. "Try to get to the inn, boys, try to get to the inn. Look out, Peter. Take care for his knife, Peter —" Suddenly he whipped a rifle out of the hands of a man and swung it, whistling. He had gone stark mad with the others.

The boy Billy, drunk from some blows and bleeding, was already. staggering toward the inn over the clearage which the wild Coleman made with the clubbed rifle. The others followed as well as they might while beating off a discouraged enemy. The remarkable innkeeper had barred his windows with strong wood shutters. He held the door by the crack for them, and they stumbled one by on through the portal. Coleman did not know why they were not all dead, nor did he understand the intrepid and generous behaviour of the innkeeper, but at any rate he felt that the fighting was suspended, and he wanted to see Marjory. The innkeeper was, doing a great pantomime in the middle of the darkened room, pointing to the outer door and then aiming his rifle at it to explain his intention of defending them at all costs. Some of the students moved to a billiard table and spread them- selves wearily upon it. Others sank down where they stood. Outside the crowd was beginning to roar. Coleman's groom crept out from under the little Coffee bar and comically saluted his master. The dragoman was not present. Coleman felt that he must see Marjory, and he made signs to the innkeeper. The latter understood quickly, and motioned that Coleman should follow him. They passed together through a dark hall and up a darker stairway, where after Coleman stepped out into a sun-lit room, saying loudly: "Oh, it's all right. It's all over. Don't worry."

Three wild people were instantly upon him. "Oh, what was it? What did happen? Is anybody hurt? Oh, tell us, quick!" It seemed at the time that it was an avalanche of three of them, and it was not until later that he recognised that Mrs. Wainwright had tumbled the largest number of questions upon him. As for Marjory, she had said nothing until the time when she cried: "Oh-he is bleeding-he is bleeding. Oh, come, quick!" She fairly dragged him out of one room into another room, where there was a jug of water. She wet her handkerchief and softly smote his wounds. "Bruises," she said, piteously, tearfully. " Bruises. Oh, dear! How they must hurt you.' The handkerchief was soon stained crimson.

When Coleman spoke his voice quavered. "It isn't anything. Really, it isn't anything." He had not known of these wonderful wounds, but he almost choked in the joy of Marjory's ministry and her half coherent exclamations. This proud and beautiful girl, this superlative creature, was reddening her handkerchief with his blood, and no word of his could have prevented her from thus attending him. He could hear the professor and Mrs. Wainwright fussing near him, trying to be of use. He would have liked to have been able to order them out of the room. Marjory's cool fingers on his face and neck had conjured within him a vision at an intimacy that was even sweeter than anything which he had imagined, and he longed to pour out to her the bubbling, impassioned speech which came to his lips. But, always doddering behind him, were the two old people, strenuous to be of help to him.

Suddenly a door opened and a youth appeared, simply red with blood. It was Peter Tounley. His first remark was cheerful. "Well, I don't suppose those people will be any too quick to look for more trouble."

Coleman felt a swift pang because he had forgotten to announce the dilapidated state of all the students. He had been so submerged by Marjory's tenderness that all else had been drowned from his mind. His heart beat quickly as he waited for Marjory to leave him and rush to Peter Tounley.

But she did nothing of the sort. "Oh, Peter," she cried in distress, and then she turned back to Coleman. It was the professor and Mrs. Wainwright who, at last finding a field for their kindly ambitions, flung them. selves upon Tounley and carried him off to another place. Peter was removed, crying: "Oh, now, look here, professor, I'm not dying or anything of the sort Coleman and Marjory were left alone. He suddenly and forcibly took one of her hands and the blood stained hankerchief dropped to the floor.

CHAPTER XXII.

From below they could hear the thunder of weapons and fits upon the door of the inn amid a great clamour of tongues. Sometimes there arose the argumtntative howl of the innkeeper. Above this roar, Coleman's quick words sounded in Marjory's ear.

"I've got to go. I've got to go back to the boys, but-I love you."

"Yes go, go," she whispered hastily. "You should be there, but-come back."

He held her close to him. "But you are mine, remember," he said fiercely and sternly. "You are mine-forever-As I am yours-remember." Her eyes half closed. She made intensely solemn answer. "Yes." He released her and was gone. In the glooming coffee room of the inn he found the students, the dragoman, the groom and the innkeeper armed with a motley collection of weapons which ranged from the rifle of the innkeeper to the table leg in the hands of Peter Tounley. The last named young student of archeology was in a position of temporary leadership and holding a great pow-bow with the innkeeper through the medium of peircing outcries by the dragoman. Coleman had not yet undestood why none of them had been either stabbed or shot in the fight in the street, but it seemed to him now that affairs were leading toward a crisis of tragedy. He thought of the possibilities of having the dragoman go to an upper window and harangue the people, but he saw no chance of success in such a plan. He saw that the crowd would merely howl at the dragoman while the dragoman howled at the crowd. He then asked if there was any other exit from the inn by which they could secretly escape. He learned that the door into the coffee room was the only door which pierced the four great walls. All he could then do was to find out from the innkeeper how much of a sicgc the place could stand, and to this the innkeeper answered volubly and with smiles that this hostelry would easily endure until the mercurial temper of the crowd had darted off in a new direction. It may be curious to note here that all of Peter Tounley's impassioned communication with the innkeeper had been devoted to an endeavour to learn what in the devil was the matter with these people, as a man about to be bitten by poisonous snakes should, first of all, furiously insist upon learning their exact species before deciding upon either his route, if he intended to run away, or his weapon if he intended to fight them.

The innkeeper was evidently convinced that this house would withstand the rage of the populace, and he was such an unaccountably gallant little chap that Coleman trusted entirely to his word. His only fear or suspicion was an occasional one as to the purity of the dragoman's translation.

Suddenly there was half a silence on the mob without the door. It is inconceivable that it could become altogether silent, but it was as near to a rational stillness of tongues as it was able. Then there was a loud knocking by a single fist and a new voice began to spin Greek, a voice that was somewhat like the rattle of pebbles in a tin box. Then a startling voice called out in English. "Are you in there, Rufus?"

Answers came from every English speaking person in the room in one great outburst. "Yes."

"Well, let us in," called Nora Black. "It is all right. We've got an officer with us."

"Open the door," said Coleman with speed. The little innkeeper labouriously unfastened the great bars, and when the door finally opened there appeared on the threshold Nora Black with Coke and an officer of infantry, Nora's little old companion, and Nora's dragoman.

"We saw your carriage in the street," cried the queen of comic opera as she swept into the room. She was beaming with delight. "What is all the row, anyway? O-o-oh, look at that student's nose. Who hit him? And look at Rufus. What have you boys been doing?"

Her little Greek officer of infantry had stopped the mob from flowing into the room. Coleman looked toward the door at times with some anxiety. Nora, noting it, waved her hand in careless reassurance; "Oh, it's, all right. Don't worry about them any more. He is perfectly devoted to me. He would die there on the threshold if I told him it would please me. Speaks splendid French. I found him limping along the road and gave him a lift. And now do hurry up and tell me exactly what happened." They all told what had happened, while Nora and Coke listened agape. Coke, by the way, had quite floated back to his old position with the students. It had been easy in the stress of excitement and wonder. Nobody had any time to think of the excessively remote incidents of the early morning. All minor interests were lost in the marvel of the present situation.

"Who landed you in the eye, Billie?" asked the awed Coke. "That was a bad one." " Oh, I don't know," said Billie. "You really couldn't tell who hit you, you know. It was a football rush. They had guns and knives, but they didn't use 'em. I don't know why Jinks! I'm getting pretty stiff. My face feels as if it were made of tin. Did they give you people a row, too?"

"No; only talk. That little officer managed them. Out-talked them, I suppose. Hear him buzz, now." The Wainwrights came down stairs. Nora Black went confidently forward to meet them. "You've added one more to your list of rescuers," She cried, with her glowing, triumphant smile. "Miss Black of the New York Daylight-at your service. How in the world do you manage to get yourselves into such dreadful Scrapes? You are the most remarkable people. You need a guardian. Why, you might have all been killed. How exciting it must seem to be regularly of your party." She had shaken cordiaily one of Mrs. Wainwright's hands without that lady indicating assent to the proceeding but Mrs. Wainwright had not felt repulsion. In fact she had had no emotion springing directly from it. Here again the marvel of the situation came to deny Mrs. Wainwright the right to resume a state of mind which had been so painfully interesting to her a few hours earlier.

The professor, Coleman and all the students were talking together. Coke had addressed Coleman civilly and Coleman had made a civil reply. Peace was upon them.

Nora slipped her arm lovingly through Marjbry's arm. "That Rufus! Oh, that Rufus," she cried joyously. " I'll give him a good scolding as soon as I see him alone. I might have foreseen that he would get you all into trouble. The old stupid ! "

Marjory did not appear to resent anything. "Oh, I don't think it was Mr. Coleman's fault at ail," she answered calmly. "I think it was more the fault of Peter Tounley, poor boy."

"Well, I'd be glad to believe it, I'd be glad to believe it," said Nora. "I want Rufus to keep out of that sort of thing, but he is so hot-headed and foolish." If she had pointed out her proprietary stamp on Coleman's cheek she could not have conveyed what she wanted with more clearness.

"Oh," said the impassive Marjory, "I don't think you need have any doubt as to whose fault it was, if there were any of our boys at fault. Mr. Coleman was inside when the fighting commenced, and only ran out to help the boys. He had just brought us safely through the mob, and, far from being hot-headed and foolish, he was utterly cool in manner, impressively cool, I thought. I am glad to be able to reassure you on these points, for I see that they worry you."

".Yes, they do worry me," said Nora, densely. They worry me night and day when he is away from me."

"Oh," responded Marjory, "I have never thought of Mr. Coleman as a man that one would worry about much. We consider him very self-reliant, able to take care of himself under almost any conditions, but then, of course, we do not know him at all in the way that you know him. I should think that you would find that he came off rather better than you expected from most of his difficulties. But then, of course, as. I said, you know him so much better than we do." Her easy indifference was a tacit dismissal of Coleman as a topic.

Nora, now thoroughly alert, glanced keenly into the other girl's face, but it was inscrutable. The actress had intended to go careering through a whole circle of daring illusions to an intimacy with,Coleman, but here, before she had really developed her attack, Marjory, with a few conventional and indifferent sentences, almost expressive of boredom, had made the subject of Coleman impossible. An effect was left upon Nora's mind that Marjory had been extremely polite in listening to much nervous talk about a person in whom she had no interest.

The actress was dazed. She did not know how it had all been done. Where was the head of this thing? And where Was the tail? A fog had mysteriously come upon all her brilliant prospects of seeing Marjory Wainwright suffer, and this fog was the product of a kind of magic with which she was not familiar. She could not think how to fight it. After being simply dubious throughout a long pause, she in the end went into a great rage. She glared furiously at Marjory, dropped her arm as if it had burned her and moved down upon Coleman. She must have reflected that at any rate she could make him wriggle. When she was come near to him, she called out: "Rufus!" In her tone was all the old insolent statement of ownership. Coleman might have been a poodle. She knew how to call his same in a way that was anything less than a public scandal. On this occasion everybody looked at him and then went silent, as people awaiting the startling denouement of a drama. " Rufus! " She was baring his shoulder to show the fleur-de-lis of the criminal. The students gaped.

Coleman's temper was, if one may be allowed to speak in that way, broken loose inside of him. He could hardly beeathe; he felt that his body was about to explode into a thousand fragments. He simply snarled out " What?" Almost at once he saw that she had at last goaded him into making a serious tactical mistake. It must be admitted that it is only when the relations between a man and a woman are the relations of wedlock, or at least an intimate resemblance to it, that the man snarls out " What?" to the woman. Mere lovers say " I beg your pardon? " It is only Cupid's finished product that spits like a cat. Nora Black had called him like a wife, and he had answered like a husband. For his cause, his manner could not possibly have been worse. He saw the professor stare at him in surprise and alarm, and felt the excitement of the eight students. These latter were diabolic in the celerity with which they picked out meanings. It was as plain to them as if Nora Black had said: "He is my property."

Coleman would have given his nose to have been able to recall that single reverberating word. But he saw that the scene was spelling downfall for him, and he went still more blind and desperate of it. His despair made him burn to make matters Worse. He did not want to improve anything at all. "What?" he demanded. "What do ye' want?"

Nora was sweetly reproachful. "I left my jacket in the carriage, and I want you to get it for me."

"Well, get it for yourself, do you see? Get it for yourself."

Now it is plainly to be seen that no one of the people listening there had ever heard a man speak thus to a woman who was not his wife. Whenever they had heard that form of spirited repartee it had come from the lips of a husband. Coleman's rude speech was to their ears a flat announcement of an extraordinary intimacy between Nora Black and the correspondent. Any other interpretation would not have occurred to them. It was so palpable that it greatly distressed them with its arrogance and boldness. The professor had blushed. The very milkiest word in his mind at the time was the word vulgarity.

Nora Black had won a great battle. It was her Agincourt. She had beaten the clever Coleman in a way that had left little of him but rags. However, she could have lost it all again if she had shown her feeling of elation. At Coleman's rudeness her manner indicated a mixture of sadness and embarrassment. Her suffering was so plain to the eye that Peter Tounley was instantly moved. "Can't I get your jacket for you, Miss Black?" he asked hastily, and at her grateful nod he was off at once.

Coleman was resolved to improve nothing. His overthrow seemed to him to be so complete that he could not in any way mend it without a sacrifice of his dearest prides. He turned away from them all and walked to an isolated corner of the room. He would abide no longer with them. He had been made an outcast by Nora Black, and he intended to be an outcast. There was no sense in attempting to stem this extraordinary deluge. It was better to acquiesce. Then suddenly he was angry with Marjory. He did not exactly see why he was angry at Marjory, but he was angry at her nevertheless. He thought of how he could revenge himself upon her. He decided to take horse with his groom and dragoman and proceed forthwith on the road, leaving the jumble as it stood. This would pain Marjory, anyhow, he hoped. She would feel it deeply, he hoped. Acting upon this plan, he went to the professor. Well, of course you are all right now, professor, and if you don't mind, I would like to leave you-go on ahead. I've got a considerable pressure of business on my mind, and I think I should hurry on to Athens, if you don't mind."

The professor did not seem to know what to say. " Of course, if you wish it-sorry, I'm sure-of course it is as you please-but you have been such a power in our favour-it seems too bad to lose you-but-if you wish it-if you insist-"

"Oh, yes, I quite insist," said Coleman, calmly. "I quite insist. Make your mind easy on that score, professor. I insist."

"Well, Mr. Coleman," stammered the old man. " Well, it seems a great pity to lose you-you have been such a power in our favour-"

"Oh, you are now only eight hours from the rail- way. It is very easy. You would not need my as- sistance, even if it were a benefit!

"But-" said the professor.

Coleman's dragoman came to him then and said: "There is one man here who says you made to take one rifle in the fight and was break his head. He was say he wants something for you was break his head. He says hurt."

"How much does he want?" asked Coleman, im- patiently.

The dragoman wrestled then evidently with a desire to protect this mine from outside fingers. "I-I think two gold piece plenty." "Take them," said Coleman. It seemed to him preposterous that this idiot with a broken head should interpolate upon his tragedy. "Afterward you and the groom get the three horses and we will start for Athens at once."

"For Athens? At once?" said Marjory's voice in his ear.

CHAPTER XXIII

"Om," said Coleman, "I was thinking of starting."

"Why?" asked Marjory, unconcernedly.

Coleman shot her a quick glance. "I believe my period of usefulness is quite ended," he said. with just a small betrayal of bitter feeling.

"It is certainly true that you have had a remark- able period of usefulness to us," said Marjory with a slow smile, "but if it is ended, you should not run away from us."

Coleman looked at her to see what she could mean. From many women, these words would have been equal, under the circumstances, to a command to stay, but he felt that none might know what impulses moved the mind behind that beautiful mask. In his misery he thought to hurt her into an expression of feeling by a rough speech. "I'm so in love with Nora Black, you know, that I have to be very careful of myself."

"Oh," said Marjory, never thought of that. I should think you would have to be careful of yourself." She did not seem moved in any way. Coleman despaired of finding her weak spot. She was a'damantine, this girl. He searched his mind for something to say which would be still more gross than his last outbreak, but when he felt that he was about to hit upon it, the professor interrupted with an agitated speech to Marjory. "You had better go to your mother, my child, and see that you are all ready to leave here as soon as the carriages come up."

"We have absolutely nothing to make ready," said Marjory, laughing. "But I'll go and see if mother needs anything before we start that I can get for her." She went away without bidding good-bye to Coleman. The sole maddening impression to him was that the matter of his going had not been of sufficient importance to remain longer than a moment upon her mind. At the same time he decided that he would go, irretrievably go.

Even then the dragoman entered the room. "We will pack everything -upon the horse?"

"Everything-yes."

Peter Tounley came afterward. "You are not going to bolt?"

"Yes, I'm off," answered Coleman recovering him- self for Peter's benefit. "See you in Athens, probably."

Presently the dragoman announced the readiness of the horses. Coleman shook hands with the students and the Professor amid cries of surprise and polite regret. "What? Going, oldman? Really? What for? Oh, wait for us. We're off in a few minutes. Sorry as the devil, old boy, to' see you go." He accepted their protestations with a somewhat sour face. He knew perfectly well that they were thinking of his departure as something that related to Nora Black. At the last, he bowed to the ladies as a collection. Marjory's answering bow was affable; the bow of Mrs. Wainwright spoke a resentment for some- thing; and Nora's bow was triumphant mockery. As he swung into the saddle an idea struck him with over whelming force. The idea was that he was a fool. He was a colossal imbecile. He touched the spur to his horse and the animal leaped superbly, making the Greeks hasten for safety in all directions. He was off ; he could no more return to retract his devious idiocy than he could make his horse fly to Athens. What was done was done. He could not mend it. And he felt like a man that had broken his own heart; perversely, childishly, stupidly broken his own heart. He was sure that Marjory was lost to him. No man could be degraded so publicly and resent it so crudely and still retain a Marjory. In his abasement from his defeat at the hands of Nora Black he had performed every imaginable block-headish act and had finally climaxed it all by a departure which left the tongue of Nora to speak unmolested into the ear of Marjory. Nora's victory had been a serious blow to his fortunes, but it had not been so serious as his own subsequent folly. He had generously muddled his own affairs until he could read nothing out of them but despair.

He was in the mood for hatred. He hated many people. Nora Black was the principal item, but he did not hesitate to detest the professor, Mrs. Wainwright, Coke and all the students. As for Marjory, he would revenge himself upon her. She had done nothing that he defined clearly but, at any rate, he would take revenge for it. As much as was possible, he would make her suffer. He would convince her that he was a tremendous and inexorable person. But it came upon his mind that he was powerless in all ways. If he hated many people they probably would not be even interested in his emotion and, as for his revenge upon Marjory, it was beyond his strength. He was nothing but the complaining victim of Nora Black and himself.

He felt that he would never again see Marjory, and while feeling it he began to plan his attitude when next they met. He would be very cold and reserved. At Agrinion he found that there would be no train until the next daybreak. The dragoman was excessively annoyed over it, but Coleman did not scold at all. As a matter of fact his heart had given a great joyus bound. He could not now prevent his being overtaken. They were only a few leagues away, and while he was waiting for the train they would easily cover the distance. If anybody expressed surprise at seeing him he could exhibit the logical reasons. If there had been a train starting at once he would have taken it. His pride would have put up with no subterfuge. If the Wainwrights overtook him it was because he could not help it. But he was delighted that he could not help it. There had been an inter- position by some specially beneficent fate. He felt like whistling. He spent the early half of the night in blissful smoke, striding the room which the dragoman had found for him. His head was full of plans and detached impressive scenes in which he figured before Marjory. The simple fact that there was no train away from Agrinion until the next daybreak had wrought a stupendous change in his outlook. He unhesitatingly considered it an omen of a good future. He was up before the darkness even contained presage of coming light, but near the railway station was a little hut where coffee was being served to several prospective travellers who had come even earlier to the rendezvous. There was no evidence of the Wainwrights.

Coleman sat in the hut and listened for the rumble of wheels. He was suddenly appalled that the Wainwrights were going to miss the train. Perhaps they had decided against travelling during the night. Perhaps this thing, and perhaps that thing. The morning was very cold. Closely muffled in his cloak, he went to the door and stared at where the road was whitening out of night. At the station stood a little spectral train, and the engine at intervals emitted a long, piercing scream which informed the echoing land that, in all probability, it was going to start after a time for the south. The Greeks in the coffee room were, of course, talking.

At last Coleman did hear the sound of hoofs and wheels. The three carriages swept up in grand procession. The first was laden with students ; in the second was the professor, the Greek officer, Nora Black's old lady and other persons, all looking marvellously unimportant and shelved. It was the third carriage at which Coleman stared. At first be thought the dim light deceived his vision, but in a moment he knew that his first leaping conception of the arrangement of the people in this vehicle had been perfectly correct. Nora Black and Mrs. Wainwright sat side by side on the back seat, while facing them were Coke and Marjory.

They looked cold but intimate.

The oddity of the grouping stupefied Coleman. It was anarchy, naked and unashamed. He could not imagine how such changes could have been consummated in the short time he had been away from them, but he laid it all to some startling necromancy on the part of Nora Black, some wondrous play which had captured them all because of its surpassing skill and because they were, in the main, rather gullible people. He was wrong. The magic had been wrought by the unaided foolishness of Mrs. Wainwfight. As soon as Nora Black had succeeded in creating an effect of intimacy and dependence between herself and Coleman, the professor had flatly stated to his wife that the presence of Nora Black in the party, in the inn, in the world, was a thing that did not meet his approval in any way. She should be abolished. As for Coleman, he would not defend him. He preferred not to talk to him. It made him sad. Coleman at least had been very indiscreet, very indiscreet. It was a great pity. But as for this blatant woman, the sooner they rid themselves of her, the sooner he would feel that all the world was not evil.

Whereupon Mrs. Wainwright had changed front with the speed of light and attacked with horse, foot and guns. She failed to see, she had declared, where this poor, lone girt was in great fault. Of course it was probable that she had listened to this snaky. tongued Rufus Coleman, but that was ever the mistake that women made. Oh, certainly ; the professor would like to let

Rufus Coleman off scot-free. That was the way with men. They defended each other in all cases. If wrong were done it was the woman who suffered. Now, since this poor girl was alone far off here in Greece, Mrs. Wainwright announced that she had such full sense of her duty to her sex that her conscience would not allow her to scorn and desert a sister, even if that sister was, approximately, the victim of a creature like Rufus Coleman. Perhaps the poor thing loved this wretched man, although it was hard to imagine any woman giving her heart to such. a monster.

The professor had then asked with considerable spirit for the proofs upon which Mrs. Wainwright named Coleman a monster, and had made a wry face over her completely conventional reply. He had told her categorically his opinion of her erudition in such matters.

But Mrs. Wainwright was not to be deterred from an exciting espousal of the cause of her sex. Upon the instant that the professor strenuously opposed her she became an apostle, an enlightened, uplifted apostle to the world on the wrongs of her sex. She had come down with this thing as if it were a disease. Nothing could stop her. Her husband, her daughter, all influences in other directions, had been overturned with a roar, and the first thing fully clear to the professor's mind had been that his wife was riding affably in the carriage with Nora Black. Coleman aroused when he heard one of the students cry out: "Why, there is Rufus Coleman's dragoman. He must be here." A moment later they thronged upon him. "Hi, old man, caught you again! Where did you break to? Glad to catch you, old boy. How are you making it? Where's your horse?"

"Sent the horses on to, Athens," said Coleman. He had not yet recovered his composure, and he was glad to find available this commonplace return to their exuberant greetings and questions. "Sent them on to Athens with the groom."

In the mean time the engine of the little train was screaming to heaven that its intention of starting was most serious. The diligencia careered to the station platform and unburdened. Coleman had had his dragoman place his luggage in a little first-class carriage and he defiantly entered it and closed the door. He had a sudden return to the old sense of downfall, and with it came the original rebellious desires. However, he hoped that somebody would intrude upon him. It was Peter Tounley. The student flung open the door and then yelled to the distance : "Here's an empty one." He clattered into the compartment. "Hello, Coleman! Didn't know you were in here!" At his heels came Nora Black, Coke and Marjory. "Oh!" they said, when they saw the occupant of the carriage. "Oh!" Coleman was furious. He could have distributed some of his traps in a way to create more room, but he did not move.

CHAPTER XXIV.

THERE was a demonstration of the unequalled facilities of a European railway carriage for rendering unpleasant things almost intolerable. These people could find no way to alleviate the poignancy of their position. Coleman did not know where to look. Every personal mannerism becomes accentuated in a European railway carriage. If you glance at a man, your glance defines itself as a stare. If you carefully look at nothing, you create for yourself a resemblance to all wooden-headed things. A newspaper is, then, in the nature of a preservative, and Coleman longed for a newspaper.

It was this abominable railway carriage which exacted the first display of agitation from Marjory. She flushed rosily, and her eyes wavered over the compartment. Nora Black laughed in a way that was a shock to the nerves. Coke seemed very angry, indeed, and Peter Tounley was in pitiful distress. Everything was acutely, painfully vivid, bald, painted as glaringly as a grocer's new wagon. It fulfilled those traditions which the artists deplore when they use their pet phrase on a picture, "It hurts." The damnable power of accentuation of the European railway carriage seemed, to Coleman's amazed mind, to be redoubled and redoubled.

It was Peter Tounley who seemed to be in the greatest agony. He looked at the correspondent beseechingly and said: "It's a very cold morning, Coleman." This was an actual appeal in the name of humanity.

Coleman came squarely. to the front and even grinned a little at poor Peter Tounley's misery. "Yes, it is a cold morning, Peter. I should say it to one of the coldest mornings in my recollection."

Peter Tounley had not intended a typical American emphasis on the polar conditions which obtained in the compartment at this time, but Coleman had given the word this meaning. Spontaneously every body smiled, and at once the tension was relieved. But of course the satanic powers of the railway carriage could not be altogether set at naught. Of course it fell to the lot of Coke to get the seat directly in front of Coleman, and thus, face to face, they were doomed to stare at each other.

Peter Tounley was inspired to begin conventional babble, in which he took great care to make an appearance of talking to all in the carriage. "Funny thing I never knew these mornings in Greece were so cold. I thought the climate here was quite tropical. It must have been inconvenient in the ancient times, when, I am told, people didn't wear near so many- er-clothes. Really, I don't see how they stood it. For my part, I would like nothing so much as a buffalo robe. I suppose when those great sculptors were doing their masterpieces, they had to wear gloves. Ever think of that? Funny, isn't it? Aren't you cold, Marjory? I am. jingo! Imagine the Spartans in ulsters, going out to meet an enemy in cape-overcoats, and being desired by their mothers to return with their ulsters or wrapped in them."

It was rather hard work for Peter Tounley. Both Marjory and Coleman tried to display an interest in his labours, and they laughed not at what he said, but because they believed it assisted him. The little train, meanwhile, wandered up a great green slope, and the day rapidly coloured the land.

At first Nora Black did not display a militant mood, but as time passed Coleman saw clearly that she was considering the advisability of a new attack. She had Coleman and Marjory in conjunction and where they were unable to escape from her. The opportunities were great. To Coleman, she seemed to be gloating over the possibilities of making more mischief. She was looking at him speculatively, as if considering the best place to hit him first. Presently she drawled : " Rufus, I wish you would fix my rug about me a little better." Coleman saw that this was a beginning. Peter Tounley sprang to his feet with speed and enthusiasm. "Oh, let me do it for you." He had her well muffled in the rug before she could protest, even if a protest had been rational. The young man had no idea of defending Coleman. He had no knowledge of the necessity for it. It had been merely the exercise of his habit of amiability, his chronic desire to see everybody comfortable. His passion in this direction was well known in Washurst, where the students had borrowed a phrase from the photographers in order to describe him fully in a nickname. They called him " Look-pleasant Tounley." This did not in any way antagonise his perfect willingness to fight on occasions with a singular desperation, which usually has a small stool in every mind where good nature has a throne.

"Oh, thank you very much, Mr. Tounley," said Nora Black, without gratitude. "Rufus is always so lax in these matters."

"I don't know how you know it," said Coleman boldly, and he looked her fearlessly in the eye. The battle had begun.

"Oh," responded Nora, airily, "I have had opportunity enough to know it, I should think, by this time."

"No," said Coleman, "since I have never paid you particular and direct attention, you cannot possibly know what I am lax in and what I am not lax in. I would be obliged to be of service at any time, Nora, but surely you do not consider that you have a right to my services superior to any other right."

Nora Black simply went mad, but fortunately part of her madness was in the form of speechlessness. Otherwise there might have been heard something approaching to billingsgate.

Marjory and Peter Tounley turned first hot and then cold, and looked as if they wanted to fly away; and even Coke, penned helplessly in with this unpleasant incident, seemed to have a sudden attack of distress. The only frigid person was Coleman. He had made his declaration of independence, and he saw with glee that the victory was complete. Nora Black might storm and rage, but he had announced his position in an unconventional blunt way which nobody in the carriage could fail to understand. He felt somewhat like smiling with confidence and defiance in Nora's face, but he still had the fear for Marjory.

Unexpectedly, the fight was all out of Nora Black. She had the fury of a woman scorned, but evidently she had perceived that all was over and lost. The remainder of her wrath dispensed itself in glares which Coleman withstood with great composure.

A strained silence fell upon the group which lasted until they arrived at the little port of Mesalonghi, whence they were to take ship for Patras. Coleman found himself wondering why he had not gone flatly at the great question at a much earlier period, indeed at the first moment when the great question began to make life exciting for him. He thought that if he had charged Nora's guns in the beginning they would have turned out to be the same incapable artillery. Instead of that he had run away and continued to run away until he was actually cornered and made to fight, and his easy victory had defined him as a person who had, earlier, indulged in much stupidity and cowardice. Everything had worked out so simply, his terrors had been dispelled so easily, that he probably was led to overestimate his success. And it occurred suddenly to him. He foresaw a fine occasion to talk privately to Marjory when all had boarded the steamer for Patras and he resolved to make use of it. This he believed would end the strife and conclusively laurel him.

The train finally drew up on a little stone pier and some boatmen began to scream like gulls. The steamer lay at anchor in the placid blue cove. The embarkation was chaotic in the Oriental fashion and there was the customary misery which was only relieved when the travellers had set foot on the deck of the steamer. Coleman did not devote any premature attention to finding Marjory, but when the steamer was fairly out on the calm waters of the Gulf of Corinth, he saw her pacing to and fro with Peter Tounley. At first he lurked in the distance waiting for an opportunity, but ultimately he decided to make his own opportunity. He approached them. "Marjory, would you let me speak to you alone for a few moments? You won't mind, will you, Peter?"

"Oh, no, certainly not," said Peter Tounley.

"Of course. It is not some dreadful revelation, is it?" said Marjory, bantering him coolly.

"No," answered Coleman, abstractedly. He was thinking of what he was going to say. Peter Tounley vanished around the corner of a deck-house and Marjory and Coleman began to pace to and fro even as Marjory and Peter Tounley had done. Coleman had thought to speak his mind frankly and once for all, and on the train he had invented many clear expressions of his feeling. It did not appear that he had forgotten them. It seemed, more, that they had become entangled in his mind in such a way that he could not unravel the end of his discourse.

In the pause, Marjory began to speak in admiration of the scenery. "I never imagined that Greece was so full of mountains. One reads so much of the Attic Plains, but aren't these mountains royal? They look so rugged and cold, whereas the bay is absolutely as blue as the old descriptions of a summer sea."

"I wanted to speak to you about Nora Black," said Coleman.

"Nora Black? Why?" said Marjory, lifting her eye-brows.

You know well enough," said Coleman, in a head. long fashion. "You must know, you must have seen it. She knows I care for you and she wants to stop it. And she has no right to-to interfere. She is a fiend, a perfect fiend. She is trying to make you feel that I care for her."

"And don't you care for her?" asked Marjory.

"No," said Coleman, vehemently. "I don't care for her at all."

"Very well," answered Marjory, simply. "I believe you." She managed to give the words the effect of a mere announcement that she believed him and it was in no way plain that she was glad or that she esteemed the matter as being of consequence.

He scowled at her in dark resentment. "You mean by that, I suppose, that you don't believe me?"

"Oh," answered Marjory, wearily, "I believe you. I said so. Don't talk about it any more."

"Then," said Coleman, slowly, "you mean that you do not care whether I'm telling the truth or not?"

"Why, of course I care," she said. "Lying is not nice."

He did not know, apparently, exactly how to deal with her manner, which was actually so pliable that-it was marble, if one may speak in that way. He looked ruefully at the sea. He had expected a far easier time. "Well—" he began.

"Really," interrupted Marjory, "this is something which I do not care to discuss. I would rather you would not speak to me at all about it. It seems too -too-bad. I can readily give you my word that I believe you, but I would prefer you not to try to talk to me about it or-anything of that sort. Mother!"

Mrs. Wainwright was hovering anxiously in the vicinity, and she now bore down rapidly upon the pair. "You are very nearly to Patras," she said reproachfully to her daughter, as if the fact had some fault of Marjory's concealed in it. She in no way acknowledged the presence of Coleman.

"Oh, are we?" cried Marjory.

"Yes," said Mrs. Wainwright. "We are."

She stood waiting as if she expected Marjory to instantly quit Coleman. The girl wavered a moment and then followed her mother. "Good-bye." she said. "I hope we may see you again in Athens." It was a command to him to travel alone with his servant on the long railway journey from Patras to Athens. It was a dismissal of a casual acquaintance given so graciously that it stung him to the depths of his pride. He bowed his adieu and his thanks. When the yelling boatmen came again, he and his man proceeded to the shore in an early boat without looking in any way after the welfare of the others.

At the train, the party split into three sections. Coleman and his man had one compartment, Nora Black and her squad had another, and the Wainwrights and students occupied two more.

The little officer was still in tow of Nora Black. He was very enthusiastic. In French she directed him to remain silent, but he did not appear to understand. " You tell him," she then said to her dragoman, " to sit in a corner and not to speak until I tell him to, or I won't have him in here." She seemed anxious to unburden herself to the old lady companion. " Do you know," she said, "that girl has a nerve like steel. I tried to break it there in that inn, but I couldn't budge her. If I am going to have her beaten I must prove myself to be a very, very artful person."

"Why did you try to break her nerve?" asked the old lady, yawning. "Why do you want to have her beaten?"

"Because I do, old stupid," answered Nora. "You should have heard the things I said to her."

"About what?"

"About Coleman. Can't you understand anything at all?"

"And why should you say anything about Coleman to her?" queried the old lady, still hopelessly befogged.

"Because," cried Nora, darting a look of wrath at her companion, "I want to prevent that marriage." She had been betrayed into this avowal by the singularly opaque mind of the old lady. The latter at once sat erect. - " Oh, ho," she said, as if a ray of light had been let into her head. "Oh, ho. So that's it, is it?"

"Yes, that's it, rejoined Nora, shortly.

The old lady was amazed into a long period of meditation. At last she spoke depressingly. "Well, how are you going to prevent it? Those things can't be done in these days at all. If they care for each other-"

Nora burst out furiously. "Don't venture opinions until you know what you are talking about, please. They don't care for each other, do you see? She cares for him, but he don't give a snap of his fingers for her."

"But," cried the bewildered lady, "if he don't care for her, there will be nothing to prevent. If he don't care for her, he won't ask her to marry him, and so there won't be anything to prevent."

Nora made a broad gesture of impatience. "Oh, can't you get anything through your head? Haven't you seen that the girl has been the only young woman in that whole party lost up there in the mountains, and that naturally more than half of the men still think they are in love with her? That's what it is. Can't you see? It always happens that way. Then Coleman comes along and makes a fool of himself with the others."

The old lady spoke up brightly as if at last feeling able to contribute something intelligent to the talk. " Oh, then, he does care for her."

Nora's eyes looked as if their glance might shrivel the old lady's hair. "Don't I keep telling you that it is no such thing? Can't you understand? It is all glamour! Fascination! Way up there in the wilderness! Only one even passable woman in sight."

"I don't say that I am so very keen," said the old lady, somewhat offended, "but I fail to see where I could improve when first you tell me he don't care for her, and then you tell me that he does care for her."

"Glamour,' ' Fascination,'" quoted Nora. "Don't you understand the meaning of the words?"

"Well," asked the other, didn't he know her, then, before he came over here?"

Nora was silent for a time, while a gloom upon her face deepened. It had struck her that the theories for which she protested so energetically might not be of such great value. Spoken aloud, they had a sudden new flimsiness. Perhaps she had reiterated to herself that Coleman was the victim of glamour only because she wished it to be true. One theory, however, re- mained unshaken. Marjory was an artful rninx, with no truth in her.

She presently felt the necessity of replying to the question of her companion. "Oh," she said, carelessly, "I suppose they were acquainted-in a way."

The old lady was giving the best of her mind to the subject. "If that's the case-" she observed, musingly, "if that's the case, you can't tell what is between 'em."

The talk had so slackened that Nora's unfortunate Greek admirer felt that here was a good opportunity to present himself again to the notice of the actress. The means was a smile and a French sentence, but his reception would have frightened a man in armour. His face blanched with horror at the storm, he had invoked, and he dropped limply back as if some one had shot him. "You tell this little snipe to let me alone! " cried Nora, to the dragoman. "If he dares to come around me with any more of those Parisian dude speeches, I-I don't know what I'll do! I won't have it, I say." The impression upon the dragoman was hardly less in effect. He looked with bulging eyes at Nora, and then began to stammer at the officer. The latter's voice could sometimes be heard in awed whispers for the more elaborate explanation of some detail of the tragedy. Afterward, he remained meek and silent in his corner, barely more than a shadow, like the proverbial husband of imperious beauty.

"Well," said the old lady, after a long and thoughtful pause, "I don't know, I'm sure, but it seems to me that if Rufus Coleman really cares for that girl, there isn't much use in trying to stop him from getting her. He isn't that kind of a man."

"For heaven's sake, will you stop assuming that he does care for her?" demanded Nora, breathlessly.

"And I don't see," continued the old lady, "what you want to prevent him for, anyhow."

CHAPTER XXV.

" I FEEL in this radiant atmosphere that there could be no such thing as war-men striving together in black and passionate hatred." The professor's words were for the benefit of his wife and daughter. ,He was viewing the sky-blue waters of the Gulf of Corinth with its background of mountains that in the sunshine were touched here and there with a copperish glare. The train was slowly sweeping along the southern shore. "It is strange to think of those men fighting up there in the north. And it is strange to think that we ourselves are but just returning from it."

"I cannot begin to realise it yet," said Mrs. Wainwright, in a high voice.

"Quite so," responded the professor, reflectively.

"I do not suppose any of us will realise it fully for some time. It is altogether too odd, too very odd."

"To think of it!" cried Mrs. Wainwright. "To think of it! Supposing those dreadful Albanians or those awful men from the Greek mountains had caught us! Why, years from now I'll wake up in the night and think of it! "

The professor mused. "Strange that we cannot feel it strongly now. My logic tells me to be aghast that we ever got into such a place, but my nerves at present refuse to thrill. I am very much afraid that this singular apathy of ours has led us to be unjust to poor Coleman." Here Mrs. Wainwright objected. "Poor Coleman! I don't see why you call him poor Coleman."

"Well," answered the professor, slowly, "I am in doubt about our behaviour. It-"

"Oh," cried the wife, gleefully," in doubt about our behaviour! I'm in doubt about his behaviour."

"So, then, you do have a doubt. of his behaviour?" " Oh, no," responded Mrs. Wainwright, hastily, " not about its badness. What I meant to say was that in the face of his outrageous conduct with that- that woman, it is curious that you should worry about our behaviour. It surprises me, Harrison."

The professor was wagging his head sadly. "I don't know I don't know It seems hard to judge * * I hesitate to-"

Mrs. Wainwright treated this attitude with disdain. "It is not hard to judge," she scoffed, "and I fail to see why you have any reason for hesitation at all. Here he brings this woman — "

The professor got angry. "Nonsense! Nonsense! I do not believe that he brought her. If I ever saw a spectacle of a woman bringing herself, it was then. You keep chanting that thing like an outright parrot."

"Well," retorted Mrs. Wainwright, bridling, "I suppose you imagine that you understand such things, Men usually think that, but I want to tell you that you seem to me utterly blind."

"Blind or not, do stop the everlasting reiteration of that sentence."

Mrs. Wainwright passed into an offended silence, and the professor, also silent, looked with a gradually dwindling indignation at the scenery.

Night was suggested in the sky before the train was near to Athens. "My trunks," sighed Mrs. Wainwright. "How glad I will be to get back to my trunks! Oh, the dust! Oh, the misery ! Do find out when we will get there, Harrison. Maybe the train is late."

But, at last, they arrived in Athens, amid a darkness which was confusing, and, after no more than the common amount of trouble, they procured carriages and were taken to the hotel. Mrs. Wainwright's impulses now dominated the others in the family. She had one passion after another. The majority of the servants in the hotel pretended that they spoke English, but, in three minutes, she drove them distracted with the abundance and violence of her requests. It came to pass that in the excitement the old couple quite forgot Marjory. It was not until Mrs. Wainwright, then feeling splendidly, was dressed for dinner, that she thought to open Marjory's door and go to render a usual motherly supervision of the girl's toilet.

There was no light: there did not seem to be any- body in the room. "Marjory ! " called the mother, in alarm. She listened for a moment and then ran hastily out again. "Harrison ! " she cried. "I can't find Marjory!" The professor had been tying his cravat. He let the loose ends fly. "What?" he ejaculated, opening his mouth wide. Then they both rushed into Marjory's room. "Marjory!" beseeched the old man in a voice which would have invoked the grave.

The answer was from the bed. "Yes?" It was low, weary, tearful. It was not like Marjory. It was dangerously the voice of a heart-broken woman. They hurried forward with outcries. "Why, Marjory! Are you ill, child? How long have you been lying in the dark? Why didn't you call us? Are you ill?"

"No," answered this changed voice, "I am not ill. I only thought I'd rest for a time. Don't bother."

The professor hastily lit the gas and then father and mother turned hurriedly to the bed. In the first of the illumination they saw that tears were flowing unchecked down Marjory's face.

The effect of this grief upon the professor was, in part, an effect of fear. He seemed afraid to touch it, to go near it. He could, evidently, only remain in the outskirts, a horrified spectator. The mother, how. ever, flung her arms about her daughter. "Oh, Marjory! " She, too, was weeping.

The girl turned her face to the pillow and held out a hand of protest. "Don't, mother! Don't!"

"Oh, Marjory! Oh, Marjory!"

"Don't, mother. Please go away. Please go away. Don't speak at all, I beg of you."

"Oh, Marjory! Oh, Marjory!"

"Don't." The girl lifted a face which appalled them. It had something entirely new in it. "Please go away, mother. I will speak to father, but I won't -I can't-I can't be pitied."

Mrs. Wainwright looked at her husband. "Yes," said the old man, trembling. "Go! " She threw up her hands in a sorrowing gesture that was not without its suggestion that her exclusion would be a mistake. She left the room.

The professor dropped on his knees at the bedside and took one of Marjory's hands. His voice dropped to its tenderest note. "Well, my Marjory?"

She had turned her face again to the pillow. At last she answered in muffled tones, "You know." Thereafter came a long silence full of sharpened pain. It was Marjory who spoke first. "I have saved my pride, daddy, but-I have-lost-everything —else." Even her sudden resumption of the old epithet of her childhood was an additional misery to the old man. He still said no word. He knelt, gripping her fingers and staring at the wall.

"Yes, I have lost-everything-else."

The father gave a low groan. He was thinking deeply, bitterly. Since one was only a human being, how was one going to protect beloved hearts assailed with sinister fury from the inexplicable zenith? In this tragedy he felt as helpless as an old grey ape. He did not see a possible weapon with which he could defend his child from the calamity which was upon her. There was no wall, no shield which could turn this sorrow from the heart of his child. If one of his hands loss could have spared her, there would have been a sacrifice of his hand, but he was potent for nothing. He could only groan and stare at the wall. He reviewed the past half in fear that he would suddenly come upon his error which was now the cause of Marjory's tears. He dwelt long upon the fact that in Washurst he had refused his consent to Marjory's marriage with Coleman, but even now he could not say that his judgment was not correct. It was simply that the doom of woman's woe was upon Marjory, this ancient woe of the silent tongue and the governed will, and he could only kneel at the bedside and stare at the wall.

Marjory raised her voice in a laugh. "Did I betray myself? Did I become the maiden all forlorn? Did I giggle to show people that I did not care? No-I did not-I did not. And it was such a long time, daddy! Oh, such a long time! I thought we would never get here. I thought I would never get where I could be alone like this, where I could-cry-if I wanted to. I am not much of - a crier, am I, daddy? But this time-this-time-"

She suddenly drew herself over near to her father and looked at him. "Oh, daddy, I want to tell you one thing. just one simple little thing." She waited then, and while she waited her father's head went lower and lower. "Of course, you know-I told you once. I love him! I love him! Yes, probably he is a rascal, but, do you know, I don't think I would mind if he was a-an assassin. This morning I sent him away, but, daddy, he didn't want to go at all. I know he didn't. This Nora Black is nothing to him. I know she is not. I am sure of it. Yes-I am sure of it. * * * I never expected to talk this way to any living creature, but-you are so good, daddy. Dear old daddy—-"

She ceased, for she saw that her father was praying.

The sight brought to her a new outburst of sobbing, for her sorrow now had dignity and solemnity from the bowed white head of her old father, and she felt that her heart was dying amid the pomp of the church. It was the last rites being performed at the death-bed. Into her ears came some imagining of the low melancholy chant of monks in a gloom.

Finally her father arose. He kissed her on the brow. "Try to sleep, dear," he said. He turned out the gas and left the room. His thought was full of chastened emotion.

But if his thought was full of chastened emotion, it received some degree of shock when he arrived in the presence of Mrs. Wainwright. "Well, what is all this about?" she demanded, irascibly. "Do you mean to say that Marjory is breaking her heart over that man Coleman? It is all your fault-" She was apparently still ruffled over her exclusion.

When the professor interrupted her he did not speak with his accustomed spirit, but from something novel in his manner she recognised a danger signal. " Please do not burst out at it in that way."

"Then it Is true?" she asked. Her voice was a mere awed whisper.

"It is true," answered the professor.

"Well," she said, after reflection, "I knew it. I alway's knew it. If you hadn't been so blind! You turned like a weather-cock in your opinions of Coleman. You never could keep your opinion about him for more than an hour. Nobody could imagine what you might think next. And now you see the result of it! I warned you! I told you what this Coleman was, and if Marjory is suffering now, you have only yourself to blame for it. I warned you! "

"If it is my fault," said the professor, drearily, "I hope God may forgive me, for here is a great wrong to my daughter."

Well, if you had done as I told you-" she began.

Here the professor revolted. "Oh, now, do not be- gin on that," he snarled, peevishly. Do not begin on that."

"Anyhow," said Mrs. Wainwright, it is time that we should be going down to dinner. Is Marjory com- ing?"

"No, she is not," answered the professor, "and I do not know as I shall go myself."

"But you must go. Think how it would look! All the students down there dining without us, and cutting up capers! You must come."

"Yes," he said, dubiously, "but who will look after Marjory? "

"She wants to be left alone," announced Mrs. Wainwright, as if she was the particular herald of this news. "She wants to be left alone."

"Well, I suppose we may as well go down." Before they went, the professor tiptoed into his daughter's room. In the darkness he could only see her waxen face on the pillow, and her two eyes gazing fixedly at the ceiling. He did not speak, but immediately withdrew, closing the door noiselessly behind him.

CHAPTER XXVI.

IF the professor and Mrs. Wainwright had descended sooner to a lower floor of the hotel, they would have found reigning there a form of anarchy. The students were in a smoking room which was also an entrance hall to the dining room, and because there was in the middle of this apartment a fountain containing gold fish, they had been moved to license and sin. They had all been tubbed and polished and brushed and dressed until they were exuberantly beyond themselves. The proprietor of the hotel brought in his dignity and showed it to them, but they minded it no more than if he had been only a common man. He drew himself to his height and looked gravely at them and they jovially said: "Hello, Whiskers." American college students are notorious in their country for their inclination to scoff at robed and crowned authority, and, far from being awed by the dignity of the hotel-keeper, they were delighted with it. It was something with which to sport. With immeasurable impudence, they copied his attitude, and, standing before him, made comic speeches, always alluding with blinding vividness to his beard. His exit disappointed them. He had not remained long under fire. They felt that they could have interested themselves with him an entire evening. "Come back, Whiskers! Oh, come back!" Out in the main hall he made a gesture of despair to some of his gaping minions and then fled to seclusion.

A formidable majority then decided that Coke was a gold fish, and that therefore his proper place was in the fountain. They carried him to it while he strug. gled madly. This quiet room with its crimson rugs and gilded mirrors seemed suddenly to have become an important apartment in hell. There being as yet no traffic in the dining room, the waiters were all at liberty to come to the open doors, where they stood as men turned to stone. To them, it was no less than incendiarism.

Coke, standing with one foot on the floor and the other on the bottom of the shallow fountain, blasphemed his comrades in a low tone, but with intention. He was certainly desirous of lifting his foot out of the water, but it seemed that all movement to that end would have to wait until he had successfully ex- pressed his opinions. In the meantime, there was heard slow footsteps and the rustle of skirts, and then some people entered the smoking room on their way to dine. Coke took his foot hastily out of the fountain.

The faces of the men of the arriving party went blank, and they turned their cold and pebbly eyes straight to the front, while the ladies, after little expressions of alarm, looked As if they wanted to run. In fact, the whole crowd rather bolted from this extraordinary scene.

"There, now," said Coke bitterly to his companions. "You see? We looked like little school-boys-"

"Oh, never mind, old man," said Peter Tounley. "We'll forgive you, although you did embarrass us. But, above everything, don't drip. Whatever you do, don't drip."

The students took this question of dripping and played upon it until they would have made quite insane anybody but another student. They worked it into all manner of forms, and hacked and haggled at Coke until he was driven to his room to seek other apparel. "Be sure and change both legs," they told him. "Remember you can't change one leg without changing both legs."

After Coke's departure, the United States minister entered the room, and instantly they were subdued. It was not his lofty station-that affected them. There are probably few stations that would have at all affected them. They became subdued because they unfeignedly liked the United States minister. They, were suddenly a group of well-bred, correctly attired young men who had not put Coke's foot in the fountain. Nor had they desecrated the majesty of the hotelkeeper.

"Well, I am delighted," said the minister, laughing as he shook hands with them all. "I was not sure I would ever see you again. You are not to be trusted, and, good boys as you are, I'll be glad to see you once and forever over the boundary of my jurisdiction. Leave Greece, you vagabonds. However, I am truly delighted to see you all safe."

"Thank you, sir," they said.

"How in the world did you get out of it? You must be remarkable chaps. I thought you were in a hopeless position. I wired and cabled everywhere I could, but I could find out nothing."

"A correspondent," said Peter Tounley. "I don't know if you have met him. His name is Coleman. He found us."

"Coleman?" asked the minister, quickly.

"Yes, sir. He found us and brought us out safely."

"Well, glory be to Coleman," exclaimed the min- ister, after a long sigh of surprise. "Glory be to Cole- man! I never thought he could do it."

The students were alert immediately. "Why, did you know about it, sir? Did he tell you he was coming after us?"

"Of course. He came tome here in Athens. and asked where you were. I told him you were in a peck of trouble. He acted quietly and somewhat queerly,. and said that he would try to look you up. He said you were friends of his. I warned him against trying it. Yes, I said it was impossible, I had no idea that he would really carry the thing out. But didn't he tell you anything about this himself?"

"No, sir'" answered Peter Tounley. "He never said much about it. I think he usually con- tended that it was mainly an accident."

"It was no accident," said the minister, sharply. "When a man starts out to do a thing and does it, you can't say it is an accident."

"I didn't say so, sir," said Peter Tounley diffidently.

"Quite true, quite true ! You didn't, but-this Coleman must be a man!"

"We think so, sir," said be who was called Billie. "He certainly brought us through in style."

"But how did he manage it?" cried the minister, keenly interested. "How did he do it?"

"It is hard to say, sir. But he did it. He met us in the dead of night out near Nikopolis-"

"Near Nikopolis?"

"Yes, sir. And he hid us in a forest while a fight was going on, and then in the morning he brought us inside the Greek lines. Oh, there is a lot to tell-"

Whereupon they told it, or as much as they could of it. In the end, the minister said: "Well, where are the professor and Mrs. Wainwright? I want you all to dine with me to-night. I am dining in the public room, but you won't mind that after Epirus." " They should be down now, sir," answered a Student.

People were now coming rapidly to dinner and presently the professor and Mrs. Wainwright appeared. The old man looked haggard and white. He accepted the minister's warm greeting with a strained pathetic smile. "Thank you. We are glad to return safely."

Once at dinner the minister launched immediately into the subject of Coleman. "He must be altogether a most remarkable man. When he told me, very quietly, that he was going to try to rescue you, I frankly warned him against any such attempt. I thought he would merely add one more to a party of suffering people. But the. boys tell- me that he did actually rescue you."

"Yes, he did," said the professor. "It was a very gallant performance, and we are very grateful."

"Of course," spoke Mrs. Wainwright, "we might have rescued ourselves. We were on the right road, and all we had to do was to keep going on."

"Yes, but I understand-" said the minister. "I understand he took you into a wood to protect you from that fight, and generally protected you from all, kinds of trouble. It seems wonderful to me, not so much because it was done as because it was done by the man who, some time ago, calmy announced to me that he was going to do it. Extraordinary."

"Of course," said Mrs. Wainwright. "Oh, of course."

"And where is he now?" asked the minister suddenly. "Has he now left you to the mercies of civilisation? "

There was a moment's curious stillness, and then Mrs. Wainwright used that high voice which-the students believed-could only come to her when she was about to say something peculiarly destructive to the sensibilities. "Oh, of course, Mr. Coleman rendered us a great service, but in his private character he is not a man whom we exactly care to associate with."

"Indeed" said the minister staring. Then he hastily addressed the students. "Well, isn't this a comic war? Did you ever imagine war could be like this?" The professor remained looking at his wife with an air of stupefaction, as if she had opened up to him visions of imbecility of which he had not even dreamed. The students loyally began to chatter at the minister. "Yes, sir, it is a queer war. After all their bragging, it is funny to hear that they are running away with such agility. We thought, of course, of the old Greek wars."

Later, the minister asked them all to his rooms for coffee and cigarettes, but the professor and Mrs. Wainwright apologetically retired to their own quarters. The minister and the students made clouds of smoke, through which sang the eloquent descriptions of late adventures.

The minister had spent days of listening to questions from the State Department at Washington as to the whereabouts of the Wainwright party. "I suppose you know that you,are very prominent people in, the United States just now? Your pictures must have been in all the papers, and there must have been columns printed about you. My life here was made almost insupportable by your friends, who consist, I should think, of about half the population of the country. Of course they laid regular siege to the department. I am angry at Coleman for only one thing. When he cabled the news of your rescue to his news. paper from Arta, he should have also wired me, if only to relieve my failing mind. My first news of your escape was from Washington-think of that."

"Coleman had us all on his hands at Arta," said Peter Tounley. "He was a fairly busy man."

"I suppose so," said the minister. "By the way," he asked bluntly, "what is wrong with him? What did Mrs. Wainwright mean?"

They were silent for a time, but it seemed plain to him that it was not evidence that his question had demoralised them. They seemed to be deliberating upon the form of answer. Ultimately Peter Tounley coughed behind his hand. "You see, sir," he began, " there is-well, there is a woman in the case. Not that anybody would care to speak of it excepting to you. But that is what is the cause of things, and then, you see, Mrs. Wainwright is-well-" He hesitated a moment and then completed his sentence in the ingenuous profanity of his age and condition. "She is rather an extraordinary old bird."

"But who is the woman?

"Why, it is Nora Blaick, the actress." "Oh," cried the minister, enlightened. "Her Why, I saw her here. She was very beautiful, but she seemed harmless enough. She was somewhat-er-confident, perhaps, but she did not alarm me. She called upon me, and I confess I-why, she seemed charming." " She's sweet on little Rufus. That's the point," said an oracular voice.

"Oh," cried the host, suddenly. "I remember. She asked me where he was. She said she had heard he was in Greece, and I told her he had gone knight- erranting off after you people. I remember now. I suppose she posted after him up to Arta, eh?"

"That's it. And so she asked you where he was?

"Yes."

"Why, that old flamingo-Mrs. Wainwright insists that it was a rendezvous."

Every one exchanged glances and laughed a little. " And did you see any actual fighting?" asked the minister.

"No. We only beard it-"

Afterward, as they were trooping up to their rooms, Peter Tounley spoke musingly. "Well, it looks to me now as if Old Mother Wainwright was just a bad-minded old hen."

"Oh, I don't know. How is one going to tell what the truth is?"

"At any rate, we are sure now that Coleman had nothing to do with Nora's debut in Epirus."

They had talked much of Coleman, but in their tones there always had been a note of indifference or carelessness. This matter, which to some people was as vital and fundamental as existence, remained to others who knew of it only a harmless detail of life, with no terrible powers, and its significance had faded greatly when had ended the close associations of the late adventure.

After dinner the professor had gone directly to his daughter's room. Apparently she had not moved. He knelt by the bedside again and took one of her hands. She was not weeping. She looked at him and smiled through the darkness. "Daddy, I would like to die," she said. "I think-yes-I would like to die."

For a long time the old man was silent, but he arose at last with a definite abruptness and said hoarsely " Wait! "

Mrs. Wainwright was standing before her mirror with her elbows thrust out at angles above her head, while her fingers moved in a disarrangement of 'her hair. In the glass she saw a reflection of her husband coming from Marjory's room, and his face was set with some kind of alarming purpose. She turned to watch him actually, but he walked toward the door into the corridor and did not in any wise heed her.

"Harrison! " she called. "Where are you going?"

He turned a troubled face upon her, and, as if she had hailed him in his sleep, he vacantly said: "What?"

"Where are you going?" she demanded with increasing trepidation.

He dropped heavily into a chair. "Going?" he repeated.

She was angry. "Yes! Going? Where are you going?"

"I am going-" he answered, "I am going to see Rufus Coleman."

Mrs. Wainwright gave voice to a muffled scream. "Not about Marjory? "

"Yes," he said, "about Marjory."

It was now Mrs. Wainwright's turn to look at her husband with an air of stupefaction as if he had opened up to her visions of imbecility of which she had not even dreamed. "About Marjory!" she gurgled. Then suddenly her wrath flamed out. "Well, upon my word, Harrison Wainwright, you are, of all men in the world, the most silly and stupid. You are absolutely beyond belief. Of all projects! And what do you think Marjory would have to say of it if she knew it? I suppose you think she would like it? Why, I tell you she would keep her right hand in the fire until it was burned off before she would allow you to do such a thing."

"She must never know it," responded the professor, in dull misery.

"Then think of yourself! Think of the shame of it! The shame of it ! "

The professor raised his eyes for an ironical glance at his wife. "Oh I have thought of the shame of it!"

"And you'll accomplish nothing," cried Mrs. Wainwright. "You'll accomplish nothing. He'll only laugh at you."

"If he laughs at me, he will laugh at nothing but a poor, weak, unworldly old man. It is my duty to go."

Mrs. Wainwright opened her mouth as if she was about to shriek. After choking a moment she said: " Your duty? Your duty to go and bend the knee to that man? Yourduty?"

"'It is my duty to go,'" he repeated humbly. "If I can find even one chance for my daughter's happiness in a personal sacrifice. He can do no more than he can do no more than make me a little sadder."

His wife evidently understood his humility as a tribute to her arguments and a clear indication that she had fatally undermined his original intention. " Oh, he would have made you sadder," she quoth grimly. "No fear! Why, it was the most insane idea I ever heard of."

The professor arose wearily. "Well, I must be going to this work. It is a thing to have ended quickly." There was something almost biblical in his manner.

"Harrison! " burst out his wife in amazed lamentation. You are not really going to do it? Not really!"

"I am going to do it," he answered.

"Well, there! " ejaculated Mrs. Wainwright to the heavens. She was, so to speak, prostrate. "Well, there! "

As the professor passed out of the door she cried beseechingly but futilely after him. "Harrison." In a mechanical way she turned then back to the mirror and resumed the disarrangement of her hair. She ad- dressed her image. "Well, of all stupid creatures under the sun, men are the very worst! " And her image said this to her even as she informed it, and afterward they stared at each other in a profound and tragic reception and acceptance of this great truth. Presently she began to consider the advisability of going to Marjdry with the whole story. Really, Harrison must not be allowed to go on blundering until the whole world heard that Marjory was trying to break her heart over that common scamp of a Coleman. It seemed to be about time for her, Mrs. Wainwright, to come into the situation and mend matters.

CHAPTER XXVII.

WHEN the professor arrived before Coleman's door, he paused a moment and looked at it. Previously, he could not have imagined that a simple door would ever so affect him. Every line of it seemed to express cold superiority and disdain. It was only the door of a former student, one of his old boys, whom, as the need arrived, he had whipped with his satire in the class rooms at Washurst until the mental blood had come, and all without a conception of his ultimately arriving before the door of this boy in the attitude of a supplicant. He would not say it; Coleman probably would not say it; but-they would both know it. A single thought of it, made him feel like running away. He would never dare to knock on that door. It would be too monstrous. And even as he decided that he was afraid to knock, he knocked.

Coleman's voice said; "Come in." The professor opened the door. The correspondent, without a coat, was seated at a paper-littered table. Near his elbow, upon another table, was a tray from which he had evidently dined and also a brandy bottle with several recumbent bottles of soda. Although he had so lately arrived at the hotel he had contrived to diffuse his traps over the room in an organised disarray which represented a long and careless occupation if it did not represent t'le scene of a scuffle. His pipe was in his mouth.

After a first murmur of surprise, he arose and reached in some haste for his coat. "Come in, professor, come in," he cried, wriggling deeper into his jacket as he held out his hand. He had laid aside his pipe and had also been very successful in flinging a newspaper so that it hid the brandy and soda. This act was a feat of deference to the professor's well known principles.

"Won't you sit down, sir?" said Coleman cordially. His quick glance of surprise had been immediately suppressed and his manner was now as if the professor's call was a common matter.

"Thank you, Mr. Coleman, I-yes, I will sit down,". replied the old man. His hand shook as he laid it on the back of the chair and steadied himself down into it. "Thank you!" -

Coleman looked at him with a great deal of ex- pectation.

"Mr. Coleman ! "

"Yes, sir."

"I —"

He halted then and passed his hand over his face. His eyes did not seem to rest once upon Coleman, but they occupied themselves in furtive and frightened glances over the room. Coleman could make neither head nor tail of the affair. He would not have believed any man's statement that the professor could act in such an extraordinary fashion. "Yes, sir," he said again suggestively. The simple strategy resulted in a silence that was actually awkward. Coleman, despite his bewilderment, hastened into a preserving gossip. "I've had a great many cables waiting for me for heaven knows- how long and others have been arriving in flocks to-night. You have no idea of the row in America, professor. Why, everybody must have gone wild over the lost sheep. My paper has cabled some things that are evidently for you. For instance, here is one that says a new puzzle-game called Find the Wainwright Party has had a big success. Think of that, would you." Coleman grinned at the professor. "Find the Wainwright Party, a new puzzle-game."

The professor had seemed grateful for Coleman's tangent off into matters of a light vein. "Yes?" he said, almost eagerly. "Are they selling a game really called that?"

"Yes, really," replied Coleman. "And of course you know that-er-well, all the Sunday papers would of course have big illustrated articles-full pages- with your photographs and general private histories pertaining mostly to things which are none of their business." "Yes, I suppose they would do that," admitted the professor. "But I dare say it may not be as bad as you suggest."

"Very like not," said Coleman. "I put it to you forcibly so that in the future the blow will not be too cruel. They are often a weird lot."

"Perhaps they can't find anything very bad about us."

"Oh, no. And besides the whole episode will probably be forgotten by the time you return to the United States."

342

They talked onin this way slowly, strainedly, until they each found that the situation would soon become insupportable. The professor had come for a distinct purpose and Coleman knew it; they could not sit there lying at each other forever. Yet when he saw the pain deepening in the professor's eyes, the correspondent again ordered up his trivialities. "Funny thing. My paper has been congratulating me, you know, sir, in a wholesale fashion, and I think-I feel sure-that they have been exploiting my name all over the country as the Heroic Rescuer. There is no sense in trying to stop them, because they don't care whether it is true or not true. All they want is the privilege of howling out that their correspondent rescued you, and they would take that privilege without in any ways worrying if I refused my consent. You see, sir? I wouldn't like you to feel that I was such a strident idiot as I doubtless am appearing now before the public."

"No," said the professor absently. It was plain that he had been a very slack listener. "I-Mr. Coleman-" he began.

"Yes, sir," answered Coleman promptly and gently.

It was obviously only a recognition of the futility of further dallying that was driving the old man on- ward. He knew, of course, that if he was resolved to take this step, a longer delay would simply make it harder for him. The correspondent, leaning forward, was watching him almost breathlessly.

"Mr. Coleman, I understand-or at least I am led to believe-that you-at one time, proposed marriage to my daughter?"

The faltering words did not sound as if either man had aught to do with them. They were an expression by the tragic muse herself. Coleman's jaw fell and he looked glassily at the professor. He said: "Yes!" But already his blood was leaping as his mind flashed everywhere in speculation.

"I refused my consent to that marriage," said the old man more easily. "I do not know if the matter has remained important to you, but at any rate, I-I retract my refusal."

Suddenly the blank expression left Coleman's face and he smiled with sudden intelligence, as if informa- tion of what the professor had been saying had just reached him. In this smile there was a sudden be. trayal, too, of something keen and bitter which had lain hidden in the man's mind. He arose and made a step towards the professor and held out his hand. "Sir, I thank you from the bottom of my heart!" And they both seemed to note with surprise that Coleman's voice had broken.

The professor had arisen to receive Coleman's hand. His nerve was now of iron and he was very formal. "I judge from your tone that I have not made a mistake-something which I feared."

Coleman did not seem to mind the professor's formality. " Don't fear anything. Won't you sit down again? Will you have a cigar. * * No, I couldn't tell you how glad I am. How glad I am. I feel like a fool. It —"

But the professor fixed him with an Arctic eye and bluntly said: "You love her?"

The question steadied Coleman at once. He looked undauntedly straight into the professor's face. He simply said: "I love her! "

"You love her?" repeated the professor.

"I love her," repeated Coleman.

After some seconds of pregnant silence, the professor arose. "Well, if she cares to give her life to you I will allow it, but I must say that I do not consider you nearly good enough. Good-night." He smiled faintly as he held out his hand.

"Good-night, sir," said Coleman. "And I can't tell, you, now-"

Mrs. Wainwright, in her room was languishing in a chair and applying to her brow a hand- kerchief wet with cologne water. She, kept her feverish glarice upon the door. Remembering well the manner of her husband when he went out she could hardly identify him when he came in. Serenity, composure, even self-satisfaction, was written upon him. He, paid no attention to her, but going to a chair sat down with a groan of contentment.

"Well?" cried Mrs. Wainwright, starting up. "Well? "

"Well-what?" he asked.

She waved her hand impatiently. "Harrison, don't be absurd. You know perfectly well what I mean. It is a pity you couldn't think of the anxiety I have been in." She was going to weep.

"Oh, I'll tell you after awhile," he said stretching out his legs with the complacency of a rich merchant after a successful day.

"No! Tell me now," she implored him. "Can't you see I've worried myself nearly to death?" She was not going to weep, she was going to wax angry.

"Well, to tell the truth," said the professor with considerable pomposity, "I've arranged it. Didn't think I could do it at first, but it turned out "

"I Arranged it,'" wailed Mrs. Wainwright. "Arranged what?"

It here seemed to strike the professor suddenly that he was not such a flaming example for diplomatists as he might have imagined. "Arranged," he stammered. "Arranged ."

"Arranged what?"

"Why, I fixed-I fixed it up."

"Fixed what up?"

"It-it-" began the professor. Then he swelled with indignation. "Why, can't you understand anything at all? I-I fixed it."

"Fixed what?"

"Fixed it. Fixed it with Coleman."

"Fixed what with Coleman?

The professor's wrath now took control of him. "Thunder and lightenin' ! You seem to jump at the conclusion that I've made some horrible mistake. For goodness' sake, give me credit for a particle of sense."

"What did you do?" she asked in a sepulchral voice.

"Well," said the professor, in a burning defiance, " I'll tell you what I did. I went to Coleman and told him that once-as he of course knew-I had re- fused his marriage with my daughter, but that now —-"

"Grrr," said Mrs. Wainwright.

"But that now-" continued the professor, "I retracted that refusal."

"Mercy on us! " cried Mrs. Wainwright, throwing herself back in the chair. "Mercy on us! What fools men are!"

"Now, wait a minute-" But Mrs. Wainwright began to croon: "Oh, if Marjory should hear of this! Oh, if she should hear of it! just let her. Hear-"

"But she must not," cried the professor, tigerishly. just you dare! " And the woman saw before her a man whose eyes were lit with a flame which almost expressed a temporary hatred.

The professor had left Coleman so abruptly that the correspondent found himself murmuring half. coherent gratitude to the closed door of his room. Amazement soon began to be mastered by exultation. He flung himself upon the brandy and soda and negotiated a strong glass. Pacing. the room with nervous steps, he caught a vision of himself in a tall mirror. He halted before it. "Well, well," he said. "Rufus, you're a grand man. There is not your equal anywhere. You are a great, bold, strong player, fit to sit down to a game with the -best."

A moment later it struck him that he had appropriated too much. If the professor had paid him a visit and made a wonderful announcement, he, Coleman, had not been the engine of it. And then he enunciated clearly something in his mind which, even in a vague form, had been responsible for much of his early elation. Marjory herself had compassed this thing. With shame he rejected a first wild and preposterous idea that she had sent her father to him. He reflected that a man who for an instant could conceive such a thing was a natural-born idiot. With an equal feeling, he rejected also an idea that she could have known anything of her father's purpose. If she had known of his purpose, there would have been no visit.

What, then, was the cause? Coleman soon decided that the professor had witnessed some demonstration of Marjory's emotion which had been sufficiently severe in its character to force him to the extraordinary visit. But then this also was wild and preposterous. That coldly beautiful goddess would not have given a demonstration of emotion over Rufus Coleman sufficiently alarming to have forced her father on such an errand. That was impossible. No, he was wrong; Marjory even indirectly, could not be connected with the visit. As he arrived at this decision, the enthusiasm passed out of him and he wore a doleful, monkish face.

"Well, what, then, was the cause?" After eliminating Marjory from the discussion waging in his mind, he found it hard to hit upon anything rational. The only remaining theory was to the effect that the professor, having a very high sense of the correspond. ent's help in the escape of the Wainwright party, had decided that the only way to express his gratitude was to revoke a certain decision which he now could see had been unfair. The retort to this theory seemed to be that if the professor had had such a fine conception of the services rendered by Coleman, he had had ample time to display his appreciation on the road to Arta and on the road down from Arta. There was no necessity for his waiting until their arrival in Athens. It was impossible to concede that the professor's emotion could be anew one; if he had it now, he must have had it in far stronger measure directly after he had been hauled out of danger.

So, it may be seen that after Coleman had eliminated Marjory from the discussion that was waging in his mind, he had practically succeeded in eliminating the professor as well. This, he thought, mournfully, was eliminating with a vengeance. If he dissolved all the factors he could hardly proceed.

The mind of a lover moves in a circle, or at least on a more circular course than other minds, some of which at times even seem to move almost in a straight line. Presently, Coleman was at the point where he bad started, and he did not pause until he reached that theory which asserted that the professor had been inspired to his visit by some sight or knowledge of Marjory in distress. Of course, Coleman was wistfully desirous of proving to himself the truth of this theory.

The palpable agitation of the professor during the interview seemed to support it. If he had come on a mere journey of conscience, he would have hardly appeared as a white and trembling old, man. But then, said Coleman, he himself probably exaggerated this idea of the professor's appearance. It might have been that he was only sour and distressed over the performance of a very disagreeable duty.

The correspondent paced his room and smoked. Sometimes he halted at the little table where was the brandy and soda. He thought so hard that sometimes it seemed that Marjory had been to him to propose marriage, and at other times it seemed that there had been no visit from any one at all.

A desire to talk to somebody was upon him. He strolled down stairs and into the smoking and reading rooms, hoping to see a man he knew, even if it were Coke. But the only occupants were two strangers, furiously debating the war. Passing the minister's room, Coleman saw that there was a light within, and he could not forbear knocking. He was bidden to enter, and opened the door upon the minister, care- fully reading his Spectator fresh from London. He looked up and seemed very glad. "How are you?" he cried. "I was tremendously anxious to see you, do you know! I looked for you to dine with me to-night, but you were not down?" "No ; I had a great deal of work."

"Over the Wainwright affair? By the way, I want you to accept my personal thanks for that work. In a week more I would have gone demented and spent the rest of my life in some kind of a cage, shaking the bars and howling out State Department messages about the Wainwrights. You see, in my territory there are no missionaries to get into trouble, and I was living a life of undisturbed and innocent calm, ridiculing the sentiments of men from Smyrna and other interesting towns who maintained that the diplomatic service was exciting. However, when the Wainwright party got lost, my life at once became active. I was all but helpless, too; which was the worst of it. I suppose Terry at Constantinople must have got grandly stirred up, also. Pity he can't see you to thank you for saving him from probably going mad. By the way," he added, while looking keenly at Coleman, "the Wainwrights don't seem to be smothering you with gratitude?"

"Oh, as much as I deserve-sometimes more," answered Coleman. "My exploit was more or less of a fake, you know. I was between the lines by accident, or through the efforts of that blockhead of a dragoman. I didn't intend it. And then, in the night, when we were waiting in the road because of a fight, they almost bunked into us. That's all."

"They tell it better," said the minister, severely. "Especially the youngsters."

"Those kids got into a high old fight at a town up there beyond Agrinion. Tell you about that, did they? I thought not. Clever kids. You have noted that there are signs of a few bruises and scratches?" " Yes, but I didn't ask-" " Well, they are from the fight. It seems the people took us for Germans, and there was an awful palaver, which ended in a proper and handsome shindig. It raised the town, I tell you."

The minister sighed in mock despair. "Take these people home, will you? Or at any rate, conduct them out of the field of my responsibility. Now, they would like Italy immensely, I am sure."

Coleman laughed, and they smoked for a time.

"That's a charming girl-Miss Wainwright," said the minister, musingly. "And what a beauty! It does my exiled eyes good to see her. I suppose all those youngsters are madly in love with her? I don't see how they could help it."

"Yes," said Coleman, glumly. "More than half of them."

The minister seemed struck with a sudden thought. "You ought to try to win that splendid prize yourself. The rescuer ! Perseus! What more fitting?"

Coleman answered calmly: "Well * * * I think I'll take your advice."

CHAPTER XXVIII.

THE next morning Coleman awoke with a sign of a resolute decision on his face, as if it had been a development of his sleep. He would see Marjory as soon as possible, see her despite any barbed-wire entanglements which might be placed in the way by her mother, whom he regarded as his strenuous enemy. And he would ask Marjory's hand in the presence of all Athens if it became necessary.

He sat a long time at his breakfast in order to see the Wainwrights enter the dining room, and as he was about to surrender to the will of time, they came in, the professor placid and self-satisfied, Mrs. Wainwright worried and injured and Marjory cool, beautiful, serene. If there had been any kind of a storm there was no trace of it on the white brow of the girl. Coleman studied her closely but furtively while his mind spun around his circle of speculation. Finally he noted the waiter who was observing him with a pained air as if it was on the tip of his tongue to ask this guest if he was going to remain at breakfast forever. Coleman passed out to the reading room where upon the table a multitude of great red guide books were crushing the fragile magazines of London and Paris. On the walls were various depressing maps with the name of a tourist agency luridly upon them, and there were also some pictures of hotels with their rates-in francs-printed beneath. The room was cold, dark, empty, with the trail of the tourist upon it.

Coleman went to the picture of a hotel in Corfu and stared at it precisely as if he was interested. He was standing before it when he heard Marjory's voice just without the door. "All right! I'll wait." He did not move for the reason that the hunter moves not when the unsuspecting deer approaches his hiding place. She entered rather quickly and was well toward the centre of the room before she perceived Coleman. "Oh," she said and stopped. Then she spoke the immortal sentence, a sentence which, curiously enough is common to the drama, to the novel, and to life. "I thought no one was here." She looked as if she was going to retreat, but it would have been hard to make such retreat graceful, and probably for this reason she stood her ground.

Coleman immediately moved to a point between her and the door. "You are not going to run away from me, Marjory Wainwright," he cried, angrily. " You at least owe it to me to tell me definitely that you don't love me-that you can't love me-"

She did not face him with all of her old spirit, but she faced him, and in her answer there was the old Marjory. "A most common question. Do you ask all your feminine acquaintances that?"

"I mean-" he said. "I mean that I love you and-"

"Yesterday-no. To-day-yes. To-morrow-who knows. Really, you ought to take some steps to know your own mind."

"Know my own mind," he retorted in a burst of indignation. "You mean you ought to take steps to know your own mind."

"My own mind! You-" Then she halted in acute confusion and all her face went pink. She had been far quicker than the man to define the scene. She lowered her head. Let me past, please-"

But Coleman sturdily blocked the way and even took one of her struggling hands. "Marjory-" And then his brain must have roared with a thousand quick sentences for they came tumbling out, one over the other. * * Her resistance to the grip of his fingers grew somewhat feeble. Once she raised her eyes in a quick glance at him. * * Then suddenly she wilted. She surrendered, she confessed without words. "Oh, Marjory, thank God, thank God-" Peter Tounley made a dramatic entrance on the gallop. He stopped, petrified. "Whoo!" he cried. "My stars! " He turned and fled. But Coleman called after him in a low voice, intense with agitation.

"Come back here, you young scoundrel! Come book here I "

Peter returned, looking very sheepish. "I hadn't the slightest idea you-"

"Never mind that now. But look here, if you tell a single soul-particularly those other young scoundrels-I'll break-"

"I won't, Coleman. Honest, I won't." He was far more embarrassed than Coleman and almost equally so with Marjory. He was like a horse tugging at a tether. "I won't, Coleman! Honest!"

"Well, all right, then." Peter escaped.

The professor and his wife were in their sitting room writing letters. The cablegrams had all been answered, but as the professor intended to prolong his journey homeward into a month of Paris and London, there remained the arduous duty of telling their friends at length exactly what had happened. There was considerable of the lore of olden Greece in the professor's descriptions of their escape, and in those of Mrs. Wainwright there was much about the lack of hair-pins and soap.

Their heads were lowered over their writing when the door into the corridor opened and shut quickly, and upon looking up they saw in the room a radiant girl, a new Marjory. She dropped to her knees by her father's chair and reached her arms to his neck. " Oh, daddy! I'm happy I I'm so happy! "

"Why-what-" began the professor stupidly.

"Oh, I am so happy, daddy!

Of course he could not be long in making his conclusion. The one who could give such joy to Marjory was the one who, last night, gave her such grief. The professor was only a moment in understanding. He laid his hand tenderly upon her head " Bless my soul," he murmured. "And so-and so-he-"

At the personal pronoun, Mrs. Wainwright lumbered frantically to her feet. "What?" she shouted. Coleman?"

"Yes," answered Marjory. "Coleman." As she spoke the name her eyes were shot with soft yet tropic flashes of light.

Mrs. Wainwright dropped suddenly back into her chair. "Well-of-all-things!" The professor was stroking his daughter's hair and although for a time after Mrs. Wainwright's outbreak there was little said, the old man and the girl seemed in gentle communion, she making him feel her happiness, he making her feel his appreciation. Providentially Mrs. Wainwright had been so stunned by the first blow that she was evidently rendered incapable of speech.

"And are you sure you will be happy with him? asked her father gently.

"All my life long," she answered.

"I am glad! I am glad! " said the father, but even as he spoke a great sadness came to blend with his joy. The hour when he was to give this beautiful and beloved life into the keeping of another had been heralded by the god of the sexes, the ruthless god that devotes itself to the tearing of children from the parental arms and casting them amid the mysteries of an irretrievable wedlock. The thought filled him with solemnity.

But in the dewy eyes of the girl there was no question. The world to her was a land of glowing promise.

"I am glad," repeated the professor.

The girl arose from her knees. "I must go away and-think all about it," she said, smiling. When the door of her room closed upon her, the mother arose in majesty.

"Harrison Wainwright," she declaimed, "you are not going to allow this monstrous thing! "

The professor was aroused from a reverie by these words. "What monstrous thing?" he growled.

"Why, this between Coleman and Marjory."

"Yes," he answered boldly.

"Harrison! That man who-"

The professor crashed his hand down on the table. "Mary! I will not hear another word of it! "

"Well," said Mrs. Wainwright, sullen and ominous, " time will tell! Time will tell!"

When Coleman bad turned from the fleeing Peter Tounley again to Marjory, he found her making the preliminary movements of a flight. "What's the matter?" he demanded anxiously.

348

"Oh, it's too dreadful"

"Nonsense," lie retorted stoutly. "Only Peter Tounley! He don't count. What of that?"

' Oh, dear! " She pressed her palm to a burning cheek. She gave him a star-like, beseeching glance. Let me go now-please."

"Well," he answered, somewhat affronted, "if you like —"

At the door she turned to look at him, and this glance expressed in its elusive way a score of things which she had not yet been able to speak. It explained that she was loth to leave him, that she asked forgiveness for leaving him, that even for a short absence she wished to take his image in her eyes, that he must not bully her, that there was something now in her heart which frightened her, that she loved him, that she was happy —

When she had gone, Coleman went to the rooms of the American minister. A Greek was there who talked wildly as he waved his cigarette. Coleman waited in well-concealed impatience for the dvapora- tion of this man. Once the minister, regarding the correspondent hurriedly, interpolated a comment. " You look very cheerful?"

"Yes," answered Coleman, "I've been taking your advice."

"Oh, ho ! " said the minister.

The Greek with the cigarette jawed endlessly. Coleman began to marvel at the enduring good manners of the minister, who continued to nod and nod in polite appreciation of the Greek's harangue, which, Coleman firmly believed, had no point of interest whatever. But at last the man, after an effusive farewell, went his way.

"Now," said the minister, wheeling in his chair tell me all about it."

Coleman arose, and thrusting his hands deep in his trousers' pockets, began to pace the room with long strides. He, said nothing, but kept his eyes on the floor.

"Can I have a drink?" he asked, abruptly pausing.

"What would you like?" asked the minister, benevolently, as he touched the bell.

"A brandy and soda. I'd like it very much. You see," he said, as he resumed his walk, "I have no kind of right to burden you with my affairs, but, to tell the truth, if I don't get this news off my mind and into somebody's ear, I'll die. It's this-I asked Marjory Wainwright to marry me, and-she accepted, and- that's all."

"Well, I am very glad," cried the minister, arising and giving his hand. "And as for burdening me with your affairs, no one has a better right, you know, since you released me from the persecution of Washington and the friends of the Wainwrights. May good luck follow you both forever. You, in my opinion, are a very, very fortunate man. And, for her part she has not done too badly."

Seeing that it was important that Coleman should have his spirits pacified in part, the minister continued: " Now, I have got to write an official letter, so you just walk up and down here and use up this surplus steam. Else you'll explode."

But Coleman was not to be detained. Now that he had informed the minister, he must rush off some. where, anywhere, and do-he knew not what.

All right," said the minister, laughing. "You have a wilder head than I thought. But look here," he called, as Coleman was making for the door. "Am I to keep this news a secret?"

Coleman with his hand on the knob, turned impressively. He spoke with deliberation. "As far as I am concerned, I would be glad to see a man paint it in red letters, eight feet high, on the front of the king's palace."

The minister, left alone, wrote steadily and did not even look up when Peter Tounley and two others entered, in response to his cry of permission. How ever, he presently found time to speak over his shoulder to them. "Hear the news?"

"No, sir," they answered.

"Well, be good boys, now, and read the papers and look at pictures until I finish this letter. Then I will tell you."

They surveyed him keenly. They evidently judged that the news was worth hearing, but, obediently, they said nothing. Ultimately the minister affixed a rapid signature to the letter, and turning, looked at the students with a smile. " Haven't heard the news, eh?"

"No, Sir."

"Well, Marjory Wainwright is engaged to marry Coleman."

The minister was amazed to see the effect of this announcement upon the three students. He had expected the crows and cackles of rather absurd merriment with which unbearded youth often greets, such news. But there was no crow or cackle. One young man blushed scarlet and looked guiltily at the floor. With a great effort he muttered: "Shes too good for him." Another student had turned ghastly pate and was staring. It was Peter Tounley who relieved the minister's mind, for upon that young man's face was a broad jack-o-lantern grin, and the minister saw that, at any rate, he had not made a complete massacre.

Peter Tounley said triumphantly: "I knew it ! "

The minister was anxious over the havoc he had wrought with the two other students, but slowly the colour abated in one face and grew in the other. To give them opportunity, the minister talked busily to Peter Tounley. "And how did you know it, you young scamp?"

Peter was jubilant. "Oh, -I knew it! I knew it I I am very clever."

The student who had blushed now addressed the minister in a slightly strained voice. "Are you positive that it is true, Mr. Gordner?,"

"I had it on the best authority," replied the minister gravely.

The student who had turned pale said: "Oh, it's true, of course."

"Well," said crudely the one who had blushed, she's a great sight too good for Coleman or anybody like him. That's all I've got to say."

"Oh, Coleman is a good fellow," said Peter Tounley, reproachfully. "You've no right to say that-exactly. You don't know where you'd. be now if it were not for Coleman."

The, response was, first, an angry gesture. "Oh, don't keep everlasting rubbing that in. For heaven's sake, let up. - Supposing I don't. know where I'd be now if,it were not for Rufus Coleman? What of it? For the rest of my life have I got to —"

The minister saw. that this was the embittered speech of a really defeated youth, so, to save scenes, he gently ejected the trio. "There, there, now ! Run along home like good boys. I'll be busy until luncheon. And I -dare say you won't find Coleman such a bad chap.'"

In the corridor, one of the students said offensively to Peter Tounley : "Say, how in hell did you find out all this so early?"

Peter's reply was amiable in tone. "You are a damned bleating little kid and you made a holy show of yourself before Mr. Gordner. There's where you stand. Didn't you see that he turned us out because he didn't know but what you were going to blubber or something. - you are a sucking pig, and if you want to know how I find out things go ask the Delphic Oracle, you blind ass."

"You better look out or you may get a punch in the eye!,"

"You take one punch in the general direction of my eye, me son," said -Peter cheerfully, "and I'll distribute your remains, over this hotel in a way that will cause your, friends years of trouble to collect you. Instead of anticipating an attack upon my eye, you had much better be engaged in improving your mind, which is at present not a fit machine to cope with exciting situations. There's Coke! Hello, Coke, hear the news? Well, Marjory Wainwright and Rufus Coleman , are engaged.. Straight? Certainly ! Go ask the minister."

Coke did not take Peter's word. "Is that so?" he asked the others.

"So the minister told us," they answered, and then these two, who seemed so unhappy, watched Coke's face to see if they could not find surprised misery there. But Coke coolly said: "Well, then, I suppose it's true."

It soon became evident that the students did not care for each other's society. Peter Tounley was probably an exception, but the others seemed to long for quiet corners. They were distrusting each other, and, in a boyish way, they were even capable of malignant things. Their excuses for separation were badly made.

"I-I think I'll go for a walk." "I'm going up stairs to read." "Well, so long, old man.'" So long." There was no heart to it.

Peter Tounley went to Coleman's door, where he knocked with noisy hilarity. "Come in I" The correspondent apparently had just come from the street, for his hat was on his head and a light top-coat was on his back. He was searching hurriedly through some, papers. "Hello, you young devil What are you doing here?

Peter's entrance was a somewhat elaborate comedy which Coleman watched in icy silence. Peter after a long,and impudent pantomime halted abruptly and fixing Coleman with his eye demanded: "Well?"

"Well-what?." said Coleman, bristling a trifle.

"Is it true?"

"Is what true?"

"Is it true?" Peter was extremely solemn. " Say, me bucko," said Coleman suddenly, "if you've. come up here to twist the beard of the patriarch, don't you think you are running a chance?"

"All right. I'll be good," said Peter, and he sat on the bed. "But-is it true?

"Is what true?"

"What the whole hotel is saying."

] "I haven't heard the hotel making any remarks lately. Been talking to the other buildings, I sup- pose."

"Well, I want to tell you that everybody knows that you and Marjory have done gone and got yourselves engaged," said Peter bluntly.

"And well?" asked Coleman imperturbably.

"Oh, nothing," replied Peter, waving his hand. "Only-I thought it might interest you."

Coleman was silent for some time. He fingered his papers. At last he burst out joyously. "And so they know it already, do they? Well-damn them- let them know it. But you didn't tell them yourself?"

"I !" quoth Peter wrathfully. "No! The minister told us."

Then Coleman was again silent for a time and Peter Tounley sat on the. bed reflectively looking at the ceiling. "Funny thing, Marjory 'way over here in Greece, and then you happening over here the way you did."

"It isn't funny at all."

"Why isn't it?"

"Because," said Coleman impressively,, "that is why I came to Greece. It was all planned. See?"

"Whirroo," exclaimed Peter. "This here is magic."

"No magic at all." Coleman displayed some complacence. " No magic at all. just pure, plain — whatever you choose to call it."

"Holy smoke," said Peter, admiring the situation. "Why, this is plum romance, Coleman. I'm blowed if it isn't."

Coleman was grinning with delight. He took a fresh cigar and his bright eyes looked at Peter through the smoke., "Seems like it, don't it? Yes. Regular romance. Have a drink, my boy, just to celebrate my good luck. And be patient if I talk a great deal of my-my-future. My head spins with it." He arose to pace the room flinging out bis arms in a great gesture. "God! When I think yesterday was not like to-day I wonder how I stood it." There was a knock at the door and a waiter left a note in Coleman's hand

"Dear Rufus:-We are going for a drive this afternoon at three, and mother wishes you to come, if you. care to. I too wish it, if you care to. Yours, " MARJORY."

With a radiant face, Coleman gave the note a little crackling flourish in the air. "Oh, you don't know what life is, kid."

"S-steady the Blues," said Peter Tounley seriously. You'll lose your head if you don't watch out."

"Not I" cried Coleman with irritation. "But a man must turn loose some times, mustn't he?"

When the four, students had separated in the corridor, Coke had posted at once to Nora Black's sitting room. His entrance was somewhat precipitate, but he cooled down almost at once, for he reflected that he was not bearing good news. He ended by perching in awkward fashion on the brink of his chair and fumbling his hat uneasily. Nora floated to him in a cloud of a white dressing gown. She gave him a plump hand. "Well, youngman? "she said, with a glowing smile. She took a chair, and the stuff of her gown fell in curves over the arms of it.,

Coke looked hot and bothered, as if he could have more than half wanted to retract his visit. "I-aw- we haven't seen much of you lately," he began, sparing. He had expected to tell his news at once.

No," said Nora, languidly. "I have been resting after that horrible journey-that horrible journey. Dear, dear! Nothing,will ever induce me to leave London, New York and Paris. I am at home there. But here I Why, it is worse than living in Brooklyn. And that journey into the wilds! No. no; not for me! "

"I suppose we'll all be glad to get home," said Coke, aimlessly.

At the moment a waiter entered the room and began to lay the table for luncheon. He kept open the door to the corridor, and he had the luncheon at a point just outside the door. His excursions to the trays were flying ones, so that, as far as Coke's purpose was concerned, the waiter was always in the room. Moreover, Coke was obliged, naturally, to depart at once. He had bungled everything.

As he arose he whispered hastily: "Does this waiter understand English?"

"Yes," answered Nora. "Why?"

"Because I have something to tell you-important."

"What is it?" whispered Nora, eagerly.

He leaned toward her and replied: "Marjory Wainwright and Coleman are engaged."

To his unfeigned astonishment, Nora Black burst into peals of silvery laughter, "Oh, indeed? And so this is your tragic story, poor, innocent lambkin? And what did you expect? That I would faint?" -

"I thought-I don't know-" murmured Coke in confusion.

Nora became suddenly business-like. "But how do you know? Are you sure? Who told you? Anyhow, stay to luncheon. Do-like a good boy. Oh, you must."

Coke dropped again into his chair. He studied her in some wonder. "I thought you'd be surprised," he said, ingenuously.

"Oh, you did, did you? Well, you see I'm not. And now tell me all about it."

"There's really nothing to tell but the plain fact. Some of the boys dropped in at the minister's rooms a little while ago, and, he told them of it. That's all."

Well, how did he know?

"I am sure I can't tell you. Got it first hand, I suppose. He likes Coleman, and Coleman is always hanging up there."

"Oh, perhaps Coleman was lying," said Nora easily. Then suddenly her face brightened and she spoke with animation. "Oh, I haven't told you how my little Greek officer has turned out. Have I? No? Well, it is simply lovely. Do you know, he belongs to one of the best families in Athens? Hedoes. And they're rich-rich as can be. My courier tells me that the marble palace where they live is enough to blind you, and that if titles hadn't gone out of style-or something-here in Greece, my little officer would be a prince! Think of that! The courier didn't know it until we got to Athens, and the little officer-the prince-gave me his card, of course. One of the oldest, noblest and richest families in Greece. Think of that! There I thought he was only a bothersome little officer who came in handy at times, and there he turns out to be a prince. I could hardly keep myself from rushing right off to find him and apologise to him for the way I treated him. It was awful! And-" added the fair Nora, pensively, "if he does meet me in Paris, I'll make him wear that title down to a shred, you can bet. What's the good of having a title unless you make it work?"

CHAPTER XXIX.

COKE did not stay to luncheon with Nora Black. He went away saying to himself either that girl don't care a straw for Coleman or she has got a heart absolutely of flint, or she is the greatest actress on earth or-there is some other reason."

At his departure, Nora turned and called into an adjoining room. "Maude I " The voice of her companion and friend answered her peevishly. "What?"

"Don't bother me. I'm reading."

"Well, anyhow, luncheon is ready, so you will have to stir your precious self," responded Nora. "You're lazy."

"I don't want any luncheon. Don't bother me. I've got a headache."

"Well, if you don't come out, you'll miss the news. That's all I've got to say."

There was a rustle in the adjoining room, and immediately the companion appeared, seeming much annoyed but curious. "Well, what is it?"

"Rufus Coleman is engaged to be married to that Wainwright girl, after all."

"Well I declare! " ejaculated the little old lady. " Well I declare." She meditated for a moment, and then continued in a tone of satisfaction. "I told you that you couldn't stop that man Coleman if he had feally made up his mind to-"

"You're a fool," said Nora, pleasantly. "Why?" said the old lady. Because you are. Don't talk to me about it. I want to think of Marco."

" 'Marco,' " quoted the old lady startled.

"The prince. The prince. Can't you understand? I mean the prince."

" ' Marco!' " again quoted the old lady, under her breath.

"Yes, 'Marco,' " cried Nora, belligerently. " 'Marco,' Do you object to the name? What's the matter with you, anyhow?"

"Well," rejoined the other, nodding her head wisely, "he may be a prince, but I've always heard that these continental titles are no good in comparison to the English titles."

"Yes, but who told you so, eh?" demanded Nora, noisily. She herself answered the question. "The English! "

"Anyhow, that little marquis who tagged after you in London is a much bigger man in every way, I'll bet, than this little prince of yours."

"But-good heavens-he didn't mean it. Why, he was only one of the regular rounders. But Marco, he is serious I He means it. He'd go through fire and water for me and be glad of the chance."

"Well," proclaimed the old lady, "if you are not the strangest woman in the world, I'd like to know! Here I thought-"

"What did you think?" demanded Nora, suspisciously. "I thought that Coleman —-"

"Bosh!" interrupted, the graceful Nora. "I tell you what, Maude; you'd better try to think as little as possible. It will suit your style of beauty better. And above all, don't think of my affairs. I myself am taking pains not to think of them. It's easier."

Mrs. Wainwright, with no spirit of intention what. ever, had sit about readjusting her opinions. It is certain that she was unconscious of any evolution. If some one had said to her that she was surrendering to the inevitable, she would have been immediately on her guard, and would have opposed forever all suggestions of a match between Marjory and Coleman. On the other hand, if some one had said to her that her daughter was going to marry a human serpent, and that there were people in Athens who would be glad to explain his treacherous character, she would have haughtily scorned the tale-bearing and would have gone with more haste into the professor's way of thinking. In fact, she was in process of undermining herself., and the work could have been. retarded or advanced by any irresponsible, gossipy tongue.

The professor, from the depths of his experience with her, arranged a course of conduct. "If I just leave her to herself she will come around all right, but if I go 'striking while the iron is hot,' or any of those things, I'll bungle it surely."

As they were making ready to go down to luncheon, Mrs. Wainwright made her speech which first indicated a changing mind. "Well, what will be, will be," she murmured with a prolonged sigh of resignation. " What will be, will be. Girls are very headstrong in these days, and there is nothing much to be done with them. They go their own roads. It wasn't so in my girlhood. - We were obliged to pay attention to our mothers wishes."

"I did not notice that you paid much attention to your mother's wishes when you married me," remarked the professor. "In fact, I thought-"

"That was another thing," retorted Mrs. Wainwright with severity. "You were a steady young man who had taken the highest honours all through your college course, and my mother's sole objection was that we were too hasty. She thought we -ought to wait until you had a penny to bless yourself with, and I can see now where she was quite right." " Well, you married me, anyhow," said the professor, victoriously.

Mrs. Wainwright allowed her husband's retort to pass over her thoughtful mood. "They say * * they say Rufus Coleman makes as much as fifteen thousand dollars a year. That's more than three times your income * * I don't know. * * It all depends on whether they try to save or not. His manner of life is, no doubt, very luxurious. I don't suppose he knows how to economise at all. That kind of a man usually doesn't. And then, in the newspaper world positions are so very precarious. Men may have valuable positions one minute and be penniless in the street the next minute. It isn't as if he had any real income, and of course he has no real ability. If he was suddenly thrown out of his position, goodness knows what would become of him. Still still fifteen thousand dollars a year is a big income while it lasts. I suppose he is very extravagant. That kind of a man usually is. And I wouldn't be surprised if he was heavily in debt; very heavily in debt. Still * * if Marjory has set her heart there is nothing to be done, I suppose. It wouldn't have happened if you had been as wise as you thought you were. * * I suppose he thinks I have been very rude to him. Well, some times I wasn't nearly so rude as I felt like being. Feeling as I did, I could hardly be very amiable. * * Of course this drive this afternoon was all your affair and Marjory's. But, of course, I shall be nice to him."

"And what of all this Nora Black business?" asked the professor, with, a display of valour, but really with much trepidation.

"She is a hussy," responded Mrs. Wainwright with energy. "Her conversation in the carriage on the way down to Agrinion sickened me! "

"I really believe that her plan was simply to break everything off between Marjory and Coleman," said the professor, "and I don't believe she had any-grounds for all that appearance of owning Coleman and the rest of it."

"Of course she didn't" assented Mrs. Wainwright. The vicious thing! "

"On the other hand," said the professor, "there might be some truth in it." "I don't think so," said Mrs. Wainwright seriously. I don't believe a word of it."

"You do not mean to say that you think Coleman a model man?" demanded the professor.

"Not at all! Not at all!" she hastily answered. "But * * one doesn't look for model men these days."

"'Who told you he made fifteen thousand a year? asked the professor.

"It was Peter Tounley this morning. We were talking upstairs after breakfast, and he remarked that he if could make fifteen thousand, a year: like Coleman, he'd-I've forgotten what-some fanciful thing."

"I doubt if it is true," muttered the old man wagging his head.

"Of course it's true," said his wife emphatically. "Peter Tounley says everybody knows it."

Well * anyhow * money is not everything."

But it's a. great deal, you know well enough. You know you are always speaking of poverty as an evil, as a grand resultant, a collaboration of many lesser evils. Well, then?

"But," began the professor meekly, when I say that I mean-"

"Well, money is money and poverty is poverty," interrupted his wife. "You don't have to be very learned to know that."

355

"I do not say that Coleman has not a very nice thing of it, but I must say it is hard to think of his getting any such sum, as you mention."

"Isn't he known as the most brilliant journalist in New York?" she demanded harshly.

"Y-yes, as long as it lasts, but then one never knows when he will be out in the street penniless. Of course he has no particular ability which would be marketable if he suddenly lost his present employment. Of course it is not as if he was a really talented young man. He might not be able to make his way at all in any new direction."

"I don't know about that," said Mrs. Wainwright in reflective protestation. "I don't know about that. I think he would."

"I thought you said a moment ago-" The professor spoke with an air of puzzled hesitancy. "I thought you said a moment ago that he wouldn't succeed in anything but journalism."

Mrs. Wainwright swam over the situation with a fine tranquility. "Well-I-I," she answered musingly, "if I did say that, I didn't mean it exactly."

"No, I suppose not," spoke the professor, and de- spite the necessity for caution he could not keep out of his voice a faint note of annoyance.

"Of course," continued the wife, "Rufus Coleman is known everywhere as a brilliant man, a very brilliant man, and he even might do well in-in politics or something of that sort."

"I have a very poor opinion of that kind of a mind which does well in American politics," said the pro- fessor, speaking as a collegian, "but I suppose there may be something in it."

"Well, at any rate," decided Mrs. Wainwright. "At any rate-"

At that moment, Marjory attired for luncheon and the drive entered from her room, and Mrs. Wainwright checked the expression of her important conclusion. Neither father or mother had ever seen her so glowing with triumphant beauty, a beauty which would carry the mind of a spectator far above physical appreciation into that realm of poetry where creatures of light move and are beautiful because they cannot know pain or a burden. It carried tears to the old father's eyes. He took her hands. "Don't be too happy, my child, don't be too happy," he admonished her tremulously. "It makes me afraid-it makes me afraid."

CHAPTER XXX

IT seems strange that the one who was the most hilarious over the engagement of Marjory and Cole- man should be Coleman's dragoman who was indeed in a state bordering on transport. It is not known how he learned the glad tidings, but it is certain that he learned them before luncheon. He told all the visible employes of the hotel and allowed them to know that the betrothal really had been his handiwork He had arranged it. He did not make quite clear how he had performed this feat, but at least he was perfectly frank in acknowledging it.

When some of the students came down to luncheon, they saw him but could not decide what ailed him. He was in the main corridor of the hotel, grinning from ear to ear, and when he perceived the students he made signs to intimate that they possessed in common a joyous secret. "What's the matter with that idiot?" asked Coke morosely. "Looks as if his wheels were going around too fast." Peter Tounley walked close to him and scanned him imperturbably, but with care. "What's up, Phidias?" The man made no articulate reply. He continued to grin and gesture. "Pain in oo tummy? Mother dead? Caught the cholera? Found out that you've swallowed a pair of hammered brass and irons in your beer? Say, who are you, anyhow? " But he could not shake this invincible glee, so he went away.

The dragoman's rapture reached its zenith when Coleman lent him to the professor and he was commissioned to bring a carriage for four people to the door at three o'clock. He himself was to sit on the box and tell the driver what was required of him. He dashed off, his hat in his hand, his hair flying, puffing, important beyond everything, and apparently babbling his mission to half the people he met on the street. In most countries he would have landed speedily in jail, but among a people who exist on a basis of jibbering, his violent gabble aroused no suspicions as to his sanity. However, he stirred several livery stables to their depths and set men running here and there wildly and for the most part futiltiy.

At fifteen minutes to three o'clock, a carriage with its horses on a gallop tore around the corner and up to the . front of the hotel, where it halted with the pomp and excitement of a fire engine. The dragoman jumped down from his seat beside the driver and scrambled hurriedly into the hoiel, in the gloom of which hemet a serene stillness which was punctuated only by the leisurely tinkle of silver and glass in the dining room. For a moment the dragoman seemed really astounded out of speech. Then he plunged into the manager's room. Was it conceivable that Monsieur Coleman was still at luncheon? Yes; in fact, it was true. But the carriage, was at the door! The carriage was at the door! The manager, undisturbed, asked for what hour Monsieur Coleman had been pleased to order a carriage. Three o'clock ! Three o'clock? The manager pointed calmly at the clock. Very well. It was now only thirteen minutes of three o'clock. Monsieur Coleman doubtless would appear at three. Until that hour the manager would not disturb Monsieur Coleman. The dragoman clutched both his hands in his hair and cast a look of agony to the ceiling. Great God! Had he accomplished the herculean task of getting a carriage for four people to the door of the hotel in time for a drive at three o'clock, only to meet with this stoniness, this inhumanity? Ah, it was unendurable? He begged the manager; he implored him. But at every word. the manager seemed to grow more indifferent, more callous. He pointed with a wooden finger at the clock-face. In reality, it is thus, that Greek meets Greek.

Professor Wainwright and Coleman strolled together out of the dining room. The dragoman rushed ecstatically upon the correspondent. "Oh, Meester Coleman! The carge is ready!"

"Well, all right," said Coleman, knocking ashes from his cigar. "Don't be in a hurry. I suppose we'll be ready, presently." The man was in despair.

The departure of the Wainwrights and Coleman on this ordinary drive was of a somewhat dramatic and public nature, No one seemed to know how to prevent its being so. In the first place, the attendants thronged out en masse for a reason which was plain at the time only to Coleman's dragoman. And, rather in the background, lurked the interested students. The professor was surprised and nervous. Coleman was rigid and angry. Marjory was flushed and some what hurried, and Mrs. Wainwright was as proud as an old turkey-hen.

As the carriage rolled away, Peter Tounley turned to his companions and said: "Now, that's official! That is the official announcement! Did you see Old Mother Wainwright? Oh, my eye, wasn't she puffed up ! Say, what in hell do you suppose all these jay hawking bell-boys poured out to the kerb for? Go back to your cages, my good people-"

As soon as the carriage wheeled into another street, its occupants exchanged easier smiles, and they must have confessed in some subtle way of glances that now at last they were upon their own mission, a mission undefined but earnest to them all. Coleman had a glad feeling of being let into the family, or becoming one of them

The professor looked sideways at him and smiled gently. "You know, I thought of driving you to some ruins, but Marjory would not have it. She flatly objected to any more ruins. So I thought we would drive down to New Phalerum." Coleman nodded and smiled as if he were immensely pleased, but of course New Phalerum was to him no more nor-less than Vladivostok or Khartoum. Neither place nor distance had interest for him. They swept along a shaded avenue where the dust lay thick on the leaves; they passed cafes where crowds were angrily shouting over the news in the little papers; they passed a hospital before which wounded men, white with bandages, were taking the sun; then came soon to the and valley flanked by gaunt naked mountains, which would lead them to the sea. Sometimes to accentuate the dry nakedness of this valley, there would be a patch of grass upon which poppies burned crimson spots. The dust writhed out from under the wheels of the carriage; in the distance the sea appeared, a blue half-disc set between shoulders of barren land. It would be common to say that Coleman was oblivious to all about him but Marjory. On the contrary, the parched land, the isolated flame of poppies, the cool air from the sea, all were keenly known to him, and they had developed an extraordinary power of blending sympathetically into his mood. Meanwhile the professor talked a great deal. And as a somewhat exhilarating detail, Coleman perceived that Ms. Wainwright was beaming upon him.

At New Phalerum-a small collection of pale square villas-they left the carriage and strolled, by the sea. The waves were snarling together like wolves amid the honeycomb rocks and from where the blue plane sprang level to the horizon, came a strong cold breeze, the kind of a breeze which moves an exulting man or a parson to take off his hat and let his locks flutter and tug back from his brow.

The professor and Mrs. Wainwright were left to themselves.

Marjory and Coleman did not speak for a time. It might have been that they did not quite know where to make a beginning. At last Marjory asked: "What has become of your splendid horse?"

"Oh, I've told the dragoman to have him sold as soon as he arrives," said Coleman absently.

"Oh. I'm sorry * * I liked that horse."

"Why?"

"Oh, because-"

"Well, he was a fine-" Then he, too, interrupted himself, for he saw plainly that they had not come to this place to talk about a horse. Thereat he made speech of matters which at least did not afford as many opportunities for coherency as would the horse. Marjory, it can't be true * * * Is it true, dearest * * I can hardly believe it. -I-"

"Oh, I know I'm not nearly good enough for you."

"Good enough for me, dear?

"They all told me so, and they were right ! Why, even the American minister said it. Everybody thinks it."

"Why, aren 't they wretches To think of them saying such a thing! As if-as if anybody could be too —"

"Do you know-" She paused and looked at him with a certain timid challenge. "I don't know why I feel it, but-sometimes I feel that I've been I've been flung at your head."

He opened his mouth in astonishment. "Flung at my head!

She held up her finger. "And if I thought you could ever believe it ! "

"Is a girl flung at a man's head when her father carries her thousands of miles away and the man follows her all these miles, and at last-"

"Her eyes were shining. "And you really came to Greece-on purpose to-to-"

"Confess you knew it all the time! Confess!" The answer was muffled. "Well, sometimes I thought you did, and at other times I thought you- didn't."

In a secluded cove, in which the sea-maids once had played, no doubt, Marjory and Coleman sat in silence. He was below her, and if he looked at her he had to turn his glance obliquely upward. She was staring at the sea with woman's mystic gaze, a gaze which men at once reverence and fear since it seems to look into the deep, simple heart of nature, and men begin to feel that their petty wisdoms are futile to control these strange spirits, as wayward as nature and as pure as nature, wild as the play of waves, sometimes as unalterable as the mountain amid the winds; and to measure them, man must perforce use a mathematical formula.

He wished that she would lay her hand upon his hair. He would be happy then. If she would only, of her own will, touch his hair lightly with her fingers-if she would do it with an unconscious air it would be even better. It would show him that she was thinking of him, even when she did not know she was thinking of him.

Perhaps he dared lay his head softly against her knee. Did he dare?

As his head touched her knee, she did not move. She seemed to be still gazing at the sea. Presently idly caressing fingers played in his hair near the forehead. He looked up suddenly lifting his arms. He breathed out a cry which was laden with a kind of diffident ferocity. "I haven't kissed you yet-"

The Monster

I

Little Jim was, for the time, engine Number 36, and he was making the run between Syracuse and Rochester. He was fourteen minutes behind time, and the throttle was wide open. In consequence, when he swung around the curve at the flower-bed, a wheel of his cart destroyed a peony. Number 36 slowed down at once and looked guiltily at his father, who was mowing the lawn. The doctor had his back to this accident, and he continued to pace slowly to and fro, pushing the mower.

Jim dropped the tongue of the cart. He looked at his father and at the broken flower. Finally he went to the peony and tried to stand it on its pins, resuscitated, but the spine of it was hurt, and it would only hang limply from his hand. Jim could do no reparation. He looked again toward his father.

He went on to the lawn, very slowly, and kicking wretchedly at the turf. Presently his father came along with the whirring machine, while the sweet new grass blades spun from the knives. In a low voice, Jim said, "Pa!"

The doctor was shaving this lawn as if it were a priest's chin. All during the season he had worked at it in the coolness and peace of the evenings after supper. Even in the shadow of the cherry-trees the grass was strong and healthy. Jim raised his voice a trifle. "Pa!"

The doctor paused, and with the howl of the machine no longer occupying the sense, one could hear the robins in the cherry-trees arranging their affairs. Jim's hands were behind his back, and sometimes his fingers clasped and unclasped. Again he said, "Pa!" The child's fresh and rosy lip was lowered.

The doctor stared down at his son, thrusting his head forward and frowning attentively. "What is it, Jimmie?"

"Pa!" repeated the child at length. Then he raised his finger and pointed at the flower-bed. "There!"

"What?" said the doctor, frowning more. "What is it, Jim?"

After a period of silence, during which the child may have undergone a severe mental tumult, he raised his finger and repeated his former word – "There!" The father had respected this silence with perfect courtesy. Afterwards his glance carefully followed the direction indicated by the child's finger, but he could see nothing which explained to him. "I don't understand what you mean, Jimmie," he said.

It seemed that the importance of the whole thing had taken away the boy's vocabulary. He could only reiterate, "There!"

The doctor mused upon the situation, but he could make nothing of it. At last he said, "Come, show me."

Together they crossed the lawn toward the flower-bed. At some yards from the broken peony Jimmie began to lag. "There!" The word came almost breathlessly.

"Where?" said the doctor.

Jimmie kicked at the grass. "There!" he replied.

The doctor was obliged to go forward alone. After some trouble he found the subject of the incident, the broken flower. Turning then, he saw the child lurking at the rear and scanning his countenance.

The father reflected. After a time he said, "Jimmie, come here." With an infinite modesty of demeanor the child came forward. "Jimmie, how did this happen?"

The child answered, "Now – I was playin' train – and – now – I runned over it."

"You were doing what?"

"I was playin' train."

The father reflected again. "Well, Jimmie," he said, slowly, "I guess you had better not play train any more today. Do you think you had better?"

"No, sir," said Jimmie.

During the delivery of the judgment the child had not faced his father, and afterwards he went away, with his head lowered, shuffling his feet.

II

It was apparent from Jimmie's manner that he felt some kind of desire to efface himself. He went down to the stable. Henry Johnson, the negro who cared for the doctor's horses, was sponging the buggy. He grinned fraternally when he saw Jimmie coming. These two were pals. In regard to almost everything in life they seemed to have minds precisely alike. Of course there were points of emphatic divergence. For instance, it was plain from Henry's talk that he was a very handsome negro, and he was known to be a light, a weight, and an eminence in the suburb of the town, where lived the larger number of the negroes, and obviously this glory was over Jimmie's horizon; but he vaguely appreciated it and paid deference to Henry for it mainly because Henry appreciated it and deferred to himself. However, on all points of conduct as related to the doctor, who was the moon, they were in complete but unexpressed understanding. Whenever Jimmie became the victim of an eclipse he went to the stable to solace himself with Henry's crimes. Henry, with the elasticity of his race, could usually provide a sin to place himself on a footing with the disgraced one. Perhaps he would remember that he had forgotten to put the hitching strap in the back of the buggy on some recent occasion, and had been reprimanded by the doctor. Then these two would commune subtly and without words concerning their moon, holding themselves sympathetically as people who had committed similar treasons. On the other hand, Henry would sometimes choose to absolutely repudiate this idea, and when Jimmie appeared in his shame would bully him most virtuously, preaching with assurance the precepts of the doctor's creed, and pointing out to Jimmie all his abominations. Jimmie did not discover that this was odious in his comrade. He accepted it and lived in its shadow with humility, merely trying to conciliate the saintly Henry with acts of deference. Won by this attitude, Henry would sometimes allow the child to enjoy the felicity of squeezing the sponge over a buggy-wheel, even when Jimmie was still gory from unspeakable deeds.

Whenever Henry dwelt for a time in sackcloth, Jimmie did not patronize him at all. This was a justice of his age, his condition. He did not know. Besides, Henry could drive a horse, and Jimmie had a full sense of this sublimity. Henry personally conducted the moon during the splendid journeys through the country roads, where farms spread on all sides, with sheep, cows, and other marvels abounding.

"Hello, Jim!" said Henry, poising his sponge. Water was dripping from the buggy. Sometimes the horses in the stalls stamped thunderingly on the pine floor. There was an atmosphere of hay and of harness.

For a minute Jimmie refused to take an interest in anything. He was very downcast. He could not even feel the wonders of wagon-washing. Henry, while at his work, narrowly observed him.

"Your pop done wallop yer, didn't he?" he said at last.

"No," said Jimmie, defensively; "he didn't."

After this casual remark Henry continued his labor, with a scowl of occupation. Presently he said: "I done tol' yer many's th' time not to go a-foolin' an' a-projjeckin' with them flowers. Yer pop don' like it nohow." As a matter of fact, Henry had never mentioned flowers to the boy.

Jimmie preserved a gloomy silence, so Henry began to use seductive wiles in this affair of washing a wagon. It was not until he began to spin a wheel on the tree, and the sprinkling water flew everywhere, that the boy was visibly moved. He had been seated on the sill of the carriage-house door, but at the beginning of this ceremony he arose and circled toward the buggy, with an interest that slowly consumed the remembrance of a late disgrace.

Johnson could then display all the dignity of a man whose duty it was to protect Jimmie from a splashing. "Look out, boy! look out! You done gwi' spile yer pants. I raikon your mommer don't 'low this foolishness, she know it. I ain't gwi' have you round yere spilin' yer pants, an' have Mis' Trescott light on me pressen'ly. 'Deed I ain't."

He spoke with an air of great irritation, but he was not annoyed at all. This tone was merely a part of his importance. In reality he was always delighted to have the child there to witness the business of the stable. For one thing, Jimmie was invariably overcome with reverence when he was told how beautifully a harness was polished or a horse groomed. Henry explained each detail of this kind with unction, procuring great joy from the child's admiration.

III

After Johnson had taken his supper in the kitchen, he went to his loft in the carriage-house and dressed himself with much care. No belle of a court circle could bestow more mind on a toilet than did Johnson. On second thought, he was more like a priest arraying himself for some parade of the church. As he emerged from his room and sauntered down the carriage drive, no one would have suspected him of ever having washed a buggy.

It was not altogether a matter of the lavender trousers, nor yet the straw hat with its bright silk band. The change was somewhere far in the interior of Henry. But there was no cake-walk hyperbole in it. He was simply a quiet, well-bred gentleman of position, wealth, and other necessary achievements out for an evening stroll, and he had never washed a wagon in his life.

In the morning, when in his working-clothes, he had met a friend – "Hello, Pete!" "Hello, Henry!" Now, in his effulgence, he encountered this same friend. His bow was not at all haughty. If it expressed anything, it expressed consummate generosity – "Good-evenin', Misteh Washington." Pete, who was very dirty, being at work in a potato-patch, responded in a mixture of abasement and appreciation – "Good-evenin', Misteh Johnsing."

The shimmering blue of the electric arc-lamps was strong in the main street of the town. At numerous points it was conquered by the orange glare of the outnumbering gas-lights in the windows of shops. Through this radiant lane moved a crowd, which culminated in a throng before the post-office, awaiting the distribution of the evening mails. Occasionally there came into it a shrill electric street-car, the motor singing like a cageful of grasshoppers, and possessing a great gong that clanged forth both warnings and simple noise. At the little theatre, which was a varnish and red-plush miniature of one of the famous New York theatres, a company of strollers was to play East Lynne. The young men of the town were mainly gathered at the corners, in distinctive groups, which expressed various shades and lines of chumship, and had little to do with any social gradations. There they discussed everything with critical insight, passing the whole town in review as it swarmed in the street. When the gongs of the electric cars ceased for a moment to harry the ears, there could be heard the sound of the feet of the leisurely crowd on the blue-stone pavement, and it was like the peaceful evening lashing at the shore of a lake. At the foot of the hill, where two lines of maples sentinelled the way, an electric lamp glowed high among the embowering branches, and made most wonderful shadow-etchings on the road below it.

When Johnson appeared amid the throng a member of one of the profane groups at a corner instantly telegraphed news of this extraordinary arrival to his companions. They hailed him. "Hello, Henry! Going to walk for a cake to-night?"

"Ain't he smooth?"

"Why, you've got that cake right in your pocket, Henry!"

"Throw out your chest a little more."

Henry was not ruffled in any way by these quiet admonitions and compliments. In reply he laughed a supremely good-natured, chuckling laugh, which nevertheless expressed an underground complacency of superior metal.

Young Griscom, the lawyer, was just emerging from Reifsnyder's barber shop, rubbing his chin contentedly. On the steps he dropped his hand and looked with wide eyes into the crowd. Suddenly he bolted back into the shop. "Wow!" he cried to the parliament; "you ought to see the coon that's coming!"

Reifsnyder and his assistant instantly poised their razors high and turned toward the window. Two belathered heads reared from the chairs. The electric shine in the street caused an effect like water to them who looked through the glass from the yellow glamour of Reifsnyder's shop. In fact, the people without resembled the inhabitants of a great aquarium that here had a square pane in it. Presently into this frame swam the graceful form of Henry Johnson.

"Chee!" said Reifsnyder. He and his assistant with one accord threw their obligations to the winds, and leaving their lathered victims helpless, advanced to the window. "Ain't he a taisy?" said Reifsnyder, marvelling.

But the man in the first chair, with a grievance in his mind, had found a weapon. "Why, that's only Henry Johnson, you blamed idiots! Come on now, Reif, and shave me. What do you think I am – a mummy?"

Reifsnyder turned, in a great excitement. "I bait you any money that vas not Henry Johnson! Henry Johnson! Rats!" The scorn put into this last word made it an explosion. "That man vas a Pullman-car porter or someding. How could that be Henry Johnson?" he demanded, turbulently. "You vas crazy."

The man in the first chair faced the barber in a storm of indignation. "Didn't I give him those lavender trousers?" he roared.

And young Griscom, who had remained attentively at the window, said: "Yes, I guess that was Henry. It looked like him."

"Oh, vell," said Reifsnyder, returning to his business, "if you think so! Oh, vell!" He implied that he was submitting for the sake of amiability.

Finally the man in the second chair, mumbling from a mouth made timid by adjacent lather, said: "That was Henry Johnson all right. Why, he always dresses like that when he wants to make a front! He's the biggest dude in town – anybody knows that."

"Chinger!" said Reifsnyder.

Henry was not at all oblivious of the wake of wondering ejaculation that streamed out behind him. On other occasions he had reaped this same joy, and he always had an eye for the demonstration. With a face beaming with happiness he turned away from the scene of his victories into a narrow side street, where the electric light still hung high, but only to exhibit a row of tumble-down houses leaning together like paralytics.

The saffron Miss Bella Farragut, in a calico frock, had been crouched on the front stoop, gossiping at long range, but she espied her approaching caller at a distance. She dashed around the corner of the house, galloping like a horse. Henry saw it all, but he preserved the polite demeanor of a guest when a waiter spills claret down his cuff. In this awkward situation he was simply perfect.

The duty of receiving Mr. Johnson fell upon Mrs. Farragut, because Bella, in another room, was scrambling wildly into her best gown. The fat old woman met him with a great ivory smile, sweeping back with the door, and bowing low. "Walk in, Misteh Johnson, walk in. How is you dis ebenin', Misteh Johnson – how is you?"

Henry's face showed like a reflector as he bowed and bowed, bending almost from his head to his ankles. "Good-evenin', Mis' Fa'gut; good-evenin'. How is you dis evenin'? Is all you' folks well, Mis' Fa'gut?"

After a great deal of kowtow, they were planted in two chairs opposite each other in the living-room. Here they exchanged the most tremendous civilities, until Miss Bella swept into the room, when there was more kowtow on all sides, and a smiling show of teeth that was like an illumination.

The cooking-stove was of course in this drawing-room, and on the fire was some kind of a long-winded stew. Mrs. Farragut was obliged to arise and attend to it from time to time. Also young Sim came in and went to bed on his pallet in the corner. But to all these domesticities the three maintained an absolute dumbness. They bowed and smiled and ignored and imitated until a late hour, and if they had been the occupants of the most gorgeous salon in the world they could not have been more like three monkeys.

After Henry had gone, Bella, who encouraged herself in the appropriation of phrases, said, "Oh, ma, isn't he divine?"

IV

A Saturday evening was a sign always for a larger crowd to parade the thoroughfare. In summer the band played until ten o'clock in the little park. Most of the young men of the town affected to be superior to this band, even to despise it; but in the still and fragrant evenings they invariably turned out in force, because the girls were sure to attend this concert, strolling slowly over the grass, linked closely in pairs, or preferably in threes, in the curious public dependence upon one another which was their inheritance. There was no particular social aspect to this gathering, save that group regarded group with interest, but mainly in silence. Perhaps one girl would nudge another girl and suddenly say, "Look! there goes Gertie Hodgson and her sister!" And they would appear to regard this as an event of importance.

On a particular evening a rather large company of young men were gathered on the sidewalk that edged the park. They remained thus beyond the borders of the festivities because of their dignity, which would not exactly allow them to appear in anything which was so much fun for the younger lads. These latter were careering madly through the crowd, precipitating minor accidents from time to time, but usually fleeing like mist swept by the wind before retribution could lay its hands upon them.

The band played a waltz which involved a gift of prominence to the bass horn, and one of the young men on the sidewalk said that the music reminded him of the new engines on the hill pumping water into the reservoir. A similarity of this kind was not inconceivable, but the young man did not say it because he disliked the band's playing. He said it because it was fashionable to say that manner of thing concerning the band. However, over in the stand, Billie Harris, who played the snare-drum, was always surrounded by a throng of boys, who adored his every whack.

After the mails from New York and Rochester had been finally distributed, the crowd from the post-office added to the mass already in the park. The wind waved the leaves of the maples, and, high in the air, the blue-burning globes of the arc lamps caused the wonderful traceries of leaf shadows on the ground. When the light fell upon the upturned face of a girl, it caused it to glow with a wonderful pallor. A policeman came suddenly from the darkness and chased a gang of obstreperous little boys. They hooted him from a distance. The leader of the band had some of the mannerisms of the great musicians, and during a period of silence the crowd smiled when they saw him raise his hand to his brow, stroke it sentimentally, and glance upward with a look of poetic anguish. In the shivering light, which gave to the park an effect like a great vaulted hall, the throng swarmed with a gentle murmur of dresses switching the turf, and with a steady hum of voices.

Suddenly, without preliminary bars, there arose from afar the great hoarse roar of a factory whistle. It raised and swelled to a sinister note, and then it sang on the night wind one long call that held the crowd in the park immovable, speechless. The band-master had been about to vehemently let fall his hand to start the band on a thundering career through a popular march, but, smitten by this giant voice from the night, his hand dropped slowly to his knee, and, his mouth agape, he looked at his men in silence. The cry died away to a wail, and then to stillness. It released the muscles of the company of young men on the sidewalk, who had been like statues, posed eagerly, lithely, their ears turned. And then they wheeled upon each other simultaneously, and, in a single explosion, they shouted, "One!"

Again the sound swelled in the night and roared its long ominous cry, and as it died away the crowd of young men wheeled upon each other and, in chorus, yelled, "Two!"

There was a moment of breathless waiting. Then they bawled, "Second district!" In a flash the company of indolent and cynical young men had vanished like a snowball disrupted by dynamite.

V

Jake Rogers was the first man to reach the home of Tuscarora Hose Company Number Six. He had wrenched his key from his pocket as he tore down the street, and he jumped at the spring-lock like a demon. As the doors flew back before his hands he leaped and kicked the wedges from a pair of wheels, loosened a tongue from its clasp, and in the glare of the electric light which the town placed before each of his hose-houses the next comers beheld the spectacle of Jake Rogers bent like hickory in the manfulness of his pulling, and the heavy cart was moving slowly towards the doors. Four men joined him at the time, and as they swung with the cart out into the street, dark figures sped towards them from the ponderous shadows back of the electric lamps. Some set up the inevitable question, "What district?"

"Second," was replied to them in a compact howl. Tuscarora Hose Company Number Six swept on a perilous wheel into Niagara Avenue, and as the men, attached to the cart by the rope which had been paid out from the windlass under the tongue, pulled madly in their fervor and abandon, the gong under the axle clanged incitingly. And sometimes the same cry was heard, "What district?"

"Second."

On a grade Johnnie Thorpe fell, and exercising a singular muscular ability, rolled out in time from the track of the on-coming wheel, and arose, dishevelled and aggrieved, casting a look of mournful disenchantment upon the black crowd that poured after the machine. The cart seemed to be the apex of a dark wave that was whirling as if it had been a broken dam. Back of the lad were stretches of lawn, and in that direction front doors were banged by men who hoarsely shouted out into the clamorous avenue, "What district?"

At one of these houses a woman came to the door bearing a lamp, shielding her face from its rays with her hands. Across the cropped grass the avenue represented to her a kind of black torrent, upon which, nevertheless, fled numerous miraculous figures upon bicycles. She did not know that the towering light at the corner was continuing its nightly whine.

Suddenly a little boy somersaulted around the corner of the house as if he had been projected down a flight of stairs by a catapultian boot. He halted himself in front of the house by dint of a rather extraordinary evolution with his legs. "Oh, ma," he gasped, "can I go? Can I, ma?"

She straightened with the coldness of the exterior mother-judgment, although the hand that held the lamp trembled slightly. "No, Willie; you had better come to bed."

Instantly he began to buck and fume like a mustang. "Oh, ma," he cried, contorting himself – "oh, ma, can't I go? Please, ma, can't I go? Can't I go, ma?"

"It's half past nine now, Willie."

He ended by wailing out a compromise: "Well, just down to the corner, ma? Just down to the corner?"

From the avenue came the sound of rushing men who wildly shouted. Somebody had grappled the bell-rope in the Methodist church, and now over the town rang this solemn and terrible voice, speaking from the clouds. Moved from its peaceful business, this bell gained a new spirit in the portentous night, and it swung the heart to and fro, up and down, with each peal of it.

"Just down to the corner, ma?"

"Willie, it's half past nine now."

VI

The outlines of the house of Dr. Trescott had faded quietly into the evening, hiding a shape such as we call Queen Anne against the pall of the blackened sky. The neighborhood was at this time so quiet, and seemed so devoid of obstructions, that Hannigan's dog thought it a good opportunity to prowl in forbidden precincts, and so came and pawed Trescott's lawn, growling, and considering himself a formidable beast. Later, Peter Washington strolled past the house and whistled, but there was no dim light shining from Henry's loft, and presently Peter went his way. The rays from the street, creeping in silvery waves over the grass, caused the row of shrubs along the drive to throw a clear, bold shade.

A wisp of smoke came from one of the windows at the end of the house and drifted quietly into the branches of a cherry-tree. Its companions followed it in slowly increasing numbers, and finally there was a current controlled by invisible banks which poured into the fruit-laden boughs of the cherry-tree. It was no more to be noted than if a troop of dim and silent gray monkeys had been climbing a grape-vine into the clouds.

After a moment the window brightened as if the four panes of it had been stained with blood, and a quick ear might have been led to imagine the fire-imps calling and calling, clan joining clan, gathering to the colors. From the street, however, the house maintained its dark quiet, insisting to a passer-by that it was the safe dwelling of people who chose to retire early to tranquil dreams. No one could have heard this low droning of the gathering clans.

Suddenly the panes of the red window tinkled and crashed to the ground, and at other windows there suddenly reared other flames, like bloody spectres at the apertures of a haunted house. This outbreak had been well planned, as if by professional revolutionists.

A man's voice suddenly shouted: "Fire! Fire! Fire!" Hannigan had flung his pipe frenziedly from him because his lungs demanded room. He tumbled down from his perch, swung over the fence, and ran shouting towards the front door of the Trescotts'. Then he hammered on the door, using his fists as if they were mallets. Mrs. Trescott instantly came to one of the windows on the second floor. Afterwards she knew she had been about to say, "The doctor is not at home, but if you will leave your name, I will let him know as soon as he comes."

Hannigan's bawling was for a minute incoherent, but she understood that it was not about croup.

"What?" she said, raising the window swiftly.

"Your house is on fire! You're all ablaze! Move quick if— " His cries were resounding in the street as if it were a cave of echoes. Many feet pattered swiftly on the stones. There was one man who ran with an almost fabulous speed. He wore lavender trousers. A straw hat with a bright silk band was held half crumpled in his hand.

As Henry reached the front door, Hannigan had just broken the lock with a kick. A thick cloud of smoke poured over them, and Henry, ducking his head, rushed into it. From Hannigan's clamor he knew only one thing, but it turned him blue with horror. In the hall a lick of flame had found the cord that supported "Signing the Declaration." The engraving slumped suddenly down at one end, and then dropped to the floor, where it burst with the sound of a bomb. The fire was already roaring like a winter wind among the pines.

At the head of the stairs Mrs. Trescott was waving her arms as if they were two reeds. "Jimmie! Save Jimmie!" she screamed in Henry's face. He plunged past her and disappeared, taking the long-familiar routes among these upper chambers, where he had once held office as a sort of second assistant house-maid.

Hannigan had followed him up the stairs, and grappled the arm of the maniacal woman there. His face was black with rage. "You must come down," he bellowed.

She would only scream at him in reply: "Jimmie! Jimmie! Save Jimmie!" But he dragged her forth while she babbled at him.

As they swung out into the open air a man ran across the lawn, and seizing a shutter, pulled it from its hinges and flung it far out upon the grass. Then he frantically attacked the other shutters one by one. It was a kind of temporary insanity.

"Here, you," howled Hannigan, "hold Mrs. Trescott – And stop – "

The news had been telegraphed by a twist of the wrist of a neighbor who had gone to the fire-box at the corner, and the time when Hannigan and his charge struggled out of the house was the time when the whistle roared its hoarse night call, smiting the crowd in the park, causing the leader of the band, who was about to order the first triumphal clang of a military march, to let his hand drop slowly to his knees.

VII

Henry pawed awkwardly through the smoke in the upper halls. He had attempted to guide himself by the walls, but they were too hot. The paper was crimpling, and he expected at any moment to have a flame burst from under his hands.

"Jimmie!"

He did not call very loud, as if in fear that the humming flames below would overhear him. "Jimmie! Oh, Jimmie!"

Stumbling and panting, he speedily reached the entrance to Jimmie's room and flung open the door. The little chamber had no smoke in it at all. It was faintly illumined by a beautiful rosy light reflected circuitously from the flames that were consuming the house. The boy had apparently just been aroused by the noise. He sat in his bed, his lips apart, his eyes wide, while upon his little white-robed figure played caressingly the light from the fire. As the door flew open he had before him this apparition of his pal, a terror-stricken negro, all tousled and with wool scorching, who leaped upon him and bore him up in a blanket as if the whole affair were a case of kidnapping by a dreadful robber chief. Without waiting to go through the usual short but complete process of wrinkling up his face, Jimmie let out a gorgeous bawl, which resembled the expression of a calf's deepest terror. As Johnson, bearing him, reeled into the smoke of the hall, he flung his arms about his neck and buried his face in the blanket. He called twice in muffled tones: "Mam-ma! Mam-ma!"

When Johnson came to the top of the stairs with his burden, he took a quick step backward. Through the smoke that rolled to him he could see that the lower hall was all ablaze. He cried out then in a howl that resembled Jimmie's former achievement. His legs gained a frightful faculty of bending sideways. Swinging about precariously on these reedy legs, he made his way back slowly, back along the upper hall. From the way of him then, he had given up almost all idea of escaping from the burning house, and with it the desire. He was submitting, submitting because of his fathers, bending his mind in a most perfect slavery to this conflagration.

He now clutched Jimmie as unconsciously as when, running toward the house, he had clutched the hat with the bright silk band.

Suddenly he remembered a little private staircase which led from a bedroom to an apartment which the doctor had fitted up as a laboratory and work-house, where he used some of his leisure, and also hours when he might have been sleeping, in devoting himself to experiments which came in the way of his study and interest.

When Johnson recalled this stairway the submission to the blaze departed instantly. He had been perfectly familiar with it, but his confusion had destroyed the memory of it.

In his sudden momentary apathy there had been little that resembled fear, but now, as a way of safety came to him, the old frantic terror caught him. He was no longer creature to the flames, and he was afraid of the battle with them. It was a singular and swift set of alternations in which he feared twice without submission, and submitted once without fear.

"Jimmie!" he wailed, as he staggered on his way. He wished this little inanimate body at his breast to participate in his tremblings. But the child had lain limp and still during these headlong charges and countercharges, and no sign came from him.

Johnson passed through two rooms and came to the head of the stairs. As he opened the door great billows of smoke poured out, but gripping Jimmie closer, he plunged down through them. All manner of odors assailed him during this flight. They seemed to be alive with envy, hatred, and malice. At the entrance to the laboratory he confronted a strange spectacle. The room was like a garden in the region where might be burning flowers. Flames of violet, crimson, green, blue, orange, and purple were blooming everywhere. There was one blaze that was precisely the hue of a delicate coral. In another place was a mass that lay merely in phosphorescent inaction like a pile of emeralds. But all these marvels were to be seen dimly through clouds of heaving, turning, deadly smoke.

Johnson halted for a moment on the threshold. He cried out again in the negro wail that had in it the sadness of the swamps. Then he rushed across the room. An orange-colored flame leaped like a panther at the lavender trousers. This animal bit deeply into Johnson. There was an explosion at one side, and suddenly before him there reared a delicate, trembling sapphire shape like a fairy lady. With a quiet smile she blocked his path and doomed him and Jimmie. Johnson shrieked, and then ducked in the manner of his race in fights. He aimed to pass under the left guard of the sapphire lady. But she was swifter than eagles, and her talons caught in him as he plunged past her. Bowing his head as if his neck had been struck, Johnson lurched forward, twisting this way and that way. He fell on his back. The still form in the blanket flung from his arms, rolled to the edge of the floor and beneath the window.

Johnson had fallen with his head at the base of an old-fashioned desk. There was a row of jars upon the top of this desk. For the most part, they were silent amid this rioting, but there was one which seemed to hold a scintillant and writhing serpent.

Suddenly the glass splintered, and a ruby-red snakelike thing poured its thick length out upon the top of the old desk. It coiled and hesitated, and then began to swim a languorous way down the mahogany slant. At the angle it waved its sizzling molten head to and fro over the closed eyes of the man beneath it. Then, in a moment, with mystic impulse, it moved again, and the red snake flowed directly down into Johnson's upturned face.

Afterwards the trail of this creature seemed to reek, and amid flames and low explosions drops like red-hot jewels pattered softly down it at leisurely intervals.

VIII

Suddenly all roads led to Dr. Trescott's. The whole town flowed toward one point. Chippeway Hose Company Number One toiled desperately up Bridge Street Hill even as the Tuscaroras came in an impetuous sweep down Niagara Avenue. Meanwhile the machine of the hook-and-ladder experts from across the creek was spinning on its way. The chief of the fire department had been playing poker in the rear room of Whiteley's cigar-store, but at the first breath of the alarm he sprang through the door like a man escaping with the kitty.

In Whilomville, on these occasions, there was always a number of people who instantly turned their attention to the bells in the churches and school-houses. The bells not only emphasized the alarm, but it was the habit to send these sounds rolling across the sky in a stirring brazen uproar until the flames were practically vanquished. There was also a kind of rivalry as to which bell should be made to produce the greatest din. Even the Valley Church, four miles away among the farms, had heard the voices of its brethren, and immediately added a quaint little yelp.

Doctor Trescott had been driving homeward, slowly smoking a cigar, and feeling glad that this last case was now in complete obedience to him, like a wild animal that he had subdued, when he heard the long whistle, and chirped to his horse under the unlicensed but perfectly distinct impression that a fire had broken out in Oakhurst, a new and rather high-flying suburb of the town which was at least two miles from his own home. But in the second blast and in the ensuing silence he read the designation of his own district. He was then only a few blocks from his house. He took out the whip and laid it lightly on the mare. Surprised and frightened at this extraordinary action, she leaped forward, and as the reins straightened like steel bands, the doctor leaned backward a trifle. When the mare whirled him up to the closed gate he was wondering whose house could be afire. The man who had rung the signal-box yelled something at him, but he already knew. He left the mare to her will.

In front of his door was a maniacal woman in a wrapper. "Ned!" she screamed at sight of him. "Jimmie! Save Jimmie!"

Trescott had grown hard and chill.

"Where?" he said. "Where?"

Mrs. Trescott's voice began to bubble. "Up – up – up – " She pointed at the second-story windows.

Hannigan was already shouting: "Don't go in that way! You can't go in that way!"

Trescott ran around the corner of the house and disappeared from them. He knew from the view he had taken of the main hall that it would be impossible to ascend from there. His hopes were fastened now to the stairway which led from the laboratory. The door which opened from this room out upon the lawn was fastened with a bolt and lock, but he kicked close to the lock and then close to the bolt. The door with a loud crash flew back. The doctor recoiled from the roll of smoke, and then bending low, he stepped into the garden of burning flowers. On the floor his stinging eyes could make out a form in a smouldering blanket near the window. Then, as he carried his son toward the door, he saw that the whole lawn seemed now alive with men and boys, the leaders in the great charge that the whole town was making. They seized him and his burden, and overpowered him in wet blankets and water.

But Hannigan was howling: "Johnson is in there yet! Henry Johnson is in there yet! He went in after the kid! Johnson is in there yet!"

These cries penetrated to the sleepy senses of Trescott, and he struggled with his captors, swearing, unknown to him and to them, all the deep blasphemies of his medical-student days. He arose to his feet and went again toward the door of the laboratory. They endeavored to restrain him, although they were much affrighted at him.

But a young man who was a brakeman on the railway, and lived in one of the rear streets near the Trescotts, had gone into the laboratory and brought forth a thing which he laid on the grass.

IX

There were hoarse commands from in front of the house. "Turn on your water, Five!" "Let 'er go, One!" The gathering crowd swayed this way and that way. The flames, towering high, cast a wild red light on their faces. There came the clangor of a gong from along some adjacent street. The crowd exclaimed at it. "Here comes Number Three!" "That's Three a-comin'!" A panting and irregular mob dashed into view, dragging a hose-cart. A cry of exultation arose from the little boys. "Here's Three!" The lads welcomed Never-Die Hose Company Number Three as if it was composed of a chariot dragged by a band of gods. The perspiring citizens flung themselves into the fray. The boys danced in impish joy at the displays of prowess. They acclaimed the approach of Number Two. They welcomed Number Four with cheers. They were so deeply moved by this whole affair that they bitterly guyed the late appearance of the hook and ladder company, whose heavy apparatus had almost stalled them on the Bridge Street hill. The lads hated and feared a fire, of course. They did not particularly want to have anybody's house burn, but still it was fine to see the gathering of the companies, and amid a great noise to watch their heroes perform all manner of prodigies.

They were divided into parties over the worth of different companies, and supported their creeds with no small violence. For instance, in that part of the little city where Number Four had its home it would be most daring for a boy to contend the superiority of any other company. Likewise, in another quarter, when a strange boy was asked which fire company was the best in Whilomville, he was expected to answer "Number One." Feuds, which the boys forgot and remembered according to chance or the importance of some recent event, existed all through the town.

They did not care much for John Shipley, the chief of the department. It was true that he went to a fire with the speed of a falling angel, but when there he invariably lapsed into a certain still mood, which was almost a preoccupation, moving leisurely around the burning structure and surveying it, puffing meanwhile at a cigar. This quiet man, who even when life was in danger seldom raised his voice, was not much to their fancy. Now old Sykes Huntington, when he was chief, used to bellow continually like a bull and gesticulate in a sort of delirium. He was much finer as a spectacle than this Shipley, who viewed a fire with the same steadiness that he viewed a raise in a large jackpot. The greater number of the boys could never understand why the members of these companies persisted in re-electing Shipley, although they often pretended to understand it, because "My father says" was a very formidable phrase in argument, and the fathers seemed almost unanimous in advocating Shipley.

At this time there was considerable discussion as to which company had gotten the first stream of water on the fire. Most of the boys claimed that Number Five owned that distinction, but there was a determined minority who contended for Number One. Boys who were the blood adherents of other companies were obliged to choose between the two on this occasion, and the talk waxed warm.

But a great rumor went among the crowds. It was told with hushed voices. Afterward a reverent silence fell even upon the boys. Jimmie Trescott and Henry Johnson had been burned to death, and Dr. Trescott himself had been most savagely hurt. The crowd did not even feel the police pushing at them. They raised their eyes, shining now with awe, towards the high flames.

The man who had information was at his best. In low tones he described the whole affair. "That was the kid's room – in the corner there. He had measles or somethin', and this coon – Johnson – was a-settin' up with 'im, and Johnson got sleepy or somethin' and upset the lamp, and the doctor he was down in his office, and he came running up, and they all got burned together till they dragged 'em out."

Another man, always preserved for the deliverance of the final judgment, was saying: "Oh, they'll die sure. Burned to flinders. No chance. Hull lot of 'em. Anybody can see." The crowd concentrated its gaze still more closely upon these flags of fire which waved joyfully against the black sky. The bells of the town were clashing unceasingly.

A little procession moved across the lawn and towards the street. There were three cots, borne by twelve of the firemen. The police moved sternly, but it needed no effort of theirs to open a lane for this slow cortège. The men who bore the cots were well known to the crowd, but in this solemn parade during the ringing of the bells and the shouting, and with the red glare upon the sky, they seemed utterly foreign, and Whilomville paid them a deep respect. Each man in this stretcher party had gained a reflected majesty. They were footmen to death, and the crowd made subtle obeisance to this august dignity derived from three prospective graves. One woman turned away with a shriek at sight of the covered body on the first stretcher, and people faced her suddenly in silent and mournful indignation. Otherwise there was barely a sound as these twelve important men with measured tread carried their burdens through the throng.

The little boys no longer discussed the merits of the different fire companies. For the greater part they had been routed. Only the more courageous viewed closely the three figures veiled in yellow blankets.

X

Old Judge Denning Hagenthorpe, who lived nearly opposite the Trescotts, had thrown his door wide open to receive the afflicted family. When it was publicly learned that the doctor and his son and the negro were still alive, it required a specially detailed policeman to prevent people from scaling the front porch and interviewing these sorely wounded. One old lady appeared with a miraculous poultice, and she quoted most damning scripture to the officer when he said that she could not pass him. Throughout the night some lads old enough to be given privileges or to compel them from their mothers remained vigilantly upon the kerb in anticipation of a death or some such event. The reporter of the Morning Tribune rode thither on his bicycle every hour until three o'clock.

Six of the ten doctors in Whilomville attended at Judge Hagenthorpe's house.

Almost at once they were able to know that Trescott's burns were not vitally important. The child would possibly be scarred badly, but his life was undoubtedly safe. As for the negro Henry Johnson, he could not live. His body was frightfully seared, but more than that, he now had no face. His face had simply been burned away.

Trescott was always asking news of the two other patients. In the morning he seemed fresh and strong, so they told him that Johnson was doomed. They then saw him stir on the bed, and sprang quickly to see if the bandages needed readjusting. In the sudden glance he threw from one to another he impressed them as being both leonine and impracticable.

The morning paper announced the death of Henry Johnson. It contained a long interview with Edward J. Hannigan, in which the latter described in full the performance of Johnson at the fire. There was also an editorial built from all the best words in the vocabulary of the staff. The town halted in its accustomed road of thought, and turned a reverent attention to the memory of this hostler. In the breasts of many people was the regret that they had not known enough to give him a hand and a lift when he was alive, and they judged themselves stupid and ungenerous for this failure.

The name of Henry Johnson became suddenly the title of a saint to the little boys. The one who thought of it first could, by quoting it in an argument, at once overthrow his antagonist, whether it applied to the subject or whether it did not.

Nigger, nigger, never die,
Black face and shiny eye.

Boys who had called this odious couplet in the rear of Johnson's march buried the fact at the bottom of their hearts.

Later in the day Miss Bella Farragut, of No. 7 Watermelon Alley, announced that she had been engaged to marry Mr. Henry Johnson.

XI

The old judge had a cane with an ivory head. He could never think at his best until he was leaning slightly on this stick and smoothing the white top with slow movements of his hands. It was also to him a kind of narcotic. If by any chance he mislaid it, he grew at once very irritable, and was likely to speak sharply to his sister, whose mental incapacity he had patiently endured for thirty years in the old mansion on Ontario Street. She was not at all aware of her brother's opinion of her endowments, and so it might be said that the judge had successfully dissembled for more than a quarter of a century, only risking the truth at the times when his cane was lost.

On a particular day the judge sat in his arm-chair on the porch. The sunshine sprinkled through the lilac-bushes and poured great coins on the boards. The sparrows disputed in the trees that lined the pavements. The judge mused deeply, while his hands gently caressed the ivory head of his cane.

Finally he arose and entered the house, his brow still furrowed in a thoughtful frown. His stick thumped solemnly in regular beats. On the second floor he entered a room where Dr. Trescott was working about the bedside of Henry Johnson. The bandages on the negro's head allowed only one thing to appear, an eye, which unwinkingly stared at the judge. The latter spoke to Trescott on the condition of the patient. Afterward he evidently had something further to say, but he seemed to be kept from it by the scrutiny of the unwinking eye, at which he furtively glanced from time to time.

When Jimmie Trescott was sufficiently recovered, his mother had taken him to pay a visit to his grandparents in Connecticut. The doctor had remained to take care of his patients, but as a matter of truth he spent most of his time at Judge Hagenthorpe's house, where lay Henry Johnson. Here he slept and ate almost every meal in the long nights and days of his vigil.

At dinner, and away from the magic of the unwinking eye, the judge said, suddenly, "Trescott, do you think it is – " As Trescott paused expectantly, the judge fingered his knife. He said, thoughtfully, "No one wants to advance such ideas, but somehow I think that that poor fellow ought to die."

There was in Trescott's face at once a look of recognition, as if in this tangent of the judge he saw an old problem. He merely sighed and answered, "Who knows?" The words were spoken in a deep tone that gave them an elusive kind of significance.

The judge retreated to the cold manner of the bench. "Perhaps we may not talk with propriety of this kind of action, but I am induced to say that you are performing a questionable charity in preserving this negro's life. As near as I can understand, he will hereafter be a monster, a perfect monster, and probably with an affected brain. No man can observe you as I have observed you and not know that it was a matter of conscience with you, but I am afraid, my friend, that it is one of the blunders of virtue." The judge had delivered his views with his habitual oratory. The last three words he spoke with a particular emphasis, as if the phrase was his discovery.

The doctor made a weary gesture. "He saved my boy's life."

"Yes," said the judge, swiftly – "yes, I know!"

"And what am I to do?" said Trescott, his eyes suddenly lighting like an outburst from smouldering peat. "What am I to do? He gave himself for – for Jimmie. What am I to do for him?"

The judge abased himself completely before these words. He lowered his eyes for a moment. He picked at his cucumbers.

Presently he braced himself straightly in his chair. "He will be your creation, you understand. He is purely your creation. Nature has very evidently given him up. He is dead. You are restoring him to life. You are making him, and he will be a monster, and with no mind."

"He will be what you like, judge," cried Trescott, in sudden, polite fury. "He will be anything, but, by God! he saved my boy."

The judge interrupted in a voice trembling with emotion: "Trescott! Trescott! Don't I know?"

Trescott had subsided to a sullen mood. "Yes, you know," he answered, acidly; "but you don't know all about your own boy being saved from death." This was a perfectly childish allusion to the judge's bachelorhood. Trescott knew that the remark was infantile, but he seemed to take desperate delight in it.

But it passed the judge completely. It was not his spot.

"I am puzzled," said he, in profound thought. "I don't know what to say."

Trescott had become repentant. "Don't think I don't appreciate what you say, judge. But – "

"Of course!" responded the judge, quickly. "Of course."

"It – " began Trescott.

"Of course," said the judge.

In silence they resumed their dinner.

"Well," said the judge, ultimately, "it is hard for a man to know what to do."

"It is," said the doctor, fervidly.

There was another silence. It was broken by the judge:

"Look here, Trescott; I don't want you to think – "

"No, certainly not," answered the doctor, earnestly.

"Well, I don't want you to think I would say anything to – It was only that I thought that I might be able to suggest to you that – perhaps – the affair was a little dubious."

With an appearance of suddenly disclosing his real mental perturbation, the doctor said: "Well, what would you do? Would you kill him?" he asked, abruptly and sternly.

"Trescott, you fool," said the old man, gently.

"Oh, well, I know, judge, but then – " He turned red, and spoke with new violence: "Say, he saved my boy – do you see? He saved my boy."

"You bet he did," cried the judge, with enthusiasm. "You bet he did." And they remained for a time gazing at each other, their faces illuminated with memories of a certain deed.

After another silence, the judge said, "It is hard for a man to know what to do."

XII

Late one evening Trescott, returning from a professional call, paused his buggy at the Hagenthorpe gate. He tied the mare to the old tin-covered post, and entered the house. Ultimately he appeared with a companion – a man who walked slowly and carefully, as if he were learning. He was wrapped to the heels in an old-fashioned ulster. They entered the buggy and drove away.

After a silence only broken by the swift and musical humming of the wheels on the smooth road, Trescott spoke. "Henry," he said, "I've got you a home here with old Alek Williams. You will have everything you want to eat and a good place to sleep, and I hope you will get along there all right. I will pay all your expenses, and come to see you as often as I can. If you don't get along, I want you to let me know as soon as possible, and then we will do what we can to make it better."

The dark figure at the doctor's side answered with a cheerful laugh. "These buggy wheels don' look like I washed 'em yesterday, docteh," he said.

Trescott hesitated for a moment, and then went on insistently, "I am taking you to Alek Williams, Henry, and I – "

The figure chuckled again. "No, 'deed! No, seh! Alek Williams don' know a hoss! 'Deed he don't. He don' know a hoss from a pig." The laugh that followed was like the rattle of pebbles.

Trescott turned and looked sternly and coldly at the dim form in the gloom from the buggy-top. "Henry," he said, "I didn't say anything about horses. I was saying – "

"Hoss? Hoss?" said the quavering voice from these near shadows. "Hoss? 'Deed I don' know all erbout a hoss! 'Deed I don't." There was a satirical chuckle.

At the end of three miles the mare slackened and the doctor leaned forward, peering, while holding tight reins. The wheels of the buggy bumped often over out-cropping bowlders. A window shone forth, a simple square of topaz on a great black hill-side. Four dogs charged the buggy with ferocity, and when it did not promptly retreat, they circled courageously around the flanks, baying. A door opened near the window in the hill-side, and a man came and stood on a beach of yellow light.

"Yah! yah! You Roveh! You Susie! Come yah! Come yah this minit!"

Trescott called across the dark sea of grass, "Hello, Alek!"

"Hello!"

"Come down here and show me where to drive."

The man plunged from the beach into the surf, and Trescott could then only trace his course by the fervid and polite ejaculations of a host who was somewhere approaching. Presently Williams took the mare by the head, and uttering cries of welcome and scolding the swarming dogs, led the equipage toward the lights. When they halted at the door and Trescott was climbing out, Williams cried, "Will she stand, docteh?"

"She'll stand all right, but you better hold her for a minute. Now, Henry." The doctor turned and held both arms to the dark figure. It crawled to him painfully like a man going down a ladder. Williams took the mare away to be tied to a little tree, and when he returned he found them awaiting him in the gloom beyond the rays from the door.

He burst out then like a siphon pressed by a nervous thumb. "Hennery! Hennery, ma ol' frien'. Well, if I ain' glade. If I ain' glade!"

Trescott had taken the silent shape by the arm and led it forward into the full revelation of the light. "Well, now, Alek, you can take Henry and put him to bed, and in the morning I will – "

Near the end of this sentence old Williams had come front to front with Johnson. He gasped for a second, and then yelled the yell of a man stabbed in the heart.

For a fraction of a moment Trescott seemed to be looking for epithets. Then he roared: "You old black chump! You old black – Shut up! Shut up! Do you hear?"

Williams obeyed instantly in the matter of his screams, but he continued in a lowered voice: "Ma Lode amassy! Who'd ever think? Ma Lode amassy!"

Trescott spoke again in the manner of a commander of a battalion. "Alek!"

The old negro again surrendered, but to himself he repeated in a whisper, "Ma Lode!" He was aghast and trembling.

As these three points of widening shadows approached the golden doorway a hale old negress appeared there, bowing. "Good-evenin', docteh! Good-evenin'! Come in! come in!" She had evidently just retired from a tempestuous struggle to place the room in order, but she was now bowing rapidly. She made the effort of a person swimming.

"Don't trouble yourself, Mary," said Trescott, entering. "I've brought Henry for you to take care of, and all you've got to do is to carry out what I tell you." Learning that he was not followed, he faced the door, and said, "Come in, Henry."

Johnson entered. "Whee!" shrieked Mrs. Williams. She almost achieved a back somersault. Six young members of the tribe of Williams made a simultaneous plunge for a position behind the stove, and formed a wailing heap.

XIII

"You know very well that you and your family lived usually on less than three dollars a week, and now that Doctor Trescott pays you five dollars a week for Johnson's board, you live like millionaires. You haven't done a stroke of work since Johnson began to board with you – everybody knows that – and so what are you kicking about?"

The judge sat in his chair on the porch, fondling his cane, and gazing down at old Williams, who stood under the lilac-bushes. "Yes, I know, jedge," said the negro, wagging his head in a puzzled manner. "'Tain't like as if I didn't 'preciate what the docteh done, but – but – well, yeh see, jedge," he added, gaining a new impetus, "it's – it's hard wuk. This ol' man nev' did wuk so hard. Lode, no."

"Don't talk such nonsense, Alek," spoke the judge, sharply. "You have never really worked in your life – anyhow, enough to support a family of sparrows, and now when you are in a more prosperous condition than ever before, you come around talking like an old fool."

The negro began to scratch his head. "Yeh see, jedge," he said at last, "my ol' 'ooman she cain't 'ceive no lady callahs, nohow."

"Hang lady callers!" said the judge, irascibly. "If you have flour in the barrel and meat in the pot, your wife can get along without receiving lady callers, can't she?"

"But they won't come ainyhow, jedge," replied Williams, with an air of still deeper stupefaction. "Noner ma wife's frien's ner noner ma frien's'll come near ma res'dence."

"Well, let them stay home if they are such silly people."

The old negro seemed to be seeking a way to elude this argument, but evidently finding none, he was about to shuffle meekly off. He halted, however. "Jedge," said he, "ma ol' 'ooman's near driv' abstracted."

"Your old woman is an idiot," responded the judge.

Williams came very close and peered solemnly through a branch of lilac. "Jedge," he whispered, "the chillens."

"What about them?"

Dropping his voice to funereal depths, Williams said, "They – they cain't eat."

"Can't eat!" scoffed the judge, loudly. "Can't eat! You must think I am as big an old fool as you are. Can't eat – the little rascals! What's to prevent them from eating?"

In answer, Williams said, with mournful emphasis, "Hennery." Moved with a kind of satisfaction at his tragic use of the name, he remained staring at the judge for a sign of its effect.

The judge made a gesture of irritation. "Come, now, you old scoundrel, don't beat around the bush any more. What are you up to? What do you want? Speak out like a man, and don't give me any more of this tiresome rigamarole."

"I ain't er-beatin' round 'bout nuffin, jedge," replied Williams, indignantly. "No, seh; I say whatter got to say right out. 'Deed I do."

"Well, say it, then."

"Jedge," began the negro, taking off his hat and switching his knee with it, "Lode knows I'd do jes 'bout as much fer five dollehs er week as ainy cul'd man, but – but this yere business is awful, jedge. I raikon 'ain't been no sleep in – in my house sence docteh done fetch 'im."

"Well, what do you propose to do about it?"

Williams lifted his eyes from the ground and gazed off through the trees. "Raikon I got good appetite, an' sleep jes like er dog, but he – he's done broke me all up. 'Tain't no good, nohow. I wake up in the night; I hear 'im, mebbe, er-whimperin' an' er-whimperin', an' I sneak an' I sneak until I try th' do' to see if he locked in. An' he keep me er-puzzlin' an' er-quakin' all night long. Don't know how 'll do in th' winter. Can't let 'im out where th' chillen is. He'll done freeze where he is now." Williams spoke these sentences as if he were talking to himself. After a silence of deep reflection he continued: "Folks go round sayin' he ain't Hennery Johnson at all. They say he's er devil!"

"What?" cried the judge.

"Yesseh," repeated Williams in tones of injury, as if his veracity had been challenged. "Yesseh. I'm er-tellin' it to yeh straight, jedge. Plenty cul'd people folks up my way say it is a devil."

"Well, you don't think so yourself, do you?"

"No. 'Tain't no devil. It's Hennery Johnson."

"Well, then, what is the matter with you? You don't care what a lot of foolish people say. Go on 'tending to your business, and pay no attention to such idle nonsense."

"'Tis nonsense, jedge; but he looks like er devil."

"What do you care what he looks like?" demanded the judge.

"Ma rent is two dollehs and er half er month," said Williams, slowly.

"It might just as well be ten thousand dollars a month," responded the judge. "You never pay it, anyhow."

"Then, anoth' thing," continued Williams, in his reflective tone. "If he was all right in his haid I could stan' it; but, jedge, he's crazier 'n er loon. Then when he looks like er devil, an' done skears all ma frien's away, an' ma chillens cain't eat, an' ma ole 'ooman jes raisin' Cain all the time, an' ma rent two dollehs an' er half er month, an' him not right in his haid, it seems like five dollehs er week – "

The judge's stick came down sharply and suddenly upon the floor of the porch. "There," he said, "I thought that was what you were driving at."

Williams began swinging his head from side to side in the strange racial mannerism. "Now hol' on a minnet, jedge," he said, defensively. "'Tain't like as if I didn't 'preciate what the docteh done. 'Tain't that. Docteh Trescott is er kind man, an' 'tain't like as if I didn't 'preciate what he done; but – but – "

"But what? You are getting painful, Alek. Now tell me this: did you ever have five dollars a week regularly before in your life?"

Williams at once drew himself up with great dignity, but in the pause after that question he drooped gradually to another attitude. In the end he answered, heroically: "No, jedge, I 'ain't. An' 'tain't like as if I was er-sayin' five dollehs wasn't er lot er money for a man like me. But, jedge, what er man oughter git fer this kinder wuk is er salary. Yesseh, jedge," he repeated, with a great impressive gesture; "fer this kinder wuk er man oughter git er Salary." He laid a terrible emphasis upon the final word.

The judge laughed. "I know Dr. Trescott's mind concerning this affair, Alek; and if you are dissatisfied with your boarder, he is quite ready to move him to some other place; so, if you care to leave word with me that you are tired of the arrangement and wish it changed, he will come and take Johnson away."

Williams scratched his head again in deep perplexity. "Five dollehs is er big price fer bo'd, but 'tain't no big price fer the bo'd of er crazy man," he said, finally.

"What do you think you ought to get?" asked the judge.

"Well," answered Alek, in the manner of one deep in a balancing of the scales, "he looks like er devil, an' done skears e'rybody, an' ma chillens cain't eat, an' I cain't sleep, an' he ain't right in his haid, an' – "

"You told me all those things."

After scratching his wool, and beating his knee with his hat, and gazing off through the trees and down at the ground, Williams said, as he kicked nervously at the gravel, "Well, jedge, I think it is wuth – " He stuttered.

"Worth what?"

"Six dollehs," answered Williams, in a desperate outburst.

The judge lay back in his great arm-chair and went through all the motions of a man laughing heartily, but he made no sound save a slight cough. Williams had been watching him with apprehension.

"Well," said the judge, "do you call six dollars a salary?"

"No, seh," promptly responded Williams. "'Tain't a salary. No, 'deed! 'Tain't a salary." He looked with some anger upon the man who questioned his intelligence in this way.

"Well, supposing your children can't eat?"

"I—"

"And supposing he looks like a devil? And supposing all those things continue? Would you be satisfied with six dollars a week?"

Recollections seemed to throng in Williams's mind at these interrogations, and he answered dubiously. "Of co'se a man who ain't right in his haid, an' looks like er devil – But six dollehs – " After these two attempts at a sentence Williams suddenly appeared as an orator, with a great shiny palm waving in the air. "I tell yeh, jedge, six dollehs is six dollehs, but if I git six dollehs for bo'ding Hennery Johnson, I uhns it! I uhns it!"

"I don't doubt that you earn six dollars for every week's work you do," said the judge.

"Well, if I bo'd Hennery Johnson fer six dollehs a week, I uhns it! I uhns it!" cried Williams, wildly.

XIV

Reifsnyder's assistant had gone to his supper, and the owner of the shop was trying to placate four men who wished to be shaved at once. Reifsnyder was very garrulous – a fact which made him rather remarkable among barbers, who, as a class, are austerely speechless, having been taught silence by the hammering reiteration of a tradition. It is the customers who talk in the ordinary event.

As Reifsnyder waved his razor down the cheek of a man in the chair, he turned often to cool the impatience of the others with pleasant talk, which they did not particularly heed.

"Oh, he should have let him die," said Bainbridge, a railway engineer, finally replying to one of the barber's orations. "Shut up, Reif, and go on with your business!"

Instead, Reifsnyder paused shaving entirely, and turned to front the speaker. "Let him die?" he demanded. "How vas that? How can you let a man die?"

"By letting him die, you chump," said the engineer. The others laughed a little, and Reifsnyder turned at once to his work, sullenly, as a man overwhelmed by the derision of numbers.

"How vas that?" he grumbled later. "How can you let a man die when he vas done so much for you?"

"'When he vas done so much for you?'" repeated Bainbridge. "You better shave some people. How vas that? Maybe this ain't a barber shop?"

A man hitherto silent now said, "If I had been the doctor, I would have done the same thing."

"Of course," said Reifsnyder. "Any man vould do it. Any man that vas not like you, you – old – flint-hearted – fish." He had sought the final words with painful care, and he delivered the collection triumphantly at Bainbridge. The engineer laughed.

The man in the chair now lifted himself higher, while Reifsnyder began an elaborate ceremony of anointing and combing his hair. Now free to join comfortably in the talk, the man said: "They say he is the most terrible thing in the world. Young Johnnie Bernard – that drives the grocery wagon – saw him up at Alek Williams's shanty, and he says he couldn't eat anything for two days."

"Chee!" said Reifsnyder.

"Well, what makes him so terrible?" asked another.

"Because he hasn't got any face," replied the barber and the engineer in duet.

"Hasn't got any face?" repeated the man. "How can he do without any face!" "He has no face in the front of his head, In the place where his face ought to grow."

Bainbridge sang these lines pathetically as he arose and hung his hat on a hook. The man in the chair was about to abdicate in his favor. "Get a gait on you now," he said to Reifsnyder. "I go out at 7.31."

As the barber foamed the lather on the cheeks of the engineer he seemed to be thinking heavily. Then suddenly he burst out. "How would you like to be with no face?" he cried to the assemblage.

"Oh, if I had to have a face like yours – " answered one customer.

Bainbridge's voice came from a sea of lather. "You're kicking because if losing faces became popular, you'd have to go out of business."

"I don't think it will become so much popular," said Reifsnyder.

"Not if it's got to be taken off in the way his was taken off," said another man. "I'd rather keep mine, if you don't mind."

"I guess so!" cried the barber. "Just think!"

The shaving of Bainbridge had arrived at a time of comparative liberty for him. "I wonder what the doctor says to himself?" he observed. "He may be sorry he made him live."

"It was the only thing he could do," replied a man. The others seemed to agree with him.

"Supposing you were in his place," said one, "and Johnson had saved your kid. What would you do?"

"Certainly!"

"Of course! You would do anything on earth for him. You'd take all the trouble in the world for him. And spend your last dollar on him. Well, then?"

"I wonder how it feels to be without any face?" said Reifsnyder, musingly.

The man who had previously spoken, feeling that he had expressed himself well, repeated the whole thing. "You would do anything on earth for him. You'd take all the trouble in the world for him. And spend your last dollar on him. Well, then?"

"No, but look," said Reifsnyder; "supposing you don't got a face!"

XV

As soon as Williams was hidden from the view of the old judge he began to gesture and talk to himself. An elation had evidently penetrated to his vitals, and caused him to dilate as if he had been filled with gas. He snapped his fingers in the air, and whistled fragments of triumphal music. At times, in his progress towards his shanty, he indulged in a shuffling movement that was really a dance. It was to be learned from the intermediate monologue that he had emerged from his trials laurelled and proud. He was the unconquerable Alexander Williams. Nothing could exceed the bold self-reliance of his manner. His kingly stride, his heroic song, the derisive flourish of his hands – all betokened a man who had successfully defied the world.

On his way he saw Zeke Paterson coming to town. They hailed each other at a distance of fifty yards.

"How do, Broth' Paterson?"

"How do, Broth' Williams?"

They were both deacons.

"Is you' folks well, Broth' Paterson?"

"Middlin', middlin'. How's you' folks, Broth' Williams?"

Neither of them had slowed his pace in the smallest degree. They had simply begun this talk when a considerable space separated them, continued it as they passed, and added polite questions as they drifted steadily apart. Williams's mind seemed to be a balloon. He had been so inflated that he had not noticed that Paterson had definitely shied into the dry ditch as they came to the point of ordinary contact.

Afterward, as he went a lonely way, he burst out again in song and pantomimic celebration of his estate. His feet moved in prancing steps.

When he came in sight of his cabin, the fields were bathed in a blue dusk, and the light in the window was pale. Cavorting and gesticulating, he gazed joyfully for some moments upon this light. Then suddenly another idea seemed to attack his mind, and he stopped, with an air of being suddenly dampened. In the end he approached his home as if it were the fortress of an enemy.

Some dogs disputed his advance for a loud moment, and then discovering their lord, slunk away embarrassed. His reproaches were addressed to them in muffled tones.

Arriving at the door, he pushed it open with the timidity of a new thief. He thrust his head cautiously sideways, and his eyes met the eyes of his wife, who sat by the table, the lamp-light defining a half of her face. "Sh!" he said, uselessly. His glance travelled swiftly to the inner door which shielded the one bed-chamber. The pickaninnies, strewn upon the floor of the living-room, were softly snoring. After a hearty meal they had promptly dispersed themselves about the place and gone to sleep. "Sh!" said Williams again to his motionless and silent wife. He had allowed only his head to appear. His wife, with one hand upon the edge of the table and the other at her knee, was regarding him with wide eyes and parted lips as if he were a spectre. She looked to be one who was living in terror, and even the familiar face at the door had thrilled her because it had come suddenly.

Williams broke the tense silence. "Is he all right?" he whispered, waving his eyes towards the inner door. Following his glance timorously, his wife nodded, and in a low tone answered, "I raikon he's done gone t'sleep."

Williams then slunk noiselessly across his threshold.

He lifted a chair, and with infinite care placed it so that it faced the dreaded inner door. His wife moved slightly, so as to also squarely face it. A silence came upon them in which they seemed to be waiting for a calamity, pealing and deadly.

Williams finally coughed behind his hand. His wife started, and looked upon him in alarm. "'Pears like he done gwine keep quiet ter-night," he breathed. They continually pointed their speech and their looks at the inner door, paying it the homage due to a corpse or a phantom. Another long stillness followed this sentence. Their eyes shone white and wide. A wagon rattled down the distant road. From their chairs they looked at the window, and the effect of the light in the cabin was a presentation of an intensely black and solemn night. The old woman adopted the attitude used always in church at funerals. At times she seemed to be upon the point of breaking out in prayer.

"He mighty quiet ter-night," whispered Williams. "Was he good ter-day?" For answer his wife raised her eyes to the ceiling in the supplication of Job. Williams moved restlessly. Finally he tip-toed to the door. He knelt slowly and without a sound, and placed his ear near the key-hole. Hearing a noise behind him, he turned quickly. His wife was staring at him aghast. She stood in front of the stove, and her arms were spread out in the natural movement to protect all her sleeping ducklings.

But Williams arose without having touched the door. "I raikon he er-sleep," he said, fingering his wool. He debated with himself for some time. During this interval his wife remained, a great fat statue of a mother shielding her children.

It was plain that his mind was swept suddenly by a wave of temerity. With a sounding step he moved towards the door. His fingers were almost upon the knob when he swiftly ducked and dodged away, clapping his hands to the back of his head. It was as if the portal had threatened him. There was a little tumult near the stove, where Mrs. Williams's desperate retreat had involved her feet with the prostrate children.

After the panic Williams bore traces of a feeling of shame. He returned to the charge. He firmly grasped the knob with his left hand, and with his other hand turned the key in the lock. He pushed the door, and as it swung portentously open he sprang nimbly to one side like the fearful slave liberating the lion. Near the stove a group had formed, the terror-stricken mother, with her arms stretched, and the aroused children clinging frenziedly to her skirts.

The light streamed after the swinging door, and disclosed a room six feet one way and six feet the other way. It was small enough to enable the radiance to lay it plain. Williams peered warily around the corner made by the door-post.

Suddenly he advanced, retired, and advanced again with a howl. His palsied family had expected him to spring backward, and at his howl they heaped themselves wondrously. But Williams simply stood in the little room emitting his howls before an open window. "He's gone! He's gone! He's gone!" His eye and his hand had speedily proved the fact. He had even thrown open a little cupboard.

Presently he came flying out. He grabbed his hat, and hurled the outer door back upon its hinges. Then he tumbled headlong into the night. He was yelling: "Docteh Trescott! Docteh Trescott!" He ran wildly through the fields, and galloped in the direction of town. He continued to call to Trescott, as if the latter was within easy hearing. It was as if Trescott was poised in the contemplative sky over the running negro, and could heed this reaching voice – "Docteh Trescott!"

In the cabin, Mrs. Williams, supported by relays from the battalion of children, stood quaking watch until the truth of daylight came as a re-enforcement and made them arrogant, strutting, swashbuckler children, and a mother who proclaimed her illimitable courage.

XVI

Theresa Page was giving a party. It was the outcome of a long series of arguments addressed to her mother, which had been overheard in part by her father. He had at last said five words, "Oh, let her have it." The mother had then gladly capitulated.

Theresa had written nineteen invitations, and distributed them at recess to her schoolmates. Later her mother had composed five large cakes, and still later a vast amount of lemonade.

So the nine little girls and the ten little boys sat quite primly in the dining-room, while Theresa and her mother plied them with cake and lemonade, and also with ice-cream. This primness sat now quite strangely upon them. It was owing to the presence of Mrs. Page. Previously in the parlor alone with their games they had overturned a chair; the boys had let more or less of their hoodlum spirit shine forth. But when circumstances could be possibly magnified to warrant it, the girls made the boys victims of an insufferable pride, snubbing them mercilessly. So in the dining-room they resembled a class at Sunday-school, if it were not for the subterranean smiles, gestures, rebuffs, and poutings which stamped the affair as a children's party.

Two little girls of this subdued gathering were planted in a settle with their backs to the broad window. They were beaming lovingly upon each other with an effect of scorning the boys.

Hearing a noise behind her at the window, one little girl turned to face it. Instantly she screamed and sprang away, covering her face with her hands. "What was it? What was it?" cried every one in a roar. Some slight movement of the eyes of the weeping and shuddering child informed the company that she had been frightened by an appearance at the window. At once they all faced the imperturbable window, and for a moment there was a silence. An astute lad made an immediate census of the other lads. The prank of slipping out and looming spectrally at a window was too venerable. But the little boys were all present and astonished.

As they recovered their minds they uttered warlike cries, and through a side-door sallied rapidly out against the terror. They vied with each other in daring.

None wished particularly to encounter a dragon in the darkness of the garden, but there could be no faltering when the fair ones in the dining-room were present. Calling to each other in stern voices, they went dragooning over the lawn, attacking the shadows with ferocity, but still with the caution of reasonable beings. They found, however, nothing new to the peace of the night. Of course there was a lad who told a great lie. He described a grim figure, bending low and slinking off along the fence. He gave a number of details, rendering his lie more splendid by a repetition of certain forms which he recalled from romances. For instance, he insisted that he had heard the creature emit a hollow laugh.

Inside the house the little girl who had raised the alarm was still shuddering and weeping. With the utmost difficulty was she brought to a state approximating calmness by Mrs. Page. Then she wanted to go home at once.

Page entered the house at this time. He had exiled himself until he concluded that this children's party was finished and gone. He was obliged to escort the little girl home because she screamed again when they opened the door and she saw the night.

She was not coherent even to her mother. Was it a man? She didn't know. It was simply a thing, a dreadful thing.

XVII

In Watermelon Alley the Farraguts were spending their evening as usual on the little rickety porch. Sometimes they howled gossip to other people on other rickety porches. The thin wail of a baby arose from a near house. A man had a terrific altercation with his wife, to which the alley paid no attention at all.

There appeared suddenly before the Farraguts a monster making a low and sweeping bow. There was an instant's pause, and then occurred something that resembled the effect of an upheaval of the earth's surface. The old woman hurled herself backward with a dreadful cry. Young Sim had been perched gracefully on a railing. At sight of the monster he simply fell over it to the ground. He made no sound, his eyes stuck out, his nerveless hands tried to grapple the rail to prevent a tumble, and then he vanished. Bella, blubbering, and with her hair suddenly and mysteriously dishevelled, was crawling on her hands and knees fearsomely up the steps.

Standing before this wreck of a family gathering, the monster continued to bow. It even raised a deprecatory claw. "Don' make no botheration 'bout me, Miss Fa'gut," it said, politely. "No, 'deed. I jes drap in ter ax if yer well this evenin', Miss Fa'gut. Don' make no botheration. No, 'deed. I gwine ax you to go to er daince with me, Miss Fa'gut. I ax you if I can have the magnifercent gratitude of you' company on that 'casion, Miss Fa'gut."

The girl cast a miserable glance behind her. She was still crawling away. On the ground beside the porch young Sim raised a strange bleat, which expressed both his fright and his lack of wind. Presently the monster, with a fashionable amble, ascended the steps after the girl.

She grovelled in a corner of the room as the creature took a chair. It seated itself very elegantly on the edge. It held an old cap in both hands. "Don' make no botheration, Miss Fa'gut. Don' make no botheration. No, 'deed. I jes drap in ter ax you if you won' do me the proud of acceptin' ma humble invitation to er daince, Miss Fa'gut."

She shielded her eyes with her arms and tried to crawl past it, but the genial monster blocked the way. "I jes drap in ter ax you 'bout er daince, Miss Fa'gut. I ax you if I kin have the magnifercent gratitude of you' company on that 'casion, Miss Fa'gut."

In a last outbreak of despair, the girl, shuddering and wailing, threw herself face downward on the floor, while the monster sat on the edge of the chair gabbling courteous invitations, and holding the old hat daintily to his stomach.

At the back of the house, Mrs. Farragut, who was of enormous weight, and who for eight years had done little more than sit in an arm-chair and describe her various ailments, had with speed and agility scaled a high board fence.

XVIII

The black mass in the middle of Trescott's property was hardly allowed to cool before the builders were at work on another house. It had sprung upward at a fabulous rate. It was like a magical composition born of the ashes. The doctor's office was the first part to be completed, and he had already moved in his new books and instruments and medicines.

Trescott sat before his desk when the chief of police arrived. "Well, we found him," said the latter.

"Did you?" cried the doctor. "Where?"

"Shambling around the streets at daylight this morning. I'll be blamed if I can figure on where he passed the night."

"Where is he now?"

"Oh, we jugged him. I didn't know what else to do with him. That's what I want you to tell me. Of course we can't keep him. No charge could be made, you know."

"I'll come down and get him."

The official grinned retrospectively. "Must say he had a fine career while he was out. First thing he did was to break up a children's party at Page's. Then he went to Watermelon Alley. Whoo! He stampeded the whole outfit. Men, women, and children running pell-mell, and yelling. They say one old woman broke her leg, or something, shinning over a fence. Then he went right out on the main street, and an Irish girl threw a fit, and there was a sort of a riot. He began to run, and a big crowd chased him, firing rocks. But he gave them the slip somehow down there by the foundry and in the railroad yard. We looked for him all night, but couldn't find him."

"Was he hurt any? Did anybody hit him with a stone?"

"Guess there isn't much of him to hurt any more, is there? Guess he's been hurt up to the limit. No. They never touched him. Of course nobody really wanted to hit him, but you know how a crowd gets. It's like – it's like – "

"Yes, I know."

For a moment the chief of the police looked reflectively at the floor. Then he spoke hesitatingly. "You know Jake Winter's little girl was the one that he scared at the party. She is pretty sick, they say."

"Is she? Why, they didn't call me. I always attend the Winter family."

"No? Didn't they?" asked the chief, slowly. "Well – you know – Winter is – well, Winter has gone clean crazy over this business. He wanted – he wanted to have you arrested."

"Have me arrested? The idiot! What in the name of wonder could he have me arrested for?"

"Of course. He is a fool. I told him to keep his trap shut. But then you know how he'll go all over town yapping about the thing. I thought I'd better tip you."

"Oh, he is of no consequence; but then, of course, I'm obliged to you, Sam."

"That's all right. Well, you'll be down to-night and take him out, eh? You'll get a good welcome from the jailer. He don't like his job for a cent. He says you can have your man whenever you want him. He's got no use for him."

"But what is this business of Winter's about having me arrested?"

"Oh, it's a lot of chin about your having no right to allow this – this – this man to be at large. But I told him to tend to his own business. Only I thought I'd better let you know. And I might as well say right now, doctor, that there is a good deal of talk about this thing. If I were you, I'd come to the jail pretty late at night, because there is likely to be a crowd around the door, and I'd bring a – er – mask, or some kind of a veil, anyhow."

XIX

Martha Goodwin was single, and well along into the thin years. She lived with her married sister in Whilomville. She performed nearly all the house-work in exchange for the privilege of existence. Every one tacitly recognized her labor as a form of penance for the early end of her betrothed, who had died of small-pox, which he had not caught from her.

But despite the strenuous and unceasing workaday of her life, she was a woman of great mind. She had adamantine opinions upon the situation in Armenia, the condition of women in China, the flirtation between Mrs. Minster of Niagara Avenue and young Griscom, the conflict in the Bible class of the Baptist Sunday-school, the duty of the United States toward the Cuban insurgents, and many other colossal matters. Her fullest experience of violence was gained on an occasion when she had seen a hound clubbed, but in the plan which she had made for the reform of the world she advocated drastic measures. For instance, she contended that all the Turks should be pushed into the sea and drowned, and that Mrs. Minster and young Griscom should be hanged side by side on twin gallows. In fact, this woman of peace, who had seen only peace, argued constantly for a creed of illimitable ferocity. She was invulnerable on these questions, because eventually she overrode all opponents with a sniff. This sniff was an active force. It was to her antagonists like a bang over the head, and none was known to recover from this expression of exalted contempt. It left them windless and conquered. They never again came forward as candidates for suppression. And Martha walked her kitchen with a stern brow, an invincible being like Napoleon.

Nevertheless her acquaintances, from the pain of their defeats, had been long in secret revolt. It was in no wise a conspiracy, because they did not care to state their open rebellion, but nevertheless it was understood that any woman who could not coincide with one of Martha's contentions was entitled to the support of others in the small circle. It amounted to an arrangement by which all were required to disbelieve any theory for which Martha fought. This, however, did not prevent them from speaking of her mind with profound respect.

Two people bore the brunt of her ability. Her sister Kate was visibly afraid of her, while Carrie Dungen sailed across from her kitchen to sit respectfully at Martha's feet and learn the business of the world. To be sure, afterwards, under another sun, she always laughed at Martha and pretended to deride her ideas, but in the presence of the sovereign she always remained silent or admiring. Kate, the sister, was of no consequence at all. Her principal delusion was that she did all the work in the upstairs rooms of the house, while Martha did it downstairs. The truth was seen only by the husband, who treated Martha with a kindness that was half banter, half deference. Martha herself had no suspicion that she was the only pillar of the domestic edifice. The situation was without definitions. Martha made definitions, but she devoted them entirely to the Armenians and Griscom and the Chinese and other subjects. Her dreams, which in early days had been of love, of meadows and the shade of trees, of the face of a man, were now involved otherwise, and they were companioned in the kitchen curiously, Cuba, the hot-water kettle, Armenia, the washing of the dishes, and the whole thing being jumbled. In regard to social misdemeanors, she who was simply the mausoleum of a dead passion was probably the most savage critic in town. This unknown woman, hidden in a kitchen as in a well, was sure to have a considerable effect of the one kind or the other in the life of the town. Every time it moved a yard, she had personally contributed an inch. She could hammer so stoutly upon the door of a proposition that it would break from its hinges and fall upon her, but at any rate it moved. She was an engine, and the fact that she did not know that she was an engine contributed largely to the effect. One reason that she was formidable was that she did not even imagine that she was formidable. She remained a weak, innocent, and pig-headed creature, who alone would defy the universe if she thought the universe merited this proceeding.

One day Carrie Dungen came across from her kitchen with speed. She had a great deal of grist. "Oh," she cried, "Henry Johnson got away from where they was keeping him, and came to town last night, and scared everybody almost to death."

Martha was shining a dish-pan, polishing madly. No reasonable person could see cause for this operation, because the pan already glistened like silver. "Well!" she ejaculated. She imparted to the word a deep meaning. "This, my prophecy, has come to pass." It was a habit.

The overplus of information was choking Carrie. Before she could go on she was obliged to struggle for a moment. "And, oh, little Sadie Winter is awful sick, and they say Jake Winter was around this morning trying to get Doctor Trescott arrested. And poor old Mrs. Farragut sprained her ankle in trying to climb a fence. And there's a crowd around the jail all the time. They put Henry in jail because they didn't know what else to do with him, I guess. They say he is perfectly terrible."

Martha finally released the dish-pan and confronted the headlong speaker. "Well!" she said again, poising a great brown rag. Kate had heard the excited new-comer, and drifted down from the novel in her room. She was a shivery little woman. Her shoulder-blades seemed to be two panes of ice, for she was constantly shrugging and shrugging. "Serves him right if he was to lose all his patients," she said suddenly, in bloodthirsty tones. She snipped her words out as if her lips were scissors.

"Well, he's likely to," shouted Carrie Dungen. "Don't a lot of people say that they won't have him any more? If you're sick and nervous, Doctor Trescott would scare the life out of you, wouldn't he? He would me. I'd keep thinking."

Martha, stalking to and fro, sometimes surveyed the two other women with a contemplative frown.

XX

After the return from Connecticut, little Jimmie was at first much afraid of the monster who lived in the room over the carriage-house. He could not identify it in any way. Gradually, however, his fear dwindled under the influence of a weird fascination. He sidled into closer and closer relations with it.

One time the monster was seated on a box behind the stable basking in the rays of the afternoon sun. A heavy crêpe veil was swathed about its head.

Little Jimmie and many companions came around the corner of the stable. They were all in what was popularly known as the baby class, and consequently escaped from school a half-hour before the other children. They halted abruptly at sight of the figure on the box. Jimmie waved his hand with the air of a proprietor.

"There he is," he said.

"O-o-o!" murmured all the little boys – "o-o-o!" They shrank back, and grouped according to courage or experience, as at the sound the monster slowly turned its head. Jimmie had remained in the van alone. "Don't be afraid! I won't let him hurt you," he said, delighted.

"Huh!" they replied, contemptuously. "We ain't afraid."

Jimmie seemed to reap all the joys of the owner and exhibitor of one of the world's marvels, while his audience remained at a distance – awed and entranced, fearful and envious.

One of them addressed Jimmie gloomily. "Bet you dassent walk right up to him." He was an older boy than Jimmie, and habitually oppressed him to a small degree. This new social elevation of the smaller lad probably seemed revolutionary to him.

"Huh!" said Jimmie, with deep scorn. "Dassent I? Dassent I, hey? Dassent I?"

The group was immensely excited. It turned its eyes upon the boy that Jimmie addressed. "No, you dassent," he said, stolidly, facing a moral defeat. He could see that Jimmie was resolved. "No, you dassent," he repeated, doggedly.

"Ho!" cried Jimmie. "You just watch! – you just watch!"

Amid a silence he turned and marched toward the monster. But possibly the palpable wariness of his companions had an effect upon him that weighed more than his previous experience, for suddenly, when near to the monster, he halted dubiously. But his playmates immediately uttered a derisive shout, and it seemed to force him forward. He went to the monster and laid his hand delicately on its shoulder. "Hello, Henry," he said, in a voice that trembled a trifle. The monster was crooning a weird line of negro melody that was scarcely more than a thread of sound, and it paid no heed to the boy.

Jimmie strutted back to his companions. They acclaimed him and hooted his opponent. Amid this clamor the larger boy with difficulty preserved a dignified attitude.

"I dassent, dassent I?" said Jimmie to him. "Now, you're so smart, let's see you do it!"

This challenge brought forth renewed taunts from the others. The larger boy puffed out his cheeks. "Well, I ain't afraid," he explained, sullenly. He had made a mistake in diplomacy, and now his small enemies were tumbling his prestige all about his ears. They crowed like roosters and bleated like lambs, and made many other noises which were supposed to bury him in ridicule and dishonor. "Well, I ain't afraid," he continued to explain through the din.

Jimmie, the hero of the mob, was pitiless. "You ain't afraid, hey?" he sneered. "If you ain't afraid, go do it, then."

"Well, I would if I wanted to," the other retorted. His eyes wore an expression of profound misery, but he preserved steadily other portions of a pot-valiant air. He suddenly faced one of his persecutors. "If you're so smart, why don't you go do it?" This persecutor sank promptly through the group to the rear. The incident gave the badgered one a breathing-spell, and for a moment even turned the derision in another direction. He took advantage of his interval. "I'll do it if anybody else will," he announced, swaggering to and fro.

Candidates for the adventure did not come forward. To defend themselves from this counter-charge, the other boys again set up their crowing and bleating. For a while they would hear nothing from him. Each time he opened his lips their chorus of noises made oratory impossible. But at last he was able to repeat that he would volunteer to dare as much in the affair as any other boy.

"Well, you go first," they shouted.

But Jimmie intervened to once more lead the populace against the large boy. "You're mighty brave, ain't you?" he said to him. "You dared me to do it, and I did – didn't I? Now who's afraid?" The others cheered this view loudly, and they instantly resumed the baiting of the large boy.

He shamefacedly scratched his left shin with his right foot. "Well, I ain't afraid." He cast an eye at the monster. "Well, I ain't afraid." With a glare of hatred at his squalling tormentors, he finally announced a grim intention. "Well, I'll do it, then, since you're so fresh. Now!"

The mob subsided as with a formidable countenance he turned toward the impassive figure on the box. The advance was also a regular progression from high daring to craven hesitation. At last, when some yards from the monster, the lad came to a full halt, as if he had encountered a stone wall. The observant little boys in the distance promptly hooted. Stung again by these cries, the lad sneaked two yards forward. He was crouched like a young cat ready for a backward spring. The crowd at the rear, beginning to respect this display, uttered some encouraging cries. Suddenly the lad gathered himself together, made a white and desperate rush forward, touched the monster's shoulder with a far-outstretched finger, and sped away, while his laughter rang out wild, shrill, and exultant.

The crowd of boys reverenced him at once, and began to throng into his camp, and look at him, and be his admirers. Jimmie was discomfited for a moment, but he and the larger boy, without agreement or word of any kind, seemed to recognize a truce, and they swiftly combined and began to parade before the others.

"Why, it's just as easy as nothing," puffed the larger boy. "Ain't it, Jim?"

"Course," blew Jimmie. "Why, it's as e-e-easy."

They were people of another class. If they had been decorated for courage on twelve battle-fields, they could not have made the other boys more ashamed of the situation.

Meanwhile they condescended to explain the emotions of the excursion, expressing unqualified contempt for any one who could hang back. "Why, it ain't nothin'. He won't do nothin' to you," they told the others, in tones of exasperation.

One of the very smallest boys in the party showed signs of a wistful desire to distinguish himself, and they turned their attention to him, pushing at his shoulders while he swung away from them, and hesitated dreamily. He was eventually induced to make furtive expedition, but it was only for a few yards. Then he paused, motionless, gazing with open mouth. The vociferous entreaties of Jimmie and the large boy had no power over him.

Mrs. Hannigan had come out on her back porch with a pail of water. From this coign she had a view of the secluded portion of the Trescott grounds that was behind the stable. She perceived the group of boys, and the monster on the box. She shaded her eyes with her hand to benefit her vision. She screeched then as if she was being murdered. "Eddie! Eddie! You come home this minute!"

Her son queruously demanded, "Aw, what for?"

"You come home this minute. Do you hear?"

The other boys seemed to think this visitation upon one of their number required them to preserve for a time the hang-dog air of a collection of culprits, and they remained in guilty silence until the little Hannigan, wrathfully protesting, was pushed through the door of his home. Mrs. Hannigan cast a piercing glance over the group, stared with a bitter face at the Trescott house, as if this new and handsome edifice was insulting her, and then followed her son.

There was wavering in the party. An inroad by one mother always caused them to carefully sweep the horizon to see if there were more coming. "This is my yard," said Jimmie, proudly. "We don't have to go home."

The monster on the box had turned its black crêpe countenance toward the sky, and was waving its arms in time to a religious chant. "Look at him now," cried a little boy. They turned, and were transfixed by the solemnity and mystery of the indefinable gestures. The wail of the melody was mournful and slow. They drew back. It seemed to spellbind them with the power of a funeral. They were so absorbed that they did not hear the doctor's buggy drive up to the stable. Trescott got out, tied his horse, and approached the group. Jimmie saw him first, and at his look of dismay the others wheeled.

"What's all this, Jimmie?" asked Trescott, in surprise.

The lad advanced to the front of his companions, halted, and said nothing. Trescott's face gloomed slightly as he scanned the scene.

"What were you doing, Jimmie?"

"We was playin'," answered Jimmie, huskily.

"Playing at what?"

"Just playin'."

Trescott looked gravely at the other boys, and asked them to please go home. They proceeded to the street much in the manner of frustrated and revealed assassins. The crime of trespass on another boy's place was still a crime when they had only accepted the other boy's cordial invitation, and they were used to being sent out of all manner of gardens upon the sudden appearance of a father or a mother. Jimmie had wretchedly watched the departure of his companions. It involved the loss of his position as a lad who controlled the privileges of his father's grounds, but then he knew that in the beginning he had no right to ask so many boys to be his guests.

Once on the sidewalk, however, they speedily forgot their shame as trespassers, and the large boy launched forth in a description of his success in the late trial of courage. As they went rapidly up the street, the little boy who had made the furtive expedition cried out confidently from the rear, "Yes, and I went almost up to him, didn't I, Willie?"

The large boy crushed him in a few words. "Huh!" he scoffed. "You only went a little way. I went clear up to him."

The pace of the other boys was so manly that the tiny thing had to trot, and he remained at the rear, getting entangled in their legs in his attempts to reach the front rank and become of some importance, dodging this way and that way, and always piping out his little claim to glory.

XXI

"By-the-way, Grace," said Trescott, looking into the dining-room from his office door, "I wish you would send Jimmie to me before school-time."

When Jimmie came, he advanced so quietly that Trescott did not at first note him. "Oh," he said, wheeling from a cabinet, "here you are, young man."

"Yes, sir."

Trescott dropped into his chair and tapped the desk with a thoughtful finger. "Jimmie, what were you doing in the back garden yesterday – you and the other boys – to Henry?"

"We weren't doing anything, pa."

Trescott looked sternly into the raised eyes of his son. "Are you sure you were not annoying him in any way? Now what were you doing, exactly?"

"Why, we – why, we – now – Willie Dalzel said I dassent go right up to him, and I did; and then he did; and then – the other boys were 'fraid; and then – you comed."

Trescott groaned deeply. His countenance was so clouded in sorrow that the lad, bewildered by the mystery of it, burst suddenly forth in dismal lamentations. "There, there. Don't cry, Jim," said Trescott, going round the desk. "Only – " He sat in a great leather reading-chair, and took the boy on his knee. "Only I want to explain to you – "

After Jimmie had gone to school, and as Trescott was about to start on his round of morning calls, a message arrived from Doctor Moser. It set forth that the latter's sister was dying in the old homestead, twenty miles away up the valley, and asked Trescott to care for his patients for the day at least. There was also in the envelope a little history of each case and of what had already been done. Trescott replied to the messenger that he would gladly assent to the arrangement.

He noted that the first name on Moser's list was Winter, but this did not seem to strike him as an important fact. When its turn came, he rang the Winter bell. "Good-morning, Mrs. Winter," he said, cheerfully, as the door was opened. "Doctor Moser has been obliged to leave town to-day, and he has asked me to come in his stead. How is the little girl this morning?"

Mrs. Winter had regarded him in stony surprise. At last she said: "Come in! I'll see my husband." She bolted into the house. Trescott entered the hall, and turned to the left into the sitting-room.

Presently Winter shuffled through the door. His eyes flashed towards Trescott. He did not betray any desire to advance far into the room. "What do you want?" he said.

"What do I want? What do I want?" repeated Trescott, lifting his head suddenly. He had heard an utterly new challenge in the night of the jungle.

"Yes, that's what I want to know," snapped Winter. "What do you want?"

Trescott was silent for a moment. He consulted Moser's memoranda. "I see that your little girl's case is a trifle serious," he remarked. "I would advise you to call a physician soon. I will leave you a copy of Doctor Moser's record to give to any one you may call." He paused to transcribe the record on a page of his note-book. Tearing out the leaf, he extended it to Winter as he moved towards the door. The latter shrunk against the wall. His head was hanging as he reached for the paper. This caused him to grasp air, and so Trescott simply let the paper flutter to the feet of the other man.

"Good-morning," said Trescott from the hall. This placid retreat seemed to suddenly arouse Winter to ferocity. It was as if he had then recalled all the truths, which he had formulated to hurl at Trescott. So he followed him into the hall, and down the hall to the door, and through the door to the porch, barking in fiery rage from a respectful distance. As Trescott imperturbably turned the mare's head down the road, Winter stood on the porch, still yelping. He was like a little dog.

XXII

"Have you heard the news?" cried Carrie Dungen, as she sped toward Martha's kitchen. "Have you heard the news?" Her eyes were shining with delight.

"No," answered Martha's sister Kate, bending forward eagerly. "What was it? What was it?"

Carrie appeared triumphantly in the open door. "Oh, there's been an awful scene between Doctor Trescott and Jake Winter. I never thought that Jake Winter had any pluck at all, but this morning he told the doctor just what he thought of him."

"Well, what did he think of him?" asked Martha.

"Oh, he called him everything. Mrs. Howarth heard it through her front blinds. It was terrible, she says. It's all over town now. Everybody knows it."

"Didn't the doctor answer back?"

"No! Mrs. Howarth – she says he never said a word. He just walked down to his buggy and got in, and drove off as co-o-o-l. But Jake gave him jinks, by all accounts."

"But what did he say?" cried Kate, shrill and excited. She was evidently at some kind of a feast.

"Oh, he told him that Sadie had never been well since that night Henry Johnson frightened her at Theresa Page's party, and he held him responsible, and how dared he cross his threshold – and – and – and – "

"And what?" said Martha.

"Did he swear at him?" said Kate, in fearsome glee.

"No – not much. He did swear at him a little, but not more than a man does anyhow when he is real mad, Mrs. Howarth says."

"O-oh!" breathed Kate. "And did he call him any names?"

Martha, at her work, had been for a time in deep thought. She now interrupted the others. "It don't seem as if Sadie Winter had been sick since that time Henry Johnson got loose. She's been to school almost the whole time since then, hasn't she?"

They combined upon her in immediate indignation. "School? School? I should say not. Don't think for a moment. School!"

Martha wheeled from the sink. She held an iron spoon, and it seemed as if she was going to attack them. "Sadie Winter has passed here many a morning since then carrying her school-bag. Where was she going? To a wedding?"

The others, long accustomed to a mental tyranny, speedily surrendered.

"Did she?" stammered Kate. "I never saw her."

Carrie Dungen made a weak gesture.

"If I had been Doctor Trescott," exclaimed Martha, loudly, "I'd have knocked that miserable Jake Winter's head off."

Kate and Carrie, exchanging glances, made an alliance in the air. "I don't see why you say that, Martha," replied Carrie, with considerable boldness, gaining support and sympathy from Kate's smile. "I don't see how anybody can be blamed for getting angry when their little girl gets almost scared to death and gets sick from it, and all that. Besides, everybody says – "

"Oh, I don't care what everybody says," said Martha.

"Well, you can't go against the whole town," answered Carrie, in sudden sharp defiance.

"No, Martha, you can't go against the whole town," piped Kate, following her leader rapidly.

"'The whole town,'" cried Martha. "I'd like to know what you call 'the whole town.' Do you call these silly people who are scared of Henry Johnson 'the whole town'?"

"Why, Martha," said Carrie, in a reasoning tone, "you talk as if you wouldn't be scared of him!"

"No more would I," retorted Martha.

"O-oh, Martha, how you talk!" said Kate. "Why, the idea! Everybody's afraid of him."

Carrie was grinning. "You've never seen him, have you?" she asked, seductively.

"No," admitted Martha.

"Well, then, how do you know that you wouldn't be scared?"

Martha confronted her. "Have you ever seen him? No? Well, then, how do you know you would be scared?"

The allied forces broke out in chorus: "But, Martha, everybody says so. Everybody says so."

"Everybody says what?"

"Everybody that's seen him say they were frightened almost to death. 'Tisn't only women, but it's men too. It's awful."

Martha wagged her head solemnly. "I'd try not to be afraid of him."

"But supposing you could not help it?" said Kate.

"Yes, and look here," cried Carrie. "I'll tell you another thing. The Hannigans are going to move out of the house next door."

"On account of him?" demanded Martha.

Carrie nodded. "Mrs. Hannigan says so herself."

"Well, of all things!" ejaculated Martha. "Going to move, eh? You don't say so! Where they going to move to?"

"Down on Orchard Avenue."

"Well, of all things! Nice house?"

"I don't know about that. I haven't heard. But there's lots of nice houses on Orchard."

"Yes, but they're all taken," said Kate. "There isn't a vacant house on Orchard Avenue."

"Oh yes, there is," said Martha. "The old Hampstead house is vacant."

"Oh, of course," said Kate. "But then I don't believe Mrs. Hannigan would like it there. I wonder where they can be going to move to?"

"I'm sure I don't know," sighed Martha. "It must be to some place we don't know about."

"Well," said Carrie Dungen, after a general reflective silence, "it's easy enough to find out, anyhow."

"Who knows – around here?" asked Kate.

"Why, Mrs. Smith, and there she is in her garden," said Carrie, jumping to her feet. As she dashed out of the door, Kate and Martha crowded at the window. Carrie's voice rang out from near the steps. "Mrs. Smith! Mrs. Smith! Do you know where the Hannigans are going to move to?"

XXIII

The autumn smote the leaves, and the trees of Whilomville were panoplied in crimson and yellow. The winds grew stronger, and in the melancholy purple of the nights the home shine of a window became a finer thing. The little boys, watching the sear and sorrowful leaves drifting down from the maples, dreamed of the near time when they could heap bushels in the streets and burn them during the abrupt evenings.

Three men walked down the Niagara Avenue. As they approached Judge Hagenthorpe's house he came down his walk to meet them in the manner of one who has been waiting.

"Are you ready, judge?" one said.

"All ready," he answered.

The four then walked to Trescott's house. He received them in his office, where he had been reading. He seemed surprised at this visit of four very active and influential citizens, but he had nothing to say of it.

After they were all seated, Trescott looked expectantly from one face to another. There was a little silence. It was broken by John Twelve, the wholesale grocer, who was worth $400,000, and reported to be worth over a million.

"Well, doctor," he said, with a short laugh, "I suppose we might as well admit at once that we've come to interfere in something which is none of our business."

"Why, what is it?" asked Trescott, again looking from one face to another. He seemed to appeal particularly to Judge Hagenthorpe, but the old man had his chin lowered musingly to his cane, and would not look at him.

"It's about what nobody talks of – much," said Twelve. "It's about Henry Johnson."

Trescott squared himself in his chair. "Yes?" he said.

Having delivered himself of the title, Twelve seemed to become more easy. "Yes," he answered, blandly, "we wanted to talk to you about it."

"Yes?" said Trescott.

Twelve abruptly advanced on the main attack. "Now see here, Trescott, we like you, and we have come to talk right out about this business. It may be none of our affairs and all that, and as for me, I don't mind if you tell me so; but I am not going to keep quiet and see you ruin yourself. And that's how we all feel."

"I am not ruining myself," answered Trescott.

"No, maybe you are not exactly ruining yourself," said Twelve, slowly, "but you are doing yourself a great deal of harm. You have changed from being the leading doctor in town to about the last one. It is mainly because there are always a large number of people who are very thoughtless fools, of course, but then that doesn't change the condition."

A man who had not heretofore spoken said, solemnly, "It's the women."

"Well, what I want to say is this," resumed Twelve: "Even if there are a lot of fools in the world, we can't see any reason why you should ruin yourself by opposing them. You can't teach them anything, you know."

"I am not trying to teach them anything." Trescott smiled wearily. "I – It is a matter of – well – "

"And there are a good many of us that admire you for it immensely," interrupted Twelve; "but that isn't going to change the minds of all those ninnies."

"It's the women," stated the advocate of this view again.

"Well, what I want to say is this," said Twelve. "We want you to get out of this trouble and strike your old gait again. You are simply killing your practice through your infernal pig-headedness. Now this thing is out of the ordinary, but there must be ways to – to beat the game somehow, you see. So we've talked it over – about a dozen of us – and, as I say, if you want to tell us to mind our own business, why, go ahead; but we've talked it over, and we've come to the conclusion that the only way to do is to get Johnson a place somewhere off up the valley, and – "

Trescott wearily gestured. "You don't know, my friend. Everybody is so afraid of him, they can't even give him good care. Nobody can attend to him as I do myself."

"But I have a little no-good farm up beyond Clarence Mountain that I was going to give to Henry," cried Twelve, aggrieved. "And if you – and if you – if you – through your house burning down, or anything – why, all the boys were prepared to take him right off your hands, and – and – "

Trescott arose and went to the window. He turned his back upon them. They sat waiting in silence. When he returned he kept his face in the shadow. "No, John Twelve," he said, "it can't be done."

There was another stillness. Suddenly a man stirred on his chair.

"Well, then, a public institution – " he began.

"No," said Trescott; "public institutions are all very good, but he is not going to one."

In the background of the group old Judge Hagenthorpe was thoughtfully smoothing the polished ivory head of his cane.

XXIV

Trescott loudly stamped the snow from his feet and shook the flakes from his shoulders. When he entered the house he went at once to the dining-room, and then to the sitting-room. Jimmie was there, reading painfully in a large book concerning giraffes and tigers and crocodiles.

"Where is your mother, Jimmie?" asked Trescott.

"I don't know, pa," answered the boy. "I think she is upstairs."

Trescott went to the foot of the stairs and called, but there came no answer. Seeing that the door of the little drawing-room was open, he entered. The room was bathed in the half-light that came from the four dull panes of mica in the front of the great stove. As his eyes grew used to the shadows he saw his wife curled in an arm-chair. He went to her. "Why, Grace," he said, "didn't you hear me calling you?"

She made no answer, and as he bent over the chair he heard her trying to smother a sob in the cushion.

"Grace!" he cried. "You're crying!"

She raised her face. "I've got a headache, a dreadful headache, Ned."

"A headache?" he repeated, in surprise and incredulity.

He pulled a chair close to hers. Later, as he cast his eye over the zone of light shed by the dull red panes, he saw that a low table had been drawn close to the stove, and that it was burdened with many small cups and plates of uncut tea-cake. He remembered that the day was Wednesday, and that his wife received on Wednesdays.

"Who was here to-day, Gracie?" he asked.

From his shoulder there came a mumble, "Mrs. Twelve."

"Was she – um," he said. "Why – didn't Anna Hagenthorpe come over?"

The mumble from his shoulder continued, "She wasn't well enough."

Glancing down at the cups, Trescott mechanically counted them. There were fifteen of them. "There, there," he said. "Don't cry, Grace. Don't cry."

The wind was whining round the house, and the snow beat aslant upon the windows. Sometimes the coal in the stove settled with a crumbling sound, and the four panes of mica flashed a sudden new crimson. As he sat holding her head on his shoulder, Trescott found himself occasionally trying to count the cups. There were fifteen of them.

The O'Ruddy

CHAPTER I

My chieftain ancestors had lived at Glandore for many centuries and were very well known. Hardly a ship could pass the Old Head of Kinsale without some boats putting off to exchange the time of day with her, and our family name was on men's tongues in half the seaports of Europe, I dare say. My ancestors lived in castles which were like churches stuck on end, and they drank the best of everything amid the joyous cries of a devoted peasantry. But the good time passed away soon enough, and when I had reached the age of eighteen we had nobody on the land but a few fisher-folk and small farmers, people who were almost law-abiding, and my father came to die more from disappointment than from any other cause. Before the end he sent for me to come to his bedside.

"Tom," he said, "I brought you into existence, and God help you safe out of it; for you are not the kind of man ever to turn your hand to work, and there is only enough money to last a gentleman five more years.

"The 'Martha Bixby,' she was, out of Bristol for the West Indies, and if it hadn't been for her we would never have got along this far with plenty to eat and drink. However, I leave you, besides the money, the two swords,—the grand one that King Louis, God bless him, gave me, and the plain one that will really be of use to you if you get into a disturbance. Then here is the most important matter of all. Here are some papers which young Lord Strepp gave me to hold for him when we were comrades in France. I don't know what they are, having had very little time for reading during my life, but do you return them to him. He is now the great Earl of Westport, and he lives in London in a grand house, I hear. In the last campaign in France I had to lend him a pair of breeches or he would have gone bare. These papers are important to him, and he may reward you, but do not you depend on it, for you may get the back of his hand. I have not seen him for years. I am glad I had you taught to read. They read considerably in England, I hear. There is one more cask of the best brandy remaining, and I recommend you to leave for England as soon as it is finished. And now, one more thing, my lad, never be civil to a king's officer. Wherever you see a red coat, depend there is a rogue between the front and the back of it. I have said everything. Push the bottle near me."

Three weeks after my father's burial I resolved to set out, with no more words, to deliver the papers to the Earl of Westport. I was resolved to be prompt in obeying my father's command, for I was extremely anxious to see the world, and my feet would hardly wait for me. I put my estate into the hands of old Mickey Clancy, and told him not to trouble the tenants too much over the rent, or they probably would split his skull for him. And I bid Father Donovan look out for old Mickey Clancy, that he stole from me only what was reasonable.

I went to the Cove of Cork and took ship there for Bristol, and arrived safely after a passage amid great storms which blew us so near Glandore that I feared the enterprise of my own peasantry. Bristol, I confess, frightened me greatly. I had not imagined such a huge and teeming place. All the ships in the world seemed to lie there, and the quays were thick with sailor-men. The streets rang with noise. I suddenly found that I was a young gentleman from the country.

I followed my luggage to the best inn, and it was very splendid, fit to be a bishop's palace. It was filled with handsomely dressed people who all seemed to be yelling, "Landlord! landlord!" And there was a little fat man in a white apron who flew about as if he were being stung by bees, and he was crying, "Coming, sir! Yes, madam! At once, your ludship!" They heeded me no more than if I had been an empty glass. I stood on one leg, waiting until the little fat man should either wear himself out or attend all the people. But it was to no purpose. He did not wear out, nor did his business finish, so finally I was obliged to plant myself in his way, but my speech was decent enough as I asked him for a chamber. Would you believe it, he stopped abruptly and stared at me with sudden suspicion. My speech had been so civil that he had thought perhaps I was a rogue. I only give you this incident to show that if later I came to bellow like a bull with the best of them, it was only through the necessity of proving to strangers that I was a gentleman. I soon learned to enter an inn as a drunken soldier goes through the breach into a surrendering city.

Having made myself as presentable as possible, I came down from my chamber to seek some supper. The supper-room was ablaze with light and well filled with persons of quality, to judge from the noise that they were making. My seat was next to a garrulous man in plum-colour, who seemed to know the affairs of the entire world. As I dropped into my chair he was saying —

"—the heir to the title, of course. Young Lord Strepp. That is he-the slim youth with light hair. Oh, of course, all in shipping. The Earl must own twenty sail that trade from Bristol. He is posting down from London, by the way, to-night."

You can well imagine how these words excited me. I half arose from my chair with the idea of going at once to the young man who had been indicated as Lord Strepp, and informing him of my errand, but I had a sudden feeling of timidity, a feeling that it was necessary to be proper with these people of high degree. I kept my seat, resolving to accost him directly after supper. I studied him with interest. He was a young man of about twenty years, with fair unpowdered hair and a face ruddy from a life in the open air. He looked generous and kindly, but just at the moment he was damning a waiter in language that would have set fire to a stone bridge. Opposite him was a clear-eyed soldierly man of about forty, whom I had heard called "Colonel," and at the Colonel's right was a proud, dark-skinned man who kept looking in all directions to make sure that people regarded him, seated thus with a lord.

They had drunk eight bottles of port, and in those days eight bottles could just put three gentlemen in pleasant humour. As the ninth bottle came on the table the Colonel cried—

"Come, Strepp, tell us that story of how your father lost his papers. Gad, that's a good story."

"No, no," said the young lord. "It isn't a good story, and besides my father never tells it at all. I misdoubt it's truth."

The Colonel pounded the table. "'Tis true. 'Tis too good a story to be false. You know the story, Forister?" said he, turning to the dark-skinned man. The latter shook his head.

"Well, when the Earl was a young man serving with the French he rather recklessly carried with him some valuable papers relating to some estates in the North, and once the noble Earl-or Lord Strepp as he was then-found it necessary, after fording a stream, to hang his breeches on a bush to dry, and then a certain blackguard of a wild Irishman in the corps came along and stole—"

But I had arisen and called loudly but with dignity up the long table, "That, sir, is a lie." The room came still with a bang, if I may be allowed that expression. Every one gaped at me, and the Colonel's face slowly went the colour of a tiled roof.

"My father never stole his lordship's breeches, for the good reason that at the time his lordship had no breeches. 'Twas the other way. My father —"

Here the two long rows of faces lining the room crackled for a moment, and then every man burst into a thunderous laugh. But I had flung to the winds my timidity of a new country, and I was not to be put down by these clowns.

"'Tis a lie against an honourable man and my father," I shouted. "And if my father hadn't provided his lordship with breeches, he would have gone bare, and there's the truth. And," said I, staring at the Colonel, "I give the lie again. We are never obliged to give it twice in my country."

The Colonel had been grinning a little, no doubt thinking, along with everybody else in the room, that I was drunk or crazy; but this last twist took the smile off his face clean enough, and he came to his feet with a bound. I awaited him. But young Lord Strepp and Forister grabbed him and began to argue. At the same time there came down upon me such a deluge of waiters and pot-boys, and, may be, hostlers, that I couldn't have done anything if I had been an elephant. They were frightened out of their wits and painfully respectful, but all the same and all the time they were bundling me toward the door. "Sir! Sir! Sir! I beg you, sir! Think of the 'ouse, sir! Sir! Sir! Sir!" And I found myself out in the hall.

Here I addressed them calmly. "Loose me and takes yourselves off quickly, lest I grow angry and break some dozen of these wooden heads." They took me at my word and vanished like ghosts. Then the landlord came bleating, but I merely told him that I wanted to go to my chamber, and if anybody inquired for me I wished him conducted up at once.

In my chamber I had not long to wait. Presently there were steps in the corridor and a knock at my door. At my bidding the door opened and Lord Strepp entered. I arose and we bowed. He was embarrassed and rather dubious.

"Aw," he began, "I come, sir, from Colonel Royale, who begs to be informed who he has had the honour of offending, sir?"

"'Tis not a question for your father's son, my lord," I answered bluntly at last.

"You are, then, the son of The O'Ruddy?"

"No," said I. "I am The O'Ruddy. My father died a month gone and more."

"Oh!" said he. And I now saw why he was embarrassed. He had feared from the beginning that I was altogether too much in the right. "Oh!" said he again. I made up my mind that he was a good lad. "That is dif—" he began awkwardly. "I mean, Mr. O'Ruddy-oh, damn it all, you know what I mean, Mr. O'Ruddy!"

I bowed. "Perfectly, my lord!" I did not understand him, of course.

"I shall have the honour to inform Colonel Royale that Mr. O'Ruddy is entitled to every consideration," he said more collectedly. "If Mr. O'Ruddy will have the goodness to await me here?"

"Yes, my lord." He was going in order to tell the Colonel that I was a gentleman. And of course he returned quickly with the news. But he did not look as if the message was one which he could deliver with a glib tongue. "Sir," he began, and then halted. I could but courteously wait. "Sir, Colonel Royale bids me say that he is shocked to find that he has carelessly and publicly inflicted an insult upon an unknown gentleman through the memory of the gentleman's dead father. Colonel Royale bids me to say, sir, that he is overwhelmed with regret, and that far from taking an initial step himself it is his duty to express to you his feeling that his movements should coincide with any arrangements you may choose to make."

I was obliged to be silent for a considerable period in order to gather head and tail of this marvellous sentence. At last I caught it. "At daybreak I shall walk abroad," I replied, "and I have no doubt that Colonel Royale will be good enough to accompany me. I know nothing of Bristol. Any cleared space will serve."

My Lord Strepp bowed until he almost knocked his forehead on the floor. "You are most amiable, Mr. O'Ruddy. You of course will give me the name of some friend to whom I can refer minor matters?"

I found that I could lie in England as readily as ever I did in Ireland. "My friend will be on the ground with me, my lord; and as he also is a very amiable man it will not take two minutes to make everything clear and fair." Me, with not a friend in the world but Father O'Donovan and Mickey Clancy at Glandore!

Lord Strepp bowed again, the same as before. "Until the morning then, Mr. O'Ruddy," he said, and left me.

I sat me down on my bed to think. In truth I was much puzzled and amazed. These gentlemen were actually reasonable and were behaving like men of heart. Neither my books nor my father's stories-great lies, many of them, God rest him! —had taught me that the duelling gentry could think at all, and I was quite certain that they never tried. "You were looking at me, sir?" "Was I, 'faith? Well, if I care to look at you I shall look at you." And then away they would go at it, prodding at each other's bellies until somebody's flesh swallowed a foot of steel. "Sir, I do not like the colour of your coat!" Clash! "Sir, red hair always offends me." Cling! "Sir, your fondness for rabbit-pie is not polite." Clang!

However, the minds of young Lord Strepp and Colonel Royale seemed to be capable of a process which may be termed human reflection. It was plain that the Colonel did not like the situation at all, and perhaps considered himself the victim of a peculiarly exasperating combination of circumstances. That an Irishman should turn up in Bristol and give him the lie over a French pair of breeches must have seemed astonishing to him, notably when he learned that the Irishman was quite correct, having in fact a clear title to speak authoritatively upon the matter of the breeches. And when Lord Strepp learned that I was The O'Ruddy he saw clearly that the Colonel was in the wrong, and that I had a perfect right to resent the insult to my father's memory. And so the Colonel probably said: "Look you, Strepp. I have no desire to kill this young gentleman, because I insulted his father's name. It is out of all decency. And do you go to him this second time and see what may be done in the matter of avoidance. But, mark you, if he expresses any wishes, you of course offer immediate accommodation. I will not wrong him twice." And so up came my Lord Strepp and hemmed and hawed in that way which puzzled me. A pair of thoughtful, honourable fellows, these, and I admired them greatly.

There was now no reason why I should keep my chamber, since if I now met even the Colonel himself there would be no brawling; only bows. I was not, indeed, fond of these latter,—replying to Lord Strepp had almost broken my back; but, any how, more bows were better than more loud words and another downpour of waiters and pot-boys.

But I had reckoned without the dark-skinned man, Forister. When I arrived in the lower corridor and was passing through it on my way to take the air, I found a large group of excited people talking of the quarrel and the duel that was to be fought at daybreak. I thought it was a great hubbub over a very small thing, but it seems that the mainspring of the excitement was the tongue of this black Forister. "Why, the Irish run naked through their native forests," he was crying. "Their sole weapon is the great knotted club, with which, however, they do not hesitate, when in great numbers, to attack lions and tigers. But how can this barbarian face the sword of an officer of His Majesty's army?"

Some in the group espied my approach, and there was a nudging of elbows. There was a general display of agitation, and I marvelled at the way in which many made it to appear that they had not formed part of the group at all. Only Forister was cool and insolent. He stared full at me and grinned, showing very white teeth. "Swords are very different from clubs, great knotted clubs," he said with admirable deliberation.

"Even so," rejoined I gravely. "Swords are for gentlemen, while clubs are to clout the heads of rogues-thus." I boxed his ear with my open hand, so that he fell against the wall. "I will now picture also the use of boots by kicking you into the inn yard which is adjacent." So saying I hurled him to the great front door which stood open, and then, taking a sort of hop and skip, I kicked for glory and the Saints.

I do not know that I ever kicked a man with more success. He shot out as if he had been heaved by a catapult. There was a dreadful uproar behind me, and I expected every moment to be stormed by the waiter-and-pot-boy regiment. However I could hear some of the gentlemen bystanding cry:

"Well done! Well kicked! A record! A miracle!"

But my first hours on English soil contained still other festivities. Bright light streamed out from the great door, and I could plainly note what I shall call the arc or arcs described by Forister. He struck the railing once, but spun off it, and to my great astonishment went headlong and slap-crash into some sort of an upper servant who had been approaching the door with both arms loaded with cloaks, cushions, and rugs.

I suppose the poor man thought that black doom had fallen upon him from the sky. He gave a great howl as he, Forister, the cloaks, cushions, and rugs spread out grandly in one sublime confusion.

Some ladies screamed, and a bold commanding voice said: "In the devil's name what have we here?" Behind the unhappy servant had been coming two ladies and a very tall gentleman in a black cloak that reached to his heels. "What have we here?" again cried this tall man, who looked like an old eagle. He stepped up to me haughtily. I knew that I was face to face with the Earl of Westport.

But was I a man for ever in the wrong that I should always be giving down and walking away with my tail between my legs? Not I; I stood bravely to the Earl:

"If your lordship pleases, 'tis The O'Ruddy kicking a blackguard into the yard," I made answer coolly.

I could see that he had been about to shout for the landlord and more waiters and pot-boys, but at my naming myself he gave a quick stare.

"The O'Ruddy?" he repeated. "Rubbish!"

He was startled, bewildered; but I could not tell if he were glad or grieved.

"'Tis all the name I own," I said placidly. "My father left it me clear, it being something that he could not mortgage. 'Twas on his death-bed he told me of lending you the breeches, and that is why I kicked the man into the yard; and if your lordship had arrived sooner I could have avoided this duel at daybreak, and, any how, I wonder at his breeches fitting you. He was a small man."

Suddenly the Earl raised his hand. "Enough," he said sternly. "You are your father's son. Come to my chamber in the morning, O'Ruddy."

There had been little chance to see what was inside the cloaks of the ladies, but at the words of the Earl there peeped from one hood a pair of bright liquid eyes-God save us all! In a flash I was no longer a free man; I was a dazed slave; the Saints be good to us!

The contents of the other hood could not have been so interesting, for from it came the raucous voice of a bargeman with a cold:

"Why did he kick him? Whom did he kick? Had he cheated at play? Where has he gone?"

The upper servant appeared, much battered and holding his encrimsoned nose.

"My lord —" he began.

But the Earl roared at him, —

"Hold your tongue, rascal, and in future look where you are going and don't get in a gentleman's way."

The landlord, in a perfect anguish, was hovering with his squadrons on the flanks. They could not think of pouncing upon me if I was noticed at all by the great Earl; but, somewhat as a precaution perhaps, they remained in form for attack. I had no wish that the pair of bright eyes should see me buried under a heap of these wretches, so I bowed low to the ladies and to the Earl and passed out of doors. As I left, the Earl moved his hand to signify that he was now willing to endure the attendance of the landlord and his people, and in a moment the inn rang with hurried cries and rushing feet.

As I passed near the taproom window the light fell full upon a railing; just beneath and over this railing hung two men. At first I thought they were ill, but upon passing near I learned that they were simply limp and helpless with laughter, the sound of which they contrived to keep muffled. To my surprise I recognized the persons of young Lord Strepp and Colonel Royale.

CHAPTER II

The night was growing, and as I was to fight at daybreak I needed a good rest; but I could not forget that in my pride I had told Lord Strepp that I was provided with a friend to attend me at the duel. It was on my mind. I must achieve a friend, or Colonel Royale might quite properly refuse to fight me on the usual grounds that if he killed me there would be present no adherent of my cause to declare that the fight was fair. And any how I had lied so thoroughly to Lord Strepp. I must have a friend.

But how was I to carve a friend out of this black Bristol at such short notice? My sense told me that friends could not be found in the road like pebbles, but some curious feeling kept me abroad, scanning by the light of the lanterns or the torches each face that passed me. A low dull roar came from the direction of the quay, and this was the noise of the sailor-men, being drunk. I knew that there would be none found there to suit my purpose, but my spirit led me to wander so that I could not have told why I went this way or that way.

Of a sudden I heard from a grassy bank beside me the sound of low and strenuous sobbing. I stopped dead short to listen, moved by instinctive recognition. Aye, I was right. It was Irish keening. Some son of Erin was spelling out his sorrow to the darkness with that profound and garrulous eloquence which is in the character of my people.

"Wirra, wirra! Sorrow the day I would be leaving Ireland against my own will and intention, and may the rocks go out to meet the lugger that brought me here! It's beginning to rain, too! Sure it never rains like this in Ireland! And me without a brass penny to buy a bed! If the Saints save me from England, 'tis al —"

"Come out of that, now!" said I.

The monologue ceased; there was a quick silence. Then the voice, much altered, said: "Who calls? 'Tis may be an Irish voice!"

"It is," said I. "I've swallowed as much peat smoke as any man of my years. Come out of that now, and let me have a look at you."

He came trustfully enough, knowing me to be Irish, and I examined him as well as I was able in the darkness. He was what I expected, a bedraggled vagabond with tear-stains on his dirty cheeks and a vast shock of hair which I well knew would look, in daylight, like a burning haycock. And as I examined him he just as carefully examined me. I could see his shrewd blue eyes twinkling.

"You are a red man," said I. "I know the strain; 'tis better than some. Your family must have been very inhospitable people." And then, thinking that I had spent enough time, I was about to give the fellow some coin and send him away. But here a mad project came into my empty head. I had ever been the victim of my powerful impulses, which surge up within me and sway me until I can only gasp at my own conduct. The sight of this red-headed scoundrel had thrust an idea into my head, and I was a lost man.

"Mark you!" said I to him. "You know what I am?"

"'Tis hard to see in the dark," he answered; "but I mistrust you are a gentleman, sir. McDermott of the Three Trees had a voice and a way with him like you, and Father Burk too, and he was a gentleman born if he could only remain sober."

"Well, you've hit it, in the dark or whatever," said I. "I am a gentleman. Indeed I am an O'Ruddy. Have you ever been hearing of my family?"

"Not of your honour's branch of it, sure," he made answer confidently. "But I have often been hearing of the O'Ruddys of Glandore, who are well known to be such great robbers and blackguards that their match is not to be found in all the south of Ireland. Nor in the west, neither, for that matter."

"Aye," said I, "I have heard that that branch of the family was much admired by the peasantry for their qualities. But let us have done with it and speak of other matters. I want a service of you."

"Yes, your honour," said he, dropping his voice. "May be 'twill not be the first time I've been behind a ditch; but the light to-night is very bad unless I am knowing him well, and I would never be forgetting how Tim Malone let fly in the dark of a night like this, thinking it was a bailiff, until she screamed out with the pain in her leg, the poor creature, and her beyond seventy and a good Catholic."

"Come out of it now!" said I impatiently. "You will be behind no ditch." And as we walked back to the inn I explained to my new man the part I wished him to play. He was amazed at it, and I had to explain fifty times; but when it once was established in his red head Paddy was wild with enthusiasm, and I had to forbid him telling me how well he would do it.

I had them give him some straw in the stable, and then retired to my chamber for needed rest. Before dawn I had them send Paddy to me, and by the light of a new fire I looked at him. Ye Saints! What hair! It must have been more than a foot in length, and the flaming strands radiated in all directions from an isolated and central spire which shot out straight toward the sky. I knew what to do with his tatters, but that crimson thatch dumfounded me. However there was no going back now, so I set to work upon him. Luckily my wardrobe represented three generations of O'Ruddy clothes, and there was a great plenty. I put my impostor in a suit of blue velvet with a flowered waistcoat and stockings of pink. I gave him a cocked hat and a fine cloak. I worked with success up to the sword-belt, and there I was checked. I had two swords, but only one belt. However, I slung the sword which King Louis had given my father on a long string from Paddy's neck and sternly bid him keep his cloak tight about him. We were ready.

"Now, Paddy," said I, "do you bow in this manner." I bowed as a gentleman should. But I will not say how I strove with him. I could do little in that brief space. If he remained motionless and kept his tongue still he was somewhat near his part, but the moment he moved he was astonishing. I depended on keeping him under my eye, and I told him to watch me like a cat. "Don't go thinking how grand you are, that way," I cried to him angrily. "If you make a blunder of it, the gentlemen will cudgel you, mark you that. Do you as I direct you. And the string, curse you. Mind your cloak!" The villain had bethought him of his flowered waistcoat, and with a comic air flung back his coat to display it. "Take your fingers out of your mouth. Stop scratching your shin with your foot. Leave your hair alone. 'Tis as good and as bad as you can make it. Come along now, and hold your tongue like a graven image if you would not be having me stop the duel to lather you."

We marched in good order out of the inn. We saw our two gentlemen awaiting us, wrapped in their cloaks, for the dawn was cold. They bowed politely, and as I returned their salute I said in a low, quick aside to Paddy:

"Now, for the love of God, bow for your life!"

My intense manner must have frightened the poor thing, for he ducked as swiftly as if he had been at a fair in Ireland and somebody had hove a cobble at his head.

"Come up!" I whispered, choking with rage. "Come up! You'll be breaking your nose on the road."

He straightened himself, looking somewhat bewildered, and said:

"What was it? Was I too slow? Did I do it well?"

"Oh, fine," said I. "Fine. You do it as well as that once more, and you will probably break your own neck, and 'tis not me will be buying masses for your soul, you thief. Now don't drop as if a gamekeeper had shot at you. There is no hurry in life. Be quiet and easy."

"I mistrusted I was going too fast," said he; "but for the life of me I couldn't pull up. If I had been the Dublin mail, and the road thick as fleas with highwaymen, I should have gone through them grand."

My Lord Strepp and Colonel Royale had not betrayed the slightest surprise at the appearance of my extraordinary companion. Their smooth, regular faces remained absolutely imperturbable. This I took to be very considerate of them, but I gave them just a little more than their due, as I afterward perceived when I came to understand the English character somewhat. The great reason was that Paddy and I were foreigners. It is not to be thought that gentlemen of their position would have walked out for a duel with an Englishman in the party of so fantastic an appearance. They would have placed him at once as a person impossible and altogether out of their class. They would have told a lackey to kick this preposterous creation into the horse-pond. But since Paddy was a foreigner he was possessed of some curious license, and his grotesque ways could be explained fully in the simple phrase, "'Tis a foreigner."

So, then, we preceded my Lord Strepp and Colonel Royale through a number of narrow streets and out into some clear country. I chose a fine open bit of green turf as a goodly place for us to meet, and I warped Paddy through the gate and moved to the middle of the field. I drew my sword and saluted, and then turned away. I had told Paddy everything which a heaven-sent sense of instruction could suggest, and if he failed I could do no more than kill him.

After I had kicked him sharply he went aside with Lord Strepp, and they indulged in what sounded like a very animated discussion. Finally I was surprised to see Lord Strepp approaching me. He said:

"It is very irregular, but I seem unable to understand your friend. He has proposed to me that the man whose head is broken first —I do not perfectly understand what he could mean by that; it does not enter our anticipations that a man could possibly have his head broken-he has proposed that the man whose head may be broken first should provide 'lashings' —I feel sure that is the word-lashings of meat and drink at some good inn for the others. Lashings is a word which I do not know. We do not know how to understand you gentlemen when you speak of lashings. I am instructed to meet any terms which you may suggest, but I find that I cannot make myself clear to your friend who speaks of nothing but lashings."

"Sir," said I, as I threw coat and waistcoat on the grass, "my friend refers to a custom of his own country. You will, I feel sure, pardon his misconception of the circumstances. Pray accept my regrets, and, if you please, I am ready."

He immediately signified that his mind was now clear, and that the incident of Paddy's lashings he regarded as closed. As for that flame-headed imp of crime, if I could have got my hands upon him he would have taken a short road to his fathers. Him and his lashings! As I stood there with a black glare at him, the impudent scoundrel repeatedly winked at me with the readable information that if I only would be patient and bide a moment he would compass something very clever. As I faced Colonel Royale I was so wild with thinking of what I would do to Paddy, that, for all I knew, I might have been crossing swords with my mother.

And now as to this duel. I will not conceal that I was a very fine fencer in both the French and Italian manners. My father was in his day one of the finest blades in Paris, and had fought with some of the most skillful and impertinent gentlemen in all France. He had done his best to give me his eye and his wrist, and sometimes he would say that I was qualified to meet all but the best in the world. He commonly made fun of the gentlemen of England, saying that a dragoon was their ideal of a man with a sword; and he would add that the rapier was a weapon which did not lend itself readily to the wood-chopper's art. He was all for the French and Italian schools.

I had always thought that my father's judgment was very good, but I could not help reflecting that if it turned out to be bad I would have a grievance as well as a sword-thrust in the body. Colonel Royale came at me in a somewhat leisurely manner, and, as I said, my mind was so full of rage at Paddy that I met the first of my opponent's thrusts through sheer force of habit. But my head was clear a moment later, and I knew that I was fighting my first duel in England and for my father's honour. It was no time to think of Paddy.

Another moment later I knew that I was the Colonel's master. I could reach him where I chose. But he did not know it. He went on prodding away with a serious countenance, evidently under the impression that he had me hard put to it. He was as grave as an owl-faced parson. And now here I did a sorry thing. I became the victim of another of my mad impulses. I was seized with an ungovernable desire to laugh. It was hideous. But laugh I did, and, of necessity, square in the Colonel's face. And to this day I regret it.

Then the real duel began. At my laugh the Colonel instantly lost his grave air, and his countenance flushed with high, angry surprise. He beset me in a perfect fury, caring no more for his guard than if he had been made of iron. Never have I seen such quick and tremendous change in a man. I had laughed at him under peculiar conditions: very well, then; he was a demon. Thrice my point pricked him to keep him off, and thrice my heart was in my mouth that he would come on regardless. The blood oozed out on his white ruffled shirt; he was panting heavily, and his eyes rolled. He was a terrible sight to face. At last I again touched him, and this time sharply and in the sword arm, and upon the instant my Lord Strepp knocked our blades apart.

"Enough," he cried sternly. "Back, Colonel! Back!"

The Colonel flung himself sobbing into his friend's arms, choking out, "O God, Strepp! I couldn't reach him. I couldn't reach him, Strepp! Oh, my God!"

At the same time I disappeared, so to speak, in the embrace of my red-headed villain, who let out an Irish howl of victory that should have been heard at Glandore. "Be quiet, rascal," I cried, flinging him off. But he went on with his howling until I was obliged forcibly to lead him to a corner of the field, where he exclaimed:

"Oh, your honour, when I seen the other gentleman, all blazing with rage, rush at you that way, and me with not so much as a tuppence for all my service to you excepting these fine clothes and the sword, although I am thinking I shall have little to do with swords if this is the way they do it, I said, 'Sorrow the day England saw me!' "

If I had a fool for a second, Colonel Royale had a fine, wise young man. Lord Strepp was dealing firmly and coolly with his maddened principal.

"I can fight with my left hand," the Colonel was screaming. "I tell you, Strepp, I am resolved! Don't bar my way! I will kill him! I will kill him!"

"You are not in condition to fight," said the undisturbed young man. "You are wounded in four places already. You are in my hands. You will fight no more to-day."

"But, Strepp!" wailed the Colonel. "Oh, my God, Strepp!"

"You fight no more to-day," said the young lord.

Then happened unexpected interruptions. Paddy told me afterward that during the duel a maid had looked over a wall and yelled, and dropped a great brown bowl at sight of our occupation. She must have been the instrument that aroused the entire county, for suddenly men came running from everywhere. And the little boys! There must have been little boys from all over England.

"What is it? What is it?"

"Two gentlemen have been fighting!"

"Oh, aye, look at him with the blood on him!"

"Well, and there is young my Lord Strepp. He'd be deep in the matter, I warrant you!"

"Look yon, Bill! Mark the gentleman with the red hair. He's not from these parts, truly. Where, think you, he comes from?"

"'Tis a great marvel to see such hair, and I doubt not he comes from Africa."

They did not come very near, for in those days there was little the people feared but a gentleman, and small wonder. However, when the little boys judged that the delay in a resumption of the fight was too prolonged, they did not hesitate to express certain unconventional opinions and commands.

"Hurry up, now!"

"Go on!"

"You're both afeared!"

"Begin! Begin!"

"Are the gentlemen in earnest?"

"Sirs, do you mean ever to fight again? Begin, begin."

But their enthusiasm waxed high after they had thoroughly comprehended Paddy and his hair.

"You're alight, sir; you're alight!"

"Water! Water!"

"Farmer Pelton will have the officers at you an you go near his hay. Water!"

Paddy understood that they were paying tribute to his importance, and he again went suddenly out of my control. He began to strut and caper and pose with the air of knowing that he was the finest gentleman in England.

"Paddy, you baboon," said I, "be quiet and don't be making yourself a laughing-stock for the whole of them."

But I could give small heed to him, for I was greatly occupied in watching Lord Strepp and the Colonel. The Colonel was listening now to his friend for the simple reason that the loss of blood had made him too weak to fight again. Of a sudden he slumped gently down through Lord Strepp's arms to the ground, and, as the young man knelt, he cast his eyes about him until they rested upon me in what I took to be mute appeal. I ran forward, and we quickly tore his fine ruffles to pieces and succeeded in quite stanching his wounds, none of which were serious. "'Tis only a little blood-letting," said my Lord Strepp with something of a smile. "'Twill cool him, perchance."

"None of them are deep," I cried hastily. "I —"

But Lord Strepp stopped me with a swift gesture. "Yes," he said, "I knew. I could see. But —" He looked at me with troubled eyes. "It is an extraordinary situation. You have spared him, and he will not wish to be spared, I feel sure. Most remarkable case."

"Well, I won't kill him," said I bluntly, having tired of this rubbish. "Damme if I will!"

Lord Strepp laughed outright. "It is ridiculous," he said. "Do you return, O'Ruddy, and leave me the care of this business. And," added he, with embarrassed manner, "this mixture is full strange; but — I feel sure any how, I salute you, sir." And in his bow he paid a sensible tribute to my conduct.

Afterward there was nought to do but gather in Paddy and return to the inn. I found my countryman swaggering to and fro before the crowd. Some ignoramus, or some wit, had dubbed him the King of Ireland, and he was playing to the part.

"Paddy, you red-headed scandal," said I, "come along now!"

When he heard me, he came well enough; but I could not help but feel from his manner that he had made a great concession.

"And so they would be taking me for the King of Ireland, and, sure, 'tis an advantage to be thought a king whatever, and if your honour would be easy 'tis you and me that would sleep in the finest beds in Bristol the night, and nothing to do but take the drink as it was handed and — I'll say no more."

A rabble followed us on our way to the inn, but I turned on them so fiercely from time to time that ultimately they ran off. We made direct for my chamber, where I ordered food and drink immediately to be served. Once alone there with Paddy I allowed my joy to take hold on me. "Eh, Paddy, my boy," said I, walking before him, "I have done grand. I am, indeed, one of the finest gentlemen in the world."

"Aye, that's true," he answered, "but there was a man at your back throughout who —"

To his extreme astonishment I buffeted him heavily upon the cheek. "And we'll have no more of that talk," said I.

CHAPTER III

"Aye!" said Paddy, holding his jowl; "'tis what one gets for serving a gentleman. 'Tis the service of a good truthful blackguard I'd be looking for, and that's true for me."

"Be quiet and mind what I tell you," I cried to him. "I'm uplifted with my success in England, and I won't be hearing anything from you while I am saying that I am one of the grandest gentlemen in all the world. I came over here with papers-papers!" said I; and then I bethought me that I would take the papers and wave them in my hand. I don't know why people wish to wave important documents in their hands, but the impulse came to me. Above all things I wished to take these papers and wave them defiantly, exultantly, in the air. They were my inheritance and my land of promise; they were everything. I must wave them even to the chamber, empty save for Paddy.

When I reached for them in the proper place in my luggage they were gone. I wheeled like a tiger upon Paddy.

"Villain," I roared, grasping him at the throat, "you have them!"

He sank in full surrender to his knees.

"I have, your honour," he wailed; "but, sure, I never thought your honour would care, since one of them is badly worn at the heel, and the other is no better than no boot at all."

I was cooled by the incontestable verity of this man. I sat heavily down in a chair by the fire.

"Aye," said I stupidly, "the boots! I did not mean the boots, although when you took them passes my sense of time. I mean some papers."

"Some papers!" cried he excitedly. "Your honour never thought it would be me that would steal papers? Nothing less than good cows would do my people, and a bit of turf now and then, but papers —"

"Peace!" said I sombrely, and began to search my luggage thoroughly for my missing inheritance. But it was all to no purpose. The papers were not there. I could not have lost them. They had been stolen. I saw my always-flimsy inheritance melt away. I had been, I thought, on the edge of success, but I now had nothing but my name, a successful duel, and a few pieces of gold. I was buried in defeat.

Of a sudden a name shot through my mind. The name of this black Forister was upon me violently and yet with perfect sureness. It was he who had stolen the papers. I knew it. I felt it in every bone. He had taken the papers.

I have since been told that it is very common for people to be moved by these feelings of omen, which are invariably correct in their particulars; but at the time I thought it odd that I should be so certain that Forister had my papers. However, I had no time to waste in thinking. I grasped my pistols. "A black man-black as the devil," cried I to Paddy. "Help me catch a little black man."

"Sure!" said Paddy, and we sallied forth.

In a moment I was below and crying to the landlord in as fine a fury as any noble:

"This villain Forister! And where be he?"

The landlord looked at me with bulging eyes. "Master Forister," he stammered. "Aye-aye-he's been agone these many hours since your lordship kicked him. He took horse, he did, for Bath, he did."

"Horses!" I roared. "Horses for two gentlemen!" And the stableyard, very respectful since my duel, began to ring with cries. The landlord pleaded something about his bill, and in my impatience I hurled to him all of my gold save one piece. The horses came soon enough, and I leaped into the saddle and was away to Bath after Forister. As I galloped out of the inn yard I heard a tumult behind me, and, looking back, I saw three hostlers lifting hard at Paddy to raise him into the saddle. He gave a despairing cry when he perceived me leaving him at such speed, but my heart was hardened to my work. I must catch Forister.

It was a dark and angry morning. The rain swept across my face, and the wind flourished my cloak. The road, glistening steel and brown, was no better than an Irish bog for hard riding.

Once I passed a chaise with a flogging post-boy and steaming nags. Once I overtook a farmer jogging somewhere on a fat mare. Otherwise I saw no travellers.

I was near my journey's end when I came to a portion of the road which dipped down a steep hill. At the foot of this hill was an oak-tree, and under this tree was a man masked and mounted, and in his hand was a levelled pistol.

"Stand!" he said. "Stand!"

I knew his meaning, but when a man has lost a documentary fortune and given an innkeeper all but his last guinea, he is sure to be filled with fury at the appearance of a third and completing misfortune. With a loud shout I drew my pistol and rode like a demon at the highwayman. He fired, but his bullet struck nothing but the flying tails of my cloak. As my horse crashed into him I struck at his pate with my pistol. An instant later we both came a mighty downfall, and when I could get my eyes free of stars I arose and drew my sword. The highwayman sat before me on the ground, ruefully handling his skull. Our two horses were scampering away into the mist.

I placed my point at the highwayman's throat.

"So, my fine fellow," cried I grandly, "you rob well. You are the principal knight of the road of all England, I would dare say, by the way in which an empty pistol overcomes you."

He was still ruefully handling his skull.

"Aye," he muttered sadly, more to himself than to me, "a true knight of the road with seven ballads written of me in Bristol and three in Bath. Ill betide me for not minding my mother's word and staying at home this day. 'Tis all the unhappy luck of Jem Bottles. I should have remained an honest sheep-stealer and never engaged in this dangerous and nefarious game of lifting purses."

The man's genuine sorrow touched me. "Cheer up, Jem Bottles," said I. "All may yet be well. 'Tis not one little bang on the crown that so disturbs you?"

"'Tis not one-no," he answered gloomily; "'tis two. The traveller riding to the east before you dealt me a similar blow-may hell catch the little black devil."

"Black!" cried I. "Forister, for my life!"

"He took no moment to tell me his name," responded the sullen and wounded highwayman. "He beat me out of the saddle and rode away as brisk as a bird. I know not what my mother will say. She be for ever telling me of the danger in this trade, and here come two gentlemen in one day and unhorse me without the profit of a sixpence to my store. When I became a highwayman I thought me I had profited me from the low estate of a sheep-stealer, but now I see that happiness in this life does not altogether depend upon —"

"Enough," I shouted in my impatience. "Tell me of the black man! The black man, worm!" I pricked his throat with my sword very carefully.

"He was black, and he rode like a demon, and he handled his weapons finely," said Jem Bottles. "And since I have told you all I know, please, good sir, move the point from my throat. This will be ill news for my mother."

I took thought with myself. I must on to Bath; but the two horses had long since scampered out of sight, and my pursuit of the papers would make small way afoot.

"Come, Jem Bottles," I cried, "help me to a horse in a comrade's way and for the sake of your mother. In another case I will leave you here a bloody corse. Come; there's a good fellow!"

He seemed moved to help me. "Now, if there comes a well-mounted traveller," he said, brightening, "I will gain his horse for you if I die for it."

"And if there comes no well-mounted traveller?"

"I know not, sir. But-perhaps he will come."

"'Tis a cheap rogue who has but one horse," I observed contemptuously. "You are only a footpad, a simple-minded marquis of the bludgeon."

Now, as I had hoped, this deeply cut his pride.

"Did I not speak of the ballads, sir?" he demanded with considerable spirit. "Horses? Aye, and have I not three good nags hid behind my mother's cottage, which is less than a mile from this spot?"

"Monsieur Jem Bottles," said I, not forgetting the French manners which my father had taught me, "unless you instantly show me the way to these horses I shall cut off your hands, your feet, and your head; and, ripping out your bowels, shall sprinkle them on the road for the first post-horses to mash and trample. Do you understand my intention, Monsieur Jem Bottles?"

"Sir," he begged, "think of my mother!"

"I think of the horses," I answered grimly. "'Tis for you to think of your mother. How could I think of your mother when I wouldn't know her from the Head of Kinsale, if it didn't happen that I know the Head of Kinsale too well to mistake it for anybody's mother?"

"You speak like a man from foreign parts, sir," he rejoined in a meek voice; "but I am able to see that your meaning is serious."

"'Tis so serious," said I, rapping him gently on the head with the butt of my pistol, "that if you don't instantly display a greedy activity you will display a perfect inability to move."

"The speeching is obscure," said he, "but the rap on the head is clear to me. Still, it was not kind of you to hit me on the same spot twice."

He now arose from his mournful seat on the ground, and, still rubbing his pate, he asked me to follow him. We moved from the highway into a very narrow lane, and for some time proceeded in silence.

"'Tis a regular dog's life," spoke Jem Bottles after a period of reflection.

By this time I had grown a strong sympathy for my scoundrel.

"Come, cheer yourself, Jem Bottles," said I. "I have known a lesser ruffian who was hanged until he was dry, whereas you march along the lane with nought to your discouragement but three cracks in your crown."

"'Tis not the cracks in the crown," he answered moodily. "'Tis what my mother will say."

"I had no thought that highwaymen had mothers," said I. I had resolved now to take care of his pride, for I saw that he was bound to be considered a great highwayman, and I did not wish to disturb his feelings until I gained possession of one of the horses. But now he grew as indignant as he dared.

"Mother? Mother, sir? Do you think me an illegitimate child? I say to you flat in your face, even if you kill me the next instant, that I have a mother. Perchance I am not of the lofty gentry who go about beating honest highwaymen to the earth, but I repulse with scorn any man's suggestion that I am illegitimate. In a quarter of an hour you shall see my mother for yourself."

"Peace, Jem Bottles," said I soothingly. "I took no thought of such a thing. I would be thinking only of the ballads, and how honourable it is that a gallant and dashing life should be celebrated in song. I, for certain, have never done anything to make a pothouse ring with my name, and I liken you to the knights of olden days who tilted in all simple fair bravery without being able to wager a brass farthing as to who was right and who was wrong. Admirable Jem Bottles," I cried enthusiastically, "tell me, if you will, of your glories; tell me with your own tongue, so that when I hear the ballads waxing furious with praise of you, I shall recall the time I marched with your historic person."

"My beginning was without pretence," said the highwayman. "Little Susan, daughter of Farmer Hants, was crossing the fields with a basket of eggs. I, a masked figure, sprang out at her from a thicket. I seized the basket. She screamed. There was a frightful tumult. But in the end I bore away this basket of eight eggs, creeping stealthily through the wood. The next day Farmer Hants met me. He had a long whip. There was a frightful tumult. But he little knew that he was laying with his whip the foundation of a career so illustrious. For a time I stole his sheep, but soon grew weary of this business. Once, after they had chased me almost to Bristol, I was so weary that I resolved to forego the thing entirely. Then I became a highwayman, whom you see before you. One of the ballads begins thus:

"What ho! the merry Jem!
Not a pint he gives for them.
All his —"

"Stop," said I, "we'll have it at Dame Bottles's fireside. Hearing songs in the night air always makes me hoarse the next morning."

"As you will," he answered without heat. "We're a'most there."

Soon a lighted window of the highwayman's humble home shone out in the darkness, and a moment later Jem Bottles was knocking at the door. It was immediately opened, and he stalked in with his blood-marks still upon his face. There was a great outcry in a feminine voice, and a large woman rushed forward and flung her arms about the highwayman.

"Oh, Jemmie, my son, my son!" she screamed, "whatever have they done to ye this time?"

"Silence, mother dear," said Bottles. "'Tis nought but a wind-broken bough fallen on my head. Have you no manners? Do you not see the gentleman waiting to enter and warm himself?"

The woman turned upon me, alarmed, but fiery and defiant. After a moment's scrutiny she demanded:

"Oh, ho, and the gentleman had nought to do of course with my Jem's broken head?"

"'Tis a priest but newly arrived from his native island of Asia," said Bottles piously; "and it ill beseems you, mother dear, to be haggling when you might be getting the holy man and I some supper."

"True, Jemmie, my own," responded Dame Bottles. "But there are so many rogues abroad that you must forgive your old mother if she grow often affrighted that her good Jemmie has been misled." She turned to me. "Pardon, my good gentleman," she said almost in tears. "Ye little know what it is to be the mother of a high-spirited boy."

"I can truthfully say that I do not, Dame Bottles," said I, with one of my father's French bows. She was immensely pleased. Any woman may fall a victim to a limber, manly, and courteous bow.

Presently we sat down to a supper of plum-stew and bread. Bottles had washed the blood from his face and now resembled an honest man.

"You may think it strange, sir," said Dame Bottles with some housewifely embarrassment, "that a highwayman of such distinction that he has had written of him in Bristol six ballads —"

"Seven," said the highwayman.

"Seven in Bristol and in Bath two."

"Three," said the highwayman.

"And three in Bath," continued the old woman. "You may think it strange, sir, that a highwayman of such distinction that he has had written of him in Bristol seven ballads, and in Bath three, is yet obliged to sit down to a supper of plum-stew and bread."

"Where is the rest of that cheese I took on last Michaelmas?" demanded Bottles suddenly.

"Jemmie," answered his mother with reproach, "you know you gave the last of it to the crippled shepherd over on the big hill."

"So I did, mother dear," assented the highwayman, "and I regret now that I let no less than three cheeses pass me on the highway because I thought we had plenty at home."

"If you let anything pass on the road because you do not lack it at the moment, you will ultimately die of starvation, Jemmie dear," quoth the mother. "How often have I told you?"

"Aye," he answered somewhat irritably, "you also often have told me to take snuff-boxes."

"And was I at fault," she retorted, "because the cheating avarice of the merchants led them to make sinful, paltry snuff-boxes that were mere pictures of the good old gold and silver? Was it my mischief? Or was it the mischief of the plotting swineherds who now find it to their interest to deal in base and imitative metals?"

"Peace, my mother," said the highwayman. "The gentleman here has not the same interest in snuff-boxes which moves us to loud speech."

"True," said Dame Bottles, "and I readily wish that my Jemmie had no reason to care if snuff-boxes were made from cabbage-leaves."

I had been turning a scheme in my mind, and here I thought I saw my opportunity to introduce it. "Dame Bottles," said I, "your words fit well with the plan which has brought me here to your house. Know you, then, that I am a nobleman —"

"Alack, poor Jemmie!" cried the woman, raising her hands.

"No," said I, "I am not a nobleman rampant. I am a nobleman in trouble, and I need the services of your son, for which I will reward him with such richness that he will not care if they make snuff-boxes out of water or wind. I am in pursuit of a man —"

"The little black man," cried the alert Bottles.

"And I want your son to ride with me to catch this thief. He need never pass through the shadow of the creeping, clanking tree. He will be on an honest hunt to recover a great property. Give him to me. Give him fourteen guineas from his store, and bid us mount his horses and away. Save your son!"

The old woman burst into tears. "Sir," she answered, "I know little of you, but, as near as I can see in the light of this one candle, you are a hangel. Take my boy! Treat him as you would your own stepson, and if snuff-boxes ever get better I will let you both hear of it."

Less than an hour later Jem Bottles and I were off for Bath, riding two very good horses.

CHAPTER IV

Now my whole mind was really bent on finding my black Forister, but yet, as Jem Bottles and I rode toward Bath, I thought of a cloaked figure and a pair of shining eyes, and it seemed to me that I recalled the curve of sweet, proud lips. I knew that I should be thinking of my papers, my future; but a quick perversity made me dwell for a long trotting time in a dream of feminine excellence, in a dream of feminine beauty which was both ascetic and deeply sensuous. I know hardly how to say that two eyes, a vision of lips, a conception of a figure, should properly move me as I bounced along the road with Jem Bottles. But it is certain that it came upon me. The eyes of the daughter of the great Earl of Westport had put in chains the redoubtable O'Ruddy. It was true. It was clear. I admitted it to myself. The admission caused a number of reflections to occur in my mind, and the chief of these was that I was a misfortunate wretch.

Jem Bottles recalled me to the immediate business.

"'Tis the lights of Bath, sir," he said, "and if it please you, sir, I shall await you under yonder tree, since the wretched balladists have rendered me so well known in the town that I dare not venture in it for fear of a popular welcome from the people who have no snuff-boxes whatever."

"I will go and listen to the ballads," I replied, "and in the mean time do you await me here under that tree."

So saying I galloped into Bath, my soul sharp to find Forister and to take him by the neck and strangle out of him those papers which were my sole reasons for living. But the landlord of the best inn met me with an unmistakable frankness.

"Mr. Forister?" said he. "Yes, your lordship, but Mr. Forister is gone back to Bristol."

I was so pleased with his calling me "your lordship" that I hesitated a moment. But I was recalled to sense by the thought that although Jem Bottles and I had fifteen guineas between us, he had fourteen and I had the one. Thanking the landlord I galloped out of Bath.

Bottles was awaiting me under the tree. "To Bristol," I cried. "Our chase lies toward Bristol. He has doubled back."

"'Twas while we were at supper," said Bottles, as he cantered up to my shoulder. "I might have had two trials at him if I had not had the honour of meeting your worship. I warrant you, sir, he would not have escaped me twice."

"Think of his crack in your skull, and be content," I replied. "And in the mean time ride for Bristol."

Within five miles of Bristol we came upon a wayside inn in which there was progressing a great commotion. Lights flashed from window to window, and we could hear women howling. To my great surprise Bottles at once became hugely excited.

"Damme, sir," he shouted, "my sweetheart is a chambermaid here, and if she be hurted I will know it."

He spurred valiantly forward, and, after futilely calling to him to check his career, I followed. He leaped from his horse at the door of the inn and bounced into the place, pistol in hand. I was too confused to understand much, but it seemed to my ears that his entrance was hailed with a roar of relief and joy. A stable-boy, fearfully anxious, grasped my bridle, crying, "Go in, sir, in God's name. They will be killing each other." Thinking that, whatever betide, it was proper to be at the back of my friend Bottles, I too sprang from my horse and popped into the inn.

A more unexpected sight never met my experienced gaze. A fat landlady, mark you, was sobbing in the arms of my villainous friend, and a pretty maid was clinging to his arm and screaming. At the same time there were about him a dozen people of both sexes who were yelling, —

"Oh, pray, Master Bottles! Good Master Bottles, do stop them. One is a great Afric chief, red as a fire, and the other is Satan, Satan himself! Oh, pray, good Master Bottles, stop them!"

My fine highwayman was puffed out like a poisoned frog. I had no thought that he could be so grand.

"What is this disturbance?" he demanded in a bass voice.

"O good Master Bottles," clamoured the people. "Satan wishes to kill the Red Giant, who has Satan barred in the best room in the inn. And they make frightful destruction of chairs and tables. Bid them cease, O good Master Bottles!"

From overhead we could hear the sound of blows upon wood mingled with threatening talk.

"Stand aside," said the highwayman in a great gruff voice which made me marvel at him. He unhesitatingly dumped the swooning form of the landlady into another pair of arms, shook off the pretty maid, and moved sublimely upon the foot of the stairs amid exclamations of joy, wonder, admiration, even reverence.

But the voice of an unseen person hailed suddenly from the head of the stairs.

"And if ye have not said enough masses for your heathen soul," remarked the voice, "you would be better mustering the neighbours this instant to go to church for you and bid them do the best they can in a short time. You will never be coming downstairs if you once come up."

Bottles hesitated; the company shuddered out: "'Tis the Red Giant."

"And I would be having one more word with you," continued the unseen person. "I have him here, and here I keep him. 'Tis not me that wants the little black rogue, what with his hammering on the door and his calling me out of my name. 'Tis no work that I like, and I would lever go in and put my heel in his face. But I was told to catch a little black man, and I have him, and him I will keep. 'Tis not me that wished to come here and catch little black men for anybody; but here I am in this foreign country, catching little black men, and I will have no interference."

But here I gave a great call of recognition.

"Paddy!"

I saw the whole thing. This wild-headed Paddy, whom I had told to catch me a little black man, had followed after me toward Bath and somehow managed to barricade in a room the very first man he saw who was small and black. At first I wished to laugh; an instant later I was furious.

"Paddy," I thundered; "come down out of that now! What would you be doing? Come down out of that now!"

The reply was sulky, but unmistakably from Paddy. Most of it was mumbled.

"Sure I've gone and caught as little and as black a man as is in the whole world, and was keeping the scoundrel here safe, and along he comes and tells me to come down out of that now with no more gratitude than if he had given me a gold goose. And yet I fought a duel for him and managed everything so finely that he came away well enough to box me on the ear, which was mere hilarity and means nothing between friends."

Jem Bottles was still halted on the stair. He and all the others had listened to Paddy's speeches in a blank amazement which had much superstition in it.

"Shall I go up, sir?" he asked, not eagerly.

"No," said I. "Leave me to deal with it. I fear a great mistake. Give me ten minutes, and I promise to empty the inn of all uproar."

A murmur of admiration arose, and as the sound leaped about my ears I moved casually and indifferently up against Paddy. It was a grand scene.

"Paddy," I whispered as soon as I had reached a place on the stairs safe from the ears of the people below. "Paddy, you have made a great blunder. You have the wrong man."

"'Tis unlikely," replied Paddy with scorn. "You wait until you see him, and if he is not little and black, then —"

"Yes, yes," said I hastily, "but it was not any little black man at all which I wanted. It was a particular little black man."

"But," said the ruffian brightly, "it would be possible this one will serve your end. He's little and he's black."

At this moment the voice of the captive came intoning through the door of a chamber.

"When I am free I will first cut out your liver and have it grilled, and feed it to you as you are dying."

Paddy had stepped forward and placed his lips within about six inches of one of the panels.

"Come now, be easy!" he said. "You know well that if you should do as you say, I would beat your head that it would have the looks of a pudding fallen from a high window, and that's the truth."

"Open the door, rascal," called the captive, "and we shall see."

"I will be opening no doors," retorted Paddy indignantly. "Remain quiet, you little black devil, or, by the mass, I'll —"

"I'll slice your heart into pieces of paper," thundered Paddy's prisoner, kicking and pounding.

By this time I was ready to interfere. "Paddy," said I, catching him by the shoulder, "you have the wrong man. Leave it to me; mind you, leave it to me."

"He's that small and black you'd think—" he began dejectedly, but I cut him short.

Jem Bottles, unable to endure the suspense, had come up from below. He was still bristling and blustering, as if all the maids were remarking him.

"And why does this fine gentleman kick and pound on the door?" he demanded in a gruff voice loud enough to be heard in all appreciative parts of the inn. "I'll have him out and slit his nose."

The thunder on the door ceased, and the captive observed:

"Ha! another scoundrel! If my ears do not play me false, there are now three waiting for me to kick them to the hangman."

Restraining Paddy and Bottles, who each wished to reply in heroic verse to this sally, I stepped to the door.

"Sir," said I civilly, "I fear a great blunder has been done. I —"

"Why," said the captive with a sneer, "'tis the Irishman! 'Tis the king of the Irelands. Open the door, pig."

My elation knew no bounds.

"Paddy," cried I, "you have the right little black man." But there was no time for celebration. I must first answer my enemy. "You will remember that I kicked you once," said I, "and if you have a memory as long as my finger be careful I do not kick you again, else even people as far away as the French will think you are a meteor. But I would not be bandying words at long range. Paddy, unbar the door."

"If I can," muttered Paddy, fumbling with a lot of machinery so ingenious that it would require a great lack of knowledge to thoroughly understand it. In the mean time we could hear Forister move away from the door, and by the sound of a leisurely scrape of a chair on the floor I judge he had taken his seat somewhere near the centre of the room. Bottles was handling his pistol and regarding me.

"Yes," said I, "if he fires, do you pepper him fairly. Otherwise await my orders. Paddy, you slug, unbar the door."

"If I am able," said Paddy, still muttering and fumbling with his contrivances. He had no sooner mouthed the words than the door flew open as if by magic, and we discovered a room bright with the light of a fire and candles. Forister was seated negligently at a table in the centre of the room. His legs were crossed, but his naked sword lay on the table at his hand. He had the first word, because I was amazed, almost stunned, by the precipitous opening of the door.

"Ho! ho!" he observed frigidly, "'tis indeed the king of the Irelands, accompanied by the red-headed duke who has entertained me for some time, and a third party with a thief's face who handles a loaded pistol with such abandon as leads me to suppose that he once may have been a highwayman. A very pretty band."

"Use your tongue for a garter, Forister," said I. "I want my papers."

CHAPTER V

"Your 'papers'?" said Forister. "Damn you and your papers. What would I know of your papers?"

"I mean," said I fiercely, "the papers that you stole out of my chamber in the inn at Bristol."

The man actually sank back in his chair and laughed me up to the roof.

"'Papers'!" he shouted. "Here's the king of the Irelands thinking that I have made off with his papers!"

"You choose a good time for laughing," said I, with more sobriety. "In a short time you will be laughing with the back of your head."

He sat up and looked at me with quick decision.

"Now, what is all this rubbish about papers?" he said sharply. "What have I to do with your filthy papers? I had one intention regarding you,—of that I am certain. I was resolved to kill you on the first occasion when we could cross swords, but—'papers'—faugh! What do you mean?"

The hoarse voice of Jem Bottles broke in from somewhere behind me. "We might easily throw him to the earth and tie him, sir, and then make search of him."

"And you would know how to go about the business, I warrant me," laughed Forister. "You muzzle-faced rogue, you!"

To my astonishment the redoubtable highwayman gave back before the easy disdain of this superior scoundrel.

"My ways may not always have been straight and narrow, master," he rejoined, almost in a whine, "but you have no call to name me muzzle-faced."

Forister turned from him contemptuously and fixed his regard with much enthusiasm upon Paddy.

"Very red," said he. "Very red, indeed. And thick as fagots, too. A very delectable head of hair, fit to be spun into a thousand blankets for the naked savages in heathen parts. The wild forests in Ireland must indeed be dark when it requires a lantern of this measure to light the lonely traveller on his way."

But Paddy was an honest man even if he did not know it, and he at once walked to Forister and held against his ear a fist the size of a pig's hind-leg.

"I cannot throw the talk back to you," he said. "You are too fast for me, but I tell you to your face that you had better change your tongue for a lock of an old witch's hair unless you intend to be battered this moment."

"Peace," said Forister calmly. "I am a man of natural wit, and I would entertain myself. Now, there is your excellent chieftain the king of the Irelands. Him I regard as a very good specimen, whose ancestors were not very long ago swinging by their tails from the lofty palms of Ireland and playing with cocoanuts to and fro." He smiled and leaned back, well satisfied with himself.

All this time I had been silent, because I had been deep in reflection upon Forister. Now I said:

"Forister, you are a great rogue. I know you. One thing is certain. You have not my papers and never did you have them."

He looked upon me with some admiration and cried:

"Aye, the cannibal shows a glimmer of reason. No, I have not your foolish papers, and I only wish I had them in order to hurl the bundle at your damned stupid head."

"For a kicked man you have a gay spirit," I replied. "But at any rate I have no time for you now. I am off to Bristol after my papers, and I only wish for the sake of ease that I had to go no farther than this chamber. Come, Paddy! Come, Jem!"

My two henchmen were manifestly disappointed; they turned reluctantly at my word.

"Have I the leave of one crack at him, your honour?" whispered Paddy earnestly. "He said my head was a lantern."

"No," said I, "leave him to his meditations."

As we passed down the corridor we heard him laugh loudly, and he called out to me,—

"When I come to Bristol I will kill you."

I had more than a mind to go back and stuff this threat into his throat, but I better knew my business, which was to recover the papers.

"Come," said I, and we passed down stairs.

The people of the inn made way for Paddy as if he had been a falling tree, and at the same time they worshipped Jem Bottles for having performed everything. I had some wonder as to which would be able to out-strut the other. I think Jem Bottles won the match, for he had the advantage of being known as one of the most dangerous men in southwestern England, whereas Paddy had only his vanity to help him.

"'Tis all arranged," said Bottles pompously. "Your devil will come forth as quiet as a rabbit."

We ordered our horses, and a small crowd of obsequious stable-boys rushed to fetch them. I marvelled when I saw them lead out Paddy's horse. I had thought from what I perceived over my shoulder when I left Bristol that he would never be able to make half a league in the saddle. Amid the flicker of lanterns, Bottles and I mounted and then I heard Paddy calling to him all the stable-boys:

"Now, when I give the word, you heave for your lives. Stand, you beast! Cannot four of you hold him by the legs? I will be giving the word in a moment. Are you all ready? Well, now, ready again—heave!"

There was a short scuffle in the darkness, and presently Paddy appeared above the heads of the others in the *mêlée*.

"There, now," said he to them, "that was well done. One would easily be telling that I was an ex-trooper of the king." He rode out to us complacently. "'Tis a good horse, if only he steered with a tiller instead of these straps," he remarked, "and he goes well before the wind."

"To Bristol," said I. "Paddy, you must follow as best you may. I have no time to be watching you, although you are interesting."

An unhappy cry came from behind Bottles, and I spurred on, but again I could not wait for my faithful countryman. My papers were still the stake for which I played. However I hoped that Paddy would now give over his ideas about catching little black men.

As we neared Bristol Jem Bottles once more became backward. He referred to the seven ballads, and feared that the unexpected presence of such a well-known character would create an excitement which would not be easy to cool. So we made a rendezvous under another tree, and I rode on alone. Thus I was separated from both my good companions. However, before parting, I took occasion to borrow five guineas from Jem's store.

I was as weary as a dog, although I had never been told that gentlemen riding amid such adventures were ever aweary. At the inn in Bristol a sleepy boy took my horse, and a sleepy landlord aroused himself as he recognized me.

"My poor inn is at your disposal, sir," he cried as he bowed. "The Earl has inquired for you to-day, or yesterday, as well as my young Lord Strepp and Colonel Royale."

"Aye?" said I carelessly. "Did they so? Show me to a chamber. I am much enwearied. I would seek a good bed and a sound sleep, for I have ridden far and done much since last I had repose."

"Yes, sir," said the landlord deferentially.

After a long hard sleep I was aroused by a constant pounding on my door. At my cry a servant entered. He was very abject. "His lordship's valet has been waiting to give you a message from his lordship, sir." I bid him let the valet enter. The man whose heroic nose had borne the brunt of Forister's swift departure from the inn when I kicked him came into my chamber with distinguished grace and dignity and informed me that his noble master cared to see me in his chamber when it would suit my convenience.

Of course the old Earl was after his papers. And what was I to tell him,—that I was all befooled and befuddled?—that after my father had kept these papers for so many years in faithful trust I had lost them on the very brink of deliverance of them to their rightful owner? What was I to speak?

I did not wish to see the Earl of Westport, but some sudden and curious courage forced me into my clothes and out to the corridor. The Earl's valet was waiting there. "I pray you, sir, follow me," he said. I followed him to an expensive part of the inn, where he knocked upon a door. It was opened by a bending serving-man. The room was a kind of parlour, and in it, to my surprise, were Lord Strepp and Colonel Royale. They gazed at me with a surprise equivalent to mine own.

Young Lord Strepp was the first one thoroughly to collect himself. Then he advanced upon me with outstretched hand.

"Mr. O'Ruddy," he cried, "believe me, we are glad to see you. We thought you had gone for all time."

Colonel Royale was only a moment behind his friend, but as he extended his hand his face flushed painfully.

"Sir," he said somewhat formally, "not long ago I lost my temper, I fear. I know I have to thank you for great consideration and generosity. I—I—you—"

Whereupon we both began to stammer and grimace. All the time I was chocking out:

"Pray-pray—, don't speak of it —a —nothing-in truth, you kindly exaggerate —I —"

It was young Lord Strepp who brought us out of our embarrassment. "Here, you two good fellows," he cried heartily, "a glass of wine with you."

We looked gratefully at him, and in the business of filling our glasses we lost our awkwardness. "To you," said Lord Strepp; and as we drained our wine I knew that I had two more friends in England.

During the drinking the Earl's valet had been hovering near my coat-tails. Afterward he took occasion to make gentle suggestion to me:

"His lordship awaits your presence in his chamber, sir, when it pleases you."

The other gentlemen immediately deferred to my obligation, and I followed the valet into a large darkened chamber. It was some moments before my eyes could discover that the Earl was abed. Indeed, a rasping voice from beneath the canopies called to me before I knew that anybody was in the chamber but myself and the valet.

"Come hither, O'Ruddy," called the Earl. "Tompkins, get out! Is it your duty to stand there mummified? Get out!"

The servant hastily withdrew, and I walked slowly to the great man's bedside. Two shining shrewd eyes looked at me from a mass of pillows, and I had a knowledge of an aged face, half smiling and yet satirical, even malignant.

"And so this is the young fortune-hunter from Ireland," he said in a hoarse sick-man's voice. "The young fortune-hunter! Ha! With his worthless papers! Ha!"

"Worthless?" cried I, starting.

"Worthless!" cried the Earl vehemently. He tried to lift himself in his bed, in order to make more emphasis. "Worthless! Nothing but straw-straw-straw!" Then he cackled out a laugh.

And this was my inheritance! I could have sobbed my grief and anger, but I took firm hold on myself and resolved upon another way of dealing with the nobleman.

"My lord," said I coolly, "My father is dead. When he was dying he gave certain papers into my hands, —papers which he had guarded for many years, —and bade me, as his son, to deliver them into the hands of an old friend and comrade; and I come to this old friend and comrade of my father, and he lies back in his bed and cackles at me like a hen. 'Tis a small foot I would have set upon England if I had known more of you, you old skate!"

But still he laughed and cried: "Straw! Straw! Nothing but straw!"

"Well, sir," said I with icy dignity, "I may be a fool of an Irishman with no title save an older one than yours; but I would be deeply sorry if there came a day when I should throw a trust back in the teeth of a dead comrade's son."

"No," said the bright-eyed old man, comforting himself amid his pillows. "Look you, O'Ruddy! You are a rascal! You came over in an attempt to ruin me! I know it!"

I was awed by this accusation. It seemed to me to be too grand, too gorgeous for my personal consumption. I knew not what to do with this colossus. It towered above me in splendour and gilt. I had never expected to be challenged with attempting to ruin earls. My father had often ruined sea-captains, but he never in his life ruined so much as a baronet. It seemed altogether too fine for my family, but I could only blurt weakly, "Yessir." I was much like a lackey.

"Aye," said the old man, suddenly feeble from the excitement, "I see you admit it, you black Irish rogue." He sank back and applied a napkin to his mouth. It seemed to come away stained with blood. "You scoundrel!"

I had a strange cowardly inclination to fling myself upon this ancient survival and squeeze his throat until it closed like a pursel. And my inclination was so strong that I stood like a stone.

The valet opened the door. "If it please your Lordship-Lady Mary," he announced, and stood aside to let a lady pass. The Earl seemed immediately to forget my presence. He began at once to make himself uncomfortable in his bed. Then he cried fretfully: "Come, Mary, what caused you to be so long? Make me easy! Ruffle my pillows! Come, daughter."

"Yes, father," answered a soothing and sweet voice. A gracious figure passed before me and bended over the bed of the Earl. I was near blinded. It was not a natural blindness. It was an artificial blindness which came from my emotion. Was she tall? I don't know. Was she short? I don't know. But I am certain that she was exactly of the right size. She was, in all ways, perfection. She was of such glory, she was so splendid, that my heart ceased to beat. I remained standing like a stone, but my sword scabbard, reminiscent of some movement, flapped gently against my leg. I thought it was a horrible sound. I sought to stay it, but it continued to tinkle, and I remember that, standing there in the room with the old Earl and my love-'til-death, I thought most of my scabbard and its inability to lay quiet at my thigh.

She smoothed his bed and coaxed him and comforted him. Never had I seen such tenderness. It was like a vision of a classic hereafter. In a second I would have exchanged my youth for the position of this doddering old nobleman who spat blood into a napkin.

Suddenly the Earl wheeled his eyes and saw me.

"Ha, Mary!" he cried feebly, "I wish to point out a rogue. There he stands! The O'Ruddy! An Irishman and a fine robber! Mark him well, and keep stern watch of your jewels."

The beautiful young lady turned upon me an affrighted glance. And I stood like a stone.

"Aye," said the old wretch, "keep stern watch of your jewels. He is a very demon for skill. He could take a ring from your finger while you were thinking he was fluttering his hands in the air."

I bowed gallantly to the young lady. "Your rings are safe, my lady. I would ill requite the kindness shown by your father to the son of an old friend if I deprived your white fingers of a single ornament."

"Clever as ever, clever as ever," chuckled the wicked old man.

The young lady flushed and looked first at me and then at her father. I thought her eye, as it rested upon me, was not without some sympathetic feeling. I adored her. All the same I wished to kill her father. It is very curious when one wishes to kill the father of the woman one adores. But I suppose the situation was made more possible for me by the fact that it would have been extremely inexpedient to have killed the Earl in his sick bed. I even grinned at him.

"If you remember my father, your lordship," said I amiably, "despite your trying hard to forget him, you will remember that he had a certain native wit which on occasion led him to be able to frustrate his enemies. It must have been a family trait, for I seem to have it. You are an evil old man! You yourself stole my papers!"

CHAPTER VI

At first I thought that my speech had given the aged Earl a stroke. He writhed on his bed, and something appeared at his lips which was like froth. His lovely daughter sprang to him with a cry of fear and woe. But he was not dying; he was only mad with rage.

"How dare you? How dare you?" he gasped. "You whelp of Satan!"

"'Tis me that would not be fearing to dare anything," I rejoined calmly. "I would not so. I came here with a mind for fair words, but you have met me with insult and something worse. We cannot talk the thing. We must act it. The papers are yours, but you took them from me unfairly. You may destroy them. Otherwise I will have them back and discover what turned you into a great rogue near the end of your days."

"Hearken!" screamed the Earl. "Hearken! He threatens." The door into the parlour flew open, and Lord Strepp and Colonel Royale appeared on the threshold, their faces blank with wonder.

"Father," cried the young lord, stepping hastily forward, "whatever is wrong?"

"That!" screamed the Earl, pointing a palsied finger at me. "That! He comes here and threatens *me*, — a peer of England."

The Lady Mary spoke swiftly to her brother and the Colonel.

"'Tis a sick man's fancy," she said. "There have been no threats. Father has had a bad day. He is not himself. He talks wildly. He —"

"Mary!" yelled the Earl as well as he was able. "Do you betray me? Do you betray your own father? Oh, a woman Judas and my daughter!"

Lord Strepp and Colonel Royale looked as if their minds were coming apart. They stared at Lady Mary, at the Earl, at me. For my part I remained silent and stiff in a corner, keeping my eye upon the swords of the other gentlemen. I had no doubt but that presently I would be engaged in a desperate attempt to preserve my life. Lady Mary was weeping. She had never once glanced in my direction. But I was thrilling with happiness. She had flung me her feeble intercession even as a lady may fling a bun to a bear in a pit, but I had the remembrance to prize, to treasure, and if both gentlemen had set upon me and the sick Earl had advanced with the warming-pan I believe my new strength would have been able to beat them off.

In the meantime the Earl was screeching meaningless rubbish in which my name, with epithets, occurred constantly. Lady Mary, still weeping, was trying to calm him.

Young Lord Strepp at last seemed to make up his mind. He approached me and remarked:

"An inexplicable situation, Mr. O'Ruddy."

"More to me than to you," I repeated suavely.

"How?" he asked, with less consideration in his manner. "I know nought of this mummery."

"At least I know no more," I replied, still suave.

"How, Mr. O'Ruddy?" he asked, frowning. "I enter and find you wrangling with my father in his sick chamber. Is there to be no word for this?"

"I dare say you will get forty from your father; a hundred, it may be," said I, always pleasant. "But from me you will get none."

He reflected for a moment. "I dare say you understand I will brook no high-handed silence in a matter of this kind. I am accustomed to ask for the reasons for certain kinds of conduct, and of course I am somewhat prepared to see that the reasons are forthcoming."

"Well, in this case, my lord," said I with a smile, "you can accustom yourself to not getting a reason for a certain kind of conduct, because I do not intend to explain myself."

But at this moment our agreeable conversation was interrupted by the old Earl who began to bay at his son. "Arthur, Arthur, fling the rascal out; fling the rascal out! He is an impostor, a thief!" He began to fume and sputter, and threw his arms wildly; he was in some kind of convulsion; his pillows tossed, and suddenly a packet fell from under them to the floor. As all eyes wheeled toward it, I stooped swiftly and picked it up.

"My papers!" said I.

On their part there was a breathless moment of indecision. Then the swords of Lord Strepp and the Colonel came wildly from their scabbards. Mine was whipped out no less speedily, but I took it and flung it on the floor at their feet, the hilt toward them. "No," said I, my hands empty save for the papers, "'tis only that I would be making a present to the fair Lady Mary, which I pray her to receive." With my best Irish bow I extended to the young lady the papers, my inheritance, which had caused her father so much foaming at the mouth.

She looked at me scornfully, she looked at her father, she looked at me pathetically, she looked at her father, she looked at me piteously; she took the papers.

I walked to the lowering and abashed points of the other men's swords, and picked my blade from the floor. I paid no heed to the glittering points which flashed near my eyes. I strode to the door; I turned and bowed; as I did so, I believe I saw something in Lady Mary's eyes which I wished to see there. I closed the door behind me.

But immediately there was a great clamour in the room I had left, and the door was thrown violently open again. Colonel Royale appeared in a high passion:

"No, no, O'Ruddy," he shouted, "you are a gallant gentleman. I would stake my life that you are in the right. Say the word, and I will back you to the end against ten thousand fiends."

And after him came tempestuously young Lord Strepp, white on the lips with pure rage. But he spoke with a sudden steadiness.

"Colonel Royale, it appears," he said, "thinks he has to protect my friend The O'Ruddy from some wrong of my family or of mine?"

The Colonel drew in his breath for a dangerous reply, but I quickly broke in:

"Come, come, gentlemen," said I sharply. "Are swords to flash between friends when there are so many damned scoundrels in the world to parry and pink? 'Tis wrong; 'tis very wrong. Now, mark you, let us be men of peace at least until to-morrow morning, when, by the way, I have to fight your friend Forister."

"Forister!" they cried together. Their jaws fell; their eyes bulged; they forgot everything; there was a silence.

"Well," said I, wishing to reassure them, "it may not be to-morrow morning. He only told me that he would kill me as soon as he came to Bristol, and I expect him to-night or in the morning. I would of course be expecting him to show here as quickly as possible after his grand speech; but he would not be entirely unwelcome, I am thinking, for I have a mind to see if the sword of an honest man, but no fighter, would be able to put this rogue to shame, and him with all his high talk about killing people who have never done a thing in life to him but kick him some number of feet out into the inn yard, and this need never to have happened if he had known enough to have kept his sense of humour to himself, which often happens in this world."

Reflectively, Colonel Royale murmured:

"One of the finest swordsmen in England."

For this I cared nothing.

Reflectively, Lord Strepp murmured: "My father's partner in the shipping trade."

This last made me open my eyes. "Your father's partner in the shipping trade, Lord Strepp? That little black rascal?"

The young nobleman looked sheepish.

"Aye, I doubt not he may well be called a little black rascal, O'Ruddy," he answered; "but in fact he is my father's partner in certain large-fairly large, you know-shipping interests. Of course that is a matter of no consequence to me personally-but —I believe my father likes him, and my mother and my sister are quite fond of him, I think. I, myself, have never been able to quite-quite understand him in certain ways. He seems a trifle odd at moments. But he certainly is a friend of the family."

"Then," said I, "you will not be able to have the felicity of seeing him kill me, Lord Strepp."

"On the contrary," he rejoined considerately, "I would regard it as usual if he asked me to accompany him to the scene of the fight."

His remark, incidentally, that his sister was fond of Forister, filled me with a sudden insolent madness.

"I would hesitate to disturb any shipping trade," I said with dignity. "It is far from me to wish that the commerce of Great Britain should be hampered by sword-thrust of mine. If it would please young Lord Strepp, I could hand my apologies to Forister all tied up in blue-silk ribbon."

But the youthful nobleman only looked at me long with a sad and reproachful gaze.

"O'Ruddy," he said mournfully, "I have seen you do two fine things. You have never seen me do anything. But, know you now, once and for all, that you may not quarrel with me."

This was too much for an Irish heart. I was moved to throw myself on this lad's neck. I wished to swear to him that I was a brother in blood, I wished to cut a vein to give him everlasting strength-but perhaps his sister Mary had something to do with this feeling.

Colonel Royale had been fidgeting. Now he said suddenly:

"Strepp, I wronged you. Your pardon, Mr. O'Ruddy; but, damme, Strepp, if I didn't think you had gone wrong for the moment."

Lord Strepp took the offered hand. "You are a stupid old firebrain," he said affectionately to the Colonel.

"Well," said the Colonel jubilantly, "now everything is clear. If Mr. O'Ruddy will have me, I will go with him to meet this Forister; and you, Strepp, will accompany Forister; and we all will meet in a friendly way-ahem!"

"The situation is intimately involved," said Lord Strepp dejectedly. "It will be a ridiculous business-watching each blade lunge toward the breast of a friend. I don't know that it is proper. Royale, let us set ourselves to part these duellists. It is indecent."

"Did you note the manner in which he kicked him out of the inn?" asked the Colonel. "Do you think a few soothing words would calm the mind of one of the finest swordsmen in England?"

I began to do some profound thinking.

"Look you, Colonel," said I. "Do you mean that this wretched little liar and coward is a fine swordsman?"

"I haven't heard what you call him," said the Colonel, "but his sword-play is regular firelight on the wall. However," he added hopefully, "we may find some way to keep him from killing you. I have seen some of the greatest swordsmen lose by chance to a novice. It is something like cards. And yet you are not an ignorant player. That, I, Clarence Royale, know full well. Let us try to beat him."

I remembered Forister's parting sentence. Could it be true that a man I had kicked with such enthusiasm and success was now about to take revenge by killing me? I was really disturbed. I was a very brave youth, but I had the most advanced ideas about being killed. On occasion of great danger I could easily and tranquilly develop a philosophy of avoidance and retirement. I had no antiquated notions about going out and getting myself killed through sheer bull-headed scorn of the other fellow's hurting me. My father had taught me this discretion. As a soldier he claimed that he had run away from nine battles, and he would have run away from more, he said, only that all the others had turned out to be victories for his side. He was admittedly a brave man, but, more than this, he had a great deal of sense. I was the child of my father. It did not seem to me profitable to be killed for the sake of a sentiment which seemed weak and dispensable. This little villain! Should I allow him to gratify a furious revenge because I was afraid to take to my heels? I resolved to have the courage of my emotions. I would run away.

But of all this I said nothing. It passed through my mind like light and left me still smiling gayly at Colonel Royale's observations upon the situation.

"Wounds in the body from Forister," quoth he academically, "are almost certain to be fatal, for his wrist has a magnificent twist which reminds one of a top. I do not know where he learned this wrist movement, but almost invariably it leads him to kill his man. Last year I saw him —I digress. I must look to it that O'Ruddy has quiet, rest, and peace of mind until the morning."

Yes; I would have great peace of mind until the morning! I saw that clearly.

"Well," said I, "at any rate we will know more to-morrow. A good day to you, Lord Strepp, and I hope your principal has no more harm come to him than I care to have come to me, which is precious little, and in which case the two of us will be little hurted."

"Good-bye, O'Ruddy," said the young man.

In the corridor the Colonel slapped my shoulder in a sudden exuberant outburst.

"O'Ruddy," he cried, "the chance of your life! Probably the best-known swordsman in all England! 'Pon my word, if you should even graze him, it would almost make you a peer. If you truly pinked him, you could marry a duchess. My eye, what an opportunity for a young and ambitious man."

"And what right has he to be such a fine swordsman?" I demanded fretfully. "Damn him! 'Tis no right of a little tadpole like him to be a great cut-throat. One could never have told from the look of him, and yet it simply teaches one to be always cautious with men."

The Colonel was bubbling over with good nature, his mind full of the prospective event.

"I saw Ponsonby kill Stewart in their great fight several years agone," he cried, rubbing his hands, "but Ponsonby was no such swordsman as Forister, and I misdoubt me that Stewart was much better than you yourself."

Here was a cheerful butcher. I eyed him coldly.

"And out of this," said I slowly, "comes a vast deal of entertainment for you, and a hole between two ribs for me. I think I need a drink."

"By all means, my boy," he answered, heartily. "Come to my chamber. A quart of port under your waistcoat will cure a certain bilious desire in you to see the worst of things, which I have detected lately in your manner. With grand sport before us, how could you be otherwise than jolly? Ha, Ha!"

So saying, he affectionately took my arm and led me along the corridor.

CHAPTER VII

When I reached my own chamber I sank heavily into a chair. My brain was in a tumult. I had fallen in love and arranged to be killed in one short day's work. I stared at my image in a mirror. Could I be The O'Ruddy? Perhaps my name was Paddy or Jem Bottles? Could I pick myself out in a crowd? Could I establish my identification? I little knew.

At first I thought of my calm friend who apparently drank blood for his breakfast. Colonel Royale to me was somewhat of a stranger, but his charming willingness to grind the bones of his friends in his teeth was now quite clear. I fight the best swordsman in England as an amusement, a show? I began to see reasons for returning to Ireland. It was doubtful if old Mickey Clancy would be able to take full care of my estate even with the assistance and prevention of Father Donovan. All properties looked better while the real owner had his eye on them. It would be a shame to waste the place at Glandore all for a bit of pride of staying in England. Never a man neglected his patrimony but that it didn't melt down to a kick in the breeches and much trouble in the courts. I perceived, in short, that my Irish lands were in danger. What could endanger them was not quite clear to my eye, but at any rate they must be saved. Moreover it was necessary to take quick measures. I started up from my chair, hastily recounting Jem Bottles's five guineas.

But I bethought me of Lady Mary. She could hardly be my good fairy. She was rather too plump to be a fairy. She was not extremely plump, but when she walked something moved within her skirts. For my part I think little of fairies, who remind me of roasted fowl's wing. Give me the less brittle beauty which is not likely to break in a man's arms.

After all, I reflected, Mickey Clancy could take care quite well of that estate at Glandore; and, if he didn't, Father Donovan would soon bring him to trouble; and, if Father Donovan couldn't, why, the place was worth very little any how. Besides, 'tis a very weak man who cannot throw an estate into the air for a pair of bright eyes.

Aye, and Lady Mary's bright eyes! That was one matter. And there was Forister's bright sword. That was another matter. But to my descendants I declare that my hesitation did not endure an instant. Forister might have an arm so supple and a sword so long that he might be able to touch the nape of his neck with his own point, but I was firm on English soil. I would meet him even if he were a *chevaux de frise*. Little it mattered to me. He might swing the ten arms of an Indian god; he might yell like a gale at sea; he might be more terrible in appearance than a volcano in its passions; still I would meet him.

There was a knock, and at my bidding a servant approached and said: "A gentleman, Mr. Forister, wishes to see you, sir."

For a moment I was privately in a panic. Should I say that I was ill, and then send for a doctor to prove that I was not ill? Should I run straightway and hide under the bed? No!

"Bid the gentleman enter," said I to the servant.

Forister came in smiling, cool and deadly. "Good day to you, Mr. O'Ruddy," he said, showing me his little teeth. "I am glad to see that you are not for the moment consorting with highwaymen and other abandoned characters who might succeed in corrupting your morals, Mr. O'Ruddy. I have decided to kill you, Mr. O'Ruddy. You may have heard that I am the finest swordsman in England, Mr. O'Ruddy?"

I replied calmly: "I have heard that you are the finest swordsman in England, Mr. Forister, whenever better swordsmen have been traveling in foreign parts, Mr. Forister, and when no visitors of fencing distinction have taken occasion to journey here, Mr. Forister."

This talk did not give him pleasure, evidently. He had entered with brave composure, but now he bit his lip and shot me a glance of hatred. "I only wished to announce," he said savagely, "that I would prefer to kill you in the morning as early as possible."

"And how may I render my small assistance to you, Mr. Forister? Have you come to request me to arise at an untimely hour?"

I was very placid; but it was not for him to be coming to my chamber with talk of killing me. Still, I thought that, inasmuch as he was there, I might do some good to myself by irritating him slightly. I continued:

"I to-day informed my friends —"

"Your friends!" said he.

"My friends," said I. "Colonel Royale in this matter."

"Colonel Royale!" said he.

"Colonel Royale," said I. "And if you are bound to talk more you had best thrust your head from the window and talk to those chimneys there, which will take far more interest in your speech than I can work up. I was telling you that to-day I informed my friends-then you interrupted me. Well, I informed them-but what the devil I informed them of you will not know very soon. I can promise you, however, it was not a thing you would care to hear with your hands tied behind you."

"Here's a cold man with a belly full of ice," said he musingly. "I have wronged him. He has a tongue on him, he has that. And here I have been judging from his appearance that he was a mere common dolt. And, what, Mr. O'Ruddy," he added, "were you pleased to say to the gentlemen which I would not care to hear with my hands tied behind me?"

"I told them why you took that sudden trip to Bristol," I answered softly.

He fairly leaped in a sudden wild rage. "You-told them?" he stuttered. "You poltroon! 'Twas a coward's work!"

"Be easy," said I, to soothe him. "'Tis no more cowardly than it is for the best swordsman in England to be fighting the worst swordsman in Ireland over a matter in which he is entirely in the wrong, although 'tis not me that cares one way or another way. Indeed, I prefer you to be in the wrong, you little black pig."

"Stop," said he, with a face as white as milk. "You told them-you told them about-about the girl at Bristol?"

"What girl at Bristol?" said I innocently. "'Tis not me to be knowing your wenches in Bristol or otherwheres."

A red flush came into the side of his neck and swelled slowly across his cheeks. "If you've told them about Nell!"

"Nell?" said I. "Nell? Yes, that's the name. Nell. Yes, Nell. And if I told them about Nell?"

"Then," he rejoined solemnly, "I shall kill you ten times if I lose my soul in everlasting hell for it."

"But after I have killed you eleven times I shall go to Bristol and have some sweet interviews with fair Nell," said I. This sting I expected to call forth a terrific outburst, but he remained scowling in dark thought. Then I saw where I had been wrong. This Nell was now more a shame than a sweetheart, and he was afraid that word had been passed by me to the brother of-Here was a chance to disturb him. "When I was making my little joke of you and your flame at Bristol," said I thoughtfully, "I believe there were no ladies present. I don't remember quite. Any how we will let that pass. 'Tis of no consequence."

And here I got him in full cry. *"God rot you!"* he shrieked. His sword sprang and whistled in the air.

"Hold," said I, as a man of peace. "'Twould be murder. My weapon is on the bed, and I am too lazy to go and fetch it. And in the mean time let me assure you that no word has crossed my lips in regard to Nell, your Bristol sweetheart, for the very excellent reason that I never knew of her existence until you yourself told me some moments ago."

Never before had he met a man like me. I thought his under-jaw would drop on the floor.

"Up to a short time ago," said I candidly, "your indecent amours were safe from my knowledge. I can be in the way of putting myself as silent as a turtle when it comes to protecting a man from his folly with a woman. In fact, I am a gentleman. But," I added sternly, "what of the child?"

"The child?" he cried jumping. "May hell swallow you! And what may you know of the child?"

I waved my hand in gentle deprecation of his excitement as I said:

"Peace, Forister; I know nothing of any child. It was only an observation by a man of natural wit who desired to entertain himself. And, pray, how old is the infant?"

He breathed heavily. "You are a fiend," he answered. Keeping his eyes on the floor, he deliberated upon his choice of conduct. Presently he sheathed his sword and turned with some of his old jauntiness toward the door. "Very good," said he. "To-morrow we shall know more of our own affairs."

"True," I replied.

"We shall learn if slyness and treachery are to be defeated by fair-going and honour."

"True," said I.

"We shall learn if a snake in the grass can with freedom bite the foot of a lion."

"True," said I.

There was a loud jovial clamour at the door, and at my cry it flew open. Colonel Royale entered precipitately, beaming with good humour.

"O'Ruddy, you rascal," he shouted, "I commanded you to take much rest, and here I find —" He halted abruptly as he perceived my other visitor. "And here I find," he repeated coldly, "here I find Mr. Forister."

Forister saluted with finished politeness. "My friend and I," he said, "were discussing the probabilities of my killing him in the morning. He seems to think that he has some small chance for his life, but I have assured him that any real betting man would not wager a grain of sand that he would see the sun go down to-morrow."

"Even so," rejoined the Colonel imperturbably.

"And I also suggested to my friend," pursued Forister, "that to-morrow I would sacrifice my ruffles for him, although I always abominate having a man's life-blood about my wrists."

"Even so," quoth the undisturbed Colonel.

"And further I suggested to my friend that if he came to the ground with a coffin on his back, it might promote expedition after the affair was over."

Colonel Royale turned away with a gesture of disgust.

I thought it was high time to play an ace at Forister and stop his babble, so I said:

"And when Mr. Forister had finished his graceful remarks we had some talk regarding Mr. Forister's affairs in Bristol, and I confess I was much interested in hearing about the little —"

Here I stopped abruptly, as if I had been interrupted by Forister; but he had given me no sign but a sickly grin.

"Eh, Forister?" said I. "What's that?"

"I was remarking that I had nothing further to say for the present," he replied, with superb insolence. "For the time I am quite willing to be silent. I bid you a good day, sirs."

CHAPTER VIII

As the door closed upon Forister, Colonel Royale beat his hand passionately against the wall. "O'Ruddy," he cried, "if you could severely maim that cold-blooded bully, I would be willing to adopt you as my legitimate grandfather. I would indeed."

"Never fear me," said I. "I shall pink him well."

"Aye," said my friend, looking at me mournfully, "I ever feared your Irish light-heartedness. 'Twill not do to be confident. He is an evil man, but a great swordsman. Now I never liked Ponsonby, and Stewart was the most lovable of men; but in the great duel Ponsonby killed —"

"No," I interrupted, "damn the duel between Ponsonby and Stewart. I'm sick of it. This is to be the duel between The O'Ruddy and Forister, and it won't be like the other."

"Eh, well," said the Colonel good-naturedly; "make your mind easy. But I hope to God you lay him flat."

"After I have finished with him," said I in measured tones, "he will be willing to sell himself as a sailor to go to the Indies; only, poor devil, he won't be able to walk, which is always a drawback after a hard fight, since it leaves one man incapable on the ground and thus discloses strong evidence of a struggle."

I could see that Colonel Royale had no admiration for my bragging air, but how otherwise was I to keep up my spirits? With all my discouragements it seemed to me that I was privileged to do a little fine lying. Had my father been in my place, he would have lied Forister into such a corner that the man would be thinking that he had the devil for an opponent. My father knew more about such matters.

Still I could not help but be thinking how misfortunate it was that I had kicked a great swordsman out of this inn at Bristol when he might have been a harmless shoemaker if I had only decent luck. I must make the best of it, and for this my only method was to talk loudly, — to myself, if need be; to others if I could. I was not the kind that is quite unable to say a good word for itself even if I was not able to lie as well as my father in his prime. In his day he could lie the coat off a man's back, or the patches off a lady's cheek, and he could lie a good dog into howling ominously. Still it was my duty to lie as well as I was able.

After a time Lord Strepp was announced and entered. Both he and Colonel Royale immediately stiffened and decided not to perceive each other. "Sir," said Lord Strepp to me, "I have the honour to present my compliments to you, and to request that you join a friend of mine, Mr. Forister, at dawn to-morrow, in the settlement of a certain small misunderstanding."

"Sir," said I, in the same manner, "I am only too happy to have this little matter adjusted."

"And of course the arrangements, sir?"

"For them I may refer you to my friend Colonel Royale."

"Ah," said the young Lord, as if he had never before seen the Colonel.

"I am at your service, sir," said Colonel Royale as if he never in his whole life had heard of Lord Strepp.

Then these two began to salaam one another, and mouth out fool phrases, and cavort and prance and caracole, until I thought them mad. When they departed there was a dreadful scene. Each refused to go through the door before the other. There was a frightful deadlock. They each bowed and scraped and waved their hands, and surrendered the doorway back and forth, until I thought they were to be in my chamber eternally. Lord Strepp gorgeously presented the right of way to Colonel Royale, and the Colonel gorgeously presented the right of way to Lord Strepp. All this time they were bending their backs at each other.

Finally I could stand it no longer. "In God's name," I shouted, "the door is wide enough for the two of you. Take it together. You will go through like grease. Never fear the door. 'Tis a good wide door."

To my surprise, they turned to glance at me and burst into great laughter. Then they passed out amiably enough together. I was alone.

Well, the first thing I did was to think. I thought with all my force. I fancied the top of my skull was coming off. I thought myself into ten thousand intricacies. I thought myself into doom and out of it, and behind it and below it, but I could not think of anything which was of service to me. It seemed that I had come among a lot of mummers, and one of these mummers was resolved to kill me, although I had never even so much as broken his leg. But I remembered my father's word, who had told me that gentlemen should properly kill each other over a matter of one liking oranges and the other not liking oranges. It was the custom among men of position, he had said, and of course a way was not clear to changing this custom at the time. However, I determined that if I lived I would insist upon all these customs being moderated and re-directed. For my part I was willing that any man should like oranges.

I decided that I must go for a walk. To sit and gloom in my room until the time of the great affair would do me no good in any case. In fact it was likely to do me much harm. I went forth to the garden in the rear of the inn. Here spread a lawn more level than a ballroom floor. There was a summer-house and many beds of flowers. On this day there was nobody abroad in the garden but an atrocious parrot, which, balancing on its stick, called out continually raucous cries in a foreign tongue.

I paced the lawn for a time, and then took a seat in the summer-house. I had been there but a moment when I perceived Lady Mary and the Countess come into the garden. Through the leafy walls of the summer-house I watched them as they walked slowly to and fro on the grass. The mother had evidently a great deal to say to the daughter. She waved her arms and spoke with a keen excitement.

But did I overhear anything? I overheard nothing! From what I knew of the proper conduct of the really thrilling episodes of life I judged that I should have been able to overhear almost every word of this conversation. Instead, I could only see the Countess making irritated speech to Lady Mary.

Moreover it was legitimate that I should have been undetected in the summer-house. On the contrary, they were perfectly aware that there was somebody there, and so in their promenade they presented it with a distinguished isolation.

No old maid ever held her ears so wide open. But I could hear nothing but a murmur of angry argument from the Countess and a murmur of gentle objection from Lady Mary. I was in possession of an ideal place from which to overhear conversation. Almost every important conversation ever held had been overheard from a position of this kind. It seemed unfair that I, of all men in literature, should be denied this casual and usual privilege.

The Countess harangued in a low voice at great length; Lady Mary answered from time to time, admitting this and admitting that, protesting against the other. It seemed certain to me that talk related to Forister, although I had no real reason for thinking it. And I was extremely angry that the Countess of Westport and her daughter, Lady Mary Strepp, should talk of Forister.

Upon my indignant meditations the parrot interpolated:

"Ho, ho!" it cried hoarsely. "A pretty lady! A pretty lady! A pretty lady! A pretty lady! —"

Lady Mary smiled at this vacuous repetition, but her mother went into a great rage, opening her old jaws like a maddened horse. "Here, landlord! Here, waiter! Here, anybody!"

So people came running from the inn, and at their head was, truly enough, the landlord. "My lady," he cried panting.

She pointed an angry and terrible finger at the parrot. "When I walk in this garden, am I to be troubled with this wretched bird?"

The landlord almost bit the turf while the servants from the inn grovelled near him. "My lady," he cried, "the bird shall be removed at once." He ran forward. The parrot was chained by its leg to a tall perch. As the innkeeper came away with the entire business, the parrot began to shout: "Old harridan! Old harridan! Old harridan!" The innkeeper seemed to me to be about to die of wild terror. It was a dreadful moment. One could not help but feel sorry for this poor wretch, whose sole offence was that he kept an inn and also chose to keep a parrot in his garden.

The Countess sailed grandly toward the door of the hotel. To the solemn protestations of six or seven servants she paid no heed. At the door she paused and turned for the intimate remark. "I cannot endure parrots," she said impressively. To this dictum the menials crouched.

The servants departed: the garden was now empty save for Lady Mary and me. She continued a pensive strolling. Now, I could see plainly that here fate had arranged for some kind of interview. The whole thing was set like a scene in a theatre. I was undoubtedly to emerge suddenly from the summer-house; the lovely maid would startle, blush, cast down her eyes, turn away. Then, when it came my turn, I would doff my hat to the earth and beg pardon for continuing a comparatively futile existence. Then she would slyly murmur a disclaimer of any ability to criticise my continuation of a comparatively futile existence, adding that she was but an inexperienced girl. The ice thus being broken, we would travel by easy stages into more intimate talk.

I looked down carefully at my apparel and flecked a handkerchief over it. I tilted my hat; I set my hip against my harbour. A moment of indecision, of weakness, and I was out of the summer-house. God knows how I hoped that Lady Mary would not run away.

But the moment she saw me she came swiftly to me. I almost lost my wits.

"'Tis the very gentleman I wished to see," she cried. She was blushing, it is true, but it was evident she intended to say nothing about inexperience or mere weak girls. "I wished to see you because —" she hesitated and then rapidly said: "It was about the papers. I wanted to thank you — I — you have no notion how happy the possession of the papers has made my father. It seemed to have given him new life. I — I saw you throw your sword on the floor with the hilt away from you. And-and then you gave me the papers. I knew you were a gallant gentleman."

All this time, I, in my confusion, was bobbing and murmuring pledges of service. But if I was confused, Lady Mary was soon cool enough in the presence of a simple bog-trotter like me. Her beautiful eyes looked at me reflectively.

"There is only one service I can render you, sir," said she softly. "'Tis advice which would have been useful in saving some men's lives if only they had received it. I mean-don't fight with Forister in the morning. 'Tis certain death."

It was now my turn once more. I drew myself up, and for the first time I looked squarely into her bright eyes.

"My lady," said I, with mournful dignity, "I was filled with pride when you said the good word to me. But what am I to think now? Am I, after all, such a poor stick that, to your mind, I could be advised to sell my honour for a mere fear of being killed?"

Even then I remembered my one-time decision to run away from the duel with Forister; but we will not be thinking of that now.

Tears came into Lady Mary's eyes. "Ah, now, I have blundered," she said. "'Tis what you would say, sir. 'Tis what you would do. I have only made matters worse. A woman's meddling often results in the destruction of those she-those she don't care to have killed."

One would think from the look of this last sentence, that with certain reason I could have felt somewhat elated without being altogether a fool. Lady Mary meant nothing of importance by her speech, but it was a little bit for a man who was hungry to have her think of him. But here I was assailed by a very demon of jealousy and distrust. This beautiful witch had some plan in her head which did not concern my welfare at all. Why should she, a great lady, take any trouble for a poor devil who was living at an inn on money borrowed from a highwayman. I had been highly honoured by an indifferent consideration born of a wish to be polite to a man who had eased the mind of her father. No; I would not deceive myself.

But her tears! Were they marking indifferent consideration? For a second I lost myself in a roseate impossible dream. I dreamed that she had spoken to me because she —

Oh, what folly! Even as I dreamed, she turned to me with splendid carriage, and remarked coldly:

"I did not wish you to suppose that I ever failed to pay a debt. I have paid this one. Proceed now, sir, in your glowing stupidity. I have done."

When I recovered myself she was placidly moving away from me toward the door of the inn.

CHAPTER IX

I had better be getting to the story of the duel. I have been hanging back with it long enough, and I shall tell it at once. I remember my father saying that the most aggravating creature in life was one who would be keeping back the best part of a story through mere reasons of trickery, although I have seen himself dawdle over a tale until his friends wished to hurl the decanters at him. However, there can be no doubting of the wisdom of my father's remark. Indeed there can be little doubting of the wisdom of anything that my father said in life, for he was a very learned man. The fact that my father did not invariably defer to his own opinions does not alter the truth of those opinions in my judgment, since even the greatest of philosophers is more likely to be living a life based on the temper of his wife and the advice of his physician than on the rules laid down in his books. Nor am I certain that my father was in a regular habit of delaying a story. I only remember this one incident, wherein he was recounting a stirring tale of a fight with a lancer, and just as the lance was within an inch of the paternal breast my father was reminded, by a sight of the walnuts, that Mickey Clancy was not serving the port with his usual rapidity, and so he addressed him. I remember the words well.

"Mickey, you spalpeen," said my father, "would you be leaving the gentlemen as dry as the bottom of Moses' feet when he crossed the Red Sea? Look at O'Mahoney there! He is as thirsty as a fish in the top of a tree. And Father Donovan has had but two small quarts, and he never takes less than five. Bad luck to you, Mickey, if it was a drink for your own stomach, you would be moving faster. Are you wishing to ruin my reputation for hospitality, you rogue you?"

And my father was going on with Mickey, only that he looked about him at this time and discovered his guests all upon their feet, one with the tongs and one with the poker, others with decanters ready to throw.

"What's this?" said he.

"The lance," said they.

"What lance?" said he.

"The lance of the lancer," said they.

"And why shouldn't he have a lance?" said my father. "Faith, 'twould be an odd lancer without a lance!"

By this time they were so angry that Mickey, seeing how things were going, and I being a mere lad, took me from the room. I never heard precisely what happened to the lancer, but he must have had the worst of it, for wasn't my father, seated there at the table, telling the story long years after?

Well, as to my duel with Forister: Colonel Royale was an extremely busy man, and almost tired my life out with a quantity of needless attentions. For my part, I thought more of Lady Mary and the fact that she considered me no more than if I had been a spud. Colonel Royale fluttered about me. I would have gruffly sent him away if it were not that everything he did was meant in kindliness and generous feeling. I was already believing that he did not have more than one brain in his head, but I could not be ungrateful for his interest and enthusiasm in getting me out to be hurt correctly. I understood, long years afterward, that he and Lord Strepp were each so particular in the negotiations that no less than eighteen bottles of wine were consumed.

The morning for the duel dawned softly warm, softly wet, softly foggy. The Colonel popped into my room the moment I was dressed. To my surprise, he was now quite mournful. It was I, now, who had to do the cheering.

"Your spirits are low, Colonel?" said I banteringly.

"Aye, O'Ruddy," he answered with an effort, "I had a bad night, with the gout. Heaven help this devil from getting his sword into your bowels."

He had made the appointment with Strepp, of course, and as we walked toward the ground he looked at me very curiously out of the ends of his eyes. "You know-ah, you have the honour of the acquaintance of Lady Mary Strepp, O'Ruddy?" said he suddenly and nervously.

"I have," I answered, stiffening. Then I said: "And you?"

"Her father and I were friends before either of you were born," he said simply. "I was a cornet in his old regiment. Little Lady Mary played at the knee of the poor young subaltern."

"Oh," said I meanly, "you are, then, a kind of uncle."

"Aye," said he, "a kind of uncle. So much of an uncle," he added with more energy, "that when she gave me this note I thought much of acting like a real uncle. From what I have unfortunately overheard, I suspect that the Earl-aw-disagrees with you on certain points."

He averted his face as he handed me the note, and eagerly I tore it open. It was unsigned. It contained but three words: "God spare you!" And so I marched in a tumult of joy to a duel wherein I was expected to be killed.

I glanced at the Colonel. His countenance was deeply mournful. "'Tis for few girls I would become a dove to carry notes between lovers," he said gloomily. "Damn you for it, O'Ruddy!"

"Nay, Colonel," said I. "'Tis no missive of love. Look you!"

But still he kept his eyes averted. "I judge it was not meant for my eyes," he said, still very gloomy.

But here I flamed up in wrath:

"And would the eye of an angel be allowed to rest upon this paper if it were not fit that it should be so?" I demanded in my anger. "Colonel, am I to hear you bleat about doves and lovers when a glance of your eye will disabuse you? Read!"

He read. "'God spare you!'" he repeated tenderly. Then he addressed me with fine candor. "Aye, I have watched her these many years, O'Ruddy. When she was a babe I have seen her in her little bath. When she was a small girl I have seen her asleep with some trinket clasped in her rosy hand on the coverlet. Since she has been a beautiful young lady I have-but no matter. You come along, named nobody, hailing from nowhere; and she-she sends me out to deliver her prayer that God may spare you!"

I was awed by this middle-aged sorrow. But, curse him! when she was a babe he had seen her in her little bath, had he? Damn his eyes! He had seen the baby naked in her tiny tub? Damn his eyes again! I was in such a fury that I longed to fight Royale on the spot and kill him, running my sword through his memory so that it would be blotted out forever, and never, never again, even in Paradise, could he recall the image in the little tub.

But the Colonel's next words took the rage out of me.

"Go in, O'Ruddy," he cried heartily. "There is no truer man could win her. As my lady says, 'God spare you!'"

"And if Forister's blade be not too brisk, I will manage to be spared," I rejoined.

"Oh, there is another thing touching the matter," said the Colonel suddenly. "Forister is your chief rival, although I little know what has passed between them. Nothing important, I think, although I am sure Forister is resolved to have her for a bride. Of that I am certain. He is resolved."

"Is he so?" said I.

I was numb and cold for a moment. Then I slowly began to boil, like a kettle freshly placed on the fire. So I was facing a rival? Well, and he would get such a facing as few men had received. And he was my rival and in the breast of my coat I wore a note —"God spare you!" Ha, ha! He little knew the advantages under which he was to play. Could I lose with "God spare you!" against my heart? Not against three Foristers!

But hold! might it not be that the gentle Lady Mary, deprecating this duel and filled with feelings of humanity, had sent us each a note with this fervid cry for God to spare us? I was forced to concede it possible. After all, I perfectly well knew that to Lady Mary I was a mere nothing. Royale's words had been so many plumes in my life's helmet, but at bottom I knew better than to set great store by them. The whole thing was now to hurry to the duelling-ground and see if I could discover from this black Forister's face if he had received a "God spare you!" I took the Colonel's arm and fairly dragged him.

"Damme, O'Ruddy!" said he, puffing; "this can be nought but genuine eagerness."

When we came to the duelling-place we found Lord Strepp and Forister pacing to and fro, while the top of a near-by wall was crowded with pleasant-minded spectators. "Aye, you've come, have ye, sirs?" called out the rabble. Lord Strepp seemed rather annoyed, and Colonel Royale grew red and stepped peremptorily toward the wall, but Forister and I had eyes only for each other. His eye for me was a glad, cruel eye. I have a dim remembrance of seeing the Colonel take his scabbard and incontinently beat many worthy citizens of Bristol; indeed, he seemed to beat every worthy citizen of Bristol who had not legs enough to get away. I could hear them squeaking out protests while I keenly studied the jubilant Forister.

Aye, it was true. He too had a "God spare you!" I felt my blood begin to run hot. My eyes suddenly cleared as if I had been empowered with miraculous vision. My arm became supple as a whip. I decided upon one thing. I would kill Forister.

I thought the Colonel never would give over chasing citizens, but at last he returned breathless, having scattered the populace over a wide stretch of country. The preliminaries were very simple. In a half-minute Forister and I, in our shirts, faced each other.

And now I passed into such a state of fury that I cannot find words to describe it; but, as I have said, I was possessed with a remarkable clearness of vision and strength of arm. These phenomena amaze me even at this day. I was so airy upon my feet that I might have been a spirit. I think great rages work thus upon some natures. Their competence is suddenly made manifold. They live, for a brief space, the life of giants. Rage is destruction active. Whenever anything in this world needs to be destroyed, nature makes somebody wrathful. Another thing that I recall is that I had not the slightest doubt of my ability to kill Forister. There were no more misgivings: no quakings. I thought of the impending duel with delight.

In all my midnight meditations upon the fight I had pictured myself as lying strictly upon the defensive and seeking a chance opportunity to damage my redoubtable opponent. But the moment after our swords had crossed I was an absolute demon of attack. My very first lunge made him give back a long pace. I saw his confident face change to a look of fierce excitement.

There is little to say of the flying, spinning blades. It is only necessary to remark that Forister dropped almost immediately to defensive tactics before an assault which was not only impetuous but exceedingly brilliant, if I may be allowed to say so. And I know that on my left a certain Colonel Royale was steadily growing happier.

The end came with an almost ridiculous swiftness. The feeling of an ugly quivering wrench communicated itself from the point of my sword to my mind; I heard Strepp and Royale cry "Hold!" I saw Forister fall; I lowered my point and stood dizzily thinking. My sight was now blurred; my arm was weak.

My sword had gone deep into Forister's left shoulder, and the bones there had given that hideous feeling of a quivering wrench. He was not injured beyond repair, but he was in exquisite agony. Before they could reach him he turned over on his elbows and managed in some way to fling his sword at me. "Damn your soul!" he cried, and he gave a sort of howl as Lord Strepp, grim and unceremonious, bounced him over again upon his back. In the mean time Colonel Royale was helping me on with my coat and waistcoat, although I hardly knew that either he or the coat or waistcoat were in existence.

I had my usual inclination to go forward and explain to everybody how it all had happened. But Royale took me forcibly by the arm, and we turned our backs on Strepp and Forister and walked toward the inn.

As soon as we were out of their sight, Colonel Royale clasped my hands with rapture. "My boy," he cried, "you are great! You are renowned! You are illustrious! What a game you could give Ponsonby! You would give him such a stir!"

"Never doubt me," said I. "But I am now your legitimate grandfather, and I should be treated with great respect."

When we came near the inn I began to glance up at the windows. I surely expected to see a face at one of them. Certainly she would care to know who was slain or who was hurt. She would be watching, I fondly hoped, to see who returned on his legs. But the front of the inn stared at us, chilly and vacant, like a prison wall.

When we entered, the Colonel bawled lustily for an immediate bottle of wine, and I joined him in its drinking, for I knew that it would be a bellows to my flagging spirits. I had set my heart upon seeing a face at the window of the inn.

CHAPTER X

And now I found out what it was to be a famous swordsman. All that day the inn seemed to hum with my name. I could not step down a corridor without seeing flocks of servants taking wing. They fled tumultuously. A silly maid coming from a chamber with a bucket saw me and shrieked. She dropped her bucket and fled back into the chamber. A man-servant saw me, gave a low moan of terror, and leaped down a convenient stairway. All attendants scuttled aside.

What was the matter with me? Had I grown in stature or developed a ferocious ugliness? No; I now was a famous swordsman. That was all. I now was expected to try to grab the maids and kiss them wantonly. I now was expected to clout the grooms on their ears if they so much as showed themselves in my sight. In fact, I was now a great blustering, overpowering, preposterous ass.

There was a crowd of people in the coffee-room, but the buzz of talk suddenly ceased as I entered.

"Is this your chair, sir?" said I civilly to a gentleman.

He stepped away from the chair as if it had tried to bite him.

"'Tis at your service, sir!" he cried hastily.

"No," said I, "I would not be taking it if it be yours, for there are just as good chairs in the sea as ever were caught, and it would ill become me to deprive a gentleman of his chair when by exercising a little energy I can gain one for myself, although I am willing to admit that I have a slight hunger upon me. 'Tis a fine morning, sir."

He had turned pale and was edging toward the door. "'Tis at your service, sir," he repeated in a low and frightened voice. All the people were staring at us.

"No, good sir," I remonstrated, stepping forward to explain. "I would not be having you think that I am unable to get a chair for myself, since I am above everything able and swift with my hands, and it is a small thing to get a chair for one's self and not deprive a worthy gentleman of his own."

"I did not think to deprive you, sir," he ejaculated desperately. "The chair is at your service, sir!"

"Plague the man!" I cried, stamping my foot impatiently; and at the stamping of my foot a waiter let fall a dish, some women screamed, three or four people disappeared through the door, and a venerable gentleman arose from his seat in a corner and in a tremulous voice said:

"Sir, let us pray you that there be no bloodshed."

"You are an old fool," said I to him. "How could there be bloodshed with me here merely despising you all for not knowing what I mean when I say it."

"We know you mean what you say, sir," responded the old gentleman. "Pray God you mean peaceably!"

"Hoity-toity!" shouted a loud voice, and I saw a great, tall, ugly woman bearing down upon me from the doorway. "Out of my way," she thundered at a waiter. The man gasped out: "Yes, your ladyship!"

I was face to face with the mother of my lovely Mary.

"Hoity-toity!" she shouted at me again. "A brawler, eh? A lively swordster, hey? A real damn-my-eyes swaggering bully!"

Then she charged upon me. "How dare you brawl with these inoffensive people under the same roof which shelters me, fellow? By my word, I would have pleasure to give you a box on the ear!"

"Madam," I protested hurriedly. But I saw the futility of it. Without devoting further time to an appeal, I turned and fled. I dodged behind three chairs and moved them hastily into a rampart.

"Madam," I cried, feeling that I could parley from my new position, "you labour under a misapprehension."

"Misapprehend me no misapprehensions," she retorted hotly. "How dare you say that I can misapprehend anything, wretch?"

She attacked each flank in turn, but so agile was I that I escaped capture, although my position in regard to the chairs was twice reversed. We performed a series of nimble manœuvres which were characterized on my part by a high degree of strategy. But I found the rampart of chairs an untenable place. I was again obliged hurriedly to retreat, this time taking up a position behind a large table.

"Madam," I said desperately, "believe me, you are suffering under a grave misapprehension."

"Again he talks of misapprehension!"

We revolved once swiftly around the table; she stopped, panting.

"And this is the blusterer! And why do you not stand your ground, coward?"

"Madam," said I with more coolness now that I saw she would soon be losing her wind, "I would esteem it very ungallant behaviour if I endured your attack for even a brief moment. My forefathers form a brave race which always runs away from the ladies."

After this speech we revolved twice around the table. I must in all candour say that the Countess used language which would not at all suit the pages of my true and virtuous chronicle; but indeed it was no worse than I often heard afterward from the great ladies of the time. However, the talk was not always addressed to me, thank the Saints!

After we had made the two revolutions, I spoke reasonably. "Madam," said I, "if we go spinning about the table in this fashion for any length of time, these gawking spectators will think we are a pair of wheels."

"Spectators!" she cried, lifting her old head high. She beheld about seventy-five interested people. She called out loudly to them:

"And is there no gentleman among you all to draw his sword and beat me this rascal from the inn?"

Nobody moved.

"Madam," said I, still reasonable, "would it not be better to avoid a possible scandal by discontinuing these movements, as the tongues of men are not always fair, and it might be said by some —"

Whereupon we revolved twice more around the table.

When the old pelican stopped, she had only enough breath left to impartially abuse all the sight-seers. As her eye fixed upon them, The O'Ruddy, illustrious fighting-man, saw his chance and bolted like a hare. The escape must have formed a great spectacle, but I had no time for appearances. As I was passing out of the door, the Countess, in her disappointed rage, threw a heavy ivory fan after me, which struck an innocent bystander in the eye, for which he apologized.

CHAPTER XI

I wasted no time in the vicinity of the inn. I decided that an interval spent in some remote place would be consistent with the behaviour of a gentleman.

But the agitations of the day were not yet closed for me. Suddenly I came upon a small, slow-moving, and solemn company of men, who carried among them some kind of a pallet, and on this pallet was the body of Forister. I gazed upon his ghastly face; I saw the large blood blotches on his shirt; as they drew nearer I saw him roll his eyes and heard him groan. Some of the men recognized me, and I saw black looks and straight-pointing fingers. At the rear walked Lord Strepp with Forister's sword under his arm. I turned away with a new impression of the pastime of duelling. Forister's pallor, the show of bloody cloth, his groan, the dark stares of men, made me see my victory in a different way, and I even wondered if it had been absolutely necessary to work this mischief upon a fellow-being.

I spent most of the day down among the low taverns of the sailors, striving to interest myself in a thousand new sights brought by the ships from foreign parts.

But ever my mind returned to Lady Mary, and to my misfortune in being pursued around chairs and tables by my angel's mother. I had also managed to have a bitter quarrel with the noble father of this lovely creature. It was hardly possible that I could be joyous over my prospects.

At noon I returned to the inn, approaching with some display of caution. As I neared it, a carriage followed by some horsemen whirled speedily from the door. I knew at once that Lady Mary had been taken from me. She was gone with her father and mother back to London. I recognized Lord Strepp and Colonel Royale among the horsemen.

I walked through the inn to the garden, and looked at the parrot. My senses were all numb. I stared at the bird as it rolled its wicked eye at me.

"Pretty lady! Pretty lady!" it called in coarse mockery.

"Plague the bird!" I muttered, as I turned upon my heel and entered the inn.

"My bill," said I. "A horse for Bath!" said I.

Again I rode forth on a quest. The first had been after my papers. The second was after my love. The second was the hopeless one, and, overcome by melancholy, I did not even spur my horse swiftly on my mission. There was upon me the deep-rooted sadness which balances the mirth of my people,—the Celtic aptitude for discouragement; and even the keening of old women in the red glow of the peat fire could never have deepened my mood.

And if I should succeed in reaching London, what then? Would the wild savage from the rocky shore of Ireland be a pleasing sight to my Lady Mary when once more amid the glamour and whirl of the fashionable town? Besides, I could no longer travel on the guineas of Jem Bottles. He had engaged himself and his purse in my service because I had told him of a fortune involved in the regaining of certain papers. I had regained those papers, and then coolly placed them as a gift in a certain lovely white hand. I had had no more thought of Jem Bottles and his five guineas than if I had never seen them. But this was no excuse for a gentleman. When I was arrived at the rendezvous I must immediately confess to Jem Bottles, the highwayman, that I had wronged him. I did not expect him to demand satisfaction, but I thought he might shoot me in the back as I was riding away.

But Jem was not at the appointed place under the tree. Not puzzled at this behaviour, I rode on. I saw I could not expect the man to stay for ever under a tree while I was away in Bristol fighting a duel and making eyes at a lady. Still, I had heard that it was always done.

At the inn where Paddy holed Forister, I did not dismount, although a hostler ran out busily. "No," said I. "I ride on." I looked at the man. Small, sharp-eyed, weazened, he was as likely a rascal of a hostler as ever helped a highwayman to know a filled purse from a man who was riding to make arrangements with his creditors.

"Do you remember me?" said I.

"No, sir," he said with great promptitude.

"Very good," said I. "I knew you did. Now I want to know if Master Jem Bottles has passed this way to-day. A shilling for the truth and a thrashing for a lie."

The man came close to my stirrup. "Master," he said, "I know you to be a friend of him. Well, in day-time he don't ride past our door. There be lanes. And so he ain't passed here, and that's the truth."

I flung him a shilling. "Now," I said, "what of the red giant?"

The man opened his little eyes in surprise. "He took horse with you gentlemen and rode on to Bristol, or I don't know."

"Very good; now I see two very fine horses champing in the yard. And who owns them?"

If I had expected to catch him in treachery I was wrong.

"Them?" said he, jerking his thumb. He still kept his voice lowered. "They belong to two gentlemen who rode out some hours agone along with some great man's carriage. The officer said some pin-pricks he had gotten in a duel had stiffened him, and made the saddle ill of ease with him, and the young lord said that he would stay behind as a companion. They be up in the Colonel's chamber, drinking vastly. But mind your life, sir, if you would halt them on the road. They be men of great spirit. This inn seldom sees such drinkers."

And so Lord Strepp and Colonel Royale were resting at this inn while the carriage of the Earl had gone on toward Bath? I had a mind to dismount and join the two in their roystering, but my eyes turned wistfully toward Bath.

As I rode away I began to wonder what had become of Jem Bottles and Paddy. Here was a fine pair to be abroad in the land. Here were two jewels to be rampaging across the country. Separately, they were villains enough, but together they would overturn England and get themselves hung for it on twin gibbets. I tried to imagine the particular roguery to which they would first give their attention.

But then all thought of the rascals faded from me as my mind received a vision of Lady Mary's fair face, her figure, her foot. It would not be me to be thinking of two such thieves when I could be dreaming of Lady Mary with her soft voice and the clear depth of her eyes. My horse seemed to have a sympathy with my feeling and he leaped bravely along the road. The Celtic melancholy of the first part of the journey had blown away like a sea-mist. I sped on gallantly toward Bath and Lady Mary.

But almost at the end of the day, when I was within a few miles of Bath, my horse suddenly pitched forward onto his knees and nose. There was a flying spray of muddy water. I was flung out of the saddle, but I fell without any serious hurt whatever. We had been ambushed by some kind of deep-sided puddle. My poor horse scrambled out and stood with lowered head, heaving and trembling. His soft nose had been cut between his teeth and the far edge of the puddle. I led him forward, watching his legs. He was lamed. I looked in wrath and despair back at the puddle, which was as plain as a golden guinea on a platter. I do not see how I could have blundered into it, for the daylight was still clear and strong. I had been gazing like a fool in the direction of Bath. And my Celtic melancholy swept down upon me again, and even my father's bier appeared before me with the pale candle-flames swaying in the gusty room, and now indeed my ears heard the loud wailing keen of the old women.

"Rubbish," said I suddenly and aloud, "and is it one of the best swordsmen in England that is to be beaten by a lame horse?" My spirit revived. I resolved to leave my horse in the care of the people of the nearest house and proceed at once on foot to Bath. The people of the inn could be sent out after the poor animal. Wheeling my eyes, I saw a house not more than two fields away, with honest hospitable smoke curling from the chimneys. I led my beast through a hole in the hedge, and I slowly made my way toward it.

Now it happened that my way led me near a haycock, and as I neared this haycock I heard voices from the other side of it. I hastened forward, thinking to find some yokels. But as I drew very close I suddenly halted and silently listened to the voices on the other side.

"Sure, I can read," Paddy was saying. "And why wouldn't I be able? If we couldn't read in Ireland, we would be after being cheated in our rents, but we never pay them any how, so that's no matter. I would be having you to know we are a highly educated people. And perhaps you would be reading it yourself, my man?"

"No," said Jem Bottles, "I be not a great scholar and it has a look of amazing hardness. And I misdoubt me," he added in a morose and envious voice, "that your head be too full of learning."

"Learning!" cried Paddy. "Why wouldn't I be learned, since my uncle was a sexton and had to know one grave from another by looking at the stones so as never to mix up the people? Learning! says you? And wasn't there a convent at Ballygowagglycuddi, and wasn't Ballygowagglycuddi only ten miles from my father's house, and haven't I seen it many a time?"

"Aye, well, good Master Paddy," replied Jem Bottles, oppressed and sullen, but still in a voice ironic from suspicion, "I never doubt me but what you are a regular clerk for deep learning, but you have not yet read a line from the paper, and I have been waiting this half-hour."

"And how could I be reading?" cried Paddy in tones of indignation. "How could I be reading with you there croaking of this and that and speaking hard of my learning? Bad cess to the paper, I will be after reading it to myself if you are never to stop your clatter, Jem Bottles."

"I be still as a dead rat," exclaimed the astonished highwayman.

"Well, then," said Paddy. "Listen hard, and you will hear such learning as would be making your eyes jump from your head. And 'tis not me either that cares to show my learning before people who are unable to tell a mile-post from a church-tower."

"I be awaiting," said Jem Bottles with a new meekness apparently born of respect for Paddy's eloquence.

"Well, then," said Paddy, pained at these interruptions. "Listen well, and maybe you will gain some learning which may serve you all your life in reading chalk-marks in taprooms; for I see that they have that custom in this country, and 'tis very bad for hard-drinking men who have no learning."

"If you would read from the paper—" began Jem Bottles.

"Now, will you be still?" cried Paddy in vast exasperation.

But here Jem Bottles spoke with angry resolution. "Come, now! Read! 'Tis not me that talks too much, and the day wanes."

"Well, well, I would not be hurried, and that's the truth," said Paddy soothingly. "Listen now." I heard a rustling of paper. "Ahem!" said Paddy, "Ahem! Are ye listening, Jem Bottles?"

"I be," replied the highwayman.

"Ahem!" said Paddy. "Ahem! Are ye listening, Jem Bottles?"

"I be," replied the highwayman.

"Then here's for it," said Paddy in a formidable voice. There was another rustling of paper. Then to my surprise I heard Paddy intone, without punctuation, the following words:

> "Dear Sister Mary I am asking the good father to write this because my hand is lame from milking the cows although we only have one and we sold her in the autumn the four shillings you owe on the pig we would like if convenient to pay now owing to the landlord may the plague take him how did your Mickey find the fishing when you see Peggy tell her —"

Here Jem Bottles's voice arose in tones of incredulity.

"And these be the papers of the great Earl!" he cried.

Then the truth flashed across my vision like the lightning. My two madmen had robbed the carriage of the Earl of Westport, and had taken, among other things, the Earl's papers-my papers-Lady Mary's papers. I strode around the haycock.

"Wretches!" I shouted. "Miserable wretches!"

For a time they were speechless. Paddy found his tongue first.

"Aye, 'tis him! 'Tis nothing but little black men and papers with him, and when we get them for him he calls us out of our names in a foreign tongue. 'Tis no service for a bright man," he concluded mournfully.

"Give me the papers," said I.

Paddy obediently handed them. I knew them. They were my papers-Lady Mary's papers.

"And now," said I, eyeing the pair, "what mischief have you two been compassing?"

Paddy only mumbled sulkily. It was something on the difficulties of satisfying me on the subjects of little black men and papers. Jem Bottles was also sulky, but he grumbled out the beginning of an explanation.

"Well, master, I bided under the tree till him here came, and then we together bided. And at last we thought, with the time so heavy, we might better work to handle a purse or two. Thinking," he said delicately, "our gentleman might have need of a little gold. Well, and as we were riding, a good lad from the-your worship knows where-tells us the Earl's carriage is halting there for a time, but will go on later without its escort of two gentlemen; only with servants. And, thinking to do our gentleman a good deed, I brought them to stand on the highway, and then he —"

"And then I," broke in Paddy proudly, "walks up to the carriage-door looking like a king's cruiser, and says I, 'Pray excuse the manners of a self-opinionated man, but I consider your purses would look better in my pocket.' And then there was a great trouble. An old owl of a woman screeched, and was for killing me with a bottle which she had been holding against her nose. But she never dared. And with that an old sick man lifted himself from hundreds of cushions and says he, 'What do you want? You can't have them,' says he, and he keeps clasping his breast. 'First of all,' says I, 'I want what you have there. What I want else I'll tell you at my leisure.' And he was all for mouthing and fuming, but he was that scared he gave me these papers-bad luck to them." Paddy cast an evil eye upon the papers in my hand.

"And then?" said I.

"The driver he tried for to whip up," interpolated Jem Bottles. "He was a game one, but the others were like wet cats."

"And says I," continued Paddy, "'now we will have the gold, if it please you.' And out it came. 'I bid ye a good journey,' says I, and I thought it was over, and how easy it was highwaying, and I liked it well, until the lady on the front seat opens her hood and shows me a prettier face than we have in all Ireland. She clasps two white hands. 'Oh, please Mister Highwayman, my father's papers —' And with that I backs away. 'Let them go,' says I to Jem Bottles, and sick I was of it, and I would be buying masses to-night if I might find a Christian church. The poor lady!"

I was no longer angry with Paddy.

"Aye," said Jem Bottles, "the poor lady was that forlorn!"

I was no longer angry with Jem Bottles.

But I now had to do a deal of thinking. It was plain that the papers were of supreme importance to the Earl. Although I had given them to Lady Mary, they had returned to me. It was fate. My father had taught me to respect these papers, but I now saw them as a sign in the sky.

However, it was hard to decide what to do. I had given the papers to Lady Mary, and they had fled back to me swifter than cormorants. Perhaps it was willed that I should keep them. And then there would be tears in the eyes of Lady Mary, who suffered through the suffering of her father. No; come good, come bad for me, for Jem Bottles, for Paddy, I would stake our fortunes on the act of returning the papers to Lady Mary.

It is the way of Irishmen. We are all of us true philanthropists. That is why we have nothing, although in other countries I have seen philanthropists who had a great deal. My own interest in the papers I staked, mentally, with a glad mind; the minor interests of Jem Bottles and Paddy I staked, mentally, without thinking of them at all. But surely it would be a tribute to fate to give anything to Lady Mary.

I resolved on a course of action. When I aroused to look at my companions I found them seated face to face on the ground like players of draughts. Between them was spread a handkerchief, and on that handkerchief was a heap of guineas. Jem Bottles was saying, "Here be my fingers five times over again." He separated a smaller heap. "Here be my fingers five times over again." He separated another little stack. "And here be my fingers five times over again and two more yet. Now can ye understand?"

"By dad," said Paddy admiringly, "you have the learning this time, Master Bottles. My uncle the sexton could not have done it better."

"What is all this?" said I.

They both looked at me deprecatingly. "'Tis, your honour," began Paddy; "'tis only some little small sum-nothing to be talked of-belonging to the old sick man in the carriage."

"Paddy and Jem Bottles," said I, "I forgive you the taking of the papers. Ye are good men and true. Now we will do great deeds."

CHAPTER XII

My plans were formed quickly. "We now have a treasure chest of no small dimensions," said I, very complacent, naturally. "We can conquer London with this. Everything is before us. I have already established myself as the grandest swordsman in the whole continent of England. Lately we have gained much treasure. And also I have the papers. Paddy, do you take care of this poor horse. Then follow me into Bath. Jem Bottles, do you mount and ride around the town, for I fear your balladists. Meet me on the London road. Ride slowly on the highway to London, and in due time I will overtake you. I shall pocket a few of those guineas, but you yourself shall be the main treasury. Hold! what of Paddy's hair? Did he rob the Earl with that great flame showing? He dare not appear in Bath."

"'Tis small tribute to my wit, sir," answered Jem Bottles. "I would as soon go poaching in company with a lighthouse as to call a stand on the road with him uncovered. I tied him in cloth until he looked no more like himself than he now does look like a parson."

"Aye," said Paddy in some bad humour, "my head was tied in a bag. My mother would not have known me from a pig going to market. And I would not be for liking it every day. My hair is what the blessed Saints sent me, and I see no such fine hair around me that people are free to throw the laugh at me."

"Peace!" said I.

Their horses were tied in an adjacent thicket. I sent Paddy off with my lame mount, giving him full instructions as to his lies. I and Jem Bottles took the other horses and rode toward Bath.

Where a certain lane turned off from the highway I parted with Jem Bottles, and he rode away between the hedges. I cantered into Bath.

The best-known inn was ablaze with fleeting lights, and people were shouting within. It was some time before I could gain a man to look after my horse. Of him I demanded the reason of the disturbance. "The Earl of Westport's carriage has been robbed on the Bristol road, sir," he cried excitedly. "There be parties starting out. I pray they catch him."

"And who would they be catching, my lad," said I.

"Jem Bottles, damn him, sir," answered the man. "But 'tis a fierce time they will have, for he stands no less than eight feet in his boots, and his eyes are no human eyes, but burn blood-red always. His hands are adrip with blood, and 'tis said that he eats human flesh, sir. He surely is a devil, sir."

"From the description I would be willing to believe it," said I. "However, he will be easy to mark. Such a monster can hardly be mistaken for an honest man."

I entered the inn, while a boy staggered under my valises. I had difficulty in finding the landlord. But in the corridor were a number of travellers, and evidently one had come that day from Bristol, for he suddenly nudged another and hurriedly whispered:

"'Tis him! The great Irish swordsman!"

Then the news spread like the wind, apparently, that the man who had beaten the great Forister was arrived in good health at the inn. There were murmurs, and a great deal of attention, and many eyes. I suddenly caught myself swaggering somewhat. It is hard to be a famous person and not show a great swollen chicken-breast to the people. They are disappointed if you do not strut and step high. "Show me to a chamber," said I splendidly. The servants bowed their foreheads to the floor.

But the great hubbub over the Earl's loss continued without abatement. Gentlemen clanked down in their spurs; there was much talk of dragoons; the tumult was extraordinary. Upstairs the landlord led me past the door of a kind of drawing-room. I glanced within and saw the Earl of Westport gesturing and declaiming to a company of gentlemen. He was propped up in a great arm-chair.

"And why would he be waving his hands that way?" said I to two servants who stood without.

"His lordship has lost many valuable papers at the hands of a miscreant, sir," answered one.

"Is it so?" said I. "Well, then, I would see his lordship."

But here this valet stiffened. "No doubt but what his lordship would be happy to see you, sir," he answered slowly. "Unfortunately, however, he has forbidden me to present strangers to his presence."

"I have very important news. Do not be an idiot," said I. "Announce me. The O'Ruddy."

"The O'Ruggy?" said he.

"The O'Ruddy," said I.

"The O'Rudgy?" said he.

"No," said I, and I told him again. Finally he took two paces within the room and sung out in a loud voice:

"The O'Rubby."

I heard the voice of the sick old Earl calling out from his great chair. "Why, 'tis the Irishman. Bid him enter. I am glad—I am always very glad-ahem!—"

As I strode into the room I was aware of another buzz of talk. Apparently here, too, were plenty of people who knew me as the famous swordsman. The Earl moved his jaw and mumbled.

"Aye," said he at last, "here is The O'Ruddy. And, do you know, Mr. O'Ruddy, I have been foully robbed, and, among other things, have lost your worthless papers?"

"I heard that you had lost them," I answered composedly. "But I refuse to take your word that they are worthless."

Many people stared, and the Earl gave me a firm scowl. But after consideration he spoke as if he thought it well to dissemble a great dislike of me. The many candles burned very brightly, and we could all see each other. I thought it better to back casually toward the wall.

"You never accomplish anything," coughed the sick Earl. "Yet you are for ever prating of yourself. I wish my son were here. My papers are gone. I shall never recover them."

"The papers are in the breast of my coat at this moment," said I coolly.

There was a great tumult. The Earl lost his head and cried:

"Seize him!" Two or three young men took steps toward me. I was back to the wall, and in a leisurely and contemptuous way I drew my sword.

"The first gentleman who advances is a dead man," said I pleasantly.

Some drew away quickly; some hesitated, and then withdrew subtilely. In the mean time the screeches of the Earl mocked them all.

"Aye, the wild Irishman brings you up to a stand, he does! Now who will have at him? In all Bath I have no friend with a stout heart?"

After looking them over I said:

"No, my Lord, you have none."

At this insult the aged peer arose from his chair. "Bring me my sword," he cried to his valet. A hush fell upon us all. We were rendered immovable by the solemn dignity of this proceeding.

It was some time before I could find my tongue.

"And if you design to cross blades with me, you will find me a sad renegade," said I. "I am holding the papers for the hands of their true owner."

"And their true owner?" he demanded.

"Lady Mary Strepp," said I.

He sank back into his seat. "This Irishman's impudence is beyond measuring," he exclaimed. The hurrying valet arrived at that moment with a sword. "Take it away! Take it away!" he cried. "Do I wish valets to be handing swords to me at any time of the day or night?"

Here a belligerent red-faced man disengaged himself abruptly from the group of gentlemen and addressed the Earl. "Westport," said he flatly, "I can ill bear your taunt concerning your Bath friends, and this is not to speak of the insolence of the person yonder."

"Oh, ho!" said I. "Well, and the person yonder remains serene in his insolence."

The Earl, smiling slightly, regarded the new speaker.

"Sir Edmund Flixton was ever a dainty swordsman, picking and choosing like a lady in a flower-bed. Perchance he is anxious to fight the gentleman who has just given Reginald Forister something he will not forget?"

At this Flixton actually turned pale and drew back. Evidently he had not yet heard the news. And, mind you, I could see that he would fight me the next moment. He would come up and be killed like a gentleman. But the name of a great conqueror had simply appalled him and smitten him back.

The Earl was gazing at me with an entirely new expression. He had cleverly eliminated all dislike from his eyes. He covered me with a friendly regard.

"O'Ruddy," he said softly, "I would have some private speech with you. Come into my chamber."

The Earl leaned on the shoulder of his valet and a little fat doctor, and walked painfully into another room. I followed, knowing that I was now to withstand a subtle, wheedling, gentle attempt to gain the papers without the name of Lady Mary being mentioned.

The Earl was slowly lowered into a great chair. After a gasp of relief he devoted a brightening attention to me. "You are not a bad fellow, O'Ruddy," he observed. "You remind me greatly of your father. Aye, he was a rare dog, a rare dog!"

"I've heard him say so, many is the day, sir," I answered.

"Aye, a rare dog!" chuckled the old man. "I have in my memory some brisk pictures of your father with his ready tongue, his what-the-devil-does-it-matter-sir, and that extraordinary swordsmanship which you seem to have inherited."

"My father told me you were great friends in France," I answered civilly, "but from some words you let drop in Bristol I judged that he was mistaken."

"Tut," said the Earl. "You are not out of temper with me, are you, O'Ruddy?"

"With me happily in possession of the papers," I rejoined, "I am in good temper with everybody. 'Tis not for me to lose my good nature when I hold all the cards."

The Earl's mouth quickly dropped to a sour expression, but almost as quickly he put on a pleasant smile. "Aye," he said, nodding his sick head. "Always jovial, always jovial. Precisely like his father. In fact it brings back an old affection."

"If the old affection had been brought back a little earlier, sir," said I, "we all would have had less bother. 'Twas you who in the beginning drew a long face and set a square chin over the business. I am now in the mood to be rather airy."

Our glances blazed across each other.

"But," said the Earl in the gentlest of voices, "you have my papers, O'Ruddy, papers entrusted to you by your dying father to give into the hands of his old comrade. Would you betray such a sacred trust? Could you wanton yourself to the base practices of mere thievery?"

"'Tis not I who has betrayed any trust," I cried boldly. "I brought the papers and wished to offer them. They arrived in your possession, and you cried 'Straw, straw!' Did you not?"

"'Twas an expedient, O'Ruddy," said the Earl.

"There is more than one expedient in the world," said I. "I am now using the expedient of keeping the papers."

And in the glance which he gave me I saw that I had been admitted behind a certain barrier. He was angry, but he would never more attempt to overbear me with grand threats. And he would never more attempt to undermine me with cheap flattery. We had measured one against the other, and he had not come away thinking out of his proportion. After a time he said:

"What do you propose to do, Mr. O'Ruddy?"

I could not help but grin at him. "I propose nothing," said I. "I am not a man for meaning two things when I say one."

"You've said one thing, I suppose?" he said slowly.

"I have," said I.

"And the one thing?" said he.

"Your memory is as good as mine," said I.

He mused deeply and at great length. "You have the papers?" he asked finally.

"I still have them," said I.

"Then," he cried with sudden vehemence, "why didn't you read the papers and find out the truth?"

I almost ran away.

"Your-your lordship," I stammered, "I thought perhaps in London-in London perhaps —I might get a —I would try to get a tutor."

CHAPTER XIII

"So that is the way of it, is it?" said the Earl, grinning. "And why did you not take it to some clerk?"

"My lord," said I with dignity, "the papers were with me in trust for you. A man may be a gentleman and yet not know how to read and write."

"'Tis quite true," answered he.

"And when I spoke of the tutor in London I did not mean to say that I would use what knowledge he imparted to read your papers. I was merely blushing for the defects in my education, although Father Donovan often said that I knew half as much as he did, poor man, and him a holy father. If you care to so direct me, I can go even now to my chamber and make shift to read the papers."

"The Irish possess a keen sense of honour," said he admiringly.

"We do," said I. "We possess more integrity and perfect sense of honour than any other country in the world, although they all say the same of themselves, and it was my own father who often said that he would trust an Irishman as far as he could see him and no more, but for a foreigner he had only the length of an eyelash."

"And what do you intend with the papers now, O'Ruddy?" said he.

"I intend as I intended," I replied. "There is no change in me."

"And your intentions?" said he.

"To give them into the hands of Lady Mary Strepp and no other," said I boldly.

I looked at him. He looked at me.

"Lady Mary Strepp, my daughter," he said in ironic musing. "Would not her mother do, O'Ruddy?" he asked softly.

I gave a start.

"She is not near?" I demanded, looking from here to there.

He laughed.

"Aye, she is. I can have her here to take the papers in one short moment."

I held up my hands.

"No-no—"

"Peace," said he with a satanic chuckle. "I was only testing your courage."

"My lord," said I gravely, "seeing a bare blade come at your breast is one thing, and running around a table is another, and besides you have no suitable table in this chamber."

The old villain laughed again.

"O'Ruddy," he cried, "I would be a well man if you were always near me. Will I have a table fetched up from below?—'twould be easy."

Here I stiffened.

"My lord, this is frivolity," I declared. "I came here to give the papers. If you do not care to take them in the only way in which I will give them, let us have it said quickly."

"They seem to be safe in your hands at present," he remarked. "Of course after you go to London and get a tutor-ahem!—"

"I will be starting at once," said I, "although Father Donovan always told me that he was a good tutor as tutors went at the time in Ireland. And I want to be saying now, my lord, that I cannot understand you. At one moment you are crying one thing of the papers; at the next moment you are crying another. At this time you are having a laugh with me over them. What do you mean? I'll not stand this shiver-shavering any longer, I'll have you to know. What do you mean?"

He raised himself among his cushions and fixed me with a bony finger.

"What do I mean? I'll tell you, O'Ruddy," said he, while his eyes shone brightly. "I mean that I can be contemptuous of your plot. You will not show these papers to any breathing creature because you are in love with my daughter. Fool, to match your lies against an ex-minister of the King."

My eyes must have almost dropped from my head, but as soon as I recovered from my dumfounderment I grew amazed at the great intellect of this man. I had told nobody, and yet he knew all about it. Yes, I was in love with Lady Mary, and he was as well informed of it as if he had had spies to watch my dreams. And I saw that in many cases a lover was a kind of an ostrich, the bird which buries its head in the sands and thinks it is secure from detection. I wished that my father had told me more about love, for I have no doubt he knew everything of it, he had lived so many years in Paris. Father Donovan, of course, could not have helped me in such instruction. I resolved, any how, to be more cautious in the future, although I did not exactly see how I could improve myself. The Earl's insight was pure mystery to me. I would not be for saying that he practised black magic, but any how, if he had been at Glandore, I would have had him chased through three parishes.

However, the Earl was grinning victoriously, and I saw that I must harden my face to a brave exterior.

"And is it so?" said I. "Is it so?"

"Yes," he said, with his grin.

"And what then?" said I bluntly.

In his enjoyment he had been back again among his cushions.

"'What then? What then?'" he snarled, rearing up swiftly. "Why, then you are an insolent fool: Begone from me! begone! be —" Here some spasm overtook him, a spasm more from rage than from the sickness. He fell back breathless, although his eyes continued to burn at me.

"My lord," said I, bowing, "I will go no poorer than when I came, save that I have lost part of the respect I once had for you."

I turned and left his chamber. Some few gentlemen yet remained in the drawing-room as I passed out into the public part of the inn. I went quietly to a chamber and sat down to think. I was for ever going to chambers and sitting down to think after these talks with the Earl, during which he was for ever rearing up in his chair and then falling back among the cushions.

But here was another tumble over the cliffs, if you like! Here was genuine disaster. I laid my head in my hands and mused before my lonely fire, drinking much and visioning my ruin. What the Earl said was true. There was trouble in the papers for the old nobleman. That he knew. That I knew. And he knew with his devilish wisdom that I would lose my head rather than see her in sorrow. Well, I could bide a time. I would go to London in company with Paddy and Jem Bottles, since they owned all the money, and if three such rogues could not devise something, then I would go away and bury myself in a war in foreign parts, occupying myself in scaling fortresses and capturing guns. These things I know I could have performed magnificently, but from the Earl I had learned that I was an ill man to conduct an affair of the heart.

I do not know how long I meditated, but suddenly there was a great tumult on the stairs near my door. There were the shouts and heavy breathings of men, struggling, and over all rang a screech as from some wild bird. I ran to the door and poked my head discreetly out; for my coat and waistcoat were off as well as my sword, and I wished to see the manner of tumult at a distance before I saw it close. As I thrust forth my head I heard a familiar voice:

"And if ye come closer, ye old hell-cat, 'tis me will be forgetting respect to my four great-grandmothers and braining you. Keep off! Am I not giving ye the word? Keep off!"

Then another familiar voice answered him in a fine high fury. "And you gallows-bird, you gallows-bird, you gallows-bird! You answer me, do you! They're coming, all, even to the hangman! You'll soon know how to dance without a fiddler! Ah, would you? Would you?"

If I had been afflicted with that strange malady of the body which sometimes causes men to fall to the ground and die in a moment without a word, my doom would have been sealed. It was Paddy and Hoity-Toity engaged in animated discussion.

"And if ye don't mind your eye, ye old cormorant —" began Paddy.

"And you would be a highwayman, would you, gallows-bird —" began the Countess.

"Cow —" began Paddy.

Here for many reasons I thought it time to interfere. "Paddy!" I cried. He gave a glance at my door, recognized my face, and, turning quickly, ran through into my chamber. I barred the door even as Hoity-Toity's fist thundered on the oak.

"It's a she-wolf," gasped Paddy, his chest pressing in and out.

"And what did you do to her?" I demanded.

"Nothing but try to run away, sure," said Paddy.

"And why would she be scratching you?"

"She saw me for one of the highwaymen robbing the coach, and there was I, devil knowing what to do, and all the people of the inn trying to put peace upon her, and me dodging, and then —"

"Man," said I, grabbing his arm, "'tis a game that ends on the —"

"Never a bit," he interrupted composedly. "Wasn't the old witch drunk, claws and all, and didn't even the great English lord, or whatever, send his servant to bring her in, and didn't he, the big man, stand in the door and spit on the floor and go in when he saw she was for battering all the servants and using worse talk than the sailors I heard in Bristol? It would not be me they were after, those men running. It would be her. And small power to them, but they were no good at it. I am for taking a stool in my hand —"

"Whist!" said I. "In England they would not be hitting great ladies with stools. Let us hearken to the brawl. She is fighting them finely."

For I had seen that Paddy spoke truth. The noble lady was engaged in battling with servants who had been in pursuit of her when she was in pursuit of Paddy. Never had I seen even my own father so drunk as she was then. But the heart-rending thing was the humble protests of the servants. "Your ladyship! Oh, your ladyship!"—as they came up one by one, or two by two, obeying orders of the Earl, to be incontinently boxed on the ears by a member of a profligate aristocracy. Probably any one of them was strong enough to throw the beldame out at a window. But such was not the manner of the time. One would think they would retreat upon the Earl and ask to be dismissed from his service. But this also was not the manner of the time. No; they marched up heroically and took their cuffs on the head and cried: "Oh, your ladyship! Please, your ladyship!" They were only pretenders in their attacks; all they could do was to wait until she was tired, and then humbly escort her to where she belonged, meanwhile pulling gently at her arms.

"She was after recognizing you then?" said I to Paddy.

"Indeed and she was," said he. He had dropped into a chair and was looking as if he needed a doctor to cure him of exhaustion. "She would be after having eyes like a sea-gull. And Jem Bottles was all for declaring that my disguise was complete, bad luck to the little man."

"Your disguise complete?" said I. "You couldn't disguise yourself unless you stood your head in a barrel. What talk is this?"

"Sure an' I looked no more like myself than I looked like a wild man with eight rows of teeth in his head," said Paddy mournfully. "My own mother would have been after taking me for a horse. 'Tis that old creature with her evil eye who would be seeing me when all the others were blind as bats. I could have walked down the big street in Cork without a man knowing me."

"That you could at any time," said I. The Countess had for some moments ceased to hammer on my door. "Hearken! I think they are managing her."

Either Hoity-Toity had lost heart, or the servants had gained some courage, for we heard them dragging her delicately down the staircase. Presently there was a silence.

After I had waited until this silence grew into the higher silence which seems like perfect safety, I rang the bell and ordered food and drink. Paddy had a royal meal, sitting on the floor by the fireplace and holding a platter on his knee. From time to time I tossed him something for which I did not care. He was very grateful for my generosity. He ate in a barbaric fashion, crunching bones of fowls between his great white teeth and swallowing everything.

I had a mind to discourse upon manners in order that Paddy might not shame me when we came to London; for a gentleman is known by the ways of his servants. If people of quality should see me attended by such a savage they would put me down small. "Paddy," said I, "mend your ways of eating."

"'My ways of eating,' your honour?" said he. "And am I not eating all that I can hold? I was known to be a good man at platter always. Sure I've seen no man in England eat more than me. But thank you kindly, sir."

"You misunderstand me," said I. "I wish to improve your manner of eating. It would not be fine enough for the sight of great people. You eat, without taking breath, pieces as big as a block of turf."

"'Tis the custom in my part of Ireland," answered Paddy.

"I understand," said I. "But over here 'tis only very low people who fall upon their meat from a window above."

"I am not in the way of understanding your honour," said he. "But any how a man may be respectable and yet have a good hunger on him."

CHAPTER XIV

It had been said that the unexpected often happens, although I do not know what learned man of the time succeeded in thus succinctly expressing a great law and any how it matters little, for I have since discovered that these learned men make one headful of brains go a long way by dint of poaching on each other's knowledge. But the unexpected happened in this case, all true enough whatever.

I was giving my man a bit of a warning.

"Paddy," said I, "you are big, and you are red, and you are Irish; but by the same token you are not the great Fingal, son of lightning. I would strongly give you the word. When you see that old woman you start for the open moors."

"Devil fear me, sir," answered Paddy promptly. "I'll not be stopping. I would be swimming to Ireland before she lays a claw on me."

"And mind you exchange no words with her," said I, "for 'tis that which seems to work most wrongfully upon her."

"Never a word out of me," said he. "I'll be that busy getting up the road."

There was another tumult in the corridor, with the same screeches by one and the same humble protests by a multitude. The disturbance neared us with surprising speed. Suddenly I recalled that when the servant had retired after bringing food and drink I had neglected to again bar the door. I rushed for it, but I was all too late. I saw the latch raise. "Paddy!" I shouted wildly. "Mind yourself!" And with that I dropped to the floor and slid under the bed.

Paddy howled, and I lifted a corner of the valance to see what was transpiring. The door had been opened, and the Countess stood looking into the room. She was no longer in a fiery rage; she was cool, deadly determined, her glittering eye fixed on Paddy. She took a step forward.

Paddy, in his anguish, chanted to himself an Irish wail in which he described his unhappiness. "Oh, mother of me, and here I am caught again by the old hell-cat, and sure the way she creeps toward me is enough to put the fear of God in the heart of a hedge-robber, the murdering old witch. And it was me was living so fine and grand in England and greatly pleased with myself. Sorrow the day I left Ireland; it is, indeed."

She was now close to him, and she seemed to be preparing for one stupendous pounce which would mean annihilation to Paddy. Her lean hands were thrust out, with the fingers crooked, and it seemed to me that her fingers were very long. In despair Paddy changed his tune and addressed her.

"Ah, now, alanna. Sure the kind lady would be for doing no harm? Be easy, now, acushla."

But these tender appeals had no effect. Suddenly she pounced. Paddy roared, and sprang backward with splendid agility. He seized a chair.

Now I am quite sure that before he came to England Paddy had never seen a chair, although it is true that at some time in his life he may have had a peep through a window into an Irish gentleman's house, where there might be a chair if the King's officers in the neighbourhood were not very ambitious and powerful. But Paddy handled this chair as if he had seen many of them. He grasped it by the back and thrust it out, aiming all four legs at the Countess. It was a fine move. I have seen a moderately good swordsman fairly put to it by a pack of scoundrelly drawers who assailed him at all points in this manner.

"An you come on too fast," quavered Paddy, "ye can grab two legs, but there will be one left for your eye and another for your brisket."

However she came on, sure enough, and there was a moment of scuffling near the end of the bed out of my sight. I wriggled down to gain another view, and when I cautiously lifted an edge of the valance my eyes met the strangest sight ever seen in all England. Paddy, much dishevelled and panting like a hunt-dog, had wedged the Countess against the wall. She was pinioned by the four legs of the chair, and Paddy, by dint of sturdily pushing at the chair-back, was keeping her in a fixed position.

In a flash my mind was made up. Here was the time to escape. I scrambled quickly from under the bed. "Bravo, Paddy!" I cried, dashing about the room after my sword, coat, waistcoat, and hat. "Devil a fear but you'll hold her, my bucko! Push hard, my brave lad, and mind your feet don't slip!"

"If your honour pleases," said Paddy, without turning his eyes from his conquest, "'tis a little help I would be wishing here. She would be as strong in the shoulder as a good plough-horse and I am not for staying here for ever."

"Bravo, my grand lad!" I cried, at last finding my hat, which had somehow gotten into a corner. From the door I again addressed Paddy in encouraging speech. "There's a stout-hearted boy for you! Hold hard, and mind your feet don't slip!"

He cast a quick agonized look in my direction, and, seeing that I was about basely to desert him, he gave a cry, dropped the chair, and bolted after me. As we ran down the corridor I kept well in advance, thinking it the best place in case the pursuit should be energetic. But there was no pursuit. When Paddy was holding the Countess prisoner she could only choke and stammer, and I had no doubt that she now was well mastered by exhaustion.

Curiously there was little hubbub in the inn. The fact that the Countess was the rioter had worked in a way to cause people to seek secluded and darkened nooks. However, the landlord raised his bleat at me. "Oh, sir, such a misfortune to befall my house just when so many grand ladies and gentlemen are here."

I took him quietly by the throat and beat his head against the wall, once, twice, thrice.

"And you allow mad ladies to molest your guests, do you?" said I.

"Sir," he stuttered, "could I have caused her to cease?"

"True," I said, releasing him. "But now do as I bid you and quickly. I am away to London. I have had my plenty of you and your mad ladies."

We started bravely to London, but we only went to another and quieter inn, seeking peace and the absence of fear. I may say we found it, and, in a chair before a good fire, I again took my comfort. Paddy sat on the floor, toasting his shins. The warmth passed him into a reflective mood.

"And I know all I need of grand ladies," he muttered, staring into the fire. "I thought they were all for riding in gold coaches and smelling of beautiful flowers, and here they are mad to be chasing Irishmen in inns. I remember old Mag Cooligan fought with a whole regiment of King's troops in Bantry, and even the drums stopped beating, the soldiers were that much interested. But, sure, everybody would be knowing that Mag was no grand lady, although Pat Cooligan, her brother, was pig-killer to half the country-side. I am thinking we were knowing little about grand ladies. One of the soldiers had his head broke by a musket because the others were so ambitious to destroy the old lady, and she scratching them all. 'Twas long remembered in Bantry."

"Hold your tongue about your betters," said I sharply. "Don't be comparing this Mag Cooligan with a real Countess."

"There would be a strange similarity any how," said he. "But, sure, Mag never fought in inns, for the reason that they would not be letting her inside."

"Remember how little you are knowing of them, Paddy," said I. "'Tis not for you to be talking of the grand ladies when you have seen only one, and you would not be knowing another from a fish. Grand ladies are eccentric, I would have you to know. They have their ways with them which are not for omadhauns like you to understand."

"Eccentric, is it?" said he. "I thought it would be some such devilment."

"And I am knowing," said I with dignity, "of one lady so fine that if you don't stop talking that way of ladies I will break your thick skull for you, and it would matter to nobody."

"'Tis an ill subject for discussion, I am seeing that," said Paddy. "But, faith, I could free Ireland with an army of ladies like one I've seen."

"Will you be holding your tongue?" I cried wrathfully.

Paddy began to mumble to himself,—"Bedad, he was under the bed fast enough without offering her a stool by the fire and a small drop of drink which would be no more than decent with him so fond of her. I am not knowing the ways of these people."

In despair of his long tongue I made try to change the talking.

"We are off for London, Paddy. How are you for it?"

"London, is it?" said he warily. "I was hearing there are many fine ladies there."

For the second time in his life I cuffed him soundly on the ear.

"Now," said I, "be ringing the bell. I am for buying you a bit of drink; but if you mention the gentry to me once more in that blackguard way I'll lather you into a resemblance to your grandfather's bones."

After a pleasant evening I retired to bed leaving Paddy snug asleep by the fire. I thought much of my Lady Mary, but with her mother stalking the corridors and her knowing father with his eye wide open, I knew there was no purpose in hanging about a Bath inn. I would go to London, where there were gardens, and walks in the park, and parties, and other useful customs. There I would win my love.

The following morning I started with Paddy to meet Jem Bottles and travel to London. Many surprising adventures were in store for us, but an account of these I shall leave until another time, since one would not be worrying people with too many words, which is a great fault in a man who is recounting his own affairs.

CHAPTER XV

As we ambled our way agreeably out of Bath, Paddy and I employed ourselves in worthy speech. He was not yet a notable horseman, but his Irish adaptability was so great that he was already able to think he would not fall off so long as the horse was old and tired.

"Paddy," said I, "how would you like to be an Englishman? Look at their cities. Sure, Skibbereen is a mud-pond to them. It might be fine to be an Englishman."

"I would not, your honour," said Paddy. "I would not be an Englishman while these grand— But never mind; 'tis many proud things I will say about the English considering they are our neighbours in one way; I mean they are near enough to come over and harm us when they wish. But any how they are a remarkable hard-headed lot, and in time they may come to something good."

"And is a hard head such a qualification?" said I.

Paddy became academic. "I have been knowing two kinds of hard heads," he said. "Mickey McGovern had such a hard skull on him no stick in the south of Ireland could crack it, though many were tried. And what happened to him? He died poor as a rat. 'Tis not the kind of hard head I am meaning. I am meaning the kind of hard head which believes it contains all the wisdom and honour in the world. 'Tis what I mean. If you have a head like that, you can go along blundering into ditches and tumbling over your own shins, and still hold confidence in yourself. 'Tis not very handsome for other men to see; but devil a bit care you, for you are warm inside with complacence."

"Here is a philosopher, in God's truth," I cried. "And where were you learning all this? In Ireland?"

"Your honour," said Paddy firmly, "you yourself are an Irishman. You are not for saying there is no education in Ireland, for it educates a man to see burning thatches and such like. One of them was my aunt's, Heaven rest her!"

"Your aunt?" said I. "And what of your aunt? What have the English to do with your aunt?"

"That's what she was asking them," said Paddy; "but they burned her house down over a little matter of seventeen years' rent she owed to a full-blooded Irishman, may the devil find him!"

"But I am for going on without an account of your burnt-thatch education," said I. "You are having more than two opinions about the English, and I would be hearing them. Seldom have I seen a man who could gain so much knowledge in so short a space. You are interesting me."

Paddy seemed pleased. "Well, your honour," said he confidentially, "'tis true for you. I am knowing the English down to their toes."

"And if you were an Englishman, what kind of an Englishman would you like to be?" said I.

"A gentleman," he answered swiftly. "A big gentleman!" Then he began to mimic and make gestures in a way that told me he had made good use of his eyes and of the society of underlings in the various inns. "Where's me man? Send me man! Oh, here you are! And why didn't you know I wanted you? What right have you to think I don't want you? What? A servant dead? Pah! Send it down the back staircase at once and get rid of it. Bedad!" said Paddy enthusiastically, "I could do that fine!" And to prove what he said was true, he cried "Pah!" several times in a lusty voice.

"I see you have quickly understood many customs of the time," said I. "But 'tis not all of it. There are many quite decent people alive now."

"'Tis strange we have never heard tell of them," said Paddy musingly. "I have only heard of great fighters, blackguards, and beautiful ladies, but sure, as your honour says, there must be plenty of quiet decent people somewhere."

"There is," said I. "I am feeling certain of it, although I am not knowing exactly where to lay my hand upon them."

"Perhaps they would be always at mass," said Paddy, "and in that case your honour would not be likely to see them."

"Masses!" said I. "There are more masses said in Ireland in one hour than here in two years."

"The people would be heathens, then?" said Paddy, aghast.

"Not precisely," said I. "But they have reformed themselves several times, and a number of adequate reformations is a fine thing to confuse the Church. In Ireland we are all for being true to the ancient faith; here they are always for improving matters, and their learned men study the Sacred Book solely with a view to making needed changes."

"'Tis heathen they are," said Paddy with conviction. "I was knowing it. Sure, I will be telling Father Corrigan the minute I put a foot on Ireland, for nothing pleases him so much as a good obstinate heathen, and he very near discourses the hair off their heads."

"I would not be talking about such matters," said I. "It merely makes my head grow an ache. My father was knowing all about it; but he was always claiming that if a heathen did his duty by the poor he was as good as anybody, and that view I could never understand."

"Sure, if a heathen gives to the poor, 'tis poison to them," said Paddy. "If it is food and they eat it, they turn black all over and die the day after. If it is money, it turns red-hot and burns a hole in their hand, and the devil puts a chain through it and drags them down to hell, screeching."

"Say no more," said I. "I am seeing you are a true theologian of the time. I would be talking on some more agreeable topic, something about which you know less."

"I can talk of fishing," he answered diffidently. "For I am a great fisherman, sure. And then there would be turf-cutting, and the deadly stings given to men by eels. All these things I am knowing well."

"'Tis a grand lot to know," said I, "but let us be talking of London. Have you been hearing of London?"

"I have been hearing much about the town," said Paddy. "Father Corrigan was often talking of it. He was claiming it to be full of loose women, and sin, and fighting in the streets during mass."

"I am understanding something of the same," I replied. "It must be an evil city. I am fearing something may happen to you, Paddy,—you with your red head as conspicuous as a clock in a tower. The gay people will be setting upon you and carrying you off. Sure there has never been anything like you in London."

"I am knowing how to be dealing with them. It will be all a matter of religious up-bringing, as Father Corrigan was saying. I have but to go to my devotions, and the devil will fly away with them."

"And supposing they have your purse?" said I. "The devil might fly away with them to an ill tune for you."

"When they are flying away with my purse," he replied suggestively, "they will be flying away with little of what could be called my ancestral wealth."

"You are natural rogues," said I, "you and Jem Bottles. And you had best not be talking of religion."

"Sure a man may take the purse of an ugly old sick monkey like him, and still go with an open face to confession," rejoined Paddy, "and I would not be backward if Father Corrigan's church was a mile beyond."

"And are you meaning that Father Corrigan would approve you in this robbery?" I cried.

"Devil a bit he would, your honour," answered Paddy indignantly. "He would be saying to me: 'Paddy, you limb of Satan, and how much did you get?' I would be telling him. 'Give fifteen guineas to the Church, you mortal sinner, and I will be trying my best for you,' he would be saying. And I would be giving them."

"You are saved fifteen guineas by being in England, then," said I, "for they don't do that here. And I am thinking you are traducing your clergy, you vagabond."

"Traducing?" said he. "That would mean giving them money. Aye, I was doing it often. One year I gave three silver shillings."

"You're wrong," said I. "By 'traducing' I mean speaking ill of your priest."

"'Speaking ill of my priest'?" cried Paddy, gasping with amazement. "Sure, my own mother never heard a word out of me!"

"However," said I, "we will be talking of other things. The English land seems good."

Paddy cast his eye over the rainy landscape. "I am seeing no turf for cutting," he remarked disapprovingly, "and the potatoes would not be growing well here. 'Tis a barren country."

At nightfall we came to a little inn which was ablaze with light and ringing with exuberant cries. We gave up our horses and entered. To the left was the closed door of the taproom, which now seemed to furnish all the noise. I asked the landlord to tell me the cause of the excitement.

"Sir," he answered, "I am greatly honoured to-night. Mr. O'Ruddy, the celebrated Irish swordsman, is within, recounting a history of his marvellous exploits."

"Indeed!" said I.

"Bedad!" said Paddy.

CHAPTER XVI

Paddy was for opening his mouth wide immediately, but I checked him. "I would see this great man," said I to the landlord, "but I am so timid by nature I fear to meet his eagle eye. Is there no way by which we could observe him in secret at our leisure?"

"There be one way," remarked the landlord after deliberation. I had passed him a silver coin. He led us to a little parlour back of the taproom. Here a door opened into the tap itself, and in this door was cut a large square window so that the good man of the inn could sometimes sit at his ease in his great chair in the snug parlour and observe that his customers had only that for which they were paying. It is a very good plan, for I have seen many a worthy man become a rogue merely because nobody was watching him. My father often was saying that if he had not been narrowly eyed all his young life, first by his mother and then by his wife, he had little doubt but what he might have been engaged in dishonest practices sooner or later.

A confident voice was doing some high talking in the taproom. I peered through the window, but at first I saw only a collection of gaping yokels, poor bent men with faces framed in straggly whiskers. Each had a pint pot clutched with a certain air of determination in his right hand.

Suddenly upon our line of vision strode the superb form of Jem Bottles. A short pipe was in his mouth, and he gestured splendidly with a pint pot. "More of the beer, my dear," said he to a buxom maid. "We be all rich in Ireland. And four of them set upon me," he cried again to the yokels. "All noblemen, in fine clothes and with sword-hilts so flaming with jewels an ordinary man might have been blinded. 'Stop!' said I. 'There be more of your friends somewhere. Call them.' And with that —"

"'And with that'?" said I myself, opening the door and stepping in upon him. "'And with that'?" said I again. Whereupon I smote him a blow which staggered him against the wall, holding his crown with both hands while his broken beer-pot rolled on the floor. Paddy was dancing with delight at seeing some other man cuffed, but the landlord and the yokels were nearly dead of terror. But they made no sound; only the buxom girl whimpered.

"There is no cause for alarm," said I amiably. "I was only greeting an old friend. 'Tis a way I have. And how wags the world with you, O'Ruddy?"

"I am not sure for the moment," replied Jem Bottles ruefully. "I must bide till it stops spinning."

"Truth," cried I. "That would be a light blow to trouble the great O'Ruddy. Come now; let us have the pots filled again, and O'Ruddy shall tell us more of his adventures. What say you, lads?"

The yokels had now recovered some of their senses, and they greeted my plan with hoarse mutterings of hasty and submissive assent.

"Begin," said I sternly to the highwayman. He stood miserably on one foot. He looked at the floor; he looked at the wall; from time to time he gave me a sheep's glance. "Begin," said I again. Paddy was wild with glee. "Begin," said I for the third time and very harshly.

"I —" gulped out the wretched man, but he could get no further.

"I am seeing I must help you," said I. "Come now, when did you learn the art of sticadoro proderodo sliceriscum fencing?"

Bottles rolled the eyes of despair at me, but I took him angrily by the shoulder. "Come now; when did you learn the art of sticadoro proderodo sliceriscum fencing?"

Jem Bottles staggered, but at last he choked out: "My mother taught me." Here Paddy retired from the room, doubled in a strong but soundless convulsion.

"Good," said I. "Your mother taught you. We are making progress any how. Your mother taught you. And now tell me this: When you slew Cormac of the Cliffs, what passado did you use? Don't be stuttering. Come now; quick with you; what passado did you use? What passado?"

With a heroism born of a conviction that in any event he was a lost man, Jem Bottles answered: "A blue one."

"Good," I cried cheerfully. "'A blue one'! We are coming on fine. He killed Cormac with a blue passado. And now I would be asking you —"

"Master," interrupted the highwayman with sudden resolution. "I will say no more. I have done. You may kill me an it pleases you."

Now I saw that enough was enough. I burst into laughter and clapped him merrily on the shoulder. "Be cheery, O'Ruddy," I cried. "Sure an Irishman like you ought to be able to look a joke in the face." He gave over his sulks directly, and I made him buy another pint each for the yokels. "'Twas dry work listening to you and your exploits, O'Ruddy," said I.

Later I went to my chamber, attended by my followers, having ordered roast fowls and wine to be served as soon as possible. Paddy and Jem Bottles sat on stools one at each side of the fireplace, and I occupied a chair between them.

Looking at my two faithful henchmen, I was suddenly struck by the thought that they were not very brisk servants for a gentleman to take to fashionable London. I had taken Paddy out of his finery and dressed him in a suit of decent brown; but his hair was still unbarbered, and I saw that unless I had a care his appearance would greatly surprise and please London. I resolved to have him shorn at the first large town.

As for Jem Bottles, his clothes were well enough, and indeed he was passable in most ways unless it was his habit, when hearing a sudden noise, to take a swift dark look to the right and to the left. Then, further, people might shrewdly note his way of always sitting with his back to the wall and his face to the door. However, I had no doubt of my ability to cure him of these tricks as soon as he was far enough journeyed from the scenes of his earlier activity.

But the idea I entertained at this moment was more to train them to be fine grand servants, such as I had seen waiting on big people in Bath. They were both willing enough, but they had no style to them. I decided to begin at once and see what I could teach them.

"Paddy," said I, taking off my sword and holding it out to him. "My sword!"

Paddy looked at it. "It is, sir," he answered respectfully.

"Bad scran to you, Paddy!" I cried angrily. "I am teaching you your duties. Take the sword! In both hands, mind you! Now march over and lay it very tenderly on the stand at the head of the bed. There now!"

I now turned my attention to Jem Bottles.

"Bottles," said I peremptorily, "my coat and waistcoat."

"Yes, sir," replied Bottles quickly, profiting by Paddy's lesson.

"There now," said I, as Bottles laid the coat and waistcoat on a dresser. "'Tis a good beginning. When supper comes I shall teach you other duties."

The supper came in due course, and after the inn's man had gone I bid Jem and Paddy stand one on either side of my chair and a little way back. "Now," said I, "stand square on your feet, and hold your heads away high, and stick your elbows out a little, and try to look as if you don't know enough to tell fire from water. Jem Bottles has it. That's it! Bedad! look at the ignorance on him! He's the man for you, Paddy! Wake up now, and look stupid. Am I not telling you?"

"Begor!" said Paddy dejectedly, "I feel like the greatest omadhaun in all the west country, and if that is not being stupid enough for your honour I can do no better."

"Shame to you, Paddy, to let an Englishman beat you so easily," said I. "Take that grin off your face, you scoundrel! Now," I added, "we are ready to begin. Wait, now. You must each have something to hold in your fist. Let me be thinking. There's only one plate and little of anything else. Ah, I have it! A bottle! Paddy, you shall hold one of the bottles. Put your right hand underneath it, and with your left hand hold it by the neck. But keep your elbows out. Jem, what the devil am I to give you to hold? Ah, I have it! Another bottle! Hold it the same as Paddy. Now! Stand square on your feet, and hold your heads away high, and stick your elbows out a little, and look stupid. I am going to eat my supper."

I finished my first and second bottles with the silence only broken by the sound of my knife-play and an occasional restless creaking of boots as one of my men slyly shifted his position.

Wishing to call for my third bottle, I turned and caught them exchanging a glance of sympathetic bewilderment. As my eye flashed upon them, they stiffened up like grenadier recruits.

But I was not for being too hard on them at first. "'Tis enough for one lesson," said I. "Put the bottles by me and take your ease."

With evident feelings of relief they slunk back to the stools by the fire, where they sat recovering their spirits.

After my supper I sat in the chair toasting my shins and lazily listening to my lads finishing the fowls. They seemed much more like themselves, sitting there grinding away at the bones and puffing with joy. In the red firelight it was such a scene of happiness that I misdoubted for a moment the wisdom of my plan to make them into fine grand numskulls.

I could see that all men were not fitted for the work. It needed a beefy person with fat legs and a large amount of inexplicable dignity, a regular God-knows-why loftiness. Truth, in those days, real talent was usually engaged in some form of rascality, barring the making of books and sermons. When one remembers the impenetrable dulness of the great mass of the people, the frivolity of the gentry, the arrogance and wickedness of the court, one ceases to wonder that many men of taste took to the highway as a means of recreation and livelihood. And there I had been attempting to turn my two frank rascals into the kind of sheep-headed rubbish whom you could knock down a great staircase, and for a guinea they would say no more. Unless I was the kicker, I think Paddy would have returned up the staircase after his assailant. Jem Bottles probably would have gone away nursing his wrath and his injury, and planning to waylay the kicker on a convenient night. But neither would have taken a guinea and said no more. Each of these simple-hearted reprobates was too spirited to take a guinea for a kick down a staircase.

Any how I had a mind that I could be a gentleman true enough without the help of Jem and Paddy making fools of themselves. I would worry them no more.

As I was musing thus my eyes closed from a sense of contented weariness, but I was aroused a moment later by hearing Paddy address Jem Bottles in a low voice. "'Tis you who are the cool one, Jem!" said he with admiration, "trying to make them think you were *him*!" Here I was evidently indicated by a sideways bob of the head. "Have you not been seeing the fine ways of him? Sure, be looking at his stride and his habit of slatting people over the head, and his grand manners with his food. You are looking more like a candlestick than you are looking like him. I wonder at you."

"But I befooled them," said Bottles proudly. "I befooled them well. It was Mr. O'Ruddy here, and Mr. O'Ruddy there, and the handsome wench she gave me many a glance of her eye, she did."

"Sorrow the day for her, then," responded Paddy, "and if you would be cozening the girls in the name of *him* there, he will be cozening you, and I never doubt it."

"'Twas only a trick to make the time go easy, it was," said Bottles gloomily. "If you remember, Master Paddy, I have spent the most of my new service waiting under oak-trees; and I will not be saying that it rained always, but oft-times it did rain most accursedly."

CHAPTER XVII

We rode on at daybreak. At the first large village I bid a little man cut Paddy's hair, and although Paddy was all for killing the little man, and the little man twice ran away, the work was eventually done, for I stood over Paddy and threatened him. Afterward the little boys were not so anxious to hoot us through the streets, calling us Africans. For it must be recalled that at this time there was great curiosity in the provinces over the Africans, because it was known that in London people of fashion often had African servants; and although London cared nothing for the provinces, and the provinces cared nothing for London, still the rumour of the strange man interested the country clodhopper so greatly that he called Paddy an African on principle, in order that he might blow to his neighbours that he had seen the fascinating biped. There was no general understanding that the African was a man of black skin; it was only understood that he was a great marvel. Hence the urchins in these far-away villages often ran at the heels of Paddy's horse, yelling.

In time the traffic on the highway became greatly thickened, and several times we thought we were entering London because of the large size and splendour of the towns to which we came. Paddy began to fear the people had been deceiving us as to the road, and that we had missed London entirely. But finally we came to a river with hundreds of boats upon it, and there was a magnificent bridge, and on the other bank was a roaring city, and through the fog the rain came down thick as the tears of the angels. "That's London," said I.

We rode out upon the bridge, all much interested, but somewhat fearful, for the noise of the city was terrible. But if it was terrible as we approached it, I hesitate to say what it was to us when we were once fairly in it. "Keep close to me," I yelled to Paddy and Jem, and they were not unwilling. And so we rode into this pandemonium, not having the least idea where we were going.

As we progressed I soon saw what occasioned the major part of the noise. Many heavy carts thundered slowly through the narrow, echoing streets, bumping their way uproariously over a miserable pavement. Added to this, of course, were the shrill or hoarse shouts of the street vendors and the apprentices at the shop-doors. To the sky arose an odour almost insupportable, for it was new to us all.

The eaves of the houses streamed with so much water that the sidewalks were practically untenable, although here and there a hardy wayfarer strode on regardless of a drenched cloak, probably being too proud to take to the street. Once our travel was entirely blocked by a fight. A butcher in a bloody apron had dashed out of his shop and attacked the driver of a brewer's sledge. A crowd gathered miraculously and cheered on this spectacle; women appeared at all the windows; urchins hooted; mongrel dogs barked. When the butcher had been worsted and chased back into his shop by the maddened brewer we were allowed to pursue our journey.

I must remark that neither of these men used aught but his hands. Mostly their fists were doubled, and they dealt each other sounding, swinging blows; but there was some hair-pulling, and when the brewer had the butcher down I believe the butcher tried to bite his opponent's ear. However they were rather high-class for their condition. I found out later that at this time in the darker parts of London the knife was a favourite weapon of the English and was as rampant as ever it is in the black alleys of an Italian city. It was no good news for me, for the Irish had long been devoted to the cudgel.

When I wish for information I always prefer making the request to a gentleman. To have speech of a boor is well enough if he would not first study you over to find, if he can, why you want the information, and, after a prolonged pause, tell you wrong entirely. I perceived a young gentleman standing in under a porch and ogling a window on the opposite side of the way. "Sir," said I, halting my horse close to him, "would you be so kind as to point to a stranger the way to a good inn?" He looked me full in the face, spat meaningly in the gutter, and, turning on his heel, walked away. And I will give oath he was not more than sixteen years old.

I sat stiff in the saddle; I felt my face going hot and cold. This new-feathered bird with a toy sword! But to save me, as it happened, from a preposterous quarrel with this infant, another man came along the sidewalk. He was an older man, with a grave mouth and a clean-cut jowl. I resolved to hail him. "And now my man," said I under my breath, "if you are as bad as the other, by the mass, I'll have a turnover here with you, London or no London."

Then I addressed him. "Sir —" I began. But here a cart roared on my other side, and I sat with my mouth open, looking at him. He smiled a little, but waited courteously for the hideous din to cease. "Sir," I was enabled to say at last, "would you be so kind as to point to a stranger the way to a good inn?" He scanned me quietly, in order, no doubt, to gain an idea what kind of inn would suit my condition. "Sir," he answered, coming into the gutter and pointing, "'tis this way to Bishopsgate Street, and there you will see the sign of the 'Pig and Turnip,' where there is most pleasurable accommodation for man and beast, and an agreeable host." He was a shop-keeper of the city of London, of the calm, steady breed that has made successive kings either love them or fearingly hate them, — the bone and the sinew of the great town.

I thanked him heartily, and we went on to the "Pig and Turnip." As we clattered into the inn yard it was full of people mounting and dismounting, but there seemed a thousand stable-boys. A dozen flung themselves at my horse's head. They quite lifted me out of the saddle in their great care that I should be put to no trouble. At the door of the inn a smirking landlord met me, bowing his head on the floor at every backward pace, and humbly beseeching me to tell how he could best serve me. I told him, and at once there was a most pretentious hubbub. Six or eight servants began to run hither and yon. I was delighted with my reception, but several days later I discovered they had mistaken me for a nobleman of Italy or France, and I was expected to pay extravagantly for graceful empty attentions rather than for sound food and warm beds.

This inn was so grand that I saw it would no longer do for Paddy and Jem to be sleeping in front of my fire like big dogs, so I nodded assent when the landlord asked if he should provide lodgings for my two servants. He packed them off somewhere, and I was left lonely in a great chamber. I had some fears having Paddy long out of my sight, but I assured myself that London had such terrors for him he would not dare any Irish mischief. I could trust Jem Bottles to be discreet, for he had learned discretion in a notable school.

Toward the close of the afternoon, the rain ceased, and, attiring myself for the street and going to the landlord, I desired him to tell me what interesting or amusing walk could now conveniently be taken by a gentleman who was a stranger to the sights of London. The man wagged his head in disapproval.

"'Twill be dark presently, sir," he answered, "and I would be an ill host if I did not dissuade a perfect stranger from venturing abroad in the streets of London of a night-time."

"And is it as bad as that?" I cried, surprised.

"For strangers, yes," said he. "For they be for ever wandering, and will not keep to the three or four streets which be as safe as the King's palace. But if you wish, sir, I will provide one man with a lantern and staff to go before you, and another man with lantern and staff to follow. Then, with two more stout lads and your own servants, I would venture —"

"No, no!" I cried, "I will not head an army on a night march when I intended merely an evening stroll. But how, pray you, am I to be entertained otherwise than by going forth?"

The innkeeper smiled with something like pity.

"Sir, every night there meets here such a company of gay gentlemen, wits and poets, as would dazzle the world did it but hear one half of what they say over their pipes and their punch. I serve the distinguished company myself, for I dare trust nobody's care in a matter so important to my house; and I assure you, sir, I have at times been so doubled with mirth there was no life in me. Why, sir, Mr. Fullbil himself comes here at times!"

"Does he, indeed?" I cried, although I never had heard of the illustrious man.

"Indeed and he does, sir," answered the innkeeper, pleased at my quick appreciation of this matter. "And then there is goings on, I warrant me. Mr. Bobbs and the other gentlemen will be in spirits."

"I never doubt you," said I. "But is it possible for a private gentleman of no wit to gain admittance to this distinguished company?"

"Doth require a little managing, sir," said he, full of meaning.

"Pray you manage it then," said I, "for I have nought to do in London for at least two days, and I would be seeing these famous men with whose names my country rings."

Early in the evening the innkeeper came to me, much pleased. "Sir, the gentlemen bid me bring you their compliments, and I am to say they would be happy to have a pleasure in the honour of your presence. Mr. Fullbil himself is in the chair to-night. You are very fortunate, sir."

"I am," said I. "Lead away, and let us hope to find the great Fullbil in high feather."

CHAPTER XVIII

The innkeeper led me down to a large room the door of which he had flung open with a flourish. "The furrin' gentleman, may it please you, sirs," he announced, and then retired.

The room was so full of smoke that at first I could see little, but soon enough I made out a long table bordered with smoking and drinking gentlemen. A hoarse voice, away at the head of the board, was growling some words which convulsed most of the gentlemen with laughter. Many candles burned dimly in the haze.

I stood for a moment, doubtful as to procedure, but a gentleman near the foot of the table suddenly arose and came toward me with great frankness and good nature. "Sir," he whispered, so that he would not interrupt the growls at the farther end of the room, "it would give me pleasure if you would accept a chair near me."

I could see that this good gentleman was moved solely by a desire to be kind to a stranger, and I, in another whisper, gave my thanks and assent to his plan. He placed me in a chair next his own. The voice was still growling from the head of the table.

Very quickly my eyes became accustomed to the smoke, especially after I was handed a filled clay pipe by my new and excellent friend. I began to study the room and the people in it. The room was panelled in new oak, and the chairs and table were all of new oak, well carved. It was the handsomest room I had ever been in.

Afterward I looked toward the growl. I saw a little old man in a chair much too big for him, and in a wig much too big for him. His head was bent forward until his sharp chin touched his breast, and out from under his darkling brows a pair of little eyes flashed angrily and arrogantly. All faces were turned toward him, and all ears were open to his growls. He was the king; it was Fullbil.

His speech was all addressed to one man, and I looked at the latter. He was a young man with a face both Roman and feminine; with that type of profile which is possessed by most of the popular actors in the reign of His Majesty of to-day. He had luxuriant hair, and, stung by the taunts of Fullbil, he constantly brushed it nervously from his brow while his sensitive mouth quivered with held-in retorts. He was Bobbs, the great dramatist.

And as Fullbil growled, it was a curiously mixed crowd which applauded and laughed. There were handsome lordlings from the very top of London cheek by cheek with sober men who seemed to have some intellectual occupation in life. The lordlings did the greater part of the sniggering. In the meantime everybody smoked hard and drank punch harder. During occasional short pauses in Fullbil's remarks, gentlemen passed ecstatic comments one to another. — "Ah, this is indeed a mental feast!" —"Did ye ever hear him talk more wittily?" —"Not I, faith; he surpasses even himself!" —"Is it not a blessing to sit at table with such a master of learning and wit?" —"Ah, these are the times to live in!"

I thought it was now opportune to say something of the same kind to my amiable friend, and so I did it. "The old corpse seems to be saying a prayer," I remarked. "Why don't he sing it?"

My new friend looked at me, all agape, like a fish just over the side of the boat. "'Tis Fullbil, the great literary master —" he began; but at this moment Fullbil, having recovered from a slight fit of coughing, resumed his growls, and my friend subsided again into a worshipping listener.

For my part I could not follow completely the words of the great literary master, but I construed that he had pounced upon the drama of the time and was tearing its ears and eyes off.

At that time I knew little of the drama, having never read or seen a play in my life; but I was all for the drama on account of poor Bobbs, who kept chewing his lip and making nervous movements until Fullbil finished, a thing which I thought was not likely to happen before an early hour of the morning. But finish he did, and immediately Bobbs, much impassioned, brought his glass heavily down on the table in a demand for silence. I thought he would get little hearing, but, much to my surprise, I heard again the ecstatic murmur: "Ah, now, we shall hear Bobbs reply to Fullbil!" —"Are we not fortunate?" —"Faith, this will be over half London to-morrow!"

Bobbs waited until this murmur had passed away. Then he began, nailing an impressive forefinger to the table:

"Sir, you have been contending at some length that the puzzling situations which form the basis of our dramas of the day could not possibly occur in real life because five minutes of intelligent explanation between the persons concerned would destroy the silly mystery before anything at all could happen. Your originality, sir, is famous-need I say it? —and when I hear you champion this opinion in all its majesty of venerable age and general acceptance I feel stunned by the colossal imbecile strength of the whole proposition. Why, sir, you may recall all the mysterious murders which occurred in England since England had a name. The truth of them remains in unfathomable shadow. But, sir, any one of them could be cleared up in five minutes' intelligent explanation. Pontius Pilate could have been saved his blunder by far, far, far less than five minutes of intelligent explanation. But-mark ye! —but who has ever heard five minutes of intelligent explanation? The complex interwoven mesh of life constantly, eternally, prevents people from giving intelligent explanations. You sit in the theatre, and you say to yourself: 'Well, I could mount the stage, and in a short talk to these people I could anticipate a further continuation of the drama.' Yes, you could; but you are an outsider. You have no relations with these characters. You arise like an angel. Nobody has been your enemy; nobody has been your mistress. You arise and give the five minutes' intelligent explanation; bah! There is not a situation in life which does not need five minutes' intelligent explanation; but it does not get it."

It could now be seen that the old man Fullbil was simply aflame with a destructive reply, and even Bobbs paused under the spell of this anticipation of a gigantic answering. The literary master began very deliberately.

"My good friend Bobbs," said he, "I see your nose gradually is turning red."

The drama immediately pitched into oblivion. The room thundered with a great shout of laughter that went to the ceiling. I could see Bobbs making angry shouts against an invulnerable bank of uncontrolled merriment. And amid his victory old Fullbil sat with a vain smile on his cracked lips.

My excellent and adjacent friend turned to me in a burst of enthusiasm.

"And did you ever hear a thing so well turned? Ha, ha! 'My good friend Bobbs,' quoth he, 'I see your nose gradually is turning red.' Ha, ha, ha! By my King, I have seldom heard a wittier answer."

"Bedad!" said I, somewhat bewildered, but resolved to appreciate the noted master of wit, "it stamped the drama down into the ground. Sure, never another play will be delivered in England after that tremendous overthrow."

"Aye," he rejoined, still shuddering with mirth, "I fail to see how the dramatists can survive it. It was like the wit of a new Shakespeare. It subsided Bobbs to nothing. I would not be surprised at all if Bobbs now entirely quit the writing of plays, since Fullbil's words so closely hit his condition in the dramatic world. A dangerous dog is this Fullbil."

"It reminds me of a story my father used to tell —" I began.

"Sir," cried my new friend hastily, "I beg of you! May I, indeed, insist? Here we talk only of the very deepest matters."

"Very good, sir," I replied amiably. "I will appear better, no doubt, as a listener; but if my father was alive —"

"Sir," beseeched my friend, "the great Fancher, the immortal critic, is about to speak."

"Let him," said I, still amiable.

A portly gentleman of middle age now addressed Bobbs amid a general and respectful silence.

"Sir," he remarked, "your words concerning the great age of what I shall call the five-minutes-intelligent-explanation theory was first developed by the Chinese, and is contemporaneous, I believe, with their adoption of the custom of roasting their meat instead of eating it raw."

"Sir, I am interested and instructed," rejoined Bobbs.

Here old Fullbil let go two or three growls of scornful disapproval.

"Fancher," said he, "my delight in your company is sometimes dimmed by my appreciation of your facilities for being entirely wrong. The great theory of which you speak so confidently, sir, was born no earlier than seven o'clock on the morning of this day. I was in my bed, sir; the maid had come in with my tea and toast. 'Stop,' said I, sternly. She stopped. And in those few moments of undisturbed reflection, sir, the thought came to life, the thought which you so falsely attribute to the Chinese, a savage tribe whose sole distinction is its ability to fly kites."

After the murmurs of glee had died away, Fancher answered with spirit:

"Sir, that you are subject to periods of reflection I will not deny, I cannot deny. Nor can I say honourably that I give my support to our dramatic friend's defence of his idea. But, sir, when you refer to the Chinese in terms which I cannot but regard as insulting, I am prepared, sir, to —"

There were loud cries of "Order! Order! Order!" The wrathful Fancher was pulled down into his chair by soothful friends and neighbours, to whom he gesticulated and cried out during the uproar.

I looked toward old Fullbil, expecting to see him disturbed, or annoyed, or angry. On the contrary he seemed pleased, as a little boy who had somehow created a row.

"The excellent Fancher," said he, "the excellent Fancher is wroth. Let us proceed, gentlemen, to more friendly topics. You, now, Doctor Chord, with what new thing in chemics are you ready to astound us?"

The speech was addressed to a little man near me, who instantly blushed crimson, mopping his brow in much agitation, and looked at the table, unable for the moment to raise his eyes or speak a word.

"One of the greatest scientists of the time," said my friend in my ear.

"Sir," faltered the little man in his bashfulness, "that part of the discourse which related to the flying of kites has interested me greatly, and I am ready to contend that kites fly, not, as many say, through the influence of a demon or spirit which inhabits the materials, but through the pressure of the wind itself."

Fancher, now himself again, said:

"I wish to ask the learned doctor whether he refers to Chinese kites?"

The little man hurriedly replied that he had not Chinese kites in his mind at all.

"Very good, then," said the great critic. "Very good."

"But, sir," said Fullbil to little Chord, "how is it that kites may fly without the aid of demons or spirits, if they are made by man? For it is known, sir, that man may not move in the air without the aid of some devilish agency, and it is also known that he may not send aloft things formed of the gross materials of the earth. How, then, can these kites fly virtuously?"

There was a general murmur of approbation of Fullbil's speech, and the little doctor cast down his eyes and blushed again, speechless.

It was a triumph for Fullbil, and he received the congratulations of his friends with his faint vain smile implying that it was really nothing, you know, and that he could have done it much better if he had thought that anybody was likely to heed it.

The little Doctor Chord was so downtrodden that for the remainder of the evening he hardly dared to raise his eyes from the table, but I was glad to see him apply himself industriously to the punch.

To my great alarm Fullbil now said: "Sirs, I fear we have suffered ourselves to forget we have with us to-night a strange gentleman from foreign parts. Your good fortune, sir," he added, bowing to me over his glass. I bowed likewise, but I saw his little piggish eyes looking wickedly at me. There went a titter around the board, and I understood from it that I was the next victim of the celebrated Fullbil.

"Sir," said he, "may I ask from what part of Italy do you come?"

"I come from Ireland, sir," I answered decently.

He frowned. "Ireland is not in Italy, sir," said he. "Are you so good as to trifle with me, sir?"

"I am not, sir," said I.

All the gentlemen murmured; some looked at me with pity, some with contempt. I began to be frightened until I remembered that if I once drew my sword I could chase the whole roomful of philosophy into the next parish. I resolved to put on a bold front.

"Probably, sir," observed Fullbil, "the people of Ireland have heard so much of me that I may expect many visits from Irish gentlemen who wish to hear what my poor mind may develop in regard to the only true philosophy of life?"

"Not in the least, sir," I rejoined. "Over there they don't know you are alive, and they are not caring."

Consternation fell upon that assembly like snow from a roof. The gentlemen stared at me. Old Fullbil turned purple at first, but his grandeur could not be made to suffer long or seriously from my impudence. Presently he smiled at me, — a smile confident, cruel, deadly.

"Ireland is a great country, sir," he observed.

"'Tis not so great as many people's ignorance of it," I replied bluntly, for I was being stirred somewhat.

"Indeed!" cried Fullbil. Then he triumphantly added: "Then, sir, we are proud to have among us one so manifestly capable of giving us instruction."

There was a loud shout of laughter at this sally, and I was very uncomfortable down to my toes; but I resolved to hold a brave face, and pretended that I was not minding their sneers. However, it was plain enough that old Fullbil had made me the butt of the evening.

"Sir," said the dramatist Bobbs, looking at me, "I understand that in Ireland pigs sit at table with even the best families."

"Sir," said the critic, Fancher, looking at me, "I understand that in Ireland the chastity of the women is so great that no child is born without a birthmark in the shape of the initials of the legal husband and father."

"Sir," said old Fullbil, "I understand that in Ireland people go naked when it rains, for fear of wetting their clothes."

Amid the uproarious merriment provoked by their speeches I sat in silence. Suddenly the embarrassed little scientist, Doctor Chord, looked up at me with a fine friendly sympathy. "A glass with you, sir," he said, and as we nodded our heads solemnly over the rims I felt that there had come to my help one poor little frightened friend. As for my first acquaintance, he, seeing me attacked not only by the redoubtable Fullbil, but also by the formidable Bobbs and the dangerous Fancher, had immediately begun to pretend that never in his life had he spoken to me.

Having a great knowledge of Irish character I could see that trouble was brewing for somebody, but I resolved to be very backward, for I hesitated to create a genuine disturbance in these philosophical circles. However, I was saved this annoyance in a strange manner. The door opened, and a newcomer came in, bowing right and left to his acquaintances, and finally taking a seat near Fullbil. I recognized him instantly; he was Sir Edmund Flixton, the gentleman who had had some thought of fighting me in Bath, but who had refrained from it upon hearing that I had worsted Forister.

However, he did not perceive me at that time. He chattered with Fullbil, telling him evidently some very exciting news, for I heard the old man ejaculate. "By my soul, can it be possible?" Later Fullbil related some amusing things to Flixton, and, upon an inquiry from Flixton, I was pointed out to him. I saw Flixton's face change; he spoke hastily to old Fullbil, who turned pale as death. Swiftly some bit of information flashed around the board, and I saw men's eyes open wide and white as they looked at me.

I have said it was the age of bullies. It was the age when men of physical prowess walked down the street shouldering lesser men into the gutter, and the lesser men had never a word to say for themselves. It was the age when if you expressed opinions contrary to those of a bully he was confidently expected to kill you or somehow maltreat you.

Of all that company of genius there now seemed to be only one gentleman who was not a-tremble. It was the little scientist Doctor Chord. He looked at me with a bright and twinkling

471

eye; suddenly he grinned broadly. I could not but burst into laughter when I noted the appetite with which he enjoyed the confusion and alarm of his friends.

"Come, Fullbil! Come, Bobbs! Come, Fancher! Where are all your pretty wits?" he cried; for this timid little man's impudence increased mightily amid all this helpless distress. "Here's the dignity and power of learning of you, in God's truth. Here's knowledge enthroned, fearless, great! Have ye all lost your tongues?"

And he was for going on to worry them, but that I called out to him, —

"Sir," said I mildly, "if it please you, I would not have the gentlemen disturbed over any little misunderstanding of a pleasant evening. As regards quarrelling, I am all milk and water myself. It reminds me of an occasion in Ireland once when —" Here I recounted a story which Father Donovan always began on after more than three bottles, and to my knowledge he had never succeeded in finishing it. But this time I finished it. "And," said I, "the fellow was sitting there drinking with them, and they had had good fun with him, when of a sudden he up and spoke. Says he: ''Tis God's truth I never expected in all my life to be an evening in the company of such a lot of scurvy rat-eaters,' he says to them. 'And,' says he, 'I have only one word for that squawking old masquerading peacock that sits at the head of the table,' says he. 'What little he has of learning I could put in my eye without going blind,' says he. 'The old curmudgeon!' says he. And with that he arose and left the room, afterward becoming the King of Galway and living to a great age."

This amusing tale created a sickly burst of applause, in the midst of which I bowed myself from the room.

CHAPTER XIX

On my way to my chamber I met the innkeeper and casually asked him after Paddy and Jem. He said that he would send to have word of them and inform me as soon as possible. Later a drawer came to my door and told me that Paddy and Jem, with three men-servants of gentlemen sleeping at the inn, had sallied out to a mug-house.

"Mug-house?" said I. "What in the devil's name is a mug-house?"

"Mug-house, sir?" said the man, staring. "Mug-house? Why, sir, 'tis —'tis a form of amusement, sir."

"It is, is it?" said I. "Very good. And does any one here know to what mug-house they went?"

"The 'Red Slipper,' I think, sir," said the man.

"And how do I get to it?" said I.

"Oh, sir," he cried, "'tis impossible!"

"Is it?" said I. "And why is it? The innkeeper said the same to me, and I would like to hear all the reasons."

"Sir," said the man, "when it becometh dark in London there walk abroad many men of evil minds who are no respecters of persons, but fall upon whomsoever they, may, beating them sorely, having no regard for that part of the Holy Book in which it is written —"

"Let go," said I. "I see what you mean." I then bade him get for me a stout lad with a cudgel and a lantern and a knowledge of the whereabouts of the "Red Slipper."

I, with the stout lad, had not been long in the street before I understood what the landlord and the waiter had meant. In fact we were scarce out of the door before the man was menacing with his cudgel two human vultures who slunk upon us out of the shadow. I saw their pale, wicked, snarling faces in the glow of the lantern.

A little later a great shindy broke out in the darkness, and I heard voices calling loudly for a rally in the name of some guild or society. I moved closer, but I could make out little save that it was a very pretty fight in which a company of good citizens were trying to put to flight a band of roughs and law-breakers. There was a merry rattling of sticks. Soon enough, answering shouts could be heard from some of the houses, and with a great slamming of doors men rushed out to do battle for the peace of the great city. Meanwhile all the high windows had been filled with night-capped heads, and some of these people even went so far as to pour water down upon the combatants. They also sent down cat-calls and phrases of witty advice. The sticks clattered together furiously; once a man with a bloody face staggered past us; he seemed to have been whacked directly on the ear by some uneducated person. It was as fine a shindy as one could hope to witness, and I was deeply interested.

Then suddenly a man called out hoarsely that he had been stabbed-murdered. There were yells from the street and screams from the windows. My lantern-bearer plucked me madly by the sleeve. I understood him, and we hastily left the neighbourhood.

I may tell now what had happened and what followed this affair of the night. A worthy citizen had been stabbed to death indeed. After further skirmishes his comrade citizens had taken several wretches into custody. They were tried for the murder and all acquitted save one. Of this latter it was proven that the brawl had started through his attempt to gain the purse of a passing citizen, and forthwith he was sentenced to be hanged for murder. His companion rascals were sent to prison for long terms on the expectation that one of them really might have been the murderer.

We passed into another street, where each well-lighted window framed one or more painted hussies who called out in jocular obscenity, but when we marched stiffly on without replying their manner changed, and they delivered at us volley after volley of language incredibly foul. There were only two of these creatures who paid no heed, and their indifference to us was due to the fact that they were deeply engaged in a duel of words, exchanging the most frightful, blood-curdling epithets. Confident drunken men jostled us from time to time, and frequently I could see small, ashy-faced, ancient-eyed youths dodging here and there with food and wine. My lantern-bearer told me that the street was not quite awake; it was waiting for the outpourings from the taverns and mug-houses. I bade him hurry me to the "Red Slipper" as soon as possible, for never have I had any stomach for these tawdry evils, fit as they are only for clerks and sailors.

We came at length to the creaking sign of the "Red Slipper." A great noise came from the place. A large company was roaring out a chorus. Without many words I was introduced into the room in which the disturbance was proceeding. It was blue with smoke, and the thundering chorus was still unfinished. I sank unnoticed into a quiet corner.

I was astonished at the appearance of the company. There were many men who looked like venerable prelates, and many men who looked like the heads of old and noble houses. I laughed in my sleeve when I remembered I had thought to find Paddy and Jem here. And at the same time I saw them up near the head of the table, if it please you. Paddy had his hand on the shoulder of a bishop, and Jem was telling some tale into the sympathetic ear of a marquis. At least this is the way matters appeared to my stupefied sense.

The singing ceased, and a distinguished peer at my elbow resumed a talk which evidently had been broken by the chorus:

"And so the Duke spoke with somewhat more than his accustomed vigour," said the distinguished peer.

My worst suspicions were confirmed. Here was a man talking of what had been said by a duke. I cast my eye toward my happy pair of rogues and wondered how I could ever extricate them from their position.

Suddenly there was a loud pounding upon the table, and in the ensuing quiet the grave and dignified voice of the chairman could be heard:

"Gentlemen," he said, "we crave your attention to a song by Mr. John Snowden."

Whereupon my very own Jem Bottles arose amid a burst of applause, and began to sing a ballad which had been written in Bristol or Bath in celebration of the notorious scoundrel Jem Bottles.

Here I could see that if impudence could serve us we would not lack success in England. The ballad was answered with wild cheers of appreciation. It was the great thing of the evening. Jem was strenuously pressed to sing again, but he buried his face in his mug and modestly refused. However, they devoted themselves to his chorus and sang it over and over with immense delight. I had never imagined that the nobility were so free and easy.

During the excitement over Jem's ballad I stole forward to Paddy. "Paddy," I whispered, "come out of this now. 'Tis no place for you here among all these reverend fathers and gentlemen of title. Shame on you!"

He saw my idea in a flash.

"Whist, sir," he answered. "There are being no reverend fathers or gentlemen of title here. They are all after being footmen and valets."

I was extremely vexed with myself. I had been in London only a brief space; and Paddy had been in the city no longer. However, he had already managed his instruction so well that he could at once tell a member of the gentry from a servant. I admired Paddy's cleverness, but at the same time I felt a certain resentment against the prelates and nobles who had so imposed upon me.

But, to be truthful, I have never seen a finer display of manners. These menials could have put courtiers to the blush. And from time to time somebody spoke out loud and clear an opinion pilfered verbatim from his master. They seldom spoke their own thoughts in their own way; they sent forth as their own whatever they could remember from the talk of their masters and other gentlemen. There was one man who seemed to be the servant of some noted scholar, and when he spoke the others were dumfounded into quiet.

"The loriot," said he with a learned frown, "is a bird. If it is looked upon by one who has the yellow jaundice, the bird straightway dies, but the sick person becomes well instantly. 'Tis said that lovage is used, but I would be luctuous to hear of anybody using this lothir weed, for 'tis no pentepharmacon, but a mere simple and not worth a caspatory."

This utterance fairly made their eyes bulge, and they sat in stunned silence. But I must say that there was one man who did not fear.

"Sir," said Paddy respectfully, but still with his own dignity, "I would be hearing more of this bird, and we all would be feeling honoured for a short description."

"In color he is ningid," said the learned valet.

"Bedad!" cried Paddy. "That's strange!"

"'Tis a question full of tenebrosity," remarked the other leaning back in his chair. "We poor scholars grow madarosis reflecting upon it. However, I may tell you that the bird is simous; yblent in the sunlight, but withal strenuous-eyed; its blood inclined to intumescence. However, I must be breviloquent, for I require an enneadecaterides to enumerate the true qualities of the loriot."

"By gor!" said Paddy, "I'll know that bird if I see him ten years from now. Thank you kindly, sir. But we would be late for breakfast if you took the required time; and that's true for me."

Afterward I reflected that I had attended the meetings of two scholarly bodies in this one evening, but for the life of me I couldn't decide which knew the least.

CHAPTER XX

By the following Sunday I judged that the Earl of Westport and his family had returned to London, and so I walked abroad in the hopes of catching a glimpse of some of them among the brilliant gentry who on this day thronged the public gardens. I had both Jem Bottles and Paddy accompany me, for I feared that they would get into mischief if I left them to themselves. The innkeeper had told me that Kensington Gardens was the place where the grand people mostly chose to walk and flirt and show their clothes on a clear Sunday. It was a long way to these Gardens, but we footed out bravely, although we stopped once to see a fight between five drunken apprentices, as well as several times for much-needed refreshment.

I had no idea that the scene at the Gardens would be so splendid. Outside, the road was a block of gleaming chariots and coaches with servants ablaze in their liveries. Here I left Paddy and Jem to amuse themselves as suited them.

But the array of carriages had been only a forecast of what my eyes would encounter in the Garden itself. I was involved at once in a swarm of fashionable people. My eyes were dazzled with myriad colours, and my nostrils, trained as they were to peat smoke, were saluted by a hundred delicious perfumes. Priceless silks and satins swept against my modest stockings.

I suffered from my usual inclination to run away, but I put it down with an iron will. I soon found a more retired spot from which I could review the assemblage at something like my leisure. All the highly fashionable flock knew each other intimately, it appeared, and they kept off with figurative pikes attempts of a certain class not quite so high and mighty, who seemed for ever trying to edge into situations which would benefit them on the social ladder. Their failures were dismal, but not so dismal as the heroic smiles with which they covered their little noiseless defeats.

I saw a lady, sumptuously arrayed, sweep slowly along with her daughter, a beautiful girl who greatly wished to keep her eyes fixed on the ground. The mother glanced everywhere with half-concealed eagerness and anxiety. Once she bowed impressively to a dame with a cold, pale aristocratic face, around whom were gathered several officers in the uniform of His Majesty's Guards. The grand dame lifted her lorgnette and stared coolly at that impressive bow; then she turned and said something amusing to one of the officers, who smilingly answered. The mother, with her beautiful daughter, passed on, both pairs of eyes now on the ground.

I had thought the rebuff would settle this poor misguided creature, but in the course of an hour I saw three more of her impressive bows thrown away against the icy faces of other women. But as they were leaving the Gardens they received attention from members of the very best society. One lordling nudged another lordling, and they stared into the face of the girl as if she had been a creature of the street. Then they leisurely looked her up and down from head to toe. No tailor could have taken her measurements so completely. Afterward they grinned at each other, and one spoke behind his hand, his insolent speculative eyes fixed on the retiring form of the girl. This was the social reward of the ambitious mother.

It has always been clear to me why the women turn out in such cohorts to any sort of a function. They wish to see the frocks, and they are insistent that their own frocks shall be seen. Moreover they take great enjoyment in hating such of their enemies as may come under their notice. They never have a really good time; but of this fact they are not aware, since women are so constituted that they are able to misinterpret almost every one of their emotions.

The men, knowing something of their own minds at times, stealthily avoid such things unless there are very special reasons. In my own modest experience I have seen many a popular hostess hunting men with a net. However it was plain why so many men came to Kensington Gardens on a Sunday afternoon. It was the display of feminine beauty. And when I say "display" I mean it. In my old age the fashion balloons a lady with such a sweep of wires and trellises that no Irishman could marry her because there is never a door in all Ireland through which his wife could pass. In my youth, however, the fashion required all dresses to be cut very low, and all skirts to cling so that if a four-legged woman entered a drawing-room everybody would know it. It would be so easy to count them. At present a woman could have eight legs and nobody be the wiser.

It was small wonder that the men came to ogle at Kensington Gardens on a fine Sunday afternoon. Upon my word, it was worth any young gentleman's time. Nor did the beauties blush under the gaze of banks of fastidious beaus who surveyed them like men about to bid at a horse-fair. I thought of my father and how he would have enjoyed the scene. I wager he would have been a gallant with the best of them, bowing and scraping, and dodging ladies' skirts. He would have been in his very element.

But as for me I had come to gain a possible glimpse of Lady Mary. Beyond that I had no warm interest in Kensington Gardens. The crowd was too high and fine; many of the people were altogether too well bred. They frightened me.

However, I turned my head by chance to the left, and saw near me a small plain man who did not frighten me at all. It was Doctor Chord, the little scientist. He was alone and seemed to be occupied in studying the crowd. I moved over to him.

"A good day to you, sir," I said, extending my hand.

When he recognized me, his face broke into a beaming smile.

"Why, sir," he cried, "I am very glad to see you, sir. Perchance, like me, you have come here for an hour's quiet musing on fashionable folly."

"That's it, sir," said I. "You've hit it exactly."

I have said that he was a bashful man, but it seemed that his timidity was likely to show itself only in the presence of other great philosophers and scientists. At any rate, he now rattled on like a little engine, surveying the people keenly and discoursing upon their faults.

"There's the old Marquis of Stubblington," observed my friend. "He beats his wife with an ebony stick. 'Tis said she always carries a little bottle of liniment in the pocket of her skirt. Poor thing, her only pleasure in life is to talk scandal; but this she does on such a heroic scale that it occupies her time completely. There is young Lord Gram walking again with that soap-boiler and candle-maker. 'Tis disgraceful! The poor devil lends Gram money, and Gram repays him by allowing him to be seen in his company. Gram gambles away the money, but I don't know what the soap-boiler does with his distinguished honours. However, you can see that the poor wretch is delighted with his bargain. There are the three Banellic girls, the most ill-tempered, ugly cats in England. But each will have a large marriage portion, so they have no fears, I warrant me. I wonder the elder has the effrontery to show her face here so soon if it is true that the waiting-woman died of her injuries. Little Wax is talking to them. He needs one of those marriage portions. Aye, he needs all three, what with his very boot-maker almost inclined to be insolent to him. I see that foreign count is talking to the Honourable Mrs. Trasky. He is no more nor less than a gambler by trade, and they say he came here from Paris because he was caught cheating there, and was kicked and caned with such intense publicity that he was forced to leave in the dead of night. However, he found many young birds here eager to be plucked and devoured. 'Tis little they care, so long as they may play till dawn. Did you hear about Lady Prefent? She went after her son to the Count's rooms at night. In her younger days she lived rather a gay life herself, 'tis rumoured, and so she was not to be taken by her son's lies as to where he spent his evenings and his money. Ha, I see the Countess Cheer. There is a citadel of virtue! It has been stormed and taken so many times that I wonder it is not in ruins, and yet here it is defiant, with banners flying. Wonderful. She—"

"Hold!" I cried. "I have enough. I would have leave to try and collect my wits. But one thing I would know at once. I thought you were a shy scholar, and here you clatter away with the tongue of an old rake. You amaze me. Tell me why you do this? Why do you use your brain to examine this muck?"

"'Tis my recreation," he answered simply. "In my boyhood I was allowed no games, and in the greater part of my manhood I have been too busy. Of late years I have more leisure, and I often have sought here a little innocent amusement, something to take one's mind off one's own affairs, and yet not of such an arduous nature as would make one's head tired."

"By my faith, it would make my head tired," I said. "What with remembering the names of the people and all the different crimes, I should go raving mad." But what still amazed me was the fact that this little man, habitually meek, frightened and easily trodden down in most ordinary matters, should be able to turn himself upon occasion into a fierce and howling wolf of scandal, baying his betters, waiting for the time when an exhausted one fell in the snow, and then burying his remorseless teeth in him. What a quaint little Doctor Chord.

"But tell me truly," said I. "Is there no virtuous lady or honest gentleman in all this great crowd?"

He stared, his jaw dropping. "Strap me, the place is full of them," he ejaculated. "They are as thick as flies in a fish-market."

"Well, then," said I, "let us talk of them. 'Tis well to furbish and burnish our minds with tales of rectitude and honour."

But the little Doctor was no longer happy. "There is nought to say," he answered gloomily. "They are as quiet as Bibles. They make no recreation for me. I have scant interest in them."

"Oh, you little rogue, you!" I cried. "What a precious little bunch of evil it is! 'They make no recreation for me,' quoth he. Here's a great, bold, outspoken monster. But, mark you, sir, I am a younger man, but I too have a bold tongue in my head, and I am saying that I have friends among ladies in London, and if I catch you so much as whispering their names in your sleep, I'll cut off your ears and eat them. I speak few words, as you may have noted, but I keep my engagements, you little brew of trouble, you!"

"Strap me," whimpered the little Doctor, plucking feverishly at the buttons of his coat, rolling his eyes wildly, not knowing at all what he did. "The man's mad! The man's mad!"

"No," said I, "my blood is cold, very cold."

The little Doctor looked at me with the light of a desperate inspiration in his eye. "If your blood is cold, sir," said he, "I can recommend a gill of port wine."

I needs must laugh. "Good," I cried, "and you will join me."

CHAPTER XXI

I don't know if it was the gill of comforting port, but at any rate I was soon enough convinced that there was no reason for speaking harshly to Doctor Chord. It served no purpose; it accomplished nothing. The little old villain was really as innocent as a lamb. He had no dream of wronging people. His prattle was the prattle of an unsophisticated maiden lady. He did not know what he was talking. These direful intelligences ran as easily off his tongue as water runs off the falling wheel. When I had indirectly informed him that he was more or less of a dangerous scandal-monger, he had cried: "The man is mad!" Yes; he was an innocent old thing.

But then it is the innocent old scandal-mongers, poor placid-minded well-protected hens, who are often the most harmful. The vicious gabblers defeat themselves very often. I remember my father once going to a fair and kissing some girls there. He kissed them all turn by turn, as was his right and his duty, and then he returned to a girl near the head of the list and kissed her five times more because she was the prettiest girl in all Ireland, and there is no shame to him there. However, there was a great hullabaloo. The girls who had been kissed only once led a regular crusade against the character of this other girl, and before long she had a bad name, and the odious sly lads with no hair on their throats winked as she passed them, and numerous mothers thanked God that their daughters were not fancied by the lord of that region. In time these tales came to the ears of my father, and he called some of his head men to meet him in the dining-room.

"I'll have no trifling," said he. "The girl is a good girl for all I know, and I have never seen her before or since. If I can trace a bad word to any man's mouth, I'll flog him till he can't move. 'Tis a shame taking away the girl's name for a few kisses by the squire at a fair with everybody looking on and laughing. What do you blackguards mean?"

Every man in the dining-room took oath he had never said a word, and they all spoke truth. But the women clamoured on without pausing for wind, and refused to take word of the men-folk, who were gifted with the power of reason. However, the vicious people defeated themselves in time. People began to say to a lass who had been kissed only once: "Ah, now, you would be angry because you were not getting the other five." Everything seemed to grow quiet, and my father thought no more about it, having thought very little about it in the first place save enough to speak a few sharp words. But, would you believe it, there was an old woman living in a hovel not a mile from the castle, who kept up the scandal for twelve more months. She had never been married, and, as far as any one knew, she had never wished to be. She had never moved beyond Father Donovan's church in one direction and a little peat-heap in the other direction. All her days she had seen nothing but the wind-swept moors, and heard nothing but the sea lashing the black rocks. I am mistaken; once she came to the castle, hearing that my mother was ill. She had a remedy with her, poor soul, and they poured it in the ashes when her back was turned. My mother bade them give her some hot porridge and an old cloth gown of her own to take home. I remember the time distinctly. Well, this poor thing couldn't tell between a real sin and an alligator. Bony, withered, aged, this crone might have been one of the highest types of human perfection. She wronged nobody; she had no power to wrong. Nobody wronged her; it was never worth it. She really was at peace with all the world. This obeys the most exalted injunctions. Every precept is kept here. But this tale of the Squire and the girl took root in her head. She must have been dazzled by the immensity of the event. It probably appealed to her as would a grand picture of the burning of Rome or a vivid statue of Lot's wife turning to look back. It reached the dimensions of great history. And so this old woman, who had always lived the life of a nun, dreamed of nothing but the colossal wrong which had come within her stunted range of vision. Before and after church she talked of no other thing for almost eighteen months. Finally my father in despair rode down to her little cottage.

"Mollie," said he, calling from the road, "Mollie, come out." She came out.

"Mollie," said my father, "you know me?"

"Ay," said she, "you are The O'Ruddy, and you are a rogue."

"True for you, Mollie," said my father pleasantly. "You know it and I know it. I am indeed a grand rogue. But why would you be tearing to tatters the name of that poor girl in Ballygoway?"

"'Tis not me that has said more than three words," she cried, astonished, "and before I speak ill of anybody I hope the devil flies away with me."

Well, my father palavered on for a long time, telling her that he would take away the pension of twenty-five shillings a year which he had given her because he by accident had shot her second cousin in the leg twelve years before that time. She steadfastly answered that she would never speak ill of anybody; but the girl was a brazen-faced wench, and he was no better. My father came away, and I have no doubt the scandal would still be alive if the old woman had not died, may the saints rest her!

And so I was no longer angry with Doctor Chord, but spoke to him pleasantly.

"Come," said I, "I would have you point me out the great swordsmen, if it pleases you. I am eager to see them, and the talk will be cleanly, also."

"Aye," said my friend. "Nothing could give me more pleasure. And now, look you! The tall, straight, grave young man there is Ponsonby, who flashes the wisest blade in England unless Reginald Forister is better. Any how, Forister is not here to-day. At least I don't see him. Ponsonby fought his last duel with a gentleman named Vellum because Vellum said flatly that Mrs. Catherine Wainescorte was a —"

"Stop there," said I, "and get to the tale of the fighting."

"Well, Ponsonby won without difficulty," said the Doctor; "but it is said that he took an unfair advantage —"

"Stop again!" I cried. "Stop again! We will talk no more of swordsmen. Somehow I have lost my interest. I am put to it to think of a subject for talk, and we may have to do with a period of silence, but that will do your jaw no injury at any rate."

But I was mistaken in thinking that the little man could forego his recreation for more than a moment. Suddenly he burst out with a great spleen:

"Titles!" he cried. "Empty titles! husks, husks, husks! 'Tis all they care for, this mob! Honourable manhood goes a-begging while the world worships at the feet of pimply lords! Pah! Lovely girls, the making of fine wives and mothers, grow old while the world worships at the feet of some old horse-headed duchess! Pah! Look at those pick-thanks and flatterers, cringing at the boots of the people of fashion. Upon my life, before I would so demean myself, I —" he ceased suddenly, his eye having caught sight of some people in the crowd. "Ah," said he, while a singularly vain and fatuous smile settled upon his countenance. "Ah, the Countess of Westport and her charming daughter, the Lady Mary, have arrived. I must go and speak to them." My eye had followed his glance quickly enough you may be sure. There, true enough, was the formidable figure of the old Countess, and at her side was the beautiful Lady Mary.

With an absent-minded murmur of apology, Doctor Chord went mincing toward them, his face still spread with its idiotic smile.

He cantered up to them with the grace of a hobbled cow. I expected him to get a rebuff that would stun him into the need of a surgeon, but to my surprise the Countess received him affably, bending her head to say some gracious words. However, I had more eyes for Lady Mary than for the capers of little Chord.

It was a great joy to be able to look at her. I suffered from a delicious trembling, and frequently my vision became dim purely from the excitement. But later I was moved by another profound emotion. I was looking at her; I must have her look at me. I must learn if her eye would light, if her expression would change, when she saw me. All this sounds very boyish, but it is not necessary to leave it out for that reason, because, as my father often said, every Irishman is a boy until he has grandchildren. I do not know if he was perfectly right in this matter, but it is a certain advantage in a love affair to have the true boyish ardour which is able to enshrine a woman in one's heart to the exclusion of everything, believing her to be perfection and believing life without her a hell of suffering and woe. No man of middle-aged experience can ever be in love. He may have his illusions. He may think he is in love. A woman may gain the power to bind him hand and foot and drag him wherever she listeth, but he is not in love. That is his mistaken idea. He is only misinterpreting his feelings. But, as my father said, it is very different with Irishmen, who are able to remain in love to a very great age. If you will note, too, climatic conditions and other unpleasant matters have practically no effect upon them; so little, indeed, that you may find streets named after the main Italian cities, and many little German children speak with a slight brogue. My father often said that one great reason for an Irishman's successes with the ladies was his perfect willingness to get married. He was seldom to be seen scouting for advantages in intrigue. If the girl be willing, be she brown, yellow, or white, he was always for the priest and the solemn words. My father also contended that in every marriage contracted on the face of the earth in which neither maid nor man could understand the other's national speech, the bridegroom was an Irishman. He was the only man who was able to make delightful love with the aid of mere signals.

However I must be going on with my story, although it is a great pleasure to talk of my country-men. They possess a singular fascination for me. I cannot forget that I too am an Irishman.

The little Doctor was still saying agreeable things; Lady Mary was smiling in gentle amusement. As I moved out to catch Lady Mary's eye, I did not at all lose sight of the fact that if the pugnacious mother of my *innamorata* took one glimpse of me there might result a scene which could end in nothing but my ignominious flight. I edged toward the group, advancing on the Countess's port quarter as she was talking animatedly over her starboard bow at the entranced little Doctor. At times Lady Mary looked about her, still smiling her smile, which no doubt was born of the ridiculous performances of Chord. Once I thought she looked squarely at me, and my heart beat like a drum so loudly that I thought people must hear. But her glance wandered on casually over the throng, and then I felt truly insignificant, like a man who could hide behind the nail of his own thumb.

Perceiving that I was so insignificant, I judged it prudent as well as advantageous to advance much closer. Suddenly Lady Mary's clear virgin eye met mine,—met it fully.

Now, I don't know what was in this glance we exchanged. I have stopped myself just on the verge of a full explanation of the thrills, quivers, hopes, fears, and dreams which assailed me as I looked back into the beautiful face of Lady Mary. I was also going to explain how the whole scene appeared. But I can see soon enough that my language would not be appropriate to the occasion. But any how we looked each other point-blank in the eye. It was a moment in which that very circling of the earth halted, and all the suns of the universe poised, ready to tumble or to rise. Then Lady Mary lowered her glance, and a pink blush suffused her neck and cheek.

The Countess, Lady Mary, and Doctor Chord moved slowly on through the throng, and I followed. The great question now was whether Lady Mary would look back. If she looked back, I would feel that I was making grand way with her. If she did not look back, I would know myself as a lost man. One can imagine how eagerly I watched her. For a long time it was plain that she had no intention whatever of looking back. I lugubriously arranged my complete downfall. Then, at the very moment of my despair, she gazed studiously off to her extreme left for a certain time, and then suddenly cast one short glance behind her. Only heaven knows what value I placed upon this brief look. It appeared for the moment to me that I had won her, won everything. I bravely forged ahead until I was quite insistently under the eye of Lady Mary, and then she again looked toward me, but it was a look so repelling and frigid that it went through me as if I had been a paper ring in the circus. I slunk away through the crowd, my thoughts busy with trying to find out what had happened to me.

For three minutes I was a miserable human being. At the end of that time I took heart again. I decided that Lady Mary had frowned at me because she was afraid that she had been too good to me with her look and smile. You know what I mean. I have seen a young girl give a young man a flower, and at the very next moment be seemingly willing to give her heart's blood to get that flower back, overcome with panic terror that she had passed-in his opinion, mind you-beyond the lines of best behaviour. Well I said to myself that Lady Mary had given me the hard look for similar reasons. It was rational to make this judgment, for certainly she had no cause for an active dislike. I had never been even so much as a nuisance to her.

Fortified with these philosophic decisions, I again followed the trio, and I was just in time to find Chord handing them into a splendid chariot. I stood out boldly, for I knew if I could not get one more look from Lady Mary I would die.

Seated beside her mother, her eye wandered eagerly over the crowd. I was right, by the saints! She was looking for me.

And now here come the stupid laws of convention. Could I yell? Could I even throw my hat in the air to guide her eye aright? No! I was doomed to stand there as still as a bottle on a shelf.

But she saw me! It was at the very last moment. There was no time for coquetry. She allowed her glance to linger, and God knows what we said to each other in this subtle communication through all the noise and hubbub of the entrance place. Then suddenly the coachman's reins tightened; there were some last bows; the chariot whirled away.

CHAPTER XXII

Chord ambled back, very proud indeed, and still wearing his fatuous smile. He was bursting with a sense of social value, and to everybody he seemed to be saying, "Did you see me?" He was overjoyed to find me waiting for him. He needed a good listener at once. Otherwise he would surely fly to pieces.

"I have been talking to the Countess of Westport and her daughter, Lady Mary Strepp," he said pompously. "The Countess tells that the Earl has been extremely indisposed during their late journey in the West."

He spoke of the Earl's illness with an air of great concern, as if the news had much upset him. He pretended that the day was quite over-gloomed for him. Dear, dear! I doubted if he would be able to eat any supper.

"Have a drop of something, old friend," said I sympathetically. "You can't really go on this way. 'Twill ruin your nerves. I am surprised that the Countess did not break the news to you more gently. She was very inconsiderate, I am sure."

"No, no, don't blame the poor lady," cried Chord. "She herself was quite distracted. The moment she saw me she ran to me-did you see her run to me?"

"I did that," said I with emphasis.

"Aye, she ran to me," said the little fool, "and says she, 'Oh, my dear Doctor, I must tell you at once the condition of the Earl.' And when I heard everything I was naturally cut up, as you remarked, being an old friend of the family, ahem! —yes, an old friend of the family."

He rattled on with his nonsensical lies, and in the mean time I made up my mind to speak plainly to him, as I intended to make him of great service to me.

"Stop a moment," said I good-naturedly. "I will hear no more of this rubbish from you, you impudent little impostor. You care no more for the Earl of Westport's illness than you do for telling the truth, and I know how much you care for that. Listen to me, and I'll see if I can't knock some sense into your little addled head. In the first place the Earl of Westport and my father were old friends and companions-in-arms in the service of the French king, and I came over from Ireland especially to take a dying message and a token from my father to the Earl. That is all you need know about that; but I would have you leave off your prate of your friend the Earl of Westport, for I understand full well you couldn't distinguish between him and a church door, although 'tis scandalously little you know of church doors. So we will stop there on that point. Then I will go on to the next point. The next point is that I am going to marry Lady Mary Strepp."

The little Doctor had been choking and stuttering in a great spasm, but my last point bid fair to flatten him out on the floor. I took the overpowered philosopher and led or carried him to another drink.

"Stap me!" he cried again and again. "The man is mad!"

I surveyed him with a bland smile.

"Let it sink into you," said I soothingly. "Don't snarl and wrangle at it. It is all heaven's truth, and in time you will come to your senses and see what I am telling you."

Well, as soon as he had fully recovered his wind, he fell upon me with thousands of questions; for one may see that he would have plenty of interest in the matter as soon as he was assured that there was much veracity involved in one way or another in my early statement. His questions I answered as it pleased me, but I made clear enough to him that, although Lady Mary was well disposed toward me, neither her father nor her mother would even so much as look at me if I applied for a position as under-footman, I was that low in their estimate.

"However," said I, "I can rearrange all that very easily. And now, my bucko, here is where your fortune meets mine. You are fitted by nature more to attend other people's affairs than to take a strict interest in your own. All kinds of meddling and interference come easily to you. Well, then, here is a chance to exercise your gifts inoffensively, and yet in a way which may make two people happy for life. I will tell you now that I don't even know where is the Earl's town house.

There is where your importance appears at once. You must show me the house. That is the first thing. After that we will arrange all the details about ladders and garden walls, and, mayhap, carrier doves. As for your reward, it will appear finally in the shape of a bowing recognition by people of fashion, which is what you most desire in the world, you funny little man."

Again I had stunned him. For a time I could see his brain swimming in a perfect sea of bewilderment. But, as before, sense gradually came to him, and he again volleyed questions at me. But what stuck in his crop was the thought that Lady Mary could prefer me. He tried his best to believe it, but he would always end up by saying: "Well, *if* Lady Mary cares for you, the affair is not too difficult." Or, "Well, if you are *sure* Lady Mary loves you —" I could have broken his head a thousand times.

"Bad luck to you, Doctor," I cried. "Don't you know such croaking would spoil the peace of any true lover? Is ever any worthy man able not to be anxious in such matters? 'Tis only foppery coxcombs who have great confidence, and they are usually misled, thank the Lord! Be quiet, now, and try to take everything for granted."

Then the spirit of the adventure came upon him, and he was all for it, heels over head. As I told him, this sort of meddling was his proper vocation. He who as a recreation revelled in the mere shadows of the intrigues of people of quality was now really part of one, an actor in it, the repository of its deep secret. I had to curb his enthusiasm. He had such a sense of the importance of my news, and of his distinction in having heard it, that I think he wanted to tell the secret to the entire world.

As soon as the afternoon grew late I suggested a walk to that part of London in which was situated the Earl's town house. I did not see why we should not be moving at once on the campaign. The Doctor assented, and we went forth to look for Paddy and Jem Bottles. We found them at an ale-house which was the resort of the chairmen, footmen, and coachmen of the grand people. The two rogues had evidently passed a pleasant afternoon. Jem Bottles was still making love to a very pretty girl, some part of whose easy affection or interest he had won; and Paddy, it seems, had had a rip-roaring fight with two lackeys, worsted them with despatch, and even pursued them some distance. To my stern interrogation in regard to the pretty girl, Jem Bottles stoutly rejoined that she was his second cousin whom he had not seen for many years. To this I made no reply, for it does no good to disturb the balance of a good liar. If at times he is led to tell the truth, he becomes very puzzling. In all the years Jem Bottles has been in my service I have never reprimanded him for lying. I would confuse matters to no purpose, inasmuch as I understand him perfectly.

"And how," said I to Paddy, "did you come to engage in this disgraceful brawl of a Sunday?"

"Your honour," answered Paddy, "there was two of these men with fat legs came here, and says one, looking hard at me, 'Here's a furriner,' he says. 'Furriner yourself, you fish-faced ditch-lurker,' says I, and with that he takes up his fists and hits me a knock. There was a little shindy, and afterward they ran away bawling, and I was pursuing them, only I feared to lose my way in these strange parts."

The walk to Lord Westport's house was a long one. It seemed that he had built a great new mansion at a place outside of the old city gates, where other nobles and great brewers had built fine houses, surrounding them all with splendid gardens.

One must not suppose that I had any idea of taking the mansion by storm. My first idea was to dream a lover's dream as I gazed upon the abode of my treasure. This, I believe, is a legitimate proceeding in all careers. Every lover worthy of the name is certain to pilgrimage, muffled in his cloak, to moon over the home of his adored one. Otherwise there can be no real attachment.

In the second place I wished to develop certain plans for gaining speech of Lady Mary. I will not deny that I purposed on a near day to scale the garden wall and hold speech of my sweetheart as she walked alone among the flowers. For my success I depended upon the absolute conventionality of the idea. In all history no lover has even been chased out of a garden by an under-gardener with a hoe.

When we arrived at the house I found that it was indeed a gorgeous mansion. It was surrounded on all sides by high brick walls, but through the elaborate tracery of one of the ironwork gates I saw Lady Mary's home standing among sweeping green lawns.

We reconnoitred all sides, and at the back I found a lonely avenue lined with oaks. Here a small door pierced the wall for the use apparently of the gardeners or grooms. I resolved that here I would make my attack.

As we passed the iron gates on our way back to town, we saw window after window light up with a golden radiance. I wondered which part of that vast edifice hid the form of my Mary.

I had asked Doctor Chord to sup with me at the inn, and on the way thither he proved somewhat loquacious.

"I see in you, sir," said he, "a certain instinct of true romance which is infrequently encountered in this humdrum commercial age. Allow me to express to you, sir, my warm admiration. I did not think that a gallant of this humdrum commercial age could prove such a free spirit. In this humdrum commercial age —"

"I am an Irishman," said I, "and in Ireland we are always humdrum, but we are never commercial, for the reason that we have not the tools."

"Aye," said he, "you must be a great people. Strangely enough, you are the first Irishman I have ever seen, although I have seen many blackamoors. However, I am edified to find you a gentleman of great learning and experience. In this humdrum commercial age —"

"Let go," said I. "I can do very well without your opinion as to my learning and experience. In regard to this being a humdrum commercial age you will find that all ages say the same thing of themselves. I am more interested in the winning of Lady Mary."

"'Twas to that subject I was just about to turn the talk," said the Doctor. "I need not express again to you the interest I feel; and if it is true, as you say, that Lady Mary really loves you —"

"May the devil fly away with you," I cried in a great rage. "Are you never to have done? You are an old frog. I asked you to help me, and you do nothing but dispirit me with these doubts. I'll not put up with it."

"I am very sorry to displease you, sir," answered my friend. "If you examine my intentions with a dispassionate eye, sir, I am convinced you will have found nothing in me which should properly cause these outbursts of disapprobation. When I say, 'If Lady Mary really loves you,' I am referring to the strange mishaps and misconstructions which attend human thought at all times, and when I say —"

"Let go again," I cried. "When I misunderstand you, don't enlighten me; for I find these explanations very hard to bear."

To my surprise the little man answered with great spirit: "I am unable to gain any approval for my deep interest in your affairs, sir," he cried. "Perchance, it would be better if I could affect a profound indifference. I am certainly at a loss for words when each sentence of mine is made the subject of wrathful objection."

"You are right," said I. "But you will understand how ten thousand emotions beset and haggle a lover, and I believe he always revenges himself upon his dearest friends. Forgive me!"

"With all my heart!" answered the little Doctor. "I am aware, sir, that at the present time you are in many ways like a highly-tightened fiddle, which any breeze frets into murmurings. Now, being absolutely certain of the devotion of your beloved, you naturally —"

"By the ten lame pipers of Ballydehob," I shouted, "let go of that talk. I can't be having it. I warn ye. 'Tis either a grave for me, or quiet for you, and I am thinking it is quiet for you."

"Inasmuch," said the Doctor, "as my most judicious speeches seem to inflame your passions, sir, I am of the opinion that a perfect silence on my part becomes almost necessary, and, to further this end, I would recommend that you refrain from making interrogations, or otherwise promulgating opportunities, when an expression of candid opinion seems expected and desired."

"You've hit it," said I. "We will have no more interrogations. However, I would much like to know how you became so intimate with Lord Westport's family."

Doctor Chord blushed with something of his earlier manner. "'Tis a matter which I did not expect to have leap at me out of the darkness in this fashion," he said bashfully. "However, I am convinced of how well you know these people, and I will traffic no more with hollow pretence. As you know, I deal much in chemical knowledge, which I am able to spread to almost every branch of human use and need."

"'Tis an ill work," said I slowly. "I doubt if Father Donovan would care to hear you be speaking in this way. He always objected to scientific improvements as things which do harm to the Church."

"In regard to the estimable friend you mention," said the Doctor, "I unhesitatingly state my profound assurances of respect."

"Quite so," I answered. "He will be pleased to hear of it. And now we will return to the other matter."

"I will obediently proceed," said he. "Five years back the Countess of Westport was thrown from her carriage. Physicians rushed to her rescue. I too appeared, being for the time out for a walk. They wished to immediately bleed her, but I waved them aside and, recognizing me as a figure in the street world of science, they fell back abashed. I prescribed a small drink of hot rum. The lady took it. Almost immediately she recovered. She offered me a guinea. I refused curtly. She inquired here and there for my condition. Afterward she apologized to me for not offering me more than a guinea. Since that time we have been warm friends. She knows me as a great scientist who came to her assistance in time of trouble when numerous quacks wished to bleed her, and I overpowered them and gave her a drink of rum. 'Tis true that after she reached her own bed the Earl's physician bled her, but she did not seem to appreciate it although he drew twenty-five ounces, I think. But she has remained always grateful for the hot rum."

CHAPTER XXIII

At supper that evening Doctor Chord amplified some of his views "A few staunch retainers could quickly aid you to scale the walls of the castle," said he. "But I have forgotten," he added blankly. "'Tis not a castle. 'Tis a house."

"If you would take some of these ancient ideas and bury them in the garden," said I, "they might grow in time to be some kind of turnip or other valuable food. But at the present moment they do not seem to me to serve much purpose. Supposing that the house is not a castle? What of that?"

"Castles—" said he. "Castles lend themselves—"

"Castles!" I cried. "Have done with castles! All castles may be Jews, as you say. But this is a house."

"I remarked that it was a house," he answered gently. "It was that point that I was making."

"Very good," said I. "We will now proceed to define matters. Do you know if Lady Mary walks in the garden? It is absolutely necessary that Lady Mary should walk in the garden."

"She does," he replied at once. "At this season of the year Lady Mary walks in the garden on every fine day at ten of the clock."

"Then," I cried, smiting the table, "our course is clear; I feel elate. My only regret is that my father is not here to give me a word now and then, for 'tis a game he would know down to the ground."

"Although I am not your father," said Doctor Chord modestly, "I may be able to suggest some expedient way of gaining entrance to the castle."

"House," said I.

"House," said he.

"However," said I, "we must lower ourselves to extremely practical matters. Can you climb a tree?"

"A tree?" said he. "Climb a tree? Strap me!"

"'Tis all very well to strap yourself in this fashion," said I rather warmly; "but the climbing of trees appears here as an important matter. In my part of Ireland there are few trees, and so climbing trees did not enter into my education. However, I am willing to attempt the climbing of a tree for the sake of my true love, and if I fall-how high is this wall? Do you remember?"

"'Twas at least ten feet," answered the Doctor. "And there is a murderous row of spikes at the top. But," he added, "the more spikes and all that make them the more convinced that the garden is perfectly safe from intrusion."

"That's a world of sense out of you," I cried. "The spikes convince them the garden is safe from intrusion, and so they give over their watchfulness. So now in the morning we will go there, and I will climb one of the oak-trees bordering the wall-may the saints aid me!"

"You were asking if I could climb a tree," remarked the Doctor. "I will point out to you that it is a question of no importance. It is you yourself who must climb the tree; for even if I succeeded in the arduous and painful task I could not pay your vows to Lady Mary, and for such purpose primarily the tree is to be climbed."

"True for you, Doctor," I answered with a sigh. "True for you. I must climb the tree. I can see that. I had some thought of making Paddy climb it, but, as you say, a man must do his own love-making, and by the same token I would break the head of any one who tried to do it for me. I would that! In this world people must climb their own trees. Now that I think of it seriously, it was ridiculous in me to plan that Paddy should climb the tree."

"'Second thoughts are always best,'" said the little Doctor piously. "'Tis a phrase from one of the greatest writers of the day. And at any rate I myself, because of age and debility, would not be able to climb a tree."

"Let us say no more of it," said I. "I see my mistake. But tell me one thing. I know you are a man with a great deal on your mind. Can you spare the time for this adventure?"

But on this point the Doctor was very clear and emphatic. I think if I had said he could not have a place in the plot he would have died immediately of a broken heart.

"'Tis true I have not yet finished my treatise proving that the touchstone is fallible," he cried eagerly; "but it would give me pleasure to delay the work indefinitely if in the meantime I can be of assistance."

"That is a man's talk," I said. "Well, then, in the morning we will go forth to do or die. And now a glass to success."

That night I slept very heartily, for some of my father's soldier training is in my veins, and on the eve of a hard or precarious work I am always able to get sound rest. My father often said that on the night before a battle in which he would stand seventy-seven chances of being killed he always slept like a dog in front of the fire.

At dawn I was up and ready. My first move was to have Paddy and Jem sent to me, and to give them such information as would lead them to an intelligent performance of their duties during the day. "Mind ye now," said I, "here's where the whole thing may be won or lost. There is a lovely lady inside the walls of that garden which I was showing you yesterday. She lives in the big house. She is the lady who made you feel ashamed when you took the old Earl's —well, never mind! I hope we are all properly repentant over it. However, I had better be getting on with the matter in hand. She lives there, and if I can find no way to gain speech of her we all three of us will have to take to the thickets, and that's the truth."

"If I could but lay my fingers on her throttle," said Jem Bottles in a blood-curdling voice, "she soon enough would —"

"Stop!" I cried. "You misunderstood me!"

"Aye, he does," spoke in Paddy. "But I know what your honour is meaning. You are meaning that the young lady-aye, didn't I see her, and didn't she give me a look of her eye? Aye, I know what your honour is meaning."

"You are knowing it precisely," said I. "The young lady is more to me than three Irelands. You understand? Well, then, in the first place I must gain speech of her. To-day we march out and see what I can accomplish by climbing trees. In the meantime you two are to lay in waiting and assist me when necessary."

"I am foreseeing that everything will be easy," cried Paddy jubilantly.

"You are an Irishman," I responded in anger.

"Aye," he replied bitterly, "and another is within reach of my stick if it weren't for my respect for my betters, although such a thing never could happen, please God!"

"No bold talk," said I. "You may do that after." I bade Jem Bottles load his pistols and carry them handy, but to keep them well concealed. Paddy preferred to campaign with only a stout stick. I took one pistol, and of course my sword.

These preparations deeply stirred Jem Bottles and Paddy.

"Your honour," said Paddy, "if I see a man pulling you by the leg when you would be climbing the tree, may I hit him one lick?"

"Aye," growled Jem Bottles, "and if I get a pistol against his head, he'll find out the difference between gunpowder and sand."

"Stop," I cried. "You have the wrong idea entirely. This talk of carnage startles me and alarms me. Remember we are in London. In London even the smallest massacre arouses great excitement. There are to be no killings, and even no sound thrashings. It is all to be done with dainty gloves. Neither one of the pair of you looks fitted for the work, but I am obliged to make you serve by hook or crook. 'Tis too late to scour the country looking for good comrades. I must put up with you, since I can get no better."

They were well pleased at the prospect of spirited adventures, although Paddy made some complaints because there was no chance of a great ogre whom he could assail. He wished to destroy a few giants in order to prove his loyalty to the cause. However, I soothed him out of this mood, showing him where he was mistaken, and presently we were all prepared and only waited for the coming of Doctor Chord.

When the little philosopher appeared, however, I must truly say that I fell back a-gasping. He had tied some sort of a red turban about his head, and pulled a black cocked hat down over it until his left eye was wickedly shaded. From beneath his sombre cloak a heavy scabbard protruded. "I have come; I am ready," said he in a deep voice.

"Bedad, you have!" cried I, sinking into a chair. "And why didn't a mob hang you on the road, little man? How did you reach here safely? London surely never could stand two glimpses of such a dangerous-looking pirate. You would give a sedan-chair the vapours."

He looked himself over ruefully. "'Tis a garb befitting the dangerous adventure upon which I engaged," said he, somewhat stiff in the lip.

"But let me make known to you," I cried, "that when a man wears a garb befitting his adventure he fails surely. He should wear something extraneous. When you wish to do something evil, you put on the coat of a parson. That is the clever way. But here you are looking like a gallows-bird of the greatest claim for the rope. Stop it; take off the red thing, tilt your hat until you look like a gentleman, and let us go to our adventure respectably."

"I was never more surprised in my life," said he sincerely. "I thought I was doing a right thing in thus arraying myself for an experience which cannot fail to be thrilling and mayhap deadly. However, I see you in your accustomed attire, and in the apparel of your men-servants I see no great change from yesterday. May I again suggest to you that the adventure upon which we proceed may be fraught with much danger?"

"A red rag around your temples marks no improvement in our risks," said I. "We will sally out as if we were off to a tea-party. When my father led the forlorn hope at the storming of Würstenhausenstaffenberg, he wore a lace collar, and he was a man who understood these matters. And I may say that I wish he was here. He would be a great help."

In time the Doctor removed his red turban and gradually and sadly emerged from the more sanguine part of his paraphernalia and appeared as a simple little philosopher. Personally I have no objection to a man looking like a brigand, but my father always contended that clothes serve no purpose in real warfare. Thus I felt I had committed no great injustice in depriving Chord of his red turban.

We set out. I put much faith in the fact that we had no definite plans, but to my great consternation Doctor Chord almost at once began to develop well-laid schemes. As we moved toward the scene of our adventure he remarked them to me.

"First of all," said he, "a strong party should be stationed at the iron gates, not only to prevent a sally of the garrison, but to prevent an intrepid retainer from escaping and alarming the city. Furthermore —"

"My gallant warrior," said I, interrupting him, "we will drop this question to the level of a humdrum commercial age. I will try to compass my purpose by the simple climbing of a tree, and to that end all I could need from you is a stout lift and a good word. Then we proceed in the established way of making signs over a wall. All this I explained to you fully. I would not have you think I am about to bombard my lady-love's house."

With a countenance of great mournfulness he grumbled: "No fascines have been prepared."

"Very good," said I. "I will climb the tree without the aid of fascines."

As luck would have it, there was a little inn not very far from the Earl's house and on the lonely avenue lined with oaks. Here I temporarily left Jem Bottles and Paddy, for I feared their earnestness, which was becoming more terrible every minute. In order to keep them pacified I gave instructions that they should keep a strict watch up the avenue, and if they saw any signs of trouble they were to come a-running and do whatever I told them. These orders suggested serious business to their minds, and so they were quite content. Their great point was that if a shindy was coming they had a moral right to be mixed up in it.

Doctor Chord and I strolled carelessly under the oaks. It was still too early for Lady Mary's walk in the garden, and there was an hour's waiting to be worn out. In the mean time I was moved to express some of my reflections.

"'Tis possible-nay, probable-that this is a bootless quest," said I dejectedly. "What shadow of an assurance have I that Lady Mary will walk in the garden on this particular morning? This whole thing is absolute folly."

"At any rate," said the Doctor, "now that you already have walked this great distance, it will be little additional trouble to climb a tree."

He had encouraged me to my work at exactly the proper moment.

"You are right," said I, taking him warmly by the hand, "I will climb the tree in any case."

As the hour approached we began to cast about for the proper oak. I am sure they were all the same to me, but Doctor Chord was very particular.

"'Tis logical to contend," said he, "that the question of the girth of the tree will enter importantly into our devices. For example, if a tree be so huge that your hands may not meet on the far side of it, a successful ascension will be impossible. On the other hand, a very slim tree is like to bend beneath your weight, and even precipitate you heavily to the ground, which disaster might retard events for an indefinite period."

"Science your science, then," said I. "And tell me what manner of tree best suits the purpose of a true lover."

"A tree," said the Doctor, "is a large vegetable arising with one woody stem to a considerable height. As to the appearance and quality of a tree, there are many diversifications, and this fact in itself constitutes the chief reason for this vegetable being of such great use to the human family. Ships are made of nought but trees, and if it were not for ships we would know but little of the great world of which these English islands form less than a half. Asia itself is slightly larger than all Scotland, and if it were not for the ships we would be like to delude ourselves with the idea that we and our neighbours formed the major part of the world."

With such wise harangues the Doctor entertained my impatience until it was time for me to climb a tree. And when this time came I went at my work without discussion or delay.

"There," said I resolutely, "I will climb this one if it kills me."

I seized the tree; I climbed. I will not say there was no groaning and puffing, but any how I at last found myself astride of a branch and looking over the wall into the Earl of Westport's garden.

But I might have made myself less labour and care by having somebody paint me a large landscape of this garden and surveyed it at my leisure. There I was high in a tree, dangling my legs, and staring at smooth lawns, ornamental copses, and brilliant flower-beds without even so much as a dog to enliven the scene. "O'Ruddy," said I to myself after a long time, "you've hung yourself here in mid-air like a bacon to a rafter, and I'll not say much to you now. But if you ever reach the ground without breaking your neck, I'll have a word with you, for my feelings are sorely stirred."

I do not know how long I sat in the tree engaged in my bitter meditation. But finally I heard a great scudding of feet near the foot of the tree, and I then saw the little Doctor bolting down the road like a madman, his hat gone, his hair flying, while his two coat-tails stuck out behind him straight as boards.

My excitement and interest in my ally's flight was so great that I near fell from my perch. It was incomprehensible that my little friend could dust the road at such speed. He seemed only to touch the ground from time to time. In a moment or two he was literally gone, like an arrow shot from the bow.

But upon casting my bewildered glance downward I found myself staring squarely into the mouth of a blunderbuss. The mouth of this blunderbuss, I may say, was of about the width of a fair-sized water-pitcher; in colour it was bright and steely. Its appearance attracted me to such an extent that I lost all idea of the man behind the gun. But presently I heard a grim, slow voice say, —

"Climb down, ye thief."

The reason for little Doctor Chord's hasty self-removal from the vicinity was now quite clear, and my interest in his departure was no longer speculative.

CHAPTER XXIV

"Climb down, ye thief," said the grim, slow voice again. I looked once more into the mouth of the blunderbuss. I decided to climb. If I had had my two feet square on the ground, I would have taken a turn with this man, artillery or no artillery, to see if I could get the upper hand of him. But neither I nor any of my ancestors could ever fight well in trees. Foliage incommodes us. We like a clear sweep for the arm, and everything on a level space, and neither man in a tree. However, a sensible man holds no long discussions with a blunderbuss. I slid to the ground, arriving in a somewhat lacerated state. I thereupon found that the man behind the gun was evidently some kind of keeper or gardener. He had a sour face deeply chiselled with mean lines, but his eyes were very bright, the lighter parts of them being steely blue, and he rolled the pair of them from behind his awful weapon.

"And for whom have you mistaken me, rascal?" I cried as soon as I had come ungracefully to the ground and found with whom I had to deal.

"Have mistaken ye for naught," replied the man proudly. "Ye be the thief of the French pears, ye be."

"French pears-French-French what?" I cried.

"Ay, ye know full well," said he, "and now ye'll just march."

Seeing now plainly that I was in the hands of one of Lord Westport's gardeners, who had mistaken me for some garden-thief for whom he had been on the look-out, I began to expostulate very pointedly. But always this man stolidly faced me with the yawning mouth of the blunderbuss.

"And now ye'll march," said he, and despite everything I marched. I marched myself through the little door in the wall, and into the gardens of the Earl of Westport. And the infernal weapon was clamped against the small of my back.

But still my luck came to me even then, like basket falling out of a blue sky. As, in obedience to my captor's orders, I rounded a bit of shrubbery, I came face to face with Lady Mary. I stopped so abruptly that the rim of the on-coming blunderbuss must have printed a fine pink ring on my back. I lost all intelligence. I could not speak. I only knew that I stood before the woman I loved, while a man firmly pressed the muzzle of a deadly firearm between my shoulder-blades. I flushed with shame, as if I really had been guilty of stealing the French pears.

Lady Mary's first look upon me was one of pure astonishment. Then she quickly recognized the quaint threat expressed in the attitude of the blunderbuss.

"Strammers," she cried, rushing forward, "what would you be doing to the gentleman?"

"'Tis no gentleman, your la'ship," answered the man confidently. "He be a low-born thief o' pears, he be."

"Strammers!" she cried again, and wrested the blunderbuss from his hands. I will confess that my back immediately felt easier.

"And now, sir," she said, turning to me haughtily, "you will please grant me an explanation of to what my father is indebted for this visit to his private grounds?"

But she knew; no fool of a gardener and a floundering Irishman could keep pace with the nimble wits of a real woman. I saw the pink steal over her face, and she plainly appeared not to care for an answer to her peremptory question. However, I made a grave reply which did not involve the main situation.

"Madam may have noticed a certain deluded man with a bell-mouthed howitzer," said I. "His persuasions were so pointed and emphatic that I was induced to invade these gardens, wherein I have been so unfortunate as to disturb a lady's privacy,—a thing which only causes me the deepest regret."

"He be a pear-thief," grumbled Strammers from a distance. "Don't ye take no word o' his, your la'ship, after me bringing 'im down from out a tree."

"From out a tree?" said Lady Mary, and she looked at me, and I looked at her.

"The man is right, Lady Mary," said I significantly. "I was in a tree looking over the garden wall."

"Strammers," said she with decision, "wait for me in the rose-garden, and speak no single word to anybody until I see you again. You have made a great mistake."

The man obediently retired, after saluting me with an air of slightly dubious apology. He was not yet convinced that I had not been after his wretched French pears.

But with the withdrawal of this Strammers Lady Mary's manner changed. She became frightened and backed away from me, still holding the gardener's blunderbuss.

"O sir," she cried in a beautiful agitation, "I beg of you to leave at once. Oh, please!"

But here I saw it was necessary to treat the subject in a bold Irish way.

"I'll not leave, Lady Mary," I answered. "I was brought here by force, and only force can make me withdraw."

A glimmer of a smile came to her face, and she raised the blunderbuss, pointing it full at my breast. The mouth was still the width of a water-jug, and in the fair inexperienced hands of Lady Mary it was like to go off at any moment and blow a hole in me as big as a platter.

"Charming mistress," said I, "shoot!"

For answer she suddenly flung the weapon to the grass, and, burying her face in her hands, began to weep. "I'm afraid it's l-l-loaded," she sobbed out.

In an instant I was upon my knees at her side and had taken her hand. Her fingers resisted little, but she turned away her head.

"Lady Mary," said I softly, "I'm a poor devil of an Irish adventurer, but—I love you! I love you so that if I was dead you could bid me rise! I am a worthless fellow; I have no money, and my estate you can hardly see for the mortgages and trouble upon it; I am no fine suitor, but I love you more than them all; I do, upon my life!"

"Here approaches Strammers in quest of his blunderbuss," she answered calmly. "Perhaps we had better give it to him."

I sprang to my feet, and, sure enough, the thick-headed ninepin of a gardener was nearing us.

"Don't ye trust 'im, your la'ship!" he cried. "I caught 'im in a tree, I did, and he be a bad lot!"

Lady Mary quelled him, and he at once went away with his blunderbuss, still muttering his many doubts. But still one cannot drop a love declaration and pick it up again with the facility of a tailor resuming his work on a waistcoat. One can't say: "Where was I? How far had I gone before this miserable interruption came?" In a word I found mysef stammering and stuttering and wasting moments too precious for words.

"Lady Mary—" I began. "Lady Mary—I love you, Lady Mary! Lady Mary—"

It was impossible for me to depart from this rigmarole and express the many things with which my heart was full. It was a maddening tongue-tie. The moments seemed for me the crisis of my existence, and yet I could only say, "Lady Mary, I love you!" I know that in many cases this statement has seemed to be sufficient, but as a matter of fact I was full of things to say, and it was plain to me that I was losing everything through the fact that my silly tongue clung to the roof of my mouth.

I do not know how long the agony endured, but at any rate it was ended by a thunderous hammering upon the little door in the garden-wall. A high Irish voice could be heard:

"And if ye be not leaving him out immediately, we will be coming over the wall if it is ten thousand feet high, ye murdering rogues."

Lady Mary turned deadly pale. "Oh, we are lost," she cried.

I saw at once that the interview was ended. If I remained doughtily I remained stupidly. I could come back some other day. I clutched Lady Mary's hand and kissed it. Then I ran for the door in the garden wall. In a moment I was out, and I heard her frantically bolting the door behind me.

I confronted Paddy and Jem. Jem had in his hands a brace of pistols which he was waving determinedly. Paddy was wetting his palms and resolutely swinging a club. But when they saw me their ferocity gave way to an outburst of affectionate emotion. I had to assert all my mastership to keep Paddy from singing. He would sing. Sure, if they had never heard an Irish song it was time they did.

"Paddy," said I, "my troubles are on me. I wish to be thinking. Remain quiet."

Presently we reached the little inn, and from there the little Doctor Chord flew out like a hawk at a sparrow.

"I thought you were dead," he shouted wildly. "I thought you were dead."

"No," said I, "I am not dead, but I am very thirsty." And, although they were murmuring this thing and that thing, I would have no word with them until I was led to the parlour of the inn and given a glass.

"Now," said I, "I penetrated to the garden and afterwards I came away and I can say no more."

The little Doctor was very happy and proud.

"When I saw the man with the blunderbuss," he recounted, "I said boldly: 'Sirrah, remove that weapon! Exclude it from the scene! Eliminate it from the situation!' But his behaviour was extraordinary. He trained the weapon in such a manner that I myself was in danger of being eliminated from the situation. I instantly concluded that I would be of more benefit to the cause if I temporarily abandoned the vicinity and withdrew to a place where the climatic conditions were more favourable to prolonged terms of human existence."

"I saw you abandoning the vicinity," said I, "and I am free to declare that I never saw a vicinity abandoned with more spirit and finish."

"I thank you for your appreciation," said the Doctor simply. Then he leaned to my ear and whispered, barring his words from Jem and Paddy, who stood respectfully near our chairs. "And the main object of the expedition?" he asked. "Was there heavy firing and the beating down of doors? And I hope you took occasion to slay the hideous monster who flourished the blunderbuss? Imagine my excitement after I had successfully abandoned the vicinity! I was trembling with anxiety for you. Still, I could adopt no steps which would not involve such opportunities for instant destruction that the thought of them brought to mind the most horrible ideas. I pictured myself lying butchered, blown to atoms by a gardener's blunderbuss. Then the spirit of self-sacrifice arose in me, and, as you know, I sent your two servants to your rescue."

The little man was looking through the window at this moment. Suddenly he started back, flinging up his hands.

"My soul, he is again upon us," he cried.

I hastily followed his glance, and saw the man Strammers making peaceful way toward the inn. Apparently he was going to the taproom for an early pint. The Doctor flurried and dove until I checked him in fear that he would stand on his head in the fireplace.

"No," said I, "calm yourself. There will be no blunderbusses. On the other hand, I see here a great chance for a master-stroke. Be quiet now, and try to hold yourself in a chair and see me deal with the situation. When it comes to a thing like this, it is all child's play for me. Paddy," said I. "Jem," said I, "there is a gardener in the taproom. Go and become his warm friends. You know what I mean. A tuppence here and there won't matter. But, of course, always treat him with the profound consideration which is due to so distinguished a gardener."

They understood me at once and grinned. But even then I was struck with their peculiar reasons for understanding at once. Jem Bottles understood at once because he had been a highwayman; Paddy understood at once because he was an Irishman. One had been all his life a rogue; the other had been born on an intelligent island. And so they comprehended me with equal facility.

They departed on their errand, and when I turned I found myself in the clutches of a maddened Doctor Chord.

"Monster," he screamed, "you have ordered him to be killed!"

"Whist," said I, "it would never do to order him to be killed. He is too valuable."

CHAPTER XXV

"You appear more at your ease when you are calm," said I to the Doctor as I squashed him into a chair. "Your ideas of murder are juvenile. Gardeners are murdered only by other gardeners, over some question of a magnolia-tree. Gentlemen of position never murder gardeners."

"You are right, sir," he responded frankly. "I see my mistake. But really, I was convinced that something dreadful was about to happen. I am not familiar with the ways of your nationality, sir, and when you gave the resolute directions to your men it was according to my education to believe that something sinister was at hand, although no one could regret more than I that I have made this foolish mistake."

"No," said I, "you are not familiar with the ways of my nationality, and it will require an indefinite number of centuries to make your country-men understand the ways of my nationality; and when they do they will only pretend that after great research they have discovered something very evil indeed. However, in this detail, I am able to instruct you fully. The gardener will not be murdered. His fluency with a blunderbuss was very annoying, but in my opinion it was not so fluent as to merit death."

"I confess," said Doctor Chord, "that all peoples save my own are great rascals and natural seducers. I cannot change this national conviction, for I have studied politics as they are known in the King's Parliament, and it has been thus proved to me."

"However, the gardener is not to be murdered," said I, "and although I am willing to cure you in that particular ignorance I am not willing to take up your general cure as a life work. A glass of wine with you."

After we had adjusted this slight misunderstanding we occupied our seats comfortably before the fire. I wished to give Paddy and Jem plenty of time to conciliate Strammers, but I must say that the wait grew irksome. Finally I arose and went into the corridor and peered into the taproom. There were Paddy and Jem with their victim, the three of them seated affectionately in a row on a bench, drinking from quart pots of ale. Paddy was clapping the gardener on the shoulder.

"Strammers," he cried, "I am thinking more of you than of my cousin Mickey, who was that gay and that gallant it would make you wonder, although I am truthful in saying they killed him for the peace of the parish. But he had the same bold air with him, and devil the girl in the country-side but didn't know who was the lad for her."

Strammers seemed greatly pleased, but Jem Bottles evinced deep disapproval of Paddy's Celtic methods.

"Let Master Strammers be," said he. "He be a-wanting a quiet draught. Let him have his ale with no talking here and there."

"Ay," said Strammers, now convinced that he was a great man and a philosopher, "a quiet draught o' old ale be a good thing."

"True for you, Master Strammers," cried Paddy enthusiastically. "It is in the way of being a good thing. There you are now. Ay, that's it. A good thing! Sure."

"Ay," said Strammers, deeply moved by this appreciation, which he had believed should always have existed. "Ay, I spoke well."

"Well would be no name for it," responded Paddy fervidly. "By gor, and I wish you were knowing Father Corrigan. He would be the only man to near match you. 'A quiet draught o' old ale is a good thing,' says you, and by the piper 'tis hard to say Father Corrigan could have done it that handily. 'Tis you that are a wonderful man."

"I have a small way o' my own," said Strammers, "which even some of the best gardeners has accounted most wise and humorous. The power o' good speech be a great gift." Whereupon the complacent Strammers lifted his arm and buried more than half his face in his quart pot.

"It is," said Paddy earnestly. "And I'm doubting if even the best gardeners would be able to improve it. And says you: 'A quiet draught o' old ale is a good thing,' 'Twould take a grand gardener to beat that word."

"And besides the brisk way of giving a word now and then," continued the deluded Strammers, "I am a great man with flowers. Some of the finest beds in London are there in my master's park."

"Are they so?" said Paddy. "I would be liking to see them."

"And ye shall," cried the gardener with an outburst of generous feeling. "So ye shall. On a Sunday we may stroll quietly and decently in the gardens, and ye shall see."

Seeing that Paddy and Jem were getting on well with the man, I returned to Doctor Chord.

"'Tis all right," said I. "They have him in hand. We have only to sit still, and the whole thing is managed."

Later I saw the three men in the road, Paddy and Jem embracing the almost tearful Strammers. These farewells were touching. Afterward my rogues appeared before me, each with a wide grin.

"We have him," said Paddy, "and 'tis us that has an invitation to come inside the wall next Sunday. 'I have some fine flowers in the gardens,' said he. 'Have you so?' said I. 'Well, then, 'tis myself will be breaking your head if you don't leave us inside to see them.' 'Master Paddy,' said he, 'you are a gentleman, or if not you are very like one, and you and your handsome friend, Master Jem, as well as another friend or two, is welcome to see the gardens whenever I can make certain the master and mistress are out.' And with that I told him he could go home."

"You are doing well," I said, letting the scoundrel see in my face that I believed his pleasant tale, and he was so pleased that he was for going on and making a regular book out of it. But I checked him. "No," said I. "I am fearing that I would become too much interested and excited. I am satisfied with what you've been telling me. 'Twas more to my mind to have beaten that glass-eyed man, but we have taken the right course. And now we will be returning to where we lodge."

During the walk back to the "Pig and Turnip" Doctor Chord took it upon himself to discourse in his usual style upon the recent events. "Of course, sir, I would care to hear of the tragic scenes which must have transpired soon after I —I —"

"Abandoned the vicinity?" said I.

"Precisely," he responded. "Although I was not in the exact neighbourhood during what must have been a most tempestuous part of your adventure, I can assure you I had lost none of my former interest in the affair."

"I am believing you," said I; "but let us talk now more of the future. I am much absorbed in the future. It appears to me that it will move at a rapid pace."

I did not tell him about my meeting with Lady Mary, because I knew, if occasion arose, he would spread the news over half London. No consideration would have been great enough to bridle the tongue of the little gossip from use of the first bit of news which he had ever received warm from the fire. Besides, after his behaviour in front of the enemy, I was quite certain that an imparting of my news could do nothing in the way of impairing his inefficiency. Consequently it was not necessary to trouble him with dramatic details.

"As to the part of the adventure which took place in the garden, you are consistently silent, I observe, sir," said the Doctor.

"I am," said I. "I come of a long line of silent ancestors. My father was particularly notable in this respect."

"And yet, sir," rejoined the Doctor, "I had gained an impression that your father was quite willing to express himself in a lofty and noble manner on such affairs as attracted his especial notice."

"He was that," said I, pleased. "He was indeed. I am only wishing I had his talent for saying all that was in his mind so fast that even the priest could not keep up with him, and goodness knows Father Donovan was no small talker."

"You prove to me the limitations of science, sir," said he. "Although I think I may boast of some small education of a scientific nature, I think I will require some time for meditation and study before I will be able to reconcile your last two statements."

"'Tis no matter," I cried amiably. "Let it pass."

For the rest of that week there was conference following conference at the "Pig and Turnip" and elsewhere. My three companions were now as eager as myself for the advent of the critical Sunday when I, with Paddy and Jem, were to attempt our visit to Strammers's flower-gardens. I had no difficulty in persuading the Doctor that his services would be invaluable at another place; for the memory of the blunderbuss seemed to linger with him. I had resolved to disguise myself slightly, for I had no mind to have complications arising from this gardener's eyes. I think a little disguise is plenty unless one stalks mysteriously and stops and peers here and there. A little unostentatious minding of one's own affairs is a good way to remain undiscovered. Then nobody looks at you and demands: "Who is this fellow?" My father always said that when he wished to disguise himself he dressed as a common man, and although this gained him many a hard knock of the fist and blow of the stick from people who were really his inferiors, he found his disguise was perfection. However, my father only disguised when on some secret mission from King Louis, for it does not become a gentleman to accept a box on the ears from anybody unless it is in the service of his sovereign.

I remember my father saying also these tours as a common man taught him he must ever afterward ride carefully through the streets of villages and towns. He was deeply impressed by the way in which men, women, and children had to scud for their lives to keep from under the hoofs of the chargers of these devil-may-care gentlemen who came like whirlwinds through narrow crowded streets. He himself often had to scramble for his life, he said.

However, that was many years back, and I did not fear any such adventures in my prospective expedition. In such a case I would have trembled for what might happen. I have no such philosophy of temper as had my father. I might take the heel of a gay cavalier and throw him out of the saddle, and then there would be a fine uproar. However, I am quite convinced that it is always best to dodge. A good dodger seldom gets into trouble in this world, and lives to a green old age, while the noble patriot and others of his kind die in dungeons. I remember an honest man who set out to reform the parish in the matter of drink. They took him and—but, no matter; I must be getting on with the main tale.

CHAPTER XXVI

On Saturday night I called the lads to my room and gave them their final instructions.

"Now, you rogues," said I to them, "let there be no drinking this night, and no trapesing of the streets, getting your heads broke just at the critical moment; for, as my father used to say, although a broken head is merrily come by, a clear head's worth two of it when business is to be transacted. So go to your beds at once, the two of you, if there's any drinking to be done, troth it's myself that'll attend to it."

With that I drove them out and sat down to an exhilarating bottle, without ever a thought of where the money was to come from to pay for it. It is one of the advantages of a public house frequented by the nobility that if you come to it with a bold front, and one or two servants behind your back, you have at least a clear week ahead before they flutter the show of a bill at you and ask to see the colour of your gold in exchange for their ink and paper.

My father used to say that a gentleman with money in his pocket might economize and no disgrace to him; but when stomach and purse are both empty, go to the best house in the town, where they will feed you, and lodge you, and drink you, before asking questions. Indeed I never shed many salt tears over the losses of a publican, for he shears so closely those sheep that have plenty of wool that he may well take care of an innocent lamb like myself, on which the crop is not yet grown.

I was drinking quietly and thinking deeply on the wisdom of my father, who knew the world better than ever his son will know it, when there was an unexpected knock at the door, and in walked Doctor Chord. I was not too pleased to see the little man, for I had feared he had changed his mind and wanted to come with us in the morning, and his company was something I had no desire for. He was a coward in a pinch, and a distrustful man in peace, ever casting doubt on the affection I was sure sometimes that Lady Mary held for me; and if he wasn't talking about that, sure he went rambling on,—great discourses on science which held little interest for a young man so deeply in love as I was. The proper study of mankind is womankind, said a philosopher that my father used to quote with approval, but whose name I'm forgetting at this moment. Nevertheless I welcomed the little Doctor and said to him:

"Draw you up a chair, and I'll draw out a cork."

The little man sat him down, and I placed an open bottle nice and convenient to his elbow.

Whether it was the prospect of good wine, or the delight of better company, or the thought of what was going to happen on the morrow, I could not tell; but it seemed to me the little Doctor laboured under a great deal of excitement, and I became more and more afraid that he would insist on bearing us company while the Earl and the Countess were away at church. Now it was enough to have on my hands two such models of stupidity as Paddy and Jem without having to look after Doctor Chord as well, and him glancing his eyes this way and that in apprehension of a blunderbuss.

"Have you made all your plans, O'Ruddy?" he inquired, setting down his cup a good deal emptier than when he lifted it.

"I have," said I.

"Are you entirely satisfied with them?" he continued.

"My plans are always perfect plans," I replied to him, "and trouble only comes in the working of them. When you have to work with such raw material as I have to put up with, the best of plans have the unlucky habit of turning round and hitting you in the eye."

"Do you expect to be hit in the eye to-morrow?" asked the Doctor, very excited, which was shown by the rattle of the bottle against the lip of his cup.

"I'm only sure of one thing for to-morrow," said I, "and that is the certainty that if there's blunder to be made one or other of my following will make it. Still, I'm not complaining, for it's good to be certain of something."

"What's to be your mode of procedure?" said the Doctor, giving me a touch of his fine language.

"We wait in the lane till the church bells have stopped ringing, then Paddy and Jem go up to the little door in the wall, and Paddy knocks nice and quietly, in the expectation that the door will be opened as quietly by Strammers, and thereupon Jem and Paddy will be let in."

"But won't ye go in with them?" inquired the little Doctor very hurriedly.

"Doctor Chord," said I, lifting up my cup, "I have the honour to drink wine with you, and to inform you that it's myself that's outlining the plan."

"I beg your pardon for interrupting," said the Doctor; then he nodded to me as he drank.

"My two villains will go in alone with Strammers, and when the door is bolted, and they have passed the time of day with each other, Paddy will look around the garden and exclaim how it excels all the gardens that ever was, including that of Eden; and then Jem will say what a pity it was they couldn't have their young friend outside to see the beauty of it. It is my expectation that Strammers will rise to this, and request the pleasure of their young friend's company; but if he hesitates Paddy will say that the young friend outside is a free-handed Irishman who would no more mind a shilling going from his pocket into that of another man than he would the crooking of an elbow when a good drink is to be had. But be that as it may, they're to work me in through the little door by the united diplomacy of England and Ireland, and, once inside of the walls, it is my hope that I can slip away from them and see something of the inside of the house as well."

"And you have the hope that you'll find Lady Mary in the withdrawing-room," said the Doctor.

"I'll find her," says I, "if she's in the house; for I'm going from room to room on a tour of inspection to see whether I'll buy the mansion or not."

"It's a very good plan," said the Doctor, drawing the back of his hand across his lips. "It's a very good plan," he repeated, nodding his head several times.

"Now, by the Old Head of Kinsale, little man," said I, "what do you mean by that remark and that motion of the head? What's wrong with the plan?"

"The plan's a good one, as I have said," reiterated the Doctor. But I saw there was something on his mind, and told him so, urging him to be out with it.

"Do you think," said I, "that Lady Mary will be in church with her father and mother?"

"I do not," muttered the Doctor, cautiously bringing his voice down to a whisper; "but I want to warn you that there's danger here in this room while you're lurking around my Earl's palace."

"How can danger harm me here when I am somewhere else?" I asked.

A very mysterious manner fell upon the little man, and he glanced, one after the other, at the four corners of the room, as if he heard a mouse moving and wanted to detect it. Then he looked sternly at the door, and I thought he was going to peer up the chimney, but instead he leaned across the table and said huskily, —

"The papers!"

"What papers?" I asked, astonished.

"Your thoughts are so intent on the young lady that you forget everything else. Have you no recollection of the papers the Earl of Westport is so anxious to put himself in possession of?"

I leaned back in my chair and gazed steadily at Chord; but his eyes would not bring themselves to meet mine, and so he made some pother about filling up his cup again, with the neck of the bottle trembling on the edge, as if its teeth were chattering.

Now my father used to say when a man is afraid to meet your eye, be prepared to have him meet your fist. I disremembered saying anything to the Doctor about these same papers, which, truth to tell, I had given but little thought to recently, with other things of more importance to crowd them out of mind.

"How come you to know anything about the papers?" I said at last.

"Oh, your memory is clean leaving you!" cried the little Doctor, as if the cup of wine he drank had brought back his courage to him. "You told me all about the papers when we were in Kensington Gardens."

"If I did," says I, "then I must have further informed you that I gave them as a present to Lady Mary herself. Surely I told you that?"

"You told me that, of course; but I thought you said they had come back into your possession again. If I'm wrong, it's no matter at all, and there's nothing to be said about them. I'm merely speaking to you by way of a friend, and I thought if you had the papers here in your room it was very unsafe to leave them unprotected by yourself or some one you can trust. I was just speaking as your well-wisher, for I don't want to hear you crying you are robbed, and us at our wit's end not getting either the thief or the booty."

He spoke with great candour and good humour, and the only thing that made me suspicious at first was that for the life of me I could not ever remember mentioning the papers to him, yet it was very likely that I did; for, as my father used to say, an Irishman talks more than the recording angel can set down in his busiest day, and therefore it is lucky that everything he says is not held against him. It seemed to me that we talked more of scandal than of papers in the park, but still I might be mistaken.

"Very good, Doctor," I cried, genially. "The papers it is, and, true for you, the Earl would like to get his old claws on them. Have you any suggestions to make?"

"Well, it seems to me, O'Ruddy, that if the Earl got wind of them it would be the easiest thing in the world to have your apartment rifled during your absence."

"That is true enough," I agreed, "so what would you do about the papers if you were in my boots?"

"If I had a friend I could trust," said Doctor Chord slowly, "I would give the papers to him and tell him to take good care of them."

"But why not carry them about in my own pocket?" I asked.

"It seemed to me they were not any too safe last time they were there," said the Doctor, pleasantly enough. "You see, O'Ruddy, you're a marked man if once the Earl gets wind of your being in town. To carry the papers about on your own person would be the unsafest thing you could do, ensuring you a stab in the back, so that little use you'd have for the papers ever after. I have no desire to be mixed further in your affairs than I am at the present moment, but nevertheless I could easily take charge of the packet for you; then you would know where it was."

"But would I be sure to know where *you* were?" said I, my first suspicion of him returning to me.

The little Doctor laughed.

"I am always very easily found," he said; "but when I offered to take the papers it was merely in case a stranger like yourself should not have a faster friend beside him than I am. If you have any such, then I advise you to give custody of the papers to him."

"I have no real friend in London that I know of," said I, "but Paddy."

"The very thing," cried the Doctor, joyously, at once putting to rest all my doubts concerning him. "The very thing. I would give the papers to Paddy and tell him to protect them with his life. I'm sure he'll do it, and you'll know where to find both them and him when you want them. But to go away from the 'Pig and Turnip' right across to the other end of the town, taking your two servants with you, leaving nobody to guard papers that are of importance to you, strikes me as the height of folly. I'll just fill up another cup, and so bid you good-night, and good luck for the morrow."

And with that the little man drained the bottle, taking his leave with great effusion, and begging my pardon for even so much as mentioning the papers, saying they had been on his mind for the last day or two, and, feeling friendly toward me, he wished to warn me not to leave them carelessly about.

After he left I thought a good deal about what the Doctor had said, and I wondered at myself that I had ever misdoubted him; for, although he was a man given greatly to talk, yet he had been exceedingly friendly with me from the very first night I had met him, and I thought shame of myself that I was losing trust in my fellow man here in this great city of London, because in Ireland we trust each other entirely; and indeed we are under some compulsion in that same matter, for there is so little money about that if you do not take a man's word now and then there's nothing else for you to take.

CHAPTER XXVII

I slept well that night, and it was broad daylight when I awoke. A most beautiful morning it seemed to me, and just the time for a lonely stroll in the beautiful gardens, so long as there was some one with you that you thought a great deal of. I made a good breakfast, and then took out the papers and placed them on the table before me. They were all safe so far. I could not comprehend how the Earl would know anything of my being in London, unless, indeed, he caught sight of me walking in his own gardens with his own daughter, and then, belike, he was so jealous a man that he would maybe come to the conclusion I was in London as well as himself.

After breakfast Paddy and Jem came in, looking as bold as Blarney Castle; and when I eyed them both I saw that neither one nor the other was a fit custodian for papers that might make the proudest Earl in England a poor man or a rich man, depending which way they went. So I put the documents in my own pocket without more ado, and gave up my thoughts to a pleasanter subject. I changed my mind about a disguise, and put on my back the best clothes that I had to wear. I wished I had the new suits I had been measured for, but the spalpeen of a tailor would not let me have them unless I paid him some of the money they cost. When I came to think over it I saw that Strammers would surely never recognize me as a gay spark of fashion when he had merely seen me once before, torn and ragged, coming down from a tree on top of his blunderbuss. So I instructed Paddy to say that he and Jem were servants of the best master in the world, who was a great lover of gardens; that he was of immense generosity, and if Strammers allowed him to come into the gardens by the little door he would be a richer man when the door was opened than he would be if he kept it shut. I had been long enough in London to learn the golden method of persuasion; any how I could not bring myself to the chance of meeting with my lady, and me dressed worse than one of her own servants.

We were all in the lane when the church bells ceased to ring, and if any one had seen us he would simply have met a comely young Irish gentleman taking the air of a Sunday morning with two faithful servants at his heels. I allowed something like ten impatient minutes to crawl past me, and then, as the lane was clear and every one for the church within its walls, I tipped a nod to Paddy, and he, with Jem by his side, tapped lightly at the door, while I stood behind the trunk of the tree up which I had climbed before. There was no sign of Doctor Chord in the vicinity, and for that I was thankful, because up to the last moment I feared the little man could not help intruding himself on what was somebody else's business.

The door was opened with some caution, letting Paddy and Jem enter; then it was closed, and I heard the bolts shot into their places. But I was speedily to hear more than bolts that Sunday morning. There was a sound of thumping sticks, and I heard a yell that might well have penetrated to the "Pig and Turnip" itself, although it was miles away. I knew Paddy's cry, and next there came some good English cursing from Jem Bottles, while a shrill voice called out: —

"Catch the red-haired one; he's the villain we want!"

In the midst of various exclamations, maledictions, and other constructions of speech, mingled, I thought, with laughter, I flung my shoulder against the door, but I might as well have tried to batter down the wall itself. The door was as firm as Macgillicuddy Reeks. I know when I am beat as well as the next man, and, losing no more time there, I ran as fast as I could along the wall, out of the lane, and so to the front of the house. The main entrance was protected by great gates of wrought iron, which were opened on occasion by a man in a little cubby of a cabin that stood for a porter's lodge. The man wasn't there, and the gates were locked; but part of one of the huge wings of wrought iron was a little gate that stood ajar. This I pushed open, and, unmolested, stepped inside.

The trees and shrubbery hid from me the scene that was taking place inside the little wooden door. I dashed through the underbrush and came to the edge of a broad lawn, and there was going on as fine a scrimmage as any man could wish to see. Jem Bottles had his back against the wooden door, and was laying about him with a stout stick; half a dozen tall fellows in livery making a great show of attack, but keeping well out of range of his weapon. Poor Paddy had the broad of his back on the turf, and it looked like they were trying to tear the clothes off him, for another half-dozen were on top of him; but I can say this in his favour, Paddy was using his big feet and doing great execution with them. Every now and then he planted a boot in the well-fed front of a footman or under-gardener, and sent him flying. The whole household seemed to be present, and one could hardly believe there was such a mob in a single mansion. The Earl of Westport was there, and who stood beside him but that little villain, Doctor Chord.

But it was the Countess herself that was directing operations. She had an ebony stick in her hands, and when Paddy kicked one of her underlings the vigorous old lady smote the overturned servant to make him to the fray again. It was an exciting scene, and Donnybrook was nothing to it. Their backs were all toward me, and I was just bubbling with joy to think what a surprise I was about to give them,—for I drew my sword and had a yell of defiance on my lips,—when a cry that nobody paid the least attention to turned my mind in another direction entirely.

One of the first-floor windows was open, and over the sill leaned Lady Mary herself, her face aflush with anger.

"Father! Mother!" she cried. "Are not you ashamed of yourselves, making this commotion on a Sunday morning? Call the servants away from there! Let the two poor men go! Oh, shame, shame upon you."

She wrung her hands, but, as I was saying, nobody paid the slightest heed to her, and I doubt if any of them heard her, for Paddy was not keeping silence by any manner of means. He was taking the worst of all the blows that fell on him in a vigorous outcry.

"Murther! murther!" he shouted. "Let me on me feet, an' I'll knock yez all into the middle of county Clare."

No one, however, took advantage of this generous offer, but they kept as clear as they could of his miscellaneous feet, and the Countess poked him in the ribs with the point of her ebony stick whenever she wasn't laying it over the backs of her servants.

Now, no man can ever say that I was a laggard when a good old-fashioned contest was going on, and the less indolence was observable on my own part when friends of mine were engaged in the fray. Sure I was always eager enough, even when it was a stranger's debate, and I wonder what my father would think of me now, to see me veer from the straight course of battle and thrust my unstruck sword once more into its scabbard. It was the face in the window that made me forget friend and foe alike. Lady Mary was the only member of the household that was not on the lawn, and was protesting unheard against the violence to two poor men who were there because they had been invited to come by the under-gardener.

I saw in the twinkling of an eye that the house had been deserted on the first outcry. Doors were left wide open for the whole world to enter. I dodged behind the trees, scuttled up the gravelled driveway, leaped the stone steps three at a time, and before you could say "Ballymuggins" I was in the most superb hall in which I ever set my foot. It was a square house with the stairway in the middle. I kept in my mind's eye the direction of the window in which Lady Mary had appeared. Quick as a bog-trotter responds to an invitation to drink, I mounted that grand stairway, turned to my right, and came to a door opposite which I surmised was the window through which Lady Mary was leaning. Against this door I rapped my knuckles, and speedily I heard the sweet voice of the most charming girl in all the world demand with something like consternation in its tones,—

"Who is there?"

"It's me, Lady Mary!" said I. "The O'Ruddy, who begs the privilege of a word with you."

I heard the slam of a window being shut, then the sound of a light step across the floor, and after that she said with a catch in her voice,—

"I'll be pleased you should come in, Mr. O'Ruddy."

I tried the door, but found it locked.

"How can I come in, Lady Mary," says I, "if you've got bolts held against me?"

"There are no bolts," said Lady Mary; "the key should be on the outside. I am locked in. Look for the key and open the door."

Was ever a more delightful sentence spoken to a man? My heart was in my throat with joy. I glanced down, and there, sure enough, stuck the key. I turned it at once, then pulled it out of the lock and opened the door.

"Lady Mary," says I, "with your permission, it seems to me a door should be locked from the inside."

With that I thrust the key through the far side of the door, closed it, and locked it. Then I turned round to face her.

The room, it was plain to be seen, was the parlour of a lady,—a boudoir, as they call it in France, a word that my father was very fond of using, having caught it when he was on the campaign in that delightful country. The boudoir was full of confections and charming little dainties in the way of lace, and easy chairs, and bookcases, and little writing-desks, and a work-basket here and there; but the finest ornament it possessed was the girl who now stood in the middle of the floor with a frown on her brow that was most becoming. Yes, there was a frown on her brow, although I expected a smile on her lips because of the cordial invitation she had given me to come in.

It would seem to either you or me that if a lady suffered the indignity of being locked in her room, just as if she was a child of six years old, she would welcome with joy the person who came and released her. Now, my father, who was the wisest man since Solomon,—and indeed, as I listened to him, I've often thought that Solomon was overpraised,—my father used to say there was no mystery at all about women. "You just think," he would say, "of what a sensible man would do on a certain occasion; then configure out in your mind the very opposite, and that's what a woman will do." A man who had been imprisoned would have held out his hand and have said, "God bless you, O'Ruddy; but I'm glad to see you." And here stood this fine lady in the middle of her room, looking at me as if I were the dirt beneath her feet, and had forced my way into her presence, instead of being invited like a man of honour to enter.

"Well, Mr. O'Ruddy," she said, throwing back her head, haughty-like, "Why do you stand dallying in a lady's bower when your followers are being beaten on the lawn outside?"

I cannot give you Lady Mary's exact words, for I was so astonished at their utterance; but I give you a very good purport of them.

"Is it the beating of my men?" I said. "Troth, that's what I pay them for. And whoever gives them a good drubbing saves me the trouble. I saw they had Paddy down on the turf, but he's a son of the ould sod, and little he'll mind being thrown on his mother. But if it's Jem Bottles you're anxious about, truth to tell I'm more sorry for those that come within range of his stick than for Jem with his back to the wall. Bottles can take care of himself in any company, for he's a highwayman in an excellent way of business."

I always like to mention anything that's in favour of a man, and so I told her what profession Bottles followed. She gave a toss of her head, and gave me a look that had something like contempt in it, which was far from being pleasant to endure. Then she began walking up and down the room, and it was plain to see that my Lady was far from being pleased with me.

"Poor fellows! Poor faithful fellows! That's what comes of having a fool for a master."

"Indeed, your ladyship," said I, drawing myself up to my full height, which wasn't so very much short of the door itself, "there are worse things than blows from a good honest cudgel. You might better say, 'This is what comes to a master with two fools for servants.'"

"And what comes to a master?" she demanded. "Sure no one asks you to be here."

"That shows how short your ladyship's memory is," said I with some irritation. "Father Donovan used to tell me that the shortest thing in the world was the interval between an insult and a blow in Ireland, but I think a lady's memory is shorter still. 'Turn the key and come in,' says you. What is that, I would like to know, but an invitation."

It appeared to me that she softened a bit, but she continued her walk up and down the room and was seemingly in great agitation. The cries outside had stopped, but whether they had murdered both Jem Bottles and Paddy I had no means at that moment of knowing, and I hope the two will forgive me when I say that my thoughts were far from them.

"You will understand," said Lady Mary, speaking still with resentment in her voice, "that the papers you held are the key to the situation. Have you no more sense than to trust them to the care of a red-headed clown from whom they can be taken as easy as if they were picked up off the street?"

"Indeed, believe me, Lady Mary, that no red-headed clown has any papers of mine."

"Indeed, and I think you speak the true word there. The papers are now in my father's possession, and he will know how to take care of them."

"Well, he didn't know that the last time he had them," I cried, feeling angry at these unjust accusations, and not being able to bear the compliment to the old man, even if he was an Earl. "The papers," said I, "are as easily picked from me as from the street, like you were saying just now; but it isn't a pack of overfed flunkeys that will lift them from me. Lady Mary, on a previous occasion I placed the papers in your hands; now, with your kind permission, I lay them at your feet,"—and, saying this with the most courteous obeisance, I knelt with one knee on the floor and placed the packet of papers where I said I would place them.

Now, ever since that, the Lady Mary denies that she kicked them to the other end of the room. She says that as she was walking to and fro the toe of her foot touched the packet and sent it spinning; and, as no real Irishman ever yet contradicted a lady, all I will say is that the precious bundle went hurtling to the other end of the room, and it is very likely that Lady Mary thought the gesture of her foot a trifle too much resembled an action of her mother, the Countess, for her manner changed in the twinkling of an eye, and she laughed like her old self again.

"Mr. O'Ruddy," she said, "you put me out of all patience. You're as simple as if you came out of Ireland yesterday."

"It's tolerably well known," said I, "by some of your expert swordsmen, that I came out the day before."

Again Lady Mary laughed.

"You're not very wise in the choice of your friends," she said.

"I am, if I can count you as one of them," I returned.

She made no direct reply to this, but continued:

"Can't you see that that little Doctor Chord is a traitor? He has been telling my father all you have been doing and all you have been planning, and he says you are almost simple enough to have given the papers into his own keeping no longer ago than last night."

"Now, look you, Lady Mary, how much you misjudged me. The little villain asked for the papers, but he didn't get them; then he advised me to give them to a man I could trust, and when I said the only man I could trust was red-headed Paddy out yonder, he was delighted to think I was to leave them in his custody. But you can see for yourself I did nothing of the kind, and if your people thought they could get anything out of Paddy by bad language and heroic kicks they were mistaken."

At that moment we had an interruption that brought our conversation to a standstill and Lady Mary to the door, outside which her mother was crying,—

"Mary, Mary! where's the key?"

"Where should it be?" said Lady Mary, "but in the door."

"It is not in the door," said the Countess wrathfully, shaking it as if she would tear it down.

"It is in the door," said Lady Mary positively; and quite right she was, for both of us were looking at it.

"It is not in the door," shouted her mother. "Some of the servants have taken it away."

Then we heard her calling over the banisters to find out who had taken away the key of Lady Mary's room. There was a twinkle in Mary's eye, and a quiver in the corners of her pretty mouth that made me feel she would burst out laughing, and indeed I had some ado to keep silence myself.

"What have you done with those two poor wretches you were maltreating out in the garden?" asked Lady Mary.

"Oh, don't speak of them," cried the Countess, evidently in no good humour. "It was all a scandal for nothing. The red-headed beast did not have the papers. That little fool, Chord, has misled both your father and me. I could wring his neck for him, and now he is palavering your father in the library and saying he will get the papers himself or die in the attempt. It serves us right for paying attention to a babbling idiot like him. I said in the first place that that Irish baboon of an O'Ruddy was not likely to give them to the ape that follows him."

"Tare-an-ounds!" I cried, clenching my fists and making for the door; but Lady Mary rattled it so I could not be heard, and the next instant she placed her snow-flake hand across my mouth, which was as pleasant a way of stopping an injudicious utterance as ever I had been acquainted with.

"Mary," said the Countess, "your father is very much agitated and disappointed, so I'm taking him out for a drive. I have told the butler to look out for the key, and when he finds it he will let you out. You've only yourself to blame for being locked in, because we expected the baboon himself and couldn't trust you in his presence."

It was now Lady Mary's turn to show confusion at the old termagant's talk, and she coloured as red as a sunset on the coast of Kerry. I forgave the old hag her discourteous appellation of "baboon" because of the joyful intimation she gave me through the door that Lady Mary was not to be trusted when I was near by. My father used to say that if you are present when an embarrassment comes to a lady it is well not to notice it, else the embarrassment will be transferred to yourself. Remembering this, I pretended not to see Lady Mary's flaming cheeks, and, begging her pardon, walked up the room and picked from the corner the bundle of papers which had, somehow or other come there, whether kicked or not. I came back to where she was standing and offered them to her most respectfully, as if they, and not herself, were the subject of discussion.

"Hush," said Lady Mary in a whisper; "sit down yonder and see how long you can keep quiet."

She pointed to a chair that stood beside a beautifully polished table of foreign wood, the like of which I had never seen before, and I, wishing very much to please her, sat down where she told me and placed the bundle of papers on the table. Lady Mary tiptoed over, as light-footed as a canary-bird, and sat down on the opposite side of the table, resting her elbows on the polished wood, and, with her chin in her hands, gazed across at me, and a most bewildering scrutiny I found it, rendering it difficult for me to keep quiet and seated, as she had requested. In a minute or two we heard the crunch of wheels on the gravel in front, then the carriage drove off, and the big gates clanked together.

Still Lady Mary poured the sunshine of her eyes upon me, and I hope and trust she found me a presentable young man, for under the warmth of her look my heart began to bubble up like a pot of potatoes on a strong fire.

"You make me a present of the papers, then?" said Lady Mary at last.

"Indeed and I do, and of myself as well, if you'll have me. And this latter is a thing I've been trying to say to you every time I met you, Mary acushla, and no sooner do the words come to my lips than some doddering fool interrupts us; but now, my darling, we are alone together, in that lover's paradise which is always typified by a locked door, and at last I can say the things —"

Just here, as I mentioned the word "door," there came a rap at it, and Lady Mary started as if some one had fired a gun.

"Your ladyship," said the butler, "I cannot find the key. Shall I send for a locksmith?"

"Oh, no," said Lady Mary, "do not take the trouble. I have letters to write, and do not wish to be disturbed until my mother returns."

"Very good, your ladyship," returned the butler, and he walked away.

"A locksmith!" said Lady Mary, looking across the table at me.

"Love laughs at them," said I.

Lady Mary smiled very sweetly, but shook her head.

"This is not a time for laughter," she said, "but for seriousness. Now, I cannot risk your staying here longer, so will tell you what I have to say as quickly as possible. Your repeatedly interrupted declaration I take for truth, because the course of true love never did run smooth. Therefore, if you want me, you must keep the papers."

At this I hastily took the bundle from the table and thrust it in my pocket, which action made Lady Mary smile again.

"Have you read them?" she asked.

"I have not."

"Do you mean to say you have carried these papers about for so long and have not read them?"

"I had no curiosity concerning them," I replied. "I have something better to look at," I went on, gazing across at her; "and when that is not with me the memory of it is, and it's little I care for a pack of musty papers and what's in them."

"Then I will tell you what they are," said Lady Mary. "There are in that packet the title-deeds to great estates, the fairest length of land that lies under the sun in Sussex. There is also a letter written by my father's own hand, giving the property to your father."

"But he did not mean my father to keep it," said I.

"No, he did not. He feared capture, and knew the ransom would be heavy if they found evidence of property upon him. Now all these years he has been saying nothing, but collecting the revenues of this estate and using them, while another man had the legal right to it."

"Still he has but taken what was his own," said I, "and my father never disputed that, always intending to come over to England and return the papers to the Earl; but he got lazy-like, by sitting at his own fireside, and seldom went farther abroad than to the house of the priest; but his last injunctions to me were to see that the Earl got his papers, and indeed he would have had them long since if he had but treated me like the son of an old friend."

"Did your father mention that the Earl would give you any reward for returning his property to him?"

"He did not," I replied with indignation. "In Ireland, when a friend does a friend's part, he doesn't expect to be paid for it."

"But don't you expect a reward for returning them?"

"Lady Mary," said I, "do you mean to be after insulting me? These papers are not mine, but the Earl of Westport's, and he can have them without saying as much as 'Thank you kindly' for them."

Lady Mary leaned back in her chair and looked at me with half-closed eyes, then she stretched forth her hand and said:

"Give me the papers."

"But it's only a minute since," I cried, perplexed, "that you held them to be the key of the situation, and said if I didn't keep them I would never get you."

"Did I say that?" asked Lady Mary with the innocence of a three-year-old child. "I had no idea we had come to such a conclusion. Now do you want a little advice about those same papers?"

"As long as the advice comes from you, Mary darling, I want it on any subject."

"You have come into England brawling, sword-playing, cudgel-flinging, and never till this moment have you given a thought to what the papers are for. These papers represent the law."

"Bad cess to it," said I. "My father used to say, have as little to do with the law as possible, for what's the use of bringing your man into the courts when a good shillelah is speedier and more satisfactory to all concerned."

"That may be true in Ireland, but it is not true in England. Now, here is my advice. You know my father and mother, and if you'll just quit staring your eyes out at me, and think for a minute, you may be able to tell when you will get their consent to pay your addresses to me without interruption." Here she blushed and looked down.

"Indeed," said I, "I don't need to take my eyes from you to answer *that* question. It'll be the afternoon following the Day of Judgment."

"Very well. You must then stand on your rights. I will give you a letter to a man in the Temple, learned in the law. He was legal adviser to my aunt, who left me all her property, and she told me that if I ever was in trouble I was to go to him; but instead of that I'll send my trouble to him with a letter of introduction. I advise you to take possession of the estate at Brede, and think no more of giving up the papers to my father until he is willing to give you something in return. You may then ask what you like of him; money, goods, or a farm," —and again a bright red colour flooded her cheeks. With that she drew toward her pen and paper and dashed off a letter which she gave to me.

"I think," she said, "it would be well if you left the papers with the man in the Temple; he will keep them safely, and no one will suspect where they are; while, if you need money, which is likely, he will be able to advance you what you want on the security of the documents you leave with him."

"Is it money?" said I, "sure I couldn't think of drawing money on property that belongs to your good father, the Earl."

"As I read the papers," replied Lady Mary, very demurely, casting down her eyes once more, "the property does not belong to my good father, the Earl, but to the good-for-nothing young man named O'Ruddy. I think that my father, the Earl, will find that he needs your signature before he can call the estate his own once more. It may be I am wrong, and that your father, by leaving possession so long in the hands of the Earl, may have forfeited his claim. Mr. Josiah Brooks will tell you all about that when you meet him in the Temple. You may depend upon it that if he advances you money your claim is good, and, your claim being good, you may make terms with even so obstreperous a man as my father."

"And if I make terms with the father," I cried, "do you think his comely daughter will ratify the bargain?"

Lady Mary smiled very sweetly, and gave me the swiftest and shyest of glances across the table from her speaking eyes, which next instant were hidden from me.

"May be," she said, "the lawyer could answer that question."

"Troth," I said, springing to my feet, "I know a better one to ask it of than any old curmudgeon poring over dry law-books, and the answer I'm going to have from your own lips."

Then, with a boldness that has ever characterized the O'Ruddys, I swung out my arms and had her inside o' them before you could say Ballymoyle. She made a bit of a struggle and cried breathlessly:

"I'll answer, if you'll sit in that chair again."

"It's not words," says I, "I want from your lips, but this," —and I smothered a little shriek with one of the heartiest kisses that ever took place out of Ireland itself, and it seemed to me that her struggle ceased, or, as one might say, faded away, as my lips came in contact with hers; for she suddenly weakened in my arms so that I had to hold her close to me, for I thought she would sink to the floor if I did but leave go, and in the excitement of the moment my own head was swimming in a way that the richest of wine had never made it swim before. Then Lady Mary buried her face in my shoulder with a little sigh of content, and I knew she was mine in spite of all the Earls and Countesses in the kingdom, or estates either, so far as that went. At last she straightened up and made as though she would push me from her, but held me thus at arms' length, while her limpid eyes looked like twin lakes of Killarney on a dreamy misty morning when there's no wind blowing.

"O'Ruddy," she said, solemnly, with a little catch in her voice, "you're a bold man, and I think you've no doubt of your answer; but what has happened makes me the more anxious for your success in dealing with those who will oppose both your wishes and mine. My dear lover, is what I call you now; you have come over in tempestuous fashion, with a sword in your hand, striving against every one who would stand up before you. After this morning, all that should be changed, for life seems to have become serious and momentous. O'Ruddy, I want your actions to be guided, not by a drawn sword, but by religion and by law."

"Troth, Mary acushla, an Irishman takes to religion of his own nature, but I much misdoubt me if it comes natural to take to the law."

"How often have you been to mass since you came to England, O'Ruddy?"

"How often?" says I, wrinkling my brow, "indeed you mean, how many times?"

"Yes; how many times?"

"Now, Mary, how could you expect me to be keeping count of them?"

"Has your attendance, then, been so regular?"

"Ah, Mary, darling; it's not me that has the face to tell you a lie, and yet I'm ashamed to say that I've never set foot in a church since I crossed the channel, and the best of luck it is for me that good old Father Donovan doesn't hear these same words."

"Then you will go to church this very day and pray for heaven's blessing on both of us."

"It's too late for the mass this Sunday, Mary, but the churches are open, and the first one I come to will have me inside of it."

With that she drew me gently to her, and herself kissed me, meeting none of that resistance which I had encountered but a short time before; and then, as bitter ill luck would have it, at this delicious moment we were startled by the sound of carriage-wheels on the gravel outside.

"Oh!" cried Lady Mary in a panic; "how time has flown!"

"Indeed," said I, "I never knew it so fast before."

And she, without wasting further time in talking, unlocked the door, whipped out the key, and placed it where I had found it in the beginning. She seemed to think of everything in a moment, and I would have left her letter and the papers on the table if it hadn't been for that cleverest of all girls, who, besides her lips of honey, had an alert mind, which is one of the things appreciated in Ireland. I then followed her quickly down a narrow back stairway and out into a glass house, where a little door at the end led us into a deliciously shaded walk, free from all observation, with a thick screen of trees on the right hand and the old stone wall on the left.

Here I sprang quickly to overtake her, but she danced away like a fairy in the moonlight, throwing a glance of mischief over her shoulder at me, with her finger on her lips. It seemed to me a pity that so sylvan a dell should merely be used for the purposes of speed, but in a jiffy Mary was at the little door in the wall and had the bolts drawn back, and I was outside before I understood what had happened, listening to bolts being thrust back again, and my only consolation was the remembrance of a little dab at my lips as I passed through, as brief and unsatisfactory as the peck of a sparrow.

CHAPTER XXVIII

It was a beautiful day, as lovely as any an indulgent Providence had ever bestowed upon an unthankful generation.

Although I wished I had had an hour or two to spend with Mary wandering up and down that green alley through which we had rushed with such indecent haste, all because two aged and angry members of the nobility might have come upon us, yet I walked through the streets of London as if I trod on the air, and not on the rough cobble-stones of the causeway. It seemed as if I had suddenly become a boy again, and yet with all the strength and vigour of a man, and I was hard put to it not to shout aloud in the sunlight, or to slap on the back the slow and solemn Englishmen I met, who looked as if they had never laughed in their lives. Sure it's a very serious country, this same land of England, where their dignity is so oppressive that it bows down head and shoulders with thinking how grand they are; and yet I'll say nothing against them, for it was an Englishwoman that made me feel like a balloon. Pondering over the sobriety of the nation, I found myself in the shadow of a great church, and, remembering what my dear Mary had said, I turned and went in through the open door, with my hat in my hand. It was a great contrast to the bright sunlight I had left, and to the busy streets with their holiday-making people. There were only a few scattered here and there in the dim silence of the church, some on their knees, some walking slowly about on tiptoe, and some seated meditating in chairs. No service was going forward, so I knelt down in the chapel of Saint Patrick himself; I bowed my head and thanked God for the day and for the blessing that had come with it. As I said, I was like a boy again, and to my lips, too long held from them, came the prayers that had been taught me. I was glad I had not forgotten them, and I said them over and over with joy in my heart. As I raised my head, I saw standing and looking at me a priest, and, rising to my feet, I made my bow to him, and he came forward, recognizing me before I recognized him.

"O'Ruddy," he said, "if you knew the joy it gives to my old heart to meet you in this sacred place and in that devout attitude, it would bring some corresponding happiness to yourself."

"Now by the piper that played before Moses, Father Donovan, and is this yourself? Sure I disrecognized you, coming into the darkness, and me just out of the glare beyond," —and I took his hand in both of mine and shook it with a heartiness he had not met since he left the old turf. "Sure and there's no one I'd rather meet this day than yourself," —and with that I dropped on one knee and asked for his blessing on me and mine.

As we walked out of the church together, his hand resting on my shoulder, I asked how such a marvel came to pass as Father Donovan, who never thought to leave Ireland, being here in London. The old man said nothing till we were down the steps, and then he told me what had happened.

"You remember Patsy O'Gorman," he said.

"I do that," I replied, "and an old thief of the world and a tight-fisted miser he is."

"Whist," said Father Donovan, quietly crossing himself. "O'Gorman is dead and buried."

"Do you tell me that!" said I, "then rest his soul. He would be a warm man and leave more money than my father did, I'm thinking."

"Yes, he left some money, and to me he left three hundred pounds, with the request that I should accomplish the desire of my life and take the pilgrimage to Rome."

"The crafty old chap, that same bit of bequestration will help him over many a rough mile in purgatory."

"Ah, O'Ruddy, it's not our place to judge. They gave a harder name to O'Gorman than he deserved. Just look at your own case. The stories that have come back to Ireland, O'Ruddy, just made me shiver. I heard that you were fighting and brawling through England, ready to run through any man that looked cross-eyed at you. They said that you had taken up with a highwayman; that you spent your nights in drink and breathing out smoke; and here I find you, a proper young man, doing credit to your country, meeting you, not in a tavern, but on your knees with bowed head in the chapel of Saint Patrick, giving the lie to the slanderer's tongue."

The good old man stopped in our walk, and with tears in his eyes shook hands with me again, and I had not the heart to tell him the truth.

"Ah well," I said, "Father Donovan, I suppose nobody, except yourself, is quite as good as he thinks, and nobody, including myself, is as bad as he appears to be. And now, Father Donovan, where are you stopping, and how long will you be in London?"

"I am stopping with an old college friend, who is a priest in the church where I found you. I expect to leave in a few days' time and journey down to the seaport of Rye, where I am to take ship that will land me either in Dunkirk or in Calais. From there I am to make my way to Rome as best I can."

"And are you travelling alone?"

"I am that, although, by the blessing of God, I have made many friends on the journey, and every one I met has been good to me."

"Ah, Father Donovan, you couldn't meet a bad man if you travelled the world over. Sure there's some that carry such an air of blessedness with them that every one they meet must, for very shame, show the best of his character. With me it's different, for it seems that where there's contention I am in the middle of it, though, God knows, I'm a man of peace, as my father was before me."

"Well," said Father Donovan slowly, but with a sweet smile on his lip, "I suppose the O'Ruddys were always men of peace, for I've known them before now to fight hard enough to get it."

The good father spoke a little doubtfully, as if he were not quite approving of our family methods, but he was a kindly man who always took the most lenient view of things. He walked far with me, and then I turned and escorted him to the place where he resided, and, bidding good-bye, got a promise from him that he would come to the "Pig and Turnip" a day later and have a bite and sup with me, for I thought with the assistance of the landlord I could put a very creditable meal before him, and Father Donovan was always one that relished his meals, and he enjoyed his drink too, although he was set against too much of it. He used to say, "It's a wise drinker that knows when geniality ends and hostility begins, and it's just as well to stop before you come to the line."

With this walking to and fro the day was near done with when I got back to the "Pig and Turnip" and remembered that neither a bit of pig nor a bit of turnip had I had all that long day, and now I was ravenous. I never knew anything make me forget my appetite before; but here had I missed my noonday meal, and not in all my life could I overtake it again. Sure there was many an experience crowded together in that beautiful Sunday, so, as I passed through the entrance to the inn I said to the obsequious landlord:

"For the love of Heaven, get placed on my table all you have in the house that's fit to eat, and a trifle of a bottle or two, to wash it down with."

So saying, I passed up the creaking old oaken stair and came to my room, where I instantly remembered there was something else I had forgotten. As I opened the door there came a dismal groan from Paddy, and something that sounded like a wicked oath from Jem Bottles. Poor lads! that had taken such a beating that day, such a cudgelling for my sake; and here I stood at my own door in a wonder of amazement, and something of fright, thinking I had heard a banshee wail. The two misused lads had slipped out of my memory as completely as the devil slipped off Macgillicuddy Reeks into the pond beneath when Saint Patrick had sent the holy words after him.

"Paddy," said I, "are you hurted? Where is it you're sore?"

"Is it sore?" he groaned. "Except the soles of my feet, which they couldn't hit with me kickin' them, there isn't an inch of me that doesn't think it's worse hurted than the rest."

"It's sorry I am to hear that," I replied, quite truthfully, "and you, Jem, how did you come off?"

"Well, I gave a better account of myself than Paddy here, for I made most of them keep their distance from me; but him they got on the turf before you could say Watch me eye, and the whole boiling of them was on top of him in the twinkling of the same."

"The whole boiling of them?" said I, as if I knew nothing of the occurrence, "then there was more than Strammers to receive you?"

"More!" shouted Jem Bottles, "there was forty if there was one."

Paddy groaned again at the remembrance, and moaned out:

"The whole population of London was there, and half of it on top of me before I could wink. I thought they would strip the clothes off me, and they nearly did it."

"And have you been here alone ever since? Have you had nothing to eat or drink since you got back?"

"Oh," said Jem, "we had too much attention in the morning, and too little as the day went on. We were expecting you home, and so took the liberty of coming up here and waiting for you, thinking you might be good enough to send out for some one who would dress our wounds; but luckily that's not needed now."

"Why is it not needed?" I asked. "I'll send at once.

"Oh, no," moaned Paddy, "there was one good friend that did not forget us."

"Well," said Jem, "he seemed mighty afeerd of coming in. I suppose he thought it was on his advice that we went where we did, and he was afeerd we thought badly of him for it; but of course we had no blame to put on the poor little man."

"In Heaven's name, who are you talking of?" said I.

"Doctor Chord," answered Jem. "He put his head inside the door and inquired for us, and inquired specially where you were; but that, of course, we couldn't tell him. He was very much put out to find us mis-handled, and he sent us some tankards of beer, which are now empty, and we're waiting for him because he promised to come back and attend to our injuries."

"Then you didn't see Doctor Chord in the gardens?"

"In what gardens?" asked Bottles.

"You didn't see him among that mob that set on you?"

"No fear," said Jem, "wherever there is a scrimmage Doctor Chord will keep away from it."

"Indeed and in that you're wrong," said I. "Doctor Chord has been the instigator of everything that has happened, and he stood in the background and helped to set them on."

Paddy sat up with wild alarm in his eyes.

"Sure, master," says he, "how could you see through so thick a wall as that?"

"I did not see through the wall at all; I was in the house. When you went through the back door, I went through the front gate, and what I am telling you is true. Doctor Chord is the cause of the whole commotion. That's why he was afraid to come in the room. He thought perhaps you had seen him, and, finding you had not, he'll be back here again when everything is over. Doctor Chord is a traitor, and you may take my word for that."

Paddy rose slowly to his feet, every red hair in his head bristling with scorn and indignation; but as he stood erect he put his hand to his side and gave a howl as he limped a step or two over the floor.

"The black-hearted villain," he muttered through his teeth. "I'll have his life."

"You'll have nothing of the sort," said I, "and we'll get some good attendance out of him, for he's a skillful man. When he has done his duty in repairing what he has inflicted upon you, then you can give him a piece of your mind."

"I'll give him a piece of my boot; all that's left of it," growled Jem Bottles, scowling.

"You may take your will of him after he has put some embrocation on your bruises," said I; and as I was speaking there came a timorous little knock at the door.

"Come in," I cried, and after some hesitation the door opened, and there stood little Doctor Chord with a big bottle under his arm. I was glad there was no supper yet on the table, for if there had been I must have asked the little man to sit down with me, and that he would do without a second's hesitation, so I could not rightly see him maltreated who had broken a crust with me.

He paid no attention to Jem or Paddy at first, but kept his cunning little eye on me.

"And where have you been to-day, O'Ruddy?" he asked.

"Oh," said I, "I accompanied these two to the door in the wall, and when they got through I heard yells fit to make a hero out of a nigger; but you know how stout the bolts are and I couldn't get to them, so I had just to go out of hearing of their bellowings. On the way back I happened to meet an old friend of mine, Father Donovan, and —"

Here Paddy, forgetting his good manners, shouted out:

"Thank God there's a holy father in this hole of perdition; for I know I'm goin' t' die to-morrow at the latest."

"Stop your nonsense," said I. "You'll have to hold on to life at least a day longer; for the good father is not coming here until two days are past. You're more frightened than hurt, and the Doctor here has a lotion that will make you meet the priest as a friend and not as a last counsellor."

"As I was saying, Doctor Chord, I met Father Donovan, and we strolled about the town, so that I have only now just come in. The father is a stranger in London, on a pilgrimage to Rome. And sure I had to show him the sights."

"It was a kindly action of you," said Doctor Chord, pulling the cork of the medicine-bottle. "Get those rags off," he called to Paddy, "and I'll rub you down as if you were the finest horse that ever followed the hounds."

There was a great smell of medicine in the air as he lubricated Paddy over the bruised places; then Jem Bottles came under his hands, and either he was not so much hurt as Paddy was, or he made less fuss about it, for he glared at the Doctor all the time he was attending him, and said nothing.

It seemed an inhospitable thing to misuse a man who had acted the good Samaritan so arduously as the little Doctor with three quarters of his bottle gone, but as he slapped the cork in it again I stepped to the door and turned the key. Paddy was scowling now and then, and groaning now and again, when the cheerful Doctor said to him, as is the way with physicians when they wish to encourage a patient:

"Oh, you're not hurt nearly as bad as you think you are. You'll be a little sore and stiff in the morning, that's all, and I'll leave the bottle with you."

"You've never rubbed me at all on the worst place," said Paddy angrily.

"Where was that?" asked Doctor Chord, —and the words were hardly out of his mouth when Paddy hit him one in the right eye that sent him staggering across the room.

"There's where I got the blow that knocked me down," cried Paddy.

Doctor Chord threw a wild glance at the door, when Jem Bottles, with a little run and a lift of his foot, gave him one behind that caused the Doctor to turn a somersault.

"Take that, you thief," said Jem; "and now you've something that neither of us got, because we kept our faces to the villains that set on us."

Paddy made a rush, but I cried:

"Don't touch the man when he's down."

"Sure," says Paddy, "that's when they all fell on me."

"Never strike a man when he's down," I cried.

"Do ye mean to say we shouldn't hit a man when he's down?" asked Jem Bottles.

"You knew very well you shouldn't," I told him. "Sure you've been in the ring before now."

"That I have," shouted Bottles, pouncing on the unfortunate Doctor. He grabbed him by the scruff of the neck and flung him to his feet, then gave him a bat on the side of the head that sent him reeling up toward the ceiling again.

"That's enough, Jem," I cautioned him.

"I'm not only following the Doctor," said Jem, "but I'm following the Doctor's advice. He told us to take a little gentle exercise and it would allay the soreness."

"The exercise you're taking will not allay the soreness on the Doctor's part. Stop it, Jem! Now leave him alone, Paddy; he's had enough to remember you by, and to learn that the way of the traitor is the rocky road to Dublin. Come now, Doctor, the door is open; get out into the passage as quick as you can, and I hope you have another bottle of that excellent lotion at home."

The threatening attitude of both Jem and Paddy seemed to paralyse the little man with fear, and he lay on the boards glaring up at them with terror in his eyes.

"I'm holding the door open for you," said I, "and remember I may not be able to hold Paddy and Jem as easily as I hold the door; so make your escape before they get into action again."

Doctor Chord rolled himself over quickly, but, not daring to get on his feet, trotted out into the passage like a big dog on his hands and knees; and just then a waiter, coming up with a tray and not counting on this sudden apparition in the hallway, fell over him; and if it were not for my customary agility and presence of mind in grasping the broad metal server, a good part of my supper would have been on the floor. The waiter luckily leaned forward when he found himself falling, holding the tray high over his head, and so, seizing it, I saved the situation and the supper.

"What are ye grovelling down there for, ye drunken beast?" shouted the angry waiter, as he came down with a thud. "Why don't you walk on your two feet like a Christian?"

Doctor Chord took the hint and his departure, running along the passage and stumbling down the stairway like a man demented. When he got down into the courtyard he shook his fist at my window and swore he would have the law of us; but I never saw the little man again, although Paddy and Jem were destined to meet him once more, as I shall tell later on.

The supper being now laid, I fell at it and I dis-remember having ever enjoyed a meal more in my life. I sent Paddy and Jem to their quarters with food and a bottle of good wine to keep them company, and I think they deserved it, for they said the lotion the Doctor had put on the outside of them was stinging, so they thought there should be something in the inside to counteract the inconvenience.

I went to sleep the moment I touched the pillow, and dreamed I was in the most umbrageous lover's walk that ever was, overhung with green branches through which the sunlight flickered, and closed in with shrubbery. There I chased a flying nymph that always just eluded me, laughing at me over her shoulder and putting her finger to her lips, and at last, when I caught her, it turned out to be Doctor Chord, whereupon I threw him indignantly into the bushes, and then saw to my dismay it was the Countess. She began giving her opinion of me so vigorously that I awoke and found it broad daylight.

CHAPTER XXIX

After a comforting and sustaining breakfast I sent for Paddy and Jem, both of whom came in limping.

"Are you no better this morning?" I asked them.

"Troth, we're worse," said Paddy with a most dismal look on his face.

"I'm sorry to hear it," said I; "but I think the trouble will wear off to-day if you lie snug and quiet in the inn. Here's this bottle of embrocation, or what is left of it, so you may take it with you and divide it fairly between you, remembering that one good rub deserves another, and that our chief duty on this earth is to help our fellow man; and as there's nothing like easy employment for making a man forget his tribulations, Jem will rub Paddy, and Paddy will rub Jem, and thus, God blessing you both, you will pass the time to your mutual benefit."

"Yer honour," sniffed Jem Bottles, "I like your own prescriptions better than Doctor Chord's. I have but small faith in the liniment; the bottle of wine you gave us last night-and I wish it had been as double as it made us see-was far better for our trouble than this stuff."

"I doubt it, Jem," said I, "for you're worse this morning than you were last night; so I'll change the treatment and go back to Doctor Chord's remedy, for sure the Doctor is a physician held in high esteem by the nobility of London. But you're welcome to a double mug of beer at my expense, only see that you don't take too much of that."

"Yer honour," said Jem, "it's only when we're sober that we fall upon affliction. We had not a drop to drink yesterday morning, and see what happened us."

"It would have made no differ," I said, "if you had been as tipsy as the Earl himself is when dinner's over. Trust in Providence, Jem, and rub hard with the liniment, and you'll be a new man by the morrow morn."

With this I took my papers and the letter of introduction, and set out as brave as you please to find the Temple, which I thought would be a sort of a church, but which I found to be a most sober and respectable place very difficult for a stranger to find his way about in. But at last I came to the place where Mr. Josiah Brooks dispensed the law for a consideration to ignorant spalpeens like myself, that was less familiar with the head that had a gray wig on than with cracking heads by help of a good shillelah that didn't know what a wig was. As it was earlier in the morning than Mr. Brooks's usual hour I had to sit kicking my heels in a dismal panelled anteroom till the great lawyer came in. He was a smooth-faced serious-looking man, rather elderly, and he passed through the anteroom without so much as casting a look at me, and was followed by a melancholy man in rusty black who had told me to take a chair, holding in his hand the letter Lady Mary had written. After a short time the man came out again, and, treating me with more deference than when he bade me be seated, asked me kindly if I would step this way and Mr. Brooks would see me.

"You are Mr. O'Ruddy, I take it," he said in a tone which I think he thought was affable.

"I am."

"Have you brought with you the papers referred to in this letter?"

"I have."

And with that I slammed them down on the table before him. He untied the bundle and sorted out the different documents, apparently placing them in their right order. After this he adjusted his glasses more to his liking and glanced over the papers rapidly until he came to one that was smaller than the rest, and this he read through twice very carefully. Then he piled them up together at his right hand very neatly, for he seemed to have a habit of old maid's precision about him. He removed his glasses and looked across the table at me.

"Are you the son of the O'Ruddy here mentioned?"

"I am."

"His eldest son?"

"His only son."

"You can prove that, I suppose?"

"Troth, it was never disputed."

"I mean there would be no difficulty in getting legal and documentary proof."

"I think not, for my father said after my first fight, that it might be questioned whether I was my mother's son or no,—there was no doubt that I was his."

The legal man drew down his brows at this, but made no comment as, in tones that betrayed little interest in the affair, he demanded:

"Why did your father not claim this property during his lifetime?"

"Well, you see, Mr. Brooks, my father was an honest man, and he never pretended the property was his. From what I remember of his conversation on the subject the Earl and him was in a tight place after a battle in France, and it was thought they would both be made prisoners. The Earl had his deeds with him, and if he were caught the enemy would demand a large ransom for him, for these would show him to be a man of property. So he made the estate over to my father, and my father ran the risk of being captured and taken for the Earl of Westport. Now that I have been made happy by the acquaintance of his lordship, I'm thinking that if my father had fallen into the hands of the enemy he might have remained there till this day without the Earl raising a hand to help him. Nobody in England would have disputed the Earl's ownership of his own place, which I understand has been in his family for hundreds of years, so they might very well have got on without the deeds, as in fact they have done. That's all I know about it."

"Then, sir," said Mr. Brooks, "do you intend to contest the ownership of the property on the strength of these documents?"

"I do," said I firmly.

"Very well. You must leave them with me for a few days until I get opinion upon them. I may say I have grave doubts of your succeeding in such litigation unless you can prove that your father gave reasonable consideration for the property made over to him."

"Troth, he'd no consideration to give except his own freedom and the loan of a pair of breeches, and it seems that the Earl never troubled his head whether he gave the first-named or not. He might have given his life for all the thanks his son got from my Lord of Westport."

"From a rapid glance at these instruments I can see that they may be of great value to his lordship, but I doubt their being of any value at all to you; in fact you might find the tables turned upon you, and be put in the position of a fraudulent claimant or a levier of blackmail."

"It's not blackmail I'm going to levy at all," cried I, "but the whitest of white mail. I have not the slightest intention of going into the courts of law; but, to tell you the plain truth about it, Lady Mary and me are going to get married in spite of all the Earls that ever drank, or all the Countesses that ever scolded. Now this dear girl has a great confidence in you, and she has sent me to you to find what's best to be done. I want nothing of this property at all. Sure I've estates enough of my own in Ireland, and a good castle forby, save that the roof leaks a little in places; but a bundle of straw will soon set that to rights, only old Patsy is so lazy through not getting his money regular. Now it struck me that if I went boldly to Brede Castle, or whatever it is, and took possession of it, there would first be the finest scrimmage any man ever saw outside of Ireland, and after that his lordship the Earl would say to me, —

"'O'Ruddy, my boy, my limbs are sore; can't we crack a bottle instead of our heads over this, and make a compromise?'

"'Earl of Westport,' I'll say to him, 'a bottle will be but the beginning of it. We'll sit down at a table and settle this debate in ten minutes if you're reasonable.'

"He'll not be reasonable, of course, but you see what I have in my mind."

"Brede Place," said the lawyer slowly, "is not exactly a castle, but it's a very strong house and might be held by a dozen determined men against an army."

"Then once let me get legally inside, and I'll hold it till the Earl gets more sense in his head than is there at the present moment."

"Possession," said Mr. Brooks, "is nine points of the law."

"It is with a woman," said I, thinking of something else.

"It is with an estate," answered Josiah severely.

"True for you," I admitted, coming back to the point at issue, for it was curious, in spite of the importance of the interview, how my mind kept wandering away to a locked room in the Earl of Westport's house, and to a shady path that ran around the edge of his garden.

"I intend to get possession of the Brede estate if I have to crack the crown of every man at present upon it. But I am an Irishman, and therefore a person of peace, and I wish to crack the crowns in accordance with the law of England, so I come to you for directions how it should be done."

"It is not my place," said Brooks, looking very sour, "to counsel a man to break either heads or the law. In fact it is altogether illegal to assault another unless you are in danger of your own life."

"The blessing of all the Saints be upon you," said I, "yet, ever since I set foot in this land, coming across the boiling seas, entirely to do a kindness to the Earl of Westport, I have gone about in fear of my life."

"You have surely not been assaulted?" demanded Mr. Brooks, raising his eyebrows in surprise.

"Assaulted, is it? I have been set upon in every manner that is possible for a peace-lover to be interfered with. To tell you the truth, no longer ago than yesterday morning, as quiet and decent a Sunday as ever came down on London, my two innocent servants, garrulous creatures that wouldn't hurt a fly, were lured into the high walled garden of the Earl of Westport to see the flowers which both of them love, and there they were pounced upon by the whole body-guard of my lord the Earl, while himself and his quiet-mannered Countess were there to urge them on. Doctor Chord, a little snobbish creature, basking in the smiles of their noble countenances, stood by and gave medical advice showing where best to hit the poor innocent unfortunates that had fallen into their hands."

"Tut, tut!" said Josiah Brooks, his face frowning like a storm-cloud over the hills of Donegal. "If such is indeed the case, an action would lie —"

"Oh, well and as far as that goes, so would Doctor Chord, and all the rest that was there. My poor lads lie now, bruised and sore, in the upper rooms of the stable at the 'Pig and Turnip.' They want no more action, I can tell you, nor lying either."

"You can prove, then," said the lawyer, "that you have suffered violence from the outset."

"Indeed and I could."

"Well, well, we must look into the matter. You recite a most curious accumulation of offences, each of which bears a serious penalty according to the law of England. But there is another matter mentioned in Lady Mary's letter which is even more grave than any yet alluded to."

"And what is that?" I asked in surprise.

"She says that she wishes to have advanced to you, upon the security of these papers, five hundred golden guineas."

"Do you tell me that now?" I cried with delight. "Sure I have always said that Mary was the most sensible girl within the boundaries of this realm."

"That may all be; but women, you see, know little of money or the methods of obtaining it."

"You're right in that," I admitted. "It's the other end of the stick they hold; they know a good deal of the way of spending it."

"You will understand," went on Mr. Brooks, "that if money is to be raised on the security of these documents, your rights in possessing them must be severely scrutinized, while-you will pardon my saying so-the security of your estates in Ireland might be looked at askance by the money-lenders of London."

"Oh, don't let the estates in Ireland trouble you, for the money-lenders of Dublin have already mortgaged them a foot deep. You can raise little on my estates in Ireland but the best turf you ever burned, and that's raised with a spade."

"Very well," said Josiah Brooks, gathering up the papers and tying them together with a bit of red ribbon which he took out of his drawer, ignoring the Irish cord that had held them through all their emergencies. "Very well, I shall seek advice and let you know the result."

"Seek advice," I cried. "Sure a man of your attainments doesn't need to seek advice of any one. Aren't you learned in the law yourself?"

"I must have counsel's opinion," said Josiah solemnly, as if he were speaking of the decisions of Providence.

"Well, you astonish me, Mr. Brooks, for I thought you knew it all, and that's why I came to you; but perhaps it's only your own modesty that makes you reluctant to speak of your attainments, though I suppose what you really mean is that you want to take a pipe in your mouth and a glass of good liquor at your elbow and read the papers at your leisure."

Mr. Josiah Brooks was a solemn man, and he did not appear to relish the picture I so graphically drew of him, when in truth I was thinking only of his own comfort; so I changed the subject with an alertness of mind which perhaps he was incapable of appreciating.

"How far from London is this estate of Brede?" I asked, "and how do you get to it?"

"It is fifty or sixty miles away," he said, "and lies in the county of Sussex, close to the sea, but not on it. If you wish to visit Brede estate," he went on, as if I had not been telling him I was going to do that very thing in force, "if you wish to visit Brede estate, the best plan is to go to Rye and there engage a guide who will lead you to it."

"Rye," said I in astonishment, wondering where I had heard the name before; then, suddenly remembering, I said:

"Rye is a seaport town, is it not?"

"It is," agreed Mr. Brooks.

"Rye is the spot," rejoined I, "where Father Donovan will embark on his pilgrimage to Rome. Sure, and I'm glad to hear that, for the good old man and I will travel there together, and the blessing of Providence will surround me, which I hope will be helpful if the Earl's cut-throats bar the way, as is more than likely."

"Very well, Mr. O'Ruddy, as you are doubtless impatient to know the result, you may call upon me to-morrow afternoon at four o'clock, and I may be in a position to give you more information than I can offer at present."

I took that as a dismissal, and, getting up, shook him warmly by the hand, although his arm was as stiff as a pump handle, and he seemed to take little pleasure in the farewell. And so I left the Temple, that was as lonely as the road between Innishannon and the sea, and trudged out into Fleet Street, which was as lively as Skibbereen Fair. I was so overjoyed to find that my journey lay in the same direction as Father Donovan's that I tramped on westward till after some trouble I found the priest's house in which he was stopping, to tell the good father that I would go part of the way to Rome with him. He was indeed delighted to see me, and introduced me to his host, Father Kilnane, nearly as fine a man and as good a priest as Father Donovan himself.

We had dinner there all together at mid-day, and I invited Father Donovan to come out and see the town with me, which he did. The peaceful father clung to my arm in a kind of terror at what he was witnessing, for he was as innocent of the ways of a big town as if he had been a gossoon from a hedge-school in Ireland. Yet he was mightily interested in all he saw, and asked me many thousand questions that day, and if I did not know the correct answer to them, it made no differ to Father Donovan, for he did not know the answer himself and took any explanation as if it was as true as the gospels he studied and preached.

Daylight was gone before we got back to the house he lodged in, and nothing would do but I must come in and have a bit of supper, although I told him that supper would be waiting for me at the "Pig and Turnip." It had been agreed between us that we would travel together as far as Rye, and that there I should see him off on his tempestuous voyage to Dunkirk or Calais, as the case might be. The old man was mightily delighted to find that our ways lay together through the south of England. He was pleased to hear that I had determined on my rights through the courts of law, with no more sword-playing and violence, which, to tell the truth, until it reached its height, the old man was always against; although, when a quarrel came to its utmost interesting point, I have seen Father Donovan fidget in his cassock, and his eyes sparkle with the glow of battle, although up till then he had done his best to prevent the conflict.

It was getting late when I neared the "Pig and Turnip," and there was a good deal of turmoil in the streets. I saw one or two pretty debates, but, remembering my new resolution to abide by law and order, I came safely past them and turned up the less-frequented street that held my inn, when at the corner, under the big lamp, a young man with something of a swagger about him, in spite of the meanness of his dress, came out from the shadow of the wall and looked me hard in the face.

"Could you direct me, sir, to a hostelry they call the 'Pig and Turnip'?" he asked with great civility.

"If you will come with me," said I, "I'll bring you to the place itself, for that's where I'm stopping."

"Is it possible," he said, "that I have the honour of addressing The O'Ruddy?"

"That great privilege is yours," said I, coming to a standstill in the middle of the street, as I saw the young man had his sword drawn and pressed close against his side to allay suspicion. I forgot all about law and order, and had my own blade free of the scabbard on the instant; but the young man spoke smoothly and made no motion of attack, which was very wise of him.

"Mr. O'Ruddy," he says, "we are both men of the world and sensible men and men of peace. Where two gentlemen, one down on his luck and the other in prosperity, have a private matter to discuss between them, I think this discussion should take place quietly and in even tones of voice."

"Sir," said I, giving my sword-hand a little shake, so that the weapon settled down into its place, "Sir, you express my sentiments exactly, and as you are a stranger to me perhaps you will be good enough to announce the subject that concerns us."

"I may say at the outset," he remarked almost in a whisper, so polite he was, "that I have eight good swordsmen at my back, who are not visible until I give the signal; therefore you see, sir, that your chances are of the slightest if I should be compelled to call upon them. I know the fame of The O'Ruddy as a swordsman, and you may take it as a compliment, sir, that I should hesitate to meet you alone. So much for saving my own skin, but I am a kindly man and would like to save your skin as well. Therefore if you will be kind enough to hand to me the papers which you carry in your pocket, you will put me under strong obligations, and at the same time sleep peaceably to-night at the 'Pig and Turnip' instead of here in the gutter, to be picked up by the watch, for I can assure you, sir, as a man that knows the town, the watch will not be here to save you whatever outcry you may make."

"I am obliged to you, sir, for your discourse and your warning, to both of which I have paid strict attention; and in the interests of that peace which we are each of us so loath to break I may announce to you that the papers you speak of are not in my possession."

"Pardon me, sir, but they must be; for we have searched your room thoroughly, and we have also searched your servants."

"A thief of the night," cried I with mighty indignation, "may easily search an honest man's room; and his poor servants, beaten and bruised by your master's orders, would fall easy victims to the strength and numbers of your ruffians; but you will find it a difficult matter to search me."

"Sir," he replied, bowing as polite as Palermo, "I grieve to state that you are in error. The searching of both your servants and your rooms was accomplished, not through the employment of force, but by the power of money. Your servants insisted they had nothing on their persons but liniment, and they accepted one gold piece each to allow me to verify their statements. Another gold piece gave me, for a time, the freedom of your room. If you have not the papers upon you, then there is no harm in allowing me to run my hand over your clothes, because the package is a bulky one and I will speedily corroborate your statement."

"Sir," said I, not to be outdone in courtesy by this gentleman of the gutter, "I will tell you truthfully that I have nothing on me but my sword, and to that you are quite welcome if you leave to me the choice of which end I hold and which I present to you," —and with that I sprang with my back to the wall, under the lamp, leaving myself partially in shadow, but having spread in front of me a semicircle of light which any assailant attacking must cross, or indeed remain in its effulgence if he would keep free of the point of my blade.

"It grieves me to find that you are a man of violence," replied the scoundrel in the mildest of tones, "and you will bear witness afterward that I did my best to keep you from harm."

"I freely acknowledge it now," said I. "Bring on your men."

To tell the truth, I had no belief at all in the existence of his force, and thought he was playing a game on me, hoping to take me unawares; for if the man knew anything at all he must have known what a swordsman I was, and it was no charge of cowardice against him that he was loath to come to close quarters with me. I speedily discovered, however, that all he said was true; for he gave a low whistle, and out of the darkness instantly sprang seven or eight as malicious-looking villains as a man would care to see, each one with a sword in his hand.

As many erroneous and exaggerated accounts of this encounter have been given in the coffee-houses, and even in the public prints, it is well that I should now tell the truth about it. No man that has the hang of his blade need fear the onset of a mob except in one case, and that is this,—if the whole eight set upon me at once with every sword extended, there was a chance that though I might, by great expertness, disable half of them, the other half would run me through. But it should never be forgotten that these men were fighting for money, and I was fighting for my life, and that makes all the difference in the world. Each man makes a show of attack, but he holds off, hoping that one of the others will dare to thrust. This is fatal to success, but not necessarily fatal to their intended victim. An active man with a wall at his back can generally account for all that comes in front of him if he is deeply in earnest and has not too much liquor in him. It astonished London that I was able to defeat eight men, each one of whom was armed as efficiently as myself; but, as my father used to say, if you are not wholly taken up with the determination to have a man's life, you may pink him in what spot you choose if you give a little thought to the matter. The great object is the disarming of the enemy. Now, if you give a man a jab in the knuckles, or if you run your blade delicately up his arm from the wrist to the elbow, this is what happens. The man involuntarily yells out, and as involuntarily drops his sword on the flags. If you prick a man on the knuckle-bone, he will leave go his sword before he has time to think, it being an action entirely unconscious on his part, just like winking your eye or drawing your breath; yet I have seen men run through the body who kept sword in hand and made a beautiful lunge with it even as they staggered across the threshold of death's door.

Now I had no desire for any of these men's lives, but I determined to have their swords. I glittered my own shining blade before their eyes, flourishing a semicircle with it, and making it dart here and there like the tongue of an angry snake; and instantly every man in front of me felt uncomfortable, not knowing where the snake was going to sting, and then, as I said before, they were fighting for money and not for honour. When I had dazzled their eyes for a moment with this sword-play and bewildered their dull brains, I suddenly changed my tactics and thrust forward quicker than you can count one, two, three, four, five, six, seven, eight,—and each man was holding a bleeding fist to his mouth, while the swords clattered on the cobbles like hail on the copper roof of a cathedral. It was the most beautiful and complete thing I ever saw. I then swept the unarmed men back a pace or two with a flirt of my weapon, and walked up the pavement, kicking the swords together till they lay in a heap at my feet. The chief ruffian stood there dazed, with his sword still in his hand, for he had stepped outside the circle, he acting as captain, and depending on the men to do the work.

"Drop that," I shouted, turning on him, and he flung his sword in the street as if it was red hot.

"Sir," said I to him, "a sword in your hand is merely an inconvenience to you; see if you don't look better with an armful of them. Pick up these nine blades in a bundle and walk on before me to the 'Pig and Turnip.' When we come into the courtyard of that tavern, you are to turn round and make me the lowest bow you can without rubbing your nose against the pavement. Then you will say, as gracefully as the words can be uttered:

"'Mr. O'Ruddy,' you say, 'these swords are yours by right of conquest. You have defeated nine armed men to-night in less than as many minutes, so I present you with the spoil.' Then you will bow to the people assembled in the courtyard,—for there is aways a mob of them there, late and early,—and you will make another low obeisance to me. If you do all this acceptably to my sense of politeness, I will let you go unmolested; but if you do otherwise, I will split your gullet for you."

"Sir," said the captain, "I accept your terms."

With that he stooped and picked up the bundle of weapons, marching on stolidly before me till he came to the "Pig and Turnip." All the rest had disappeared in the darkness, and had gone to their dens, very likely to nurse sore knuckles and regret the loss of good stout blades.

Our coming to the tavern caused a commotion, as you may well imagine; and although I don't make too much of the encounter, yet it is my belief that such an incident never happened in London before. The captain carried out his part of the presentation with an air of deference and a choice of good language that charmed me; then he backed out under the archway to the street, bowing six or seven times as he went. I had never any fault to find with the man's manner. Paddy and Jem, now seemingly quite recovered from their misusage of Sunday, stood back of the group with eyes and mouths open, gazing upon me with an admiration I could not but appreciate.

"Come out of that," said I, "and take this cutlery up to my room," and they did.

I sat down at the table and wrote a letter to Mr. Brooks.

"Sir," said I in it, "I don't know whether I am plaintiff or defendant in the suit that's coming on, but whichever it is here's a bundle of legal evidence for your use. You mentioned the word 'violence' to me when I had the pleasure of calling on you. This night I was set upon by nine ruffians, who demanded from me the papers now in your possession. I took their knives from them, so they would not hurt themselves or other people, and I send you these knives to be filed for reference."

I tied up the swords in two bundles, and in the morning sent Paddy and Jem off with them and the letter to the Temple, which caused great commotion in that peaceable quarter of the city, and sent forth the rumour that all the lawyers were to be at each other's throats next day.

CHAPTER XXX

In the afternoon I went slowly to the Temple, thinking a good deal on the way. It's truth I tell, that in spite of the victory of the night before I walked to the Temple rather downhearted. Whether Josiah Brooks was an attorney, or a barrister, or a solicitor, or a plain lawyer, I don't know to this day, and I never could get my mind to grasp the distinction that lies between those names in that trade; but whichever it was it seemed to me he was a cold, unenthusiastic man, and that he thought very little indeed of my game. There is small pleasure in litigation in England as compared with the delight of the law in the old Ark. If I had gone to see a lawyer in Dublin or Cork he would have been wild with excitement before I had got half through my story. He would have slapped me on the back and shook me by the hand, and cried "Whurroo" at the prospect of a contest. My quarrel would have been his before I had been ten minutes in his presence, and he would have entered into the spirit of the fight as if he were the principal in it instead of merely acting for him; but in this gloomy country of England, where they engage upon a lawsuit, not with delight, but as if they were preparing for a funeral; there is no enjoyment in the courts at all at all. I wished I could transfer the case to the old turf, where there is more joy in being defeated than there is in winning in England; for I have seen the opposing lawyers rise from the most gentlemanly and elegant language you ever heard to a heated debate; then fling books at each other, and finally clench, while the judge stood up and saw fair play. But this man Brooks was so calm and collected and uninterested that he fairly discouraged me, and I saw that I was going to get neither the money I needed nor the support I expected from him.

As I went up his dark stairway in the Temple and came to the passage that led to the outer room, I saw standing in a corner the two bundles of swords I had sent him, as if he had cast them out, which indeed he had done. After some delay in the outer room, the melancholy man in rusty black asked me, would I go in, and there sat Josiah Brooks at his table as if he had never left it since I took my departure the day before. He looked across at me with a scrutiny which seemed to be mingled with dislike and disapproval.

"Mr. O'Ruddy," he said, quiet-like, "it is not customary to send to a law office a number of swords, which are entirely out of place in such rooms. They have been counted and are found to number nine. I shall be obliged if you sign this receipt for them, accept delivery of the same, and remove them from the premises at your earliest convenience."

So I signed the receipt without a word and handed it back to him. Then I said, —

"I will send my servant for the swords as soon as I return to the inn."

He inclined his head the merest trifle, drew some papers toward him, and adjusted his glasses.

"It is my duty to tell you, Mr. O'Ruddy, that if you go into the courts with this case you will assuredly be defeated, and the costs will follow. There is also a possibility that when the civil proceedings are determined a criminal action against yourself may ensue."

"I told you, sir," said I, with my heart sinking, "I had no intention of troubling the courts at all at all. In the land I come from we are more inclined to settle a case with a good stout blackthorn than with the aid of a lawyer's wig. These papers say in black and white that I am the owner of Brede estate, and I intend to take possession of it."

"It is only right to add," continued Brooks, with that great air of calm I found so exasperating, "it is only right to add that you are in a position to cause great annoyance to the Earl of Westport. You can at least cast doubt on his title to the estate; and he stands this jeopardy, that if contrary to opinion your cause should prove successful, —and we must never forget that the law is very uncertain, —the Earl would have to account for the moneys he has drawn from the estate, which would run into many thousands of pounds, and, together with the loss of the property, would confront his lordship with a most serious situation. Your case, therefore, though weak from a strictly legal point of view, is exceptionally strong as a basis for compromise."

These words cheered me more than I can say, and it is an extraordinary fact that his frozen, even tone, and his lack of all interest in the proceedings had an elevating effect upon my spirits which I could not have believed possible.

"As it is a compromise that I'm after," said I, "what better case can we want?"

"Quite so," he resumed; "but as there is no encouragement in the strictly legal aspect of the plea, you will understand that no money-lender in London will advance a farthing on such unstable security. Even though I am acting in your interests, I could not take the responsibility of advising any capitalist to advance money on such uncertain tenure."

This threw me into the depths again; for, although I never care to meet trouble half way, I could not conceal from myself the fact that my bill at the "Pig and Turnip" had already reached proportions which left me no alternative but to slip quietly away in liquidation of the account. This was a thing I never liked to do; and when I am compelled to make that settlement I always take note of the amount, so that I may pay it if I am ever that way again and have more money than I need at the moment. Even if I succeeded in getting away from the inn, what could I do at Brede with no money at all? —for in that part of the country they would certainly look upon the Earl of Westport as the real owner of the property, and on me as a mere interloper; and if I could not get money on the documents in London, there was little chance of getting credit even for food at Brede.

"It is rather a blue look-out then," said I as cheerfully as I could.

"From a legal standpoint it is," concurred Mr. Brooks, as unconcerned as if his own payment did not depend on my raising the wind with these papers. "However, I have been instructed by a person who need not be named, who has indeed stipulated that no name shall be mentioned, to advance you the sum of five hundred guineas, which I have here in my drawer, and which I will now proceed to count out to you if you, in the mean time, will sign this receipt, which acquits me of all responsibility and certifies that I have handed the money over to you without rebate or reduction."

And with that the man pulled open a drawer and began to count out the glittering gold.

I sprang to my feet and brought my fist down on the table with a thump. "Now, by the Great Book of Kells, what do you mean by chopping and changing like a rudderless lugger in a ten-knot breeze? If the expedition is possible, and you had the money in your drawer all the time, why couldn't you have spoken it out like a man, without raising me to the roof and dropping me into the cellar in the way you've done?"

The man looked unruffled across the table at me. He pushed a paper a little farther from him, and said without any trace of emotion:

"Will you sign that receipt at the bottom, if you please?"

I sat down and signed it, but I would rather have jabbed a pen between his close-set lips to give him a taste of his own ink. Then I sat quiet and watched him count the gold, placing it all in neat little pillars before him. When it was finished, he said:

"Will you check the amount?"

"Is that gold mine?" I asked him.

"It is," he replied.

So I rose up without more ado and shovelled it into my pockets, and he put the receipt into the drawer after reading it over carefully, and arched his eyebrows without saying anything when he saw me pocket the coins uncounted.

"I wish you good afternoon," said I.

"I have to detain you one moment longer," he replied. "I have it on the most trustworthy information that the Earl of Westport is already aware of your intention to proceed to the country estate alleged to be owned by him. Your outgoings and incomings are watched, and I have to inform you that unless you proceed to Rye with extreme caution there is likelihood that you may be waylaid, and perchance violence offered to you."

"In that case I will reap a few more swords; but you need not fear, I shall not trouble you with them."

"They are out of place in a solicitor's chamber," he murmured gently. "Is there anything further I can do for you?"

"Yes," I said, "there is one thing more. I would be obliged if you could make me a bundle of legal-looking papers that are of no further use to you: a sheet of that parchment, and some of the blue stuff like what I carried. The Earl seems determined to have a packet of papers from me, and I would like to oblige him, as he's going to be my father-in-law, although he doesn't know it. I'd like some writing on these papers, —Latin for preference."

Josiah Brooks thought steadily for a few moments, then he called out and the melancholy rusty man came in. He took a few instructions and went out again. After a long time he entered once more and placed on the table a packet I would have sworn was my own. This the lawyer handed to me without a word, and the rusty man held open the door for me. So, with the bogus papers in my pocket, not to mention the genuine gold, I took my leave of Josiah and the Temple.

As soon as I was outside I saw at once that there was no time to be lost. If the Earl had guessed my intention, as was hinted, what would he do? Whenever I wish to answer a question like that to myself, I think what would I do if I were in the position of the other man. Now what I would have done, was this, if I were the Earl of Westport. I would send down to Brede all the ruffians at my disposal and garrison the house with them; and if the Earl did this, I would be on the outside, and he on the inside with advantage over me accordingly. Most men fight better behind stone walls than out in the open; and, besides, a few men can garrison a barracks that five hundred cannot take by assault. However, as it turned out, I was crediting the Earl with brains equal to my own, which in truth neither he nor any of his followers had below their bonnets. He trusted to intercepting me on the highway, just as if he hadn't already failed in that trick. But it takes a score of failures to convince an Englishman that he is on the wrong track altogether, while an Irishman has so many plans in his head that there's never time to try one of them twice in succession. But if I was wrong about the Earl, I was right about his daughter, when I suspected that she gave the lawyer the information about the Earl's knowledge of my plans, and I was also right when I credited the dear girl with drawing on her own funds to give me the golden guineas, —"and may each one of them," said I to myself, "prove a golden blessing on her head."

At any rate, there was no time to be lost, so I made straight to Father Donovan and asked him would he be ready to begin the journey to Rye after an early breakfast with me at the "Pig and Turnip."

You never saw a man in your life so delighted at the prospect of leaving London as was Father Donovan, and indeed I was glad to get away from the place myself. The good father said the big town confused him; and, although he was glad to have seen it, he was more happy still to get out of it and breathe a breath of fresh country air once more. So it was arranged that he would come to the "Pig and Turnip" next morning between six and seven o'clock. I then turned back to the shop of a tailor who for a long time had had two suits of clothing waiting for me that were entirely elegant in their design. The tailor, however, would not take the word of a gentleman that payment would follow the delivery of the costumes; for a little later would be more convenient for me to give him the money, and this made me doubt, in spite of the buttons and gold lace, if the garments were quite the fashionable cut, because a tailor who demands money on the spot shows he is entirely unaccustomed to deal with the upper classes; but I needed these clothes, as the two suits I possessed were getting a little the worse for wear.

When I went into his shop he was inclined to be haughty, thinking I had come to ask credit again; but when he saw the glitter of the money the man became obsequious to a degree that I never had witnessed before. I was affable to him, but distant; and when he offered me everything that was in his shop, I told him I would take time and consider it. He sent a servant following behind me with the goods, and so I came once more to the "Pig and Turnip," where I ordered Paddy and Jem to go to the Temple and fetch away the swords.

There seemed to be a pleased surprise on the face of the landlord when I called for my bill and paid it without question, chiding him for his delay in not sending it before. I engaged a horse for Father Donovan to ride on the following morning, and ordered breakfast ready at six o'clock, although I gave my commands that I was to be wakened an hour before daylight.

I spent the rest of the day in my room with Paddy and Jem, trying to knock into their heads some little notion of geography, wishing to make certain that they would sooner or later arrive in Rye without stumbling in on Belfast while on the way. My own knowledge of the face of the country was but meagre, so the landlord brought in a rough map of the south of England, and I cautioned the lads to get across London Bridge and make for the town of Maidstone, from where they could go due south, and if they happened on the coast they were to inquire for Rye and stay there until further orders. Jem Bottles, who thought he had brains in his head, said he would not be so open in telling every one we were going to Rye if he was me, because he was sure the Earl had people on the look-out, and money was plenty with his lordship. If every one knew when we were taking our departure, there would be no difficulty in following us and overcoming us on some lonely part of the road.

"Jem," said I, "that's all very true; but when they attacked us before they got very little change for their trouble; and if you are afraid of some slight commotion on the road, then you can stay back here in London."

"I am not afraid at all," said Jem, "but if there's anything particular you would like to see in Rye, there's no use in blocking the road to it."

"Sure, Jem, then be quiet about it."

Turning to the landlord, who was standing by, I said to him:

"My men fear we are going to be intercepted, so I think if I began the journey some time before daylight, and they followed me soon after, I might slip away unnoticed."

The landlord scratched his head and crinkled up his brow, for to think was unusual with him.

"I don't see," he said at last, "what you have to gain by going separately. It seems to me it would be better to go in a body, and then, if you are set on, there are three instead of one."

"Very well," said I, "I'll take your caution into consideration, and act upon it or not as seems best when the time comes."

I told Paddy and Jem to sleep that night on the floor of my own room, and cautioned them to wake me an hour before daylight at the latest. Jem slept through until I had to kick him into consciousness; but poor Paddy, on the other hand, wakened me four times during the night,—the first time two hours after I had gone to sleep, and I could have cudgelled him for his pains, only I knew the lad's intentions were good. The last time I could stand it no longer, although it was still earlier than the hour I had said, so I got up and dressed myself in one of my new suits.

"And here, Paddy," said I, "you will wear the costume I had on yesterday."

"I couldn't think of it," said Paddy, drawing back from the grandeur.

"You are not to think, you impudent gossoon, but to do as I tell you. Put them on, and be as quick as you can."

"Troth, yer honour," said Paddy, still shrinking from them, "they're too grand for the likes o' me, an' few will be able to tell the differ atween us."

"You conceited spalpeen, do ye think there's no difference between us but what the clothes make? Get into them. I intend certain other people to take you for me in the dark, and I can warrant you these clothes, grand as you think them, will be very soundly beaten before this day is done with."

"Ochone, ochone," moaned Paddy, "am I to get another beating already, and some of the bruises not yet off my flesh?"

"Put on the coat now, and don't do so much talking. Sure it's all in the day's work, and I promise you before long you'll have your revenge on them."

"It's not revenge I'm after," wailed Paddy, "but a whole skin."

"Now you're transformed into a gentleman," said I, "and many a lad would take a beating for the privilege of wearing such gorgeous raiment. Here is a packet of paper that you're to keep in your pocket till it's taken away from you. And now I'll help you to saddle the horse, and once you're across London Bridge you'll likely come upon Maidstone and Rye some time in your life, for you can't get back over the river again except by the same bridge, so you'll know it when you come to it."

And so I mounted Paddy in the courtyard; the sleepy watchman undid the bolts in the big gate in the archway; and my man rode out into the darkness in no very cheerful humour over his journey. I came back and took forty winks more in the arm-chair, then, with much difficulty, I roused Jem Bottles. He also, without a murmur, but with much pride in his dressing, put on the second of my discarded suits, and seemed to fancy himself mightily in his new gear. With plenty of cord I tied and retied the two bundles of swords and placed them across the horse in front of his saddle, and it was not yet daylight when Jem jingled out into the street like a moving armoury. Two huge pistols were in his holsters, loaded and ready to his hand.

"By the Saints," said Jem proudly, "the man that meddles with me shall get hot lead or cold steel for his breakfast," and with that he went off at a canter, waking the echoes with the clash of his horse's shoes on the cobble-stones.

I went up stairs again and threw myself down on the bed and slept peacefully with no Paddy to rouse me until half-past-six, when a drawer knocked at the door and said that a priest that was downstairs would be glad to see me. I had him up in a jiffy, and a hot breakfast following fast on his heels, which we both laid in in quantities, for neither of us knew where our next meal was to be. However, the good father paid little thought to the future as long as the present meal was well served and satisfactory. He had no more idea than a spring lamb how we were to get to Rye, but thought perhaps a coach set out at that hour in the morning. When I told him I had a horse saddled and waiting for him, he was pleased, for Father Donovan could scamper across the country in Ireland with the best of them. So far as I could judge, the coast was clear, for every one we met between the "Pig and Turnip" and the bridge seemed honest folk intent on getting early to their work. It was ten minutes past seven when we clattered across the bridge and set our faces toward Rye.

CHAPTER XXXI

Looking back over my long life I scarcely remember any day more pleasant than that I spent riding side by side with Father Donovan from London to Rye. The fine old man had a fund of entertaining stories, and although I had heard them over and over again there was always something fresh in his way of telling them, and now and then I recognized a narrative that had once made two separate stories, but which had now become welded into one in the old man's mind. There was never anything gloomy in these anecdotes, for they always showed the cheerful side of life and gave courage to the man that wanted to do right; for in all of Father Donovan's stories the virtuous were always made happy. We talked of our friends and acquaintances, and if he ever knew anything bad about a man he never told it; while if I mentioned it he could always say something good of him to balance it, or at least to mitigate the opinion that might be formed of it. He was always doing some man a good turn or speaking a comforting word for him.

"O'Ruddy," he said, "I spent most of the day yesterday writing letters to those that could read them in our part of Ireland, setting right the rumours that had come back to us, which said you were fighting duels and engaged in brawls, but the strangest story of all was the one about your forming a friendship with a highwayman, who, they said, committed robberies on the road and divided the spoil with you, and here I find you without a servant at all at all, leading a quiet, respectable life at a quiet, respectable inn. It's not even in a tavern that I first come across you, but kneeling devoutly, saying a prayer in your mother church. I see you leaving your inn having paid your bill like a gentleman, when they said you took night-leave of most of the hostelries in England. Dear me, and there was the landlord bowing to you as if you were a prince, and all his servants in a row with the utmost respect for you. Ah, O'Ruddy, it's men like you that gives the good name to Ireland, and causes her to be looked up to by all the people of the world."

I gave Father Donovan heartfelt thanks for his kindness, and prayed to myself that we would not come upon Jem Bottles on the road, and that we would be left unmolested on our journey until we saw the sea-coast. Of course, if we were set upon, it would not be my fault, and it's not likely he would blame me; but if we came on Bottles, he was inclined to be very easy in conversation, and, in spite of my warnings, would let slip words that would shock the old priest. But when a day begins too auspiciously, its luck is apt to change before the sun sets, as it was with me.

It was nearing mid-day, and we were beginning to feel a trifle hungry, yet were in a part of the country that gave little promise of an inn, for it was a lonely place with heath on each side of the road, and, further on, a bit of forest. About half-way through this wooded plain an astonishing sight met my eyes. Two saddled horses were tied to a tree, and by the side of the road appeared to be a heap of nine or ten saddles, on one of which a man was sitting, comfortably eating a bit of bread, while on another a second man, whose head was tied up in a white cloth, lay back in a recumbent position, held upright by the saddlery. Coming closer, I was disturbed to see that the man eating was Jem Bottles, while the other was undoubtedly poor Paddy, although his clothes were so badly torn that I had difficulty in recognizing them as my own. As we drew up Jem stood and saluted with his mouth full, while Paddy groaned deeply. I was off my horse at once and ran to Paddy.

"Where are ye hurted?" said I.

"I'm killed," said Paddy.

"I've done the best I could for him," put in Jem Bottles. "He'll be all right in a day or two."

"I'll not," said Paddy, with more strength than one would suspect; "I'll not be all right in a day or two, nor in a week or two, nor in a month or two, nor in a year or two; I'm killed entirely."

"You're not," said Bottles. "When I was on the highway I never minded a little clip like that."

"Hush, Bottles," said I, "you talk altogether too much. Paddy," cried I, "get on your feet, and show yer manners here to Father Donovan."

Paddy got on his feet with a celerity which his former attitude would not have allowed one to believe possible.

"My poor boy!" said the kindly priest; "who has misused you?" and he put his two hands on the sore head.

"About two miles from here," said Paddy, "I was set on by a score of men —"

"There was only nine of them," interrupted Jem, "count the saddles."

"They came on me so sudden and unexpected that I was off my horse before I knew there was a man within reach. They had me down before I could say my prayers, and cudgelled me sorely, tearing my clothes, and they took away the packet of papers you gave me, sir. Sure I tried to guard it with my life, an' they nearly took both."

"I am certain you did your best, Paddy," said I; "and it's sorry I am to see you injured."

"Then they rode away, leaving me, sore wounded, sitting on the side of the road," continued Paddy. "After a while I come to myself, for I seemed dazed; and, my horse peacefully grazing beside me, I managed to get on its back, and turned toward London in the hope of meeting you; but instead of meeting you, sir, I came upon Jem with his pile of saddles, and he bound up my head and did what he could to save me, although I've a great thirst on me at this moment that's difficult to deal with."

"There's a ditch by the side of the road," said the priest.

"Yes," said Paddy sadly; "I tried some of that."

I went to my pack on the horse and took out a bottle and a leather cup. Paddy drank and smacked his lips with an ecstasy that gave us hope for his ultimate recovery. Jem Bottles laughed, and to close his mouth I gave him also some of the wine.

"I hope," said Father Donovan with indignation, "that the miscreant who misused you will be caught and punished."

"I punished them," said Jem, drawing the back of his hand across his mouth.

"We'll hear about it another time," said I, having my suspicions.

"Let the good man go on," begged Father Donovan, who is not without human curiosity.

Jem needed no second bidding.

"Your Reverence," he said, "I was jogging quietly on as a decent man should, when, coming to the edge of this forest, I saw approach me a party of horsemen, who were very hilarious and laughed loudly. If you look up and down the road and see how lonely it is, and then look at the wood, with no hedge between it and the highway, you'll notice the place was designed by Providence for such a meeting."

"Sure the public road is designed as a place for travellers to meet," said the father, somewhat bewildered by the harangue.

"Your Reverence is right, but this place could not afford better accommodation if I had made it myself. I struck into the wood before they saw me, tore the black lining from my hat, punched two holes in it for the eyes, and tied it around my forehead, letting it hang down over my face; then I primed my two pistols and waited for the gentlemen. When they were nearly opposite, a touch of the heels to my horse's flank was enough, and out he sprang into the middle of the road.

"'Stand and deliver!' I cried, pointing the pistols at them, the words coming as glibly to my lips as if I had said them no later ago than yesterday. 'Stand and deliver, ye —'" and here Jem glibly rattled out a stream of profane appellatives which was disgraceful to listen to.

"Tut, tut, Jem," I said, "you shouldn't speak like that. Any way we'll hear the rest another time."

"That's what I called them, sir," said Jem, turning to me with surprise, "you surely would not have me tell an untruth."

"I wouldn't have you tell anything. Keep quiet. Father Donovan is not interested in your recital."

"I beg your pardon, O'Ruddy," said Father Donovan, looking at me reproachfully; "but I am very much interested in this man's narrative."

"As any good man should be," continued Jem, "for these were arrant scoundrels; one of them I knew, and his name is Doctor Chord. He fell off his horse on the roadway at once and pleaded for mercy. I ordered the others instantly to hold their hands above their heads, and they did so, except one man who began fumbling in his holster, and then, to show him what I could do with a pistol, I broke his wrist. At the sound of the shot the horses began to plunge, nearly trampling Doctor Chord into the dust.

"'Clasp your hands above your heads, ye —'"

Here went on another stream of terrible language again, and in despair I sat down on the pile of saddles, allowing things to take their course. Jem continued:

"The lesson of the pistol was not misread by my gentlemen, when they noticed I had a second loaded one; so, going to them one after the other I took their weapons from them and flung them to the foot of that tree, where, if you look, you may see them now. Then I took a contribution from each one, just as you do in church, your Reverence. I'm sure you have a collection for the poor, and that was the one I was taking up this day. I have not counted them yet," said the villain turning to me, "but I think I have between sixty and seventy guineas, which are all freely at your disposal, excepting a trifle for myself and Paddy there. There's no plaster like gold for a sore head, your Reverence. I made each one of them dismount and take off his saddle and throw it in the pile; then I had them mount again and drove them with curses toward London, and very glad they were to escape."

"He did not get the papers again," wailed Paddy, who was not taking as jubilant a view of the world as was Jem at that moment.

"I knew nothing of the papers," protested Bottles. "If you had told me about the papers, I would have had them, and if I had been carrying the papers these fellows would not have made away with them."

"Then," said the horrified priest, "you did not commit this action in punishment for the injury done to your friend? You knew nothing of that at the time. You set on these men thinking they were simple travellers."

"O, I knew nothing of what happened to Paddy till later, but you see, your Reverence, these men themselves were thieves and robbers. In their case it was nine men against one poor half-witted Irish lad —"

"Half-witted yourself," cried Paddy angrily.

"But you, sir," continued his Reverence, "were simply carrying out the action of a highwayman. Sir, you *are* a highwayman."

"I was, your Reverence, but I have reformed."

"And this pile of saddles attests your reformation!" said the old man, shaking his head.

"But you see, your Reverence, this is the way to look at it —"

"Keep quiet, Jem!" cried I in disgust.

"How can I keep quiet," urged Bottles, "when I am unjustly accused? I do not deny that I was once a highwayman, but Mr. O'Ruddy converted me to better ways —"

"Highways," said Paddy, adding, with a sniff, "Half-witted!"

"Your Reverence, I had no more intention of robbing those men than you have at this moment. I didn't know they were thieves themselves. Then what put it into my head to jump into the wood and on with a mask before you could say, Bristol town? It's the mysterious ways of Providence, your Reverence. Even I didn't understand it at the time, but the moment I heard Paddy's tale I knew at once I was but an instrument in the hand of Providence, for I had not said, 'Stand and deliver!' this many a day, nor thought of it."

"It may be so; it may be so," murmured the priest, more to himself than to us; but I saw that he was much troubled, so, getting up, I said to Paddy:

"Are you able to ride farther on to-day?"

"If I'd another sup from the cup, sir, I think I could," whereat Jem Bottles laughed again, and I gave them both a drink of wine.

"What are you going to do with all this saddlery?" said I to Bottles.

"I don't know anything better than to leave it here; but I think, your honour, the pistols will come handy, for they're all very good ones, and Paddy and me can carry them between us, or I can make two bags from these leather packs, and Paddy could carry the lot in them, as I do the swords."

"Very well," I said. "Make your preparations as quickly as you can and let us be off, for this latest incident, in spite of you, Jem, may lead to pursuit and get us into trouble before we are ready for it."

"No fear, sir," said Jem confidently. "One thief does not lay information against another. If they had been peaceable travellers, that would be another thing; but, as I said, Providence is protecting us, no doubt because of the presence of his Reverence here, and not for our own merits."

"Be thankful it is the reward of some one else's merits you, reap, Bottles, instead of your own. No more talk now, but to horse and away."

For some miles Father Donovan rode very silently. I told him something of my meeting with Jem Bottles and explained how I tried to make an honest man of him, while this was the first lapse I had known since his conversion. I even pretended that I had some belief in his own theory of the interposition of Providence, and Father Donovan was evidently struggling to acquire a similar feeling, although he seemed to find some difficulty in the contest. He admitted that this robbery appeared but even justice; still he ventured to hope that Jem Bottles would not take the coincidence as a precedent, and that he would never mistake the dictates of Providence for the desires of his own nature.

"I will speak with the man later," he said, "and hope that my words will make some impression upon him. There was a trace of exaltation in his recital that showed no sign of a contrite spirit."

On account of the delay at the roadside it was well past twelve o'clock before we reached Maidstone, and there we indulged in a good dinner that put heart into all of us, while the horses had time to rest and feed. The road to Rye presented no difficulties whatever, but under ordinary conditions I would have rested a night before travelling to the coast. There would be a little delay before the Earl discovered the useless nature of the papers which he had been at such expense to acquire, but after the discovery there was no doubt in my mind that he would move upon Brede as quickly as horses could carry his men, so I insisted upon pressing on to Rye that night, and we reached the town late with horses that were very tired. It was a long distance for a man of the age of Father Donovan to travel in a day, but he stood the journey well, and enjoyed his supper and his wine with the best of us.

We learned that there was no boat leaving for France for several days, and this disquieted me, for I would have liked to see Father Donovan off early next morning, for I did not wish to disclose my project to the peace-loving man. I must march on Brede next day if I was to get there in time, and so there was no longer any possibility of concealing my designs. However, there was no help for it, and I resolved to be up bright and early in the morning and engage a dozen men whom I could trust to stand by me. I also intended to purchase several cartloads of provisions, so that if a siege was attempted we could not be starved out. All this I would accomplish at as early an hour as possible, get the carts on their way to Brede, and march at the head of the men myself; so I went to bed with a somewhat troubled mind, but fell speedily into a dreamless sleep nevertheless, and slept till broad daylight.

CHAPTER XXXII

I found Rye a snug little town, and so entirely peaceable-looking that when I went out in the morning I was afraid there would be nobody there who would join me in the hazardous task of taking possession of the place of so well-known a man as the Earl of Westport. But I did not know Rye then as well as I do now: it proved to be a great resort for smugglers when they were off duty and wished to enjoy the innocent relaxation of a town after the comparative loneliness of the sea-coast, although, if all the tales they tell me are true, the authorities sometimes made the sea-shore a little too lively for their comfort. Then there were a number of seafaring men looking for a job, and some of them had the appearance of being pirates in more prosperous days.

As I wandered about I saw a most gigantic ruffian, taking his ease with his back against the wall, looking down on the shipping.

"If that man's as bold as he's strong," said I to myself, "and I had half a dozen more like him, we'd hold Brede House till the day there's liberty in Ireland;" so I accosted him.

"The top o' the morning to you," said I genially.

He eyed me up and down, especially glancing at the sword by my side, and then said civilly:

"The same to you, sir. You seem to be looking for some one?"

"I am," said I, "I'm looking for nine men."

"If you'll tell me their names I'll tell you where to find them, for I know everybody in Rye."

"If that's the case you'll know their names, which is more than I do myself."

"Then you're not acquainted with them?"

"I am not; but if you'll tell me your name I think then I'll know one of them."

There was a twinkle in his eye as he said:

"They call me Tom Peel."

"Then Tom," said I, "are there eight like you in the town of Rye?"

"Not quite as big perhaps," said Tom, "but there's plenty of good men here, as the French have found out before now, —yes, and the constables as well. What do you want nine men for?"

"Because I have nine swords and nine pistols that will fit that number of courageous subjects."

"Then it's not for the occupation of agriculture you require them?" said Peel with the hint of a laugh. "There's a chance of a cut in the ribs, I suppose, for swords generally meet other swords."

"You're right in that; but I don't think the chance is very strong."

"And perhaps a term in prison when the scrimmage is ended?"

"No fear of that at all at all; for if any one was to go to prison it would be me, who will be your leader, and not you, who will be my dupes, do you see?"

Peel shrugged his shoulders.

"My experience of the world is that the man with gold lace on his coat goes free, while they punish the poor devil in the leather jacket. But, turn the scheme out bad or ill, how much money is at the end of it?"

"There'll be ten guineas at the end of it for each man, win or lose."

"And when will the money be paid?"

"Half before you leave Rye, the other half in a week's time, and perhaps before, —a week's time at the latest; but I want men who will not turn white if a blunderbuss happens to go off."

The rascallion smiled and spat contemptuously in the dust before him.

"If you show me the guineas," said he, "I'll show you the men."

"Here's five of them, to begin with, that won't be counted against you. There'll be five more in your pocket when we leave Rye, and a third five when the job's ended."

His big hand closed over the coins.

"I like your way of speaking," he said. "Now where are we to go?"

"To the strong house of Brede, some seven or eight miles from here. I do not know how far exactly, nor in what direction."

"I am well acquainted with it," said Peel. "It was a famous smuggler's place in its time."

"I don't mean a smuggler's place," said I. "I am talking of the country house of the Earl of Westport."

"Yes, curse him, that's the spot I mean. Many a nobleman's house is put to purposes he learns little of, although the Earl is such a scoundrel he may well have been in with the smugglers and sold them to the government."

"Did he sell them?"

"Somebody sold them."

There was a scowl on Peel's face that somehow encouraged me, although I liked the look of the ruffian from the first.

"You're an old friend of his lordship's, then?" said I.

"He has few friends in Rye or about Rye. If you're going to do anything against Westport, I'll get you a hundred men for nothing if there's a chance of escape after the fight."

"Nine men will do me, if they're the right stuff. You will have good cover to sleep under, plenty to eat and drink, and then I expect you to hold Brede House against all the men the Earl of Westport can bring forward."

"That's an easy thing," said Peel, his eye lighting up. "And if worse comes to the worst I know a way out of the house that's neither through door or window nor up a chimney. Where will I collect your men?"

"Assemble them on the road to Brede, quietly, about half a mile from Rye. Which direction is Brede from here?"

"It lies to the west, between six and seven miles away as the crow flies."

"Very well, collect your men as quickly as you can, and send word to me at the 'Anchor.' Tell your messenger to ask for The O'Ruddy."

Now I turned back to the tavern sorely troubled what I would do with Father Donovan. He was such a kindly man that he would be loath to shake hands with me at the door of the inn, as he had still two or three days to stop, so I felt sure he would insist on accompanying me part of the way. I wished I could stop and see him off on his ship; but if we were to get inside of Brede's House unopposed, we had to act at once. I found Paddy almost recovered from the assault of the day before. He had a bandage around his forehead, which, with his red hair, gave him a hideous appearance, as if the whole top of his head had been smashed. Poor Paddy was getting so used to a beating each day that I wondered wouldn't he be lonesome when the beatings ceased and there was no enemy to follow him.

Father Donovan had not yet appeared, and the fire was just lit in the kitchen to prepare breakfast, so I took Jem and Paddy with me to the eating shop of the town, and there a sleepy-looking shop-keeper let us in, mightily resenting this early intrusion, but changed his demeanour when he understood the size of the order I was giving him, and the fact that I was going to pay good gold; for it would be a fine joke on The O'Ruddy if the Earl surrounded the house with his men and starved him out. So it was no less than three cartloads of provisions I ordered, though one of them was a cartload of drink, for I thought the company I had hired would have a continuous thirst on them, being seafaring men and smugglers, and I knew that strong, sound ale was brewed in Rye.

The business being finished, we three went back to the "Anchor," and found an excellent breakfast and an excellent man waiting for me, the latter being Father Donovan, although slightly impatient for closer acquaintance with the former.

When breakfast was done with, I ordered the three horses saddled, and presently out in the courtyard Paddy was seated on his nag with the two sacks of pistols before him, and Jem in like manner with his two bundles of swords. The stableman held my horse, so I turned to Father Donovan and grasped him warmly by the hand.

"A safe journey across the Channel to you, Father Donovan, and a peaceful voyage from there to Rome, whichever road you take. If you write to me in the care of the landlord of this inn I'll be sending and sending till I get your letter, and when you return I'll be standing and watching the sea, at whatever point you land in England, if you'll but let me know in time. And so good-bye to you, Father Donovan, and God bless you, and I humbly beseech your own blessing in return."

The old man's eyes grew wider and wider as I went on talking and talking and shaking him by the hand.

"What's come over you, O'Ruddy?" he said, "and where are you going?"

"I am taking a long journey to the west and must have an early start."

"Nonsense," cried Father Donovan, "it's two or three days before I can leave this shore, so I'll accompany you a bit of the way."

"You mustn't think of it, Father, because you had a long day's ride yesterday, and I want you to take care of yourself and take thought on your health."

"Tush, I'm as fresh as a boy this morning. Landlord, see that the saddle is put on that horse I came into Rye with."

The landlord at once rushed off and gave the order, while I stood there at my wit's end.

"Father Donovan," said I, "I'm in great need of haste at this moment, and we must ride fast, so I'll just bid good-bye to you here at this comfortable spot, and you'll sit down at your ease in that big arm-chair."

"I'll do nothing of the kind, O'Ruddy. What's troubling you, man? and why are you in such a hurry this morning, when you said nothing of it yesterday?"

"Father, I said nothing of it yesterday, but sure I acted it. See how we rode on and on in spite of everything, and did the whole journey from London to Rye between breakfast and supper. Didn't that give you a hint that I was in a hurry?"

"Well, it should have done, it should have done, O'Ruddy; still, I'll go a bit of the way with you and not delay you."

"But we intend to ride very fast, Father."

"Ah, it's an old man you're thinking I'm getting to be. Troth, I can ride as fast as any one of the three of you, and a good deal faster than Paddy."

At this moment the landlord came bustling in.

"Your Reverence's horse is ready," he said.

And so there was nothing for it but to knock the old man down, which I hadn't the heart to do. It is curious how stubborn some people are; but Father Donovan was always set in his ways, and so, as we rode out of Rye to the west, with Paddy and Jem following us, I had simply to tell his Reverence all about it, and you should have seen the consternation on his countenance.

"Do you mean to tell me you propose to take possession of another man's house and fight him if he comes to claim his own?"

"I intend that same thing, your Reverence;" for now I was as stubborn as the old gentleman himself, and it was not likely I was going to be put off my course when I remembered the happiness that was ahead of me; but there's little use in trying to explain to an aged priest what a young man is willing to do for the love of the sweetest girl in all the land.

"O'Ruddy," he said, "you'll be put in prison. It's the inside of a gaol, and not the inside of a castle, you'll see. It's not down the aisle of a church you'll march with your bride on your arm, but its hobbling over the cobbles of a Newgate passage you'll go with manacles on your legs. Take warning from me, my poor boy, who would be heart-broken to see harm come to you, and don't run your neck into the hangman's noose, thinking it the matrimonial halter. Turn back while there's yet time, O'Ruddy."

"Believe me, Father Donovan, it grieves me to refuse you anything, but I cannot turn back."

"You'll be breaking the law of the land."

"But the law of the land is broken every day in our district of Ireland, and not too many words said about it."

"Oh, O'Ruddy, that's a different thing. The law of the land in Ireland is the law of the alien."

"Father, you're not logical. It's the alien I'm going to fight here,"—but before the father could reply we saw ahead of us the bulky form of Tom Peel, and ranged alongside of the road, trying to look very stiff and military-like, was the most awkward squad of men I had ever clapped eyes on; but determined fellows they were, as I could see at a glance when I came fornenst them, and each man pulled a lock of his hair by way of a salute.

"Do you men understand the use of a sword and a pistol?" said I.

The men smiled at each other as though I was trying some kind of a joke on them.

"They do, your honour," answered Tom Peel on their behalf. "Each one of them can sling a cutlass to the king's taste, and fire a pistol without winking, and there are now concealed in the hedge half a dozen blunderbusses in case they should be needed. They make a loud report and have a good effect on the enemy, even when they do no harm."

"Yes, we'll have the blunderbusses," said I, and with that the men broke rank, burst through the hedge, and came back with those formidable weapons. "I have ammunition in the carts," I said, "did you see anything of them?"

"The carts have gone on to the west, your honour; but we'll soon overtake them," and the men smacked their lips when they thought of the one that had the barrels in it. Now Paddy came forward with the pistols, and Bottles followed and gave each man a blade, while I gave each his money.

"O dear! O dear!" groaned Father Donovan.

"There's just a chance we may be attacked before we get to Brede, and, Father, though I am loath to say good-bye, still it must be said. It's rare glad I'll be when I grip your hand again."

"All in good time; all in good time," said Father Donovan; "I'll go a bit farther along the road with you and see how your men march. They would fight better and better behind a hedge than in the open, I'm thinking."

"They'll not have to fight in the open, Father," said I, "but they'll be comfortably housed if we get there in time. Now, Peel, I make you captain of the men, as you've got them together, and so, Forward, my lads."

They struck out along the road, walking a dozen different kinds of steps, although there were only nine of them; some with the swords over their shoulders, some using them like walking-sticks, till I told them to be more careful of the points; but they walked rapidly and got over the ground, for the clank of the five guineas that was in each man's pocket played the right kind of march for them.

"Listen to reason, O'Ruddy, and even now turn back," said Father Donovan.

"I'll not turn back now," said I, "and, sure, you can't expect it of me. You're an obstinate man yourself, if I must say so, Father."

"It's a foolhardy exploit," he continued, frowning. "There's prison at the end of it for some one," he murmured.

"No, it's the House of Brede, Father, that's at the end of it."

"Supposing the Earl of Westport brings a thousand men against you,—what are you going to do?"

"Give them the finest fight they have ever seen in this part of England."

In spite of himself I saw a sparkle in Father Donovan's eye. The nationality of him was getting the better of his profession.

"If it were legitimate and lawful," at last he said, "it would be a fine sight to see."

"It will be legitimate and lawful enough when the Earl and myself come to terms. You need have no fear that we're going to get into the courts, Father."

"Do you think he'll fight?" demanded the father suddenly, with a glint in his eyes that I have seen in my own father's when he was telling us of his battles in France.

"Fight? Why of course he'll fight, for he's as full of malice as an egg's full of meat; but nevertheless he's a sensible old curmudgeon, when the last word's said, and before he'll have it noised over England that his title to the land is disputed he'll give me what I want, although at first he'll try to master me."

"Can you depend on these men?"

"I think I can. They're old smugglers and pirates, most of them."

"I wonder who the Earl will bring against you?" said Father Donovan, speaking more to himself than to me. "Will it be farmers or regular soldiers?"

"I expect they will be from among his own tenantry; there's plenty of them, and they'll all have to do his bidding."

"But that doesn't give a man courage in battle?"

"No, but he'll have good men to lead them, even if he brings them from London."

"I wouldn't like to see you attacked by real soldiers; but I think these men of yours will give a good account of themselves if there's only peasantry brought up against them. Sure, the peasantry in this country is not so warlike as in our own," —and there was a touch of pride in the father's remark that went to my very heart.

After riding in silence for a while, meditating with head bowed, he looked suddenly across at me, his whole face lighted up with delicious remembrance.

"Wouldn't you like to have Mike Sullivan with you this day," he cried, naming the most famous fighter in all the land, noted from Belfast to our own Old Head of Kinsale.

"I'd give many a guinea," I said, "to have Mike by my side when the Earl comes on."

The old father suddenly brought down his open hand with a slap on his thigh.

"I'm going to stand by you, O'Ruddy," he said.

"I'm glad to have your blessing on the job at last, Father," said I; "for it was sore against me to go into this business when you were in a contrary frame of mind."

"You'll not only have my blessing, O'Ruddy, but myself as well. How could I sail across the ocean and never know which way the fight came out? and then, if it is to happen in spite of me, the Lord pity the frailness of mankind, but I'd like to see it. I've not seen a debate since the Black Fair of Bandon."

By this time we had overtaken the hirelings with their carts, and the men were swinging past them at a good pace.

"Whip up your horses," said I to the drivers, "and get over the ground a little faster. It's not gunpowder that's in those barrels, and when we reach the house there will be a drink for every one of you."

There was a cheer at this, and we all pushed on with good hearts. At last we came to a lane turning out from the main road, and then to the private way through fields that led to Brede House. So far there had been no one to oppose us, and now, setting spurs to our horses, we galloped over the private way, which ran along the side of a gentle hill until one end of the mansion came into view. It seemed likely there was no suspicion who we were, for a man digging in the garden, stood up and took off his cap to us. The front door looked like the Gothic entrance of a church, and I sprang from my horse and knocked loudly against the studded oak. An old man opened the door without any measure of caution, and I stepped inside. I asked him who he was, and he said he was the caretaker.

"How many beside yourself are in this house?"

He said there was only himself, his wife, and a kitchen wench, and two of the gardeners, while the family was in London.

"Well," said I, "I'd have you know that I'm the family now, and that I'm at home. I am the owner of Brede estate."

"You're not the Earl of Westport!" said the old man, his eyes opening wide.

"No, thank God, I'm not!"

He now got frightened and would have shut the door, but I gently pushed him aside. I heard the tramp of the men, and, what was more, the singing of a sea song, for they were nearing the end of their walk and thinking that something else would soon pass their lips besides the tune. The old man was somewhat reassured when he saw the priest come in; but dismay and terror took hold of him when the nine men with their blunderbusses and their swords came singing around a corner of the house and drew up in front of it. By and by the carts came creaking along, and then every man turned to and brought the provisions inside of the house and piled them up in the kitchen in an orderly way, while the old man, his wife, the wench, and the two gardeners stood looking on with growing signs of panic upon them.

"Now, my ancient caretaker," said I to the old man, in the kindest tones I could bring to my lips, so as not to frighten him more than was already the case, "what is the name of that little village over yonder?" and I pointed toward the west, where, on the top of a hill, appeared a church and a few houses.

"That, sir," he said, with his lips trembling, "is the village of Brede."

"Is there any decent place there where you five people can get lodging; for you see that this house is now filled with men of war, and so men of peace should be elsewhere? Would they take you in over at the village?"

"Yes, sir, it is like they would."

"Very well. Here is three guineas to divide among you, and in a week or thereabouts you will be back in your own place, so don't think disaster has fallen on you."

The old man took the money, but seemed in a strange state of hesitancy about leaving.

"You will be unhappy here," I said, "for there will be gun-firing and sword-playing. Although I may not look it, I am the most bloodthirsty swordsman in England, with a mighty uncertain temper on me at times. So be off, the five of you!"

"But who is to be here to receive the family?" he asked.

"What family?"

"Sir, we had word last night that the Earl of Westport and his following would come to this house to-day at two of the clock, and we have much ado preparing for them; for the messenger said that he was bringing many men with him. I thought at first that you were the men, or I would not have let you in."

"Now the Saints preserve us," cried I, "they'll be on us before we get the windows barricaded. Tom Peel," I shouted, "set your men to prepare the defence at once, and you'll have only a few hours to do it in. Come, old man, take your wife and your gardeners, and get away."

"But the family, sir, the family," cried the old man, unable to understand that they should not be treated with the utmost respect.

"I will receive the family. What is that big house over there in the village?"

"The Manor House, sir."

"Very well, get you gone, and tell them to prepare the Manor House for the Earl of Westport and his following; for he cannot lodge here to-night," —and with that I was compelled to drag them forth, the old woman crying and the wench snivelling in company. I patted the ancient wife on the shoulder and told her there was nothing to be feared of; but I saw my attempt at consolation had little effect.

Tom Peel understood his business; he had every door barred and stanchioned, and the windows protected, as well as the means to his hand would allow. Up stairs he knocked out some of the diamond panes so that the muzzle of a blunderbuss would go through. He seemed to know the house as if it was his own; and in truth the timbers and materials for defence which he conjured up from the ample cellars or pulled down from the garret seemed to show that he had prepared the place for defence long since.

"Your honour," he said, "two dangers threaten this house which you may not be aware of."

"And what are those, Tom?" I asked.

"Well, the least serious one is the tunnel. There is a secret passage from this house down under the valley and out and up near the church. If it was not guarded they could fill this house unknown to you. I will stop this end of it with timber if your honour gives the word. There's not many knows of it, but the Earl of Westport is certain to have the knowledge, and some of his servants as well."

"Lead me to this tunnel, Tom," said I, astonished at his information.

We came to a door in one of the lower rooms that opened on a little circular stone stairway, something like a well, and, going down to the bottom, we found a tunnel in which a short man could stand upright.

"Thunder and turf, Tom!" said I, "what did they want this for?"

"Well, some thought it was to reach the church, but no one ever lived in this house that was so anxious to get to church that he would go underground to it. Faith, they've been a godless lot in Brede Place until your honour came, and we were glad to see you bring a priest with you. It put new heart in the men; they think he'll keep off Sir Goddard Oxenbridge."

"Does he live near here? What has he to do with the place?"

"He is dead long since, sir, and was owner of this house. Bullet wouldn't harm him, nor steel cut him, so they sawed him in two with a wooden saw down by the bridge in front. He was a witch of the very worst kind, your honour. You hear him groaning at the bridge every night, and sometimes he walks through the house himself in two halves, and then every body leaves the place. And that is our most serious danger, your honour. When Sir Goddard takes to groaning through these rooms at night, you'll not get a man to stay with you, sir; but as he comes up from the pit by the will of the Devil we expect his Reverence to ward him off."

Now this was most momentous news, for I would not stop in the place myself if a ghost was in the habit of walking through it; but I cheered up Tom Peel by telling him that no imp of Satan could appear in the same county as Father Donovan, and he passed on the word to the men, to their mighty easement.

We had a splendid dinner in the grand hall, and each of us was well prepared for it; Father Donovan himself, standing up at the head of the table, said the holy words in good Latin, and I was so hungry that I was glad the Latins were in the habit of making short prayers.

Father Donovan and I sat at table with a bottle for company, and now that he knew all about the situation, I was overjoyed to find him an inhabitant of the same house; for there was no gentleman in all the company, except himself, for me to talk with.

Suddenly there was a blast of a bugle, and a great fluttering outside. The lower windows being barricaded, it was not possible to see out of them, and I was up the stair as quick as legs could carry me; and there in front were four horses harnessed to a great carriage, and in it sat the old Earl and the Countess, and opposite them who but Lady Mary herself, and her brother, Lord Strepp. Postilions rode two of the horses, and the carriage was surrounded by a dozen mounted men.

Everybody was looking at the house and wondering why nobody was there to welcome them, and very forbidding this stronghold must have seemed to those who expected to find the doors wide open when they drove up. I undid the bolts of one of the diamond-paned windows, and, throwing it open, leaned with my arms on the sill, my head and shoulders outside.

"Good day to your ladyship and your lordship," I cried,—and then all eyes were turned on me,—"I have just this day come into my inheritance, and I fear the house is not in a state to receive visitors. The rooms are all occupied by desperate men and armed; but I have given orders to your servants to prepare the Manor House in the village for your accommodation; so, if you will be so good as to drive across the valley, you will doubtless meet with a better reception than I can give you at this moment. When you come again, if there are no ladies of the party, I can guarantee you will have no complaint to make of the warmth of your reception."

His lordship sat dumb in his carriage, and for once her ladyship appeared to find difficulty in choosing words that would do justice to her anger. I could not catch a glimpse of Lady Mary's face at all at all, for she kept it turned toward the village; but young Lord Strepp rose in the carriage, and, shaking his fist at me, said:

"By God, O'Ruddy, you shall pay for this;" but the effect of the words was somewhat weakened by reason that his sister, Lady Mary, reached out and pulled him by the coat-tails, which caused him to be seated more suddenly than he expected; then she gave me one rapid glance of her eye and turned away her face again.

Now his lordship, the great Earl of Westport, spoke, but not to me.

"Drive to the village," he said to the postilions; then horsemen and carriage clattered down the hill.

We kept watch all that night, but were not molested. In the southern part of the house Father Donovan found a well-furnished chapel, and next morning held mass there, which had a very quieting effect on the men, especially as Oxenbridge had not walked during the night. The only one of them who did not attend mass was Jem Bottles, who said he was not well enough and therefore would remain on watch. Just as mass was finished Jem appeared in the gallery of the chapel and shouted excitedly:

"They're coming, sir; they're coming!"

I never before saw a congregation dismiss themselves so speedily. They were at their posts even before Tom Peel could give the order. The opposing party was leaving the village and coming down the hill when I first caught sight of them from an upper window. There seemed somewhere between half a dozen and a dozen horsemen, and behind them a great mob of people on foot that fairly covered the hillside. As they crossed the brook and began to come up, I saw that their leader was young Lord Strepp himself, and Jem whispered that the horsemen behind him were the very men he had encountered on the road between London and Maidstone. The cavalry were well in advance, and it seemed that the amateur infantry took less and less pleasure in their excursion the nearer they drew to the gloomy old house, so much so that Lord Strepp turned back among them and appeared to be urging them to make haste. However, their slow progress may be explained by the fact that a certain number of them were carrying a huge piece of timber, so heavy that they had to stagger along cautiously.

"That," said Tom Peel, who stood at my elbow, "is to batter in the front door and take us by storm. If you give the word, your honour, we can massacre the lot o' them before they get three blows struck."

"Give command to the men, Peel," said I, "not to shoot any one if they can help it. Let them hold their fire till they are within fifty yards or so of the front, then pass the word to fire into the gravel of the terrace; and when you shoot let every man yell as if he were a dozen, and keep dead silence till that moment. I'll hold up my hand when I want you to fire."

There was a deep stillness over all the beautiful landscape. The bushes and the wood, however, were an exception to this, although the songs of the birds among the trees and singing of the larks high in the air seemed not to disturb the silence; but the whole air of the country-side was a suggestion of restful peace, at great variance with the designs of the inhabitants, who were preparing to attack each other.

Father Donovan stood beside me, and I saw his lips moving in prayer; but his eyes were dancing with irredeemable delight, while his breath came quick and expectant.

"I'm afraid those chaps will run at the first volley," he said, smiling at me. "They come on very slowly and must be a great trial to the young lord that's leading them."

It was indeed a trial to the patience of all of us, for the time seemed incredibly long till they arrived at the spot where I had determined they should at least hear the report of the blunderbusses, although I hoped none of them would feel the effects of the firing. Indeed, the horsemen themselves, with the exception of Lord Strepp, appeared to take little comfort in their position, and were now more anxious to fall behind and urge on the others on foot than to lead the band with his lordship.

I let them all get very close, then held up my hand, and you would think pandemonium was let loose. I doubt if all the cannon in Cork would have made such a noise, and the heathen Indians we read of in America could not have given so terrifying a yell as came from my nine men. The blunderbusses were more dangerous than I supposed, and they tore up the gravel into a shower of small stones that scattered far and wide, and made many a man fall down, thinking he was shot. Then the mob ran away with a speed which made up for all lost time coming the other direction. Cries of anguish were heard on every side, which made us all laugh, for we knew none of them were hurted. The horses themselves seemed seized with panic; they plunged and kicked like mad, two riders being thrown on the ground, while others galloped across the valley as if they were running away; but I suspect that their owners were slyly spurring them on while pretending they had lost control of them. Lord Strepp and one or two others, however, stood their ground, and indeed his lordship spurred his horse up opposite the front door. One of my men drew a pistol, but I shouted at him:

"Don't shoot at that man, whatever he does," and the weapon was lowered.

I opened the window and leaned out.

"Well, Lord Strepp," cried I, "'tis a valiant crowd you have behind you."

"You cursed highwayman," he cried, "what do you expect to make by this?"

"I expect to see some good foot-racing; but you are under an error in your appellation. I am not a highwayman; it is Jem Bottles here who stopped nine of your men on the Maidstone road and piled their saddles by the side of it. Is it new saddlery you have, or did you make a roadside collection?"

"I'll have you out of that, if I have to burn the house over your head."

"I'll wager you'll not get any man, unless it's yourself, to come near enough to carry a torch to it. You can easily have me out of this without burning the house. Tell your father I am ready to compromise with him."

"Sir, you have no right in my father's house; and, to tell you the truth, I did not expect such outlawry from a man who had shown himself to be a gentleman."

"Thank you for that, Lord Strepp; but, nevertheless, tell your father to try to cultivate a conciliatory frame of mind, and let us talk the matter over as sensible men should."

"We cannot compromise with you, O'Ruddy," said Lord Strepp in a very determined tone, which for the first time made me doubt the wisdom of my proceedings; for of course it was a compromise I had in mind all the time, for I knew as well as Father Donovan that if he refused to settle with me my position was entirely untenable.

"We cannot compromise with you," went on the young man. "You have no right, legal or moral, to this place, and you know it. I have advised my father to make no terms with you. Good day to you, sir."

And with that he galloped off, while I drew a very long face as I turned away.

"Father Donovan," I said, when I had closed the window, "I am not sure but your advice to me on the way here was nearer right than I thought at the time."

"Oh, not a bit of it," cried Father Donovan cheerfully. "You heard what the young man said, that he had advised his father not to make any terms with you. Very well, that means terms have been proposed already; and this youth rejects the wisdom of age, which I have known to be done before."

"You think, then, they will accept a conference?"

"I am sure of it. These men will not stand fire, and small blame to them. What chance have they? As your captain says, he could annihilate the lot of them before they crushed in the front door. The men who ran away have far more sense than that brainless spalpeen who led them on, although I can see he is brave enough. One or two more useless attacks will lead him to a more conciliatory frame of mind, unless he appeals to the law, which is what I thought he would do; for I felt sure a sheriff would be in the van of attack. Just now you are opposed only to the Earl of Westport; but, when the sheriff comes on, you're fornenst the might of England."

This cheered me greatly, and after a while we had our dinner in peace. The long afternoon passed slowly away, and there was no rally in the village, and no sign of a further advance; so night came on and nothing had been done. After supper I said good-night to Father Donovan, threw myself, dressed as I was, on the bed, and fell into a doze. It was toward midnight when Tom Peel woke me up; that man seemed to sleep neither night nor day; and there he stood by my bed, looking like a giant in the flicker of the candle-light.

"Your honour," he said, "I think there's something going on at the mouth of the tunnel. Twice I've caught the glimpse of a light there, although they're evidently trying to conceal it."

I sat up in bed and said:

"What do you propose to do?"

"Well, there's a man inside here that knows the tunnel just as well as I do,—every inch of it,—and he's up near the other end now. If a company begins coming in, my man will run back without being seen and let us know. Now, sir, shall I timber this end, or shall we deal with them at the top of the stair one by one as they come up. One good swordsman at the top of the stair will prevent a thousand getting into the house."

"Peel," said I, "are there any stones outside, at the other end of the tunnel?"

"Plenty. There's a dyke of loose stones fronting it."

"Very well; if your man reports that any have entered the tunnel, they'll have left one or two at the other end on guard; take you five of your most trusted men, and go you cautiously a roundabout way until you are within striking distance of the men on guard. Watch the front upper windows of this house; and if you see two lights displayed, you will know they are in the tunnel. If you waited here till your man comes back, you would be too late; so go now, and, if you see the two lights, overpower the men at the mouth of the tunnel unless they are too many for you. If they are, then there's nothing to do but retreat. When you have captured the guard, make them go down into the tunnel; then you and your men tear down the dyke and fill the hole full of stones; I will guard this end of the passage."

Tom Peel pulled his forelock and was gone at once, delighted with his task. I knew that if I got them once in the tunnel there would no longer be any question of a compromise, even if Lord Strepp himself was leading them. I took two lighted candles with me and sat patiently at the head of the stone stairway that led, in circular fashion, down into the depths. Half an hour passed, but nothing happened, and I began to wonder whether or not they had captured our man, when suddenly his face appeared.

"They are coming, sir," he cried, "by the dozen. Lord Strepp is leading them."

"Will they be here soon, do you think?"

"I cannot tell. First I saw torches appear, then Lord Strepp came down and began giving instructions, and, after counting nearly a score of his followers, I came back as quick as I could."

"You've done nobly," said I. "Now stand here with this sword and prevent any man from coming up."

I took one of the candles, leaving him another, and lighted a third. I went up the stair and set them in the front window; then I opened another window and listened. The night was exceedingly still, —not even the sound of a cricket to be heard. After a few minutes, however, there came a cry, instantly smothered, from the other side of the valley; another moment and I heard the stones a rolling, as if the side of a wall had tumbled over, which indeed was the case; then two lights were shown on the hill and were waved up and down; and although Peel and I had arranged no signal, yet this being the counterpart of my own, I took to signify that they had been successful, so, leaving the candles burning there, in case there might have been some mistake, I started down the stair to the man who was guarding the secret passage.

"Has anything happened?"

"Nothing, sir."

I think the best part of an hour must have passed before there was sign or sound. Of course I knew if the guards were flung down the hole, they would at once run after their comrades and warn them that both ends of the tunnel were in our possession. I was well aware that the imprisoned men might drag away the stones and ultimately win a passage out for themselves; but I trusted that they would be panic-stricken when they found themselves caught like rats in a trap. In any case it would be very difficult to remove stones from below in the tunnel, because the space was narrow and few could labour at a time; then there was every chance that the stones might jam, when nothing could be done. However, I told the man beside me to go across the valley and ask Peel and his men to pile on rocks till he had a great heap above the entrance, and, if not disturbed, to work till nearly daylight, so I sat on the top of the circular stair step with my rapier across my knees, waiting so long that I began to fear they all might be smothered, for I didn't know whether the stopping of air at one end would prevent it coming in at the other, for I never heard my father say what took place in a case like that. Father Donovan was in bed and asleep, and I was afraid to leave the guarding of the stair to any one else. It seemed that hours and hours passed, and I began to wonder was daylight never going to come, when the most welcome sound I ever heard was the well-known tones of a voice which came up from the bottom of the well.

"Are you there, Mr. O'Ruddy?"

There was a subdued and chastened cadence in the inquiry that pleased me.

"I am, and waiting for you."

"May I come up?"

"Yes, and very welcome; but you'll remember, Lord Strepp, that you come up as a prisoner."

"I quite understand that, Mr. O'Ruddy."

So, as I held the candle, I saw the top of his head coming round and round and round, and finally he stood before me stretching out his sword, hilt forward.

"Stick it in its scabbard," said I, "and I'll do the same with mine." Then I put out my hand, "Good morning to your lordship," I said. "It seems to me I've been waiting here forty days and forty nights. Will you have a sup of wine?"

"I would be very much obliged to you for it, Mr. O'Ruddy."

With that I called the nearest guard and bade him let nobody up the stair without my knowing it.

"I suppose, my lord, you are better acquainted with this house than I am; but I know a spot where there's a drop of good drink."

"You have discovered the old gentleman's cellar, then?"

"Indeed, Lord Strepp, I have not. I possess a cellar of my own. It's you that's my guest, and not me that's yours on this occasion."

I poured him out a flagon, and then one for myself, and as we stood by the table I lifted it high and said:

"Here's to our better acquaintance."

His lordship drank, and said with a wry face, as he put down the mug:

"Our acquaintance seems to be a somewhat tempestuous one; but I confess, Mr. O'Ruddy, that I have as great a respect for your generalship as I have for your swordsmanship. The wine is good and revivifying. I've been in that accursed pit all night, and I came to this end of it with greater reluctance than I expected to when I entered the other. We tried to clear away the stones; but they must have piled all the rocks in Sussex on top of us. Are your men toiling there yet?"

"Yes, they're there, and I gave them instructions to work till daylight."

"Well, Mr. O'Ruddy, my poor fellows are all half dead with fright, and they fancy themselves choking; but although the place was foul enough when we entered it, I didn't see much difference at the end. However, I did see one thing, and that was that I had to come and make terms. I want you to let the poor devils go, Mr. O'Ruddy, and I'll be parole that they won't attack you again."

"And who will give his parole that Lord Strepp will not attack me again?"

"Well, O'Ruddy,"—I took great comfort from the fact that he dropped the Mr.,—"Well, O'Ruddy, you see we cannot possibly give up this estate. You are not legally entitled to it. It is ours and always has been."

"I'm not fighting for any estate, Lord Strepp."

"Then, in Heaven's name, what are you fighting for?"

"For the consent of the Earl and Countess of Westport to my marriage with Lady Mary, your sister."

Lord Strepp gave a long whistle; then he laughed and sat down in the nearest chair.

"But what does Mary say about it?" he asked at last.

"The conceit of an Irishman, my lord, leads me to suspect that I can ultimately overcome any objections she may put forward."

"Oho! that is how the land lies, is it? I'm a thick-headed clod, or I would have suspected something of that sort when Mary pulled me down so sharply as I was cursing you at the front door." Then, with a slight touch of patronage in his tone, he said:

"There is some difference in the relative positions of our families, Mr. O'Ruddy."

"Oh, I'm quite willing to waive that," said I. "Of course it isn't usual for the descendant of kings, like myself, to marry a daughter of the mere nobility; but Lady Mary is so very charming that she more than makes up for any discrepancy, whatever may be said for the rest of the family."

At this Lord Strepp threw back his head and laughed again joyously, crying, —

"King O'Ruddy, fill me another cup of your wine, and I'll drink to your marriage."

We drank, and then he said:

"I'm a selfish beast, guzzling here when those poor devils think they're smothering down below. Well, O'Ruddy, will you let my unlucky fellows go?"

"I'll do that instantly," said I, and so we went to the head of the circular stair and sent the guard down to shout to them to come on, and by this time the daylight was beginning to turn the upper windows grey. A very bedraggled stream of badly frightened men began crawling up and up and up the stairway, and as Tom Peel had now returned I asked him to open the front door and let the yeomen out. Once on the terrace in front, the men seemed not to be able to move away, but stood there drawing in deep breaths of air as if they had never tasted it before. Lord Strepp, in the daylight, counted the mob, asking them if they were sure every one had come up, but they all seemed to be there, though I sent Tom Peel down along the tunnel to find if any had been left behind.

Lord Strepp shook hands most cordially with me at the front door.

"Thank you for your hospitality, O'Ruddy," he said, "although I came in by the lower entrance. I will send over a flag of truce when I've seen my father; then I hope you will trust yourself to come to the Manor House and have a talk with him."

"I'll do it with pleasure," said I.

"Good morning to you," said Lord Strepp.

"And the top o' the morning to you, which is exactly what we are getting at this moment, though in ten minutes I hope to be asleep."

"So do I," said Lord Strepp, setting off at a run down the slope.

CHAPTER XXXIII

Once more I went to my bed, but this time with my clothes off, for if there was to be a conference with the Earl and the Countess at the Manor House, not to speak of the chance of seeing Lady Mary herself, I wished to put on the new and gorgeous suit I had bought in London for that occasion, and which had not yet been on my back. I was so excited and so delighted with the thought of seeing Lady Mary that I knew I could not sleep a wink, especially as daylight was upon me, but I had scarcely put my head on the pillow when I was as sound asleep as any of my ancestors, the old Kings of Kinsale. The first thing I knew Paddy was shaking me by the shoulder just a little rougher than a well-trained servant should.

"Beggin' your pardon," says he, "his lordship, the great Earl of Westport, sends word by a messenger that he'll be pleased to have account with ye, at your early convenience, over at the Manor House beyond."

"Very well, Paddy," said I, "ask the messenger to take my compliments to the Earl and say to him I will do myself the honour of calling on him in an hour's time. Deliver that message to him; then come back and help me on with my new duds."

When Paddy returned I was still yawning, but in the shake of a shillelah he had me inside the new costume, and he stood back against the wall with his hand raised in amazement and admiration at the glory he beheld. He said after that kings would be nothing to him, and indeed the tailor had done his best and had won his guineas with more honesty than you'd expect from a London tradesman. I was quietly pleased with the result myself.

I noticed with astonishment that it was long after mid-day, so it occurred to me that Lord Strepp must have had a good sleep himself, and sure the poor boy needed it, for it's no pleasure to spend life underground till after you're dead, and his evening in the tunnel must have been very trying to him, as indeed he admitted to me afterward that it was.

I called on Father Donovan, and he looked me over from head to foot with wonder and joy in his eye.

"My dear lad, you're a credit to the O'Ruddys," he said, "and to Ireland," he said, "and to the Old Head of Kinsale," he said.

"And to that little tailor in London as well," I replied, turning around so that he might see me the better.

In spite of my chiding him Paddy could not contain his delight, and danced about the room like an overgrown monkey.

"Paddy," said I, "you're making a fool of yourself."

Then I addressed his Reverence.

"Father Donovan," I began, "this cruel war is over and done with, and no one hurt and no blood shed, so the Earl—"

At this moment there was a crash and an unearthly scream, then a thud that sounded as if it had happened in the middle of the earth. Father Donovan and I looked around in alarm, but Paddy was nowhere to be seen. Toward the wall there was a square black hole, and, rushing up to it, we knew at once what had happened. Paddy had danced a bit too heavy on an old trap-door, and the rusty bolts had broken. It had let him down into a dungeon that had no other entrance; and indeed this was a queer house entirely, with many odd nooks and corners about it, besides the disadvantage of Sir Goddard Oxenbridge tramping through the rooms in two sections.

"For the love of Heaven and all the Saints," I cried down this trap-door, "Paddy, what has happened to you?"

"Sure, sir, the house has fallen on me."

"Nothing of the kind, Paddy. The house is where it always was. Are you hurted?"

"I'm dead and done for completely this time, sir. Sure I feel I'm with the angels at last."

"Tut, tut, Paddy, my lad; you've gone in the wrong direction altogether for them."

"Oh, I'm dying, and I feel the flutter of their wings," and as he spoke two or three ugly blind bats fluttered up and butted their stupid heads against the wall.

"You've gone in the right direction for the wrong kind of angels, Paddy; but don't be feared, they're only bats, like them in my own tower at home, except they're larger."

I called for Tom Peel, as he knew the place well.

"Many a good cask of brandy has gone down that trap-door," said he, "and the people opposite have searched this house from cellar to garret and never made the discovery Paddy did a moment since."

He got a stout rope and sent a man down, who found Paddy much more frightened than hurt. We hoisted both of them up, and Paddy was a sight to behold.

"Bad luck to ye," says I; "just at the moment I want a presentable lad behind me when I'm paying my respects to the Earl of Westport, you must go diving into the refuse heap of a house that doesn't belong to you, and spoiling the clothes that does. Paddy, if you were in a seven years' war, you would be the first man wounded and the last man killed, with all the trouble for nothing in between. Is there anything broken about ye?"

"Every leg and arm I've got is broken," he whimpered, but Father Donovan, who was nearly as much of a surgeon as a priest, passed his hand over the trembling lad, then smote him on the back, and said the exercise of falling had done him good.

"Get on with you," said I, "and get off with those clothes. Wash yourself, and put on the suit I was wearing yesterday, and see that you don't fall in the water-jug and drown yourself."

I gave the order for Tom Peel to saddle the four horses and get six of his men with swords and pistols and blunderbusses to act as an escort for me.

"Are you going back to Rye, your honour?" asked Peel.

"I am not. I am going to the Manor House."

"That's but a step," he cried in surprise.

"It's a step," said I, "that will be taken with dignity and consequence."

So, with the afternoon sun shining in our faces, we set out from the house of Brede, leaving but few men to guard it. Of course I ran the risk that it might be taken in our absence; but I trusted the word of Lord Strepp as much as I distrusted the designs of his father and mother, and Strepp had been the captain of the expedition against us; but if I had been sure the mansion was lost to me, I would have evaded none of the pomp of my march to the Manor House in the face of such pride as these upstarts of Westports exhibited toward a representative of a really ancient family like the O'Ruddy. So his Reverence and I rode slowly side by side, with Jem and Paddy, also on horseback, a decent interval behind us, and tramping in their wake that giant, Tom Peel, with six men nearly as stalwart as himself, their blunderbusses over their shoulders, following him. It struck panic in the village when they saw this terrible array marching up the hill toward them, with the sun glittering on us as if we were walking jewellery. The villagers, expecting to be torn limb from limb, scuttled away into the forest, leaving the place as empty as a bottle of beer after a wake. Even the guards around the Manor House fled as we approached it, for the fame of our turbulence had spread abroad in the land. Lord Strepp tried to persuade them that nothing would happen to them, for when he saw the style in which we were coming he was anxious to make a show from the Westport side and had drawn up his men in line to receive us. But we rode through a silent village that might have been just sacked by the French. I thought afterward that this desertion had a subduing effect on the old Earl's pride, and made him more easy to deal with. In any case his manner was somewhat abated when he received me. Lord Strepp himself was there at the door, making excuses for the servants, who he said had gone to the fields to pick berries for their supper. So, leaving Paddy to hold one horse and Jem the other, with the seven men drawn up fiercely in front of the Manor House, Father Donovan and myself followed Lord Strepp into a large room, and there, buried in an arm-chair, reclined the aged Earl of Westport, looking none too pleased to meet his visitors. In cases like this it's as well to be genial at the first, so that you may remove the tension in the beginning.

"The top of the morning —I beg your pardon-the tail of the afternoon to you, sir, and I hope I see you well."

"I am very well," said his lordship, more gruffly than politely.

"Permit me to introduce to your lordship, his Reverence, Father Donovan, who has kindly consented to accompany me that he may yield testimony to the long-standing respectability of the House of O'Ruddy."

"I am pleased to meet your Reverence," said the Earl, although his appearance belied his words. He wasn't pleased to meet either of us, if one might judge by his lowering countenance, in spite of my cordiality and my wish to make his surrender as easy for him as possible.

I was disappointed not to see the Countess and Lady Mary in the room, for it seemed a pity that such a costume as mine should be wasted on an old curmudgeon, sitting with his chin in his breast in the depths of an easy-chair, looking daggers though he spoke dumplings.

I was just going to express my regret to Lord Strepp that no ladies were to be present in our assemblage, when the door opened, and who should sail in, like a full-rigged man-o'-war, but the Countess herself, and Lady Mary, like an elegant yacht floating in tow of her. I swept my bonnet to the boards of the floor with a gesture that would have done honour to the Court of France; but her Ladyship tossed her nose higher in the air, as if the man-o'-war had encountered a huge wave. She seated herself with emphasis on a chair, and says I to myself, "It's lucky for you, you haven't Paddy's trap-door under you, or we'd see your heels disappear, coming down like that."

Lady Mary very modestly took up her position standing behind her mother's chair, and, after one timid glance at me, dropped her eyes on the floor, and then there were some moments of silence, as if every one was afraid to begin. I saw I was going to have trouble with the Countess, and although I think it will be admitted by my enemies that I'm as brave a man as ever faced a foe, I was reluctant to throw down the gage of battle to the old lady.

It was young Lord Strepp that began, and he spoke most politely, as was his custom.

"I took the liberty of sending for you, Mr. O'Ruddy, and I thank you for responding so quickly to my invitation. The occurrences of the past day or two, it would be wiser perhaps to ignore —"

At this there was an indignant sniff from the Countess, and I feared she was going to open her batteries, but to my amazement she kept silent, although the effort made her red in the face.

"I have told my father and mother," went on Lord Strepp, "that I had some conversation with you this morning, and that conditions might be arrived at satisfactory to all parties concerned. I have said nothing to my parents regarding the nature of these conditions, but I gained their consent to give consideration to anything you might say, and to any proposal you are good enough to make."

The old gentleman mumbled something incomprehensible in his chair, but the old lady could keep silence no longer.

"This is an outrage," she cried, "the man's action has been scandalous and unlawful. If, instead of bringing those filthy scoundrels against our own house, those cowards that ran away as soon as they heard the sound of a blunderbuss, we had all stayed in London, and you had had the law of him, he would have been in gaol by this time and not standing brazenly there in the Manor House of Brede."

And after saying this she sniffed again, having no appreciation of good manners.

"Your ladyship has been misinformed," I said with extreme deference. "The case is already in the hands of dignified men of law, who are mightily pleased with it."

"Pleased with it, you idiot," she cried. "They are pleased with it simply because they know somebody will pay them for their work, even it's a beggar from Ireland, who has nothing on him but rags."

"Your ladyship," said I, not loath to call attention to my costume, "I assure you these rags cost golden guineas in London."

"Well, you will not get golden guineas from Brede estate," snapped her ladyship.

"Again your ladyship is misinformed. The papers are so perfect, and so well do they confirm my title to this beautiful domain, that the money-lenders of London simply bothered the life out of me trying to shovel gold on me, and both his lordship and your ladyship know that if a title is defective there is no money to be lent on it."

"You're a liar," said the Countess genially, although the Earl looked up in alarm when I mentioned that I could draw money on the papers. Again I bowed deeply to her ladyship, and, putting my hands in my pockets, I drew out two handfuls of gold, which I strewed up and down the floor as if I were sowing corn, and each guinea was no more than a grain of it.

"There is the answer to your ladyship's complimentary remark," said I with a flourish of my empty hands; and, seeing Lady Mary's eyes anxiously fixed on me, I dropped her a wink with the side of my face farthest from the Countess, at which Lady Mary's eyelids drooped again. But I might have winked with both eyes for all the Countess, who was staring like one in a dream at the glittering pieces that lay here and there and gleamed all over the place like the little yellow devils they were. She seemed struck dumb, and if anyone thinks gold cannot perform a miracle, there is the proof of it.

"Is it gold?" cried I in a burst of eloquence that charmed even myself, "sure I could sow you acres with it by the crooking of my little finger from the revenues of my estate at the Old Head of Kinsale."

"O'Ruddy, O'Ruddy," said Father Donovan very softly and reprovingly, for no one knew better than him what my ancestral revenues were.

"Ah well, Father," said I, "your reproof is well-timed. A man should not boast, and I'll say no more of my castles and my acres, though the ships on the sea pay tribute to them. But all good Saints preserve us, Earl of Westport, if you feel proud to own this poor estate of Brede, think how little it weighed with my father, who all his life did not take the trouble to come over and look at it. Need I say more about Kinsale when you hear that? And as for myself, did I attempt to lay hands on this trivial bit of earth because I held the papers? You know I tossed them into your daughter's lap because she was the finest-looking girl I have seen since I landed on these shores."

"Well, well, well, well," growled the Earl, "I admit I have acted rashly and harshly in this matter, and it is likely I have done wrong to an honourable gentleman, therefore I apologize for it. Now, what have you to propose?"

"I have to propose myself as the husband of your daughter, Lady Mary, and as for our dowry, there it is on the floor for the picking up, and I'm content with that much if I get the lady herself."

His lordship slowly turned his head around and gazed at his daughter, who now was looking full at me with a frown on her brow. Although I knew I had depressed the old people, I had an uneasy feeling that I had displeased Lady Mary herself by my impulsive action and my bragging words. A curious mildness came into the harsh voice of the old Earl, and he said, still looking at his daughter:

"What does Mary say to this?"

The old woman could not keep her eyes from the gold, which somehow held her tongue still, yet I knew she was hearing every word that was said, although she made no comment. Lady Mary shook herself, as if to arouse herself from a trance, then she said in a low voice:

"I can never marry a man I do not love."

"What's that? what's that?" shrieked her mother, turning fiercely round upon her, whereat Lady Mary took a step back. "Love, love? What nonsense is this I hear? You say you will not marry this man to save the estate of Brede?"

"I shall marry no man whom I do not love," repeated Lady Mary firmly.

As for me, I stood there, hat in hand, with my jaw dropped, as if Sullivan had given me a stunning blow in the ear; then the old Earl said sternly:

"I cannot force my daughter: this conference is at an end. The law must decide between us."

"The law, you old dotard," cried the Countess, rounding then on him with a suddenness that made him seem to shrink into his shell. "The law! Is a silly wench to run us into danger of losing what is ours? He *shall* marry her. If you will not force her, then I'll coerce her;" and with that she turned upon her daughter, grasped her by her two shoulders and shook her as a terrier shakes a rat. At this Lady Mary began to weep, and indeed she had good cause to do so.

"Hold, madam," shouted I, springing toward her. "Leave the girl alone. I agree with his lordship, no woman shall be coerced on account of me."

My intervention turned the Countess from her victim upon me.

"You agree with his lordship, you Irish baboon? Don't think she'll marry you because of any liking for you, you chattering ape, who resemble a monkey in a show with those trappings upon you. She'll marry you because I say she'll marry you, and you'll give up those papers to me, who have sense enough to take care of them. If I have a doddering husband, who at the same time lost his breeches and his papers, I shall make amends for his folly."

"Madam," said I, "you shall have the papers; and as for the breeches, by the terror you spread around you, I learn they are already in your possession."

I thought she would have torn my eyes out, but I stepped back and saved myself.

"To your room, you huzzy," she cried to her daughter, and Mary fled toward the door. I leaped forward and opened it for her. She paused on the threshold, pretending again to cry, but instead whispered:

"My mother is the danger. Leave things alone," she said quickly. "We can easily get poor father's consent."

With that she was gone. I closed the door and returned to the centre of the room.

"Madam," said I, "I will not have your daughter browbeaten. It is quite evident she refuses to marry me."

"Hold your tongue, and keep to your word, you idiot," she rejoined, hitting me a bewildering slap on the side of the face, after which she flounced out by the way her daughter had departed.

The old Earl said nothing, but gazed gloomily into space from out the depths of his chair. Father Donovan seemed inexpressibly shocked, but my Lord Strepp, accustomed to his mother's tantrums, laughed outright as soon as the door was closed. All through he had not been in the least deceived by his sister's pretended reluctance, and recognized that the only way to get the mother's consent was through opposition. He sprang up and grasped me by the hand and said:

"Well, O'Ruddy, I think your troubles are at an end, or," he cried, laughing again, "just beginning, but you'll be able to say more on that subject this time next year. Never mind my mother; Mary is, and always will be, the best girl in the world."

"I believe you," said I, returning his handshake as cordially as he had bestowed it.

"Hush!" he cried, jumping back into his seat again. "Let us all look dejected. Hang your head, O'Ruddy!" and again the door opened, this time the Countess leading Lady Mary, her long fingers grasping that slim wrist.

"She gives her consent," snapped the Countess, as if she were pronouncing sentence. I strode forward toward her, but Mary wrenched her wrist free, slipped past me, and dropped at the feet of Father Donovan, who had risen as she came in.

"Your blessing on me, dear Father," she cried, bowing her head, "and pray on my behalf that there may be no more turbulence in my life."

The old father crossed his hands on her shapely head, and for a moment or two it seemed as if he could not command his voice, and I saw the tears fill his eyes. At last he said simply and solemnly: —

"May God bless you and yours, my dear daughter."

We were married by Father Donovan with pomp and ceremony in the chapel of the old house, and in the same house I now pen the last words of these memoirs, which I began at the request of Lady Mary herself, and continued for the pleasure she expressed as they went on. If this recital is disjointed in parts, it must be remembered I was always more used to the sword than to the pen, and that it is difficult to write with Patrick and little Mary and Terence and

Kathleen and Michael and Bridget and Donovan playing about me and asking questions, but I would not have the darlings sent from the room for all the writings there is in the world.